British Empire
Adventure Stories

British Empire

Adventure Stories

THE MAN WHO WOULD
BE KING
Rudyard Kipling

KING SOLOMON'S MINES
Sir H Rider Haggard

WITH CLIVE IN INDIA
G A Henty

PRION

THIS IS A CARLTON BOOK

This edition published in 2008 by
Carlton Books Limited
20 Mortimer Street
London W1T 3JW

10 9 8 7 6 5 4 3 2 1

A CIP catalogue record for this book is available from the
British Library.

ISBN 978-1-85375-660-3

Typeset by Ellipsis, Glasgow

Printed in Thailand

CONTENTS

King Solomon's Mines

THIS FAITHFUL BUT UNPRETENDING RECORD
OF A REMARKABLE ADVENTURE
IS HEREBY RESPECTFULLY DEDICATED
BY THE NARRATOR
ALLAN QUATERMAIN
TO ALL THE BIG AND LITTLE BOYS
WHO READ IT

Author's Note

THE author ventures to take this opportunity to thank his readers for the kind reception they have accorded to the successive editions of this tale during the last twelve years. He hopes that in its present form it will fall into the hands of an even wider public, and that it may in years to come continue to afford amusement to those who are still young enough at heart to love a story of treasure, war, and wild adventure.

DITCHINGHAM,
11th March 1898.

Post Scriptum

Now, in 1905, I can only add how glad I am that my romance should continue to please so many readers. Imagination has been verified by fact; the King Solomon's Mines I dreamed of have been discovered, and are putting out their gold once more, and, according to the latest reports, their diamonds also; the Kukuanas or, rather, the Matabele, have been tamed by the white man's bullets, but still there seem to be many who find pleasure in these simple pages. That they may continue so to do, even to the third and fourth generation, or perhaps longer still, would, I am sure, be the hope of our old and departed friend, ALLAN QUATERMAIN.

H. RIDER HAGGARD.
DITCHINGHAM,
15th July 1905.

INTRODUCTION

Now that this book is printed, and about to be given to the world, a sense of its shortcomings, both in style and contents, weighs very heavily upon me. As regards the latter, I can only say that it does not pretend to be a full account of everything we did and saw. There are many things connected with our journey into Kukuanaland that I should have liked to dwell upon at length, which, as it is, have been scarcely alluded to. Amongst these are the curious legends which I collected about the chain armour that saved us from destruction in the great battle of Loo, and also about the 'Silent Ones' or Colossi at the mouth of the stalactite cave. Again, if I had given way to my own impulses, I should have wished to go into the differences, some of which are to my mind very suggestive, between the Zulu and Kukuana dialects. Also a few pages might have been given up profitably to the consideration of the indigenous flora and fauna of Kukuanaland.* Then there remains the most interesting subject – that, as it is, has only been touched on incidentally – of the magnificent system of military organization in force in that country, which, in my opinion, is much superior to that inaugurated by Chaka in Zululand, inasmuch as it permits of even more rapid mobilization, and does not necessitate the employment of the pernicious system of forced celibacy. Lastly, I have scarcely spoken of the domestic and family customs of the Kukuanas, many of which are exceedingly quaint, or of their proficiency

* I discovered eight varieties of antelope, with which I was previously totally unacquainted, and many new species of plants, for the most part of the bulbous tribe – A. Q.

7

in the art of smelting and welding metals. This science they carry to considerable perfection, of which a good example is to be seen in their 'tollas,' or heavy throwing knives, the backs of these weapons being made of hammered iron, and the edges of beautiful steel welded with great skill on to the iron frames. The fact of the matter is, I thought, with Sir Henry Curtis and Captain Good, that the best plan would be to tell my story in a plain, straight-forward manner, and to leave these matters to be dealt with subsequently in whatever way ultimately may appear to be desirable. In the meanwhile I shall, of course, be delighted to give all information in my power to anybody interested in such things.

And now it only remains for me to offer apologies for my blunt way of writing. I can but say in excuse of it that I am more accustomed to handle a rifle than a pen, and cannot make any pretence to the grand literary flights and flourishes which I see in novels – for sometimes I like to read a novel. I suppose they – the flights and flourishes – are desirable, and I regret not being able to supply them; but at the same time I cannot help thinking that simple things are always the most impressive, and that books are easier to understand when they are written in plain language, though perhaps I have no right to set up an opinion on such a matter. 'A sharp spear,' runs the Kukuana saying, 'needs no polish'; and on the same principle I venture to hope that a true story, however strange it may be, does not require to be decked out in fine words.

ALLAN QUATERMAIN

Chapter I

I MEET SIR HENRY CURTIS

It is a curious thing that at my age – fifty-five last birthday – I should find myself taking up a pen to try to write a history. I wonder what sort of a history it will be when I have finished it, if ever I come to the end of the trip! I have done a good many things in my life, which seems a long one to me, owing to my having begun work so young, perhaps. At an age when other boys are at school I was earning my living as a trader in the old Colony. I have been trading, hunting, fighting, or mining ever since. And yet it is only eight months ago that I made my pile. It is a big pile now that I have got it – I don't yet know how big – but I do not think I would go through the last fifteen or sixteen months again for it; no, not if I knew that I should come out safe at the end, pile and all. But then I am a timid man, and dislike violence; moreover, I am fairly sick of adventure. I wonder why I am going to write this book: it is not in my line. I am not a literary man, though very devoted to the Old Testament and also to the 'Ingoldsby Legends.' Let me try to set down my reasons, just to see if I have any.

First reason: Because Sir Henry Curtis and Captain John Good asked me.

Second reason: Because I am laid up here at Durban with the pain in my left leg. Ever since that confounded lion got hold of me I have been liable to this trouble, and being rather bad just now, it makes me limp more than ever. There must be some poison in a lion's teeth, otherwise how is it that when your wounds are healed they break out again, generally, mark you, at the same time of year that you got your mauling? It is a hard thing when one has shot sixty-five lions and more, as I have in the course of my life, that the sixty-sixth should chew your leg like a quid of tobacco. It breaks the routine of the thing, and putting other considerations aside, I am an orderly man and don't like that. This is by the way.

Third reason: Because I want my boy Harry, who is over there at the hospital in London studying to become a doctor, to have something to amuse him and keep him out of mischief for a week or so. Hospital work must sometimes pall and grow rather dull, for even of cutting up dead bodies there may come satiety, and as this history will not be dull, whatever else it may be, it will put a little life into things for a day or two while Harry is reading it.

Fourth reason and last: Because I am going to tell the strangest story that I know of. It may seem a queer thing to say, especially considering that there is no woman in it – except Foulata. Stop, though! there is Gagaoola, if she was a woman and not a fiend. But she was a hundred at least, and therefore not marriageable, so I don't count her. At any rate, I can safely say that there is not a *petticoat* in the whole history.

Well, I had better come to the yoke. It is a stiff place, and I feel as though I were bogged up to the axle. But '*sutjes, sutjes*,' as the Boers say – I am sure I don't know how they spell it – softly does it. A strong team will come through at last, that is, if they are not too poor. You can never do anything with poor oxen. Now to begin.

I, Allan Quatermain, of Durban, Natal, Gentleman, make oath and say – That's how I began my deposition before the magistrate about poor Khiva's and Ventvögel's sad deaths; but somehow it doesn't seem quite the right way to begin a book. And, besides, am I a gentleman? What is a gentleman? I don't quite know, and yet I have had to do with niggers – no, I will scratch out that word 'niggers,' for I do not like it. I've known natives who *are*, and so you will say, Harry, my boy, before you have done with this tale, and I have known mean whites with lots of money and fresh out from home, too, who *are not*.

At any rate, I was born a gentleman, though I have been nothing but a poor travelling trader and hunter all my life. Whether I have remained so I know not, you must judge of that. Heaven knows I've tried. I have killed many men in my time, yet I have never slain wantonly or stained my hand in innocent blood, but only in self-defence.

The Almighty gave us our lives and I suppose He meant us to defend them, at least I have always acted on that, and I hope it will not be brought up against me when my clock strikes. There, there, it is a cruel and wicked world, and for a timid man I have been mixed up in a deal of slaughter. I cannot tell the rights of it, but at any rate I have never stolen, though once I cheated a Kafir out of a herd of cattle. But then he had done me a dirty turn, and it has troubled me ever since into the bargain.

Well, it is eighteen months or so ago since first I met Sir Henry Curtis and Captain Good. It was in this way. I had been up elephant hunting beyond Bamangwato, and had met with bad luck. Everything went wrong that trip, and to top up with I got the fever badly. So soon as I was well enough I trekked down to the Diamond Fields, sold such ivory as I had, together with my wagon and oxen, discharged my hunters, and took the postcart to the Cape. After spending a week in Cape Town, finding that they overcharged me at the hotel, and having seen everything there was to see, including the botanical gardens, which seem to me likely to confer a great benefit on the country, and the new Houses of Parliament, which I expect will do nothing of the sort, I determined to go back to Natal by the *Dunkeld*, then lying at the docks waiting for the *Edinburgh Castle* due in from England. I took my berth and went aboard, and that afternoon the Natal passengers from the *Edinburgh Castle* transhipped and we weighed and put out to sea.

Among these passengers who came on board were two who excited my curiosity. One, a gentleman of about thirty, was perhaps the biggest-chested and longest-armed man I ever saw. He had yellow hair, a thick yellow beard, clear-cut features, and large grey eyes set deep in his head. I never saw a finer-looking man, and somehow he reminded me of an ancient Dane. Not that I know much of ancient Danes, though I knew a modern Dane who did me out of ten pounds; but I remember once seeing a picture of some of those gentry, who, I take it, were a kind of white Zulus. They were drinking out of big horns, and their long hair hung down their backs. As I looked at my friend standing there by the companion-ladder, I thought that if he only let his hair grow a little, put one of those chain shirts on to his great shoulders, and took hold of a battle-axe and a horn mug, he might have sat as a model for that picture. And by the way it is a curious thing, and just shows how the blood will out,

I discovered afterwards that Sir Henry Curtis, for that was the big man's name, is of Danish blood.* He also reminded me strongly of somebody else, but at the time I could not remember who it was.

The other man who stood talking to Sir Henry was short, stout, and dark, and of quite a different cut. I suspected at once that he was a naval officer; I don't know why, but it is difficult to mistake a navy man. I have gone on shooting trips with several of them in the course of my life, and they have always proved themselves the best and bravest and nicest fellows I ever met, though sadly given, some of them, to the use of profane language. I asked a page or two back, what is a gentleman? I'll answer the question now: a Royal Naval officer is, in a general sort of way, though of course there may be a black sheep among them here and there. I fancy it is just the wide seas and the breath of God's winds that wash their hearts and blow the bitterness out of their minds and make them what men ought to be.

Well, to return, I was right again; I ascertained that the dark man *was* a naval officer, a lieutenant of thirty-one, who, after seventeen years' service, had been turned out of Her Majesty's employ with the barren honour of a commander's rank, because it was impossible that he should be promoted. This is what people who serve the Queen have to expect: to be shot out into the cold world to find a living just when they are beginning to really understand their work, and to reach the prime of life. I suppose they don't mind it, but for my own part I had rather earned my bread as a hunter. One's halfpence are as scarce perhaps, but you do not get so many kicks.

The officer's name I found out – by referring to the passengers' list – was Good – Captain John Good. He was broad, of medium height, dark, stout, and rather a curious man to look at. He was so very neat and so very clean-shaved, and he always wore an eye-glass in his right eye. It seemed to grow there, for it had no string, and he never took it out except to wipe it. At first I thought he used to sleep with it, but afterwards I found that this was a mistake. He put it in his trousers pocket when he went to bed, together with his false teeth, of which he had two beautiful sets that,

---

* Mr. Quatermain's ideas about ancient Danes seem to be rather confused; we have always understood that they were dark-haired people. Probably he was thinking of Saxons. – *Editor*.

my own being none of the best, have often caused me to break the tenth commandment. But I am anticipating.

Soon after we had got under way evening closed in, and brought with it very dirty weather. A keen breeze sprung up off land, and a kind of aggravated Scotch mist soon drove everybody from the deck. As for the *Dunkeld*, she is a flat-bottomed punt, and going up light as she was, she rolled very heavily. It almost seemed as though she would go right over, but she never did. It was quite impossible to walk about, so I stood near the engines where it was warm, and amused myself with watching the pendulum, which was fixed opposite to me, swinging slowly backwards and forwards as the vessel rolled, and marking the angle she touched at each lurch.

'That pendulum's wrong; it is not properly weighted,' suddenly said a somewhat testy voice at my shoulder. Looking round I saw the naval officer whom I had noticed when the passengers came aboard.

'Indeed, now what makes you think so?' I asked.

'Think so. I don't think at all. Why there' – as she righted herself after a roll – 'if the ship had really rolled to the degree that thing pointed to then she would never have rolled again, that's all. But it is just like these merchant skippers, they always are so confoundedly careless.'

Just then the dinner bell rung, and I was not sorry, for it is a dreadful thing to have to listen to an officer of the Royal Navy when he gets on to that subject. I only know one worse thing, and it is to hear a merchant skipper express his candid opinion of officers of the Royal Navy.

Captain Good and I went down to dinner together, and there we found Sir Henry Curtis already seated. He and Captain Good were placed together, and I sat opposite to them. The captain and I soon fell into talk about shooting and what not; he asking me many questions, and I answering them as well as I could. Presently he got on to elephants.

'Ah, sir,' called out somebody who was sitting near me, 'you've reached the right man for that; Hunter Quatermain should be able to tell you about elephants if anybody can.'

Sir Henry, who had been sitting quite quiet listening to our talk, started visibly.

'Excuse me, sir,' he said, leaning forward across the table, and speaking in a low deep voice, a very suitable voice, it seemed to me, to come out of those great lungs. 'Excuse me, sir, but is your name Allan Quatermain?'

I said that it was.

The big man made no further remark, but I heard him mutter 'fortunate' into his beard.

Presently dinner came to an end, and as we were leaving the saloon Sir Henry strolled up and asked me if I would come into his cabin to smoke a pipe. I accepted, and he led the way to the *Dunkeld* deck cabin, and a very good cabin it is. It had been two cabins, but when Sir Garnet or one of those big swells went down the coast in the *Dunkeld*, they knocked away the partition and have never put it up again. There was a sofa in the cabin, and a little table in front of it. Sir Henry sent the steward for a bottle of whisky, and the three of us sat down and lit our pipes.

'Mr. Quatermain,' said Sir Henry Curtis, when the steward had brought the whisky and lit the lamp, 'the year before last about this time you were, I believe, at a place called Bamangwato, to the north of the Transvaal.'

'I was,' I answered, rather surprised that this gentleman should be so well acquainted with my movements, which were not, so far as I was aware, considered of general interest.

'You were trading there, were you not?' put in Captain Good, in his quick way.

'I was. I took up a wagon-load of goods, made a camp outside the settlement, and stopped till I had sold them.'

Sir Henry was sitting opposite to me in a Madeira chair, his arms leaning on the table. He now looked up, fixing his large grey eyes full upon my face. There was a curious anxiety in them I thought.

'Did you happen to meet a man called Neville there?'

'Oh, yes; he outspanned alongside of me for a fortnight to rest his oxen before going on to the interior. I had a letter from a lawyer a few months back, asking me if I knew what had become of him, which I answered to the best of my ability at the time.'

'Yes,' said Sir Henry, 'your letter was forwarded to me. You said in it that the gentleman called Neville left Bamangwato at the beginning of May in a wagon with a driver, a voorlooper, and a Kafir hunter called Jim, announcing his intention of trekking if possible as far as Inyati, the extreme trading post in the Matabele country, where he would sell his wagon and proceed on foot. You also said that he did sell his wagon, for six months afterwards you saw the wagon in the possession of a Portuguese trader, who told you that he had bought it at Inyati from a white man whose name he had forgotten, and that he believed the white man with the native servant had started off for the interior on a shooting trip.'

'Yes.'

Then came a pause.

'Mr. Quatermain,' said Sir Henry suddenly, 'I suppose you know or can guess nothing more of the reasons of my – of Mr. Neville's journey to the northward, or as to what point that journey was directed?'

'I heard something,' I answered, and stopped. The subject was one which I did not care to discuss.

Sir Henry and Captain Good looked at each other, and Captain Good nodded.

'Mr. Quatermain,' went on the former, 'I am going to tell you a story, and ask your advice, and perhaps your assistance. The agent who forwarded me your letter told me that I might rely upon it implicitly, as you were,' he said, 'well known and universally respected in Natal, and especially noted for your discretion.'

I bowed and drank some whisky and water to hide my confusion, for I am a modest man – and Sir Henry went on.

'Mr. Neville was my brother.'

'Oh,' I said, starting, for now I knew who Sir Henry had reminded me of when first I saw him. His brother was a much smaller man and had a dark beard, but now that I thought of it, he possessed eyes of the same shade of grey and with the same keen look in them; the features too were not unlike.

'He was,' went on Sir Henry, 'my only and younger brother, and till five years ago I do not suppose that we were ever a month away from each other. But just about five years ago a misfortune befell us, as sometimes does happen in families. We quarrelled bitterly, and I behaved unjustly to my brother in my anger.'

Here Captain Good nodded his head vigorously to himself. The ship gave a big roll just then so that the looking-glass, which was fixed opposite us to starboard, was for a moment nearly over our heads, and as I was sitting with my hands in my pockets and staring upwards, I could see him nodding like anything.

'As I daresay you know,' went on Sir Henry, 'if a man dies intestate, and has no property but land, real property it is called in England, it all descends to his eldest son. It so happened that just at the time when we quarrelled our father died intestate. He had put off making his will until it was too late. The result was that my brother, who had not been brought up to any profession, was left without a penny. Of course it would have been my duty to provide for him, but at the time the quarrel between us was so bitter that I did not – to my shame I say it (and he sighed deeply) – offer to do anything. It was not that I grudged him justice, but I waited for him to make advances, and he made none. I am sorry to trouble you with all this, Mr. Quatermain, but I must to make things clear, eh, Good?'

'Quite so, quite so,' said the captain. 'Mr. Quatermain will, I am sure, keep this history to himself.'

'Of course,' said I, for I rather pride myself on my discretion, for which, as Sir Henry had heard, I have some repute.

'Well,' went on Sir Henry, 'my brother had a few hundred pounds to his account at the time. Without saying anything to me he drew out this paltry sum, and, having adopted the name of Neville, started off for South Africa in the wild hope of making a fortune. This I learned afterwards. Some three years passed, and I heard nothing of my brother, though I wrote several times. Doubtless the letters never reached him. But as time went on I grew more and more troubled about him. I found out, Mr. Quatermain, that blood is thicker than water.'

'That's true,' said I, thinking of my boy Harry.

'I found out, Mr. Quatermain, that I would have given half my fortune to know that my brother George, the only relation I possess, was safe and well, and that I should see him again.'

'But you never did, Curtis,' jerked out Captain Good, glancing at the big man's face.

'Well, Mr. Quatermain, as time went on I became more and more anxious to find out if my brother was alive or dead, and if alive to get him home again. I set inquiries on foot, and your letter was one of the results. So far as it went it was satisfactory, for it showed that till lately George was alive, but it did not go far enough. So, to cut a long story short, I made up my mind to come out and look for him myself, and Captain Good was so kind as to come with me.'

'Yes,' said the captain; 'nothing else to do, you see. Turned out by my Lords of the Admiralty to starve on half-pay. And now, perhaps, sir, you will tell us what you know or have heard of the gentleman called Neville.'

Chapter II

THE LEGEND OF SOLOMON'S MINES

'What was it that you heard about my brother's journey at Bamangwato?' said Sir Henry, as I paused to fill my pipe before answering Captain Good.

'I heard this,' I answered, 'and I have never mentioned it to a soul till to-day. I heard that he was starting for Solomon's Mines.'

'Solomon's Mines?' ejaculated both my hearers at once. 'Where are they?'

'I don't know,' I said; 'I know where they are said to be. Once I saw the peaks of the mountains that border them, but there were a hundred and thirty miles of desert between me and them, and I am not aware that any white man ever got across it save one. But perhaps the best thing I can do is to tell you the legend of Solomon's Mines as I know it, you passing your word not to reveal anything I tell you without my permission. Do you agree to that? I have my reasons for asking it.'

Sir Henry nodded, and Captain Good replied, 'Certainly, certainly.'

'Well,' I began, 'as you may guess, generally speaking, elephant hunters are a rough set of men who do not trouble themselves with much beyond the facts of life and the ways of Kafirs. But here and there you meet a man who takes the trouble to collect traditions from the natives, and tries to make out a little piece of the history of this dark land. It was such a man as this who first told me the legend of Solomon's Mines, now a matter of nearly thirty years ago. That was when I was on my first elephant hunt in the Matabele country. His name was Evans, and he was killed the following year, poor fellow, by a wounded buffalo, and lies buried near the Zambesi Falls. I was telling Evans one night, I remember, of some wonderful workings I had found whilst hunting koodoo and eland in what is now the Lydenburg district of the Transvaal. I see they have come across these workings again lately in prospecting for gold, but I knew of them years ago. There is a great wide wagon road cut out of the solid rock, and leading to the mouth of the working or gallery. Inside the mouth of this gallery are stacks of gold quartz piled up ready for roasting, which shows that the workers, whoever they are, must have left in a hurry. Also, about twenty paces in, the gallery is built across, and a beautiful bit of masonry it is.

"'Ay,' said Evans, "but I will spin you a queerer yarn than that;" and he went on to tell me how he had found in the far interior a ruined city, which he believed to be the Ophir of the Bible, and, by the way, other more learned men have said the same long since poor Evans's time. I was, I remember, listening open-eared to all these wonders, for I was young at the time, and this story of an ancient civilization and of treasures which those old Jewish or Phœnician adventurers used to extract from a country long since lapsed into the darkest barbarism took a great hold upon my imagination, when suddenly he said to me, 'Lad, did you ever hear of the Suliman Mountains up to the north-west of the Mashukulumbwe country?' I told him I never had. 'Ah, well,' he said, 'that is where Solomon really had his mines, his diamond mines, I mean.'

"'How do you know that?" I asked.

"'Know it! why what is 'Suliman' but a corruption of Solomon?* And, besides, an old Isanusi or witch doctoress up in the Manica country told me all about it. She said that the people who lived across those mountains were a 'branch' of the Zulus, speaking a dialect of Zulu, but finer and bigger men even; that there lived among them great wizards, who had learned their art from white men when 'all the world was dark,' and who had the secret of a wonderful mine of 'bright stones.'"

'Well, I laughed at this story at the time, though it interested me, for the Diamond Fields were not discovered then, but poor Evans went off and was killed, and for twenty years I never thought any more of the matter. However, just twenty

* Suliman is the Arabic form of Solomon. – *Editor.*

years afterwards – and that is a long time, gentlemen; an elephant hunter does not often live for twenty years at his business – I heard something more definite about Suliman's Mountains and the country which lies behind them. I was up beyond the Manica country, at a place called Sitanda's Kraal, and a miserable place it was, for a man could get nothing to eat, and there was but little game about. I had an attack of fever, and was in a bad way generally, when one day a Portugese arrived with a single companion – a half-breed. Now I know your low-class Delagoa Portugee well. There is no greater devil unhung in a general way, battening as he does upon human agony and flesh in the shape of slaves. But this was quite a different type of man to the mean fellows whom I have been accustomed to meet; indeed, in appearance he reminded me more of the polite doms I have read about, for he was tall and thin, with large dark eyes and curling grey mustachios. We talked together a little, for he could speak broken English, and I understood a little Portugese, and he told me that his name was José Silvestre, and that he had a place near Delagoa Bay. When he went on next day with his half-breed companion, he said 'Good-bye,' taking off his hat quite in the old style.

'"Good-bye, señor," he said; "if ever we meet again I shall be the richest man in the world, and I will remember you." I laughed a little – I was too weak to laugh much – and watched him strike out for the great desert to the west, wondering if he was mad, or what he thought he was going to find there.

'A week passed, and I got the better of my fever. One evening I was sitting on the ground in front of the little tent I had with me, chewing the last leg of a miserable fowl I had bought from a native for a bit of cloth worth twenty fowls, and staring at the hot red sun sinking down over the desert, when suddenly I saw a figure, apparently that of a European, for it wore a coat, on the slope of the rising ground opposite to me, about three hundred yards away. The figure crept along on its hands and knees, then it got up and staggered forward a few yards on its legs, only to fall and crawl again. Seeing that it must be somebody in distress, I sent one of my hunters to help him, and presently he arrived, and whom do you suppose it turned out to be?'

'José Silvestre, of course,' said Captain Good.

'Yes, José Silvestre, or rather his skeleton and a little skin. His face was bright yellow with bilious fever, and his large dark eyes stood nearly out of his head, for all the flesh had gone. There was nothing but yellow parchment-like skin, white hair, and the gaunt bones sticking up beneath.

"'Water! for the sake of Christ, water!" he moaned, and I saw that his lips were cracked, and his tongue, which protruded between them, was swollen and blackish.

'I gave him water with a little milk in it, and he drank it in great gulps, two quarts or so, without stopping. I would not let him have any more. Then the fever took him again, and he fell down and began to rave about Suliman's Mountains, and the diamonds, and the desert. I carried him into the tent and did what I could for him, which was little enough; but I saw how it must end. About eleven o'clock he grew quieter and I lay down for a little rest and went to sleep. At dawn I woke again, and in the half light saw Silvestre sitting up, a strange, gaunt form, and gazing out towards the desert. Presently the first ray of the sun shot right across the wide plain before us till it reached the faraway crest of one of the tallest of the Suliman Mountains more than a hundred miles away

'There it is!' cried the dying man in Portuguese, and pointing with his long, thin arm, 'but I shall never reach it, never. No one will ever reach it!'

'Suddenly he paused, and seemed to take a resolution. "Friend," he said, turning towards me, "are you there? My eyes grow dark."

"'Yes," I said; "yes, lie down now, and rest."

"'Ay," he answered, "I shall rest soon, I have time to rest – all eternity. Listen, I am dying! You have been good to me. I will give you the writing. Perhaps you will get there if you can live to pass the desert, which has killed my poor servant and me."

'Then he groped in his shirt and brought out what I thought was a Boer tobacco pouch made of the skin of the Swart-vet-pens or sable antelope. It was fastened with a little strip of hide, what we call a rimpi, and this he tried to loose, but could not. He handed it to me. "Untie it," he said. I did so, and extracted a bit of torn yellow linen, on which something was written in rusty letters. Inside this rag was a paper.

'Then he went on feebly, for he was growing weak: "The paper has all that is on the linen. It took me years to read. Listen: my ancestor, a political refugee from Lisbon, and one of the first Portuguese who landed on these shores, wrote that when he was dying on those mountains which no white foot ever pressed before or since. His name was José da Silvestra, and he lived three hundred years ago. His slave, who waited for him on this side of the mountains, found him dead, and brought the writing home to Delagoa. It has been in the family ever since, but none have cared to read it, till at last I did. And I have lost my life over it, but another may succeed, and become the richest man in the world – the richest man in the world. Only give it to no one, señor; go yourself!" Then he began to wander again, and in an hour it was all over.

'God rest him! he died very quietly, and I buried him deep, with big boulders on his breast; so I do not think that the jackals can have dug him up. And then I came away.'

'Ay, but the document?' said Sir Henry, in a tone of deep interest.

'Yes, the document; what was in it?' added the captain.

'Well, gentlemen, if you like I will tell you. I have never showed it to anybody yet except to a drunken old Portuguese trader who translated it for me, and had forgotten all about it by the next morning. The original rag is at my home in Durban, together with poor Dom José's translation, but I have the English rendering in my pocket-book, and a facsimile of the map, if it can be called a map. Here it is.'

'I, José da Silvestra, who am now dying of hunger in the little cave where no snow is on the north side of the nipple of the southern-most of the two mountains I have named Sheba's Breasts, write this in the year 1590 with a cleft bone upon a remnant of my raiment, my blood being the ink. If my slave should find it when he comes, and should bring it to Delagoa, let my friend (name illegible) bring the matter to the knowledge of the king, that he may send an army which, if they live through the desert and the mountains, and can overcome the brave Kukuanes and their devilish arts, to which end many priests should be brought, will make him the richest king since Solomon. With my own eyes have I seen the countless diamonds stored in Solomon's treasure chamber behind the white Death; but through the treachery of Gagool the witch-finder I might bring nought away, scarcely my life. Let him who comes follow the map, and climb the snow of Sheba's left breast till he reaches the nipple, on the

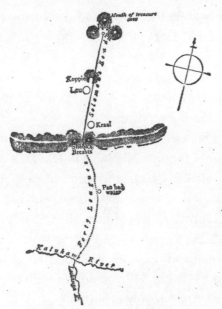

Sketch Map of the Route to King Solomon's Mines.

north side of which is the great road Solomon made, from whence three days' journey to the King's Palace. Let him kill Gagool. Pray for my soul. Farewell.

JOSÉ DA SILVESTRA."

* Eu José da Silvestra que estou morrendo de fome ná pequena cova onde não ha ncve ao lado norte do bico mais ao sul das duas montanhas que chamei seio de Sheba; escrevo isto no anno 1590; escrevo isto com um pedaço d' ôsso n' um farrapo de minha roupa e com sangue meu por tinta; se o meu escravo dér com isto quando venha ao levar para Lourenzo Marquez, que o meu amigo—leve a cousa ao conhecimento d' El Rei, para que possa mandar um exercito que, se desfiler pelo deserto e pelas montanhas e mesmo sobrepujar os bravos Kukuanes e suas artes diabolicas, pelo que se deviam trazer muitos padres Fara o Rei mais rico depois de Salomão. Com meus proprios olhos vé os di amantes sem conto guardados nas camaras do thesouro de Salomão a traz da morte branca, mas pela traição de Gagoa a feiticeira achadora, nada poderia levar, e apenas a minha vida. Quem vier siga o mappa e trepe pela neve de Sheba peito à esquerda até chegar ao bico, do lado norte do qual està a grande estrada do Solomão por elle feita, donde ha tre dias de jornada até ao Palacio do Rei. Mate Gagoal. Reze por minha alma. Adeos.

JOSÉ DA SILVESTRA.

When I had finished reading the above, and shown the copy of the map, drawn by the dying hand of the old Dom with his blood for ink, there followed a silence of astonishment.

'Well,' said Captain Good, 'I have been round the world twice, and put in at most ports, but may I be hung for a mutineer if ever I heard a yarn like this out of a story book, or in it either, for the matter of that.'

'It's a queer tale, Mr. Quatermain,' said Sir Henry. 'I suppose you are not hoaxing us? It is, I know, sometimes thought allowable to take in a greenhorn.'

'If you think that, Sir Henry,' I said, much put out, and pocketing my paper, for I do not like to be thought one of those silly fellows who consider it witty to tell lies, and who are for ever boasting to newcomers of extraordinary hunting adventures which never happened, 'why, there is an end of the matter,' and I rose to go.

Sir Henry laid his large hand upon my shoulder. 'Sit down, Mr. Quatermain,' he said, 'I beg your pardon; I see very well you do not wish to deceive us, but the story sounded so strange that I could hardly believe it.'

'You shall see the original map and writing when we reach Durban,' I answered, somewhat mollified, for really when I came to consider the question it was scarcely wonderful that he should doubt my good faith. 'But I have not told you about your brother. I knew the man Jim who was with him. He was a Bechuana by birth, a good hunter, and for a native a very clever man. That morning on which Mr. Neville was starting I saw Jim standing by my wagon and cutting up tobacco on the disselboom.

'"Jim," said I, "where are you off to this trip? Is it elephants?"

'"No, Baas," he answered, "we are after something worth much more than ivory."

'"And what might that be?" I said, for I was curious. "Is it gold?"

'"No, Baas, something worth more than gold," and he grinned.

'I asked no more questions, for I did not like to lower my dignity by seeming inquisitive, but I was puzzled. Presently Jim finished cutting his tobacco.

'"Baas," said he.

'I took no notice.

'"Baas," said he again.

'"Eh, boy, what is it?" I asked.

'"Baas, we are going after diamonds."

'"Diamonds! why, then, you are steering in the wrong direction; you should head for the Fields."

'"Baas, have you ever heard of Suliman's Berg?" – that is, Solomon's Mountains, Sir Henry.

'"Ay!"

'"Have you ever heard of the diamonds there?"

'"I have heard a foolish story, Jim."

'"It is no story, Baas. I once knew a woman who came from there, and reached Natal with her child, she told me: – she is dead now."

'"Your master will feed the aasvögels" – that is, vultures – "Jim, if he tries to reach Suliman's country, and so will you if they can get any pickings off your worthless old carcass," said I.

'He grinned. "Mayhap, Baas. Man must die; I'd rather like to try a new country myself; the elephants are getting worked out about here."

'"Ah! my boy," I said, "you wait till the 'pale old man' gets a grip of your yellow throat, and then we shall hear what sort of a tune you sing."

'Half an hour after that I saw Neville's wagon move off. Presently Jim came back running. "Good-bye, Baas," he said. "I didn't like to start without bidding you good-bye, for I daresay you are right, and that we shall never trek south again."

'"Is your master really going to Suliman's Berg, Jim, or are you lying?"

'"No," he answered, "he is going. He told me he was bound to make his fortune somehow, or try to; so he might as well have a fling for the diamonds."

'"Oh!" I said; "wait a bit, Jim; will you take a note to your master, Jim, and promise not to give it to him till you reach Inyati?" which was some hundred miles off.

'"Yes, Baas."

'So I took a scrap of paper, and wrote on it, "Let him who comes . . . climb the snow of Sheba's left breast, till he reaches the nipple, on the north side of which is Solomon's great road."

'"Now, Jim," I said, "when you give this to your master, tell him he had better follow

25

the advice on it implicitly. You are not to give it to him now, because I don't want him back asking me questions which I won't answer. Now be off, you idle fellow, the wagon is nearly out of sight."

'Jim took the note and went, and that is all I know about your brother, Sir Henry; but I am much afraid—'

'Mr. Quatermain,' said Sir Henry, 'I am going to look for my brother; I am going to trace him to Suliman's Mountains and over them if necessary, till I find him, or until I know that he is dead. Will you come with me?'

I am, as I think I have said, a cautious man, indeed a timid one, and this suggestion frightened me. It seemed to me that to undertake such a journey would be to go to certain death, and putting other considerations aside, as I had a son to support, I could not afford to die just then.

'No, thank you, Sir Henry, I think I had rather not,' I answered. 'I am too old for wild-goose chases of that sort, and we should only end up like my poor friend Silvestre. I have a son dependent on me, so I cannot afford to risk my life.'

Both Sir Henry and Captain Good looked very disappointed.

'Mr. Quatermain,' said the former, 'I am well off, and I am bent upon this business. You may put the remuneration for your services at whatever figure you like in reason, and it shall be paid over to you before we start. Moreover, I will arrange in the event of anything untoward happening to us or to you, that your son shall be suitably provided for. You will see from this offer how necessary I think your presence. Also if by chance we should reach this place and find diamonds, they shall belong to you and Good equally. I do not want them. But of course that promise is worth nothing at all, though the same thing would apply to any ivory we might get. You may pretty well make your own terms with me, Mr. Quatermain; and of course I shall pay all expenses.'

'Sir Henry,' said I, 'this is the most liberal proposal I ever had, and one not to be sneezed at by a poor hunter and trader. But the job is the biggest I have come across, and I must take time to think over it. I will give you my answer before we get to Durban.'

'Very good,' answered Sir Henry, and then I said good-night and turned in, and dreamt about poor long-dead Silvestre and the diamonds.

Chapter III

UMBOPA ENTERS OUR SERVICE

It takes from four to five days, according to the speed of the vessel and the state of the weather, to run up from the Cape to Durban. Sometimes, if the landing is bad at East London, where they have not yet made that wonderful harbour they talk so much of, and sink such a mint of money in, a ship is delayed for twenty-four hours before the cargo boats can get out to take off the goods. But on this occasion we had not to wait at all, for there were no breakers on the bar to speak of, and the tugs came out at once with the long strings of ugly flat-bottomed boats behind them, into which the packages were bundled with a crash. It did not matter what they might be, over they went slap bang; whether they contained china or woollen goods they met with the same treatment. I saw one case holding four dozen champagne smashed all to bits, and there was the champagne fizzing and boiling about in the bottom of the dirty cargo boat. It was a wicked waste, and evidently so the Kafirs in the boats thought, for they found a couple of unbroken bottles, and knocking the necks off drank the contents. But they had not allowed for the expansion caused by the fizz in the wine, and, feeling themselves swelling, rolled about in the bottom of the boat, calling out that the good liquor was 'tagati' – that is, bewitched. I spoke to them from the vessel and told them it was the white man's strongest medicine, and that they were as good as dead men. Those Kafirs went to the shore in a very great fright, and I do not think that they will touch champagne again.

Well, all the time that we were running up to Natal I was thinking over Sir Henry

Curtis's offer. We did not speak any more on the subject for a day or two, though I told them many hunting yarns, all true ones. There is no need to tell lies about hunting, for so many curious things happen within the knowledge of a man whose business it is to hunt; but this is by the way.

At last, one beautiful evening in January, which is our hottest month, we steamed past the coast of Natal expecting to make Durban Point by sunset. It is a lovely coast all along from East London, with its red sandhills and wide sweeps of vivid green, dotted here and there with Kafir kraals, and bordered by a ribbon of white surf, which spouts up in pillars of foam where it hits the rocks. But just before you come to Durban there is a peculiar richness about the landscape. There are the sheer kloofs cut in the hills by the rushing rains of centuries, down which the rivers sparkle; there is the deepest green of the bush, growing as God planted it, and the other greens of the mealie gardens and the sugar patchnes, while here and there a white house, smiling out at the placid sea, puts a finish and gives an air of homeliness to the scene. For to my mind, however beautiful a view may be, it requires the presence of man to make it complete, but perhaps that is because I have lived so much in the wilderness, and therefore know the value of civilization, though to be sure it drives away the game. The Garden of Eden, no doubt, was fair before man was, but I always think it must have been fairer when Eve was walking about it.

To return, we had miscalculated a little, and the sun was well down before we dropped anchor off the Point, and heard the gun which told the good folks of Durban that the English mail was in. It was too late to think of getting over the bar that night, so we went comfortably to dinner, after seeing the mails carried off in the lifeboat.

When we came up again the moon was out, and shining so brightly over sea and shore that she almost paled the quick large flashes from the lighthouse. From the shore floated sweet spicy odours that always remind me of hymns and missionaries, and in the windows of the houses on the Berea sparkled a hundred lights. From a large brig lying near came the music of the sailors as they worked at getting the anchor up in order to be ready for the wind. Altogether it was a perfect night, such a night as you sometimes get in Southern Africa, and it threw a garment of peace over everybody as the moon threw a garment of silver over everything. Even the great bull-dog, belonging to a sporting passenger, seemed to yield to its gentle influences, and forgetting his yearning to come to close quarters with the baboon in a cage on the fo'c'sle, snored happily in the door of the cabin, dreaming no doubt that he had finished him, and happy in his dream.

We three – that is, Sir Henry Curtis, Captain Good, and myself – went and sat by the wheel, and were quiet for a while.

'Well, Mr. Quatermain,' said Sir Henry presently, 'have you been thinking about my proposals?'

'Ay,' echoed Captain Good, 'what do you think of them, Mr. Quatermain? I hope that you are going to give us the pleasure of your company so far as Solomon's Mines, or wherever the gentleman you knew as Neville may have got to.'

I rose and knocked out my pipe before I answered. I had not made up my mind, and wanted an additional moment to complete it. Before the burning tobacco had fallen into the sea it was completed; just that little extra second did the trick. It is often the way when you have been bothering a long time over a thing.

'Yes, gentlemen,' I said, sitting down again, 'I will go, and by your leave I will tell you why, and on what conditions. First for the terms which I ask.

'1. You are to pay all expenses, and any ivory or other valuables we may get is to be divided between Captain Good and myself.

'2. That you pay me £500 for my services on the trip before we start, I undertaking to serve you faithfully till you choose to abandon the enterprise, or till we succeed, or disaster overtakes us.

'3. That before we trek you execute a deed agreeing, in the event of my death or disablement, to pay my boy Harry, who is studying medicine over there in London, at Guy's Hospital, a sum of £200 a year for five years, by which time he ought to be able to earn a living for himself if he is worth his salt. That is all, I think, and I daresay you will say quite enough too.'

'No,' answered Sir Henry, 'I accept them gladly. I am bent upon this project, and would pay more than that for your help, considering the peculiar and exclusive knowledge which you possess.'

'Pity I did not ask it, then, but I won't go back on my word. And now that I have got my terms I will tell you my reasons for making up my mind to go. First of all, gentlemen, I have been observing you both for the last few days, and if you will not think me impertinent I may say that I like you, and I believe that we shall come up well to the yoke together. That is something, let me tell you, when one has a long journey like this before one.

'And now as to the journey itself, I tell you flatly, Sir Henry and Captain Good, that I do not think it probable we can come out of it alive, that is, if we attempt to cross the Suliman Mountains. What was the fate of the old Dom da Silvestra three hundred years ago? What was the fate of his descendant twenty years ago? What has been your brother's fate? I tell you frankly, gentlemen, that as their fates were so I believe ours will be.'

I paused to watch the effect of my words. Captain Good looked a little uncomfortable, but Sir Henry's face did not change. 'We must take our chance,' he said.

'You may perhaps wonder,' I went on, 'why, if I think this, I, who am, as I told you, a timid man, should undertake such a journey. It is for two reasons. First I am a fatalist, and believe that my time is appointed to come quite without reference to my own movements and will, and that if I am to go to Suliman's Mountains to be killed, I shall go there and shall be killed. God Almighty, no doubt, knows His mind about me, so I need not trouble on that point. Secondly, I am a poor man. For nearly forty years I have hunted and traded, but I have never made more than a living. Well, gentlemen, I don't know if you are aware that the average life of an elephant hunter from the time he takes to the trade is between four to five years. So you see I have lived through about seven generations of my class, and I should think that my time cannot be far off anyway. Now, if anything were to happen to me in the ordinary course of business, by the time my debts are paid there would be nothing left to support my son Harry whilst he was getting in the way of earning a living, whereas now he will be provided for for five years. There is the whole affair in a nutshell.'

'Mr. Quatermain,' said Sir Henry, who had been giving me his most serious attention, 'your motives for undertaking an enterprise which you believe can only end in disaster reflect a great deal of credit on you. Whether or not you are right, of course time and the event alone can show. But whether you are right or wrong, I may as well tell you at once that I am going through with it to the end, sweet or bitter. If we are to be knocked on the head, all I have to say is, that I hope we get a little shooting first, eh, Good?'

'Yes, yes,' put in the captain. 'We have all three of us been accustomed to face danger, and to hold our lives in our hands in various ways, so it is no good turning back now. And now I vote we go down to the saloon and take an observation just for luck, you know.' And we did – through the bottom of a tumbler.

Next day we went ashore, and I put up Sir Henry and Captain Good at the little shanty I have built on the Berea, and which I call my home. There are only three rooms and a kitchen in it, and it is constructed of green brick with a galvanized iron roof, but there is a good garden with the best loquot trees in it that I know, and some nice young mangoes, of which I hope great things. The curator of the botanical gardens gave them to me. It is looked after by an old hunter of mine named Jack, whose thigh was so badly broken by a buffalo cow in Sikukuni's country that he will never hunt again. But he can potter about and garden, being a Griqua by birth. You will never persuade a Zulu to take much interest in gardening. It is a peaceful art, and peaceful arts are not in his line.

Sir Henry and Good slept in a tent pitched in my little grove of orange trees at the end of the garden, for there was no room for them in the house, and what with the smell of the bloom, and the sight of the green and golden fruit – in Durban you will see all three on the tree together – I daresay it is a pleasant place enough, for we have few mosquitos here on the Berea, unless there happens to come an unusually heavy rain.

Well, to get on – for unless I do, Harry, you will be tired of my story before we ever fetch up at Suliman's Mountains – having once made up my mind to go I set about making the necessary preparations. First I secured the deed from Sir Henry, providing for you, my boy, in case of accidents. There was some difficulty about its legal execution, as Sir Henry was a stranger here and the property to be charged is over the water; but it was ultimately got over with the help of a lawyer, who charged £20 for the job – a price that I thought outrageous. Then I pocketed my cheque for £500.

Having paid this tribute to my bump of caution, I bought a wagon and a span of oxen on Sir Henry's behalf, and beauties they were. It was a twenty-two-foot wagon with iron axles, very strong, very light, and built throughout of stink wood; not quite a new one, having been to the diamond fields and back, but in my opinion, all the better for that, for I could see that the wood was well seasoned. If anything is going to give in a wagon, or if there is green wood in it, it will show out on the first trip. This particular vehicle was what we call a 'half-tented' wagon, that is to say, only covered in over the after twelve feet, leaving all the front part free for the necessaries we had to carry with us. In this after part were a hide 'cartle,' or bed, on which two people could sleep, also racks for rifles, and many other little conveniences. I gave £125 for it, and think that it was cheap at the price.

Then I bought a beautiful team of twenty salted Zulu oxen, which I had kept my eye on for a year or two. Sixteen oxen are the usual number for a team, but I took four extra to allow for casualties. These Zulu cattle are small and light, not more than half the size of the Africander oxen, which are generally used for transport purposes; but they will live where the Africanders would starve, and with a moderate load can make five miles a day better going, being quicker and not so liable to become footsore. What is more, this lot were thoroughly 'salted,' that is, they had worked all over South Africa, and so had become proof, comparatively speaking, against red water, which so frequently destroys whole teams of oxen when they get on to strange 'veldt' or grass country. As for 'lung sick,' which is a dreadful form of pneumonia, very prevalent in this country, they had all been inoculated against it. This is done by cutting a slit in the tail of an ox, and binding in a piece of the diseased lung of an animal which has died of the sickness. The result is that the ox sickens, takes the disease in a mild form, which causes its tail to drop off, as a rule about a foot from the root, and becomes proof against future attacks. It seems cruel to rob the animal of his tail, especially in a country where there are so many flies, but it is better to sacrifice the tail and keep the ox than to lose both tail and ox, for a tail without an ox is not much good, except to dust with. Still it does look odd to trek along behind twenty stumps, where there ought to be tails. It seems as though Nature had made a trifling mistake, and stuck the stern ornaments of a lot of prize bull-dogs on to the rumps of the oxen.

Next came the question of provisioning and medicines, one which required the most careful consideration, for what we had to do was to avoid lumbering the wagon, and yet to take everything absolutely necessary. Fortunately, it turned out that Good is a bit of a doctor, having at some period in his previous career managed to pass through a course of medical and surgical instruction, which he has more or less kept up. He is not, of course, qualified, but he knows more about it than many a man who can write M.D. after his name, as we found out afterwards, and he had a splendid travelling medicine chest and a set of instruments. Whilst we were at Durban he cut off a Kafir's big toe in a way which it was a pleasure to see. But he was quite nonplussed when the Kafir, who had sat stolidly watching the operation, asked him to put on another, saying that a 'white one' would do at a pinch.

There remained, when these questions were satisfactorily settled, two further important points for consideration, namely, that of arms and that of servants. As to the arms I cannot do better than put down a list of those which we finally decided on from among the ample store that Sir Henry had brought with him from England, and those which I owned. I copy it from my pocket-book, where I made the entry at the time.

'Three heavy breech-loading double-eight elephant guns, weighing about fifteen pounds each, to carry a charge of eleven drachms of black powder.' Two of these were by a well-known London firm, most excellent makers, but I do not know by whom mine, which is not so highly finished, was made. I have used it on several trips, and shot a good many elephants with it, and it has always proved a most superior weapon, thoroughly to be relied on.

'Three double-500 Expresses, constructed to stand a charge of six drachms,' sweet weapons, and admirable for medium-sized game, such as eland or sable antelope, or for men, especially in an open country and with the semi-hollow bullet.

'One double No. 12 central-fire Keeper's shotgun, full choke both barrels.' This gun proved of the greatest service to us afterwards in shooting game for the pot.

'Three Winchester repeating rifles (not carbines), spare guns.

'Three single-action Colt's revolvers, with the heavier, or American pattern of cartridge.'

This was our total armament, and doubtless the reader will observe that the weapons of each class were of the same make and calibre, so that the cartridges were interchangeable, a very important point. I make no apology for detailing it at length, for every experienced hunter will know how vital a proper supply of guns and ammunition is to the success of an expedition.

Now as to the men who were to go with us. After much consultation we decided that their number should be limited to five, namely, a driver, a leader, and three servants.

The driver and leader I found without much difficulty, two Zulus, named respectively Goza and Tom; but to get the servants proved a more difficult matter. It was necessary that they should be thoroughly trustworthy and brave men, as in a business of this sort our lives might depend upon their conduct. At last I secured two, one a Hottentot called Ventvögel or 'wind-bird,' and one a little Zulu named Khiva, who had the merit of speaking English perfectly. Ventvögel I had known before; he was one of the most perfect 'spoorers,' that is, game trackers, I ever had to do with, and tough as whipcord. He never seemed to tire. But he had one failing, so common with his race, drink. Put him within reach of a bottle of grog and you could not trust him. However, as we were going beyond the region of grog-shops this little weakness of his did not so much matter.

Having secured these two men I looked in vain for a third to suit my purpose, so we determined to start without one, trusting to luck to find a suitable man on our way up country. But, as it happened, on the evening before the day we had fixed for our departure the Zulu Khiva informed me that a Kafir was waiting to see me. Accordingly, when we had done dinner, for we were at table at the time, I told Khiva to bring him in. Presently a tall, handsome-looking man, somewhere about thirty years of age, and very light-coloured for a Zulu, entered, and lifting his knob-stick by way of salute, squatted himself down in the corner on his haunches, and sat silent. I did not take any notice of him for a while, for it is a great mistake to do so. If you rush into conversation at once a Zulu is apt to think you a person of little dignity or consideration. I observed, however, that he was a 'Keshla' or ringed man, that is, he wore on his head the black ring, made of a species of gum polished with fat and worked up in the hair, which is usually assumed by Zulus on attaining a certain age or dignity. Also it struck me that his face was familiar to me.

'Well,' I said at last, 'what is your name?'

'Umbopa,' answered the man in a slow, deep voice.

'I have seen your face before.'

'Yes; the Inkoosi, the chief, my father, saw my face at the place of the Little Hand' – that is, Isandhlwana – 'on the day before the battle.'

Then I remembered. I was one of Lord Chelmsford's guides in that unlucky Zulu War, and took part in the battle, which I had the good fortune to survive. I will say nothing about it here, indeed the subject is painful to me. On the day before it happened, however, I fell into conversation with this man, who held some small command among the native auxiliaries, and he had expressed to me his doubts of the safety of the camp. At the time I told him to hold his tongue, and leave such matters to wiser heads; but afterwards I thought of his words.

'I remember,' I said; 'what is it you want?'

'It is this, "Macumazahn."' That is my Kafir name, and means the man who gets up in the middle of the night, or, in vulgar English, he who keeps his eyes open. 'I hear that you go on a great expedition far into the North with the white chiefs from over the water. Is it a true word?'

'It is.'

'I hear that you go even to the Lukanga River, a moon's journey beyond the Manica country. Is this so also, Macumazahn?'

'Why do you ask whither we go? What is it to you?' I answered suspiciously, for the objects of our journey had been kept a dead secret.

'It is this, O white men, that if indeed you travel so far I would travel with you.'

There was a certain assumption of dignity in the man's mode of speech, and especially in his use of the words 'O white men,' instead of 'O Inkosis,' or chiefs, which struck me.

'You forget yourself a little,' I said. 'Your words run out unawares. That is not the way to speak. What is your name, and where is your kraal? Tell us, that we may know with whom we have to deal.'

35

'My name is Umbopa. I am of the Zulu people, yet not of them. The house of my tribe is in the far North; it was left behind when the Zulus came down here a "thousand years ago," long before Chaka reigned in Zululand. I have no kraal. I have wandered for many years. I came from the North as a child to Zululand. I was Cetewayo's man in the Nkomabakosi Regiment, serving there under the Captain, Umslopogaasi of the Axe, who taught my hands to fight. Afterwards I ran away from Zululand and came to Natal because I wanted to see the white man's ways. Then I fought against Cetewayo in the war. Since then I have been working in Natal. Now I am tired, and would go North again. Here is not my place. I want no money, but I am a brave man, and am worth my place and meat. I have spoken.'

I was rather puzzled by this man and his way of speech. It was evident to me from his manner that in the main he was telling the truth, but somehow he was different from the ordinary run of Zulus, and I rather mistrusted his offer to come without pay. Being in a difficulty, I translated his words to Sir Henry and Good, and asked them their opinion.

Sir Henry told me to ask him to stand up. Umbopa did so, at the same time slipping off the long military great coat which he wore, and revealing himself naked except for the moocha round his centre and a necklace of lions' claws. Certainly he was a magnificent-looking man; I never saw a finer native. Standing about six foot three high he was broad in proportion, and very shapely. In that light, too, his skin looked scarcely more than dark, except here and there where deep black scars marked old assegai wounds. Sir Henry walked up to him and looked into his proud, handsome face.

'They make a good pair, don't they?' said Good; 'one as big as the other.'

'I like your looks, Mr. Umbopa, and I will take you as my servant,' said Sir Henry in English.

Umbopa evidently understood him, for he answered in Zulu, 'It is well;' and then added, with a glance at the white man's great stature and breadth, 'We are men, thou and I.'

Chapter IV

AN ELEPHANT HUNT

Now I do not propose to narrate at full length all the incidents of our long travel up to Sitanda's Kraal, near the junction of the Lukanga and Kalukwe Rivers, a journey of more than a thousand miles from Durban, the last three hundred or so of which we had to make on foot, owing to the frequent presence of the dreadful 'tsetse' fly, whose bite is fatal to all animals except donkeys and men.

We left Durban at the end of January, and it was in the second week of May that we camped near Sitanda's Kraal. Our adventures on the way were many and various, but as they were of the sort which befall every African hunter – with one exception to be presently detailed – I shall not set them down here, lest I should render this history too wearisome.

At Inyati, the outlying trading station in the Matabele country, of which Lobengula (a great scoundrel) is king, with many regrets we parted from our comfortable wagon. Only twelve oxen remained to us out of the beautiful span of twenty which I had bought at Durban. One we lost from the bite of a cobra, three had perished from 'poverty' and the want of water, one strayed, and the other three died from eating the poisonous herb called 'tulip.' Five more sickened from this cause, but we managed to cure them with doses of an infusion made by boiling down the tulip leaves. If administered in time this is a very effective antidote.

The wagon and oxen we left in the immediate charge of Goza and Tom, our driver and leader, both of them trustworthy boys, requesting a worthy Scotch missionary who lived in this distant place to keep an eye to it. Then, accompanied by Umbopa, Khiva, Ventvögel, and half a dozen bearers whom we hired on the spot, we started off on foot upon our wild quest. I remember we were all a little silent on the occasion of this departure, and I think that each of us was wondering if we should ever see our wagon again; for my part I never expected to do so. For a while we tramped on in silence, till Umbopa, who was marching in front, broke into a Zulu chant about how some brave men, tired of life and the tameness of things, started off into a great wilderness to find new things, or die, and how, lo and behold! when they had travelled far into the wilderness, they found that it was not a wilderness at all, but a beautiful place full of young wives and fat cattle, of game to hunt and enemies to kill.

Then we all laughed and took it for a good omen. Umbopa was a cheerful savage, in a dignified sort of way, when he was not suffering from one of his fits of brooding, and he had a wonderful knack of keeping up our spirits. We all grew very fond of him.

And now for the one adventure to which I am going to treat myself, for I do dearly love a hunting yarn.

About a fortnight's march from Inyati we came across a peculiarly beautiful bit of well-watered woodland country. The kloofs in the hills were covered with dense bush, 'idoro' bush as the natives call it, and in some places, with the 'wachteen-beche,' or 'wait-a-little thorn,' and there were great quantities of the lovely 'machabell' tree, laden with refreshing yellow fruit having enormous stones. This tree is the elephant's favourite food, and there were not wanting signs that the great brutes had been about, for not only was their spoor frequent, but in many places the trees were broken down and even uprooted. The elephant is a destructive feeder.

One evening, after a long day's march, we came to a spot of great loveliness. At the foot of a bush-clad hill lay a dry river-bed, in which, however, were to be found pools of crystal water all trodden round with the hoof-prints of game. Facing this hill was a park-like plain, where grew clumps of flat-topped mimosa, varied with occasional glossy-leaved machabells, and all round stretched the sea of pathless, silent bush.

As we emerged into this river-bed path suddenly we started a troop of tall giraffes, who galloped, or rather sailed off, in their strange gait, their tails screwed up over their backs, and their hoofs rattling like castanets. They were about three hundred yards from us, and therefore practically out of shot, but Good, who was walking ahead and had an express loaded with solid ball in his hand, could not resist temptation. Lifting his gun, he let drive at the last, a young cow. By some extraordinary chance the ball struck it full on the back of the neck, shattering the spinal column, and that giraffe went rolling head over heels just like a rabbit. I never saw a more curious thing.

'Curse it!' said Good – for I am sorry to say he had a habit of using strong language when excited – contracted, no doubt, in the course of his nautical career; 'curse it! I've killed him.'

'*Ou*, Bougwan,' ejaculated the Kafirs; '*ou! ou!*'

They called Good 'Bougwan,' or Glass Eye, because of his eye-glass.

'Oh, "Bougwan"!' re-echoed Sir Henry and I, and from that day Good's reputation as a marvellous shot was established, at any rate among the Kafirs. Really he was a bad one, but whenever he missed we overlooked it for the sake of that giraffe.

Having set some of the 'boys' to cut off the best of the giraffe meat, we went to work to build a 'scherm' near one of the pools and about a hundred yards to the right of it. This is done by cutting a quantity of thorn bushes and piling them in the shape of a circular hedge. Then the space enclosed is smoothed, and dry tambouki grass, if obtainable, is made into a bed in the centre, and a fire or fires lighted.

By the time the 'scherm' was finished the moon peeped up, and our dinner of giraffe steaks and roasted marrow bones was ready. How we enjoyed those marrow-bones, though it was rather a job to crack them! I know of no greater luxury than giraffe marrow, unless it is elephant's heart, and we had that on the morrow. We ate our simple meal by the light of the moon, pausing at times to thank Good for his wonderful shot; then we began to smoke and yarn and a curious picture we must have made squatting there round the fire. I, with my short grizzled hair sticking up straight, and Sir Henry with his yellow locks, which were getting rather long, were rather a contrast, especially as I am thin, and short and dark, weighing only nine stone and a half, and Sir Henry is tall, and broad, and fair, and weighs fifteen. But perhaps the most curious-looking of the three, taking all the circumstances of the case into consideration, was Captain John Good, R.N. There he sat upon a leather bag, looking just as though he had come in from a comfortable day's shooting in a civilized country, absolutely clean, tidy, and well dressed. He wore a shooting suit of brown tweed, with a hat to match, and neat gaiters. As usual, he was beautifully shaved, his eye-glass and his false teeth appeared to be in perfect order, and altogether the neatest man I ever had to do with in the wilderness. He even sported a collar, of which he had a supply, made of white guttapercha.

'You see, they weigh so little,' he said to me innocently, when I expressed my astonishment at the fact; 'and I always like to turn out like a gentleman.' Ah! if he could have foreseen the future and the raiment prepared for him.

Well, there we three sat yarning away in the beautiful moonlight, and watching the Kafirs a few yards off sucking their intoxicating 'daccha' from a pipe of which the mouthpiece was made of the horn of an eland, till one by one they rolled themselves up in their blankets and went to sleep by the fire, that is, all except Umbopa, who sat a little apart, his chin resting on his hand, and thinking deeply. I noticed that he never mixed much with the other Kafirs.

Presently from the depths of the bush behind us, came a loud '*woof, woof!*' "That's a lion," said I, and we started up to listen. Hardly had we done so, when from the pool, about a hundred yards off, we heard the strident trumpeting of an elephant. '*Unkungunklovo! Indlovu!*" "Elephant! Elephant!" whispered the Kafirs; and a few minutes afterwards we saw a succession of vast shadowy forms moving slowly from the direction of the water towards the bush.

Up jumped Good, burning for slaughter, and thinking, perhaps, that it was as easy to kill elephant as he had found it to shoot a giraffe, but I caught him by the arm and pulled him down.

'It's no good,' I whispered, 'let them go.'

'It seems that we are in a paradise of game. I vote we stop here a day or two, and have a go at them,' said Sir Henry presently.

I was rather surprised, for hitherto Sir Henry had always been for pushing on as fast as possible, more especially since we ascertained at Inyati that about two years ago an Englishman of the name of Neville *had* sold his wagon there, and gone on up country. But I suppose his hunter instincts got the better of him for a while.

Good jumped at the idea, for he was longing to have a shot at those elephants; and so, to speak the truth, did I, for it went against my conscience to let such a herd as that escape without a pull at them.

'All right, my hearties,' said I. 'I think we want a little recreation. And now let's turn in, for we ought to be off by dawn, and then perhaps we may catch them feeding before they move on.'

The others agreed, and we proceeded to make our preparations. Good took off his clothes, shook them, put his eye-glass and his false teeth into his trousers pocket, and folding each article neatly, placed it out of the dew under a corner of his mackintosh sheet. Sir Henry and I contented ourselves with rougher arrangements, and soon were curled up in our blankets, and dropping off into the dreamless sleep that rewards the traveller.

Going, going, go – What was that?

Suddenly from the direction of the water came sounds of violent scuffing, and next instant there broke upon our ears a succession of the most awful roars. There was no mistaking their origin; only a lion could make such a noise as that. We all jumped up and looked towards the water, in the direction of which we saw a confused mass, yellow and black in colour, staggering and struggling towards us. We seized our rifles, and slipping on our veldtschoons, that is shoes made of untanned hide, ran out of the scherm towards it. By this time the mass had fallen, and was rolling over and over on the ground, and when we reached the spot it struggled no longer, but lay quite still.

Now we saw what it was. On the grass there lay a sable antelope bull – the most beautiful of all the African antelopes – quite dead, and transfixed by its great curved horns was a magnificent black-maned lion, also dead. Evidently what had happened was this. The sable antelope had come down to drink at the pool where the lion – no doubt the same which we had heard – was lying in wait. While the antelope drank, the lion had sprung upon him, to be received upon the sharp curved horns and transfixed. Once before I saw a similar thing happen. Then the lion, unable to free himself, had torn and bitten at the back and neck of the bull, which, maddened with fear and pain, had rushed on until it dropped dead.

As soon as we had examined the dead beasts sufficiently we called the Kafirs, and between us managed to drag their carcasses up to the scherm. After that we went in and lay down, to wake no more till dawn.

With the first light we were up and making ready for the fray. We took with us the three eight-bore rifles, a good supply of ammunition, and our large water-bottles, filled with weak cold tea, which I have always found the best stuff to shoot on. After swallowing a little breakfast we started, Umbopa, Khiva, and Ventvögel accompanying us. The other Kafirs we left with instructions to skin the lion and the sable antelope and to cut up the latter.

We had no difficulty in finding the broad elephant trail, which Ventvögel, after examination, pronounced to have been made by between twenty and thirty elephants, most of them full-grown bulls. But the herd had moved on some way during the night, and it was nine o'clock, and already very hot, before, from the broken trees, bruised leaves and bark, and smoking droppings, we knew that we could not be far off them.

Presently we caught sight of the herd, which numbered, as Ventvögel had said, between twenty and thirty, standing in a hollow, having finished their morning meal, and flapping their great ears. It was a splendid sight, for they were only about two hundred yards from us. Taking a handful of dry grass, I threw it into the air to see how the wind was; for if once they winded us I knew they would be off before we could get a shot. Finding that, if anything, it blew from the elephants to us, we crept on stealthily, and thanks to the cover managed to get within forty yards or so of the great brutes. Just in front of us and broadside on, stood three splendid bulls, one of them with enormous tusks. I whispered to the others that I would take the middle one; Sir Henry covering the elephant to the left, and Good the bull with the big tusks.

'Now,' I whispered.

Boom! boom! boom! went the three heavy rifles, and down came Sir Henry's elephant, dead as a hammer, shot right through the heart. Mine fell on to its knees, and I thought that he was going to die, but in another moment he was up and off, tearing along straight past me. As he went I gave him the second barrel in the ribs, and this brought him down in good earnest. Hastily slipping in two fresh cartridges I ran close up to him and a ball through the brain put an end to the poor brute's struggles. Then I turned to see how Good had fared with the big bull, which I had heard screaming with rage and pain as I gave mine its quietus. On reaching the captain I found him in a great state of excitement. It appeared that on receiving the bullet the bull had turned and come straight for his assailant, who had barely time to get out of his way, and then charged blindly on past him, in the direction of our encampment. Meanwhile the herd had crashed off in wild alarm in the other direction.

For a while we doubted whether to go after the wounded bull or to follow the herd, and finally deciding for the latter alternative, departed, thinking that we had seen the last of those big tusks. I have often wished since that we had. It was easy work to follow the elephants, for they had left a trail like a carriage road behind them, crushing down the thick bush in their furious flight as though it were tambouki grass.

But to come up with them was another matter, and we had struggled on under a broiling sun for over two hours before we found them. With the exception of one bull, they were standing together, and I could see, from their unquiet way and the manner in which they kept lifting their trunks to test the air, that they were on the look-out for mischief. The solitary bull stood fifty yards or so to this side of the herd, over which he was evidently keeping sentry, and about sixty yards from us. Thinking that he would see or wind us, and that it would probably start them off again if we tried to get nearer, especially as the ground was rather open, we all aimed at this bull, and at my whispered word, we fired. The three shots took effect, and down he went, dead. Again the herd started, but unfortunately for them about a hundred yards further on was a nullah, or dried water track, with steep banks, a place very much resembling the one where the Prince Imperial was killed in Zululand. Into this the elephants plunged, and when we reached the edge we found them struggling in wild confusion to get up the other bank, filling the air with their screams, and trumpeting as they pushed one another aside in their selfish panic, just like so many human beings. Now was our opportunity, and firing away as quickly as we could load, we killed five of the poor beasts, and no doubt should have bagged the whole herd, had they not suddenly given up their attempts to climb the bank and rushed headlong down the nullah. We were too tired to follow them, and perhaps also a little sick of slaughter, eight elephants being a pretty good bag for one day.

So after we were rested a little, and the Kafirs had cut out the hearts of two of the dead elephants for supper, we started homewards, very well pleased with ourselves, having made up our minds to send the bearers on the morrow to chop out the tusks.

Shortly after we re-passed the spot where Good had wounded the patriarchal bull we came across a herd of eland, but did not shoot at them, as we had plenty of meat. They trotted past us, and then stopped behind a little patch of bush about a hundred yards away, wheeling round to look at us. As Good was anxious to get a near view of them, never having seen an eland close, he handed his rifle to Umbopa, and, followed by Khiva, strolled up to the patch of bush. We sat down and waited for him, not sorry of the excuse for a little rest.

The sun was just going down in its reddest glory, and Sir Henry and I were admiring the lovely scene, when suddenly we heard an elephant scream, and saw its huge and rushing form with uplifted trunk and tail silhouetted against the great red globe of the sun. Next second we saw something else, and that was Good and Khiva tearing back towards us with the wounded bull – for it was he – charging after them. For a moment we did not dare to fire – though at that distance it would have been of little use if we had done so – for fear of hitting one of them, and the next a dreadful thing happened – Good fell a victim to his passion for civilized dress. Had he consented to discard his trousers and gaiters like the rest of us, and to hunt in a flannel shirt and a pair of veldtschoons, it would have been all right. But as it was, his trousers cumbered him in that desperate race, and presently, when he was about sixty yards from us, his boot, polished by the dry grass, slipped, and down he went on his face right in front of the elephant.

We gave a gasp, for we knew that he must die, and ran as hard as we could towards him. In three seconds it had ended, but not as we thought. Khiva, the Zulu boy, saw his master fall, and brave lad as he was, had turned and flung his assegai straight into the elephant's face. It stuck in his trunk.

With a scream of pain, the brute seized the poor Zulu, hurled him to the earth, and placing one huge foot on to his body about the middle, twined its trunk round his upper part and *tore him in two*.

We rushed up mad with horror, and fired again and again, till presently the elephant fell upon the fragments of the Zulu.

As for Good, he rose and wrung his hands over the brave man who had given his life to save him, and, though I am an old hand, I felt a lump grow in my throat. Umbopa stood contemplating the huge dead elephant and the mangled remains of poor Khiva.

'Ah, well,' he said presently, 'he is dead, but he died like a man!'

Chapter V

OUR MARCH INTO THE DESERT

We had killed nine elephants, and it took us two days to cut out the tusks, and having brought them into camp, to bury them carefully in the sand under a large tree, which made a conspicuous mark for miles round. It was a wonderfully fine lot of ivory. I never saw a better, averaging as it did between forty and fifty pounds a tusk. The tusks of the great bull that killed poor Khiva scaled one hundred and seventy pounds the pair, so nearly as we could judge.

As for Khiva himself, we buried what remained of him in an ant-bear hole, together with an assegai to protect himself with on his journey to a better world. On the third day we marched again, hoping that we might live to return to dig up our buried ivory, and in due course, after a long and wearisome tramp, and many adventures which I have not space to detail, we reached Sitanda's Kraal, near the Lukanga River, the real starting-point of our expedition. Very well do I recollect our arrival at that place. To the right was a scattered native settlement with a few stone cattle kraals and some cultivated lands down by the water, where these savages grew their scanty supply of grain, and beyond it stretched great tracts of waving 'veldt' covered with tall grass, over which herds of the smaller game were wandering. To the left lay the vast desert. This spot appears to be the outpost of the fertile country, and it would be difficult to say to what natural causes such an abrupt change in the character of the soil is due. But so it is.

Just below our encampment flowed a little stream, on the farther side of which is a stony slope, the same down which, twenty years before, I had seen poor Silvestre creeping back after his attempt to reach Solomon's Mines, and beyond that slope begins the waterless desert, covered with a species of karoo scrub.

It was evening when we pitched our camp, and the great ball of the sun was sinking into the desert, sending glorious rays of many-coloured light flying over all its vast expanse. Leaving Good to superintend the arrangement of our little camp, I took Sir Henry with me, and walking to the top of the slope opposite, we gazed across the desert. The air was very clear, and far, far away I could distinguish the faint blue outlines here and there capped with white of the Suliman Berg.

'There,' I said, 'there is the wall round Solomon's Mines, but God knows if we shall ever climb it.'

'My brother should be there, and if he is, I shall reach him somehow,' said Sir Henry, in that tone of quiet confidence which marked the man.

'I hope so,' I answered, and turned to go back to the camp, when I saw that we were not alone. Behind us, also gazing earnestly towards the far-off mountains, stood the great Kafir Umbopa.

The Zulu spoke when he saw that I had observed him, addressing Sir Henry, to whom he had attached himself.

'Is it to that land that thou wouldst journey, Incubu?' (a native word meaning, I believe, an elephant, and the name given to Sir Henry by the Kafirs) he said, pointing towards the mountains with his broad assegai.

I asked him sharply what he meant by addressing his master in that familiar way. It is very well for natives to have a name for one among themselves, but it is not decent that they should call a white man by their heathenish appellations to his face. The Zulu laughed a quiet little laugh which angered me.

'How dost thou know that I am not the equal of the Inkosi whom I serve!' he said. 'He is of a royal house, no doubt; one can see it in his size and by his mien; so, mayhap, am I. At least I am as great a man. Be my mouth, O Macumazahn, and say my words to the Inkoos Incubu, my master, for I would speak to him and to thee.'

I was angry with the man, for I am not accustomed to be talked to in that way by Kafirs, but somehow he impressed me, and besides I was curious to know what he had to say. So I translated, expressing my opinion at the same time that he was an impudent fellow, and that his swagger was outrageous.

'Yes, Umbopa,' answered Sir Henry, 'I would journey there.'

'The desert is wide and there is no water in it, the mountains are high and covered with snow, and man cannot say what lies beyond them behind the place where the sun sets; how shalt thou come thither, Incubu, and wherefore dost thou go?'

I translated again.

'Tell him,' answered Sir Henry, 'that I go because I believe that a man of my blood, my brother, has gone there before me, and I journey to seek him.'

'That is so, Incubu; a Hottentot I met on the road told me that a white man went out into the desert two years ago towards those mountains with one servant, a hunter. They never came back.'

'How do you know it was my brother?' asked Sir Henry.

'Nay, I know not. But the Hottentot, when I asked what the white man was like, said that he had thy eyes and a black beard. He said, too, that the name of the hunter with him was Jim; that he was a Bechuana hunter and wore clothes.'

'There is no doubt about it,' said I, 'I knew Jim well.'

Sir Henry nodded. 'I was sure of it,' he said. 'If George set his mind upon a thing he generally did it. It was always so from his boyhood. If he meant to cross the Suliman Berg he has crossed it, unless some accident overtook him, and we must look for him on the other side.'

Umbopa understood English, though he rarely spoke it.

'It is a far journey, Incubu,' he put in, and I translated his remark.

'Yes,' answered Sir Henry, 'it is far. But there is no journey upon this earth that a man may not make if he sets his heart to it. There is nothing, Umbopa, that he cannot do, there are no mountains he may not climb, there are no deserts he cannot cross, save a mountain and a desert of which you are spared the knowledge, if love leads him and he holds his life in his hand counting it as nothing, ready to keep it or lose it as Heaven may order.'

I translated.

'Great words, my father,' answered the Zulu – I always called him a Zulu, though he was not really one – 'great swelling words fit to fill the mouth of a man. Thou art right, my father Incubu. Listen! what is life? It is a feather, it is the seed of the grass, blown hither and thither, sometimes multiplying itself and dying in the act, sometimes carried away into the heavens. But if the seed be good and heavy it may perchance travel a little way on the road it wills. It is well to try and journey one's road and to fight with the air. Man must die. At the worst he can but die a little sooner. I will go with thee across the desert and over the mountains, unless perchance I fall to the ground on the way, my father.'

He paused a while, and then went on with one of those strange bursts of rhetorical eloquence that Zulus sometimes indulge in, which to my mind, full though they are of vain repetitions, show that the race is by no means devoid of poetic instinct and of intellectual power.

'What is life? Tell me, O white men, who are wise, who know the secrets of the world, and the world of stars, and the world that lies above and around the stars; who flash your words from afar without a voice; tell me, white men, the secret of our life – whither it goes and whence it comes!

'You cannot answer me; you know not. Listen, I will answer. Out of the dark we came, into the dark we go. Like a storm-driven bird at night we fly out of the Nowhere; for a moment our wings are seen in the light of the fire, and, lo! we are gone again into the Nowhere. Life is nothing. Life is all. It is the Hand with which we hold off Death. It is the glow-worm that shines in the night-time and is black in the morning; it is the white breath of the oxen in winter; it is the little shadow that runs across the grass and loses itself at sunset.'

'You are a strange man,' said Sir Henry, when he had ceased.

Umbopa laughed. 'It seems to me that we are much alike, Incubu. Perhaps I seek a brother over the mountains.'

I looked at him suspiciously. 'What dost thou mean?' I asked; 'what dost thou know of those mountains?'

'A little; a very little. There is a strange land yonder, a land of witchcraft and beautiful things; a land of brave people, and of trees, and streams, and snow peaks, and a great white road. I have heard of it. But what is the good of talking? It grows dark. Those who live to see will see.'

Again I looked at him doubtfully. The man knew too much.

'You not need fear me, Macumazahn,' he said, interpreting my look. 'I dig no holes for you to fall in. I make no plots. If ever we cross those mountains behind the sun I will tell what I know. But Death sits upon them. Be wise and turn back. Go and hunt elephants, my masters. I have spoken.'

And without another word he lifted his spear in salutation, and returned towards the camp, where shortly afterwards we found him cleaning a gun like any other Kafir.

'That is an odd man,' said Sir Henry.

'Yes,' answered I, 'too odd by half. I don't like his little ways. He knows something, and will not speak out. But I suppose it is no use quarrelling with him. We are in for a curious trip, and a mysterious Zulu won't make much difference one way or another.'

Next day we made our arrangements for starting. Of course it was impossible to drag our heavy elephant rifles and other kit with us across the desert, so dismissing our bearers we made an arrangement with an old native who had a kraal close by to take care of them till we returned. It went to my heart to leave such things as those sweet tools to the tender mercies of an old thief of a savage whose greedy eyes I could see gloating over them. But I took some precautions.

First of all I loaded all the rifles, placing them at full cock, and informed him that if he touched them they would go off. He tried the experiment instantly with my eight-bore, and it did go off, and blew a hole right through one of his oxen, which was just then being driven up to the kraal, to say nothing of knocking him head over heels with the recoil. He got up considerably startled, and not at all pleased at the loss of the ox, which he had the impudence to ask me to pay for, and nothing would induce him to touch the guns again.

'Put the live devils out of the way up there in the thatch,' he said, 'or they will kill us all.'

Then I told him that, when we came back, if one of those things was missing I would kill him and all his people by witchcraft; and if we died and he tried to steal the rifles I would come and haunt him and turn his cattle mad and his milk sour till life was a weariness, and would make the devils in the guns come out and talk to him in a way he did not like, and generally gave him a good idea of judgment to come. After that he swore he would look after them as though they were his father's spirit. He was a very superstitious old Kafir and a great villain.

Having thus disposed of our superfluous gear we arranged the kit we five – Sir Henry, Good, myself, Umbopa, and the Hottentot Ventvögel – were to take with us on our journey. It was small enough, but do what we would we could not get its weight down under about forty pounds a man. This is what it consisted of: –

The three express rifles and two hundred rounds of ammunition.

The two Winchester repeating rifles (for Umbopa and Ventvögel), with two hundred rounds of cartridge.

Three 'Colt' revolvers and sixty rounds of cartridge.

Five Cochrane's water-bottles, each holding four pints.

Five blankets.

Twenty-five pounds' weight of biltong – *i.e.* sun-dried game flesh.

Ten pounds' weight of best mixed beads for gifts.

A selection of medicine, including an ounce of quinine, and one or two small surgical instruments.

Our knives, a few sundries, such as a compass, matches, a pocket filter, tobacco, a trowel, a bottle of brandy, and the clothes we stood in.

This was our total equipment, a small one indeed for such a venture, but we dared not attempt to carry more. Indeed, that load was a heavy one per man with which to travel across the burning desert, for in such places every additional ounce tells. But try as we would we could not see our way to reducing it. There was nothing taken but what was absolutely necessary.

With great difficulty, and by the promise of a present of a good hunting-knife each, I succeeded in persuading three wretched natives from the village to come with us for the first stage, twenty miles, and to carry a large gourd holding a gallon of water apiece. My object was to enable us to refill our water bottles after the first night's march, for we determined to start in the cool of the evening. I gave out to these natives that we were going to shoot ostriches, with which the desert abounded. They jabbered and shrugged their shoulders, saying that we were mad and should perish of thirst, which I must say seemed probable; but being desirous of obtaining the knives, which were almost unknown treasures up there, they consented to come, having probably reflected that, after all, our subsequent extinction would be no affair of theirs.

All next day we rested and slept, and at sunset ate a hearty meal of fresh beef washed down with tea, the last, as Good sadly remarked, we were likely to drink for many a long day. Then, having made our final preparations, we lay down and waited for the moon to rise. At last about nine o'clock up she came in all her glory, flooding the wild country with light, and throwing a silver sheen on the expanse of rolling desert before us, which looked as solemn and quiet and as alien to man as the star-studded firmament above. We rose up, and in a few minutes were ready, and yet we hesitated a little, as human nature is prone to hesitate on the threshold of an irrevocable step. We three white men stood by ourselves. Umbopa, assegai in hand and a rifle across his shoulders, looked out fixedly across the desert a few paces ahead of us; while the hired natives, with the gourds of water, and Ventvögel, were gathered in a little knot behind.

'Gentlemen,' said Sir Henry presently, in his deep voice, 'we are going on about as strange a journey as men can make in this world. It is very doubtful if we can succeed in it. But we are three men who will stand together for good or for evil to the last. And now before we start let us for a moment pray to the Power who shapes the destinies of men, and who ages since has marked out our paths, that it may please Him to direct our steps in accordance with His will.'

Taking off his hat, for the space of a minute or so, he covered his face with his hands, and Good and I did likewise.

I do not say that I am a first-rate praying man, few hunters are, and as for Sir Henry I never heard him speak like that before, and only once since, though deep down in his heart I believe that he is very religious. Good too is pious, though apt to swear. Anyhow I do not remember, excepting on one single occasion, ever putting in a better prayer in my life than I did during that minute, and somehow I felt the happier for it. Our future was so completely unknown, and I think the unknown and the awful always bring a man nearer to his Maker.

'And now,' said Sir Henry, '*trek!*'

So we started.

We had nothing to guide ourselves by except the distant mountains and old José da Silvestra's chart, which, considering that it was drawn by a dying and half-distraught man on a fragment of linen three centuries ago, was not a very satisfactory sort of thing to work with. Still, such as it was, our sole hope of success depended upon it. If we failed in finding that pool of bad water which the old Dom marked as being situated in the middle of the desert, about sixty miles from our starting-point, and as far from the mountains, in all probability we must perish miserably of thirst. And to my mind the chances of our finding it in that great sea of sand and karoo scrub seemed almost infinitesimal. Even supposing that da Silvestra had marked the pool right, what was there to prevent its having been dried up by the sun generations ago, or trampled in by game, or filled with the drifting sand?

On we tramped silently as shades through the night and in the heavy sand. The karoo bushes caught our feet and retarded us, and the sand worked into our veldtschoons and Good's shooting boots, so that every few miles we had to stop and empty them; but still the night kept fairly cool, though the atmosphere was thick and heavy, giving a sort of creamy feel to the air, and we made fair progress. It was very silent and lonely there in the desert, oppressively so indeed. Good felt this, and once began to whistle 'The Girl I left behind me,' but the notes sounded lugubrious in that vast place, and he gave it up.

Shortly afterwards a little incident occurred which, though it startled us at the time, gave rise to a laugh. Good was leading, as the holder of the compass, which, being a sailor, of course he understood thoroughly, and we were toiling along in single file behind him, when suddenly we heard the sound of an exclamation, and he vanished. Next second there arose all around us a most extraordinary hubbub, snorts, groans, and wild sounds of rushing feet. In the faint light, too, we could descry dim galloping forms half hidden by wreaths of sand. The natives threw down their loads and prepared to bolt, but remembering that there was nowhere to run to, they cast themselves upon the ground and howled out that it was the devil. As for Sir Henry and myself we stood amazed; nor was our amazement lessened when we perceived the form of Good careering off in the direction of the mountains, apparently mounted on the back of a horse and halloaing wildly. In another second he threw up his arms, and we heard him come to the earth with a thud.

Then I saw what had happened; we had stumbled upon a herd of sleeping quagga, on to the back of one of which Good actually had fallen, and the brute naturally enough got up and made off with him. Calling out to the others that it was all right, I ran towards Good, much afraid lest he should be hurt, but to my great relief I found him sitting in the sand, his eye-glass still fixed firmly in his eye, rather shaken and very much frightened, but not in any way injured.

After this we travelled on without any further misadventure till about one o'clock, when we called a halt, and having drunk a little water, not much, for water was precious, and rested for half an hour, we started again.

On, on we went, till at last the east began to blush like the cheek of a girl. Then there came faint rays of primrose light, that changed presently to golden bars, through which the dawn glided out across the desert. The stars grew pale and paler still till at last they vanished; the golden moon waxed wan, and her mountain ridges stood out against her sickly face like the bones on the cheek of a dying man. Then came spear upon spear of light flashing far away across the boundless wilderness, piercing and firing the veils of mist, till the desert was draped in a tremulous golden glow, and it was day.

Still we did not halt, though by this time we should have been glad enough to do so, for we knew that when once the sun was fully up it would be almost impossible for us to travel. At length, about an hour later, we spied a little pile of boulders rising out of the plain, and to this we dragged ourselves. As luck would have it, here we found an overhanging slab of rock carpeted beneath with smooth sand, which afforded a most grateful shelter from the heat. Underneath this we crept, and each of us having drunk some water and eaten a bit of biltong, we lay down and soon were sound asleep.

It was three o'clock in the afternoon before we woke, to find our bearers preparing to return. They had seen enough of the desert already, and no number of knives would have tempted them to come a step farther. So we took a hearty drink, and having emptied our water-bottles, filled them up again from the gourds that they had brought with them, and then watched them depart on their twenty miles' tramp home.

At half-past four we also started. It was lonely and desolate work, for, with the exception of a few ostriches, there was not a single living creature to be seen on all the vast expanse of sandy plain. Evidently it was too dry for game, and with the exception of a deadly-looking cobra or two, we saw no reptiles. One insect, however, we found abundant, and that was the common or house fly. There they came, 'not as single spies, but in battalions,' as I think the Old Testament* says somewhere. He is an extraordinary animal is the house fly. Go where you will you find him, and so it must have been always. I have seen him enclosed in amber, which is, I was told, quite half a million years old, looking exactly like his descendant of to-day, and I have little doubt but that when the last man lies dying on the earth he will be buzzing round – if this event should happen to occur in summer – watching for an opportunity to settle on his nose.

At sunset we halted, waiting for the moon to rise. At last she came up, beautiful and serene as ever, and, with one halt about two o'clock in the morning, we trudged on wearily through the night, till at last the welcome sun put a period to our labours. We drank a little and flung ourselves down on the sand, thoroughly tired out, and soon were all asleep. There was no need to set a watch, for we had nothing to fear from anybody or anything in that vast untenanted plain. Our only enemies were heat, thirst, and flies, but far rather would I have faced any danger from man and beast than that awful trinity. This time we were not so lucky as to find a sheltering rock to guard us from the glare of the sun, with the result that about seven o'clock we woke up experiencing the exact sensations one would attribute to a beef-steak on a gridiron. We were literally being baked through and through. The burning sun seemed to be sucking our very blood out of us. We sat up and gasped.

* Readers must beware of accepting Mr. Quatermain's references as accurate, as, it has been found, some are prone to do. Although his reading evidently was limited, the impression produced by it upon his mind was mixed. Thus to him the Old Testament and Shakespeare were interchangeable authorities. – *Editor.*

'Phew,' said I, grabbing at the halo of flies, which buzzed cheerfully round my head. The heat did not affect *them*.

'My word!' said Sir Henry.

'It *is* hot!' echoed Good.

It was hot indeed, and there was not a bit of shelter to be found. Look where we would there was no rock or tree, nothing but an unending glare, rendered dazzling by the heated air that danced over the surface of the desert as it dances over a red-hot stove.

'What is to be done?' asked Sir Henry, 'we can't stand this for long.'

We looked at each other blankly.

'I have it,' said Good, 'we must dig a hole, get in it, and cover ourselves with the karoo bushes.'

It did not seem a very promising suggestion, but at least it was better than nothing, so we set to work, and, with the trowel we had brought with us and the help of our hands, in about an hour we succeeded in delving out a patch of ground some ten feet long by twelve wide to the depth of two feet. Then we cut a quantity of low scrub with our hunting-knives, and creeping into the hole, pulled it over us all, with the exception of Ventvögel, on whom, being a Hottentot, the heat had no particular effect. This gave us some slight shelter from the burning rays of the sun, but the atmosphere in that amateur grave can be better imagined than described. The Black Hole of Calcutta must have been a fool to it; indeed, to this moment I do not know how we lived through the day. There we lay panting, and every now and again moistening our lips from our scanty supply of water. Had we followed our inclination we should have finished all we possessed in the first two hours, but we were forced to exercise the most rigid care, for if our water failed us we knew that very soon we must perish miserably.

But everything has an end, if only you live long enough to see it, and somehow that miserable day wore on towards evening. About three o'clock in the afternoon we determined that we could bear it no longer. It would be better to die walking than to be killed slowly by heat and thirst in this dreadful hole. So taking each of us a little drink from our fast diminishing supply of water, now warmed to about the same temperature as a man's blood, we staggered forward.

We had then covered some fifty miles of wilderness. If the reader will refer to the rough copy and translation of old da Silvestra's map, he will see that the desert is marked as measuring forty leagues across, and the 'pan bad water,' is set down as being about in the middle of it. Now forty leagues is one hundred and twenty miles, consequently we ought at the most to be within twelve or fifteen miles of the water if any should really exist.

Through the afternoon we crept slowly and painfully along, scarcely doing more than a mile and a half an hour. At sunset we rested again, waiting for the moon, and after drinking a little managed to get some sleep.

Before we lay down, Umbopa pointed out to us a slight and indistinct hillock on the flat surface of the plain about eight miles away. At the distance it looked like an ant-hill, and as I was dropping off to sleep I fell to wondering what it could be.

With the moon we marched again, feeling dreadfully exhausted, and suffering tortures from thirst and prickly heat. Nobody who has not felt it can know what we went through. We walked no longer, we staggered, now and again falling from exhaustion, and being obliged to call a halt every hour or so. We had scarcely energy left in us to speak. Up to this Good had chatted and joked, for he is a merry fellow; but now he had not a joke in him.

At last, about two o'clock, utterly worn out in body and mind, we came to the foot of the queer hill, or sand koppie, which at first sight resembled a gigantic ant-heap about a hundred feet high, and covering at the base nearly two acres of ground.

Here we halted, and driven to it by our desperate thirst, sucked down our last drops of water. We had but half a pint a head, and each of us could have drunk a gallon.

Then we lay down. Just as I was dropping off to sleep I heard Umbopa remark to himself in Zulu –

'If we cannot find water we shall all be dead before the moon rises to-morrow.'

I shuddered, hot as it was. The near prospect of such an awful death is not pleasant, but even the thought of it could not keep me from sleeping.

Chapter VI

WATER! WATER!

In two hours' time, that is, about four o'clock, I woke up. So soon as the first heavy demand of bodily fatigue had been satisfied, the torturing thirst from which I was suffering asserted itself. I could sleep no more. I had been dreaming that I was bathing in a running stream, with green banks and trees upon them, and I awoke to find myself in this arid wilderness, and to remember, as Umbopa had said, that if we did not find water this day we must perish miserably. No human creature could live without water in that heat. I sat up and rubbed my grimy face with my dry and horny hands. My lips and eyelids were stuck together, and it was only after some rubbing and with an effort that I was able to open them. It was not far from dawn, but there was none of the bright feel of dawn in the air, which was thick with a hot murkiness I cannot describe. The others were still sleeping. Presently it began to grow light enough to read, so I drew out a little pocket copy of the 'Ingoldsby Legends' I had brought with me, and read 'The Jackdaw of Rheims.' When I got to where

> 'A nice little boy held a golden ewer,
> Embossed, and filled with water as pure
> As any that flows between Rheims and Namur,'

literally I smacked my cracked lips, or rather tried to smack them. The mere thought of that pure water made me mad. If the Cardinal had been there with his bell, book, and candle, I would have whipped in and drank his water up, yes, even if he had filled it already with the suds of soap worthy of washing the hands of the Pope, and I knew that the whole concentrated curse of the Catholic Church should fall upon me for so doing. I almost think that I must have been a little light-headed with thirst and weariness and the want of food; for I fell to thinking how astonished the Cardinal and his nice little boy and the jackdaw would have looked to see a burnt-up, brown-eyed, grizzly-haired little elephant hunter suddenly bound in and put his dirty face into the basin, and swallow every drop of the precious water. The idea amused me so much that I laughed or rather cackled aloud, which woke the others, and they began to rub *their* dirty faces and get *their* gummed-up lips and eyelids apart.

As soon as we were all well awake we began to discuss the situation, which was serious enough. Not a drop of water was left. We turned the water-bottles upside down, and licked the tops, but it was a failure, they were dry as a bone. Good, who had charge of the bottle of brandy, got it out and looked at it longingly; but Sir Henry promptly took it away from him, for to drink raw spirit would only have been to precipitate the end.

'If we do not find water we shall die,' he said.

'If we can trust to the old Dom's map there should be some about,' I said; but nobody seemed to derive much satisfaction from this remark. It was so evident that no great faith could be put in the map. Now it was gradually growing light, and as we sat staring blankly at each other, I observed the Hottentot Ventvögel rise and begin to walk about with his eyes on the ground. Presently he stopped short, and uttering a guttural exclamation, pointed to the earth.

'What is it?' we exclaimed; and simultaneously we rose and went to where he was standing staring at the ground.

'Well,' I said, 'it is pretty fresh springbok spoor; what of it?'

'Springbucks do not go far from water,' he answered in Dutch.

'No,' I answered, 'I forgot; and thank God for it.'

This little discovery put new life into us; it is wonderful, when a man is in a desperate position, how he catches at the slightest hope, and feels almost happy in it. On a dark night a single star is better than nothing.

Meanwhile Ventvögel was lifting his snub nose, and sniffing the hot air for all the world like an old Impala ram who scents danger. Presently he spoke again.

'I *smell* water,' he said.

Then we felt quite jubilant, for we knew what a wonderful instinct these wild-bred men possess.

Just at that moment the sun came up gloriously and revealed so grand a sight to our astonished eyes that for a moment or two we even forgot our thirst.

For there, not more than forty or fifty miles from us, glittering like silver in the early rays of the morning sun, soared Sheba's Breasts, and stretching away for hundreds of miles on each side of them was the great Suliman Berg. Now that, sitting here, I attempt to describe the extraordinary grandeur and beauty of that sight, language seems to fail me. I am impotent even before its memory. Straight before us, rose two enormous mountains, the like of which are not, I believe, to be seen in Africa, if indeed there are any such other in the world, measuring each of them at least fifteen thousand feet in height, standing not more than a dozen miles apart, linked together by a precipitous cliff of rock, and towering in awful white solemnity straight into the sky. These mountains placed thus, like the pillars of a gigantic gateway, are shaped after the fashion of a woman's breasts, and at times the mists and shadows beneath them take the form of a recumbent woman, veiled mysteriously in sleep. Their bases swell gently from the plain, looking at that distance perfectly round and smooth; and on the top of each is a vast hillock covered with snow, exactly corresponding to the nipple on the female breast. The stretch of cliff that connects them appear to be some thousand feet in height, and perfectly precipitous, and on each side of them, so far as the eye can reach, extend similar lines of cliff, broken only here and there by flat table-topped mountains, something like the world-famed one at Cape Town; a formation, by the way, very common in Africa.

To describe the comprehensive grandeur of that view is beyond my powers. There was something so inexpressibly solemn and overpowering about those huge volcanoes – for doubtless they are extinct volcanoes – that it quite took our breath away. For a while the morning lights played upon the snow and the brown swelling masses beneath, and then, as though to veil the majestic sight from our curious eyes, strange mists and clouds gathered and increased around the mountains, till presently we could only trace their pure and gigantic outlines, showing ghostlike through the fleecy envelope. Indeed, as we afterwards discovered, usually they were wrapped in this gauzy mist, which doubtless accounted for our not having made them out more clearly before.

Sheba's Breasts had scarcely vanished into cloud-clad privacy, before our thirst – literally a burning question – reasserted itself.

It was all very well for Ventvögel to say that he smelt water, but look which way we would we could see no signs of it. So far as the eye might reach there was nothing but arid sweltering sand and karoo scrub. We walked round the hillock and gazed about anxiously on the other side, but it was the same story, not a drop of water could be seen; there was no indication of a pan, a pool, or a spring.

'You are a fool,' I said angrily to Ventvögel; 'there is no water.'

But still he lifted his ugly snub nose and sniffed.

'I smell it. Baas,' he answered; 'it is somewhere in the air.'

'Yes,' I said, 'no doubt it is in the clouds, and about two months hence it will fall and wash our bones.'

Sir Henry stroked his yellow beard thoughtfully. 'Perhaps it is on the top of the hill,' he suggested.

'Rot,' said Good, 'whoever heard of water being found at the top of a hill!'

'Let us go and look,' I put in, and hopelessly enough we scrambled up the sandy sides of the hillock, Umbopa leading. Presently he stopped as though he was petrified.

'*Nanzia manzie!*' that is, 'Here is water,' he cried with a loud voice.

We rushed up to him, and there, sure enough, in a deep cut or indentation on the very top of the sand koppie, was an undoubted pool of water. How it came to be in such a strange place we did not stop to inquire, nor did we hesitate at its black and unpleasant appearance. It was water, or a good imitation of it, and that was enough for us. We gave a bound and a rush, and in another second we were all down on our stomachs sucking up the uninviting fluid as though it were nectar fit for the gods. Heavens, how we did drink! Then when we had done drinking we tore off our clothes and sat down in the pool, absorbing the moisture through our parched skins. You, Harry my boy, who have only to turn on a couple of taps to summon 'hot' and 'cold' from an unseen vasty boiler, can have little idea of the luxury of that muddy wallow in brackish tepid water.

After a while we rose from it, refreshed indeed, and fell to on our 'biltong,' of which we had scarcely been able to touch a mouthful for twenty-four hours, and ate our fill. Then we smoked a pipe, and lay down by the side of that blessed pool, under the overhanging shadow of its bank, and slept till mid-day.

All that day we rested there by the water, thanking our stars that we had been lucky enough to find it, bad as it was, and not forgetting to render a due share of gratitude to the shade of the long-departed da Silvestra, who set its position down so accurately on the tail of his shirt. The wonderful thing to us was that the pan should have lasted so long, and the only way in which I can account for this is on the supposition that it is fed by some spring deep down in the sand.

Having filled both ourselves and our water-bottles as full as possible, in far better spirits we started off again with the moon. That night we covered nearly five-and-twenty miles, but, needless to say, found no more water, though we were lucky enough on the following day to get a little shade behind some ant-heaps. When the sun rose, and, for a while, cleared away the mysterious mists, Suliman's Berg with the two majestic Breasts, now only about twenty miles off, seemed to be towering right above us, and looked grander than ever. At the approach of evening we marched again, and, to cut a long story short, by daylight next morning found ourselves upon the lowest slopes of Sheba's left breast, for which we had been steadily steering. By this time our water was exhausted once more, and we were suffering severely from thirst, nor indeed could we see any chance of relieving it till we reached the snow line far above us. After resting an hour or two, driven to it by our torturing thirst, we went on toiling painfully in the burning heat up the lava slopes, for we found that the huge base of the mountain was composed entirely of lava beds belched from the bowels of the earth in some far past age.

By eleven o'clock we were utterly exhausted, and, generally speaking, in a very bad state indeed. The lava clinker, over which we must drag ourselves, though smooth compared with some clinker I have heard of, such as that on the Island of Ascension, for instance, was yet rough enough to make our feet very sore, and this, together with our other miseries, had pretty well finished us. A few hundred yards above us were some large lumps of lava, and towards these we steered with the intention of lying down beneath their shade. We reached them, and to our surprise so far as we had a capacity for surprise left in us, on a little plateau or ridge close by we saw that the clinker was covered with a dense green growth. Evidently soil formed of decomposed lava had rested there, and in due course had become the receptacle of seeds deposited by birds. But we did not take much further interest in the green growth, for one cannot live on grass like Nebuchadnezzar. That requires a special dispensation of Providence and peculiar digestive organs. So we sat down under the rocks and groaned, and for one I wished heartily that we had never started on this fool's errand. As we were sitting there I saw Umbopa get up and hobble towards the patch of green, and a few minutes afterwards, to my great astonishment, I perceived that usually very dignified individual dancing and shouting like a maniac, waving something green as he did so. Off we all scrambled towards him as fast as our wearied limbs would carry us, hoping that he had found water.

'What is it, Umbopa, son of a fool?' I shouted in Zulu.

'It is food and water, Macumazahn,' and again he waved the green thing.

Then I saw what he had found. It was a melon. We had hit upon a patch of wild melons, thousands of them, and dead ripe.

'Melons!' I yelled to Good, who was next to me; and in another second his false teeth were fixed in one of them.

I think we ate about six each before we had done, and poor fruit as they were, I doubt if I ever thought anything nicer.

But melons are not very nutritious, and when we had satisfied our thirst with their pulpy substance, and put a stock to cool by the simple process of cutting them in two and setting them on end in the hot sun to grow cold by evaporation, we began to feel exceedingly hungry. We had still some biltong left, but our stomachs turned from biltong, and besides we were obliged to be very sparing of it, for we could not say when we should find more food. Just at this moment a lucky thing chanced. Looking across the desert I saw a flock of about ten large birds flying straight towards us.

'*Skit, Baas, skit!*' 'Shoot, master, shoot!' whispered the Hottentot, throwing himself on his face, an example which we all followed.

Then I saw that the birds were a flock of *pauw* or bustards, and that they would pass within fifty yards of my head. Taking one of the repeating Winchesters I waited till they were nearly over us, and then jumped to my feet. On seeing me the *pauw* bunched up together, as I expected that they would, and I fired two shots straight into the thick of them, and, as luck would have it, brought one down, a fine fellow, that weighed about twenty pounds. In half an hour we had a fire made of dry melon stalks, and he was toasting over it, and we made such a feed as we had not tasted for a week. We ate that *pauw;* nothing was left of him but his leg-bones and his beak, and felt not a little the better afterwards.

That night we went on again with the moon, carrying as many melons as we could with us. As we ascended we found the air grow cooler and cooler, which was a great relief to us, and at dawn, so far as we could judge, we were not more than half a dozen miles from the snow line. Here we found more melons, and so had no longer any anxiety about water, for we knew that we should soon get plenty of snow. But the ascent had now become very precipitous, and we made but slow progress, not more than a mile an hour. Also that night we ate our last morsel of biltong. As yet, with the exception of the *pauw*, we had seen no living thing on the mountain, nor had we come across a single spring or stream of water, which struck us as very odd, considering the snow above us, which must, we thought, melt sometimes. But as we afterwards discovered, owing to a cause which is quite beyond my power to explain, all the streams flowed upon the north side of the mountains.

Now we began to grow very anxious about food. We had escaped death by thirst, but it seemed probable that it was only to die of hunger. The events of the next three miserable days are best described by copying the entries made at the time in my note-book.

'21st May. – Started 11 a.m., finding the atmosphere quite cold enough to travel by day, and carrying some water-melons with us. Struggled on all day, but found no more melons, having evidently passed out of their district. Saw no game of any sort. Halted for the night. At sundown, having had no food for many hours. Suffered much during the night from cold.

'22nd. – Started at sunrise again, feeling very faint and weak. Only made about five miles all day; found some patches of snow, of which we ate, but nothing else. Camped at night under the edge of a great plateau. Cold bitter. Drank a little brandy each, and huddled ourselves together, each wrapped up in his blanket to keep ourselves alive. Are now suffering frightfully from starvation and weariness. Thought that Ventvögel would have died during the night.

'23rd. – Struggled forward once more as soon as the sun was well up, and had thawed our limbs a little. We are now in a dreadful plight, and I fear that unless we get food this will be our last day's journey. But little brandy left. Good, Sir Henry, and Umbopa bear up wonderfully, but Ventvögel is in a very bad way. Like most Hottentots, he cannot stand cold. Pangs of hunger not so bad, but have a sort of numb feeling about the stomach. Others say the same. We are now on a level with the precipitous chain, or wall of lava, linking the two Breasts, and the view is glorious. Behind us the glowing desert rolls away to the horizon, and before us lie mile upon mile of smooth hard snow almost level, but swelling gently upwards, out of the centre of which the nipple of the mountain, that appears to be some miles in circumference, rises about four thousand feet into the sky. Not a living thing is to be seen. God help us, I fear that our time is come.'

And now I will drop the journal, partly because it is not very interesting reading, and also because what follows requires telling rather more fully.

All that day – the 23rd May – we struggled slowly up the incline of snow, lying down from time to time to rest. A strange gaunt crew we must have looked, while, laden as we were, we dragged our weary feet over the dazzling plain, glaring round us with hungry eyes. Not that there was much use in glaring, for we could see nothing to eat. We did not accomplish more than seven miles that day. Just before sunset we found ourselves exactly under the nipple of Sheba's left breast, which towered thousands of feet into the air, a vast smooth hillock of frozen snow. Weak as we were, we could not but appreciate the wonderful scene, made even more splendid by the flying rays of sunlight from the setting sun, which here and there stained the snow blood-red, and crowned the great dome above us with a diadem of glory.

'I say,' gasped Good, presently, 'we ought to be somewhere near that cave the old gentleman wrote about.'

'Yes,' said I, 'if there is a cave.'

'Come, Quatermain,' groaned Sir Henry, 'don't talk like that; I have every faith in the Dom; remember the water! We shall find the place soon.'

'If we don't find it before dark we are dead men, that is all about it,' was my consolatory reply.

For the next ten minutes we trudged in silence, when suddenly Umbopa, who was marching along beside me, wrapped in his blanket, and with a leather belt strapped so tightly round his stomach, to 'make his hunger small,' as he said, that his waist looked like a girl's, caught me by the arm.

'Look!' he said, pointing towards the springing slope of the nipple.

I followed his glance, and some two hundred yards from us perceived what appeared to be a hole in the snow.

'It is the cave,' said Umbopa.

We made the best of our way to the spot, and found sure enough that the hole was the mouth of a cave, no doubt the same as that of which da Silvestra wrote. We were not too soon, for just as we reached shelter the sun went down with startling rapidity, leaving the world nearly dark. In these latitudes there is but little twilight. So we crept into the cave, which did not appear to be very big, and huddling ourselves together for warmth, swallowed what remained of our brandy – barely a mouthful each – and tried to forget our miseries in sleep. But the cold was too intense to allow us to do so, for I am convinced that at this great altitude the thermometer cannot have marked less than fourteen or fifteen degrees below freezing-point. What such a temperature meant to us, enervated as we were by hardship, want of food, and the great heat of the desert, the reader may imagine better than I can describe. Suffice it to say that it was something as near death from exposure as I have ever felt. There we sat hour after hour through the still and bitter night, feeling the frost wander round and nip us now in the finger, now in the foot, now in the face. In vain did we huddle closer and closer; there was no warmth in our miserable starved carcasses. Sometimes one of us would drop into an uneasy slumber for a few minutes, but we could not sleep much, and perhaps it was fortunate, for if we had I doubt if we should ever have woke again. I believe it was only by the force of will that we kept ourselves alive at all.

Not very long before dawn I heard the Hottentot Ventvögel, whose teeth had been chattering all night like castanets, give a deep sigh. Then his teeth stopped chattering. I did not think anything of it at the time, concluding that he had gone to sleep. His back was resting against mine, and it seemed to grow colder and colder, till at last it felt like ice.

At length the air began to grow grey with light, then golden arrows sped across the snow, and at last the glorious sun peeped above the lava wall and looked in upon our half-frozen forms, and also upon Ventvögel, sitting there amongst us *stone dead*. No wonder his back felt cold, poor fellow. He had died when I heard him sigh, and was now frozen almost stiff. Shocked beyond measure we dragged ourselves from the corpse – how strange is that horror we mortals have of the companionship of a dead body – and left it sitting there, its arms clasped about its knees.

By this time the sunlight was pouring its cold rays, for here they were cold, straight into the mouth of the cave. Suddenly I heard an exclamation of fear from someone, and turned my head.

And this is what I saw. Sitting at the end of the cavern – it was not more than twenty feet long – was another form, of which the head rested on its chest and the long arms hung down. I stared at it, and saw that this too was a *dead man*, and, what was more, a white man.

The others saw also, and the sight proved too much for our shattered nerves. One and all we scrambled out of the cave as fast as our half-frozen limbs would allow.

Chapter VII

SOLOMON'S ROAD

Outside the cavern we halted, feeling rather foolish.

'I am going back,' said Sir Henry.

'Why?' asked Good.

'Because it has struck me that – what we saw – may be my brother.'

This was a new idea, and we re-entered the place to put it to the proof. After the bright light outside, our eyes, weak as they were with staring at the snow, could not pierce the gloom of the cave for a while. Presently, however, they grew accustomed to the semi-darkness, and we advanced towards the dead man.

Sir Henry knelt down and peered into his face.

'Thank God,' he said, with a sigh of relief, 'it is *not* my brother.'

Then I drew near and looked. The body was that of a tall man in middle life with aquiline features, grizzled hair, and a long black moustache. The skin was perfectly yellow, and stretched tightly over the bones. Its clothing, with the exception of what seemed to be the remains of a woollen pair of hose, had been removed, leaving the skeleton-like frame naked. Round the neck of the corpse, which was frozen perfectly stiff, hung a yellow ivory crucifix.

'Who on earth can it be?' said I.

'Can't you guess?' asked Good.

I shook my head.

'Why, the old Dom, José da Silvestra, of course – who else?'

'Impossible,' I gasped, 'he died three hundred years ago.'

'And what is there to prevent him lasting for three thousand years in this atmosphere, I should like to know?' asked Good. 'If only the temperature is sufficiently low, flesh and blood will keep fresh as New Zealand mutton for ever, and Heaven knows it is cold enough here. The sun never gets in here; no animal comes here to tear or destroy. No doubt his slave, of whom he speaks on the writing, took off his clothes and left him. He could not have buried him alone. Look!' he went on stooping down to pick up a queerly-shaped bone scraped at the end into a sharp point, 'here is the "cleft bone" that Silvestra used to draw the map with.'

We gazed for a moment astonished, forgetting our own miseries in this extraordinary and, as it seemed to us, semi-miraculous sight.

'Ay,' said Sir Henry, 'and this is where he got his ink from,' and he pointed to a small wound on the dead Dom's left arm. 'Did ever man see such a thing before!'

There was no longer any doubt about the matter, which for my own part I confess perfectly appalled me. There he sat, the dead man, whose directions, written some ten generations ago, had led us to this spot. Here in my own hand was the rude pen with which he had written them, and about his neck hung the crucifix that his dying lips had kissed. Gazing at him, my imagination could reconstruct the last scene of the drama, the traveller dying of cold and starvation, yet striving to convey to the world the great secret which he had discovered – the awful loneliness of his death, of which the evidence sat before us. It even seemed to me that I could trace on his strongly-marked features a likeness to those of my poor friend Silvestre his descendant, who had died twenty years before in my arms, but perhaps that was fancy. At any rate, there he sat, a sad memento of the fate that so often overtakes those who would penetrate into the unknown; and there doubtless he will still sit, crowned with the dread majesty of death, for centuries yet unborn, to startle the eyes of wanderers like ourselves, if ever any such should come again to invade his loneliness. The thing overpowered us, already nearly done to death as we were with cold and hunger.

'Let us go,' said Sir Henry in a low voice; 'stay, we will give him a companion,' and lifting up the dead body of the Hottentot Ventvögel, he placed it near to that of the old Dom. Then he stopped, and with a jerk broke the rotten string of the crucifix which hung round da Silvestra's neck, for his fingers were too cold to attempt to unfasten it. I believe that he still has it. I took the bone pen, and it is before me as I write – sometimes I sign my name with it.

Then leaving these two, the proud white man of a past age, and the poor Hottentot, to keep their eternal vigil in the midst of the eternal snows, we crept out of the cave into the welcome sunshine and resumed our path, wondering in our hearts how many hours it would be before we were even as they are.

When we had walked about half a mile we came to the edge of the plateau, for the nipple of the mountain does not rise out of its exact centre, though from the desert side it seemed to do so. What lay before us we could not see, for the landscape was wreathed in billows of morning fog. Presently, however, the higher layers of mist cleared a little, and revealed, at the end of a long slope of snow, a patch of green grass, some five hundred yards beneath us, through which a stream was running. Nor was this all. By the stream, basking in the bright sun, stood and lay a group of from ten to fifteen *large antelopes* – at that distance we could not see of what species.

The sight filled us with an unreasoning joy. There was food in plenty if only we could get it. But the question was how to get it. The beasts were fully six hundred yards off, a very long shot, and one not to be depended on when our lives hung on the result.

Rapidly we discussed the advisability of trying to stalk the game, but in the end reluctantly dismissed it. To begin with, the wind was not favourable, and further, we must certainly be perceived, however careful we were, against the blinding background of snow, which we should be obliged to traverse.

'Well, we must have a try from where we are,' said Sir Henry. 'Which shall it be, Quatermain, the repeating rifles or the expresses?'

Here again was a question. The Winchester repeaters – of which we had two, Umbopa carrying poor Ventvögel's as well as his own – were sighted up to a thousand yards, whereas the expresses were only sighted to three hundred and fifty, beyond which distance shooting with them was more or less guesswork. On the other hand, if they did hit, the express bullets, being 'expanding,' were much more likely to bring the game down. It was a knotty point, but I made up my mind that we must risk it and use the expresses.

'Let each of us take the buck opposite to him. Aim well at the point in his shoulder and high up,' said I; 'and, Umbopa, do you give the word, so that we may all fire together.'

Then came a pause, each of us aiming his level best, as indeed a man is likely to do when he knows that life itself depends upon the shot.

'Fire!' said Umbopa in Zulu, and at almost the same instant the three rifles rang out loudly; three clouds of smoke hung for a moment before us, and a hundred echoes went flying over the silent snow. Presently the smoke cleared, and revealed – oh, joy! – a great buck lying on its back and kicking furiously in its death agony. We gave a yell of triumph – we were saved – we should not starve. Weak as we were, we rushed down the intervening slope of snow, and in ten minutes from the time of shooting, that animal's heart and liver were lying before' us. But now a new difficulty arose – we had no fuel, and therefore could make no fire to cook them. We gazed at each other in dismay.

'Starving men should not be fanciful,' said Good; 'we must eat raw meat.'

There was no other way out of the dilemma, and our gnawing hunger made the proposition less distasteful than it would otherwise have been. So we took the heart and liver and buried them for a few minutes in a patch of snow to cool them. Then we washed them in the ice-cold water of the stream, and lastly ate them greedily. It sounds horrible enough, but honestly, I never tasted anything so good as that raw meat. In a quarter of an hour we were changed men. Our life and vigour came back to us, our feeble pulses grew strong again, and the blood went coursing through our veins. But mindful of the results of over-feeding on starving stomachs, we were careful not to eat too much, stopping whilst we were still hungry.

'Thank Heaven!' said Sir Henry; 'that brute has saved our lives. What is it, Quatermain?'

I rose and went to look at the antelope, for I was not certain. It was about the size of a donkey, with large curved horns. I had never seen one like it before, the species was new to me. It was brown in colour, with faint red stripes, and grew a thick coat.

I afterwards discovered that the natives of that wonderful country call these bucks 'Inco.' They are very rare, and only found at a great altitude where no other game will live. This animal was fairly shot high up in the shoulder, though whose bullet brought it down we could not, of course, discover. I believe that Good, mindful of his marvellous shot at the giraffe, secretly set it down to his own prowess, and we did not contradict him.

We had been so busy satisfying our starving stomachs that hitherto we had not found time to look about us. But now, having set Umbopa to cut off as much of the best meat as we were likely to be able to carry, we began to inspect our surroundings. The mist had cleared away, for it was eight o'clock, and the sun sucked it up, so we were able to take in all the country before us at a glance. I know not how to describe the glorious panorama which unfolded itself to our gaze. I have never seen anything like it before, nor shall, I suppose, again.

Behind and over us towered Sheba's snowy Breasts, and below, some five thousand feet beneath where we stood, lay league on league of the most lovely champaign country. Here were dense patches of lofty forest, there a great river wound its silvery way. To the left stretched a vast expanse of rich undulating veldt or grass land, on which we could just make out countless herds of game or cattle; at that distance we could not tell which. This expanse appeared to be ringed in by a wall of distant mountains. To the right the country was more or less mountainous; that is, solitary hills stood up from its level, with stretches of cultivated land between, amongst which we could see groups of dome-shaped huts. The landscape lay before us as a map, in which rivers flashed like silver snakes, and Alp-like peaks crowned with wildly twisted snow wreaths rose in grandeur, whilst over all was the glad sunlight, and the breath of Nature's happy life.

Two curious things struck us as we gazed. First, that the country before us must lie at least three thousand feet higher than the desert we had crossed, and secondly, that all the rivers flowed from south to north. As we had painful reason to know, there was no water upon the southern side of the vast range on which we stood, but on the northern face were many streams, most of which appeared to unite with the great river we could see winding away farther than we could follow it.

We sat down for a while and gazed in silence at this wonderful view. Presently Sir Henry spoke.

'Isn't there something on the map about Solomon's Great Road?' he said.

I nodded, my eyes still gazing out over the far country.

'Well, look; there it is!' and he pointed a little to our right.

Good and I looked accordingly, and there, winding away towards the plain, was what appeared to be a wide turnpike road. We had not seen it at first because, on reaching the plain, it turned behind some broken country. We did not say anything, at least, not much; we were beginning to lose the sense of wonder. Somehow it did not seem particularly unnatural that we should find a sort of Roman road in this strange land. We accepted the fact, that was all.

'Well,' said Good, 'it must be quite near us if we cut off to the right. Hadn't we better be making a start?'

This was sound advice, and as soon as we had washed our faces and hands in the stream we acted on it. For a mile or more we made our way over boulders and across patches of snow, till suddenly, on reaching the top of the little rise we found the road at our feet. It was a splendid road cut out of the solid rock, at least fifty feet wide, and apparently well kept; but the odd thing about it was that it seemed to begin there. We walked down and stood on it, but one single hundred paces behind us, in the direction of Sheba's Breasts, it vanished, the entire surface of the mountain being strewn with boulders interspersed with patches of snow.

'What do you make of this, Quatermain?' asked Sir Henry.

I shook my head. I could make nothing of it.

'I have it,' said Good; 'the road no doubt ran right over the range and across the desert on the other side, but the sand there has covered it up, and above us it has been obliterated by some volcanic eruption of molten lava.'

This seemed a good suggestion; at any rate, we accepted it, and proceeded down the mountain. It proved a very different business travelling along down hill on that magnificent pathway with full stomachs to what it was travelling uphill over the snow quite starved and almost frozen. Indeed, had it not been for melancholy recollections of poor Ventvögel's sad fate, and of that grim cave where he kept company with the old Dom, we should have felt positively cheerful, notwithstanding the sense of unknown dangers before us. Every mile we walked the atmosphere grew softer and balmier, and the country before us shone with a yet more luminous beauty. As for the road itself, I never saw such an engineering work, though Sir Henry said that the great road over the St. Gothard in Switzerland is very like it. No difficulty had been too great for the Old World engineer who designed it. At one place we came to a ravine three hundred feet broad and at least a hundred deep. This vast gulf was actually filled in with huge blocks of dressed stone, having arches pierced through them at the bottom for a waterway, over which the road went on sublimely. At another place it was cut in zigzags out of the side of a precipice five hundred feet deep, and in a third it tunnelled through the base of an intervening ridge, a space of thirty yards or more.

Here we noticed the sides of the tunnel were covered with quaint sculptures, mostly of mailed figures driving in chariots. One, which was exceedingly beautiful, represented a whole battle scene with a convoy of captives being marched off in the distance.

'Well,' said Sir Henry, after inspecting this ancient work of art, 'it is very well to call this Solomon's Road, but my humble opinion is that the Egyptians have been here before Solomon's people ever set a foot on it. If this isn't Egyptian handiwork, I must say that it is very like it.'

By midday we had advanced sufficiently down the mountain to reach the region where wood was to be met with. First we came to scattered bushes which grew more and more frequent, till at last we found the road winding through a vast grove of silver trees similar to those which are to be seen on the slopes of Table Mountain at Cape Town. I had never before met with them in all my wanderings except at the Cape, and their appearance here astonished me greatly.

'Ah!' said Good, surveying these shining-leaved trees with evident enthusiasm, 'here is lots of wood; let us stop and cook some dinner; I have about digested that raw liver.'

Nobody objected to this, so leaving the road we made our way to a stream which was babbling away not far off, and soon had a goodly fire of dry boughs blazing. Cutting off some substantial hunks from the flesh of the *inco* which we had brought with us we proceeded to toast them on the end of sharp sticks, as one sees the Kafirs do, and ate them with relish. After filling ourselves, we lit our pipes and gave ourselves up to enjoyment, which, compared with the hardships we had recently undergone, seemed almost heavenly.

The brook, of which the banks were clothed with dense masses of a gigantic species of maiden-hair fern interspersed with feathery tufts of wild asparagus, babbled merrily at our side, the soft air murmured through the leaves of the silver trees, doves cooed around, and bright-winged birds flashed like living gems from bought to bough. It was a Paradise.

The magic of the place combined with an overwhelming sense of dangers left behind, and of the Promised Land reached at last, seemed to charm us into silence. Sir Henry and Umbopa sat conversing in a mixture of broken English and kitchen Zulu in a low voice, but earnestly enough, and I lay, with my eyes half shut, upon that fragrant bed of fern and watched them.

Presently I missed Good, and I looked to see what had become of him. Soon I observed him sitting by the bank of the stream, in which he had been bathing. He had nothing on but his flannel shirt, and his natural habits of extreme neatness having reasserted themselves, he was actively employed in making a most elaborate toilet. He had washed his gutta-percha collar, had thoroughly shaken out his trousers, coat and waistcoat, and was now folding them up neatly till he was ready to put them on, shaking his head sadly as he scanned the numerous rents and tears in them, which naturally had resulted from our frightful journey. Then he took his boots, scrubbed them with a handful of fern, and finally rubbed them over with a piece of fat, which he had carefully saved from the *inco* meat, till they looked, comparatively speaking, respectable. Having inspected them judiciously through his eye-glass, he put the boots on and began a fresh operation. From a little bag that he carried he produced a pocket-comb in which was fixed a tiny looking-glass, and in this he surveyed himself. Apparently he was not satisfied, for he proceeded to do his hair with great care. Then came a pause whilst he again contemplated the effect; still it was not satisfactory. He felt his chin, on which the accumulated scrub of a ten days' beard was flourishing.

'Surely,' thought I, 'he is not going to try to shave.'

But it was so. Taking the piece of fat with which he had greased his boots, Good washed it thoroughly in the stream. Then diving again into the bag he brought out a little pocket razor with a guard to it, such as are bought by people who are afraid of cutting themselves, or by those about to undertake a sea voyage. Then he scrubbed his face and chin vigorously with the fat and began. But evidently it proved a painful process, for he groaned very much over it, and I was convulsed with inward laughter as I watched him struggling with that stubbly beard. It seemed so very odd that a man should take the trouble to shave himself with a piece of fat in such a place and in our circumstances. At last he succeeded in getting the worst of the scrub off the right side of his face and chin, when suddenly I, who was watching, became aware of a flash of light that passed by his head.

Good sprang up with a profane exclamation (if it had not been a safety razor he would certainly have cut his throat), and so did I, without the exclamation, and this was what I saw. Standing not more than twenty paces from where I was, and ten from Good, were a group of men. They were very tall and copper-coloured, and some of them wore great plumes of black feathers and short cloaks of leopard skins; this was all I noticed at the moment. In front of them stood a youth of about seventeen, his hand still raised and his body bent forward in the attitude of a Grecian statue of a spear-thrower. Evidently the flash of light had been caused by a weapon, and he had hurled it.

As I looked an old soldier-like man stepped forward out of the group, and catching the youth by the arm said something to him. Then they advanced upon us.

Sir Henry, Good, and Umbopa by this time had seized their rifles and lifted them threateningly. The party of natives still came on. It struck me that they could not know what rifles were, or they would not have treated them with such contempt.

'Put down your guns!' I halloed to the others, seeing that our only chance of safety lay in conciliation. They obeyed, and walking to the front I addressed the elderly man who had checked the youth.

'Greeting,' I said in Zulu, not knowing what language to use. To my surprise I was understood.

'Greeting,' answered the man, not, indeed, in the same tongue, but in a dialect so closely allied to it that neither Umbopa nor myself had any difficulty in understanding it. Indeed, as we afterwards found out, the language spoken by this people is an old-fashioned form of the Zulu tongue, bearing about the same relationship to it that the English of Chaucer does to the English of the nineteenth century.

'Whence come you?' he went on, 'who are you? and why are the faces of three of you white, and the face of the fourth as the face of our mother's sons?' and he pointed to Umbopa. I looked at Umbopa as he said it, and it flashed across me that he was right. The face of Umbopa was like the faces of the men before me, and so was his great form like their forms. But I had not time to reflect on this coincidence.

'We are strangers, and come in peace,' I answered, speaking very slowly, so that he might understand me, 'and this man is our servant.'

'Ye lie,' he answered; 'no strangers can cross the mountains where all things perish. But what do your lies matter? – if ye are strangers then ye must die, for no strangers may live in the land of the Kukuanas. It is the king's law. Prepare then to die, O strangers!'

I was slightly staggered at this, more especially as I saw the hands of some of the men steal down to their sides, where hung on each what looked to me like a large and heavy knife.

'What does that beggar say?' asked Good.

'He says we are going to be killed,' I answered grimly.

'Oh, Lord!' groaned Good; and, as was his way when perplexed, he put his hand to his false teeth, dragging the top set down and allowing them to fly back to his jaw with a snap. It was a most fortunate move, for next second the dignified crowd of Kukuanas uttered a simultaneous yell of horror, and bolted back some yards.

'What's up?' said I.

'It's his teeth,' whispered Sir Henry excitedly. 'He moved them. Take them out, Good, take them out!'

He obeyed, slipping the set into the sleeve of his flannel shirt.

In another second curiosity had overcome fear, and the men advanced slowly. Apparently they had now forgotten their amiable intention of killing us.

'How is it, O strangers,' asked the old man solemnly, 'that this fat man (pointing

to Good, who was clad in nothing but boots and a flannel shirt, and had only half
finished his shaving) whose body is clothed, and whose legs are bare, who grows hair
on one side of his sickly face and not on the other, and who wears one shining and
transparent eye, has teeth that move of themselves, coming away from the jaws and
returning of their own free will?'

'Open your mouth,' I said to Good, who promptly curled up his lips and grinned
at the old gentleman like an angry dog, revealing to his astonished gaze two thin
red lines of gum as utterly innocent of ivories as a new-born elephant. The audience
gasped.

'Where are his teeth?' they shouted; 'with our eyes we saw them.'

Turning his head slowly and with a gesture of ineffable contempt, Good swept
his hand across his mouth. Then he grinned again, and lo, there were two rows of
lovely teeth.

Now the young man who had flung the knife threw himself down on the grass
and gave vent to a prolonged howl of terror; and as for the old gentleman, his knees
knocked together with fear.

'I see ye are spirits,' he said faltering; 'did ever man born of woman have hair on
one side of his face and not on the other, or a round and transparent eye, or teeth
which moved and melted away and grew again? Pardon us, O my lords.'

Here was luck indeed, and, needless to say, I jumped at the chance.

'It is granted,' I said with an imperial smile. 'Nay, ye shall know the truth. We come
from another world, though we are men such as ye; we come,' I went on, 'from the
biggest star that shines at night.'

'Oh! oh!' groaned the chorus of astonished aborigines.

'Yes,' I went on, 'we do, indeed;' and again I smiled beningly as I uttered that
amazing lie. 'We come to stay with you a little while, and to bless you by our sojourn.
Ye will see, O friends, that I have prepared myself for this visit by the learning of
your language.'

'It is so, it is so,' said the chorus.

'Only, my lord,' put in the old gentleman, 'thou hast learnt it very badly.'

I cast an indignant glance at him, and he quailed.

'Now, friends,' I continued, 'ye might think that after so long a journey we should find it in our hearts to avenge such a reception, mayhap to strike cold in death the impious hand that – that, in short – threw a knife at the head of him whose teeth come and go.'

'Spare him, my lords,' said the old man in supplication; 'he is the king's son, and I am his uncle. If anything befalls him his blood will be required at my hands.'

'Yes, that is certainly so,' put in the young man with great emphasis.

'Ye may perhaps doubt our power to avenge,' I went on, heedless of this byplay. 'Stay, I will show you. Here, thou dog and slave (addressing Umbopa in a savage tone), give me the magic tube that speaks;' and I tipped a wink towards my express rifle.

Umbopa rose to the occasion, and with something as nearly resembling a grin as I have ever seen on his dignified face, he handed me the gun.

'It is here, O Lord of Lords,' he said with a deep obeisance.

Now just before I had asked for the rifle I perceived a little *klipspringer* antelope standing on a mass of rock about seventy yards away, and had determined to risk a shot at it.

'Ye see that buck,' I said, pointing the animal out to the party before me. 'Tell me, is it possible for a man born of woman to kill it from here with a noise?'

'It is not possible, my lord,' answered the old man.

'Yet shall I kill it,' I said quietly.

The old man smiled. 'That my lord cannot do,' he answered.

I raised the rifle and covered the buck. It was a small animal, and one which a man might well be excused for missing, but I knew that it would not do to miss.

I drew a deep breath, and slowly pressed on the trigger. The buck stood still as a stone.

'Bang! thud!' The antelope sprang into the air and fell on the rock dead as a door nail.

A groan of terror burst from the group before us.

'If ye want meat,' I remarked coolly, 'go fetch that buck.'

The old man made a sign, and one of his followers departed, and presently returned bearing the *klipspringer*. I noticed, with satisfaction, that I had hit it fairly behind the shoulder. They gathered round the poor creature's body, gazing at the bullet-hole in consternation.

'Ye see,' I said, 'I do not speak empty words.'

There was no answer.

'If ye doubt our power,' I went on, 'let one of you stand upon that rock that I may make him as this buck.'

None of them seemed at all inclined to take the hint, till at last the king's son spoke.

'It is well said. Do thou, my uncle, go stand upon the rock. It is but a buck that the magic has killed. Surely it cannot kill a man.'

The old gentleman did not take the suggestion in good part. Indeed, he seemed hurt.

'No! no!' he ejaculated hastily, 'my old eyes have seen enough. These are wizards, indeed. Let us bring them to the king. Yet if any wish a further proof, let *him* stand upon the rock, that the magic tube may speak with him.'

There was a most general and hasty expression of dissent.

'Let not good magic be wasted on our poor bodies,' said one, 'we are satisfied. All the witchcraft of our people cannot show the like of this.'

'It is so,' remarked the old gentleman, in a tone of intense relief; 'without any doubt it is so. Listen, children of the Stars, children of the shining eye and the movable teeth, who roar out in thunder and slay from afar. I am Infadoos, son of Kafa, once king of the Kukuana people. This youth is Scragga.'

'He nearly scragged me,' murmured Good.

'Scragga, son of Twala, the great king – Twala, husband of a thousand wives, chief and lord paramount of the Kukuanas, keeper of the great Road, terror of his enemies, student of the Black Arts, leader of an hundred thousand warriors, Twala the One-eyed, the Black, the Terrible.'

'So,' said I superciliously, 'lead us then to Twala. We do not talk with low people and underlings.'

'It is well, my lords, we will lead you, but the way is long. We are hunting three days' journey from the place of the king. But let my lords have patience, and we will lead them.'

'So be it,' I said carelessly; 'all time is before us, for we do not die. We are ready, lead on. But, Infadoos, and thou, Scragga, beware! Play us no tricks, set for us no snares, for before your brains of mud have thought of them we shall know and avenge them. The light from the transparent eye of him with the bare legs and the half-haired face shall destroy you, and go through your land; his vanishing teeth shall fix themselves fast in you and eat you up, you and your wives and children; the magic tubes shall talk with you loudly, and make you sieves. Beware!'

This magnificent address did not fail of its effect indeed, it was hardly needed, so deeply were our friends already impressed with our powers.

The old man made a deep obeisance, and murmured the words '*Koom, Koom,*' which I afterwards discovered was their royal salute, corresponding to the '*Bayéte*' of the Zulus, and turning, addressed his followers. They at once proceeded to lay hold of all our goods and chattels, in order to bear them for us, excepting only the guns, which they would on no account touch. They even seized Good's clothes, that, as the reader may remember, were neatly folded up beside him.

He saw and made a dive for them, and a loud altercation ensued.

'Let not my lord of the transparent Eye and the melting Teeth touch them,' said the old man. 'Surely his slaves shall carry the things.'

'But I want to put 'em on!' roared Good, in nervous English.

Umbopa translated.

'Nay, my lord,' answered Infadoos, 'would my lord cover up his beautiful white legs (although he is so dark Good has a singularly white skin) from the eyes of his servants? Have we offended my lord that he should do such a thing?'

Here I nearly exploded with laughing; and meanwhile one of the men started on with the garments.

'Damn it!' roared Good, 'that black villain has got my trousers.'

'Look here, Good,' said Sir Henry, 'you have appeared in this country in a certain character, and you must live up to it. It will never do for you to put on trousers again. Henceforth you must exist in a flannel shirt, a pair of boots, and an eye-glass.'

'Yes,' I said, 'and with whiskers on one side of your face and not on the other. If you change any of these things the people will think that we are impostors. I am very sorry for you, but, seriously, you must do it. If they once begin to suspect us our lives will not be worth a brass farthing.'

'Do you really think so?' said Good gloomily.

'I do, indeed. Your "beautiful white legs" and your eye-glass are now *the* features of our party, and as Sir Henry says, you must live up to them. Be thankful that you have got your boots on, and that the air is warm.'

Good sighed, and said no more, but it took him a fortnight to become accustomed to his new and scant attire.

Chapter VIII

WE ENTER KUKUANALAND

All that afternoon we travelled along the magnificent roadway, which trended steadily in a north-westerly direction. Infadoos and Scragga walked with us, but their followers marched about one hundred paces ahead.

'Infadoos,' I said at length, 'who made this road?'

'It was made, my lord, of old time, none know how or when, not even the wise woman Gagool, who has lived for generations. We are not old enough to remember its making. None can make such roads now, but the king suffers no grass to grow upon it.'

'And whose are the writings on the wall of the caves through which we have passed on the road?' I asked, referring to the Egyptian-like sculptures that we had seen.

'My lord, the hands that made the road wrote the wonderful writings. We know not who wrote them.'

'When did the Kukuana people come into this country?'

'My lord, the race came down here like the breath of a storm ten thousand thousand moons ago, from the great lands which lie there beyond,' and he pointed to the north. 'They could travel no further because of the high mountains which ring in the land, so say the old voices of our fathers that have descended to us the children, and so says Gagool, the wise woman, the smeller out of witches,' and again he pointed to the snow-clad peaks. 'The country, too, was good, so they settled here and grew strong and powerful, and now our numbers are like the sea sand, and when Twala

83

the king calls up his regiments their plumes cover the plain so far as the eye of man can reach.'

'And if the land is walled in with mountains, who is there for the regiments to fight with?'

'Nay, my lord, the country is open there towards the north, and now and again warriors sweep down upon us in clouds from a land we know not, and we slay them. It is the third part of the life of a man since there was a war. Many thousands died in it, but we destroyed those who came to eat us up. So since then there has been no war.'

'Your warriors must grow weary of resting on their spears, Infadoos.'

'My lord, there was one war, just after we destroyed the people that came down upon us, but it was a civil war; dog ate dog.'

'How was that?'

'My lord, the king, my half-brother, had a brother born at the same birth, and of the same woman. It is not our custom, my lord, to suffer twins to live, the weaker must always die. But the mother of the king hid away the feebler child, which was born the last, for her heart yearned over it, and that child is Twala the king. I am his younger brother, born of another wife.'

'Well?'

'My lord, Kafa, our father, died when we came to manhood, and my brother Imotu was made king in his place, and for a space reigned and had a son by his favourite wife. When the babe was three years old, just after the great war, during which no man could sow or reap, a famine came upon the land, and the people murmured because of the famine, and looked round like a starved lion for something to rend. Then it was that Gagool the wise and terrible woman, who does not die, made a proclamation to the people. "The king Imotu is no king." And at the time Imotu was sick with a wound, and lay in his kraal not able to move.

'Then Gagool went into a hut and led out Twala, my half-brother, and twin brother to the king, whom she had hidden since he was born among the caves and rocks, and stripping the "moocha" (waist-cloth) off his loins, showed the people of the Kukuanas the mark of the sacred snake coiled round his middle, wherewith the eldest son of the king is marked at birth, and cried out loud, "Behold, your king whom I have saved for you even to this day!"

'Now the people being mad with hunger, and altogether bereft of reason and the knowledge of truth, cried out – *The king! The king!*" but I knew that it was not so, for Imotu my brother was the elder of the twins, and our lawful king. Then just as the tumult was at its height Imotu the king, though he was very sick, crawled from his hut holding his wife by the hand, and followed by his little son Ignosi – that is, by interpretation, the lightning.

'"What is this noise?" he asked; "Why cry ye *The king! The king!*"

'Then Twala, his own brother, born of the same woman, and in the same hour, ran to him, and taking him by the hair, stabbed him through the heart with his knife. And the people being fickle, and ever ready to worship the rising sun, clapped their hands and cried, "*Twala is king!* Now we know that Twala is king!"'

'And what became of his wife and her son Ignosi? Did Twala kill them too?'

'Nay, my lord. When she saw that her lord was dead the queen seized the child with a cry, and ran away. Two days afterwards she came to a kraal very hungry, and none would give her milk or food, now that her lord the king was dead, for all men hate the unfortunate. But at nightfall a little child, a girl, crept out and brought her corn to eat, and she blessed the child, and went on towards the mountains with her boy before the sun rose again, and there she must have perished, for none have seen her since, nor the child Ignosi.'

'Then if this child Ignosi had lived he would be the true king of the Kukuana people?'

'That is so, my lord; the sacred snake is round his middle. If he lives he is king; but, alas! he is long dead.'

'See, my lord,' and Infadoos pointed to a vast collection of huts surrounded by a fence, which was in its turn encircled by a great ditch, that lay on the plain beneath us. 'That is the kraal where the wife of Imotu was last seen with the child Ignosi. It is there that we shall sleep tonight, if, indeed,' he added doubtfully, 'my lords sleep at all upon this earth.'

'When we are among the Kukuanas, my good friend Infadoos, we do as the Kukuanas do,' I said majestically, and turned round quickly to address Good, who was tramping along sullenly behind, his mind fully occupied with unsatisfactory attempts to prevent his flannel shirt from flapping in the evening breeze. To my astonishment I butted into Umbopa, who was walking along immediately behind me, and very evidently had been listening with the greatest interest to my conversation with Infadoos. The expression on his face was most curious, and gave me the idea of a man who was struggling with partial success to bring something long ago forgotten back into his mind.

All this while we had been pressing on at a good rate towards the undulating plain beneath us. The mountains we had crossed now loomed high above our heads, and Sheba's Breasts were veiled modestly in diaphanous wreaths of mist. As we went the country grew more and more lovely. The vegetation was luxuriant, without being tropical; the sun was bright and warm, but not burning; and a gracious breeze blew softly along the odorous slopes of the mountains. Indeed, this new land was little less than an earthly paradise; in beauty, in natural wealth, and in climate I have never seen its like. The Transvaal is a fine country, but it is nothing to Kukuanaland.

So soon as we started, Infadoos had despatched a runner to warn the people of the kraal, which, by the way, was in his military command, of our arrival. This man had departed at an extraordinary speed, which Infadoos informed me he would keep up all the way, as running was an exercise much practised among his people.

The result of this message now became apparent. When we arrived within two miles of the kraal we could see that company after company of men were issuing from its gates and marching towards us.

Sir Henry laid his hand upon my arm, and remarked that it looked as though we were going to meet with a warm reception. Something in his tone attracted Infadoos' attention.

'Let not my lords be afraid,' he said hastily, 'for in my breast there dwells no guile. This regiment is one under my command, and comes out by my orders to greet you.'

I nodded easily, though I was not quite easy in my mind.

About half a mile from the gates of this kraal is a long stretch of rising ground sloping gently upwards from the road, and here the companies formed up. It was a splendid sight to see them, each company about three hundred strong, charging swiftly up the rise, with flashing spears and waving plumes, to take their appointed place. By the time we reached the slope twelve such companies, or in all three thousand six hundred men, had passed out and taken up their positions along the road.

Presently we came to the first company, and were able to gaze in astonishment on the most magnificent set of warriors that I have ever seen. They were all men of mature age, mostly veterans of about forty, and not one of them was under six feet in height, whilst many stood six feet three or four. They wore upon their heads heavy black plumes of sakabools feathers, like those which adorned our guides. Round their waists and also beneath the right knees were bound circlets of white ox tails, and in their left hands they carried round shields measuring about twenty inches across. These shields are very curious. The framework is made of an iron plate beaten out thin, over which is stretched milk-white ox-hide. The weapons that each man wore were simple, but most effective, consisting of a short and very heavy two-edged spear with a wooden shaft, the blade being about six inches across at the widest part. These spears are not used for throwing, but like the Zulu *bangwan*, or stabbing assegai, are for close quarters only, when the wound inflicted by them is terrible. In addition to his *bangwan* every man carried three large and heavy knives, each knife weighing about two pounds. One knife was fixed in the ox-tail girdle, and the other two at the back of the round shield. These knives, which are called '*tollas*' by the Kukuanas, take the place of the throwing assegai of the Zulus. The Kukuana warriors can cast them with great accuracy to a distance of fifty yards, and it is their custom on charging to hurl a volley of them at the enemy as they come to close quarters.

Each company remained still as a collection of bronze statues till we were opposite to it, when at a signal given by its commanding officer, who, distinguished by a leopard skin cloak, stood some paces in front, every spear was raised into the air, and from three hundred throats sprang forth with a sudden roar the royal salute of '*Koom*.' Then, so soon as we had passed, the company formed up behind us and followed us towards the kraal, till at last the whole regiment of the 'Greys' – so called from their white shields – the crack corps of the Kukuana people, was marching in our rear with a tread that shook the ground.

At length, branching off from Solomon's Great Road, we came to the wide fosse surrounding the kraal, which is at least a mile round, and fenced with a strong palisade of piles formed of the trunks of trees. At the gateway this fosse is spanned by a primitive drawbridge, which was let down by the guard to allow us to pass in. The kraal is exceedingly well laid out. Through the centre runs a wide pathway intersected at right angles by other pathways so arranged as to cut the huts into square blocks, each block being the quarters of a company. The huts are dome-shaped, and built, like those of the Zulus, of a framework of wattle, beautifully thatched with grass; but, unlike the Zulu huts, they have doorways through which we could walk. Also, they are much larger, and surrounded by a veranda about six feet wide, beautifully paved with powdered lime trodden hard.

All along each side of this wide pathway that pierces the kraal were ranged hundreds of women, brought out by curiosity to look at us. These women, for a native race, are exceedingly handsome. They are tall and graceful, and their figures are wonderfully fine. The hair, though short, is rather curly than woolly, the features are frequently aquiline, and the lips are not unpleasantly thick as is the case among African races. But what struck us most was their exceedingly quiet and dignified air. They were as well-bred in their way as the habituées of a fashionable drawing-room, and in this respect they differ from Zulu women, and their cousins the Masai who inhabit the district behind Zanzibar. Their curiosity had brought them out to see us, but they allowed no rude expressions of astonishment or savage criticism to pass their lips as we trudged wearily in front of them. Not even when old Infadoos with a surreptitious motion of the hand pointed out the crowning wonder of poor Good's 'beautiful white legs,' did they suffer the feeling of intense admiration which evidently mastered their minds to find expression. They fixed their dark eyes upon this new and snowy loveliness, for, as I think I have said, Good's skin is exceedingly white, and that was all. But it was quite enough for Good, who is modest by nature.

When we reached the centre of the kraal, Infadoos halted at the door of a large hut, which was surrounded at a distance by a circle of smaller ones.

'Enter, Sons of the Stars,' he said, in a magniloquent voice, 'and deign to rest awhile in our humble habitations. A little food shall be brought to you, so that ye shall have no need to draw your belts tight from hunger; some honey and some milk, and an ox or two, and a few sheep; not much, my lords, but still a little food.'

'It is good,' said I, 'Infadoos, we are weary with travelling through realms of air; now let us rest.'

Accordingly we entered into the hut, which we found amply prepared for our comfort. Couches of tanned skins were spread for us to lie on, and water was placed for us to wash in.

Presently we heard a shouting outside, and stepping to the door, saw a line of damsels bearing milk and roasted mealies, and honey in a pot. Behind these were some youths driving a fat young ox. We received the gifts, and then one of the young men took the knife from his girdle and dexterously cut the ox's throat. In ten minutes it was dead, skinned, and jointed. The best of the meat was then cut off for us, and the rest, in the name of our party, I presented to the warriors round us, who took it and distributed the 'white lords' gift.'

Umbopa set to work, with the assistance of an extremely prepossessing young woman, to boil our portion in a large earthenware pot over a fire which was built outside the hut, and when it was nearly ready we sent a message to Infadoos, and asked him and Scragga, the king's son, to join us.

Presently they came, and sitting down upon little stools, of which there were several about the hut, for the Kukuanas do not in general squat upon their haunches like the Zulus, they helped us to get through our dinner. The old gentleman was most affable and polite, but it struck me that the young one regarded us with doubt. Together with the rest of the party, he had been overawed by our white appearance and by our magic properties; but it seemed to me that, on discovering that we ate, drank, and slept like other mortals, his awe was beginning to wear off, and to be replaced by a sullen suspicion – which made me feel rather uncomfortable.

In the course of our meal Sir Henry suggested to me that it might be well to try to discover if our hosts knew anything of his brother's fate, or if they had ever seen or heard of him; but, on the whole, I thought that it would be wiser to say nothing of the matter at this time.

After supper we filled our pipes and lit them; a proceeding which filled Infadoos and Scragga with astonishment. The Kukuanas were evidently unacquainted with the divine uses of tobacco-smoke. The herb is grown among them extensively; but, like the Zulus, they only use it for snuff, and quite failed to identity it in its new form.

Presently I asked Infadoos when we were to proceed on our journey, and was delighted to learn that preparations had been made for us to leave on the following morning, messengers having already left to inform Twala the king of our coming. It appeared that Twala was at his principal place, known as Loo, making ready for the great annual feast which was to be held in the first week of June. At this gathering all the regiments, with the exception of certain detachments left behind for garrison purposes, are brought up and paraded before the king; and the great annual witch-hunt, of which more by-and-by, is held.

We were to start at dawn; and Infadoos, who was to accompany us, expected that we should reach Loo on the night of the second day, unless we were detained by accident or by swollen rivers.

When they had given us this information our visitors bade us good-night; and, having arranged to watch turn and turn about, three of us flung ourselves down and slept the sweet sleep of the weary, whilst the fourth sat up on the look-out for possible treachery.

Chapter IX

TWALA THE KING

It will not be necessary for me to detail at length the incidents of our journey to Loo. It took two full days' travelling along Solomon's Great Road, which pursued its even course right into the heart of Kukuanaland. Suffice it to say that as we went the country seemed to grow richer and richer, and the kraals, with their wide surrounding belts of cultivation, more and more numerous. They were all built upon the same principles as the first camp which we had reached, and were guarded by ample garrisons of troops. Indeed, in Kukuanaland, as among the Germans, the Zulus, and the Masai, every able-bodied man is a soldier, so that the whole force of the nation is available for its wars, offensive or defensive. As we travelled along we were overtaken by thousands of warriors hurrying up to Loo to be present at the great annual review and festival, and more splendid troops I never saw.

At sunset on the second day we stopped to rest awhile upon the summit of some heights over which the road ran, and there on a beautiful and fertile plain before us lay Loo itself. For a native town it is an enormous place, quite five miles round, I should say, with outlying kraals jutting out from it, that serve on grand occasions as cantonments for the regiments, and a curious horse-shoe-shaped hill, with which we were destined to become better acquainted, about two miles to the north. It is beautifully situated, and through the centre of the kraal, dividing it into two portions, runs a river, which appeared to be bridged in several places, the same indeed that we had seen from the slopes of Sheba's Breasts. Sixty or seventy miles away three great snow-capped mountains, placed at the points of a triangle, started out of the level plain. The conformation of these mountains is unlike that of Sheba's Breasts, being sheer and precipitous, instead of smooth and rounded.

Infadoos saw us looking at them, and volunteered a remark.

'The road ends there,' he said, pointing to the mountains known among the Kukuanas as the 'Three Witches.'

'Why does it end?' I asked.

'Who knows?' he answered with a shrug; 'the mountains are full of caves, and there is a great pit between them. It is there that the wise men of old time used to go to get whatever it was they came to this country for, and it is there now that our kings are buried in the Place of Death.'

'What was it they came for?' I asked eagerly.

'Nay, I know not. My lords who have dropped from the Stars should know,' he answered with a quick look. Evidently he knew more than he chose to say.

'Yes,' I went on, 'you are right, in the Stars we learn many things. I have heard, for instance, that the wise men of old came to these mountains to get bright stones, pretty playthings, and yellow iron.'

'My lord is wise,' he answered coldly; 'I am but a child and cannot talk with my lord on such matters. My lord must speak with Gagool the old, at the king's place, who is wise even as my lord,' and he went away.

So soon as he was gone I turned to the others, and pointed out the mountains. 'There are Solomon's diamond mines,' I said.

Umbopa was standing with them, apparently plunged in one of the fits of abstraction which were common to him, and caught my words.

'Yes, Macumazahn,' he put in, in Zulu, 'the diamonds are surely there, and you shall have them since you white men are so fond of toys and money.'

'How dost thou know that, Umbopa?' I asked sharply, for I did not like his mysterious ways.

He laughed. 'I dreamed it in the night, white men,' and then he too turned upon his heel and went.

'Now what,' said Sir Henry, 'is our black friend at? He knows more than he chooses to say, that is clear. By the way, Quatermain, has he heard anything of – of my brother?'

'Nothing; he has asked everyone he has become friendly with, but they all declare that no white man has ever been seen in the country before.'

'Do you suppose that he got here at all?' suggested Good; 'we have only reached the place by a miracle; is it likely he could have reached it without the map?'

'I don't know,' said Sir Henry gloomily, 'but somehow I think that I shall find him.'

Slowly the sun sank, and then suddenly darkness rushed down on the land like a tangible thing. There was no breathing-space between the day and night, no soft transformation scene, for in these latitudes twilight does not exist. The change from day to night is as quick and as absolute as the change from life to death. The sun sank and the world was wreathed in shadows. But not for long, for see in the west there is a glow, then come rays of silver light, and at last the full and glorious moon lights up the plain and shoots its gleaming arrows far and wide, filling the earth with a faint refulgence.

We stood and watched the lovely sight, whilst the stars grew pale before this chastened majesty, and felt our hearts lifted up in the presence of a beauty that I cannot describe. Mine has been a rough life, but there are a few things I am thankful to have lived for, and one of them is to have seen that moon shine on Kukuanaland.

Presently our meditations were broken in upon by our polite friend Infadoos.

'If my lords are rested we will journey on to Loo, where a hut is made ready for my lords to-night. The moon is now bright, so that we shall not fall by the way.'

We assented, and in an hour's time were at the outskirts of the town, of which the extent, mapped out as it was by thousands of camp fires, appeared absolutely endless. Indeed, Good, who is always fond of a bad joke, christened it 'Unlimited Loo.' Soon we came to a moat with a drawbridge, where we were met by the rattling of arms and the hoarse challenge of a sentry. Infadoos gave some password that I could not catch, which was met with a salute, and we passed on through the central street of the great grass city. After nearly half an hour's tramp, past endless lines of huts, Infadoos halted at last by the gate of a little group of huts which surrounded a small courtyard of powdered limestone, and informed us that these were to be our 'poor' quarters.

We entered, and found that a hut had been assigned to each of us. These huts were superior to any that we had yet seen, and in each was a most comfortable bed made of tanned skins, spread upon mattresses of aromatic grass. Food too was ready for us, and so soon as we had washed ourselves with water which stood ready in earthenware jars, some young women of handsome appearance brought us roasted meats, and mealie cobs daintily served on wooden platters, and presented them to us with deep obeisances.

We ate and drank, and then the beds having been all moved into one hut by our request, a precaution at which the amiable young ladies smiled, we flung ourselves down to sleep, thoroughly wearied with our long journey.

When we woke it was to find the sun high in the heavens, and the female attendants, who did not seem to be troubled by any false shame, already standing inside the hut, having been ordered to attend and help us to 'make ready.'

'Make ready, indeed,' growled Good; 'when one has only a flannel shirt and a pair of boots, that does not take long. I wish you would ask them for my trousers, Quatermain.'

I asked accordingly, but was informed that these sacred relics had already been taken to the king, who would see us in the forenoon.

Somewhat to their astonishment and disappointment, having requested the young ladies to step outside, we proceeded to make the best toilet that the circumstances admitted of. Good even went the length of again shaving the right side of his face; the left, on which now appeared a very fair crop of whiskers, we impressed upon him he must on no account touch. As for ourselves, we were contented with a good wash and combing our hair. Sir Henry's yellow locks were now almost upon his shoulders, and he looked more like an ancient Dane than ever, while my grizzled scrub was fully an inch long, instead of half an inch, which in a general way I considered my maximum length.

By the time that we had eaten our breakfasts, and smoked a pipe, a message was brought to us by no less a personage than Infadoos himself that Twala the king was ready to see us, if we would be pleased to come.

We remarked in reply that we should prefer to wait till the sun was a little higher, we were yet weary with our journey, etc., etc. It is always well, when dealing with uncivilized people, not to be in too great a hurry. They are apt to mistake politeness for awe or servility. So, although we were quite as anxious to see Twala as Twala could be to see us, we sat down and waited for an hour, employing the interval in preparing such presents as our slender stock of goods permitted – namely the Winchester rifle which had been used by poor Ventvögel, and some beads. The rifle and ammunition we determined to present to his Royal Highness, and the beads were for his wives and courtiers. We had already given a few to Infadoos and Scragga, and found that they were delighted with them, never having seen anything like them before. At length we declared that we were ready, and guided by Infadoos, started off to the audience, Umbopa carrying the rifle and beads.

After walking a few hundred yards we came to an enclosure, something like that surrounding the huts which had been allotted to us, only fifty times as big, for it could not have covered less than six or seven acres of ground. All round the outside fence stood a row of huts, which were the habitations of the king's wives. Exactly opposite the gateway, on the further side of the open space, was a very large hut, built by itself, in which his majesty resided. All the rest was open ground; that is to say, it would have been open had it not been filled by company after company of warriors, who were mustered there to the number of seven or eight thousand. These men stood still as statues as we advanced through them, and it would be impossible to give an adequate idea of the grandeur of the spectacle which they presented, with their waving plumes, their glancing spears, and iron-backed ox-hide shields.

The space in front of the large hut was empty, but before it were placed several stools. On three of these, at a sign from Infadoos, we seated ourselves, Umbopa standing behind us. As for Infadoos, he took up a position by the door of the hut. So we waited for ten minutes or more in the midst of a dead silence, but conscious that we were the object of the concentrated gaze of some eight thousand pairs of eyes. It was a somewhat trying ordeal, but we carried it off as best we could. At length the door of the hut opened, and a gigantic figure, with a splendid tiger-skin karross flung over its shoulders, stepped out, followed by the boy Scragga, and what appeared to us to be a withered-up monkey, wrapped in a fur cloak. The figure seated itself upon a stool, Scragga took his stand behind it, and the withered-up monkey crept on all fours into the shade of the hut and squatted down.

Still there was silence.

Then the gigantic figure slipped off the karross and stood up before us, a truly alarming spectacle. It was that of an enormous man with the most entirely repulsive countenance we had ever beheld. The man's lips were thick as a negro's, the nose was flat, he had but one gleaming black eye, for the other was represented by a hollow in the face, and his whole expression was cruel and sensual to a degree. From the large head rose a magnificent plume of white ostrich feathers, his body was clad in a shirt of shining chain armour, whilst round the waist and right knee were the usual garnishes of white ox-tail. In his right hand was a huge spear, about the neck a thick torque of gold, and bound on to the forehead shone dully a single and enormous uncut diamond.

Still there was silence; but not for long. Presently the man, whom we rightly guessed to be the king, raised the great javelin in his hand. Instantly eight thousand spears were lifted in answer, and from eight thousand throats rang out the royal salute of '*Koom.*' Three times this was repeated, and each time the earth shook with the noise, that can only be compared to the deepest notes of thunder.

'Be humble, O people,' piped out a thin voice which seemed to come from the monkey in the shade, 'it is the king.'

'*It is the king,*' boomed out eight thousand throats in answer. '*Be humble, O people, it is the king.*'

Then there was dead silence again – dead silence. Presently, however, it was broken. A soldier on our left dropped his shield, which fell with a clatter on to the limestone flooring.

Twala turned his cold eye in the direction of the noise.

'Come hither, thou,' he said in a cold voice.

A fine young man stepped out of the ranks, and stood before him.

'It was thy shield that fell, thou awkward dog. Wilt thou make me a reproach in the eyes of these strangers from the Stars? What hast thou to say?'

We saw the poor fellow turn pale under his dusky skin.

'It was by chance, O Calf of the Black Cow,' he murmured.

'Then it is a chance for which thou must pay. Thou hast made me foolish; prepare for death.'

'I am the king's ox,' was the low answer.

'Scragga,' roared the king, 'let me see how thou canst use thy spear. Kill me this awkward dog.'

Scragga stepped forward with an ill-favoured grin, and lifted his spear. The poor victim covered his eyes with his hand and stood still. As for us, we were petrified with horror.

'Once, twice,' he waved the spear and then struck, ah! right home – the spear stood out a foot behind the soldier's back. He flung up his hands and dropped dead. From the multitude about us rose something like a murmur, it rolled round and round, and died away. The tragedy was finished; there lay the corpse, and we had not yet realized that it had been enacted. Sir Henry sprang up and swore a great oath, then, overpowered by the sense of silence, sat down again.

'The thrust was a good one,' said the king; 'take him away.'

Four men stepped out of the ranks, and lifting the body of the murdered man, carried it thence.

'Cover up the blood-stains, cover them up,' piped out the thin voice that proceeded from the monkey-like figure; 'the king's word is spoken, the king's doom is done!'

Thereupon a girl came forward from behind the hut, bearing a jar filled with powdered lime, which she scattered over the red mark, blotting it from sight.

Sir Henry meanwhile was boiling with rage at what had happened; indeed, it was with difficulty that we could keep him still.

'Sit down, for heaven's sake,' I whispered; 'our lives depend on it.'

He yielded and remained quiet.

Twala sat silent until the traces of the tragedy had been removed, then he addressed us.

'White people,' he said, 'who come hither, whence I know not, and why I know not, greeting.'

'Greeting, Twala, King of the Kukuanas,' I answered.

'White people, whence come ye, and what seek ye?'

'We come from the Stars, ask us not how. We come to see this land.'

'Ye journey from far to see a little thing. And that man with you,' pointing to Umbopa, 'does he also come from the Stars?'

'Even so; there are people of thy colour in the heavens above; but ask not of matters too high for thee, Twala the king.'

'Ye speak with a loud voice, people of the Stars,' Twala answered in a tone which I scarcely liked. 'Remember that the stars are far off, and ye are here. How if I make you as him whom they bore away?'

I laughed out loud, though there was little laughter in my heart.

'O king,' I said, 'be careful, walk warily over hot stones, lest thou shouldst burn thy feet; hold the spear by the handle, lest thou shouldst cut thy hands. Touch but one hair of our heads, and destruction shall come upon thee. What, have not these' – pointing to Infadoos and Scragga, who, young villain that he was, was employed in cleaning the blood of the soldier off his spear – 'told thee what manner of men we are? Hast thou seen the like of us?' and I pointed to Good, feeling quite sure that he had never seen anybody before who looked in the least like *him* as he then appeared.

'It is true, I have not,' said the king, surveying Good.

'Have they not told thee how we strike with death from afar?' I went on.

'They have told me, but I believe them not. Let me see you kill. Kill me a man among those who stand yonder' – and he pointed to the opposite side of the kraal – 'and I will believe.'

'Nay,' I answered; 'we shed no blood of men except in just punishment; but if thou wilt see, bid thy servants drive in an ox through the kraal gates, and before he has run-twenty paces I will strike him dead.'

'Nay,' laughed the king, 'kill me a man and I will believe.'

'Good, O king, so be it,' I answered coolly; 'do thou walk across the open space, and before thy feet reach the gate thou shalt be dead; or if thou wilt not, send thy son Scragga' (whom at that moment it would have given me much pleasure to shoot).

On hearing this suggestion Scragga uttered a sort of howl, and bolted into the hut.

Twala frowned majestically; the suggestion did not please him.

'Let a young ox be driven in,' he said.

Two men at once departed, running swiftly.

'Now, Sir Henry,' said I, 'do you shoot. I want to show this ruffian that I am not the only magician of the party.'

Sir Henry accordingly took the express, and made ready.

'I hope I shall make a good shot,' he groaned.

'You must,' I answered. 'If you miss with the first barrel, let him have the second. Sight for 150 yards, and wait till the beast turns broadside on.'

Then came a pause, until presently we caught sight of an ox running straight for the kraal gate. It came on through the gate, and then, catching sight of the vast concourse of people, stopped stupidly, turned round, and bellowed.

'Now's your time,' I whispered.

Up went the rifle.

Bang! *thud!* and the ox was kicking on his back, shot in the ribs. The semi-hollow bullet had done its work well, and a sigh of astonishment went up from the assembled thousands.

I turned round coolly –

'Have I lied, O king?'

'Nay, white man, it is the truth,' was the somewhat awed answer.

'Listen, Twala,' I went on. 'Thou hast seen. Now know we come in peace, not in war. See,' and I held up the Winchester repeater; 'there is a hollow staff that shall enable thee to kill even as we kill, only I lay this charm upon it, thou shalt kill no man with it. If thou liftest it against a man, it shall kill thee. Stay, I will show thee. Bid a soldier step forty paces and place the shaft of a spear in the ground so that the flat blade looks towards us.'

In a few seconds it was done.

'Now see, I will break yonder spear.'

Taking a careful sight I fired. The bullet struck the flat of the spear, and shattered the blade into fragments.

Again the sigh of astonishment went up.

'Now, Twala, we give this magic tube to thee, and by-and-by I will show thee how to use it; but beware how thou turnest the magic of the Stars against a man of earth,' and I handed him the rifle.

The king took it very gingerly, and laid it down at his feet. As he did so I observed the wizened monkey-like figure creeping from the shadow of the hut. It crept on all fours, but when it reached the place where the king sat it rose upon its feet, and throwing the furry covering from its face, revealed a most extraordinary and weird countenance. Apparently it was that of a woman of great age, so shrunken that in size it seemed no larger than the face of a year-old child, although made up of a number of deep and yellow wrinkles. Set in these wrinkles was a sunken slit, that represented the mouth, beneath which the chin curved outwards to a point. There was no nose to speak of; indeed, the visage might have been taken for that of a sun-dried corpse had it not been for a pair of large black eyes, still full of fire and intelligence, which gleamed and played under the snow-white eye-brows, and the projecting parchment-coloured skull, like jewels in a charnel-house. As for the head itself, it was perfectly bare, and yellow in hue, while its wrinkled scalp moved and contracted like the hood of a cobra.

The figure to which this fearful countenance belonged, a countenance so fearful, indeed, that it caused a shiver of fear to pass through us as we gazed on it, stood still for a moment. Then suddenly it projected a skinny claw armed with nails nearly an inch long, and laying it on the shoulder of Twala the king, began to speak in a thin and piercing voice –

'Listen, O king! Listen, O warriors! Listen, O mountains and plains and rivers, home of the Kukuana race! Listen, O skies and sun, O rain and storm and mist! Listen, O men and women, O youths and maidens, and O ye babes unborn! Listen, all things that live and must die! Listen, all dead things that shall live again – again to die! Listen, the spirit of life is in me, and I prophesy. I prophesy! I prophesy!'

The words died away in a faint wail, and terror seemed to seize upon the hearts of all who heard them, including our own. This old woman was very terrible.

'*Blood! blood! blood!* rivers of blood; blood everywhere. I see it, I smell it, I taste it – it is salt! it runs red upon the ground, it rains down from the skies.

'*Footsteps! footsteps! footsteps!* the tread of the white man coming from afar. It shakes the earth; the earth trembles before her master.

'Blood is good, the red blood is bright; there is no smell like the smell of new-shed blood. The lions shall lap it up and roar, the vultures shall wash their wings in it and shriek with joy.

'I am old! I am old! I have seen much blood; *ha, ha!* but I shall see more ere I die, and be merry. How old am I, think ye! Your fathers knew me, and *their* fathers knew me, and *their* father's fathers. I have seen the white man and know his desires. I am old, but the mountains are older than I. Who made the great road, tell me? Who wrote the pictures on the rocks, tell me? Who reared up the three Silent Ones yonder, that gaze across the pit, tell me?' and she pointed towards the three precipitous mountains which we had noticed on the previous night.

'Ye know not, but I know. It was a white people who were before ye are, who shall be when ye are not, who shall eat you up and destroy you. *Yea! Yea! Yea!*

'And what came they for, the White Ones, the Terrible Ones, the skilled in magic and all learning, the strong, the unswerving? What is that bright stone upon thy forehead, O king? Whose hands made the iron garments upon thy breast, O king? Ye know not, but I know. I the Old One, I the Wise One, I the *Isanust*, the witch doctress!'

Then she turned her bald vulture-head towards us.

'What seek ye, white men of the Stars – ah, yes, of the Stars? Do ye seek a lost one? Ye shall not find him here. He is not here. Never for ages upon ages has a white foot pressed this land; never except once, and he left it but to die. Ye come for bright stones; I know it – I know it; ye shall find them when the blood is dry; but shall ye return whence ye came, or shall ye stop with me? *Ha! ha! ha!*

'And thou, thou with the dark skin and the proud bearing,' and she pointed her skinny finger at Umbopa, 'who art *thou*, and what seekest *thou*? Not stones that shine, not yellow metal that gleams, these thou leavest to "white men from the Stars." Methinks I know thee; methinks I can smell the smell of the blood in thy heart. Strip off the girdle—'

Here the features of this extraordinary creature became convulsed, and she fell to the ground foaming in an epileptic fit, and was carried into the hut.

*　　　*　　　*

The king rose up trembling, and waved his hand. Instantly the regiments began to file off, and in ten minutes, save for ourselves, the king, and a few attendants, the great space was left empty.

'White people,' he said, 'it passes in my mind to kill you. Gagool has spoken strange words. What say ye?'

I laughed. 'Be careful, O king, we are not easy to slay. Thou hast seen the fate of the ox; wouldst thou be as the ox is?'

The king frowned. 'It is not well to threaten a king.'

'We threaten not, we speak what is true. Try to kill us, O king, and learn.'

The great savage put his hand to his forehead and thought.

'Go in peace,' he said at length. 'To-night is the great dance. Ye shall see it. Fear not that I shall set a snare for you. To-morrow I will think.'

'It is well, O king,' I answered unconcernedly, and then, accompanied by Infadoos, we rose and went back to our kraal.

Chapter X

THE WITCH-HUNT

On reaching our hut I motioned to Infadoos to enter with us.

'Now, Infadoos,' I said, 'we would speak with thee.'

'Let my lords say on.'

'It seems to us, Infadoos, that Twala the king is a cruel man.'

'It is so, my lords. Alas! the land cries out because of his cruelties. To-night ye shall see. It is the great witch-hunt, and many will be smelt out as wizards and slain. No man's life is safe. If the king covets a man's cattle, or a man's wife, or if he fears a man that he should excite a rebellion against him, then Gagool, whom ye saw, or some of the witch-finding women whom she has taught, will smell that man out as a wizard, and he will be killed. Many must die before the moon grows pale to-night. It is ever so. Perhaps I too shall be killed. As yet I have been spared because I am skilled in war, and beloved by the soldiers; but I know not how long I have to live. The land groans at the cruelties of Twala the king; it is wearied of him and his red ways.'

'Then why is it, Infadoos, that the people do not cast him down?'

'Nay, my lords, he is the king, and if he were killed Scragga would reign in his place, and the heart of Scragga is blacker than the heart of Twala his father. If Scragga were king the yoke upon our neck would be heavier than the yoke of Twala. If Imotu had never been slain, or if Ignosi his son had lived, it might have been otherwise; but they are both dead.'

'How knowest thou that Ignosi is dead?' said a voice behind us. We looked round astonished to see who spoke. It was Umbopa.

'What meanest thou, boy?' asked Infadoos; 'who told thee to speak?'

'Listen, Infadoos,' was the answer, 'and I will tell thee a story. Years ago the king Imotu was killed in this country and his wife fled with the boy Ignosi. Is it not so?'

'It is so.'

'It was said that the woman and her son died upon the mountains. Is it not so?'

'It is even so.'

'Well, it came to pass that the mother and the boy Ignosi did not die. They crossed the mountains, and were led by a tribe of wandering desert men across the sands beyond, till at last they came to water and grass and trees again.'

'How knowest thou this?'

'Listen. They travelled on and on, many months' journey, till they reached a land where a people called the Amazulu, who also are of the Kukuana stock, live by war, and with them they tarried many years, till at length the mother died. Then the son Ignosi became a wanderer again, and journeyed into a land of wonders, where white people live, and for many more years he learned the wisdom of the white people.'

'It is a pretty story,' said Infadoos incredulously.

'For years he lived there working as a servant and a soldier, but holding in his heart all that his mother had told him of his own place, and casting about in his mind to find how he might get back thither to see his people and his father's house before he died. For long years he lived and waited, and at last the time came, as it ever comes to him who can wait for it, and he met some white men who would seek this unknown land and joined himself to them. The white men started and journeyed on and on, seeking for one who is lost. They crossed the burning desert, they crossed the snow-clad mountains, and reached the land of the Kukuanas, and there they found *thee*, O Infadoos.'

'Surely thou art mad to talk thus,' said the astonished old soldier.

'Thou thinkest so; see, I will show Thee, O my uncle.

I am Ignosi, rightful king of the Kukuanas!'

Then with a single movement Umbopa slipped off his 'moocha' or girdle, and stood naked before us.

'Look,' he said; 'what is this?' and he pointed to the picture of a great snake tattooed in blue round his middle, its tail disappearing into its open mouth just above where the thighs are set into the body.

Infadoos looked, his eyes starting nearly out of his head, and then fell upon his knees.

'*Koom! Koom!*' he ejaculated; 'it is my brother's son; it is the king.'

'Did I not tell thee so, my uncle? Rise; I am not yet the king, but with thy help, and with the help of these brave white men, who are my friends, I shall be. Yet the old witch Gagool was right, the land shall run with blood first, and hers shall run with it, if she has any, for she killed my father with her words, and drove my mother forth. And now, Infadoos, choose thou. Wilt thou put thy hands between my hands and be my man? Wilt thou share the dangers that lie before me, and help me to overthrow this tyrant and murderer, or wilt thou not? Choose thou.'

The old man put his hand to his head and thought. Then he rose, and advancing to where Umbopa, or rather Ignosi, stood, he knelt before him and took his hand.

'Ignosi, rightful king of the Kukuanas, I put my hand between thy hands, and am thy man till death. When thou wast a babe I dandled thee upon my knees, now shall my old arm strike for thee and freedom.'

'It is well, Infadoos; if I conquer, thou shalt be the greatest man in the kingdom after the king. If I fail, thou canst only die, and death is not far off from thee. Rise, my uncle.

'And ye, white men, will ye help me? What have I to offer you! The white stones! If I conquer and can find them, ye shall have as many as ye can carry hence. Will that suffice you?'

I translated this remark.

'Tell him,' answered Sir Henry, 'that he mistakes an Englishman. Wealth is good, and if it comes in our way we will take it; but a gentleman does not sell himself for wealth. Still, speaking for myself, I say this. I have always liked Umbopa, and so far as lies in me will stand by him in this business. It will be very pleasant to me to

105

try to square matters with that cruel devil Twala. What do you say, Good, and you, Quatermain?'

'Well,' said Good, 'to adopt the language of hyperbole, in which all these people seem to indulge, you can tell him that a row is surely good, and warms the cockles of the heart, and that so far as I am concerned I'm his boy. My only stipulation is that he allows me to wear trousers.'

I translated the substance of these answers.

'It is well, my friends,' said Ignosi, late Umbopa; 'and what sayest thou, Macumazahn, art thou also with me, old hunter, cleverer than a wounded buffalo?'

I thought awhile and scratched my head.

'Umbopa, or Ignosi,' I said, 'I don't like revolutions. I am a man of peace, and a bit of a coward' – here Umbopa smiled – 'but, on the other hand, I stick to my friends, Ignosi. You have stuck to us and played the part of a man, and I will stick by you. But mind you, I am a trader, and have to make my living, so I accept your offer about those diamonds in case we should ever be in a position to avail ourselves of it. Another thing: we came, as you know, to look for Incubu's (Sir Henry's) lost brother. You must help us to find him.'

'That I will do,' answered Ignosi. 'Stay, Infadoos, by the sign of the snake about my middle; tell me the truth. Has any white man to thy knowledge set his foot within the land?'

'None, O Ignosi.'

'If any white man had been seen or heard of, wouldst thou have known it?'

'I should certainly have known.'

'Thou hearest, Incubu,' said Ignosi to Sir Henry; 'he has not been here.'

'Well, well,' said Sir Henry, with a sigh; 'there it is; I suppose that he never got so far. Poor fellow, poor fellow! So it has all been for nothing. God's will be done.'

'Now for business,' I put in, anxious to escape from a painful subject. 'It is very well to be a king by right divine, Ignosi, but how dost thou propose to become a king indeed?'

'Nay, I know not. Infadoos, hast thou a plan?'

'Ignosi, Son of the Lightning,' answered his uncle, 'to-night is the great dance and witch-hunt. Many shall be smelt out and perish, and in the hearts of many others there will be grief and anguish and anger against the king Twala. When the dance is over, then I will speak to some of the great chiefs, who in turn, if I can win them over, will speak to their regiments. I shall speak to the chiefs softly at first, and bring them to see that thou art indeed the king, and I think that by to-morrow's light thou shalt have twenty thousand spears at thy command. And now I must go and think, and hear, and make ready. After the dance is done, if I am yet alive, and we are all alive, I will meet thee here, and we can talk. At the best there must be war.'

At this moment our conference was interrupted by the cry that messengers had come from the king. Advancing to the door of the hut we ordered that they should be admitted, and presently three men entered, each bearing a shining shirt of chain armour, and a magnificent battle-axe.

'The gifts of my lord the king to the white men from the Stars!' said a herald who came with them.

'We thank the king,' I answered; 'withdraw.'

The men went, and we examined the armour with great interest. It was the most wonderful chain work that we had ever seen. A whole coat fell together so closely that it formed a mass of links scarcely too big to be covered with both hands.

'Do you make these things in this country, Infadoos?' I asked; 'they are very beautiful.'

'Nay, my lord, they came down to us from our forefathers. We know not who made them, and there are but few left.' None but those of royal blood may be clad in them. They are magic coats through which no spear can pass, and those who wear them are well-nigh safe in the battle. The king is well pleased or much afraid, or he would not have sent these garments of steel. Clothe yourselves in them to-night, my lords.'

The rest of that day we spent quietly, resting and talking over the situation, which was sufficiently exciting. At last the sun went down, the thousand watch fires glowed out, and through the darkness we heard the tramp of many feet and the clashing of

* In the Soudan, swords and coats of mail are still worn by Arabs, whose ancestors must have stripped them from the bodies of Crusaders. – *Editor.*

hundreds of spears, as the regiments passed to their appointed places to be ready for the great dance. Then the full moon shone out in splendour, and as we stood watching her rays, Infadoos arrived, clad in his war dress and accompanied by a guard of twenty men to escort us to the dance. As he recommended, we had already donned the shirts of chain armour which the king had sent us, putting them on under our ordinary clothing, and finding to our surprise that they were neither very heavy nor uncomfortable. These steel shirts, which evidently had been made for men of a very large stature, hung somewhat loosely upon Good and myself, but Sir Henry's fitted his magnificent frame like a glove. Then strapping our revolvers round our waists, and taking in our hands the battle-axes which the king had sent with the armour, we started.

On arriving at the great kraal, where we had that morning been received by the king, we found that it was closely packed with some twenty thousand men arranged round it in regiments. These regiments were in turn divided into companies, and between each company ran a little path to allow space for the witch-finders to pass up and down. Anything more imposing than the sight that was presented by this vast and orderly concourse of armed men it is impossible to conceive. There they stood perfectly silent, and the moon poured her light upon the forest of their raised spears, upon their majestic forms, waving plumes, and the harmonious shading of their various-coloured shields. Wherever we looked were line upon line of dim faces surmounted by range upon range of shimmering spears.

'Surely,' I said to Infadoos, 'the whole army is here?'

'Nay, Macumazahn,' he answered, 'but a third of it. One third part is present at this dance each year, another third is mustered outside in case there should be trouble when the killing begins, ten thousand more garrison the outposts round Loo, and the rest watch at the kraals in the country. Thou seest it is a great people.'

'They are very silent,' said Good; and indeed the intense stillness among such a vast concourse of living men was almost overpowering.

'What says Bougwan?' asked Infadoos.

I translated.

'Those over whom the shadow of Death is hovering are silent,' he answered grimly.

'Will many be killed?'

'Very many.'

'It seems,' I said to the others, 'that we are going to assist at a gladiatorial show arranged regardless of expense.'

Sir Henry shivered, and Good said he wished that we could get out of it.

'Tell me,' I asked Infadoos, 'are we in danger?'

'I know not, my lords, I trust not; but do not seem afraid. If ye live through the night all may go well. The soldiers murmur against the king.'

All this while we had been advancing steadily towards the centre of the open space, in the midst of which were placed some stools. As we proceeded we perceived another small party coming from the direction of the royal hut.

'It is the king, Twala, Scragga his son, and Gagool the old; and see, with them are those who slay,' and Infadoos pointed to a little group of about a dozen gigantic and savage-looking men, armed with spears in one hand and heavy kerries in the other.

The king seated himself upon the centre stool, Gagool crouched at his feet, and the others stood behind him.

'Greeting, white lords,' Twala cried, as we came up; 'be seated, waste not precious time – the night is all too short for the deeds that must be done. Ye come in a good hour, and shall see a glorious show. Look round, white lords; look round,' and he rolled his one wicked eye from regiment to regiment. 'Can the Stars show you such a sight as this? See how they shake in their wickedness, all those who have evil in their hearts and fear the judgment of "Heaven above."'

'*Begin! begin!*' piped Gagool, in her thin piercing voice; 'the hyænas are hungry, they howl for food. *Begin! begin!*'

Then for a moment there was intense stillness, made horrible by a presage of what was to come.

The king lifted his spear, and suddenly twenty thousand feet were raised, as though they belonged to one man, and brought down with a stamp upon the earth. This was repeated three times, causing the solid ground to shake and tremble. Then from a far point of the circle a solitary voice began a wailing song, of which the refrain ran something as follows: –

'What is the lot of man born of woman?'

Back came the answer rolling out from every throat in that vast company –

'Death!'

Gradually, however, the song was taken up by company after company, till the whole armed multitude were singing it, and I could no longer follow the words, except in so far as they appeared to represent various phases of human passions, fears, and joys. Now it seemed to be a love song, now a majestic swelling war chant, and last of all a death dirge ending suddenly in one heartbreaking wail that went echoing and rolling away in a volume of blood-curdling sound.

Again silence fell upon the place, and again it was broken by the king lifting his hand. Instantly we heard a pattering of feet, and from out of the masses of warriors strange and awful figures appeared running towards us. As they drew near we saw that these were women, most of them aged, for their white hair, ornamented with small bladders taken from fish, streamed out behind them. Their faces were painted in stripes of white and yellow; down their backs hung snake-skins, and round their waists rattled circlets of human bones, while each held a small forked wand in her shrivelled hand. In all there were ten of them. When they arrived in front of us they halted, and one of them pointing with her wand towards the crouching figure of Gagool, cried out –

'Mother, old mother, we are here.'

'Good! good! good!' answered that aged Iniquity. 'Are your eyes keen, *Isanusis* [witch doctresses], ye seers in dark places?'

'Mother, they are keen.'

'Good! good! good! Are your ears open, *Isanusis*, ye who hear words that come not from the tongue?'

'Mother, they are open.'

'Good! good! good! Are your senses awake, *Isanusis* – can ye smell blood, can ye purge the land of the wicked ones who compass evil against the king and against their neighbours? Are ye ready to do the justice of "Heaven above," ye whom I have taught, who have eaten of the bread of my wisdom, and drunk of the water of my magic?'

'Mother, we can.'

'Then go! Tarry not, ye vultures; see, the slayers' – pointing to the ominous group of executioners behind – 'make sharp their spears; the white men from afar are hungry to see. *Go!*'

With a wild yell Gagool's horrid ministers broke away in every direction, like fragments from a shell, the dry bones round their waists rattling as they ran, and headed for various points of the dense human circle. We could not watch them all, so we fixed our eyes upon the *Isanusi* nearest to us. When she came to within a few paces of the warriors she halted and began to dance wildly, turning round and round with an almost incredible rapidity, and shrieking out sentences such as 'I smell him, the evil-doer!' 'He is near, he who poisoned his mother!' 'I hear the thoughts of him who thought evil of the king!'

Quicker and quicker she danced, till she lashed herself into such a fury of excitement that the foam flew in flecks from her gnashing jaws, till her eyes seemed to start from her head, and her flesh to quiver visibly. Suddenly she stopped dead and stiffened all over, like a pointer dog when he scents game, and with outstretched wand she began to creep stealthily towards the soldiers before her. It seemed to us that as she came their stoicism gave way, and that they shrank from her. As for ourselves, we followed her movements with a horrible fascination. Presently, still creeping and crouching like a dog, the *Isanusi* was before them. Then she halted and pointed and again crept on a pace or two.

Suddenly the end came. With a shriek she sprang in and touched a tall warrior with her forked wand. Instantly two of his comrades, those standing immediately next to him, seized the doomed man, each by one arm, and advanced with him towards the king.

He did not resist, but we saw that he dragged his limbs as though they were paralysed, and that his fingers, from which the spear had fallen, were limp like those of a man newly dead.

As he came, two of the villainous executioners stepped forward to meet him. Presently they met, and the executioners turned round, looking towards the king as though for orders.

'*Kill!*' said the king.

'*Kill!*' squeaked Gagool.

'*Kill!*' re-echoed Scragga, with a hollow chuckle.

Almost before the words were uttered the horrible deed was done. One man had driven his spear into the victim's heart, and to make assurance doubly sure, the other had dashed out his brains with a great club.

'*One,*' counted Twala the king, just like a black Madame Defarge, as Good said, and the body was dragged a few paces away and stretched out.

Hardly was the thing done before another poor wretch was brought up, like an ox to the slaughter. This time we could see, from the leopard-skin cloak, that the man was a person of rank. Again the awful syllables were spoken, and the victim fell dead.

'*Two,*' counted the king.

And so the deadly game went on, till about a hundred bodies were stretched in rows behind us. I have heard of the gladiatorial shows of the Cæsars, and of the Spanish bull-fights, but I take the liberty of doubting if they were either of them half so horrible as this Kukuana witch-hunt. Gladiatorial shows and Spanish bull-fights, at any rate, contributed to the public amusement, which certainly was not the case here. The most confirmed sensation-monger would fight shy of sensation if he knew that it was well on the cards that he would, in his own proper person, be the subject of the next 'event.'

Once we rose and tried to remonstrate, but were sternly repressed by Twala.

'Let the law take its course, white men. These dogs are magicians and evil-doers; it is well that they should die,' was the only answer vouchsafed to us.

About half-past ten there was a pause. The witch finders gathered themselves together, apparently exhausted with their bloody work, and we thought that the performance was done with. But it was not so, for presently, to our surprise, the ancient woman, Gagool, rose from her crouching position, and supporting herself with a stick, staggered off into the open space. It was an extraordinary sight to see this frightful vulture-headed old creature, bent nearly double with extreme age, gather strength by degrees, until at last she rushed about almost as actively as her ill-omened pupils. To and fro she ran, chanting to herself, till suddenly she made a dash at a tall man standing in front of one of the regiments, and touched him. As she did this a sort of groan went up from the regiment which he evidently commanded. But all the same, two of its officers seized him and brought him up for execution. We learned afterwards that he was a man of great wealth and importance, being indeed a cousin of the king's.

He was slain, and the king counted one hundred and three. Then Gagool again sprang to and fro, gradually drawing nearer and nearer to ourselves.

'Hang me if I don't believe she is going to try her games on us,' ejaculated Good in horror.

'Nonsense!' said Sir Henry.

As for myself, when I saw that old fiend dancing nearer and nearer, my heart positively sank into my boots. I glanced behind us at the long rows of corpses, and shivered.

Nearer and nearer waltzed Gagool, looking for all the world like an animated crooked stick, her horrid eyes gleaming and glowing with a most unholy lustre.

Nearer she came, and yet nearer, every creature in that vast assemblage watching her movements with intense anxiety. At last she stood still and pointed.

'Which is it to be?' asked Sir Henry to himself.

In a moment all doubts were set at rest, for the old hag had rushed in and touched Umbopa, alias Ignosi, on the shoulder.

'I smell him out,' she shrieked. 'Kill him, kill him, he is full of evil; kill him, the stranger, before blood flows for him. Slay him, O king.'

There was a pause, which I instantly took advantage of.

'O king,' I called out, rising from my seat, 'this man is the servant of thy guests, he is their dog; whosoever sheds the blood of our dog sheds our blood. By the sacred law of hospitality I claim protection for him.'

'Gagool, mother of the witch-finders, has smelt him out; he must die, white men,' was the sullen answer.

'Nay, he shall not die,' I replied; 'he who tries to touch him shall die indeed.'

'Seize him!' roared Twala to the executioners, who stood around red to the eyes with the blood of their victims.

They advanced towards us, and then hesitated. As for Ignosi, he clutched his spear, and raised it as though determined to sell his life dearly.

'Stand back, ye dogs!' I shouted, 'if ye would see to-morrow's light. Touch one hair of his head and your king dies,' and I covered Twala with my revolver. Sir Henry and Good also drew their pistols, Sir Henry pointing his at the leading executioner, who was advancing to carry out the sentence, and Good taking a deliberate aim at Gagool.

Twala winced perceptibly as my barrel came in a line with his broad chest.

'Well,' I said, 'what is it to be, Twala?'

Then he spoke.

'Put away your magic tubes,' he said; 'ye have adjured me in the name of hospitality, and for that reason, but not from fear of what ye can do, I spare him. Go in peace.'

'It is well,' I answered unconcernedly; 'we are weary of slaughter, and would sleep. Is the dance ended?'

'It is ended,' Twala answered sulkily. 'Let these dead dogs,' pointing to the long row of corpses, 'be flung out to the hyænas and the vultures,' and he lifted his spear.

Instantly the regiments began to defile through the kraal gateway in perfect silence, a fatigue party only remaining behind to drag away the corpses of those who had been sacrificed.

Then we rose also, and making our salaam to his majesty, which he hardly deigned to acknowledge, we departed to our huts.

'Well,' said Sir Henry, as we sat down, having first lit a lamp of the sort used by the Kukuanas, of which the wick is made from the fibre of a species of palm leaf, and the oil from clarified hippopotamus fat, 'well, I feel uncommonly inclined to be sick.'

'If I had any doubts about helping Umbopa to rebel against that infernal black-guard,' put in Good, 'they are gone now. It was as much as I could do to sit still while that slaughter was going on. I tried to keep my eyes shut, but they would open just at the wrong time. I wonder where Infadoos is. Umbopa, my friend, you ought to be grateful to us; your skin came near to having an air-hole made in it.'

'I am grateful, Bougwan,' was Umbopa's answer, when I had translated, 'and I shall not forget. As for Infadoos, he will be here by-and-by. We must wait.'

So we lit our pipes and waited.

Chapter XI

WE GIVE A SIGN

For a long while – two hours, I should think – we sat there in silence, being too much overwhelmed by the recollection of the horrors we had seen to talk. At last, just as we were thinking of turning in – for the night drew nigh to dawn – we heard a sound of steps. Then came the challenge of a sentry posted at the kraal gate, which apparently was answered, though not in an audible tone, for the steps still advanced; and in another second Infadoos had entered the hut, followed by some half-dozen stately-looking chiefs.

'My lords,' he said, 'I have come according to my word. My lords and Ignosi, rightful king of the Kukuanas, I have brought with me these men,' pointing to the row of chiefs, 'who are great men among us, having each one of them the command of three thousand soldiers, that live but to do their bidding, under the king's. I have told them of what I have seen, and what my ears have heard. Now let them also behold the sacred snake around thee, and hear thy story, Ignosi, that they may say whether or no they will make cause with thee against Twala the king.'

By way of answer, Ignosi again stripped off his girdle and exhibited the snake tattooed about him. Each chief in turn drew near and examined the sign by the dim light of the lamp, and without saying a word passed on to the other side.

Then Ignosi resumed his moocha, and addressing them, repeated the history he had detailed in the morning.

'Now ye have heard, chiefs,' said Infadoos, when he had done, 'what say ye; will ye stand by this man and help him to his father's throne, or will ye not? The land cries out against Twala, and the blood of the people flows like the waters in spring. Ye have seen to-night. Two other chiefs there were with whom I had it in my mind to speak, and where are they now. The hyænas howl over their corpses. Soon shall ye be as they are if ye strike not. Choose then, my brothers.'

The eldest of the six men, a short, thick-set warrior, with white hair, stepped forward a pace and answered –

'Thy words are true, Infadoos; the land cries out. My own brother is among those who died to-night; but this is a great matter, and the thing is hard to believe. How know we that if we lift our spears it may not be for a cheat and a liar? It is a great matter, I say, and none can see the end of it. For of this be sure, blood will flow in rivers before the deed is done; many will still cleave to the king, for men worship the sun that still shines bright in the heavens, rather than that which has not risen. These white men from the stars, their magic is great, and Ignosi is under the cover of their wing. If he be indeed the rightful king, let them give us a sign, and let the people have a sign, that all may see. So shall men cleave to us, knowing that the white man's magic is with them.'

'Ye have the sign of the snake,' I answered.

'My lord, it is not enough. The snake may have been placed there since the man's childhood. Show us the sign. We will not move without a sign.'

The others gave a decided assent, and I turned in perplexity to Sir Henry and Good, and explained the situation.

'I think that I have it,' said Good exultingly; 'ask them to give us a moment to think.'

I did so, and the chiefs withdrew. So soon as they had gone Good went to the little box where he kept his medicines, unlocked it, and took out a note-book, in the fly-leaves of which was an almanack. 'Now look here, you fellows, isn't to-morrow the 4th of June?' he said.

We had kept a careful note of the days, so were able to answer that it was.

'Very good; then here we have it – "4 June, total eclipse of the moon commences at 8.15 Greenwich time, visible in Teneriffe – *South Africa*, etc." There's a sign for you. Tell them we will darken the moon to-morrow night.'

The idea was a splendid one; indeed, the only weak spot about it was the fear lest Good's almanack might be incorrect. If we made a false prophecy on such a subject, our prestige would be gone for ever, and so would Ignosi's chance of the throne of the Kukuanas.

'Suppose the almanack is wrong,' suggested Sir Henry to Good, who was busily employed in working out something on a blank page of the book.

'I see no reason to suppose anything of the sort,' was his answer. 'Eclipses always come up to time; at least that is my experience of them, and it especially states that this one will be visible in South Africa. I have worked out the reckonings as well as I can, without knowing our exact position; and I make out that the eclipse should begin here about ten o'clock to-morrow night, and last till half-past twelve. For an hour and a half or so there should be almost total darkness.'

'Well,' said Sir Henry, 'I suppose we had better risk it.'

I acquiesced, though doubtfully, for eclipses are queer cattle to deal with – it might be a cloudy night, for instance – and sent Umbopa to summon the chiefs back. Presently they came, and I addressed them thus –

'Great men of the Kukuanas, and thou, Infadoos, listen. We love not to show our powers, for to do so is to interfere with the course of nature, and plunge the world into fear and confusion. But since this matter is a great one, and as we are angered against the king because of the slaughter we have seen, and because of the act of the *Isanusi* Gagool, who would have put our friend Ignosi to death, we have determined to break the rule, and to give such a sign that all men may see. Come hither;' and I led them to the door of the hut and pointed to the red ball of the fading moon. 'What see ye there?'

'We see the dying moon,' answered the spokesman of the party.

'It is so. Now tell me, can any mortal man put out that moon before her hour of setting, and bring the curtain of black night down on to the land?'

The chief laughed a little. 'No, my lord, that no man can do. The moon is stronger than man who looks on her, nor can she vary in her courses.'

'Ye say so. Yet I tell you that to-morrow night, two hours before midnight, will we cause the moon to be eaten up for the space of an hour and half an hour. Yes, deep darkness shall cover the earth, and it shall be for a sign that Ignosi is indeed king of the Kukuanas. If we do this thing will ye be satisfied?'

'Yea, my lords,' answered the old chief with a smile, which was reflected on the faces of his companions; '*if* ye do this thing we will be satisfied indeed.'

'It shall be done; we three, Incubu, Bougwan, and Macumazahn, have said it, and it shall be done. Dost thou hear, Infadoos?'

'I hear, my lord, but it is a wonderful thing that ye promise, to put out the moon, the mother of the world, when she is at her full.'

'Yet shall we do it, Infadoos.'

'It is well, my lords. To-day, two hours after sunset, Twala will send for my lords to witness the girls dance, and one hour after the dance begins the girl whom Twala thinks the fairest shall be killed by Scragga, the king's son, as a sacrifice to the silent Stone Ones, who sit and keep watch by the mountains yonder,' and he pointed towards the three strange-looking peaks where Solomon's road was supposed to end. 'Then let my lords darken the moon, and save the maiden's life, and the people will believe indeed.'

'Ay,' said the old chief, still smiling a little, 'the people will believe indeed.'

'Two miles from Loo,' went on Infadoos, 'there is a hill curved like a new moon, a stronghold, where my regiment, and three other regiments which these chiefs command, are stationed. This morning we will make a plan whereby two or three other regiments may be moved there also. Then if in truth my lords can darken the moon, in the darkness I will take my lords by the hand and lead them out of Loo to this place, where they shall be safe, and thence we can make war upon Twala the king.'

'It is good,' said I. 'Now leave us to sleep awhile and to make ready our magic.'

Infadoos rose, and, having saluted us, departed with the chiefs.

'My friends,' said Ignosi, as soon as they were gone, 'can ye do this wonderful thing, or were ye speaking empty words to the men?'

'We believe that we can do it, Umbopa – Ignosi, I mean.'

'It is strange,' he answered, 'and had ye not been Englishmen I would not have believed it; but I have learned that English "gentlemen" tell no lies. If we live through the matter, be sure that I will repay you.'

'Ignosi,' said Sir Henry, 'promise me one thing.'

'I will promise, Incubu, my friend, even before I hear it,' answered the big man with a smile. 'What is it?'

'This: that if ever you come to be king of this people you will do away with the smelling out of wizards such as we saw last night; and that the killing of men without trial shall no longer take place in the land.'

Ignosi thought for a moment after I had translated this request, and then answered –

'The ways of black people are not as the ways of white men, Incubu, nor do we value life so highly. Yet I will promise it. If it be in my power to hold them back, the witch-finders shall hunt no more, nor shall any man die the death without trial and judgment.'

'That's a bargain then,' said Sir Henry; 'and now let us get a little rest.'

Thoroughly wearied out, we were soon sound asleep, and slept till Ignosi woke us about eleven o'clock. Then we rose, washed, and ate a hearty breakfast. After that we went outside the hut and walked about, amusing ourselves with examining the structure of the Kukuana huts and observing the customs of the women.

'I hope that eclipse will come off,' said Sir Henry presently.

'If it does not it will soon be all up with us,' I answered mournfully; 'for so sure as we are living men some of those chiefs will tell the whole story to the king, and then there will be another sort of eclipse, and one that we shall not like.'

Returning to the hut we ate some dinner, and passed the rest of the day in receiving visits of ceremony and curiosity. At length the sun set, and we enjoyed a couple of hours of such quiet as our melancholy forebodings would allow to us. Finally, about half-past eight, a messenger came from Twala to bid us to the great annual 'dance of girls' which was about to be celebrated.

Hastily we put on the chain shirts that the king had sent to us, and taking our rifles and ammunition with us, so as to have them handy in case we had to fly, as suggested by Infadoos, we started boldly enough, though with inward fear and trembling. The great space in front of the king's kraal bore a very different appearance from that which it had presented on the previous evening. In place of the grim ranks of serried warriors were company after company of Kukuana girls, not over-dressed, so far as clothing went, but each crowned with a wreath of flowers, and holding a palm leaf in one hand and a white arum lily in the other. In the centre of the open moonlit space sat Twala the king, with old Gagool at his feet, attended by Infadoos, the boy Scragga, and twelve guards. There were also present about a score of chiefs, amongst whom I recognized most of our friends of the night before.

Twala greeted us with much apparent cordiality, though I saw him fix his one eye viciously on Umbopa.

'Welcome, white men from the Stars,' he said; 'this is another sight from that which your eyes gazed on by the light of last night's moon, but it is not so good a sight. Girls are pleasant, and were it not for such as these,' and he pointed round him, 'we should none of us be here this day; but men are better. Kisses and the tender words of women are sweet, but the sound of the clashing of the spears of warriors, and the smell of men's blood, are sweeter far! Would ye have wives from among our people, white men? If so, choose the fairest here, and ye shall have them, as many as ye will,' and he paused for an answer.

As the prospect did not seem to be without attractions for Good, who, like most sailors, is of a susceptible nature, being elderly and wise, and foreseeing the endless complications that anything of the sort would involve, for women bring trouble so surely as the night follows the day, I put in a hasty answer –

'Thanks to thee, O king, but we white men wed only with white women like ourselves. Your maidens are fair, but they are not for us!'

The king laughed. 'It is well. In our land there is a proverb which runs, "Women's eyes are always bright, whatever the colour," and another that says, "Love her who is present, for be sure she who is absent is false to thee;" but perhaps these things are not so in the Stars. In a land where men are white all things are possible. So be it, white men; the girls will not go begging! Welcome again; and welcome, too, thou black one; if Gagool here had won her way, thou wouldst have been stiff and cold by now. It is lucky for thee that thou too camest from the Stars; ha! ha!'

'I can kill thee before thou killest me, O king,' was Ignosi's calm answer, 'and thou shalt be stiff before my limbs cease to bend.'

Twala started. 'Thou speakest boldly, boy,' he replied angrily; 'presume not too far.'

'He may well be bold in whose lips are truth. The truth is a sharp spear which flies home and misses not. It is a message from the "Stars," O king.'

Twala scowled, and his one eye gleamed fiercely, but he said nothing more.

'Let the dance begin,' he cried, and then the flower-crowned girls sprang forward in companies, singing a sweet song and waving the delicate palms and white lilies. On they danced, looking faint and spiritual in the delicate sad light of the risen moon; now whirling round and round, now meeting in mimic warfare, swaying, eddying here and there, coming forward, falling back in an ordered confusion delightful to witness. At last they paused, and a beautiful young woman sprang out of the ranks and began to pirouette in front of us with a grace and vigour which would have put most ballet girls to shame. At length she retired exhausted, and another took her place, then another and another, but none of them, either in grace, skill, or personal attractions, came up to the first.

When the chosen girls had all danced, the king lifted his hand.

'Which deem ye the fairest, white men?' he asked.

'The first,' said I unthinkingly. Next second I regretted it, for I remembered that Infadoos had told us that the fairest woman must be offered up as a sacrifice.

'Then is my mind as your minds, and my eyes are your eyes. She is the fairest; and a sorry thing it is for her, for she must die!'

'*Ay, must die!*' piped out Gagool, casting a glance of her quick eyes in the direction of the poor girl, who, as yet ignorant of the awful fate in store for her, was standing some ten yards off in front of a company of maidens, engaged in nervously picking a flower from her wreath to pieces, petal by petal.

'Why, O king?' said I, restraining my indignation with difficulty; 'the girl has danced well, and pleased us; she is fair too; it would be hard to reward her with death.'

Twala laughed as he answered –

'It is our custom, and the figures who sit in stone yonder,' and he pointed towards the three distant peaks, 'must have their due. Did I fail to put the fairest girl to death to-day, misfortune would fall upon me and my house. Thus runs the prophecy of my people: 'If the king offer not a sacrifice of a fair girl, on the day of the dance of maidens, to the Old Ones who sit and watch on the mountains, then shall he fall, and his house.' Look ye, white men, my brother who reigned before me offered not the sacrifice, because of the tears of the woman, and he fell, and his house, and I reign in his stead. It is finished; she must die!' Then turning to the guards – 'Bring her hither; Scragga, make sharp thy spear.'

Two of the men stepped forward, and as they advanced, the girl, for the first time realizing her impending fate, screamed aloud and turned to fly. But the strong hands caught her fast, and brought her, struggling and weeping, before us.

'What is thy name, girl?' piped Gagool. 'What! wilt thou not answer? Shall the king's son do his work at once?'

At this hint, Scragga, looking more evil than ever, advanced a step and lifted his great spear, and at that moment I saw Good's hand creep to the revolver. The poor girl caught the faint glint of steel through her tears, and it sobered her anguish. She ceased struggling, and clasping her hands convulsively, stood shuddering from head to foot.

'See,' cried Scragga in high glee, 'she shrinks from the sight of my little plaything even before she has tasted it,' and he tapped the broad blade of his spear.

'If ever I get the chance you shall pay for that, you young hound!' I heard Good mutter beneath his breath.

'Now that thou art quiet, give us thy name, my dear. Come, speak out, and fear not,' said Gagool in mockery.

'Oh, mother,' answered the girl, in trembling accents, 'my name is Foulata, of the house of Suko. Oh, mother, why must I die? I have done no wrong!'

'Be comforted,' went on the old woman in her hateful tone of mockery. 'Thou must die, indeed, as a sacrifice to the Old Ones who sit yonder,' and she pointed to the peaks; 'but it is better to sleep in the night than to toil in the daytime; it is better to die than to live, and thou shalt die by the royal hand of the king's own son.'

The girl Foulata wrung her hands in anguish, and cried out aloud, 'Oh, cruel! and I so young! What have I done that I should never again see the sun rise out of the night, or the stars come following on his track in the evening, that I may no more gather the flowers when the dew is heavy, or listen to the laughing of the waters? Woe is me, that I shall never see my father's hut again, nor feel my mother's kiss, nor tend the lamb that is sick! Woe is me, that no lover shall put his arm around me and look into my eyes, nor shall men children be born of me! Oh, cruel, cruel!'

And again she wrung her hands and turned her tear-stained, flower-crowned face to heaven, looking so lovely in her despair – for she was indeed a beautiful woman – that assuredly the sight of her would have melted the heart of any less cruel than were the three fiends before us. Prince Arthur's appeal to the ruffians who came to blind him was not more touching than that of this savage girl.

But it did not move Gagool or Gagool's master, though I saw signs of pity among the guards behind, and on the faces of the chiefs; and as for Good, he gave a fierce snort of indignation, and made a motion as though to go to her assistance. With all a woman's quickness, the doomed girl interpreted what was passing in his mind, and by a sudden movement flung herself before him, and clasped his 'beautiful white legs' with her hands.

'Oh, white father from the Stars!' she cried, 'throw over me the mantle of thy protection; let me creep into the shadow of thy strength, that I may be saved. Oh, keep me from these cruel men and from the mercies of Gagool!'

'All right, my hearty, I'll look after you,' sang out Good, in nervous Saxon.

'Come, get up, there's a good girl,' and he stooped and caught her hand.

Twala turned and motioned to his son, who advanced with his spear lifted.

'Now's your time,' whispered Sir Henry to me; 'what are you waiting for?'

'I am waiting for that eclipse,' I answered; 'I have had my eye on the moon for the last half-hour, and I never saw it look healthier.'

'Well, you must risk it now, or the girl will be killed. Twala is losing patience.'

Recognizing the force of the argument, and having cast one more despairing look at the bright face of the moon, for never did the most ardent astronomer with a theory to prove await a celestial event with such anxiety, I stepped with all the dignity that I could command between the prostrate girl and the advancing spear of Scragga.

'King,' I said, 'it shall not be; we will not endure this thing; let the girl go in safety.'

Twala rose from his seat in wrath and astonishment, and from the chiefs and serried ranks of maidens who had closed in slowly upon us in anticipation of the tragedy came a murmur of amazement.

'*Shall not be!* thou white dog, that yappest at the lion in his cave; *shall not be!* art thou mad? Be careful lest this chicken's fate overtake thee, and those with thee. How canst thou save her or thyself? Who art thou that thou settest thyself between me and my will? Back, I say. Scragga, kill her! Ho! guards, seize these men.'

At this cry armed men ran swiftly from behind the hut, where they had evidently been placed beforehand.

Sir Henry, Good, and Umbopa ranged themselves alongside of me, and lifted their rifles.

'Stop!' I shouted boldly, though at the moment my heart was in my boots. 'Stop! we, the white men from the Stars, say that it shall not be. Come but one pace nearer, and we will put out the moon, as we who dwell in her House can do, and plunge the land in darkness. Dare to disobey, and ye shall taste of our magic.'

My threat produced an effect; the men halted, and Scragga stood still before us, his spear lifted.

'Hear him! hear him!' piped Gagool; 'hear the liar who says that he will put out the moon like a lamp. Let him do it, and the girl shall be spared. Yes, let him do it, or die by the girl, he and those with him.'

I glanced up at the moon despairingly, and now to my intense joy and relief saw that we – or rather the almanack – had made no mistake. On the edge of the great orb lay a faint rim of shadow, while a smoky hue grew and gathered upon its bright surface.

Then I lifted my hand solemnly towards the sky, an example which Sir Henry and Good followed, and quoted a line or two from the 'Ingoldsby Legends' at it in the most impressive tones that I could command. Sir Henry followed suit with a verse out of the Old Testament, whilst Good addressed the Queen of Night in a volume of the most classical bad language which he could think of.

Slowly the penumbra, the shadow of a shadow, crept on over the bright surface, and as it crept I heard deep gasps of fear rising from the multitude around.

'Look, O king!' I cried; 'look, Gagool! Look, chiefs and people and women, and see if the white men from the Stars keep their word, or they be but empty liars!

'The moon grows black before your eyes; soon there will be darkness – ay, darkness in the hour of the full moon. Ye have asked for a sign; it is given to you. Grow dark, O Moon! withdraw thy light, thou pure and holy one; bring the proud heart to the dust, and eat up the world with shadows.'

A groan of terror burst from the onlookers. Some stood petrified with dread, others threw themselves upon their knees and cried aloud. As for the king, he sat still and turned pale beneath his dusky skin. Only Gagool kept her courage.

'It will pass,' she cried; 'I have seen the like before; no man can put out the moon; lose not heart; sit still – the shadow will pass.'

'Wait, and ye shall see,' I replied, hopping with excitement. 'O Moon! Moon! Moon! wherefore art thou so cold and fickle?' This appropriate quotation was from the pages of a popular romance that I chanced to have read recently, though now I come to think of it, it was ungrateful of me to abuse the Lady of the Heavens, who was showing herself to be the truest of friends to us, however she may have behaved to the impassioned lover in the novel. Then I added: 'Keep it up, Good, I can't remember any more poetry. Curse away, there's a good fellow.'

Good responded nobly to this tax upon his inventive faculties. Never before had I the faintest conception of the breadth and depth and height of a naval officer's objurgatory powers. For ten minutes he went on without stopping, and he scarcely ever repeated himself.

Meanwhile the dark ring crept on, and that great assembly fixed their eyes upon the sky and stared and stared in fascinated silence. Strange and unholy shadows encroached upon the moonlight, an ominous quiet filled the place. Everything grew still as death. Slowly and in the midst of this most solemn silence the minutes sped away, and while they sped the full moon passed deeper and deeper into the shadow of the earth, as the inky segment of its circle slid in awful majesty across the lunar craters. The great pale orb seemed to draw near and to grow in size. She turned a coppery hue, then that portion of her surface which was unobscured as yet grew grey and ashen, and at length, as totality approached, her mountains and her plains were to be seen glowing luridly through a crimson gloom.

On, yet on, crept the ring of darkness; it was now more than half across the blood-red orb. The air grew thick, and still more deeply tinged with dusky crimson. On, yet on, till we could scarcely see the fierce faces of the group before us. No sound rose now from the spectators, and Good stopped swearing.

'The moon is dying – the white wizards have killed the moon,' yelled the prince Scragga at last. 'We shall all perish in the dark,' and animated by fear or fury, or by both, he lifted his spear and drove it with all his force at Sir Henry's breast. But he had forgotten the mail shirts that the king had given us, and which we wore beneath our clothing. The steel rebounded harmless, and before he could repeat the blow Curtis had snatched the spear from his hand and sent it straight through him. Scragga dropped dead.

At the sight, and driven mad with fear of the gathering darkness, and of the unholy shadow which, as they believed, was swallowing the moon, the companies of girls broke up in wild confusion, and ran screeching for the gateways. Nor did the panic stop there. The king himself, followed by his guards, some of the chiefs, and Gagool, who hobbled after them with marvellous alacrity, fled for the huts, so that in another minute we ourselves, the would-be victim Foulata, Infadoos, and most of the chiefs who had interviewed us on the previous night, were left alone upon the scene, together with the dead body of Scragga, Twala's son.

'Chiefs,' I said, 'we have given you the sign. If ye are satisfied let us fly swiftly to the place ye spoke of. The charm cannot now be stopped. It will work for an hour and the half of an hour. Let us cover ourselves in the darkness.'

'Come,' said Infadoos, turning to go, an example which was followed by the awed captains, ourselves, and the girl Foulata, whom Good took by the arm.

Before we reached the gate of the kraal the moon went out utterly, and from every quarter of the firmament the stars rushed forth into the inky sky.

Holding each other by the hand we stumbled on through the darkness.

Chapter XII

BEFORE THE BATTLE

Luckily for us, Infadoos and the chiefs knew all the pathways of the great town perfectly, so that notwithstanding the gloom we made fair progress.

For an hour or more we journeyed on, till at length the eclipse began to pass, and that edge of the moon which had disappeared the first became again visible. Suddenly, as we watched, there burst from it a silver streak of light, accompanied by a wondrous ruddy glow, which hung upon the blackness of the sky like a celestial lamp, and a wild and lovely sight it was. In another five minutes the stars began to fade, and there was sufficient light to see our whereabouts. We then discovered that we were clear of the town of Loo and approaching a large flat-topped hill, measuring some two miles in circumference. This hill, which is of a formation common in South Africa, is not very high; indeed, its greatest elevation is not more than 200 feet, but it is shaped like a horseshoe, and its sides are rather precipitous and strewn with boulders. On the grass table-land at its summit is ample camping-ground, which had been utilized as a military cantonment of no mean strength. Its ordinary garrison was one regiment of three thousand men, but as we toiled up the steep side of the mountain in the returning moonlight we perceived that there were several of such regiments upon it.

Reaching the table-land at last, we found crowds of men roused from their sleep, shivering with fear and huddled up together in the utmost consternation at the natural phenomenon which they were witnessing. Passing through these without a word, we gained a hut in the centre of the ground, where we were astonished to find two men waiting, laden with our few goods and chattels, which of course we had been obliged to leave behind in our hasty flight.

'I sent for them,' explained Infadoos; 'also for these,' and he lifted up Good's long-lost trousers.

With an exclamation of rapturous delight Good sprang at them, and instantly proceeded to put them on.

'Surely my lord will not hide his beautiful white legs!' exclaimed Infadoos regretfully.

But Good persisted, and once only did the Kukuana people get the chance of seeing his beautiful legs again. Good is a very modest man. Henceforward they had to satisfy their æsthetic longings with his one whisker, his transparent eye, and his movable teeth.

Still gazing with fond remembrance at Good's trousers, Infadoos next informed us that he had commanded the regiments to muster so soon as the day broke, in order to explain to them fully the origin and circumstances of the rebellion which was decided on by the chiefs, and to introduce to them the rightful heir to the throne, Ignosi.

Accordingly, when the sun was up, the troops – in all nearly twenty thousand men, and the flower of the Kukuana army – were mustered on a large open space, to which we went. The men were drawn up in three sides of a dense square, and presented a magnificent spectacle. We took our station on the open side of the square, and were speedily surrounded by all the principal chiefs and officers.

These, after silence had been proclaimed, Infadoos proceeded to address. He narrated to them in vigorous and graceful language – for, like most Kukuanas of high rank, he was a born orator – the history of Ignosi's father, and of how he had been basely murdered by Twala the king, and his wife and child driven out to starve. Then he pointed out that the people suffered and groaned under Twala's cruel rule, instancing the proceedings of the previous night, when under pretence of their being evil-doers, many of the noblest in the land had been dragged forth and wickedly done to death. Next he went on to say that the white lords from the Stars, looking down upon their country, had perceived its trouble, and determined, at great personal inconvenience, to alleviate its lot: That they had accordingly taken the real king of the Kukuanas, Ignosi, who was languishing in exile, by the hand, and led him over the mountains: That they had seen the wickedness of Twala's doings, and for a sign to the wavering, and to save the life of the girl Foulata actually, by the exercise of their high power, had put out the moon and slain the young fiend Scragga; and that they were prepared to stand by them, and assist them to overthrow Twala, and set up the rightful king, Ignosi, in his place.

He finished his discourse amidst a murmur of approbation. Then Ignosi stepped forward and began to speak. Having reiterated all that Infadoos his uncle had said, he concluded a powerful speech in these words: –

'O chiefs, captains, soldiers, and people, ye have heard my words. Now must ye make choice between me and him who sits upon my throne, the uncle who killed his brother, and hunted his brother's child forth to die in the cold and the night. That I am indeed the king these' – pointing to the chiefs – 'can tell you, for they have seen the snake about my middle. If I were not the king, would these white men be on my side with all their magic? Tremble, chiefs, captains, soldiers, and people! Is not the darkness they have brought upon the land to confound Twala and cover our flight, darkness even in the hour of the full moon, yet before your eyes?'

'It is,' answered the soldiers.

'I am the king; I say to you, I am the king,' went on Ignosi, drawing up his great stature to its full, and lifting his broad-bladed battle-axe above his head. 'If there be any man among you who says that it is not so, let him stand forth and I will fight him now, and his blood shall be a red token that I tell you true. Let him stand forth, I say;' and he shook the great axe till it flashed in the sunlight.

As nobody seemed inclined to respond to this heroic version of 'Dilly, Dilly, come and be killed,' our late henchman proceeded with his address.

'I am indeed the king, and should ye stand by my side in the battle, if I win the day, ye shall go with me to victory and honour. I will give you oxen and wives, and ye shall take place of all the regiments; and if ye fall, I will fall with you.

'And, behold, I give you this promise, that when I sit upon the seat of my fathers, bloodshed shall cease in the land. No longer shall ye cry for justice to find slaughter, no longer shall the witch-finder hunt you out so that ye may be slain without a cause. No man shall die save he who offends against the laws. The 'eating up' of your kraals shall cease; each one of you shall sleep secure in his own hut and fear naught, and justice shall walk blindfold throughout the land. Have ye chosen, chiefs, captains, soldiers, and people?'

'We have chosen, O king,' came back the answer.

'It is well. Turn your heads and see how Twala's messengers go forth from the great town, east and west, and north and south, to gather a mighty army to slay me and you, and these my friends and protectors. To-morrow, or perchance the next day, he will come against us with all who are faithful to him. Then I shall see the man who is indeed my man, the man who fears not to die for his cause; and I tell you that he shall not be forgotten in the time of spoil. I have spoken, O chiefs, captains, soldiers, and people. Now go to your huts and make you ready for war.'

There was a pause, till presently one of the chiefs lifted his hand, and out rolled the royal salute, '*Koom*.' It was a sign that the soldiers accepted Ignosi as their king. Then they marched off in battalions.

Half an hour afterwards we held a council of war, at which all the commanders of regiments were present. It was evident to us that before very long we should be attacked in overwhelming force. Indeed from our point of vantage on the hill we could see troops mustering, and messengers going forth from Loo in every direction, doubtless to summon soldiers to the king's assistance. We had on our side about twenty thousand men, composed of seven of the best regiments in the country. Twala, so Infadoos and the chiefs calculated, had at least thirty to thirty-five thousand on whom he could rely at present assembled in Loo, and they thought that by midday on the morrow he would be able to gather another five thousand or more to his aid. It was, of course, possible that some of his troops would desert and come over to us, but it was not a contingency which could be reckoned on. Meanwhile, it was clear that active preparations were being made to subdue us. Already strong bodies of armed men were patrolling round and round the foot of the hill, and there were other signs of coming assault.

Infadoos and the chiefs, however, were of opinion that no attack would take place that day, which would be devoted to preparation and to the removal by every available means of the moral effect produced upon the minds of the soldiery by the supposed magical darkening of the moon. The onslaught would be on the morrow, they said, and they proved to be right.

Meanwhile, we set to work to strengthen the position in all ways possible. Almost every man was turned out, and in the course of a day, which seemed far too short, much was done. The paths up the hill – that was rather a sanatorium than a fortress, being used generally as the camping place of regiments suffering from recent service in unhealthy portions of the country – were carefully blocked with masses of stones, and every other approach was made as impregnable as time would allow. Piles of boulders were collected at various spots to be rolled down upon an advancing enemy, stations were appointed to the different regiments, and all preparation was made which our joint ingenuity could suggest.

Just before sundown, as we rested after our toil, we perceived a small company of men advancing towards us from the direction of Loo, one of whom bore a palm leaf in his hand for a sign that he came as a herald.

As he drew near, Ignosi, Infadoos, one or two chiefs and ourselves, went down to the foot of the mountain to meet him. He was a gallant-looking fellow, wearing the regulation leopard-skin cloak.

'Greeting!' he cried, as he came; 'the king's greeting to those who make unholy war against the king; the lion's greeting to the jackals that snarl around his heels.'

'Speak,' I said.

'These are the king's words. Surrender to the king's mercy erc a worse thing befall you. Already the shoulder has been torn from the black bull, and the king drives him bleeding about the camp.'*

'What are Twala's terms?' I asked from curiosity.

'His terms are merciful, worthy of a great king. These are the words of Twala, the one-eyed, the mighty, the husband of a thousand wives, lord of the Kukuanas, keeper

---

* This cruel custom is not confined to the Kukuanas, but is by no means uncommon amongst African tribes on the occasion of the outbreak of war or any other important public event. – A. Q.

of the Great Road (Solomon's Road), beloved of the Strange Ones who sit in silence at the mountains yonder (the Three Witches), Calf of the black Cow, Elephant whose tread shakes the earth, Terror of the evil-doer, Ostrich whose feet devour the desert, huge One, black One, wise One, king from generation to generation! these are the words of Twala: 'I will have mercy and be satisfied with a little blood. One in every ten shall die, the rest shall go free; but the white man Incubu, who slew Scragga my son, and the black man his servant, who pretends to my throne, and Infadoos my brother, who brews rebellion against me, these shall die by torture as an offering to the Silent Ones. Such are the merciful words of Twala.'

After consulting with the others a little, I answered him in a loud voice, so that the soldiers might hear, thus –

'Go back, thou dog, to Twala, who sent thee, and say that we, Ignosi, veritable king of the Kukuanas, Incubu, Bougwan, and Macumazahn, the wise ones from the Stars, who make dark the moon, Infadoos, of the royal house, and the chiefs, captains, and people here gathered, make answer and say, "That we will not surrender; that before the sun has gone down twice, Twala's corpse shall stiffen at Twala's gate, and Ignosi, whose father Twala slew, shall reign in his stead." Now go, ere we whip thee away, and beware how thou dost lift a hand against such as we are.'

The herald laughed loudly. 'Ye frighten not men with such swelling words,' he cried out. 'Show yourselves as bold to-morrow, O ye who darken the moon. Be bold, fight, and be merry, before the crows pick your bones till they are whiter than your faces. Farewell; perhaps we may meet in the fight; fly not to the Stars but wait for me, I pray, white men.' With this shaft of sarcasm he retired, and almost immediately the sun sank.

That night was a busy one, for weary as we were, so far as was possible by the moonlight all preparations for the morrow's fight were continued, and messengers were constantly coming and going from the place where we sat in council. At last about an hour after midnight, everything that could be done was done, and the camp, save for the occasional challenge of a sentry, sank into silence. Sir Henry and I, accompanied by Ignosi and one of the chiefs, descended the hill and made a round of the outposts. As we went, suddenly, from all sorts of unexpected places spears gleamed out in the moonlight, only to vanish again when we uttered the password. It was clear to us that none were sleeping at their posts. Then we returned, picking our way through thousands of sleeping warriors, many of whom were taking their last earthly rest.

The moonlight flickering along their spears played upon their features and made them ghastly; the chilly night wind tossed their tall and hearse-like plumes. There they lay in wild confusion, with arms outstretched and twisted limbs; their stern, stalwart forms looking weird and unhuman in the moonlight.

'How many of these do you suppose will be alive at this time to-morrow?' asked Sir Henry.

I shook my head and looked again at the sleeping men, and to my tired and yet excited imagination it seemed as though Death had already touched them. My mind's eye singled out those who were sealed to slaughter, and there rushed in upon my heart a great sense of the mystery of human life, and an overwhelming sorrow at its futility and sadness. To-night these thousands slept their healthy sleep, to-morrow they, and many others with them, ourselves perhaps among them, would be stiffening in the cold; their wives would be widows, their children fatherless, and their place know them no more for ever. Only the old moon would shine on serenely, the night wind would stir the grasses, and the wide earth would take its rest, even as it did æons before we were, and will do æons after we have been forgotten.

Yet man dies not whilst the world, at once his mother and his monument, remains. His name is lost, indeed, but the breath he breathed still stirs the pine-tops on the mountains, the sound of the words he spake yet echoes on through space; the thoughts his brain gave birth to we have inherited to-day; his passions are our cause of life; the joys and sorrows that he knew are our familiar friends – the end from which he fled aghast will surely overtake us also!

Truly the universe is full of ghosts, not sheeted churchyard spectres, but the inextinguishable elements of individual life, which having once been, can never *die*, though they blend and change, and change again for ever.

All sorts of reflections of this nature passed through my mind – for as I grow older

I regret to say that a detestable habit of thinking seems to be getting a hold of me – while I stood and stared at those grim yet fantastic lines of warriors, sleeping, as their saying goes, 'upon their spears.'

'Curtis,' I said, 'I am in a condition of pitiable fear.'

Sir Henry stroked his yellow beard and laughed, as he answered –

'I have heard you make that sort of remark before, Quatermain.'

'Well, I mean it now. Do you know, I very much doubt if one of us will be alive to-morrow night. We shall be attacked in overwhelming force, and it is quite a chance if we can hold this place.'

'We'll give a good account of some of them, at any rate. Look here, Quatermain, this business is a nasty one, and one with which, properly speaking, we ought not to be mixed up, but we are in for it, so we must make the best of it. Speaking personally, I had rather be killed fighting than any other way, and now that there seems little chance of our finding my poor brother, it makes the idea easier to me. But fortune favours the brave, and we may succeed. Anyway, the battle will be awful, and having a reputation to keep up, we shall need to be in the thick of it.'

He made this last remark in a mournful voice, but there was a gleam in his eye which belied its melancholy. I have an idea Sir Henry Curtis actually likes fighting.

After this we went to sleep for a couple of hours.

Just about dawn we were awakened by Infadoos, who came to say that great activity was to be observed in Loo, and that parties of the king's skirmishers were driving in our outposts.

We got up and dressed ourselves for the fray, each putting on his chain armour shirt, for which garments at the present juncture we felt exceedingly thankful. Sir Henry went the whole length about the matter, and dressed himself like a native warrior. 'When you are in Kukuanaland, do as the Kukuanas do,' he remarked, as he drew the shining steel over his broad breast, which it fitted like a glove. Nor did he stop there. At his request Infadoos had provided him with a complete set of native war uniform. Round his throat he fastened the leopard-skin cloak of a commanding officer, on his brows he bound the plume of black ostrich feathers worn only by generals of high rank, and about his middle a magnificent moocha of white ox-tails.

A pair of sandals, a leglet of goat's hair, a heavy battle-axe, with a rhinoceros-horn handle, a round iron shield covered with white ox-hide, and the regulation number of *tollas*, or throwing knives, made up his equipment, to which, however, he added his revolver. The dress was, no doubt, a savage one, but I am bound to say that I seldom saw a finer sight than Sir Henry Curtis presented in this disguise. It showed off his magnificent physique to the greatest advantage, and when Ignosi arrived presently, arrayed in a similar costume, I thought to myself that I had never before seen two such splendid men.

As for Good and myself, the armour did not suit us nearly so well. To begin with, Good insisted upon keeping on his new-found trousers, and a stout, short gentleman with an eyeglass, and one half of his face shaved, arrayed in a mail shirt, carefully tucked into a very seedy pair of corduroys, looks more remarkable than imposing. In my case, the chain shirt being too big for me, I put it on over all my clothes, which caused it to bulge in a somewhat ungainly fashion. I discarded my trousers, however, retaining only my veldtschoons, having determined to go into battle with bare legs in order to be the lighter for running, in case it became necessary to retire quickly. The mail coat, a spear, a shield, that I did not know how to use, a couple of *tollas*, a revolver, and a huge plume, which I pinned into the top of my shooting hat, in order to give a bloodthirsty finish to my appearance, completed my modest equipment. In addition to all these articles, of course we had our rifles, but as ammunition was scarce, and as they would be useless in case of a charge, we arranged that they should be carried behind us by bearers.

When at length we had equipped ourselves, we swallowed some food hastily, and then started out to see how things were going on. At one point in the table-land of the mountain, there was a little koppie of brown stone, which served the double purpose of headquarters and of a conning tower. Here we found Infadoos surrounded by his own regiment, the Greys, which was undoubtedly the finest in the Kukuana army, and the same that we had first seen at the outlying kraal. This regiment, now three thousand five hundred strong, was being held in reserve, and the men were lying down on the grass in companies, and watching the king's forces creep out of Loo in long ant-like columns. There seemed to be no end to the length of these columns – three in all, and each of them numbering at least eleven or twelve thousand men.

As soon as they were clear of the town the regiments formed up. Then one body marched off to the right, one to the left, and the third came on slowly towards us.

'Ah,' said Infadoos, 'they are going to attack us on three sides at once.'

This seemed rather serious news, for our position on the top of the mountain, which measured a mile and a half in circumference, being an extended one, it was important to us to concentrate our comparatively small defending force as much as possible. But since it was impossible for us to dictate in what way we should be attacked, we had to make the best of it, and accordingly sent orders to the various regiments to prepare to receive the separate onslaughts.

Chapter XIII

THE ATTACK

Slowly, and without the slightest appearance of haste or excitement, the three columns crept on. When within about five hundred yards of us, the main or centre column halted at the root of a tongue of open plain which ran up into the hill, to give time to the other divisions to circumvent our position, which was shaped more or less in the form of a horseshoe, with its two points facing towards the town of Loo. The object of this manœuvre was that the threefold assault should be delivered simultaneously.

'Oh, for a gatling!' groaned Good, as he contemplated the serried phalanxes beneath us. 'I would clear that plain in twenty minutes.'

'We have not got one, so it is no use yearning for it; but suppose you try a shot, Quatermain,' said Sir Henry. 'See how near you can go to that tall fellow who appears to be in command. Two to one you miss him, and an even sovereign, to be honestly paid if ever we get out of this, that you don't drop the bullet within five yards.'

This piqued me, so, loading the express with solid ball, I waited till my friend walked some ten yards out from his force, in order to get a better view of our position, accompanied only by an orderly; then, lying down and resting the express upon a rock, I covered him. The rifle, like all expresses, was only sighted to three hundred and fifty yards, so to allow for the drop in trajectory I took him half-way down the neck, which ought, I calculated, to find him in the chest. He stood quite still and gave me every opportunity, but whether it was the excitement or the wind, or the fact of the man being a long shot, I don't know, but this was what happened. Getting dead on, as I thought, a fine sight, I pressed, and when the puff of smoke had cleared away, to my disgust, I saw my man standing unharmed, whilst his orderly, who was at least three paces to the left, was stretched upon the ground apparently dead. Turning swiftly, the officer I had aimed at began to run towards his men in evident alarm.

'Bravo, Quatermain!' sang out Good; 'you've frightened him.'

This made me very angry, for, if possible to avoid it, I hate to miss in public. When a man is master of only one art he likes to keep up his reputation in that art. Moved quite out of myself at my failure, I did a rash thing. Rapidly covering the general as he ran, I let drive with the second barrel. Instantly the poor man threw up his arms, and fell forward on to his face. This time I had made no mistake; and – I say it as a proof of how little we think of others when our own safety, pride, or reputation are in question – I was brute enough to feel delighted at the sight.

The regiments who had seen the feat cheered wildly at this exhibition of the white man's magic, which they took as an omen of success, while the force the general had belonged to – which, indeed, as we ascertained afterwards, he had commanded – fell back in confusion. Sir Henry and Good now took up their rifles and began to fire, the latter industriously 'browning' the dense mass before him with a Winchester repeater, and I also had another shot or two, with the result, so far as we could judge, that we put some six or eight men *hors de combat* before they were out of range.

Just as we stopped firing there came an ominous roar from our far right, then a similar roar rose on our left. The two other divisions were engaging us.

At the sound, the mass of men before us opened out a little, and advanced towards the hill and up the spit of bare grass land at a slow trot, singing a deep-throated song as they ran. We kept up a steady fire from our rifles as they came, Ignosi joining in occasionally, and accounted for several men, but of course we produced no more effect upon that mighty rush of armed humanity than he who throws pebbles does on the breaking wave.

On they came, with a shout and the clashing of spears; now they were driving in the outposts we had placed among the rocks at the foot of the hill. After that the advance was a little slower, for though as yet we had offered no serious opposition, the attacking forces must climb up hill, and they came slowly to save their breath. Our first line of defence was about half-way down the side of the slope, our second fifty yards further back, while our third occupied the edge of the plateau.

On they stormed, shouting their war-cry, '*Twala! Twala! Chiele! Chiele!*' (Twala! Twala! Smite! Smite!) '*Ignosi! Ignosi! Chiele! Chiele!*' answered our people. They were quite close now, and the *tollas*, or throwing-knives, began to flash backwards and forwards, and now with an awful yell the battle closed in.

To and fro swayed the mass of struggling warriors, men falling fast as leaves in an autumn wind; but before long the superior weight of the attacking force began to tell, and our first line of defence was slowly pressed back, till it merged into the second. Here the struggle was very fierce, but again our people were driven back and up, till at length, within twenty minutes of the commencement of the fight, our third line came into action.

But by this time the assailants were much exhausted, and besides had lost many men killed and wounded, and to break through that third impenetrable hedge of spears proved beyond their powers. For a while the seething lines of savages swung backwards and forwards, in the fierce ebb and flow of battle, and the issue was doubtful. Sir Henry watched the desperate struggle with a kindling eye, and then without a word he rushed off, followed by Good, and flung himself into the hottest of the fray. As for myself, I stopped where I was.

The soldiers caught sight of his tall form as he plunged into the battle, and there rose a cry of –

'*Nanzia Incubu! Nanzia Unkungunklovo!*' (Here is the Elephant!) '*Chiele! Chiele!*'

From that moment the end was no longer in doubt. Inch by inch, fighting with splendid gallantry, the attacking force was pressed back down the hillside, till at last it retreated upon its reserves in something like confusion. At that instant, too, a messenger arrived to say that the left attack had been repulsed; and I was just beginning to congratulate myself, believing that the affair was over for the present, when, to our horror, we perceived our men who had been engaged in the right defence being driven towards us across the plain, followed by swarms of the enemy, who had evidently succeeded at this point.

Ignosi, who was standing by me, took in the situation at a glance, and issued a rapid order. Instantly the reserve regiment around us, the Greys, extended itself.

Again Ignosi gave a word of command, which was taken up and repeated by the captains, and in another second, to my intense disgust, I found myself involved in a furious onslaught upon the advancing foe. Getting as much as I could behind Ignosi's huge frame, I made the best of a bad job, and toddled along to be killed as though I liked it. In a minute or two – the time seemed all too short to me – we were plunging through the flying groups of our men, who at once began to re-form behind us, and then I am sure I do not know what happened. All I can remember is a dreadful noise of the meeting of shields, and the sudden apparition of a huge ruffian, whose eyes seemed literally to be starting out of his head, making straight at me with a bloody spear. But – I say it with pride – I rose – or rather sank – to the occasion. It was one before which most people would have collapsed once and for all. Seeing that if I stood where I was I must be killed, as the horrid apparition came I flung myself down in front of him so cleverly that, being unable to stop himself, he took a header right over my prostrate form. Before he could rise again, I had risen and settled the matter from behind with my revolver.

Shortly after this somebody knocked me down, and I remember no more of that charge.

When I came to I found myself back at the koppie, with Good bending over me holding some water in a gourd.

'How do you feel, old fellow?' he asked, anxiously.

I got up and shook myself before replying.

'Pretty well, thank you,' I answered.

'Thank Heaven! When I saw them carry you in, I felt quite sick; I thought that you were done for.'

'Not this time, my boy. I fancy I only got a rap on the head, which knocked me stupid. How has it ended?'

'They are repulsed at every point for a while. The loss is dreadfully heavy; we have quite two thousand killed and wounded, and they must have lost three. Look, there's a sight!' and he pointed to long lines of men advancing by fours.

In the centre of every group of four, and being borne by it, was a kind of hide tray, of which a Kukuana force always carries a quantity, with a loop for a handle at each corner. On these trays – and their number seemed endless – lay wounded men, who as they arrived were hastily examined by the medicine men, of whom ten were attached to the regiment. If the wound was not of a fatal character the sufferer was taken away and attended to as carefully as circumstances would allow. But if, on the other hand, the injured man's condition proved hopeless, what followed was very dreadful, though doubtless it may have been the truest mercy. One of the doctors, under pretence of carrying out an examination, swiftly opened an artery with a sharp knife, and in a minute or two the sufferer expired painlessly. There were many cases that day in which this was done. In fact, it was done in the majority of cases when the wound was in the body, for the gash made by the entry of the enormously broad spears used by the Kukuanas generally rendered recovery impossible. In most instances the poor sufferers were already unconscious, and in others the fatal 'nick' of the artery was inflicted so swiftly and painlessly that they did not seem to notice it. Still it was a ghastly sight, and one from which we were glad to escape; indeed, I never remember anything of the kind that affected me more than seeing those gallant soldiers thus put out of pain by the red-handed medicine men, except, indeed, on one occasion when, after an attack, I saw a force of Swazis burying their hopelessly wounded, *alive.*

Hurrying from this dreadful scene to the further side of the koppie, we found Sir Henry, who still held a battle-axe in his hand, Ignosi, Infadoos, and one or two of the chiefs in deep consultation.

'Thank Heaven, here you are, Quatermain! I can't quite make out what Ignosi wants to do. It seems that though we have beaten off the attack, Twala is now receiving large reinforcements, and is showing a disposition to invest us, with the view of starving us out.'

'That's awkward.'

'Yes; especially as Infadoos says that the water supply has given out.'

'My lord, that is so,' said Infadoos; 'the spring cannot supply the wants of so great a multitude, and it is failing rapidly. Before night we shall all be thirsty. Listen,

Macumazahn. Thou art wise, and hast doubtless seen many wars in the lands from whence thou camest – that is if indeed they make wars in the Stars. Now tell us, what shall we do? Twala has brought up many fresh men to take the place of those who have fallen. Yet Twala has learnt his lesson; the hawk did not think to find the heron ready; but our beak has pierced his breast; he fears to strike at us again. We too are wounded, and he will wait for us to die; he will wind himself round us like a snake round a buck, and fight the fight of "sit down."'

'I hear thee,' I said.

'So, Macumazahn, thou seest we have no water here, and but a little food, and we must choose between these three things – to languish like a starving lion in his den, or to strive to break away towards the north, or' – and here he rose and pointed towards the dense mass of our foes – 'to launch ourselves straight at Twala's throat. Incubu, the great warrior – for to-day he fought like a buffalo in a net, and Twala's soldiers went down before his axe like young corn before the hail; with these eyes I saw it – Incubu says "Charge"; but the Elephant is ever prone to charge. Now what says Macumazahn, the wily old fox, who has seen much, and loves to bite his enemy from behind? The last word is in Ignosi the king, for it is a king's right to speak of war; but let us hear thy voice, O Macumazahn, who watchest by night, and the voice too of him of the transparent eye.'

'What sayest thou, Ignosi?' I asked.

'Nay, my father,' answered our quondam servant, who now, clad as he was in the full panoply of savage war, looked every inch a warrior king, 'do thou speak, and let me, who am but a child in wisdom beside thee, hearken to thy words.'

Thus adjured, after taking hasty counsel with Good and Sir Henry, I delivered my opinion briefly to the effect that, being trapped, our better chance, especially in view of the failure of our water supply, was to initiate an attack upon Twala's forces. Then I recommended that the attack should be delivered at once, 'before our wounds grew stiff,' and also before the sight of Twala's overpowering force caused the hearts of our soldiers 'to wax small like fat before a fire.' Otherwise, I pointed out, some of the captains might change their minds, and, making peace with Twala, desert to him, or even betray us into his hands.

This expression of opinion seemed, on the whole, to be favourably received; indeed, among the Kukuanas my utterances met with a respect which has never been accorded to them before or since. But the real decision as to our plans lay with Ignosi, who, since he had been recognized a rightful king, could exercise the almost unbounded rights of sovereignty, including, of course, the final decision on matters of generalship, and it was to him that all eyes were now turned.

At length, after a pause, during which he appeared to be thinking deeply, he spoke.

'Incubu, Macumazahn, and Bougwan, brave white men, and my friends; Infadoos, my uncle, and chiefs; my heart is fixed. I will strike at Twala this day, and set my fortunes on the blow, ay, and my life – my life and your lives also. Listen; thus will I strike. Ye see how the hill curves round like the half-moon, and how the plain runs like a green tongue towards us within the curve?'

'We see,' I answered.

'Good; it is now mid-day, and the men eat and rest after the toil of battle. When the sun has turned and travelled a little way towards the darkness, let thy regiment, my uncle, advance with one other down to the green tongue; and it shall be that when Twala sees it he will hurl his force at it to crush it. But the spot is narrow, and the regiments can come against thee one at a time only; so may they be destroyed one by one, and the eyes of all Twala's army shall be fixed upon the struggle the like of which has not been seen by living man. And with thee, my uncle, shall go Incubu my friend, that when Twala sees his battle-axe flashing in the first rank of the Greys his heart may grow faint. And I will come with the second regiment, that which follows thee, so that if ye are destroyed, as it might happen, there may yet be a king left to fight for; and with me shall come Macumazahn the wise.'

'It is well, O king,' said Infadoos, apparently contemplating the certainty of the complete annihilation of his regiment with perfect calmness. Truly these Kukuanas are a wonderful people. Death has no terrors for them when it is incurred in the course of duty.

'And whilst the eyes of the multitude of Twala's soldiers are thus fixed upon the fight,' went on Ignosi, 'behold, one-third of the men who are left alive to us (*i.e.* about

6,000) shall creep along the right horn of the hill and fall upon the left flank of Twala's force. And one-third shall creep along the left horn and fall upon Twala's right flank. And when I see that the horns are ready to toss Twala, then will I, with the men who remain to me, charge home in Twala's face, and if fortune goes with us the day will be ours, and before Night drives her black oxen from the mountains to the mountains we shall sit in peace at Loo. And now let us eat and make ready; and, Infadoos, do thou prepare, that the plan be carried out without fail; and stay, let my white father Bougwan go with the right horn, that his shining eye may give courage to the captains.'

The arrangements for attack thus briefly indicated were set in motion with a rapidity that spoke well for the perfection of the Kukuana military system. Within little more than an hour rations had been served out to the men and devoured, the three divisions were formed, the scheme of onslaught was explained to the leaders, and the whole force, now numbering about 18,000 men in all, was ready to be put in motion, with the exception of a guard left in charge of the wounded.

Presently Good came up to Sir Henry and myself

'Good-bye, you fellows,' he said; 'I am off with the right wing according to orders; and so I have come to shake hands, in case we should not meet again, you know,' he added significantly.

We shook hands in silence, and not without the exhibition of as much emotion as Englishmen are wont to show.

'It is a queer business,' said Sir Henry, his deep voice shaking a little, 'and I confess I never expect to see to-morrow's sun. So far as I can make out, the Greys, with whom I am to go, are to fight until they are wiped out in order to enable the wings to slip round unawares and outflank Twala. Well, so be it; at any rate, it will be a man's death! Good-bye, old fellow. God bless you! I hope you will pull through and live to collar the diamonds; but if you do, take my advice and don't have anything more to do with Pretenders!'

In another second Good had wrung us both by the hand and gone; and then Infadoos came up and led off Sir Henry to his place in the forefront of the Greys, whilst, with many misgivings, I departed with Ignosi to my station in the second attacking regiment.

Chapter XIV

THE LAST STAND OF THE GREYS

In a few more minutes the regiments destined to carry out the flanking movements had tramped off in silence, keeping carefully under the lee of the rising ground in order to conceal their advance from the keen eyes of Twala's scouts.

Half an hour or more was allowed to elapse between the setting out of the horns or wings of the army before any stir was made by the Greys and their supporting regiment, known as the Buffaloes, which formed its chest, and were destined to bear the brunt of the battle.

Both of these regiments were almost perfectly fresh, and full of strength, the Greys having been in reserve in the morning, and having lost but a small number of men in sweeping back that part of the attack which had proved successful in breaking the line of defence, on the occasion when I charged with them and was knocked silly for my pains. As for the Buffaloes, they had formed the third line of defence on the left, and since the attacking force at that point had not succeeded in breaking through the second, they had scarcely come into action at all.

Infadoos, who was a wary old general, and knew the absolute importance of keeping up the spirits of his men on the eve of such a desperate encounter, employed the pause in addressing his own regiment, the Greys, in poetical language; explaining to them the honour that they were receiving in being put thus in the forefront of the battle, and having the great white warrior from the Stars to fight with them in their

145

ranks; and promising large rewards of cattle and promotion to all who survived in the event of Ignosi's arms being successful.

I looked down the long lines of waving black plumes and stern faces beneath them, and sighed to think that within one short hour most, if not all, of those magnificent veteran warriors, not a man who was under forty years of age, would be laid dead or dying in the dust. It could not be otherwise; they were being condemned, with that wise recklessness of human life which marks the great general, and often saves his forces and attains his ends, to certain slaughter, in order to give their cause and the remainder of the army a chance of success. They were foredoomed to die, and they knew it. It was to be their task to engage regiment after regiment of Twala's army on the narrow strip of green beneath us, till they were exterminated, or till the wings found a favourable opportunity for their onslaught. And yet they never hesitated, nor could I detect a sign of fear upon the face of a single warrior. There they were – going to certain death, about to quit the blessed light of day for ever, and yet able to contemplate their doom without a tremor. Even at that moment I could not help contrasting their state of mind with my own, which was far from comfortable, and breathing a sigh of envy and admiration. Never before had I seen such an absolute devotion to the idea of duty, and such a complete indifference to its bitter fruits.

'Behold your king!' ended old Infadoos, pointing to Ignosi; 'go fight and fall for him, as is the duty of brave men, and cursed and shameful for ever be the name of him who shrinks from death for his king, or who turns his back from the foe. Behold your king, chiefs, captains, and soldiers! Now do your homage to the sacred Snake, and then follow on, that Incubu and I may show you a road to the heart of Twala's forces.'

There was a moment's pause, then suddenly a murmur arose from the serried phalanxes before us, a sound like the distant whisper of the sea, caused by the gentle tapping of the handles of six thousand spears against their holders' shields. Slowly it swelled, till its growing volume deepened and widened into a roar of rolling noise, that echoed like thunder against the mountains, and filled the air with heavy waves of sound. Then it decreased and by faint degrees died away into nothing and suddenly out crashed the royal salute.

Ignosi, I thought to myself, might well be a proud man that day, for no Roman emperor ever had such a salutation from gladiators 'about to die.'

Ignosi acknowledged this magnificent act of homage by lifting his battle-axe, and then the Greys filed off in a triple-line formation, each line containing about one thousand fighting men, exclusive of officers. When the last companies had advanced some five hundred yards, Ignosi put himself at the head of the Buffaloes, which regiment was drawn up in a similar threefold formation, and gave the word to march, and off we went, I, needless to say, uttering the most heartfelt prayers that I might come out of that job with a whole skin. Many a queer position have I found myself in, but never before in one quite so unpleasant as the present, or one in which my chance of coming off safe was smaller.

By the time that we reached the edge of the plateau the Greys were already half-way down the slope ending in the tongue of grass land that ran up into the bend of the mountain, something as the frog of a horse's foot runs up into the shoe. The excitement in Twala's camp on the plain beyond was very great, and regiment after regiment was starting forward at a long swinging trot in order to reach the root of the tongue of land before the attacking force could emerge into the plain of Loo.

This tongue, which was some three hundred yards in depth, even at its root or widest part was not more than four hundred and fifty paces across, while at its tip it scarcely measured ninety. The Greys, who, in passing down the side of the hill and on to the tip of the tongue had formed into column, on reaching the spot where it broadened out again, reassumed their triple-line formation and halted dead.

Then we – that is, the Buffaloes – moved down the tip of the tongue and took our stand in reserve, about one hundred yards behind the last line of the Greys, and on slightly higher ground. Meanwhile we had leisure to observe Twala's entire force, which evidently had been reinforced since the morning attack, and could not now, notwithstanding their losses, number less than forty thousand, moving swiftly up towards us. But as they drew near the root of the tongue they hesitated, having discovered that only one regiment could advance into the gorge at a time, and that there, some seventy yards from the mouth of it, unassailable except in front, on account of the high walls of boulder-strewn ground on each side, stood the famous regiment of Greys, the pride and glory of the Kukuana army, ready to hold the way against their forces as the three Romans once held the bridge against thousands.

They hesitated, and finally stopped their advance; there was no eagerness to cross spears with these three grim ranks of warriors who stood so firm and ready. Presently, however, a tall general, wearing the customary head-dress of nodding ostrich plumes, appeared attended by a group of chiefs and orderlies, being, I thought, none other than Twala himself. He gave an order, and the first regiment, raising a shout, charged up towards the Greys, who remained perfectly still and silent till the attacking troops were within forty yards and a volley of *tollas*, or throwing-knives, came rattling among their ranks.

Then suddenly with a bound and a roar, they sprang forward with uplifted spears, and the regiments met in deadly strife. Next second the roll of the meeting shields came to our ears like the sound of thunder, and the plain seemed to be alive with flashes of light reflected from the shimmering spears. To and fro swung the surging mass of struggling, stabbing humanity, but not for long. Suddenly the attacking lines began to grow thinner, and then with a slow, long heave the Greys passed over them, just as a great wave heaves up its bulk and passes over a sunken ridge. It was done; that regiment was completely destroyed, but the Greys had but two lines left now; a third of their number were dead.

Closing up shoulder to shoulder, once more they halted in silence and awaited attack; and I was rejoiced to catch sight of Sir Henry's yellow beard as he moved to and fro arranging the ranks. So he was yet alive!

Meanwhile we moved on to the ground of the encounter, which was cumbered by about four thousand prostrate human beings, dead, dying, and wounded, and literally stained red with blood. Ignosi issued an order, which was rapidly passed down the ranks, to the effect that none of the enemy's wounded were to be killed, and so far as we could see this command was scrupulously carried out. It would have been a shocking sight, if we had found time to think of it.

But now a second regiment, distinguished by white plumes, kilts, and shields, was moving to the attack of the two thousand remaining Greys, who stood waiting in the same ominous silence as before, till the foe was within forty yards or so, when they hurled themselves with irresistible force upon them. Again there came the awful roll of the meeting shields, and as we watched the tragedy repeated itself.

But this time the issue was left longer in doubt; indeed, it seemed for a while almost impossible that the Greys should again prevail. The attacking regiment, which was formed of young men, fought with the utmost fury, and at first seemed by sheer weight to be driving the veterans back. The slaughter was truly awful, hundreds falling every minute; and from among the shouts of the warriors and the groans of the dying, set to the music of clashing spears, came a continuous hissing undertone of '*S'gee, s'gee,*' the note of triumph of each victor as he passed his assegai through and through the body of his fallen foe.

But perfect discipline and steady and unchanging valour can do wonders, and one veteran soldier is worth two young ones, as soon became apparent in the present case. For just when we thought that it was all over with the Greys, and were preparing to take their place so soon as they made room by being destroyed, I heard Sir Henry's deep voice ringing out through the din, and caught a glimpse of his circling battle-axe as he waved it high above his plumes. Then came a change; the Greys ceased to give; they stood still as a rock, against which the furious waves of spearmen broke again and again, only to recoil. Presently they began to move once more – forward this time; as they had no firearms there was no smoke, so we could see it all. Another minute and the onslaught grew fainter.

'Ah, these are *men* indeed; they will conquer again,' called out Ignosi, who was grinding his teeth with excitement at my side. 'See, it is done!'

Suddenly, like puffs of smoke from the mouth of a cannon, the attacking regiment broke away in flying groups, their white head-dresses streaming behind them in the wind, and left their opponents victors, indeed, but, alas! no more a regiment. Of the gallant triple line, which forty minutes before had gone into action three thousand strong, there remained at most some six hundred blood-bespattered men; the rest were underfoot. And yet they cheered and waved their spears in triumph, and then, instead of falling back upon us as we expected, they ran forward, for a hundred yards or so, after the flying groups of foemen, took possession of a rising knoll of ground, and, resuming their triple formation, formed a threefold ring around it. And there, thanks be to Heaven, standing on the top of the mound for a minute, I saw Sir Henry, apparently unharmed, and with him our old friend Infadoos. Then Twala's regiments rolled down upon the doomed band, and once more the battle closed in.

As those who read this history will probably long ago have gathered, I am, to be honest, a bit of a coward, and certainly in no way given to fighting, though somehow it has often been my lot to get into unpleasant positions, and to be obliged to shed a man's blood. But I have always hated it, and kept my own blood as undiminished in quantity as possible, sometimes by a judicious use of my heels. At this moment, however, for the first time in my life, I felt my bosom burn with martial ardour. Warlike fragments from the 'Ingoldsby Legends,' together with numbers of sanguinary verses in the Old Testament, sprang up in my brain like mushrooms in the dark; my blood, which hitherto had been half-frozen with horror, went beating through my veins, and there came upon me a savage desire to kill and spare not. I glanced round at the serried ranks of warriors behind us, and somehow, all in an instant, I began to wonder if my face looked like theirs. There they stood, their heads craned forward over their shields, the hands twitching, the lips apart, the fierce features instinct with the hungry lust of battle, and in the eyes a look like the glare of a bloodhound when he sights his quarry.

Only Ignosi's heart, to judge from his comparative self-possession, seemed, to all appearance, to beat as calmly as ever beneath his leopard-skin cloak, though even *he* still ground his teeth. I could bear it no longer.

'Are we to stand here till we put out roots, Umbopa – Ignosi, I mean – while Twala swallows our brothers yonder?' I asked.

'Nay, Macumazahn,' was the answer; 'see now is the ripe moment: let us pluck it.'

As he spoke a fresh regiment rushed past the ring upon the little mound, and wheeling round, attacked it from the hither side.

Then, lifting his battle-axe, Ignosi gave the signal to advance, and, raising the Kukuana war-cry, the Buffaloes charged home with a rush like the rush of the sea.

What followed immediately on this it is out of my power to tell. All I can remember is a wild yet ordered advance, that seemed to shake the ground; a sudden change of front and forming up on the part of the regiment against which the charge was directed; then an awful shock, a dull roar of voices, and a continuous flashing of spears, seen through a red mist of blood.

When my mind cleared I found myself standing inside the remnant of the Greys near the top of the mound, and just behind no less a person than Sir Henry himself. How I got there I had at the moment no idea, but Sir Henry afterwards told me that I was borne up by the first furious charge of the Buffaloes almost to his feet, and then left, as they in turn were pressed back. Thereon he dashed out of the circle and dragged me into it.

As for the fight that followed, who can describe it? Again and again the multitudes surged against our momentarily lessening circle, and again and again we beat them back.

> 'The stubborn spearmen still made good
> The dark impenetrable wood,
> Each stepping where his comrade stood
> The instant that he fell,'

as someone or other beautifully puts it.

It was a splendid thing to see those brave battalions come on time after time over the barriers of their dead, sometimes holding corpses before them to receive our spear thrusts, only to leave their own corpses to swell the rising piles. It was a gallant sight to see that sturdy old warrior, Infadoos, as cool as though he were on parade, shouting out orders, taunts, and even jests, to keep up the spirit of his few remaining men, and then, as each charge rolled on, stepping forward to wherever the fighting was thickest, to bear his share in repelling it. And yet more gallant was the vision of Sir Henry, whose ostrich plumes had been shorn off by a spear stroke, so that his long yellow hair streamed out in the breeze behind him. There he stood, the great Dane, for he was nothing else, his hands, his axe, and his armour, all red with blood, and none could live before his stroke. Time after time I saw it sweeping down, as some great warrior ventured to give him battle, and as he struck he shouted 'O-hoy!

O-hoy!' like his Berserkir forefathers, and the blow went crashing through shield and spear, through head-dress, hair, and skull, till at last none would of their own will come near the great white '*umtagati*,' the wizard, who killed and failed not.

But suddenly there rose a cry of '*Twala, y' Twala*,' and out of the press sprang forward none other than the gigantic one-eyed king himself, also armed with battle-axe and shield, and clad in chain armour.

'Where art thou, Incubu, thou white man, who slewest Scragga my son – see if thou canst slay me!' he shouted, and at the same time hurled a *tolla* straight at Sir Henry, who fortunately saw it coming, and caught it on his shield, which it transfixed, remaining wedged in the iron plate behind the hide.

Then, with a cry, Twala sprang forward straight at him, and with his battle-axe struck him such a blow upon the shield that the mere force and shock of it brought Sir Henry, strong man as he is, down upon his knees.

But at this time the matter went no further, for that instant there rose from the regiments pressing round us something like a shout of dismay, and on looking up I saw the cause.

To the right and to the left the plain was alive with the plumes of charging warriors. The outflanking squadrons had come to our relief. The time could not have been better chosen. All Twala's army, as Ignosi predicted would be the case, had fixed their attention on the bloody struggle which was raging round the remnant of the Greys and that of the Buffaloes, who were now carrying on a battle of their own at a little distance, which two regiments had formed the chest of our army. It was not until our horns were about to close upon them that they had dreamed of their approach. And now, before they could even assume a proper formation for defence, the outflanking *Impis* had leapt, like greyhounds, on their flanks.

In five minutes the fate of the battle was decided. Taken on both flanks, and dismayed at the awful slaughter inflicted upon them by the Greys and Buffaloes, Twala's regiments broke into flight, and soon the whole plain between us and Loo was scattered with groups of running soldiers making good their retreat. As for the forces that had so recently surrounded us and the Buffaloes, they melted away as though by magic, and presently we were left standing there like a rock from which the sea has retreated. But what a sight it was! Around us the dead and dying lay in heaped-up masses, and of the gallant Greys there remained but ninety-five men upon their feet. More than three thousand four hundred had fallen in this one regiment, most of them never to rise again.

'Men,' said Infadoos calmly, as between the intervals of binding a wound in his arm he surveyed what remained to him of his corps, 'ye have kept up the reputation of your regiment, and this day's fighting will be well spoken of by your children's children.' Then he turned round and shook Sir Henry Curtis by the hand. 'Thou art a great man, Incubu,' he said simply; 'I have lived a long life among warriors, and known many a brave one, yet have I never seen a man like unto thee.'

At this moment the Buffaloes began to march past our position on the road to Loo, and as they went a message was brought to us from Ignosi requesting Infadoos, Sir Henry, and myself to join him. Accordingly, orders having been issued to the remaining ninety men of the Greys to employ themselves in collecting the wounded, we joined Ignosi, who informed us that he was pressing on to Loo to complete the victory by capturing Twala, if that should be possible. Before we had gone far, suddenly we discovered the figure of Good sitting on an ant-heap about one hundred paces from us. Close beside him was the body of a Kukuana.

'He must be wounded,' said Sir Henry anxiously. As he made the remark, an untoward thing happened. The dead body of the Kukuana soldier, or rather what had appeared to be his dead body, suddenly sprang up, knocked Good head over heels off the ant-heap, and began to spear him. We rushed forward in terror, and as we drew near we saw the brawny warrior making dig after dig at the prostrate Good, who at each prod jerked all his limbs into the air. Seeing us coming, the Kukuana gave one final and most vicious dig, and with a shout of 'Take that, wizard!' bolted away. Good did not move, and we concluded that our poor comrade was done for. Sadly we came towards him, and were astonished to find him pale and faint indeed, but with a serene smile upon his face, and his eyeglass still fixed in his eye.

'Capital armour this,' he murmured, on catching sight of our faces bending over him. 'How sold that beggar must have been,' and then he fainted. On examination we discovered that he had been seriously wounded in the leg by a *tolla* in the course of the pursuit, but that the chain armour had prevented his last assailant's spear from doing anything more than bruise him badly. It was a merciful escape. As nothing could be done for him at the moment, he was placed on one of the wicker shields used for the wounded, and carried along with us.

On arriving before the nearest gate of Loo we found one of our regiments watching it in obedience to orders received from Ignosi. The other regiments were in the same way guarding the different exits to the town. The officer in command of this regiment saluted Ignosi as king, and informed him that Twala's army had taken refuge in the town, whither Twala himself had also escaped, but he thought that they were thoroughly demoralized, and would surrender. Thereupon Ignosi, after taking counsel with us, sent forward heralds to each gate ordering the defenders to open, and promising on his royal word life and forgiveness to every soldier who laid down his arms. This message was not without its effect. Presently, amid the shouts and cheers of the Buffaloes, the bridge was dropped across the fosse, and the gates upon the further side were flung open.

Taking due precautions against treachery, we marched on into the town. All along the roadways stood dejected warriors, their heads drooping, and their shields and spears at their feet, who, as Ignosi passed, saluted him as king. On we marched, straight to Twala's kraal. When we reached the great space, where a day or two previously we had seen the review and the witch hunt, we found it deserted. No, not quite deserted, for there, on the further side, in front of his hut, sat Twala himself, with but one attendant – Gagool.

It was a melancholy sight to see him seated, his battle-axe and shield by his side, his chin upon his mailed breast, with but one old crone for companion, and notwithstanding his cruelties and misdeeds, a pang of compassion shot through me as I looked upon Twala thus 'fallen from his high estate.' Not a soldier of all his armies, not a courtier out of the hundreds who had cringed round him, not even a solitary wife, remained to share his fate or halve the bitterness of his fall. Poor savage! he was learning the lesson which Fate teaches to most of us who live long enough, that the eyes of mankind are blind to the discredited, and that he who is defenceless and fallen finds few friends and little mercy. Nor, indeed, in this case did he deserve any.

Filing through the kraal gate, we marched across the open space to where the ex-king sat. When within about fifty yards of him the regiment was halted, and accompanied only by a small guard we advanced towards him, Gagool reviling us bitterly as we came. As we drew near, Twala, for the first time, lifted his plumed head, and fixed his one eye, which seemed to flash with suppressed fury almost as brightly as the great diamond bound round his forehead, upon his successful rival – Ignosi.

'Hail, O king!' he said, with bitter mockery; 'thou who hast eaten of my bread, and now by the aid of the white men's magic hast seduced my regiments and defeated mine army, hail! What fate hast thou for me, O king?'

'The fate thou gavest to my father, whose throne thou hast sat on these many years!' was the stern answer.

'It is good. I will show thee how to die, that thou mayest remember it against thine own time. See, the sun sinks in blood,' and he pointed with his battle-axe towards the setting orb; 'it is well that my sun should go down with it. And now, O king! I am ready to die, but I crave the boon of the Kukuana royal House* to die fighting. Thou canst not refuse it, or even those cowards who fled to-day will hold thee shamed.'

'It is granted. Choose – with whom wilt thou fight? Myself I cannot fight with thee, for the king fights not except in war.'

Twala's sombre eye ran up and down our ranks, and I felt, as for a moment it rested on myself, that the position had developed a new horror. What if he chose to begin by fighting *me*? What chance should I have against a desperate savage six feet five high, and broad in proportion? I might as well commit suicide at once. Hastily I made up my mind to decline the combat, even if I were hooted out of Kukuanaland as a consequence. It is, I think, better to be hooted than to be quartered with a battle-axe.

Presently Twala spoke.

---

* It is a law amongst the Kukuanas that no man of the royal blood can be put to death unless by his own consent, which is, however, never refused. He is allowed to choose a succession of antagonists, to be approved by the king, with whom he fights, till one of them kills him. – A. Q.

'Incubu, what sayest thou, shall we end what we began to-day, or shall I call thee coward, white – even to the liver?'

'Nay,' interposed Ignosi hastily; 'thou shalt not fight with Incubu.'

'Not if he is afraid,' said Twala.

Unfortunately Sir Henry understood this remark, and the blood flamed up into his cheeks.

'I will fight him,' he said; 'he shall see if I am afraid.'

'For Heaven's sake,' I entreated, 'don't risk your life against that of a desperate man. Anybody who saw you to-day will know that you are not a coward.'

'I will fight him,' was the sullen answer. 'No living man shall call me a coward. I am ready now!' and he stepped forward and lifted his axe.

I wrung my hands over this absurd piece of Quixotism; but if he was determined on fighting, of course I could not stop him.

'Fight not, my white brother,' said Ignosi, laying his hand affectionately on Sir Henry's arm; 'thou hast fought enough, and if aught befell thee at his hands it would cut my heart in twain.'

'I will fight, Ignosi,' was Sir Henry's answer.

'It is well, Incubu; thou art a brave man. It will be a good fight. Behold, Twala, the Elephant is ready for thee.'

The ex-king laughed savagely, and stepping forward faced Curtis. For a moment they stood thus, and the light of the sinking sun caught their stalwart frames and clothed them both in fire. They were a well-matched pair.

Then they began to circle round each other, their battle-axes raised.

Suddenly Sir Henry sprang forward and struck a fearful blow at Twala, who stepped to one side. So heavy was the stroke that the striker half overbalanced himself, a circumstance of which his antagonist took a prompt advantage. Circling his massive battle-axe round his head, he brought it down with tremendous force. My heart jumped into my mouth; I thought that the affair was already finished. But no; with a quick upward movement of the left arm Sir Henry interposed his shield between himself and the axe, with the result that its outer edge was shorn away, the axe falling on his left shoulder, but not heavily enough to do any serious damage. In another moment Sir Henry got in a second blow, which was also received by Twala upon his shield. Then followed blow upon blow, that were, in turn, either received upon the shields or avoided. The excitement grew intense; the regiment which was watching the encounter forgot its discipline, and, drawing near, shouted and groaned at every stroke. Just at this time, too, Good, who had been laid upon the ground by me, recovered from his faint, and, sitting up, perceived what was going on. In an instant he was up, and catching hold of my arm, hopped about from place to place on one leg, dragging me after him, and yelling encouragements to Sir Henry –

'Go it, old fellow!' he hallooed. 'That was a good one! Give it him amidships,' and so on.

Presently Sir Henry, having caught a fresh stroke upon his shield, hit out with all his force. The blow cut through Twala's shield and through the tough chain armour behind it, gashing him in the shoulder. With a yell of pain and fury Twala returned the blow with interest, and, such was his strength, shore right through the rhinoceros' horn handle of his antagonist's battle-axe, strengthened as it was with bands of steel, wounding Curtis in the face.

A cry of dismay rose from the Buffaloes as our hero's broad axe-head fell to the ground; and Twala, again raising his weapon, flew at him with a shout. I shut my eyes. When I opened them again it was to see Sir Henry's shield lying on the ground, and Sir Henry himself with his great arms twined round Twala's middle. To and fro they swung, hugging each other like bears, straining with all their mighty muscles for dear life, and dearer honour. With a supreme effort Twala swung the Englishman clean off his feet, and down they came together, rolling over and over on the lime paving, Twala striking out at Curtis's head with the battle-axe, and Sir Henry trying to drive the *tolla* he had drawn from his belt through Twala's armour.

It was a mighty struggle, and an awful thing to see.

'Get his axe!' yelled Good; and perhaps our champion heard him.

At any rate, dropping the *tolla*, he snatched at the axe, which was fastened to Twala's wrist by a strip of buffalo hide, and still rolling over and over, they fought for it like wild cats, drawing their breath in heavy gasps. Suddenly the hide string burst, and then, with a great effort, Sir Henry freed himself, the weapon remaining in his hand. Another second and he was upon his feet, the red blood streaming from the wound in his face, and so was Twala. Drawing the heavy *tolla* from his belt, he reeled straight at Curtis and struck him upon the breast. The stab came home true and strong, but whoever it was who made that chain armour, he understood his art, for it withstood the steel. Again Twala struck out with a savage yell, and again the sharp knife rebounded, and Sir Henry went staggering back. Once more Twala came on, and as he came our great Englishman gathered himself together, and swinging the big axe round his head, hit at him with all his force. There was a shriek of excitement from a thousand throats, and, behold! Twala's head seemed to spring from his shoulders; then it fell and came rolling and bounding along the ground towards Ignosi, stopping just at his feet. For a second the corpse stood upright; then with a dull crash it came to the earth, and the gold torque from its neck rolled away across the pavement. As it did so Sir Henry, overpowered by faintness and loss of blood, fell heavily across the body of the dead king.

In a second he was lifted up, and eager hands were pouring water on his face. Another minute, and the grey eyes opened wide.

He was not dead.

Then I, just as the sun sank, stepping to where Twala's head lay in the dust, unloosed the diamond from the dead brows, and handed it to Ignosi.

'Take it,' I said, 'lawful king of the Kukuanas – king by birth and victory.'

Ignosi bound the diadem upon his brows. Then advancing, he placed his foot upon the broad chest of his headless foe and broke out into a chant, or rather a pæan of triumph, so beautiful, and yet so utterly savage, that I despair of being able to give an adequate idea of it. Once I heard a scholar with a fine voice read aloud from the Greek poet Homer, and I remember that the sound of the rolling lines seemed to make my blood stand still. Ignosi's chant, uttered as it was in a language as beautiful and sonorous as the old Greek, produced exactly the same effect on me, although I was exhausted with toil and many emotions.

'*Now,*' he began, '*now is our rebellion swallowed up in victory, and our evil-doing is justified by strength.*

'In the morning the oppressors arose and shook themselves; they bound on their plumes and made them ready to war.

'They rose up and grasped their spears: the soldiers called to the captains, "Come, lead us" – and the captains cried to the king, "Direct thou the battle."

'They arose in their pride, twenty thousand men, and yet a twenty thousand.

'Their plumes covered the earth as the plumes of a bird cover her nest; they shook their spears and shouted, yea, they hurled their spears into the sunlight; they lusted for the battle and were glad.

'They came up against me; their strong ones ran swiftly to slay me; they cried, "Ha! ha! he is as one already dead."

'Then breathed I on them, and my breath was as the breath of a storm, and lo! they were not.

'My lightnings pierced them; I licked up their strength with the lightning of my spears; I shook them to the earth with the thunder of my shouting.

'They broke – they scattered – they were gone as the mists of the morning.

'They are food for the crows and the foxes, and the place of battle is fat with their blood.

'Where are the mighty ones who rose up in the morning?

'Where are the proud ones who tossed their plumes and cried, "He is as one already dead?"

'They bow their heads, but not in sleep; they are stretched out, but not in sleep.

'They are forgotten; they have gone into the blackness, and will not return; yea, others shall lead away their wives, and their children shall remember them no more.

'And I – I! the king – like an eagle I have found my eyrie.

'Behold! far have I wandered in the night time, yet have I returned to my young at the daybreak.

'Creep ye under the shadow of my wings, O people, and I will comfort you, and ye shall not be dismayed.

'Now is the good time, the time of spoil.

'Mine are the cattle in the valleys, mine also are the virgins in the kraals.

'The winter is overpast, the summer is come.

'Now shall Evil cover up her face, and Mercy and Joy shall dwell in the land.

'Rejoice, rejoice, my people!

'Let all the world rejoice in that the tyranny is trodden down, in that I am the king.'

Ignosi ceased, and out of the gathering gloom came back the deep reply –

'Thou art the king!'

Thus was my prophecy to the herald fulfilled, and within the forty-eight hours Twala's headless corpse was stiffening at Twala's gate.

Chapter XV

GOOD FALLS SICK

After the fight was ended, Sir Henry and Good were carried into Twala's hut, where I joined them. They were both utterly exhausted by exertion and loss of blood, and, indeed, my own condition was little better. I am very wiry, and can stand more fatigue than most men, probably on account of my light weight and long training; but that night I was fairly done up, and, as is always the case with me when exhausted, that old wound which the lion gave me began to pain me. Also my head was aching violently from the blow I had received in the morning, when I was knocked senseless. Altogether, a more miserable trio than we were that evening it would have been difficult to discover; and our only comfort lay in the reflection that we were exceedingly fortunate to be there to feel miserable, instead of being stretched dead upon the plain, as so many thousands of brave men were that night, who had risen well and strong in the morning.

Somehow, with the assistance of the beautiful Foulata, who, since we had been the means of saving her life, had constituted herself our handmaiden, and especially Good's, we managed to get off the chain shirts, which had certainly saved the lives of two of us that day. As I expected, we found that the flesh underneath was terribly contused, for though the steel links had kept the weapons from entering, they had not prevented them from bruising. Both Sir Henry and Good were a mass of contusions, and I was by no means free. As a remedy Foulata brought us some pounded green leaves, with an aromatic odour, which, when applied as a plaster, gave us considerable relief.

But though the bruises were painful, they did not give us such anxiety as Sir Henry's and Good's wounds. Good had a hole right through the fleshy part of his 'beautiful white leg,' from which he had lost a great deal of blood; and Sir Henry, with other hurts, had a deep cut over the jaw, inflicted by Twala's battle-axe. Luckily Good is a very decent surgeon, and so soon as his small box of medicines was forthcoming, having thoroughly cleansed the wounds, he managed to stitch up first Sir Henry's and then his own pretty satisfactorily, considering the imperfect light given by the primitive Kukuana lamp in the hut. Afterwards he plentifully smeared the injured places with some antiseptic ointment, of which there was a pot in the little box, and we covered them with the remains of a pocket-handkerchief which we possessed.

Meanwhile Foulata had prepared us some strong broth, for we were too weary to eat. This we swallowed, and then threw ourselves down on the piles of magnificent karrosses, or fur rugs, which were scattered about the dead king's great hut. By a very strange instance of the irony of fate, it was on Twala's own couch, and wrapped in Twala's own particular karross, that Sir Henry, the man who had slain him, slept that night.

I say slept; but after that day's work sleep was indeed difficult. To begin with, in very truth the air was full

> 'Of farewells to the dying
> And mournings for the dead.'

From every direction came the sound of the wailing of women whose husbands, sons, and brothers had perished in the fight. No wonder that they wailed, for over twelve thousand men, or nearly a fifth of the Kukuana army, had been destroyed in that awful struggle. It was heart-rending to lie and listen to their cries for those who would never return; and it made me understand the full horror of the work done that day to further man's ambition. Towards midnight, however, the ceaseless crying of the women grew less frequent, till at length the silence was only broken at intervals of a few minutes by a long piercing howl that came from a hut in our immediate rear, which, as I afterwards discovered, proceeded from Gagool 'keening' over the dead king Twala.

After that I got a little fitful sleep, only to wake from time to time with a start, thinking that I was once more an actor in the terrible events of the last twenty-four hours. Now I seemed to see that warrior whom my hand had sent to his last account charging at me on the mountain-top; now I was once more in that glorious ring of Greys, which made its immortal stand against all Twala's regiments upon the little mound; and now again I saw Twala's plumed and gory head roll past my feet with gnashing teeth and glaring eye.

At last, somehow or other, the night passed away; but when dawn broke I found that my companions had slept no better than myself. Good, indeed, was in a high fever, and very soon afterwards began to grow light-headed, and also, to my alarm, to spit blood, the result, no doubt, of some internal injury, inflicted by the desperate efforts made by the Kukuana warrior on the previous day to force his big spear through the chain armour. Sir Henry, however, seemed pretty fresh, notwithstanding his wound on the face, which made eating difficult and laughter an impossibility, though he was so sore and stiff that he could scarcely stir.

About eight o'clock we had a visit from Infadoos, who appeared but little the worse – tough old warrior that he was – for his exertions in the battle, although he informed us that he had been up all night. He was delighted to see us, but much grieved at Good's condition, and shook our hands cordially. I noticed, however, that he addressed Sir Henry with a kind of reverence, as though he were something more than man; and, indeed, as we afterwards found out, the great Englishman was looked on throughout Kukuanaland as a supernatural being. No man, the soldiers said, could have fought as he fought, or, at the end of a day of such toil and bloodshed, could have slain Twala, who, in addition to being the king, was supposed to be the strongest warrior in the country, in single combat, shearing through his bull-neck at a stroke. Indeed, that stroke became proverbial in Kukuanaland, and any extraordinary blow or feat of strength was henceforth known as 'Incubu's blow.'

Infadoos told us also that all Twala's regiments had submitted to Ignosi, and that like submissions were beginning to arrive from chiefs in the out-lying country. Twala's death at the hands of Sir Henry had put an end to all further chance of disturbance;

for Scragga had been his only son, and there was no rival claimant to the throne left alive.

I remarked that Ignosi had swum to power through blood. The old chief shrugged his shoulders. 'Yes,' he answered; 'but the Kukuana people can only be kept cool by letting their blood flow sometimes. Many were killed, indeed, but the women were left, and others would soon grow up to take the places of the fallen. After this the land would be quiet for a while.'

Afterwards, in the course of the morning we had a short visit from Ignosi, on whose brows the royal diadem was now bound. As I contemplated him advancing with kingly dignity, an obsequious guard following his steps, I could not help recalling to my mind the tall Zulu who had presented himself to us at Durban some few months back, asking to be taken into our service, and reflecting on the strange revolutions of the wheel of fortune.

'Hail, O king!' I said, rising.

'Yes, Macumazahn. King at last, by the might of your three right hands,' was the ready answer.

All was, he said, going on well; and he hoped to arrange a great feast in two weeks' time in order to show himself to the people.

I asked him what he had settled to do with Gagool.

'She is the evil genius of the land,' he answered, 'and I shall kill her, and all the witch-doctors with her! She has lived so long that none can remember when she was not old, and she it is who has always trained the witch-hunters, and made the land wicked in the sight of the heavens above.'

'Yet she knows much,' I replied; 'it is easier to destroy knowledge, Ignosi, than to gather it.'

'That is so,' he said thoughtfully. 'She, and she only, knows the secret of the "Three Witches," yonder, whither the great road runs, where the kings are buried, and the Silent Ones sit.'

'Yes, and the diamonds are. Forget not thy promise, Ignosi; thou must lead us to the mines, even, if thou hast to spare Gagool alive to show the way.'

'I will not forget, Macumazahn, and I will think on what thou sayest.'

After Ignosi's visit I went to see Good, and found him quite delirious. The fever set up by his wound seemed to have taken a firm hold of his system, and to be complicated with an internal injury. For four or five days his condition was most critical; indeed, I believe firmly that had it not been for Foulata's indefatigable nursing he must have died.

Women are women, all the world over, whatever their colour. Yet somehow it seemed curious to watch this dusky beauty bending night and day over the fevered man's couch and performing all the merciful errands of a sick-room swiftly, gently, and with as fine an instinct as that of a trained hospital nurse. For the first night or two I tried to help her, and so did Sir Henry as soon as his stiffness allowed him to move, but Foulata bore our interference with impatience, and finally insisted upon our leaving him to her, saying that our movements made him restless, which I think was true. Day and night she watched him and tended him, giving him his only medicine, a native cooling drink made of milk, in which was infused juice from the bulb of a species of tulip, and keeping the flies from settling on him. I can see the whole picture now as it appeared night after night by the light of our primitive lamp; Good tossing to and fro, his features emaciated, his eyes shining large and luminous, and jabbering nonsense by the yard; and seated on the ground by his side, her back resting against the wall of the hut, the soft-eyed, shapely Kukuana beauty, her face, weary as it was, animated by a look of infinite compassion – or was it something more than compassion?

For two days we thought that he must die, and crept about with heavy hearts.

Only Foulata would not believe it.

'He will live,' she said.

For three hundred yards or more around Twala's chief hut, where the sufferer lay, there was silence; for by the king's order all who lived in the habitations behind it, except Sir Henry and myself, had been removed, lest any noise should come to the sick man's ears. One night, it was the fifth of Good's illness, as was my habit, I went across to see how he was getting on before turning in for a few hours.

I entered the hut carefully. The lamp placed upon the floor showed the figure of Good, tossing no more, but lying quite still.

So it had come at last! In the bitterness of my heart I gave something like a sob. 'Hush – h – h!' came from the patch of dark shadow behind Good's head.

Then, creeping closer, I saw that he was not dead, but sleeping soundly, with Foulata's tapered fingers clasped tightly in his poor white hand. The crisis had passed, and he would live. He slept like that for eighteen hours; and I scarcely like to say it, for fear I should not be believed, but during the entire period did this devoted girl sit by him, fearing that if she moved and drew away her hand it would wake him. What she must have suffered from cramp and weariness, to say nothing of want of food, nobody will ever know; but it is the fact that, when at last he woke, she had to be carried away – her limbs were so stiff that she could not move them.

After the turn had once been taken, Good's recovery was rapid and complete. It was not till he was nearly well that Sir Henry told him of all he owed to Foulata; and when he came to the story of how she sat by his side for eighteen hours, fearing lest by moving she should wake him, the honest sailor's eyes filled with tears. He turned and went straight to the hut where Foulata was preparing the mid-day meal, for we were back in our old quarters now, taking me with him to interpret in case he could not make his meaning clear to her, though I am bound to say that she understood him marvellously as a rule, considering how extremely limited was his foreign vocabulary.

'Tell her,' said Good, 'that I owe her my life, and that I will never forget her kindness.'

I interpreted, and under her dark skin she actually seemed to blush.

Turning to him with one of those swift and graceful motions that in her always reminded me of the flight of a wild bird, Foulata answered softly, glancing at him with her large brown eyes –

'Nay, my lord; my lord forgets! Did he not save *my* life, and am I not my lord's hand-maiden?'

It will be observed that the young lady appeared entirely to have forgotten the share which Sir Henry and myself had taken in her preservation from Twala's clutches. But that is the way of women! I remember my dear wife was just the same. Well, I retired from that little interview sad at heart. I did not like Miss Foulata's soft glances, for I knew the fatal amorous propensities of sailors in general, and of Good in particular.

There are two things in the world, as I have found it, which cannot be prevented; you cannot keep a Zulu from fighting, or a sailor from falling in love upon the slightest provocation!

It was a few days after this last occurrence that Ignosi held his great 'indaba,' or council, and was formally recognized as king by the 'indunas,' or head men, of Kukuanaland. The spectacle was a most imposing one, including as it did a grand review of troops. On this day the remaining fragments of the Greys were formally paraded, and in the face of the army thanked for their splendid conduct in the great battle. To each man the king made a large present of cattle, promoting them one and all to the rank of officers in the new corps of Greys which was in process of formation. An order was also promulgated throughout the length and breadth of Kukuanaland that, whilst we honoured the country by our presence, we three were to be greeted with the royal salute, and to be treated with the same ceremony and respect that was by custom accorded to the king. Also the power of life and death was publicly conferred upon us. Ignosi, too, in the presence of his people, reaffirmed the promises which he had made, to the effect that no man's blood should be shed without trial, and that witch-hunting should cease in the land.

When the ceremony was over we waited upon Ignosi, and informed him that we were now anxious to investigate the mystery of the mines to which Solomon's Road ran, asking him if he had discovered anything about them.

'My friends,' he answered, 'I have discovered this. It is there that the three great figures sit, who here are called the "Silent Ones," and to whom Twala would have offered the girl Foulata as a sacrifice. It is there, too, in a great cave deep in the mountain, that the kings of the land are buried; there ye shall find Twala's body, sitting with those who went before him. There, also, is a deep pit, which, at some time, long-dead men dug out, mayhap for the stones ye speak of, such as I have heard men in Natal tell of at Kimberley. There, too, in the Place of Death is a secret chamber, known to none but the king and Gagool. But Twala who knew it, is dead, and I know it not, nor know I what is in it. Yet there is a legend in the land that once, many generations gone, a white man crossed the mountains, and was led by a woman to the secret chamber, and shown the wealth hidden in it. But before he could take it, she betrayed him, and he was driven by the king of that day back to the mountains, and since then no man has entered the place.'

'The story is surely true, Ignosi, for on the mountains we found the white man,' I said.

'Yes, we found him. And now I have promised you that if ye can come to that chamber, and the stones are there—'

'The gem upon thy forehead proves that they are there,' I put in, pointing to the great diamond I had taken from Twala's dead brows.

'Mayhap; if they are there,' he said, 'ye shall have as many as ye can take hence – if indeed ye would leave me, my brothers.'

'First we must find the chamber,' said I.

'There is but one who can show it to thee – Gagool.'

'And if she will not?'

'Then she must die,' said Ignosi sternly. 'I have saved her alive but for this. Stay, she shall choose,' and calling to a messenger he ordered Gagool to be brought before him.

In a few minutes she came, hurried along by two guards, whom she was cursing as she walked.

'Leave her,' said the king to the guards.

So soon as their support was withdrawn, the withered old bundle – for she looked more like a bundle than anything else, out of which her two bright and wicked eyes gleamed like those of a snake – sank in a heap on to the floor.

'What will ye with me, Ignosi?' she piped. 'Ye dare not touch me. If ye touch me I will slay you as ye sit. Beware of my magic.'

'Thy magic could not save Twala, old she-wolf, and it cannot hurt me,' was the answer. 'Listen; I will this of thee, that thou reveal to us the chamber where are the shining stones.'

'Ha! ha!' she piped, 'none know its secret but I, and I will never tell thee. The white devils shall go hence empty-handed.'

'Thou shalt tell me. I will make thee tell me.'

'How, O king? Thou art great, but can thy power wring the truth from a woman?'

'It is difficult, yet will I do it.'

'How, O king?'

'Nay, thus; if thou tellest not thou shalt slowly die.'

'Die!' she shrieked, in terror and fury; 'ye dare not touch me – man, ye know not who I am. How old think ye am I? I knew your fathers, and your fathers' fathers' fathers. When the country was young I was here; when the country grows old I shall still be here. I cannot die unless I be killed by chance, for none dare slay me.'

'Yet will I slay thee. See, Gagool, mother of evil, thou art so old that thou canst no longer love thy life. What can life be to such a hag as thou, who hast no shape, nor form, nor hair, nor teeth – hast naught, save wickedness and evil eyes? It will be mercy to make an end of thee, Gagool.'

'Thou fool,' shrieked the old fiend, 'thou accursed fool, deemest thou that life is sweet only to the young? It is not so, and naught thou knowest of the heart of man to think it. To the young, indeed, death is sometimes welcome, for the young can feel. They love and suffer, and it wrings them to see their beloved pass to the land of shadows. But the old feel not, they love not, and, *ha! ha!* they laugh to see another go out into the dark; *ha! ha!* they laugh to see the evil that is done under the sun. All they love is life, the warm, warm sun, and the sweet, sweet air. They are afraid of the cold, afraid of the cold and the dark, *ha! ha! ha!*' and the old hag writhed in ghastly merriment on the ground.

'Cease thine evil talk and answer me,' said Ignosi angrily. 'Wilt thou show the place where the stones are, or wilt thou not? If thou wilt not thou diest, even now,' and he seized a spear and held it over her.

'I will not show it; thou darest not kill me, darest not! He who slays me will be accursed for ever.'

Slowly Ignosi brought down the spear till it pricked the prostrate heap of rags.

With a wild yell Gagool sprang to her feet, then fell again and rolled upon the floor.

'Nay, I will show it. Only let me live, let me sit in the sun and have a bit of meat to suck, and I will show thee.'

'It is well. I thought that I should find a way to reason with thee. To-morrow shalt thou go with Infadoos and my white brothers to the place, and beware how thou failest, for if thou showest it not, then thou shalt slowly die. I have spoken.'

'I will not fail, Ignosi. I always keep my word – *ha! ha! ha!* Once before a woman showed the chamber to a white man, and, behold! evil befell him,' and here her wicked eyes glinted. 'Her name was Gagool also. Perchance I was that woman.'

'Thou liest,' I said, 'that was ten generations gone.'

'Mayhap, mayhap; when one lives long one forgets. Perhaps it was my mother's mother who told me, surely her name was Gagool also. But mark, ye will find in the place where the bright playthings are a bag of hide full of stones. The man filled that bag, but he never took it away. Evil befell him, I say, evil befell him! Perhaps it was my mother's mother who told me. It will be a merry journey – we can see the bodies of those who died in the battle as we go. Their eyes will be gone by now, and their ribs will be hollow. *Ha! ha! ha!*'

Chapter XVI

THE PLACE OF DEATH

It was already dark on the third day after the scene described in the previous chapter when we camped in some huts at the foot of the 'Three Witches,' as the triangle of mountains were called to which Solomon's Great Road ran. Our party consisted of our three selves and Foulata, who waited on us – especially on Good – Infadoos, Gagool, who was borne along in a litter, inside which she could be heard muttering and cursing all day long, and a party of guards and attendants. The mountains, or rather the three peaks of the mountain, for the mass was evidently the result of a solitary upheaval, were, as I have said, in the form of a triangle, of which the base was towards us, one peak being on our right, one on our left, and one straight in front of us. Never shall I forget the sight afforded by those three towering peaks in the early sunlight of the following morning. High, high above us, up into the blue air, soared their twisted snow-wreaths. Beneath the snow-line the peaks were purple with heaths, and so were the wild moors that ran up the slopes towards them. Straight before us the white ribbon of Solomon's Great Road stretched away uphill to the foot of the centre peak, about five miles from us, and there stopped. It was its terminus.

I had better leave the feelings of intense excitement with which we set out on our march that morning to the imagination of those who read this history. At last we were drawing near to the wonderful mines that had been the cause of the miserable death of the old Portuguese Dom three centuries ago, of my poor friend, his ill-starred descendant, and also, as we feared, of George Curtis, Sir Henry's brother. Were we destined, after all that we have gone through, to fare any better? Evil befell them, as that old fiend Gagool said; would it also befall us? Somehow, as we were marching up that last stretch of beautiful road, I could not help feeling a little superstitious about the matter, and so I think did Good and Sir Henry.

For an hour and a half or more we tramped on up the heather-fringed way, going so fast in our excitement that the bearers of Gagool's hammock could scarcely keep pace with us, and its occupant piped out to us to stop.

'Walk more slowly, white men,' she said, projecting her hideous shrivelled countenance between the grass curtains, and fixing her gleaming eyes upon us; 'why will ye run to meet the evil that shall befall you, ye seekers after treasure?' and she laughed that horrible laugh which always sent a cold shiver down my back, and for a while quite took the enthusiasm out of us.

However, on we went, till we saw before us, and between ourselves and the peak, a vast circular hole with sloping sides, three hundred feet or more in depth, and quite half a mile round.

'Can't you guess what this is?' I said to Sir Henry and Good, who were staring in astonishment at the awful pit before us.

They shook their heads.

'Then it is clear that you have never seen the diamond diggings at Kimberley. You may depend on it that this is Solomon's Diamond Mine. Look there,' I said, pointing to the strata of stiff blue clay which were yet to be seen among the grass and bushes that clothed the sides of the pit, 'the formation is the same. I'll be bound that if we went down there we should find "pipes" of soapy brecciated rock. Look, too,' and I pointed to a series of worn flat slabs of stone that were placed on a gentle slope below the level of a watercourse which in some past age had been cut out of the solid rock; 'if those are not tables once used to wash the "stuff," I'm a Dutchman.'

At the edge of this vast hole, which was none other than the pit marked on the old Dom's map, the Great Road branched into two and circumvented it. In many places, by the way, this surrounding road was built entirely of blocks of stone, apparently with the object of supporting the edges of the pit and preventing falls of reef. Along this path we pressed, driven by curiosity to see what the three towering objects were which we could discern from the hither side of the great gulf. As we drew nearer we perceived that they were Colossi of some sort or another, and rightly conjectured that before us sat the three 'Silent Ones' that are held in such awe by the Kukuana people. But it was not until we were quite close to them that we recognized the full majesty of these 'Silent Ones.'

There, upon huge pedestals of dark rock, sculptured with rude emblems of the Phallic worship, separated from each other by a distance of twenty paces, and looking down the road which crossed some sixty miles of plain to Loo, were three colossal seated forms – two male and one female – each measuring about eighteen feet from the crown of its head to the pedestal.

The female form, which was nude, was of great though severe beauty, but unfortunately the features had been injured by centuries of exposure to the weather. Rising from either side of her head were the points of a crescent. The two male Colossi, on the contrary, were draped, and presented a terrifying cast of features, especially the one to our right, which had the face of a devil. That to our left was serene in countenance, but the calm upon it was dreadful. It was the calm of that inhuman cruelty, Sir Henry remarked, which the ancients attributed to beings potent for good, who could yet watch the sufferings of humanity, if not with rejoicing, at least without sorrow. These three statues from a most awe-inspiring trinity, as they sit there in their solitude, and gaze out across the plain for ever.

Contemplating these 'Silent Ones,' as the Kukuanas call them, an intense curiosity again seized us to know whose were the hands which had shaped them, who it was that had dug the pit and made the road. Whilst I was gazing and wondering, suddenly it occurred to me – being familiar with the Old Testament – that Solomon went astray after strange gods, the names of three of whom I remembered – 'Ashtoreth, the goddess of the Zidonians, Chemosh, the god of the Moabites, and Milcom, the god of the children of Ammon' – and I suggested to my companions that the figures before us might represent these false and exploded divinities.

'Hum,' said Sir Henry, who is a scholar, having taken a high degree in classics at college, 'there may be something in that; Ashtoreth of the Hebrews was the Astarte of the Phœnicians, who were the great traders of Solomon's time. Astarte, who afterwards became the Aphrodite of the Greeks, was represented with horns like the half-moon, and there on the brow of the female figure are distinct horns. Perhaps these Colossi were designed by some Phœnician official who managed the mines. Who can say?"

Before we had finished examining these extraordinary relics of remote antiquity, Infadoos came up, and having saluted the 'Silent Ones' by lifting his spear, asked us if we intended entering the 'Place of Death' at once, or if we would wait till after we had taken food at mid-day. If we were ready to go at once, Gagool had announced her willingness to guide us. As it was not later than eleven o'clock – driven to it by a burning curiosity – we announced our intention of proceeding instantly, and I suggested that, in case we should be detained in the cave, we should take some food with us. Accordingly Gagool's litter was brought up, and that lady herself assisted out of it. Meanwhile Foulata, at my request, stored some 'biltong,' or dried game-flesh, together with a couple of gourds of water, in a reed basket. Straight in front of us, at a distance of some fifty paces from the backs of the Colossi, rose a sheer wall of rock, eighty feet or more in height, that gradually sloped upwards till it formed the base of the lofty snow-wreathed peak, which soared into the air three thousand feet above us. As soon as she was clear of her hammock Gagool cast one evil grin upon us, and then, leaning on a stick, hobbled off towards the face of this wall. We followed her till we came to a narrow portal solidly arched that looked like the opening of a gallery of a mine.

Here Gagool was waiting for us, still with that evil grin upon her horrid face.

'Now, white men from the Stars,' she piped; 'great warriors, Incubu, Bougwan, and Macumazahn the wise, are ye ready? Behold, I am here to do the bidding of my lord the king, and to show you the store of bright stones. *Ha! ha! ha!*'

'We are ready,' I said.

---

* Compare Milton, 'Paradise Lost,' Book I.: –
'With these in troop Came Ashtoreth, whom the Phœnicians called
Astarté, Queen of Heaven, with crescent horns
To whose bright image nightly by the moon
Sidonian virgins paid their vows and songs.'

'Good! good! Make strong your hearts to bear what ye shall see. Comest thou too, Infadoos, thou who didst betray thy master?'

Infadoos frowned as he answered –

'Nay, I come not; it is not for me to enter there. But thou, Gagool, curb thy tongue, and beware how thou dealest with my lords. At thy hands will I require them, and if a hair of them be hurt, Gagool, be'st thou fifty times a witch, thou shalt die. Hearest thou?'

'I hear, Infadoos; I know thee, thou didst ever love big words; when thou wast a babe I remember thou didst threaten thine own mother. That was but the other day. But fear not, fear not, I live only to do the bidding of the king. I have done the bidding of many kings, Infadoos, till in the end they did mine. *Ha! ha!* I go to look upon their faces once more, and Twala's also! Come on, come on, here is the lamp,' and she drew a large gourd full of oil, and fitted with a rush wick, from under her fur cloak.

'Art thou coming, Foulata?' asked Good in his villainous kitchen Kukuana, in which he had been improving himself under that young lady's tuition.

'I fear, my lord,' the girl answered timidly.

'Then give me the basket.'

'Nay, my lord, whither thou goest there will I go also.'

'The deuce you will!' thought I to myself; 'that may be rather awkward if ever we get out of this.'

Without further ado Gagool plunged into the passage, which was wide enough to admit of two walking abreast, and quite dark. We followed the sound of her voice as she piped to us to come on, in some fear and trembling, which was not allayed by the flutter of a sudden rush of wings.

'Hullo! what's that?' halloed Good; 'somebody hit me in the face.'

'Bats,' said I; 'on you go.'

When, so far as we could judge, we had gone some fifty paces, we perceived that the passage was growing faintly light. Another minute, and we were in perhaps the most wonderful place that the eyes of living man have beheld.

Let the reader picture to himself the hall of the vastest cathedral he ever stood in, windowless indeed, but dimly lighted from above, presumably by shafts connected with the outer air and driven in the roof, which arched away a hundred feet above our heads, and he will get some idea of the size of the enormous cave in which we found ourselves, with the difference that this cathedral designed by nature was loftier and wider than any built by man. But its stupendous size was the least of the wonders of the place, for running in rows down its length were gigantic pillars of what looked like ice, but were, in reality, huge stalactites. It is impossible for me to convey any idea of the overpowering beauty and grandeur of these pillars of white spar, some of which were not less than twenty feet in diameter at the base, and sprang up in lofty and yet delicate beauty sheer to the distant roof. Others again were in process of formation. On the rock floor there was in these cases what looked, Sir Henry said, exactly like a broken column in an old Grecian temple, whilst high above, depending from the roof, the point of a huge icicle could be dimly seen.

Even as we gazed we could hear the process going on, for presently with a tiny splash a drop of water would fall from the far-off icicle on to the column below. On some columns the drops only fell once in two or three minutes, and in these cases it would be an interesting calculation to discover how long, at that rate of dripping, it would take to form a pillar, say eighty feet high by ten in diameter. That the process, in at least one instance, was incalculably slow, the following example will suffice to show. Cut on one of these pillars we discovered the rude likeness of a mummy, by the head of which sat what appeared to be the figure of an Egyptian god, doubtless the handiwork of some old-world labourer in the mine. This work of art was executed at the natural height at which an idle fellow, be he Phœnician workman or British cad, is in the habit of trying to immortalize himself at the expense of nature's masterpieces, namely, about five feet from the ground. Yet at the time that we saw it, which *must* have been nearly three thousand years after the date of the execution of the carving, the column was only eight feet high, and was still in process of formation, which gives a rate of growth of a foot to a thousand years, or an inch and a fraction to a century. This we knew because, as we were standing by it, we heard a drop of water fall.

Sometimes the stalagmites took strange forms, presumably where the dropping of the water had not always been on the same spot. Thus, one huge mass, which must have weighed a hundred tons or so, was in the shape of a pulpit, beautifully fretted over outside with a design that looked like lace. Others resembled strange beasts, and on the sides of the cave were fan-like ivory tracings, such as the frost leaves upon a pane.

Out of the vast main aisle there opened here and there smaller caves, exactly, Sir Henry said, as chapels open out of great cathedrals. Some were large, but one or two – and this is a wonderful instance of how nature carries out her handiwork by the same unvarying laws, utterly irrespective of size – were tiny. One little nook, for instance, was no larger than an unusually big doll's house, and yet it might have been a model of the whole place, for the water dropped, tiny icicles hung, and spar columns were forming in just the same way.

We had not, however, enough time to examine this beautiful cavern so thoroughly as we should have liked to do, for unfortunately Gagool seemed to be indifferent to stalactites, and only anxious to get her business over. This annoyed me the more, as I was particularly anxious to discover, if possible, by what system the light was admitted into the cave, and whether it was by the hand of man or by that of nature that this was done, also if the place had been used in any way in ancient times, as seemed probable. However, we consoled ourselves with the idea that we would investigate it thoroughly on our return, and followed on after our uncanny guide.

On she led us, straight to the top of the vast and silent cave, where we found another doorway, not arched as the first was, but square at the top, something like the doorways of Egyptian temples.

'Are ye prepared to enter the Place of Death, White Men?' asked Gagool, evidently with a view to making us feel uncomfortable.

'Lead on, Macduff,' said Good solemnly, trying to look as though he was not at all alarmed, as indeed we all did except Foulata, who caught Good by the arm for protection.

'This is getting rather ghastly,' said Sir Henry, peeping into the dark doorway. 'Come on, Quatermain – *seniores priores*. Don't keep the old lady waiting!' and he politely made way for me to lead the van, for which inwardly I did not bless him.

Tap, tap, went old Gagool's stick down the passage, as she trotted along, chuckling hideously; and still overcome by some unaccountable presentiment of evil, I hung back.

'Come, get on, old fellow,' said Good, 'or we shall lose our fair guide.'

Thus adjured, I started down the passage, and after about twenty paces found myself in a gloomy apartment some forty feet long, by thirty broad, and thirty high, which in some past age evidently had been hollowed, by hand labour, out of the mountain. This apartment was not nearly so well lighted as the vast stalactite ante-cave, and at the first glance all I could discern was a massive stone table running down its length, with a colossal white figure at its head, and life-sized white figures all round it. Next I discovered a brown thing, seated on the table in the centre, and in another moment my eyes grew accustomed to the light, and I saw what all these things were, and was tailing out of the place as hard as my legs would carry me.

I am not a nervous man in a general way, and very little troubled with superstitions, of which I have lived to see the folly; but I am free to own that this sight quite upset me, and had it not been that Sir Henry caught me by the collar and held me, I do honestly believe that in another five minutes I should have been outside the stalactite cave, and that a promise of all the diamonds in Kimberley would not have induced me to enter it again. But he held me tight, so I stopped because I could not help myself. Next second, however, *his* eyes became focused to the light, and he let go of me, and began to mop the perspiration off his forehead. As for Good, he swore feebly, while Foulata threw her arms round his neck and shrieked.

Only Gagool chuckled loud and long.

It *was* a ghastly sight. There at the end of the long stone table, holding in his skeleton fingers a great white spear, sat *Death* himself, shaped in the form of a colossal human skeleton, fifteen feet or more in height. High above his head he held the spear, as though in the act to strike; one bony hand rested on the stone table before him, in the position a man assumes on rising from his seat, whilst his frame was bent forward so that the vertebræ of the neck and the grinning, gleaming skull projected towards us, and fixed its hollow eye-places upon us, the jaws a little open, as though it were about to speak.

'Great heavens!' said I faintly, at last, 'what can it be?'

'And what are *those things?*' asked Good, pointing to the white company round the table.

'And what on earth is *that thing?*' said Sir Henry, pointing to the brown creature seated on the table.

'*Hee! hee! hee!*' laughed Gagool. 'To those who enter the Hall of the Dead, evil comes. *Hee! hee! hee! ha! ha!*'

'Come, Incubu, brave in battle, come and see him thou slewest;' and the old creature caught Curtis's coat in her skinny fingers, and led him away towards the table. We followed.

Presently she stopped and pointed at the brown object seated on the table. Sir Henry looked, and started back with an exclamation; and no wonder, for there, quite naked, seated on the table, the head which Curtis's battle-axe had shorn from the body resting on its knees, was the gaunt corpse of Twala, the last king of the Kukuanas. Yes, there, the head perched upon the knees, it sat in all its ugliness, the vertebræ projecting a full inch above the level of the shrunken flesh of the neck, for all the world like a black double of Hamilton Tighe.* Over the surface of the corpse there was gathered a thin glassy film, that made its appearance yet more appalling, for which we were, at the moment, quite unable to account, till presently we observed that from the roof of the chamber the water fell steadily, *drip! drip! drip!* on to the neck of the corpse, whence it ran down over the entire surface, and finally escaped into the rock through a tiny hole in the table. Then I guessed what the film was – *Twala's body was being transformed into a stalactite.*

A look at the white forms seated on the stone bench which ran round that ghastly board confirmed this view. They were human bodies indeed, or rather they had been human; now they were *stalactites.* This was the way in which the Kukuana people had from time immemorial preserved their royal dead. They petrified them. What the exact system might be, if there was any, beyond the placing of them for a long

* 'Now haste ye, my handmaidens, haste and see
How he sits there and glowers with his head on his knee.'

179

period of years under the drip, I never discovered, but there they sat, iced over and preserved for ever by the silicious fluid.

Anything more awe-inspiring than the spectacle of this long line of departed royalties (there were twenty-seven of them, the last being Ignosi's father), wrapped, each of them, in a shroud of ice-like spar, through which the features could be dimly made out and seated round that in hospitable board, with Death himself for a host, it is impossible to imagine. That the practice of thus preserving their kings must have been an ancient one is evident from the number, which, allowing for an average reign of fifteen years, supposing that every king who reigned was placed here – an improbable thing, as some are sure to have perished in battle far from home – would fix the date of its commencement at four and a quarter centuries back.

But the colossal Death, who sits at the head of the board, is far older than that, and, unless I am much mistaken, owes his origin to the same artist who designed the three Colossi. He is hewn out of a single stalactite, and, looked at as a work of art, is most admirably conceived and executed. Good, who understands anatomy, declared that, so far as he could see, the anatomical design of the skeleton is perfect down to the smallest bones.

My own idea is, that this terrific object was a freak of fancy on the part of some old-world sculptor, and that its presence had suggested to the Kukuanas the idea of placing their royal dead under its awful presidency. Or perhaps it was set there to frighten away any marauders who might have designs upon the treasure chamber beyond. I cannot say. All I can do is to describe it as it is, and the reader must form his own conclusion.

Such, at any rate, was the White Death and such were the White Dead!

Chapter XVII

SOLOMON'S TREASURE CHAMBER

While we were engaged in recovering from our fright, and in examining the grisly wonders of the Place of Death, Gagool had been differently occupied. Somehow or other – for she was marvellously active when she chose – she had scrambled on to the great table, and made her way to where our departed friend Twala was placed, under the drip, to see, suggested Good, how he was 'pickling,' or for some dark purpose of her own. Then she hobbled back, stopping now and again to address a remark, the tenor of which I could not catch, to one or other of the shrouded forms, just as you or I might greet an old acquaintance. Having gone through this mysterious and horrible ceremony, she squatted herself down on the table immediately under the White Death, and began, so far as I could make out, to offer up prayers to it. The spectacle of this wicked old creature pouring out supplications, evil ones, no doubt, to the arch enemy of mankind, was so uncanny that it caused us to hasten our inspection.

'Now, Gagool,' said I, in a low voice – somehow one did not dare to speak above a whisper in that place – 'lead us to the chamber.'

The old creature promptly scrambled down off the table.

'My lords are not afraid?' she said, leering up into my face.

'Lead on.'

'Good, my lords;' and she hobbled round to the back of the great Death. 'Here is the chamber; let my lords light the lamp, and enter,' and she placed the gourd full of oil upon the floor, and leaned herself against the side of the cave. I took out a match, of which we had still a few in a box, and lit a rush wick, and then looked for the doorway, but there was nothing before us except the solid rock. Gagool grinned. 'The way is there, my lords. *Ha! ha! ha!*'

'Do not jest with us,' I said sternly.

'I jest not, my lords. See!' and she pointed at the rock.

As she did so, on holding up the lamp we perceived that a mass of stone was rising slowly from the floor and vanishing into the rock above, where doubtless there is a cavity prepared to receive it. The mass was of the width of a good-sized door, about ten feet high and not less than five feet thick. It must have weighed at least twenty or thirty tons, and was clearly moved upon some simple balance principle of counter-weights, probably the same as that by which the opening and shutting of an ordinary modern window is arranged. How the principle was set in motion, of course, none of us saw; Gagool was careful to avoid this; but I have little doubt that there was some very simple lever, which was moved ever so little by pressure on a secret spot, thereby throwing additional weight on to the hidden counterbalances, and causing the whole mass to be lifted from the ground.

Very slowly and gently the great stone raised itself, until at last it had vanished altogether, and a dark hole presented itself to us in the place which the door had filled.

Our excitement was so intense, as we saw the way to Solomon's treasure chamber thrown open at last, that I for one began to tremble and shake. Would it prove a hoax after all, I wondered, or was old Da Silvestra right? and were there vast hoards of wealth stored in that dark place, hoards which would make us the richest men in the whole world? We should know in a minute or two.

'Enter, white men from the Stars,' said Gagool, advancing into the doorway; 'but first hear your servant, Gagool the old. The bright stones that ye will see were dug out of the pit over which the Silent Ones are set, and stored here, I know not by whom. But once has this place been entered since the time that those who stored the stones departed in haste, leaving them behind. The report of the treasure went down indeed among the people who lived in the country from age to age, but none knew where the chamber was, nor the secret of the door. But it happened that a white man reached this country from over the mountains – perchance he too came "from the Stars" – and was well received by the king of that day. He it is who sits yonder,' and she pointed to the fifth king at the table of the Dead. 'And it came to pass that he and a woman of the country who was with him journeyed to this place, and that by chance the woman learnt the secret of the door – a thousand years might ye search, but ye should never find it. Then the white man entered with the woman and found the stones, and filled with stones the skin of a small goat, which the woman had with her to hold food. And as he was going from the chamber he took up one more stone, a large one, and held it in his hand.' Here she paused.

'Well,' I asked, breathless with interest as we all were, 'what happened to Da Silvestra?'

The old hag started at the mention of the name.

'How knowest thou the dead man's name?' she asked sharply; and then, without waiting for an answer, went on –

'None know what happened; but it came about that the white man was frightened, for he flung down the goat-skin, with the stones, and fled out with only the one stone in his hand, and that the king took, and it is the stone which thou, Macumazahn, didst take from Twala's brow.'

'Have none entered here since?' I asked, peering again down the dark passage.

'None, my lords. Only the secret of the door has been kept, and every king has opened it, though he has not entered. There is a saying, that those who enter there will die within a moon, even as the white man died in the cave upon the mountain, where ye found him, Macumazahn, and therefore the kings do not enter. *Ha! ha!* mine are true words.'

Our eyes met as she said it, and I turned sick and cold. How did the old hag know all these things?

'Enter, my lords. If I speak truth, the goat-skin with the stones will lie upon the floor; and if there is truth as to whether it is death to enter here, that will ye learn afterwards. *Ha! ha! ha!*' and she hobbled through the doorway, bearing the light with her; but I confess that once more I hesitated about following.

'Oh, confound it all!' said Good; 'here goes. I am not going to be frightened by that old devil;' and followed by Foulata, who, however, evidently did not at all like the business, for she was shivering with fear, he plunged into the passage after Gagool – an example which we quickly followed.

A few yards down the passage, in the narrow way hewn out of the living rock, Gagool had paused, and was waiting for us.

'See, my lords,' she said, holding the light before her, 'those who stored the treasure here fled in haste, and bethought them to guard against any who should find the secret of the door, but had not the time,' and she pointed to large square blocks of stone, which, to the height of two courses (about two feet three), had been placed across the passage with a view to walling it up. Along the side of the passage were similar blocks ready for use, and, most curious of all, a heap of mortar and a couple of trowels, which tools, so far as we had time to examine them, appeared to be of a similar shape and make to those used by workmen to this day.

Here Foulata, who had been in a state of great fear and agitation throughout, said that she felt faint and could go no farther, but would wait there. Accordingly we set her down on the unfinished wall, placing the basket of provisions by her side, and left her to recover.

Following the passage for about fifteen paces farther, we came suddenly to an elaborately painted wooden door. It was standing wide open. Whoever was last there had either not found the time, or had forgotten, to shut it.

Across the threshold of this door lay a skin bag, formed of a goat-skin, that appeared to be full of pebbles.

'*Hee! hee!* white men,' sniggered Gagool, as the light from the lamp fell upon it. 'What did I tell you, that the white man who came here fled in haste, and dropped the woman's bag – behold it!'

Good stooped down and lifted it. It was heavy and jingled.

'By Jove! I believe it's full of diamonds,' he said, in an awed whisper; and, indeed, the idea of a small goat-skin full of diamonds is enough to awe anybody.

'Go on,' said Henry impatiently. 'Here, old lady, give me the lamp,' and taking it from Gagool's hand, he stepped through the doorway and held it high above his head.

We pressed in after him, forgetful for the moment of the bag of diamonds, and found ourselves in Solomon's treasure chamber.

At first, all that the somewhat faint light given by the lamp revealed was a room hewn out of the living rock, and apparently not more than ten feet square. Next there came into sight, stored one on the other to the arch of the roof, a splendid collection of elephant-tusks. How many of them there were we did not know, for of course we could not see to what depth they went back, but there could not have been less than the ends of four or five hundred tusks of the first quality visible to our eyes. There, alone, was enough ivory before us to make a man wealthy for life. Perhaps, I thought, it was from this very store that Solomon drew the raw material for his 'great throne of ivory,' of which 'there was not the like made in any kingdom.'

On the opposite side of the chamber were about a score of wooden boxes, something like Martini-Henry ammunition boxes, only rather larger, and painted red.

'There are the diamonds,' cried I; 'bring the light.'

Sir Henry did so, holding it close to the top box, of which the lid, rendered rotten by time even in that dry place, appeared to have been smashed in, probably by Da Silvestra himself. Pushing my hand through the hole in the lid I drew it out full, not of diamonds, but of gold pieces, of a shape that none of us had seen before, and with what looked like Hebrew characters stamped upon them.

'Ah!' I said, replacing the coin, 'we sha'n't go back empty-handed, anyhow. There must be a couple of thousand pieces in each box, and there are eighteen boxes. I suppose this was the money to pay the workmen and merchants.'

'Well,' put in Good, 'I think that is the lot; I don't see any diamonds, unless the old Portuguee put them all into his bag.'

'Let my lords look yonder where it is darkest, if they would find the stones,' said Gagool, interpreting our looks. 'There my lords will find a nook, and three stone chests in the nook, two sealed and one open.'

Before translating this to Sir Henry, who carried the light, I could not resist asking how she knew these things, if no one had entered the place since the white man, generations ago.

'Ah, Macumazahn, the watcher by night,' was the mocking answer, 'ye who live in the stars, do ye not know that some have eyes which can see through rock? *Ha! ha! ha!*'

'Look in that corner, Curtis,' I said, indicating the spot Gagool had pointed out.

'Hullo, you fellows,' he cried, 'here's a recess. Great heavens! see here.'

We hurried up to where he was standing in a nook, shaped something like a small bow window. Against the wall of this recess were placed three stone chests, each about two feet square. Two were fitted with stone lids, the lid of the third rested against the side of the chest, which was open.

'*See!*' he repeated hoarsely, holding a lamp over the open chest. We looked, and for a moment could make nothing out, on account of a silvery sheen that dazzled us. When our eyes grew used to it we saw that the chest was three parts full of uncut diamonds, most of them of considerable size. Stooping, I picked some up. Yes, there was no doubt of it, there was the unmistakable soapy feel about them.

I fairly gasped as I dropped them.

'We are the richest men in the whole world,' I said. 'Monte Cristo was a fool to us.'

'We shall flood the market with diamonds,' said Good.

'Got to get them there first,' suggested Sir Henry.

We stood still with pale faces and stared at each other, the lantern in the middle and the glimmering gems below, as though we were conspirators about to commit a crime, instead of being, as we thought, the most fortunate men on earth.

'Hee! hee! hee!' cackled old Gagool behind us, as she flitted about like a vampire bat. 'There are the bright stones ye love, white men, as many as ye will; take them, run them through your fingers, *eat* of them, hee! hee; *drink* of them, ha! ha!'

At that moment there was something so ridiculous to my mind in the idea of eating and drinking diamonds, that I began to laugh outrageously, an example which the others followed, without knowing why. There we stood and shrieked with laughter over the gems that were ours, which had been found for *us* thousands of years ago by the patient delvers in the great hole yonder, and stored for *us* by Solomon's long-dead overseer, whose name, perchance, was written in the characters stamped on the faded wax that yet adhered to the lids of the chests. Solomon never got them, nor David, nor Da Silvestra, nor anybody else. *We* had got them: there before us were millions of pounds' worth of diamonds, and thousands of pounds' worth of gold and ivory only waiting to be taken away.

Suddenly the fit passed off, and we stopped laughing.

'Open the other chests, white men,' croaked Gagool, 'there are surely more therein. Take your fill, white lords! *Ha! ha!* take your fill.'

Thus adjured, we set to work to pull up the stone lids on the other two, first – not without a feeling of sacrilege – breaking the seals that fastened them.

Hoorah! they were full too, full to the brim; at least, the second one was; no wretched Da Silvestra had been filling goat-skins out of that. As for the third chest, it was only about a fourth full, but the stones were all picked ones; none less than twenty carats, and some of them as large as pigeon-eggs. A good many of these bigger ones, however, we could see by holding them up to the light, were a little yellow, 'off coloured,' as they call it at Kimberley.

What we did *not* see, however, was the look of fearful malevolence that old Gagool favoured us with as she crept, crept like a snake, out of the treasure chamber and down the passage towards the door of solid rock.

*   *   *   *   *

Hark! Cry upon cry comes ringing up the vaulted path. It is Foulata's voice!

'*Oh, Bougwan! help! help! the stone falls!*'

'Leave go, girl! Then—'

'*Help! help! she has stabbed me!*'

By now we are running down the passage, and this is what the light from the lamp shows us. The door of rock is closing down slowly; it is not three feet from the floor. Near it struggle Foulata and Gagool. The red blood of the former runs to her knee, but still the brave girl holds the old witch, who fights like a wild cat. Ah! she is free! Foulata falls, and Gagool throws herself on the ground, to twist like a snake through the crack of the closing stone. She is under – ah! God! too late! too late! The stone nips her, and she yells in agony. Down, down, it comes, all the thirty tons of it, slowly pressing her old body against the rock below. Shriek upon shriek, such as we never heard, then a long sickening *crunch*, and the door was shut just as, rushing down the passage, we hurled ourselves against it.

It was all done in four seconds.

Then we turned to Foulata. The poor girl was stabbed in the body, and I saw that she could not live long.

'Ah! Bougwan, I die!' gasped the beautiful creature. 'She crept out – Gagool; I did not see her, I was faint – and the door began to fall; then she came back, and was looking up the path – I saw her come in through the slowly falling door, and caught her and held her, and she stabbed me, and I *die*, Bougwan!'

'Poor girl! poor girl!' Good cried; and then, as he could do nothing else, he fell to kissing her.

'Bougwan,' she said, after a pause, 'is Macumazahn there? It grows so dark, I cannot see.'

'Here I am, Foulata.'

'Macumazahn, be my tongue for a moment, I pray thee, for Bougwan cannot understand me, and before I go into the darkness I would speak a word.'

'Say on, Foulata, I will render it.'

'Say to my lord, Bougwan, that – I love him, and that I am glad to die because I know that he cannot cumber his life with such as I am, for the sun may not mate with the darkness, nor the white with the black.

'Say that, since I saw him, at times I have felt as though there were a bird in my bosom, which would one day fly hence and sing elsewhere. Even now, though I cannot lift my hand, and my brain grows cold, I do not feel as though my heart were dying; it is so full of love that it could live a thousand years, and yet be young. Say that if I live again, mayhap I shall see him in the Stars, and that – I will search them all, though perchance there I should still be black and he would – still be white. Say – nay, Macumazahn, say no more, save that I love – Oh, hold me closer, Bougwan, I cannot feel thine arms – *oh! oh!*'

'She is dead – she is dead!' exclaimed Good, rising in grief, the tears running down his honest face.

'You need not let that trouble you, old fellow,' said Sir Henry.

'Eh!' said Good; 'what do you mean?'

'I mean that you will soon be in a position to join her. *Man, don't you see that we are buried alive?*'

Until Sir Henry uttered these words I do not think that the full horror of what had happened had come home to us, pre-occupied as we were with the sight of poor Foulata's end. But now we understood. The ponderous mass of rock had closed, probably for ever, for the only brain which knew its secret was crushed to powder beneath it. This was a door that none could hope to force with anything short of dynamite in large quantities. And we were the wrong side of it!

For a few minutes we stood horrified there over the corpse of Foulata. All the manhood seemed to have gone out of us. The first shock of this idea of the slow and miserable end that awaited us was overpowering. We saw it all now; that fiend Gagool had planned this snare for us from the first. It must have been just the jest that her evil mind would have rejoiced in, the idea of the three white men, whom, for some reason of her own, she had always hated, slowly perishing of thirst and hunger in the company of the treasure they had coveted. Now I saw the point of that sneer of hers about eating and drinking the diamonds. Perhaps somebody had tried to serve the poor old Dom in the same way, when he abandoned the skin full of jewels.

'This will never do,' said Sir Henry hoarsely; 'the lamp will soon go out. Let us see if we can't find the spring that works the rock.'

We sprang forward with desperate energy, and, standing in a bloody ooze, began to feel up and down the door and the sides of the passage. But no knob or spring could we discover.

'Depend on it,' I said, 'it does not work from the inside; if it did Gagool would not have risked trying to crawl underneath the stone. It was the knowledge of this that made her try to escape at all hazards, curse her.'

'At all events,' said Sir Henry with a hard little laugh, 'retribution was swift; hers was almost as awful an end as ours is likely to be. We can do nothing with the door; let us go back to the treasure room.'

We turned and went, and as we passed it I perceived by the unfinished wall across the passage the basket of food which poor Foulata had carried. I took it up, and brought it with me to the accursed treasure chamber that was to be our grave. Then we returned and reverently bore in Foulata's corpse, laying it on the floor by the boxes of coins.

Next we seated ourselves, leaning our backs against the three stone chests of price-less treasure.

'Let us divide the food,' said Sir Henry, 'so as to make it last as long as possible.' Accordingly we did so. It would, we reckoned, make four infinitesimally small meals for each of us, enough, say, to support life for a couple of days. Besides the 'biltong,' or dried game-flesh, there were two gourds of water, each holding about a quart.

'Now,' said Sir Henry grimly, 'let us eat and drink, for to-morrow we die.'

We each ate a small portion of the 'biltong,' and drank a sip of water. Needless to say, we had but little appetite, though we were sadly in need of food, and felt better after swallowing it. Then we got up and made a systematic examination of the walls of our prison-house, in the faint hope of finding some means of exit, sounding them and the floor carefully.

There was none. It was not probable that there would be any to a treasure chamber.

The lamp began to burn dim. The fat was nearly exhausted.

'Quatermain,' said Sir Henry, 'what is the time – your watch goes?'

I drew it out and looked at it. It was six o'clock; we had entered the cave at eleven.

'Infadoos will miss us,' I suggested. 'If we do not return to-night he will search for us in the morning, Curtis.'

'He may search in vain. He does not know the secret of the door nor even where it is. No living person knew it yesterday, except Gagool. To-day no one knows it. Even if he found the door he could not break it down. All the Kukuana army could not break through five feet of living rock. My friends, I see nothing for it but to bow ourselves to the will of the Almighty. The search for treasure has brought many to a bad end; we shall go to swell their number.'

The lamp grew dimmer yet.

Presently it flared up and showed the whole scene in strong relief, the great mass of white tusks, the boxes of gold, the corpse of poor Foulata stretched before them, the goat-skin full of treasure, the dim glimmer of the diamonds, and the wild, wan faces of us three white men seated there awaiting death by starvation.

Then the flame sank and expired.

Chapter XVIII

WE ABANDON HOPE

I can give no adequate description of the horrors of the night which followed. Mercifully they were to some extent mitigated by sleep, for even in such a position as ours wearied nature will sometimes assert itself. But I, at any rate found it impossible to sleep much. Putting aside the terrifying thought of our impending doom – for the bravest man on earth might well quail from such a fate as awaited us, and I never made any pretensions to be brave – the *silence* itself was too great to allow of it. Reader, you may have lain awake at night and thought the silence oppressive, but I say with confidence that you can have no idea what a vivid, tangible thing is perfect silence. On the surface of the earth there is always some sound or motion, and though it may in itself be imperceptible, yet it deadens the sharp edge of absolute silence. But here there was none. We were buried in the bowels of a huge snow-clad peak. Thousands of feet above us the fresh air rushed over the white snow, but no sound of it reached us. We were separated by a long tunnel and five feet of rock even from the awful chamber of the Dead; and the dead make no noise. The crashing of all the artillery of earth and heaven could not have come to our ears in our living tomb. We were cut off from every echo of the world – we were as men already dead.

And then the irony of the situation forced itself upon me. There around us lay treasures enough to pay off a moderate national debt, or to build a fleet of ironclads, and yet we would have bartered them all gladly for the faintest chance of escape. Soon, doubtless, we should be rejoiced to exchange them for a bit of food or a cup of water, and, after that, even for the privilege of a speedy close to our sufferings. Truly wealth, which men spend their lives in acquiring, is a valueless thing at the last.

And so the night wore on.

'Good,' said Sir Henry's voice at last, and it sounded awful in the intense stillness, 'how many matches have you in the box?'

'Eight, Curtis.'

'Strike one and let us see the time.'

He did so, and in contrast to the dense darkness the flame nearly blinded us. It was five o'clock by my watch. The beautiful dawn was now blushing on the snow-wreaths far over our heads, and the breeze would be stirring the night mists in the hollows.

'We had better eat something and keep up our strength,' I suggested.

'What is the good of eating?' answered Good; 'the sooner we die and get it over the better.'

'While there is life there is hope,' said Sir Henry.

Accordingly we ate and sipped some water, and another period of time passed. Then Sir Henry suggested that it might be well to get as near the door as possible and halloa, on the faint chance of somebody catching a sound outside. Accordingly Good, who, from long practice at sea, has a fine piercing note, groped his way down the passage and began. I must say that he made a most diabolical noise. I never heard such yells; but it might have been a mosquito buzzing for all the effect they produced.

After a while he gave it up and came back very thirsty, and had to drink some water. Then we stopped yelling, as it encroached on the supply of water.

So we sat down once more against the chests of useless diamonds in that dreadful inaction, which was one of the hardest circumstances of our fate; and I am bound to say that, for my part, I gave way in despair. Laying my head against Sir Henry's broad shoulder I burst into tears; and I think that I heard Good gulping away on the other side, and swearing hoarsely at himself for doing so.

Ah, how good and brave that great man was! Had we been two frightened children, and he our nurse, he could not have treated us more tenderly. Forgetting his own share of miseries, he did all he could to soothe our broken nerves, telling stories of men who had been in somewhat similar circumstances, and miraculously escaped; and when these failed to cheer us, pointing out how, after all, it was only anticipating an end which must come to us all, that it would soon be over, and that death from exhaustion was a merciful one (which is not true). Then, in a diffident sort of way, as once before I had heard him do, he suggested that we should throw ourselves on the mercy of a higher power, which for my part I did with great vigour.

His is a beautiful character, very quiet, but very strong.

And so somehow the day went as the night had gone, if, indeed, one can use these terms where all was densest night, and when I lit a match to see the time it was seven o'clock.

Once more we ate and drank, and as we did so an idea occurred to me.

'How is it,' said I, 'that the air in this place keeps fresh? It is thick and heavy, but it is perfectly fresh.'

'Great heavens!' said Good, starting up, 'I never thought of that. It can't come through the stone door, for it's air-tight, if ever a door was. It must come from somewhere. If there were no current of air in the place we should have been stifled when we first came in. Let us have a look.'

It was wonderful what a change this mere spark of hope wrought in us. In a moment we were all three groping about on our hands and knees, feeling for the slightest indication of a draught. Presently my ardour received a check. I put my hand on something cold. It was poor Foulata's dead face.

For an hour or more we went on feeling about, till at last Sir Henry and I gave it up in despair, having been considerably hurt by constantly knocking our heads against tusks, chests, and the sides of the chamber. But Good still persevered, saying, with an approach to cheerfulness, that it was better than doing nothing.

'I say, you fellows,' he said presently, in a constrained sort of voice, 'come here.'

Needless to say we scrambled towards him quickly enough.

'Quatermain, put your hand here where mine is. Now, do you feel anything?'

'I *think* I feel air coming up.'

'Now listen.' He rose and stamped upon the place, and a flame of hope shot up in our hearts. *It rang hollow.*

With trembling hands I lit a match. I had only three left, and we saw that we were in the angle of the far corner of the chamber, a fact that accounted for our not having noticed the hollow sound of the place during our former exhaustive examination. As the match burnt we scrutinized the spot. There was a join in the solid rock floor, and, great heavens! there, let in level with the rock, was a stone ring. We said no word, we were too excited, and our hearts beat too wildly with hope to allow us to speak. Good had a knife, at the back of which was one of those hooks that are made to extract stones from horses' hoofs. He opened it, and scratched round the ring with it. Finally he worked it under, and levered away gently for fear of breaking the hook. The ring began to move. Being of stone it had not got set fast in all the centuries it had lain there, as would have been the case had it been of iron. Presently it was upright. Then he thrust his hands into it and tugged with all his force, but nothing budged.

'Let me try,' I said impatiently, for the situation of the stone, right in the angle of the corner, was such that it was impossible for two to pull at once. I took hold and strained away, but no results.

Then Sir Henry tried and failed.

Taking the hook again, Good scratched all round the crack where we felt the air coming up.

'Now, Curtis,' he said, 'tackle on, and put your back into it; you are as strong as two. Stop,' and he took off a stout black silk handkerchief, which, true to his habits of neatness, he still wore, and ran it through the ring. 'Quatermain, get Curtis round the middle and pull for dear life when I give the word. *Now.*'

Sir Henry put out all his enormous strength, and Good and I did the same, with such power as nature had given us.

'Heave! heave! it's giving,' gasped Sir Henry; and I heard the muscles of his great back cracking. Suddenly there was a grating sound, then a rush of air, and we were all on our backs on the floor with a heavy flag-stone upon the top of us. Sir Henry's strength had done it, and never did muscular power stand a man in better stead.

'Light a match, Quatermain,' he said, so soon as we had picked ourselves up and got our breath; 'carefully, now.'

I did so, and there before us, Heaven be praised! was the *first step of a stone stair.*

'Now what is to be done?' asked Good.

'Follow the stair, of course, and trust to Providence.'

'Stop!' said Sir Henry; 'Quatermain, get the bit of biltong and the water that are left; we may want them.'

I went, creeping back to our place by the chests for that purpose, and as I was coming away an idea struck me. We had not thought much of the diamonds for the last twenty-four hours or so; indeed, the very idea of diamonds was nauseous, seeing what they entailed upon us; but, reflected I, I may as well pocket a few in case we ever should get out of this ghastly hole. So I just put my fist into the first chest and filled all the available pockets of my old shooting coat, topping up – this was a happy thought – with a couple of handfuls of big ones out of the third chest.

'I say, you fellows,' I sang out, 'won't you take some diamonds with you? I've filled my pockets.'

'Oh! hang the diamonds!' said Sir Henry. 'I hope that I may never see another.'

As for Good, he made no answer. He was, I think, taking his last farewell of all that was left of the poor girl who had loved him so well. And curious as it may seem to you, my reader, sitting at home at ease, and reflecting on the vast, indeed the immeasurable, wealth which we were thus abandoning, I can assure you that if you had passed some twenty-eight hours with next to nothing to eat and drink in that place, you would not have cared to cumber yourself with diamonds whilst plunging down into the unknown bowels of the earth, in the wild hope of escape from an agonizing death. If from the habits of a lifetime, it had not become a sort of second nature with me never to leave anything worth having behind if there was the slightest chance of my being able to carry it away, I am sure that I should not have bothered to fill my pockets.

'Come on, Quatermain,' said Sir Henry who was already standing on the first step of the stone stair. 'Steady, I will go first.'

'Mind where you put your feet, there may be some awful hole underneath,' I answered.

'Much more likely to be another room,' said Sir Henry, while he descended slowly, counting the steps as he went.

When he got to 'fifteen' he stopped. 'Here's the bottom,' he said. 'Thank goodness! I think it's a passage. Come on down.'

Good went next, and I followed last, and on reaching the bottom lit one of the two remaining matches. By its light we could just see that we were standing in a narrow tunnel, which ran right and left at right angles to the staircase we had descended. Before we could make out any more, the match burnt my fingers and went out. Then arose the delicate question of which way to go. Of course, it was impossible to know what the tunnel was, or where it ran to, and yet to turn one way, might lead us to safety, and the other to destruction. We were utterly perplexed, till suddenly it struck Good that when I had lit the match the draught of the passage blew the flame to the left.

'Let us go against the draught,' he said; 'air draws inwards, not outwards.'

We took this suggestion, and feeling along the wall with the hand, whilst trying the ground before us at every step, we departed from that accursed treasure chamber on our terrible quest for life. If ever it should be entered again by living man, which I do not think probable, he will find tokens of our visit in the open chests of jewels, the empty lamp, and the white bones of poor Foulata.

When we had groped our way for about a quarter of an hour along the passage, suddenly it took a sharp turn, or else was bisected by another, which we followed, only in course of time to be led into a third. And so it went on for some hours. We seemed to be in a stone labyrinth which led nowhere. What all these passages are, of course I cannot say, but we thought that they must be the ancient workings of a mine, of which the various shafts and adits travelled hither and thither as the ore led them. This is the only way in which we could account for such a multitude of galleries.

At length we halted, thoroughly worn out with fatigue and with that hope deferred which maketh the heart sick, and ate up our poor remaining piece of biltong and drank our last sup of water, for our throats were like limekilns. It seemed to us that we had escaped death in the darkness of the chamber only to meet him in the darkness of the tunnels. As we stood, once more utterly depressed, I thought that I caught a sound, to which I called the attention of the others. It was very faint and very far off, but it *was* a sound, a faint, murmuring sound, for the others heard it too, and no words can describe the blessedness of it after all those hours of utter, awful stillness.

'By heaven! it's running water,' said Good. 'Come on.'

Off we started again in the direction from which the faint murmur seemed to come, groping our way as before along the rocky walls. As we went it became more and more audible, till at last it seemed quite loud in the quiet. On, yet on; now we could distinctly make out the unmistakable swirl of rushing water. And yet how could there be running water in the bowels of the earth? Now we were quite near to it, and Good, who was leading, swore that he could smell it.

'Go gently, Good,' said Sir Henry, 'we must be close.' *Splash!* and a cry from Good.

He had fallen in.

'Good! Good! where are you?' we shouted, in terrified distress. To our intense relief an answer came back in a choky voice.

'All right; I've got hold of a rock. Strike a light to show me where you are.'

Hastily I lit the last remaining match. Its faint gleam discovered to us a dark mass of water running at our feet. How wide it was we could not see, but there, some way out, was the dark form of our companion hanging on to a projecting rock.

'Stand clear to catch me,' sung out Good. 'I must swim for it.'

Then we heard a splash, and a great struggle. Another minute and he had grabbed at and caught Sir Henry's outstretched hand, and we had pulled him up high and dry into the tunnel.

'My word!' he said, between his gasps, 'that was touch and go. If I hadn't caught that rock, and known how to swim, I should have been done. It runs like a mill-race, and I could feel no bottom.'

We dared not follow the banks of the subterranean river for fear lest we should fall into it again in the darkness. So after Good had rested a while, and we had drunk our fill of the water, which was sweet and fresh, and washed our faces, that needed it sadly, as well as we could, we started from the banks of this African Styx, and began to retrace our steps along the tunnel, Good dripping unpleasantly in front of us. At length we came to another gallery leading to our right.

'We may as well take it,' said Sir Henry wearily; 'all roads are alike here; we can only go on till we drop.'

Slowly, for a long, long while, we stumbled, utterly exhausted, along this new tunnel, Sir Henry now leading the way.

Suddenly he stopped, and we bumped up against him.

'Look!' he whispered, 'is my brain going, or is that light?'

We stared with all our eyes, and there, yes, there, far ahead of us, was a faint, glimmering spot, no larger than a cottage window pane. It was so faint, that I doubt if any eyes, except those which, like ours, had for days seen nothing but blackness, could have perceived it at all.

With a gasp of hope we pushed on. In five minutes there was no longer any doubt; it *was* a patch of faint light. A minute more and a breath of real live air was fanning us. On we struggled. All at once the tunnel narrowed. Sir Henry went on his knees. Smaller yet it grew, till it was only the size of a large fox's earth – it was *earth* now, mind you; the rock had ceased.

A squeeze, a struggle, and Sir Henry was out, and so was Good, and so was I, and there above us were the blessed stars, and in our nostrils was the sweet air. Then suddenly something gave, and we were all rolling over and over and over through grass and bushes and soft wet soil.

I caught at something and stopped. Sitting up I halloed lustily. An answering shout came from just below, where Sir Henry's wild career had been stopped by some level ground. I scrambled to him, and found him unhurt, though breathless. Then we looked for Good. A little way off we discovered him also, jammed in a forked root. He was a good deal knocked about, but soon came to himself.

We sat down together there on the grass, and the revulsion of feeling was so great that really I think we cried for joy. We had escaped from that awful dungeon, which was so near to becoming our grave. Surely some merciful Power guided our footsteps to the jackal hole, for that is what it must have been, at the termination of the tunnel. And see, yonder on the mountains the dawn we had never thought to look upon again was blushing rosy red.

Presently the grey light stole down the slopes, and we saw that we were at the bottom, or rather, nearly at the bottom, of the vast pit in front of the entrance to the cave. Now we could make out the dim forms of the three Colossi who sat upon its verge. Doubtless those awful passages, along which we had wandered the livelong night, had been originally in some way connected with the great diamond mine. As for the subterranean river in the bowels of the mountain, Heaven only knows what it is, or whence it flows, or whither it goes. I, for one, have no anxiety to trace its course.

Lighter it grew, and lighter yet. We could see each other now, and such a spectacle as we presented I have never set eyes on before or since. Gaunt-cheeked, hollow-eyed wretches, smeared all over with dust and mud, bruised, bleeding, the long fear of imminent death yet written on our countenances, we were, indeed, a sight to frighten the daylight. And yet it is a solemn fact that Good's eye-glass was still fixed in Good's eye. I doubt whether he had ever taken it out at all. Neither the darkness, nor the plunge in the subterranean river, nor the roll down the slope, had been able to separate Good and his eye-glass.

Presently we rose, fearing that our limbs would stiffen if we stopped there longer, and commenced with slow and painful steps to struggle up the sloping sides of the great pit. For an hour or more we toiled steadfastly up the blue clay, dragging ourselves on by the help of the roots and grasses with which it was clothed.

At last it was done, and we stood by the great road, on the side of the pit opposite to the Colossi.

At the side of the road, a hundred yards off, a fire was burning in front of some huts, and round the fire were figures. We staggered towards them, supporting one another, and halting every few paces. Presently one of the figures rose, saw us and fell on to the ground, crying out for fear.

'Infadoos, Infadoos! it is we, thy friends.'

He rose; he ran to us, staring wildly, and still shaking with fear.

'Oh, my lords, my lords, it is indeed you come back from the dead! – come back from the dead!'

And the old warrior flung himself down before us, and clasping Sir Henry's knees, he wept aloud for joy.

Chapter XIX

IGNOSI'S FAREWELL

Ten days from that eventful morning found us once more in our old quarters at Loo; and, strange to say, but little the worse for our terrible experience, except that my stubbly hair came out of the treasure cave about three shades greyer than it went in, and that Good never was quite the same after Foulata's death, which seemed to move him very greatly. I am bound to say, looking at the thing from the point of view of an oldish man of the world, that I consider her removal was a fortunate occurrence, since, otherwise, complications would have been sure to ensue. The poor creature was no ordinary native girl, but a person of great, I had almost said stately, beauty, and of considerable refinement of mind. But no amount of beauty or refinement could have made an entanglement between Good and herself a desirable occurrence; for, as she herself put it, 'Can the sun mate with the darkness, or the white with the black?'

I need hardly state that we never again penetrated into Solomon's treasure chamber. After we had recovered from our fatigues, a process which took us forty-eight hours, we descended into the great pit in the hope of finding the hole by which we had crept out of the mountain, but with no success. To begin with, rain had fallen, and obliterated our spoor; and what is more, the sides of the vast pit were full of ant-bear and other holes. It was impossible to say to which of these we owed our salvation. Also, on the day before we started back to Loo, we made a further examination of the wonders of the stalactite cave, and, drawn by a kind of restless feeling, even penetrated once more into the Chamber of the Dead. Passing beneath the spear of the White Death we gazed, with sensations which it would be quite impossible for me to describe, at the mass of rock that had shut us off from escape, thinking the while of the priceless treasures beyond, of the mysterious old hag whose flattened fragments lay crushed beneath it, and of the fair girl of whose tomb it was the portal. I say gazed at the 'rock,' for, examine as we would, we could find no traces of the join of the sliding door; nor, indeed, could we hit upon the secret, now utterly lost, that worked it, though we tried for an hour or more. It is certainly a marvellous bit of mechanism, characteristic, in its massive and yet inscrutable simplicity, of the age which produced it; and I doubt if the world has such another to show.

At last we gave it up in disgust; though, if the mass had suddenly risen before our eyes, I doubt if we should have screwed up courage to step over Gagool's mangled remains, and once more enter the treasure chamber, even in the sure and certain hope of unlimited diamonds. And yet I could have cried at the idea of leaving all that treasure, the biggest treasure probably that in the world's history has ever been accumulated in one spot. But there was no help for it. Only dynamite could force its way through five feet of solid rock. And so we left it. Perhaps, in some remote unborn century, a more fortunate explorer may hit upon the 'Open Sesame,' and flood the world with gems. But, myself, I doubt it. Somehow, I seem to feel that the millions of pounds' worth of jewels that lie in the three stone coffers will never shine round the neck of an earthly beauty. They and Foulata's bones will keep cold company till the end of all things.

With a sigh of disappointment we made our way back, and next day started for Loo. And yet it was really very ungrateful of us to be disappointed; for, as the reader will remember, by a lucky thought, I had taken the precaution to fill the pockets of my old shooting coat with gems before we left our prison house. A good many of these fell out in the course of our roll down the side of the pit, including most of the big ones, which I had crammed in on the top. But, comparatively speaking, an enormous quantity still remained, including eighteen large stones ranging from about one hundred to thirty carats in weight. My old shooting coat still held sufficient treasure to make us all, if not millionaires, at least exceedingly wealthy men, and yet to keep enough stones each to make the three finest sets of gems in Europe. So we had not done so badly.

On arriving at Loo we were most cordially received by Ignosi, whom we found well, and busily engaged in consolidating his power, and reorganizing the regiments which had suffered most in the great struggle with Twala.

He listened with intense interest to our wonderful story; but when we told him of old Gagool's frightful end he grew thoughtful.

'Come hither,' he called, to a very old Induna or councillor, who was sitting with others in a circle round the king, but out of ear-shot. The ancient man rose, approached, saluted, and seated himself.

'Thou art aged,' said Ignosi.

'Ay, my lord the king! Thy father's father and I were born on the same day.'

'Tell me, when thou wast little, didst thou know Gagaoola the witch doctress?'

'Ay, my lord the king!'

'How was she then – young, like thee?'

'Not so, my lord the king! She was even as she is now and as she was in the days of my grandfather before me; old and dried, very ugly, and full of wickedness.'

'She is no more; she is dead.'

'So, O king! then is an ancient curse taken from the land.'

'Go!'

'*Koom!* I go, black Puppy, who tore out the old dog's throat. *Koom!*'

'Ye see, my brothers,' said Ignosi, 'this was a strange woman, and I rejoice that she is dead. She would have let you die in the dark place, and mayhap afterwards she had found a way to slay me, as she found a way to slay my father, and set up Twala, whom her heart loved, in his place. Now go on with the tale; surely there never was its like!'

After I had narrated all the story of our escape, as we had agreed between ourselves that I should, I took the opportunity to address Ignosi as to our departure from Kukuanaland.

'And now, Ignosi,' I said, 'the time has come for us to bid thee farewell, and start to see our own land once more. Behold, Ignosi, thou camest with us a servant, and now we leave thee a mighty king. If thou art grateful to us, remember to do even as thou didst promise; to rule justly, to respect the law, and to put none to death without a cause. So shalt thou prosper. To-morrow, at break of day, Ignosi, thou wilt give us an escort who shall lead us across the mountains. Is it not so, O king?'

Ignosi covered his face with his hands for a while before answering.

'My heart is sore,' he said at last; 'your words split my heart in twain. What have I done to you, Incubu, Macumazahn, and Bougwan, that ye should leave me desolate? Ye who stood by me in rebellion and in battle, will ye leave me in the day of peace and victory? What will ye – wives? Choose from among the maidens! A place to live in? Behold, the land is yours as far as ye can see. The white man's houses? Ye shall teach my people how to build them. Cattle for beef and milk? Every married man shall bring you an ox or a cow. Wild game to hunt? Does not the elephant walk through my forests, and the river-horse sleep in the reeds? Would ye make war? My Impis wait your word. If there is anything more which I can give, that will I give you.'

'Nay, Ignosi, we want none of these things,' I answered; 'we would seek our own place.'

'Now do I learn,' said Ignosi bitterly, and with flashing eyes, 'that ye love the bright stones more than me, your friend. Ye have the stones; now ye would go to Natal and across the moving black water and sell them, and be rich, as it is the desire of a white man's heart to be. Cursed for your sake be the white stones, and cursed he who seeks them. Death shall it be to him who sets foot in the Place of Death to find them. I have spoken. White men, ye can go.'

I laid my hand upon his arm. 'Ignosi,' I said, 'tell us, when thou didst wander in Zululand, and among the white people in Natal, did not thine heart turn to the land thy mother told thee of, thy native land, where thou didst see the light, and play when thou wast little, the land where thy place was?'

'It was even so, Macumazahn.'

'In like manner, Ignosi, do our hearts turn to our land and to our own place.'

Then came a silence. When Ignosi broke it, it was in a different voice.

'I do perceive that now as ever thy words are wise and full of reason, Macumazahn; that which flies in the air loves not to run along the ground; the white man loves not to live on the level of the black. Well, ye must go, and leave my heart sore, because ye will be as dead to me, since from where ye are no tidings can come to me.

'But listen, and let all the white men know my words. No other white man shall cross the mountains, even if any man live to come so far. I will see no traders with their guns and rum. My people shall fight with the spear, and drink water, like their forefathers before them. I will have no praying-men to put a fear of death into men's hearts, to stir them up against the law of the king, and make a path for the white men who follow to run on. If a white man comes to my gates I will send him back; if a hundred come I will push them back; if armies come, I will make war on them with all my strength, and they shall not prevail against me. None shall ever seek for the shining stones: no, not an army, for if they come I will send a regiment and fill up the pit, and break down the white columns in the caves and choke them with rocks, so that none can reach even to that door of which you speak, and whereof the way to move it is lost. But for you three, Incubu, Macumazahn, and Bougwan, the path is always open; for behold ye are dearer to me than aught that breathes.

'And ye would go. Infadoos, my uncle, and my Induna, shall take you by the hand and guide you with a regiment. There is, as I have learned, another way across the mountains that he shall show you. Farewell, my brothers, brave white men. See me no more, for I have no heart to bear it. Behold, I make a decree, and it shall be published from the mountains to the mountains; your names, Incubu, Macumazahn, and Bougwan, shall be 'hlonipa' even as the names of dead kings, and he who speaks them shall die.* So shall your memory be preserved in the land for ever.

'Go now, ere my eyes rain tears like a woman's. At times as ye look back down the path of life, or when ye are old and gather yourselves together to crouch before the fire, because for you the sun has no more heat, ye will think of how we stood

---

* This extraordinary and negative way of showing intense respect is by no means unknown among African people, and the result is that if, as is usual, the name in question has a significance, the meaning must be expressed by an idiom or another word. In this way a memory is preserved for generations, or until the new word utterly supplants the old one. – A. Q.

shoulder to shoulder in that great battle which thy wise words planned, Macumazahn; of how thou wast the point of the horn that galled Twala's flank, Bougwan; whilst thou stoodst in the ring of the Greys, Incubu, and men went down before thine axe like corn before a sickle; ay, and of how thou didst break that wild bull Twala's strength, and bring his pride to dust. Fare ye well for ever, Incubu, Macumazahn, and Bougwan, my lords and my friends.'

Ignosi rose and looked earnestly at us for a few seconds. Then he threw the corner of his karross over his head, so as to cover his face from us.

We went in silence.

Next day at dawn we left Loo, escorted by our old friend Infadoos, who was heart-broken at our departure, and by the regiment of Buffaloes. Early as was the hour, all the main street of the town was lined with multitudes of people, who gave us the royal salute as we passed at the head of the regiment, while the women blessed us for having rid the land of Twala, throwing flowers before us as we went. It was really very affecting, and not the sort of thing one is accustomed to meet with from natives.

One ludicrous incident occurred, however, which I rather welcomed, as it gave us something to laugh at.

Just before we reached the confines of the town, a pretty young girl, with some lovely lilies in her hand, ran forward and presented them to Good – somehow they all seemed to like Good; I think his eye-glass and solitary whisker gave him a ficti-tious value – and then said that she had a boon to ask.

'Speak on,' he answered.

'Let my lord show his servant his beautiful white legs, that his servant may look on them, and remember them all her days, and tell of them to her children; his servant has travelled four days' journey to see them, for the fame of them has gone throughout the land.'

'I'll be hanged if I do!' exclaimed Good excitedly.

'Come, come, my dear fellow,' said Sir Henry, 'you can't refuse to oblige a lady.'

'I won't,' replied Good obstinately; 'it is positively indecent.'

However, in the end he consented to draw up his trousers to the knee, amidst notes of rapturous admiration from all the women present, especially the gratified young lady, and in this guise he had to walk till we got clear of the town.

Good's legs, I fear, will never be so greatly admired again. Of his melting teeth, and even of his 'transparent eye,' the Kukuanas wearied more or less, but of his legs never.

As we travelled, Infadoos told us that there was another pass over the mountains to the north of the one followed by Solomon's Great Road, or rather that there was a place where it is possible to climb down the wall of cliff which separates Kukuanaland from the desert, and is broken by the towering shapes of Sheba's Breasts. It appeared, too, that rather more than two years previously a party of Kukuana hunters had descended this path into the desert in search of ostriches, whose plumes are much prized among them for war head-dresses, and that in the course of their hunt they had been led far from the mountains and were much troubled by thirst. Seeing trees on the horizon, however, they walked towards them, and discovered a large and fertile oasis some miles in extent, and plentifully watered. It was by way of this oasis that Infadoos suggested that we should return, and the idea seemed to us a good one, for it appeared that we should thus escape the rigours of the mountain pass. Also some of the hunters were in attendance to guide us to the oasis, from which, they stated, they could perceive other fertile spots far away in the desert.*

Travelling easily, on the night of the fourth day's journey we found ourselves once more on the crest of the mountains that separate Kukuanaland from the desert, which rolled away in sandy billows at our feet, and about twenty-five miles to the north of Sheba's Breasts.

* It often puzzled all of us to understand how it was possible that Ignosi's mother, bearing the child with her, should have survived the dangers of her journey across the mountains and the desert, dangers which so nearly proved fatal to ourselves. It has since occurred to me, and I give the idea to the reader for what it is worth, that she must have taken this second route, and wandered out like Hagar into the wilderness. If she did so, there is no longer anything inexplicable about the story, since, as Ignosi himself related, she may well have been picked up by some ostrich hunters before she or the child was exhausted, and led by them to the oasis, and thence by stages to the fertile country, and so on by slow degrees southwards to Zululand. – A. Q.

At dawn on the following day, we were led to the edge of a very precipitous chasm, by which we were to descend the precipice, and gain the plain two thousand and more feet below.

Here we bade farewell to that true friend and sturdy old warrior, Infadoos, who solemnly wished all good upon us, and nearly wept with grief. 'Never, my lords,' he said, 'shall mine old eyes see the like of you again. Ah! the way that Incubu cut his men down in the battle! Ah! for the sight of that stroke with which he swept off my brother Twala's head! It was beautiful – beautiful! I may never hope to see such another, except perchance in happy dreams.'

We were very sorry to part from him; indeed, Good was so moved that he gave him as a souvenir – what do you think? – an *eye-glass;* afterwards we discovered that it was a spare one. Infadoos was delighted, foreseeing that the possession of such an article would increase his prestige enormously, and after several vain attempts he actually succeeded in screwing it into his own eye. Anything more incongruous than the old warrior looked with an eye-glass I never saw. Eye-glasses do not go well with leopard-skin cloaks and black ostrich plumes.

Then, after seeing that our guides were well laden with water and provisions, and having received a thundering farewell salute from the Buffaloes, we wrung Infadoos by the hand, and began our downward climb. A very arduous business it proved to be, but somehow that evening we found ourselves at the bottom without accident.

'Do you know,' said Sir Henry that night, as we sat by our fire and gazed up at the beetling cliffs above us, 'I think that there are worse places than Kukuanaland in the world, and that I have known unhappier times than the last month or two, though I have never spent such queer ones. Eh! you fellows?'

'I almost wish I were back,' said Good, with a sigh.

As for myself, I reflected that all's well that ends well; but in the course of a long life of shaves, I never had such shaves as those which I had recently experienced. The thought of that battle still makes me feel cold all over, and as for our experience in the treasure chamber—!

Next morning we started on a toilsome trudge across the desert, having with us a good supply of water carried by our five guides, and camped that night in the open, marching again at dawn on the morrow.

By noon of the third day's journey we could see the trees of the oasis of which the guides spoke and within an hour of sundown we were walking once more upon grass and listening to the sound of running water.

Chapter XX

FOUND

And now I come to perhaps the strangest adventure that happened to us in all this strange business, and one which shows how wonderfully things are brought about.

I was walking along quietly, some way in front of the other two, down the banks of the stream which runs from the oasis till it is swallowed up in the hungry desert sands, when suddenly I stopped and rubbed my eyes, as well I might. There, not twenty yards in front of me, placed in a charming situation, under the shade of a species of fig-tree, and facing to the stream, was a cosy hut, built more or less on the Kafir principle with grass and withes, but having a full-length door instead of a bee-hole.

'What the dickens,' said I to myself, 'can a hut be doing here?' Even as I said it the door of the hut opened, and there limped out of it a *white man* clothed in skins, and with an enormous black beard. I thought that I must have got a touch of the sun. It was impossible. No hunter ever came to such a place as this. Certainly no hunter would ever settle in it. I stared and stared, and so did the other man, and just at that juncture Sir Henry and Good walked up.

'Look here, you fellows,' I said, 'is that a white man, or am I mad?'

Sir Henry looked, and Good looked, and then all of a sudden the lame white man with a black beard uttered a great cry, and began hobbling towards us. When he was close he fell down in a sort of faint.

209

With a spring Sir Henry was by his side.

'Great Powers!' he cried, '*it is my brother George!*'

At the sound of the disturbance, another figure, also clad in skins, emerged from the hut, a gun in his hand, and ran towards us. On seeing me he too gave a cry.

'Macumazahn,' he halloed, 'don't you know me, Baas? I'm Jim the hunter. I lost the note you gave me to give to the Baas, and we have been here nearly two years.' And the fellow fell at my feet, and rolled over and over, weeping for joy.

'You careless scoundrel!' I said; 'you ought to be well hided.'

Meanwhile the man with the black beard had recovered and risen, and he and Sir Henry were pump-handling away at each other, apparently without a word to say. But whatever they had quarrelled about in the past – I suspect it was a lady, though I never asked – it was evidently forgotten now.

'My dear old fellow,' burst out Sir Henry at last, 'I thought that you were dead. I have been over Solomon's Mountains to find you, and now I come across you perched in the desert, like an old *aasvögel*.'*

'I tried to go over Solomon's Mountains nearly two years ago,' was the answer, spoken in the hesitating voice of a man who has had little recent opportunity of using his tongue, 'but when I got here a boulder fell on my leg and crushed it, and I have been able to go neither forward nor back.'

Then I came up. 'How do you do, Mr. Neville?' I said; 'do you remember me?'

'Why,' he said, 'isn't it Quatermain, eh, and Good too? Hold on a minute, you fellows, I am getting dizzy again. It is all so very strange, and, when a man has ceased to hope, so very happy!'

That evening, over the camp fire, George Curtis told us his story, which, in its way, was almost as eventful as our own, and, put shortly, amounted to this. A little less than two years before, he had started from Sitanda's Kraal, to try to reach Suliman's Berg. As for the note I had sent him by Jim, that worthy had lost it, and he had never heard of it till to-day. But, acting upon information he received from the natives, he headed not for Sheba's Breasts, but for the ladder-like descent of the mountains

* Vulture.

down which we had just come, which is clearly a better route than that marked out in old Dom Silvestra's plan. In the desert he and Jim suffered great hardships, but finally they reached this oasis, where a terrible accident befell George Curtis. On the day of their arrival he was sitting by the stream, and Jim was extracting the honey from the nest of a stingless bee which is to be found in the desert, on the top of a bank immediately above him. In so doing he loosened a great boulder of rock, which fell upon George Curtis's right leg, crushing it frightfully. From that day he had been so lame that he found it impossible to go either forward or back, and had preferred to take the chances of dying on the oasis to the certainty of perishing in the desert.

As for food, however, they got on pretty well, for they had a good supply of ammunition, and the oasis was frequented, especially at night, by large quantities of game, which came thither for water. These they shot, or trapped in pitfalls, using the flesh for food, and, after their clothes wore out, the hides for clothing.

'And so,' George Curtis ended, 'we have lived for nearly two years, like a second Robinson Crusoe and his man Friday, hoping against hope that some natives might come here to help us away, but none have come. Only last night we settled that Jim should leave me, and try to reach Sitanda's Kraal to get assistance. He was to go to-morrow, but I had little hope of ever seeing him back again. And now *you*, of all people in the world, *you*, who as I fancied had long ago forgotten all about me, and were living comfortably in old England, turn up in a promiscuous way and find me where you least expected. It is the most wonderful thing that I ever heard of, and the most merciful too.'

Then Sir Henry set to work and told him the main facts of our adventures, sitting till late into the night to do it.

'By Jove!' he said, when I showed him some of the diamonds: 'well, at least you have got something for your pains, besides my worthless self.'

Sir Henry laughed. 'They belong to Quatermain and Good. It was a part of the bargain that they should divide any spoils there might be.'

This remark set me thinking, and having spoken to Good, I told Sir Henry that it was our joint wish that he should take a third portion of the diamonds, or, if he would not, that his share should be handed to his brother, who had suffered even more than ourselves on the chance of getting them. Finally we prevailed upon him to consent to this arrangement, but George Curtis did not know of it until some time afterwards.

And here, at this point, I think that I shall end my history. Our journey across the desert back to Sitanda's Kraal was most arduous, especially as we had to support George Curtis, whose right leg was very weak indeed, and continually threw out splinters of bone. But we did accomplish it somehow, and to give its details would only be to reproduce much of what happened to us on the former occasion.

Six months from the date of our re-arrival at Sitanda's, where we found our guns and other goods quite safe, though the old scoundrel in charge was much disgusted at our surviving to claim them, saw us all once more safe and sound at my little place on the Berea, near Durban, where I am now writing. Thence I bid farewell to all who have accompanied me throughout the strangest trip I ever made in the course of a long and varied experience.

P.S. – Just as I had written the last word, a Kafir came up my avenue of orange trees, carrying a letter in a cleft stick, which he had brought from the post. It turned out to be from Sir Henry, and as it speaks for itself I give it in full.

'October 1st, 1884.
'Brayley Hall, Yorkshire.

'My dear Quatermain,
'I sent you a line a few mails back to say that the three of us, George, Good and myself, fetched up all right in England. We got off the boat at Southampton, and went up to town. You should have seen what a swell Good turned out the very next day, beautifully shaved, frock coat fitting like a glove, brand new eye-glass, etc., etc. I went and walked in the park with him, where I met some people I know, and at once told them the story of his "beautiful white legs."
'He is furious, especially as some ill-natured person has printed it in a society paper.

'To come to business, Good and I took the diamonds to Streeter's to be valued, as we arranged, and really I am afraid to tell you what they put them at, it seems so enormous. They say that of course it is more or less guesswork, as such stones have never to their knowledge been put on the market in anything like such quantities. It appears that (with the exception of one or two of the largest) they are of the finest water, and equal in every way to the best Brazilian stones. I asked them if they would buy them, but they said that it was beyond their power to do so, and recommended us to sell by degrees, for fear lest we should flood the market. They offer, however, a hundred and eighty thousand for a small portion of them.

'You must come home, Quatermain, and see about these things, especially if you insist upon making the magnificent present of the third share, which does not belong to me, to my brother George. As for Good, he is no good. His time is too much occupied in shaving and other matters connected with the vain adorning of the body. But I think he is still down on his luck about Foulata. He told me that since he had been home, he hadn't seen a woman to touch her, either as regards her figure or the sweetness of her expression.

'I want you to come home, my dear old comrade, and to buy a house near here. You have done your day's work, and have lots of money now, and there is a place for sale quite close which would suit you admirably. Do come; the sooner the better; you can finish writing the story of our adventures on board ship. We have refused to tell the tale till it is written by you, for fear lest we shall not be believed. If you start on receipt of this you will reach here by Christmas, and I book you to stay with me for that. Good is coming, and George; and so, by the way, is your boy Harry (there's a bribe for you). I have had him down for a week's shooting, and like him. He is a cool young hand; he shot me in the leg, cut out the pellets, and then remarked upon the advantages of having a medical student with every shooting party.

'Good-bye, old boy; I can't say any more, but I know that you will come, if it is only to oblige

'Your sincere friend,

'Henry Curtis.

213

'*P.S. – The tusks of the great bull that killed poor Khiva have now been put up in the hall here, over a pair of buffalo horns you gave me, and look magnificent; and the axe with which I chopped off Twala's head is fixed above my writing-table. I wish that we could have managed to bring away the coats of chain armour.*
    '*H. C.*'

To-day is Tuesday. There is a steamer going on Friday, and I really think that I must take Curtis at his word, and sail by her for England, if it is only to see you, Harry, my boy, and to look after the printing of this history, which is a task that I do not like to trust to anybody else.

ALLAN QUATERMAIN.

THE MAN WHO WOULD BE KING
and Other Stories

THE EDUCATION OF OTIS YEERE

One

In the pleasant orchard-closes
'God bless all our gains,' say we;
But 'May God bless all our losses,'
Better suits with our degree.
The Lost Bower

This is the history of a failure; but the woman who failed said that it might be an instructive tale to put into print for the benefit of the younger generation. The younger generation does not want instruction, being perfectly willing to instruct if anyone will listen to it. None the less, here begins the story where every right-minded story should begin, that is to say at Simla, where all things begin and many come to an evil end.

The mistake was due to a very clever woman making a blunder and not retrieving it. Men are licensed to stumble, but a clever woman's mistake is outside the regular course of Nature and Providence; since all good people know that a woman is the only infallible thing in this world, except Government Paper of the '79 issue, bearing interest at four and a half per cent. Yet, we have to remember that six consecutive days of rehearsing the leading part of *The Fallen Angel*, at the New Gaiety Theatre where the plaster is not yet properly dry, might have brought about an unhingement of spirits which, again, might have led to eccentricities.

Mrs Hauksbee came to 'The Foundry' to tiffin with Mrs Mallowe, her one bosom friend, for she was in no sense 'a woman's woman.' And it was a woman's tiffin, the door shut to all the world; and they both talked *chiffons*, which is French for Mysteries.

'I've enjoyed an interval of sanity,' Mrs Hauksbee announced, after tiffin was over and the two were comfortably settled in the little writing-room that opened out of Mrs Mallowe's bedroom.

'My dear girl, what has *he* done?' said Mrs Mallowe sweetly. It is noticeable that ladies of a certain age call each other 'dear girl,' just as commissioners of twenty-eight years' standing address their equals in the Civil List as 'my boy.'

'There's no *he* in the case. Who am I that an imaginary man should be always credited to me? Am I an Apache?'

'No, dear, but somebody's scalp is generally drying at your wigwam-door. Soaking rather.'

This was an allusion to the Hawley Boy, who was in the habit of riding all across Simla in the Rains, to call on Mrs Hauksbee. That lady laughed.

'For my sins, the Aide at Tyrconnel last night told me off to The Mussuck. Hsh! Don't laugh. One of my most devoted admirers. When the duff came – someone really ought to teach them to make puddings at Tyrconnel – The Mussuck was at liberty to attend to me.'

'Sweet soul! I know his appetite,' said Mrs Mallowe. 'Did he, oh *did* he, begin his wooing?'

'By a special mercy of Providence, *no*. He explained his importance as a Pillar of the Empire. I didn't laugh.'

'Lucy, I don't believe you.'

'Ask Captain Sangar; he was on the other side. Well, as I was saying, The Mussuck dilated.'

'I think I can see him doing it,' said Mrs Mallowe pensively, scratching her fox-terrier's ears.

'I was properly impressed. Most properly. I yawned openly. "Strict supervision, and play them off one against the other," said The Mussuck, shovelling down his ice by *tureenfuls*, I assure you. "*That*, Mrs Hauksbee, is the secret of our Government."'

Mrs Mallowe laughed long and merrily. 'And what did you say?'

'Did you ever know me at loss for an answer yet? I said: "So I have observed in my dealings with you." The Mussuck swelled with pride. He is coming to call on me tomorrow. The Hawley Boy is coming too.'

'"Strict supervision and play them off one against the other. *That*, Mrs Hauksbee, is the secret of *our* Government." And I daresay if we could get to The Mussuck's heart, we should find that he considers himself a man of the world.'

'As he is of the other two things. I like The Mussuck, and I won't have you call him names. He amuses me.'

'He has reformed you, too, by what appears. Explain the interval of sanity, and hit Tim on the nose with the paper-cutter, please. That dog is too fond of sugar. Do you take milk in yours?'

'No, thanks. Polly, I'm wearied of this life. It's hollow.'

'Turn religious, then. I always said that Rome would be your fate.'

'Only exchanging half-a-dozen *attachés* in red for one in black, and if I fasted, the wrinkles would come, and never, *never* go. Has it ever struck you, dear, that I'm getting old?'

'Thanks for your courtesy. I'll return it. Ye-es, we are both not exactly – how shall I put it?'

'What we have been. "I feel it in my bones," as Mrs Crossley says. Polly, I've wasted my life.'

'As how?'

'Never mind how. I feel it. I want to be a Power before I die.'

'Be a Power then. You've wits enough for anything – and beauty!'

Mrs Hauksbee pointed a teaspoon straight at her hostess. 'Polly, if you heap compliments on me like this, I shall cease to believe that you're a woman. Tell me how I am to be a Power.'

'Inform The Mussuck that he is the most fascinating and slimmest man in Asia, and he'll tell you anything and everything you please.'

'Bother The Mussuck! I mean an intellectual Power – not a gas-power. Polly, I'm going to start a *salon*.'

Mrs Mallowe turned lazily on the sofa and rested her head on her hand. 'Hear the words of the Preacher, the son of Baruch,' she said.

'*Will* you talk sensibly?'

'I will, dear, for I see that you are going to make a mistake.'

'I never made a mistake in my life – at least, never one that I couldn't explain away afterwards.'

'Going to make a mistake,' went on Mrs Mallowe composedly. 'It is impossible to start a *salon* in Simla. A bar would be much more to the point.'

'Perhaps, but why? It seems so easy.'

'Just what makes it so difficult. How many clever women are there in Simla?'

'Myself and yourself,' said Mrs Hauksbee, without a moment's hesitation.

'Modest woman! Mrs Feardon would thank you for that. And how many clever men?'

'Oh – er – hundreds,' said Mrs Hauksbee vaguely.

'What a fatal blunder! Not one. They are all bespoke by the Government. Take my husband, for instance. Jack *was* a clever man, though I say so who shouldn't. Government has eaten him up. All his ideas and powers of conversation – he really used to be a good talker, even to his wife, in the old days – are taken from him by this – this kitchen-sink of a Government. That's the case with every man up here who is at work. I don't suppose a Russian convict under the knout is able to amuse the rest of his gang; and all our men-folk here are gilded convicts.'

'But there are scores –'

'I know what you're going to say. Scores of idle men up on leave. I admit it, but they are all of two objectionable sets. The Civilian who'd be delightful if he had the military man's knowledge of the world and style, and the military man who'd be adorable if he had the Civilian's culture.'

'Detestable word! *Have* Civilians culchaw? I never studied the breed deeply.'

'Don't make fun of Jack's Service. Yes. They're like the teapoys in the Lakka Bazar – good material but not polished. They can't help themselves, poor dears.

A Civilian only begins to be tolerable after he has knocked about the world for fifteen years.'

'And a military man?'

'When he has had the same amount of service. The young of both species are horrible. You would have scores of them in your *salon*.'

'I would *not*!' said Mrs Hauksbee fiercely. 'I would tell the bearer to *darwaza band* them. I'd put their own colonels and commissioners at the door to turn them away. I'd give them to the Topsham Girl to play with.'

'The Topsham Girl would be grateful for the gift. But to go back to the *salon*. Allowing that you had gathered all your men and women together, what would you do with them? Make them talk? They would all with one accord begin to flirt. Your *salon* would become a glorified Peliti's – a "Scandal Point" by lamplight.'

'There's a certain amount of wisdom in that view.'

'There's all the wisdom in the world in it. Surely, twelve Simla seasons ought to have taught you that you can't focus anything in India; and a *salon*, to be any good at all, must be permanent. In two seasons your roomful would be scattered all over Asia. We are only little bits of dirt on the hillsides – here one day and blown down the *khud* the next. We have lost the art of talking – at least our men have. We have no cohesion –'

'George Eliot in the flesh,' interpolated Mrs Hauksbee wickedly.

'And collectively, my dear scoffer, we, men and women alike, have *no* influence. Come into the verandah and look at the Mall!'

The two looked down on the now rapidly filling road, for all Simla was abroad to steal a stroll between a shower and a fog.

'How do you propose to fix that river? Look! There's The Mussuck – head of goodness knows what. He is a power in the land, though he *does* eat like a coster-monger. There's Colonel Blone, and General Grucher, and Sir Dugald Delane, and Sir Henry Haughton, and Mr Jellalatty. All Heads of Departments, and all powerful.'

'And all my fervent admirers,' said Mrs Hauksbee piously. 'Sir Henry Haughton raves about me. But go on.'

'One by one, these men are worth something. Collectively, they're just a mob of Anglo-Indians. Who cares for what Anglo-Indians say? Your *salon* won't weld the

Departments together and make you mistress of India, dear. And these creatures won't talk administrative "shop" in a crowd – your *salon* – because they are so afraid of the men in the lower ranks overhearing it. They have forgotten what of Literature and Art they ever knew, and the women –'

'Can't talk about anything except the last Gymkhana, or the sins of their last nurse. I was calling on Mrs Derwills this morning.'

'You admit that? They can talk to the subalterns though, and the subalterns can talk to them. Your *salon* would suit their views admirably, if you respected the religious prejudices of the country and provided plenty of *kala juggahs*.'

'Plenty of *kala juggahs*. Oh my poor little idea! *Kala juggahs* in a *salon!* But who made you so awfully clever?'

'Perhaps I've tried myself; or perhaps I know a woman who has. I have preached and expounded the whole matter and the conclusion thereof –'

'You needn't go on. "Is Vanity." Polly, I thank you. These vermin' – Mrs Hauksbee waved her hand from the verandah to two men in the crowd below who had raised their hats to her – 'these vermin shall not rejoice in a new Scandal Point or an extra Pelit's. I will abandon the notion of a *salon*. It did seem so tempting, though. But what shall I do? I must do something.'

'Why? Are not Abana and Pharpar –'

'Jack has made you nearly as bad as himself! I want to, of course. I'm tired of everything and everybody, from a moonlight picnic at Seepee to the blandishments of The Mussuck.'

'Yes – that comes, too, sooner or later. Have you nerve enough to make your bow yet?'

Mrs Hauksbee's mouth shut grimly. Then she laughed. 'I think I see myself doing it. Big pink placards on the Mall: "Mrs Hauksbee! Positively her last appearance on *any* stage! This is to give notice!" No more dances; no more rides; no more luncheons; no more theatricals with supper to follow; no more sparring with one's dearest, dearest friend; no more fencing with an inconvenient man who hasn't wit enough to clothe what he's pleased to call his sentiments in passable speech; no more parading of The Mussuck while Mrs Tarkass calls all round Simla, spreading horrible stories about me! No more of anything that is thoroughly wearying, abominable and detestable, but, all the same, makes life worth the having. Yes! I see it all! Don't interrupt, Polly, I'm inspired. A mauve and white striped "cloud" round my excellent shoulders, a seat in the fifth row of the Gaiety, and *both* horses sold. Delightful vision! A comfortable arm-chair, situated in three different draughts, at every ballroom; and nice, large, sensible shoes for all the couples to stumble over as they go into the verandah! Then at supper. Can't you imagine the scene? The greedy mob gone away. Reluctant subaltern, pink all over like a newly-powdered baby, – they really ought to *tan* subalterns before they are exported, Polly, – sent back by the hostess to do his duty. Slouches up to me across the room, tugging at a glove two sizes too large for him – I *hate* a man who wears gloves like overcoats – and trying to look as if he'd thought of it from the first. "May I ah-have the pleasure 'f takin' you 'nt' supper?" Then I get up with a hungry smile. Just like this.'

'Lucy, how *can* you be so absurd?'

'And sweep out on his arm. So! After supper I shall go away early, you know, because I shall be afraid of catching cold. No one will look for my 'rickshaw. *Mine*, so please you! I shall stand, always with that mauve and white "cloud" over my head, while the wet soaks into my dear, old, venerable feet, and Tom swears and shouts for the *memsahib's gharri*. Then home to bed at half-past eleven! Truly excellent life – helped out by the visits of the *Padri*, just fresh from burying somebody down below there.' She pointed through the pines toward the Cemetery, and continued with vigorous dramatic gesture –

'Listen! I see it all – down, down even to the stays! *Such* stays! Six-eight a pair, Polly, with red flannel – or list, is it? – that they put into the tops of those fearful things. I can draw you a picture of them.'

'Lucy, for Heaven's sake, don't go waving your arms about in that idiotic manner! Recollect everyone can see you from the Mall.'

'Let them see! They'll think I am rehearsing for *The Fallen Angel*. Look! There's the Mussuck. How badly he rides. There!'

She blew a kiss to the venerable Indian administrator with infinite grace.

'Now,' she continued, 'he'll be chaffed about that at the Club in the delicate manner those brutes of men affect, and the Hawley Boy will tell me all about it – softening the details for fear of shocking me. That boy is too good to live, Polly. I've serious thoughts of recommending him to throw up his commission and go into the Church. In his present frame of mind he would obey me. Happy, happy child!'

'Never again,' said Mrs Mallowe, with an affectation of indignation, 'shall you tiffin here! "Lucindy your behaviour is scand'lus."'

'All your fault,' retorted Mrs Hauksbee, 'for suggesting such a thing as my abdication. No! *jamais!* nevaire! I will act, dance, ride, frivol, talk scandal, dine out, and appropriate the legitimate captives of any woman I choose, until I d-r-r-rop, or a better woman than I puts me to shame before all Simla, – and it's dust and ashes in my mouth while I'm doing it!'

She swept into the drawing-room. Mrs Mallowe followed and put an arm round her waist.

'I'm *not!*' said Mrs Hauksbee defiantly, rummaging for her handkerchief. 'I've been dining out the last ten nights, and rehearsing in the afternoon. You'd be tired yourself. It's only because I'm tired.'

Mrs Mallowe did not offer Mrs Hauksbee any pity or ask her to lie down, but gave her another cup of tea, and went on with the talk.

'I've been through that too, dear,' she said.

'I remember,' said Mrs Hauksbee, a gleam of fun on her face. 'In '84, wasn't it? You went out a great deal less next season.'

Mrs Mallowe smiled in a superior and Sphinx-like fashion.

'I became an Influence,' said she.

'Good gracious, child, you didn't join the Theosophists and kiss Buddha's big toe, did you? I tried to get into their set once, but they cast me out for a sceptic – without a chance of improving my poor little mind, too.'

No, I didn't Theosophilander. Jack says –'

'Never mind Jack. What a husband says is known before. What did you do?'

I made a lasting impression.'

'So have I – for four months. But that didn't console me in the least. I hated the man. *Will* you stop smiling in that inscrutable way and tell me what you mean?'

Mrs Mallowe told.

'And – you – mean – to – say that it is absolutely Platonic on both sides?'

'Absolutely, or I should never have taken it up.'

'And his last promotion was due to you?'

Mrs Mallowe nodded.

'And you warned him against the Topsham Girl?'

Another nod.

'And told him of Sir Dugald Delane's private memo about him?'

A third nod.

'*Why?*'

'What a question to ask a woman! Because it amused me at first. I am proud of my property now. If I live, he shall continue to be successful. Yes, I will put him upon the straight road to Knighthood, and everything else that a man values. The rest depends upon himself.'

'Polly, you are a most extraordinary woman.'

'Not in the least. I'm concentrated, that's all. You diffuse yourself, dear; and though all Simla knows your skill in managing a team –'

'Can't you choose a prettier word?'

'*Team*, of half-a-dozen, from The Mussuck to the Hawley Boy, you gain nothing by it. Not even amusement.'

'And you?'

'Try my recipe. Take a man, not a boy, mind, but an almost mature, unattached man, and be his guide, philosopher, and friend. You'll find it *the* most interesting occupation that you ever embarked on. It can be done – you needn't look like that – because I've done it.'

'There's an element of risk about it that makes the notion attractive. I'll get such a man and say to him, "Now, understand that there must be no flirtation. Do exactly what I tell you, profit by my instruction and counsels, and all will yet be well." Is that the idea?'

'More or less,' said Mrs Mallowe, with an unfathomable smile. 'But be sure he understands.'

Two

Dribble-dribble – trickle-trickle –
What a lot of raw dust!
My dollie's had an accident
And out came all the sawdust!

Nursery Rhyme

So Mrs Hauksbee, in 'The Foundry' which overlooks Simla Mall, sat at the feet of Mrs Mallowe and gathered wisdom. The end of the Conference was the Great Idea upon which Mrs Hauksbee so plumed herself.

'I warn you,' said Mrs Mallowe, beginning to repent of her suggestion, 'that the matter is not half so easy as it looks. Any woman – even the Topsham Girl – can catch a man, but very, *very* few know how to manage him when caught.'

'My child,' was the answer, 'I've been a female St Simon Stylites looking down upon men for these – these years past. Ask The Mussuck whether I can manage them.'

Mrs Hauksbee departed humming, '*I'll go to him and say to him in manner most ironical.*' Mrs Mallowe laughed to herself. Then she grew suddenly sober. 'I wonder whether I've done well in advising that amusement? Lucy's a clever woman, but a thought too careless.'

A week later the two met at a Monday Pop. 'Well?' said Mrs Mallowe.

'I've caught him!' said Mrs Hauksbee: her eyes were dancing with merriment.

'Who is it, mad woman? I'm sorry I ever spoke to you about it.'

'Look between the pillars. In the third row; fourth from the end. You can see his face now. Look!'

'Otis Yeere! Of *all* the improbable and impossible people! I don't believe you.'

'Hsh! Wait till Mrs Tarkass begins murdering Milton Wellings; and I'll tell you all about it. *S-s-ss!* That woman's voice always reminds me of an Underground train coming into Earl's Court with the brakes on. Now listen. It is *really* Otis Yeere.'

'So I see, but does it follow that he is your property!'

'He *is*! By right of trove. I found him, lonely and unbefriended, the very next night after our talk, at the Dugald Delanes' *burra-khana*. I liked his eyes, and I talked to him. Next day he called. Next day we went for a ride together and today he's tied to my 'rickshaw-wheels hand and foot. You'll see when the concert's over. He doesn't know I'm here yet.'

'Thank goodness you haven't chosen a boy. What are you going to do with him, assuming that you've got him?'

'Assuming, indeed! Does a woman – do *I* – ever make a mistake in that sort of thing? First' – Mrs Hauksbee ticked off the items ostentatiously on her little gloved fingers – 'First, my dear, I shall dress him properly. At present his raiment is a disgrace, and he wears a dress-shirt like a crumpled sheet of the *Pioneer*. Secondly, after I have made him presentable, I shall form his manners – his morals are above reproach.'

'You seem to have discovered a great deal about him considering the shortness of your acquaintance.'

'Surely *you* ought to know that the first proof a man gives of his interest in a woman is by talking to her about his own sweet self. If the woman listens without yawning, he begins to like her. If she flatters the animal's vanity, he ends by adoring her.'

'In some cases.'

'Never mind the exceptions. I know which one you are thinking of. Thirdly, and lastly, after he is polished and made pretty, I shall, as you said, be his guide, philosopher, and friend, and he shall become a success – as great a success as your friend. I always wondered how that man got on. *Did* The Mussuck come to you with the Civil List and, dropping on one knee – no, two knees, *à la Gibbon* – hand it to you and say, "Adorable angel, choose your friend's appointment"?'

'Lucy, your long experiences of the Military Department have demoralised you. One doesn't do that sort of thing on the Civil Side.'

'No disrespect meant to Jack's Service, my dear. I only asked for information. Give me three months, and see what changes I shall work in my prey.'

'Go your own way since you must. But I'm sorry that I was weak enough to suggest the amusement.'

'"I am all discretion, and may be trusted to an in-fin-ite extent,"' quoted Mrs Hauksbee from *The Fallen Angel*; and the conversation ceased with Mrs Tarkass's last, long-drawn war-whoop.

Her bitterest enemies – and she had many – could hardly accuse Mrs Hauksbee of wasting her time. Otis Yeere was one of those wandering 'dumb' characters, foredoomed through life to be nobody's property. Ten years in Her Majesty's Bengal Civil Service, spent, for the most part, in undesirable Districts, had given him little to be proud of, and nothing to bring confidence. Old enough to have lost the first fine careless rapture that showers on the immature 'Stunt imaginary Commissionerships and Stars, and sends him into the collar with coltish earnestness and abandon; too young to be yet able to look back upon the progress he had made, and thank Providence that under the conditions of the day he had come even so far, he stood upon the dead-centre of his career. And when a man stands still he feels the slightest impulse from without. Fortune had ruled that Otis Yeere should be, for the first part of his service, one of the rank and file who are ground up in the wheels of the Administration; losing heart and soul, and mind and strength, in the process. Until steam replaces manual power in the working of the Empire, there must always be this percentage – must always be the men who are used up, expended, in the mere mechanical routine. For these promotion is far off and the mill-grind of every day very instant. The Secretariats know them only by name; they are not the picked men of the Districts with Divisions and Collectorates awaiting them. They are simply the rank and file – the food for fever – sharing with the *ryot* and the plough-bullock the honour of being the plinth on which the State rests. The older ones have lost their aspirations; the younger are putting theirs aside with a sigh. Both learn to endure patiently until the end of the day. Twelve years in the rank and file, men say, will sap the hearts of the bravest and dull the wits of the most keen.

Out of this life Otis Yeere had fled for a few months; drifting, in the hope of a little masculine society, into Simla. When his leave was over he would return to his swampy, sour-green, undermanned Bengal district; to the native Assistant, the native Doctor, the native Magistrate, the steaming, sweltering Station, the ill-kempt City, and the undisguised insolence of the Municipality that babbled away the lives of men. Life was cheap, however. The soil spawned humanity, as it bred frogs in the Rains, and the gap of the sickness of one season was filled to overflowing by the fecundity of the next. Otis was unfeignedly thankful to lay down his work for a little while and escape from the seething, whining, weakly hive, impotent to help itself, but strong in its power to cripple, thwart, and annoy the sunken-eyed man who, by official irony, was said to be 'in charge' of it.

'I knew there were women-dowdies in Bengal. They come up here sometimes. But I didn't know that there were men-dowds, too.'

Then, for the first time, it occurred to Otis Yeere that his clothes wore rather the mark of the ages. It will be seen that his friendship with Mrs Hauksbee had made great strides.

As that lady truthfully says, a man is never so happy as when he is talking about himself. From Otis Yeere's lips Mrs Hauksbee, before long, learned everything that she wished to know about the subject of her experiment: learned what manner of life he had led in what she vaguely called 'those awful cholera districts'; learned, too, but this knowledge came later, what manner of life he had purposed to lead and what dreams he had dreamed in the year of grace '77, before the reality had knocked the heart out of him. Very pleasant are the shady bridle-paths round Prospect Hill for the telling of such confidences.

'Not yet,' said Mrs Hauksbee to Mrs Mallowe. 'Not yet. I must wait until the man is properly dressed, at least. Great heavens, is it possible that he doesn't know what an honour it is to be taken up by *Me*!'

Mrs Hauksbee did not reckon false modesty as one of her failings.

'Always with Mrs Hauksbee!' murmured Mrs Mallowe, with her sweetest smile, to Otis. 'Oh you men, you men! Here are our Punjabis growling because you've monopolised the nicest woman in Simla. They'll tear you to pieces on the Mall, some day, Mr Yeere.'

Mrs Mallowe rattled downhill, having satisfied herself, by a glance through the fringe of her sunshade, of the effect of her words.

The shot went home. Of a surety Otis Yeere was somebody in this bewildering whirl of Simla – had monopolised the nicest woman in it, and the Punjabis were growling. The notion justified a mild glow of vanity. He had never looked upon his acquaintance with Mrs Hauksbee as a matter for general interest.

The knowledge of envy was a pleasant feeling to the man of no account. It was intensified later in the day when a luncher at the Club said spitefully, 'Well, for a debilitated Ditcher, Yeere, you *are* going it. Hasn't any kind friend told you that she's the most dangerous woman in Simla?'

Yeere chuckled and passed out. When, oh, when would his new clothes be ready? He descended into the Mall to inquire; and Mrs Hauksbee, coming over the Church Ridge in her 'rickshaw, looked down upon him approvingly. 'He's learning to carry himself as if he were a man, instead of a piece of furniture, – and,' she screwed up her eyes to see the better through the sunlight – 'he *is* a man when he holds himself like that. O blessed Conceit, what should we be without you?'

With the new clothes came a new stock of self-confidence. Otis Yeere discovered that he could enter a room without breaking into a gentle perspiration – could cross one, even to talk to Mrs Hauksbee, as though rooms were meant to be crossed. He was for the first time in nine years proud of himself, and contented with his life, satisfied with his new clothes, and rejoicing in the friendship of Mrs Hauksbee.

'Conceit is what the poor fellow wants,' she said in confidence to Mrs Mallowe. 'I believe they must use Civilians to plough the fields with in Lower Bengal. You see I have to begin from the very beginning – haven't I? But you'll admit, won't you, dear, that he is immensely improved since I took him in hand. Only give me a little more time and he won't know himself.'

Indeed, Yeere was rapidly beginning to forget what he had been. One of his own rank and file put the matter brutally when he asked Yeere, in reference to nothing, 'And who has been making *you* a Member of Council, lately? You carry the side of half-a-dozen of 'em.'

'I – I'm awf'ly sorry. I didn't mean it, you know,' said Yeere apologetically.

'There'll be no holding you,' continued the old stager grimly. 'Climb down, Otis – climb down, and get all that beastly affectation knocked out of you with fever! Three thousand a month wouldn't support it.'

Yeere repeated the incident to Mrs Hauksbee. He had come to look upon her as his Mother Confessor.

'And you apologised!' she said. 'Oh, shame! I *hate* a man who apologises. Never apologise for what your friend called "side." *Never*! It's a man's business to be insolent and overbearing until he meets with a stronger. Now, you bad boy, listen to me.'

Simply and straightforwardly, as the 'rickshaw loitered round Jakko, Mrs Hauksbee preached to Otis Yeere the Great Gospel of Conceit, illustrating it with living pictures encountered during their Sunday afternoon stroll.

'Good gracious!' she ended with the personal argument, 'you'll apologise next for being my *attaché*!'

'Never!' said Otis Yeere. 'That's another thing altogether. I shall always be –'

'What's coming?' thought Mrs Hauksbee.

'Proud of that,' said Otis.

'Safe for the present,' she said to herself.

'But I'm afraid I have grown conceited. Like Jeshurun, you know. When he waxed fat, then he kicked. It's the having no worry on one's mind and the Hill air, I suppose.'

'Hill air, indeed!' said Mrs Hauksbee to herself. 'He'd have been hiding in the Club till the last day of his leave, if I hadn't discovered him.' And aloud –

'Why shouldn't you be? You have every right to.'

'I! Why?'

'Oh, hundreds of things. I'm not going to waste this lovely afternoon by explaining; but I know you have. What was that heap of manuscript you showed me about the grammar of the aboriginal – what's their names?'

'*Gullals. A* piece of nonsense. I've far too much work to do to bother over *Gullals* now. You should see my District. Come down with your husband some day and I'll show you round. Such a lovely place in the Rains! A sheet of water with the railway-embankment and the snakes sticking out, and, in the summer, green flies and green squash. The people would die of fear if you shook a dogwhip at 'em. But they know you're forbidden to do that, so they conspire to make your life a burden to you. My District's worked by some man at Darjiling, on the strength of a native pleader's false reports. Oh, it's a heavenly place!'

Otis Yeere laughed bitterly.

'There's not the least necessity that you should stay in it. Why do you?'

'Because I must. How'm I to get out of it?'

'How! In a hundred and fifty ways. If there weren't so many people on the road I'd like to box your ears. Ask, my dear boy, *ask*! Look! There is young Hexarly with six years' service and half your talents. He asked for what he wanted, and he got it. See, down by the Convent! There's McArthurson, who has come to his present position by asking – sheer, downright asking – after he had pushed himself out of the rank and file. One man is as good as another in your service – believe me. I've seen Simla for more seasons than I care to think about. Do you suppose men are chosen for appointments because of their special fitness *beforehand*? You have all passed a high test – what do you call it? – in the beginning, and, except for the few who have gone altogether to the bad, you can all work hard. Asking does the rest. Call it cheek, call it insolence, call it anything you like, but *ask*! Men argue – yes, I know what men say – that a man, by the mere audacity of his request, *must* have some good in him. A weak man doesn't say: "Give me this and that." He whines: "Why haven't I been given this and that?" If you were in the Army, I should say learn to spin plates or play a tambourine with your toes. As it is – *ask*! You belong to a Service that ought to be able to command the Channel Fleet, or set a leg at twenty minutes' notice, and *yet* you hesitate over asking to escape from a squashy green district where you *admit* you are not master. Drop the Bengal Government altogether. Even Darjiling is a little out-of-the-way hole. I was there once, and the rents were extortionate. Assert yourself. Get the Government of India to take you over. Try to get on the Frontier, where *every* man has a grand chance if he can trust himself. *Go* somewhere! *Do* something! You have twice the wits and three times the presence of the men up here, and, and' – Mrs Hauksbee paused for breath; then continued – 'and in *any* way you look at it, you *ought* to. *You* who could go so far!'

'I don't know,' said Yeere, rather taken aback by the unexpected eloquence. 'I haven't such a good opinion of myself.'

It was not strictly Platonic, but it was Policy. Mrs Hauksbee laid her hand lightly upon the ungloved paw that rested on the turned-back 'rickshaw hood, and, looking the man full in the face, said tenderly, almost too tenderly, '*I* believe in you if you mistrust yourself. Is that enough, my friend?

'It is enough,' answered Otis very solemnly.

He was silent for a long time, redreaming the dreams that he had dreamed eight years ago, but through them all ran, as sheet-lightning through golden cloud, the light of Mrs Hauksbee's violet eyes.

Curious and impenetrable are the mazes of Simla life – the only existence in this desolate land worth the living. Gradually it went abroad among men and women, in the pauses between dance, play, and Gymkhana, that Otis Yeere, the man with the newly-lit light of self-confidence in his eyes, had 'done something decent' in the wilds whence he came. He had brought an erring Municipality to reason, appropriated the funds on his own responsibility, and saved the lives of hundreds. He knew more about the *Gullals* than any living man. Had a vast knowledge of the aboriginal tribes; was, in spite of his juniority, the greatest authority on the aboriginal *Gullals*. No one quite knew who or what the *Gullals* were till The Mussuck, who had been calling on Mrs Hauksbee, and prided himself upon picking people's brains, explained they were a tribe of ferocious hillmen, somewhere near Sikkim, whose friendship even the Great Indian Empire would find it worth her while to secure. Now we know that Otis Yeere had showed Mrs Hauksbee his MS. notes of six years' standing on these same *Gullals*. He had told her, too, how, sick and shaken with the fever their negligence had bred, crippled by the loss of his pet clerk, and savagely angry at the desolation in his charge, he had once damned the collective eyes of his 'intelligent local board' for a set of *haramzadas*. Which act of 'brutal and tyrannous oppression' won him a Reprimand Royal from the Bengal Government; but in the anecdote as amended for Northern consumption we find no record of this. Hence we are forced to conclude that Mrs Hauksbee edited his reminiscences before sowing them in idle ears, ready, as she well knew, to exaggerate good or evil. And Otis Yeere bore himself as befitted the hero of many tales.

'You can talk to *me* when you don't fall into a brown study. Talk now, and talk your brightest and best,' said Mrs Hauksbee.

Otis needed no spur. Look to a man who has the counsel of a woman of or above the world to back him. So long as he keeps his head, he can meet both sexes on equal ground – an advantage never intended by Providence, who fashioned Man on one day and Woman on another, in sign that neither should know more than a very little of the other's life. Such a man goes far, or, the counsel being withdrawn, collapses suddenly while his world seeks the reason.

Generalled by Mrs Hauksbee, who, again, had all Mrs Mallowe's wisdom at her disposal, proud of himself and, in the end, believing in himself because he was believed in, Otis Yeere stood ready for any fortune that might befall, certain that it would be good. He would fight for his own hand, and intended that this second struggle should lead to better issue than the first helpless surrender of the bewildered 'Stunt.

What might have happened it is impossible to say. This lamentable thing befell, bred directly by a statement of Mrs Hauksbee that she would spend the next season in Darjiling.

'Are you certain of that?' said Otis Yeere.

'Quite. We're writing about a house now.'

Otis Yeere 'stopped dead,' as Mrs Hauksbee put it in discussing the relapse with Mrs Mallowe.

'He has behaved,' she said angrily, 'just like Captain Kerrington's pony – only Otis is a donkey – at the last Gymkhana. Planted his forefeet and refused to go on another step. Polly, my man's going to disappoint me. What shall I do?'

As a rule, Mrs Mallowe does not approve of staring, but on this occasion she opened her eyes to the utmost.

'You have managed cleverly so far,' she said. 'Speak to him, and ask him what he means.'

'I will – at tonight's dance.'

'No-o, not at a dance,' said Mrs Mallowe cautiously. 'Men are never themselves quite at dances. Better wait till tomorrow morning.'

'Nonsense. If he's going to 'vert in this insane way there isn't a day to lose. Are you going? No? Then sit up for me, there's a dear. I shan't stay longer than supper under any circumstances.'

Mrs Mallowe waited through the evening, looking long and earnestly into the fire, and sometimes smiling to herself.

'Oh! oh! oh! The man's an idiot! A raving, positive idiot! I'm sorry I ever saw him!'

Mrs Hauksbee burst into Mrs Mallowe's house, at midnight, almost in tears.

'What in the world has happened?' said Mrs Mallowe, but her eyes showed that she had guessed an answer.

'Happened! Everything has happened! He was there. I went to him and said, "Now, what does this nonsense mean?" Don't laugh, dear, I can't bear it. But you know what I mean I said. Then it was a square, and I sat it out with him and wanted an explanation, and *he* said – Oh! I haven't patience with such idiots! You know what I said about going to Darjiling next year? It doesn't matter to me *where* I go. I'd have changed the Station and lost the rent to have saved this. He said, in so many words, that he wasn't going to try to work up any more, because – because he would be shifted into a province away from Darjiling, and his own District, where these creatures are, is within a day's journey –'

'Ah – hh!' said Mrs Mallowe, in a tone of one who has successfully tracked an obscure word through a large dictionary.

'Did you ever *hear* of anything so mad – so absurd? And he had the ball at his feet. He had only to kick it! I would have made him *anything!* Anything in the wide world. He could have gone to the world's end. I would have helped him. I made him, didn't I, Polly? Didn't I *create* that man? Doesn't he owe everything to me? And to reward me, just when everything was nicely arranged, by this lunacy that spoilt everything!'

'Very few men understand your devotion thoroughly.'

'Oh, Polly, *don't* laugh at me! I give men up from this hour. I could have killed him then and there. What *right* had this man – this *Thing* I had picked out of his filthy paddy-fields – to make love to me?'

'He did that, did he?'

'He did. I don't remember half he said, I was so angry. Oh, but such a funny thing happened! I can't help laughing at it now, though I felt nearly ready to cry with rage.

He raved and I stormed – I'm afraid we must have made an awful noise in our *kala juggah*. Protect my character, dear, if it's all over Simla by tomorrow – and then he bobbed forward in the middle of this insanity – *firmly* believe the man's demented – and kissed me.'

'Morals above reproach,' purred Mrs Mallowe.

'So they were – so they are! It was the most absurd kiss. I don't believe he'd ever kissed a woman in his life before. I threw my head back, and it was a sort of slidy, pecking dab, just on the end of the chin – here.' Mrs Hauksbee tapped her masculine little chin with her fan. 'Then, of course, I was *furiously* angry, and told him that he was no gentleman, and I was sorry I'd ever met him, and so on. He was crushed so easily then I couldn't be *very* angry. Then I came away straight to you.'

'Was this before or after supper?'

'Oh! before – oceans before. Isn't it perfectly disgusting?'

'Let me think. I withhold judgment till tomorrow. Morning brings counsel.'

But morning brought only a servant with a dainty bouquet of Annandale roses for Mrs Hauksbee to wear at the dance at Viceregal Lodge that night.

'He doesn't seem to be very penitent,' said Mrs Mallowe. 'What's the *billet-doux* in the centre?'

Mrs Hauksbee opened the neatly-folded note, – another accomplishment that she had taught Otis, – read it, and groaned tragically.

'Last wreck of a feeble intellect! Poetry! Is it his own, do you think? Oh, that I ever built my hopes on such a maudlin idiot!'

'No. It's a quotation from Mrs Browning, and in view of the facts of the case, as Jack says, uncommonly well chosen. Listen –

> 'Sweet, thou hast trod on a heart,
> Pass! There's a world full of men;
> And women as fair as thou art
> Must do such things now and then.

'Thou only hast stepped unaware –
Malice not one can impute;
And why should a heart have been there,
In the way of a fair woman's foot?'

'I didn't – I didn't – I didn't!' – said Mrs Hauksbee angrily, her eyes filling with tears; 'there was no malice at all. Oh, it's *too* vexatious!'

'You've misunderstood the compliment,' said Mrs Mallowe. 'He clears you completely and – ahem – I should think by this, that *he* has cleared completely too! My experience of men is that when they begin to quote poetry they are going to flit. Like swans singing before they die, you know.'

'Polly, you take my sorrows in a most unfeeling way.'

'Do I? Is it so terrible? If he's hurt your vanity, I should say that you've done a certain amount of damage to his heart.'

'Oh, you can never tell about a man!' said Mrs Hauksbee.

AT THE PIT'S MOUTH

Men say it was a stolen tide –
The Lord that sent it He knows all,
But in mine ear will aye abide
The message that the bells let fall,
And awesome bells they were to me,
That in the dark rang, 'Enderby.'
                                        Jean Ingelow

Once upon a time there was a Man and his Wife and a Tertium Quid.
         All three were unwise, but the Wife was the unwisest. The Man should have
looked after his Wife, who should have avoided the Tertium Quid who, again, should
have married a wife of his own, after clean and open flirtations, to which nobody
can possibly object, round Jakko or Observatory Hill. When you see a young man
with his pony in a white lather and his hat on the back of his head, flying downhill
at fifteen miles an hour to meet a girl who will be properly surprised to meet him,
you naturally approve of that young man, and wish him Staff appointments, and
take an interest in his welfare, and, as the proper time comes, give them sugar-tongs
or side-saddles according to your means and generosity.

         The Tertium Quid flew downhill on horseback, but it was to meet the Man's

Wife; and when he flew uphill it was for the same end. The Man was in the Plains, earning money for his Wife to spend on dresses and four-hundred-rupee bracelets, and inexpensive luxuries of that kind. He worked very hard, and sent her a letter or a post-card daily. She also wrote to him daily, and said that she was longing for him to come up to Simla. The Tertium Quid used to lean over her shoulder and laugh as she wrote the notes. Then the two would ride to the Post-office together.

Now, Simla is a strange place and its customs are peculiar; nor is any man who has not spent at least ten seasons there qualified to pass judgment on circumstantial evidence, which is the most untrustworthy in the Courts. For these reasons, and for others which need not appear, I decline to state positively whether there was anything irretrievably wrong in the relations between the Man's Wife and the Tertium Quid. If there was, and hereon you must form your own Opinion, it was the Man's Wife's fault. She was kittenish in her manners, wearing generally an air of soft and fluffy innocence. But she was deadly learned and evil-instructed; and, now and again, when the mask dropped, men saw this, shuddered and – almost drew back. Men are occasionally particular, and the least particular men are always the most exacting.

Simla is eccentric in its fashion of treating friendships. Certain attachments which have set and crystallised through half-a-dozen seasons acquire almost the sanctity of the marriage bond, and are revered as such. Again, certain attachments equally old, and, to all appearance, equally venerable, never seem to win any recognised official status; while a chance-sprung acquaintance, not two months born, steps into the place which by right belongs to the senior. There is no law reducible to print which regulates these affairs.

Some people have a gift which secures them infinite toleration, and others have not. The Man's Wife had not. If she looked over the garden wall, for instance, women taxed her with stealing their husbands. She complained pathetically that she was not allowed to choose her own friends. When she put up her big white muff to her lips, and gazed over it and under her eyebrows at you as she said this thing, you felt that she had been infamously misjudged, and that all the other women's instincts were all wrong; which was absurd. She was not allowed to own the Tertium Quid in peace; and was so strangely constructed that she would not have enjoyed peace had she been so permitted. She preferred some semblance of intrigue to cloak even her most commonplace actions.

After two months of riding, first round Jakko, then Elysium, then Summer Hill, then Observatory Hill, then under Jutogh, and lastly up and down the Cart Road as far as the Tara Devi gap in the dusk, she said to the Tertium Quid, 'Frank, people say we are too much together, and people are so horrid.'

The Tertium Quid pulled his moustache, and replied that horrid people were unworthy of the consideration of nice people.

'But they have done more than talk – they have written – written to my hubby – I'm sure of it,' said the Man's Wife, and she pulled a letter from her husband out of her saddle-pocket and gave it to the Tertium Quid.

It was an honest letter, written by an honest man, then stewing in the Plains on two hundred rupees a month (for he allowed his wife eight hundred and fifty), and in a silk banian and cotton trousers. It said that, perhaps, she had not thought of the unwisdom of allowing her name to be so generally coupled with the Tertium Quid's; that she was too much of a child to understand the dangers of that sort of thing; that he, her husband, was the last man in the world to interfere jealously with her little amusements and interests, but that it would be better were she to drop the Tertium Quid quietly and for her husband's sake. The letter was sweetened with many pretty little pet names, and it amused the Tertium Quid considerably. He and She laughed over it, so that you, fifty yards away, could see their shoulders shaking while the horses slouched along side by side.

Their conversation was not worth reporting. The upshot of it was that, next day, no one saw the Man's Wife and the Tertium Quid together. They had both gone down to the Cemetery, which, as a rule, is only visited officially by the inhabitants of Simla.

A Simla funeral with the clergyman riding, the mourners riding, and the coffin creaking as it swings between the bearers, is one of the most depressing things on this earth, particularly when the procession passes under the wet, dank dip beneath the Rockcliffe Hotel, where the sun is shut out, and all the hill streams are wailing and weeping together as they go down the valleys.

Occasionally folk tend the graves, but we in India shift and are transferred so often that, at the end of the second year, the Dead have no friends – only acquaintances who are far too busy amusing themselves up the hill to attend to old partners. The idea of using a Cemetery as a rendezvous is distinctly a feminine one. A man would have said simply, 'Let people talk. We'll go down the Mall.' A woman is made differently, especially if she be such a woman as the Man's Wife. She and the Tertium Quid enjoyed each other's society among the graves of men and women whom they had known and danced with aforetime.

They used to take a big horse-blanket and sit on the grass a little to the left of the lower end, where there is a dip in the ground, and where the occupied graves stop short and the ready-made ones are not ready. Each well-regulated Indian Cemetery keeps half-a-dozen graves permanently open for contingencies and incidental wear and tear. In the Hills these are more usually baby's size, because children who come up weakened and sick from the Plains often succumb to the effects of the Rains in the Hills or get pneumonia from their *ayahs* taking them through damp pine-woods after the sun has set. In Cantonments, of course, the man's size is more in request; these arrangements varying with the climate and population.

One day when the Man's Wife and the Tertium Quid had just arrived in the Cemetery, they saw some coolies breaking ground. They had marked out a full-size grave, and the Tertium Quid asked them whether any *Sahib* was sick. They said that they did not know; but it was an order that they should dig a *Sahib's* grave.

'Work away,' said the Tertium Quid, 'and let's see how it's done.'

The coolies worked away, and the Man's Wife and the Tertium Quid watched and talked for a couple of hours while the grave was being deepened. Then a coolie, taking the earth in baskets as it was thrown up, jumped over the grave.

'That's queer,' said the Tertium Quid. 'Where's my ulster?'

'What's queer?' said the Man's Wife.

'I have got a chill down my back – just as if a goose had walked over my grave.'

'Why do you look at the thing, then?' said the Man's Wife. 'Let us go.'

The Tertium Quid stood at the head of the grave, and stared without answering for a space. Then he said, dropping a pebble down, 'It is nasty – and cold: horribly cold. I don't think I shall come to the Cemetery any more. I don't think grave-digging is cheerful.'

The two talked and agreed that the Cemetery was depressing. They also arranged for a ride next day out from the Cemetery through the Mashobra Tunnel up to Fagoo and back, because all the world was going to a garden-party at Viceregal Lodge, and all the people of Mashobra would go too.

Coming up the Cemetery road, the Tertium Quid's horse tried to bolt uphill, being tired with standing so long, and managed to strain a back sinew.

'I shall have to take the mare tomorrow,' said the Tertium Quid, 'and she will stand nothing heavier than a snaffle.'

They made their arrangements to meet in the Cemetery, after allowing all the Mashobra people time to pass into Simla. That night it rained heavily, and, next day, when the Tertium Quid came to the trysting-place, he saw that the new grave had a foot of water in it, the ground being a tough and sour clay.

''Jove! That looks beastly,' said the Tertium Quid. 'Fancy being boarded up and dropped into that well!'

They then started off to Fagoo, the mare playing with the snaffle and picking her way as though she were shod with satin, and the sun shining divinely. The road below Mashobra to Fagoo is officially styled the Himalayan-Thibet road; but in spite of its name it is not much more than six feet wide in most places, and the drop into the valley below may be anything between one and two thousand feet.

'Now we're going to Thibet,' said the Man's Wife merrily, as the horses drew near to Fagoo. She was riding on the cliff-side.

'Into Thibet,' said the Tertium Quid, 'ever so far from people who say horrid things, and hubbies who write stupid letters. With you – to the end of the world!'

A coolie carrying a log of wood came round a corner, and the mare went wide to avoid him – forefeet in and haunches out, as a sensible mare should go.

'To the world's end,' said the Man's Wife, and looked unspeakable things over her near shoulder at the Tertium Quid.

He was smiling, but, while she looked, the smile froze stiff as it were on his face, and changed to a nervous grin – the sort of grin men wear when they are not quite easy in their saddles. The mare seemed to be sinking by the stern, and her nostrils cracked while she was trying to realise what was happening. The rain of the night before had rotted the drop-side of the Himalayan-Thibet road, and it was giving way under her. 'What are you doing?' said the Man's Wife. The Tertium Quid gave no answer. He grinned nervously and set his spurs into the mare, who rapped with her forefeet on the road, and the struggle began. The Man's Wife screamed, 'Oh, Frank, get off!'

But the Tertium Quid was glued to the saddle – his face blue and white – and he looked into the Man's Wife's eyes. Then the Man's Wife clutched at the mare's head and caught her by the nose instead of the bridle. The brute threw up her head and went down with a scream, the Tertium Quid upon her, and the nervous grin still set on his face.

The Man's Wife heard the tinkle-tinkle of little stones and loose earth falling off the roadway, and the sliding roar of the man and horse going down. Then everything was quiet, and she called on Frank to leave his mare and walk up. But Frank did not answer. He was underneath the mare, nine hundred feet below, spoiling a patch of Indian corn.

As the revellers came back from Viceregal Lodge in the mists of the evening, they met a temporarily insane woman, on a temporarily mad horse, swinging round the corners, with her eyes and her mouth open, and her head like the head of a Medusa. She was stopped by a man at the risk of his life, and taken out of the saddle, a limp heap, and put on the bank to explain herself. This wasted twenty minutes, and then she was sent home in a lady's 'rickshaw, still with her mouth open and her hands picking at her riding-gloves.

She was in bed through the following three days, which were rainy; so she missed attending the funeral of the Tertium Quid, who was lowered into eighteen inches of water, instead of the twelve to which he had first objected.

A WAYSIDE COMEDY

Because to every purpose there is time and judgment, therefore the misery of man is great upon him.

Eccles. viii. 6

Fate and the Government of India have turned the Station of Kashima into a prison; and, because there is no help for the poor souls who are now lying there in torment, I write this story, praying that the Government of India may be moved to scatter the European population to the four winds.

Kashima is bounded on all sides by the rock-tipped circle of the Dosehri hills. In Spring, it is ablaze with roses; in Summer, the roses die and the hot winds blow from the hills; in Autumn, the white mists from the *jbils* cover the place as with water, and in Winter the frosts nip everything young and tender to earth-level. There is but one view in Kashima – a stretch of perfectly flat pasture and plough-land, running up to the gray-blue scrub of the Dosehri hills.

There are no amusements, except snipe and tiger shooting; but the tigers have been long since hunted from their lairs in the rock-caves, and the snipe only come once a year. Narkarra – one hundred and forty-three miles by road – is the nearest station to Kashima. But Kashima never goes to Narkarra, where there are at least twelve English people. It stays within the circle of the Dosehri hills.

244

All Kashima acquits Mrs Vansuythen of any intention to do harm; but all Kashima knows that she, and she alone, brought about their pain.

Boulte, the Engineer, Mrs Boulte, and Captain Kurrell know this. They are the English population of Kashima, if we except Major Vansuythen, who is of no importance whatever, and Mrs Vansuythen, who is the most important of all.

You must remember, though you will not understand, that all laws weaken in a small and hidden community where there is no public opinion. When a man is absolutely alone in a Station he runs a certain risk of falling into evil ways. This risk is multiplied by every addition to the population up to twelve – the Jury-number. After that, fear and consequent restraint begin, and human action becomes less grotesquely jerky.

There was deep peace in Kashima till Mrs Vansuythen arrived. She was a charming woman, everyone said so everywhere; and she charmed everyone. In spite of this, or, perhaps, because of this, since Fate is so perverse, she cared only for one man, and he was Major Vansuythen. Had she been plain or stupid, this matter would have been intelligible to Kashima. But she was a fair woman, with very still gray eyes, the colour of a lake just before the light of the sun touches it. No man who had seen those eyes could, later on, explain what fashion of woman she was to look upon. The eyes dazzled him. Her own sex said that she was 'not bad-looking, but spoilt by pretending to be so grave.' And yet her gravity was natural. It was not her habit to smile. She merely went through life, looking at those who passed; and the women objected while the men fell down and worshipped.

She knows and is deeply sorry for the evil she has done to Kashima; but Major Vansuythen cannot understand why Mrs Boulte does not drop in to afternoon tea at least three times a week. 'When there are only two women in one Station, they ought to see a great deal of each other,' says Major Vansuythen.

Long and long before ever Mrs Vansuythen came out of those faraway places where there is society and amusement, Kurrell had discovered that Mrs Boulte was the one woman in the world for him and – you dare not blame them. Kashima was as out of the world as Heaven or the Other Place, and the Dosehri hills kept their secret well. Boulte had no concern in the matter. He was in camp for a fortnight at a time. He was a hard, heavy man, and neither Mrs Boulte nor Kurrell pitied him. They had all Kashima and each other for their very, very own; and Kashima was the Garden of Eden in those days. When Boulte returned from his wanderings he would slap Kurrell between the shoulders and call him 'old fellow,' and the three would dine together. Kashima was happy then when the judgment of God seemed almost as distant as Narkarra or the railway that ran down to the sea. But the Government sent Major Vansuythen to Kashima, and with him came his wife.

The etiquette of Kashima is much the same as that of a desert island. When a stranger is cast away there, all hands go down to the shore to make him welcome. Kashima assembled at the masonry platform close to the Narkarra Road, and spread tea for the Vansuythens. That ceremony was reckoned a formal call, and made them free of the Station, its rights and privileges. When the Vansuythens settled down they gave a tiny house-warming to all Kashima; and that made Kashima free of their house, according to the immemorial usage of the Station.

Then the Rains came, when no one could go into camp, and the Narkarra Road was washed away by the Kasun River, and in the cup-like pastures of Kashima the cattle waded knee-deep. The clouds dropped down from the Dosehri hills and covered everything.

At the end of the Rains Boulte's manner towards his wife changed and became demonstratively affectionate. They had been married twelve years, and the change startled Mrs Boulte, who hated her husband with the hate of a woman who has met with nothing but kindness from her mate, and, in the teeth of this kindness, has done him a great wrong. Moreover, she had her own trouble to fight with – her watch to keep over her own property, Kurrell. For two months the Rains had hidden the Dosehri hills and many other things besides; but, when they lifted, they showed Mrs Boulte that her man among men, her Ted – for she called him Ted in the old days when Boulte was out of earshot – was slipping the links of the allegiance.

'The Vansuythen Woman has taken him,' Mrs Boulte said to herself; and when Boulte was away, wept over her belief, in the face of the over-vehement blandish-ments of Ted. Sorrow in Kashima is as fortunate as Love because there is nothing to weaken it save the flight of Time. Mrs Boulte had never breathed her suspicion to

Kurrell because she was not certain; and her nature led her to be very certain before she took steps in any direction. That is why she behaved as she did.

Boulte came into the house one evening, and leaned against the door-posts of the drawing-room, chewing his moustache. Mrs Boulte was putting some flowers into a vase. There is a pretence of civilisation even in Kashima.

'Little woman,' said Boulte quietly, 'do you care for me?'

'Immensely,' said she, with a laugh. 'Can you ask it?'

'But I'm serious,' said Boulte. '*Do* you care for me?'

Mrs Boulte dropped the flowers, and turned round quickly. 'Do you want an honest answer?'

'Ye-es, I've asked for it.'

Mrs Boulte spoke in a low, even voice for five minutes, very distinctly, that there might be no misunderstanding her meaning. When Samson broke the pillars of Gaza, he did a little thing, and one not to be compared to the deliberate pulling down of a woman's homestead about her own ears. There was no wise female friend to advise Mrs Boulte, the singularly cautious wife, to hold her hand. She struck at Boulte's heart, because her own was sick with suspicion of Kurrell, and worn out with the long strain of watching alone through the Rains. There was no plan or purpose in her speaking. The sentences made themselves; and Boulte listened, leaning against the door-post with his hands in his pockets. When all was over, and Mrs Boulte began to breathe through her nose before breaking out into tears, he laughed and stared straight in front of him at the Dosehri hills.

'Is that all?' he said. 'Thanks, I only wanted to know, you know.'

'What are you going to do?' said the woman, between her sobs.

'Do! Nothing. What should I do? Kill Kurrell, or send you Home, or apply for leave to get a divorce? It's two days' *dâk* into Narkarra.' He laughed again and went on: 'I'll tell you what *you* can do. You can ask Kurrell to dinner tomorrow – no, on Thursday, that will allow you time to pack – and you can bolt with him. I give you my word I won't follow.'

He took up his helmet and went out of the room, and Mrs Boulte sat till the moonlight streaked the floor, thinking and thinking and thinking. She had done her best upon the spur of the moment to pull the house down; but it would not fall. Moreover, she could not understand her husband, and she was afraid. Then the folly of her useless truthfulness struck her, and she was ashamed to write to Kurrell, saying, 'I have gone mad and told everything. My husband says that I am free to elope with you. Get a *dâk* for Thursday, and we will fly after dinner.' There was a cold-bloodedness about that procedure which did not appeal to her. So she sat still in her own house and thought.

At dinner-time Boulte came back from his walk, white and worn and haggard, and the woman was touched at his distress. As the evening wore on she muttered some expression of sorrow, something approaching to contrition. Boulte came out of a brown study and said, 'Oh, *that*! I wasn't thinking about that. By the way, what does Kurrell say to the elopement?'

'I haven't seen him,' said Mrs Boulte. 'Good God, is that all?'

But Boulte was not listening and her sentence ended in a gulp.

The next day brought no comfort to Mrs Boulte, for Kurrell did not appear, and the new life that she, in the five minutes' madness of the previous evening, had hoped to build out of the ruins of the old, seemed to be no nearer.

Boulte ate his breakfast, advised her to see her Arab pony fed in the verandah, and went out. The morning wore through, and at midday the tension became unendurable. Mrs Boulte could not cry. She had finished her crying in the night, and now she did not want to be left alone. Perhaps the Vansuythen Woman would talk to her; and, since talking opens the heart, perhaps there might be some comfort to be found in her company. She was the only other woman in the Station.

In Kashima there are no regular calling-hours. Every one can drop in upon everyone else at pleasure. Mrs Boulte put on a big *terai* hat, and walked across to the Vansuythens' house to borrow last week's *Queen*. The two compounds touched, and instead of going up the drive, she crossed through the gap in the cactus-hedge, entering the house from the back. As she passed through the dining-room, she heard, behind the *purdah* that cloaked the drawing-room door, her husband's voice, saying –

'But on my Honour! On my Soul and Honour, I tell you she doesn't care for me. She told me so last night. I would have told you then if Vansuythen hadn't been with you. If it is for *her* sake that you'll have nothing to say to me, you can make your mind easy. It's Kurrell –'

'What?' said Mrs Vansuythen, with a hysterical little laugh. 'Kurrell! Oh, it can't be! You two must have made some horrible mistake. Perhaps you – you lost your temper, or misunderstood, or something. Things *can't* be as wrong as you say.'

Mrs Vansuythen had shifted her defence to avoid the man's pleading, and was desperately trying to keep him to a side-issue.

'There must be some mistake,' she insisted, 'and it can be all put right again.'

Boulte laughed grimly.

'It can't be Captain Kurrell! He told me that he had never taken the least – the least interest in your wife, Mr Boulte. Oh, *do* listen! He said he had not. He swore he had not,' said Mrs Vansuythen.

The *purdah* rustled, and the speech was cut short by the entry of a little thin woman, with big rings round her eyes. Mrs Vansuythen stood up with a gasp.

'What was that you said?' asked Mrs Boulte. 'Never mind that man. What did Ted say to you? What did he say to you? What did he say to you?'

Mrs Vansuythen sat down helplessly on the sofa, overborne by the trouble of her questioner.

'He said – I can't remember exactly what he said – but I understood him to say – that is – But, really, Mrs Boulte, isn't it rather a strange question?'

'*Will* you tell me what he said?' repeated Mrs Boulte. Even a tiger will fly before a bear robbed of her whelps, and Mrs Vansuythen was only an ordinarily good woman. She began in a sort of desperation: 'Well, he said that he never cared for you at all, and, of course, there was not the least reason why he should have, and – and – that was all.'

'You said he *swore* he had not cared for me. Was that true?'

'Yes,' said Mrs Vansuythen very softly.

Mrs Boulte wavered for an instant where she stood, and then fell forward fainting.

'What did I tell you?' said Boulte, as though the conversation had been unbroken. 'You can see for yourself. She cares for *him*.' The light began to break into his dull mind, and he went on – 'And he – what was *he* saying to you?'

But Mrs Vansuythen, with no heart for explanations or impassioned protestations, was kneeling over Mrs Boulte.

'Oh, you brute!' she cried. 'Are *all* men like this? Help me to get her into my room – and her face is cut against the table. Oh, *will* you be quiet, and help me to carry her? I hate you, and I hate Captain Kurrell. Lift her up carefully, and now – go! Go away!'

Boulte carried his wife into Mrs Vansuythen's bedroom, and departed before the storm of that lady's wrath and disgust, impenitent and burning with jealousy. Kurrell had been making love to Mrs Vansuythen – would do Vansuythen as great a wrong as he had done Boulte, who caught himself considering whether Mrs Vansuythen would faint if she discovered that the man she loved had forsworn her.

In the middle of these meditations, Kurrell came cantering along the road and pulled up with a cheery 'Good-mornin'. 'Been mashing Mrs Vansuythen as usual, eh? Bad thing for a sober, married man, that. What will Mrs Boulte say?'

Boulte raised his head and said slowly, – 'Oh, you liar!' Kurrell's face changed. 'What's that?' he asked quickly.

'Nothing much,' said Boulte. 'Has my wife told you that you two are free to go off whenever you please? She has been good enough to explain the situation to me. You've been a true friend to me, Kurrell – old man – haven't you?'

Kurrell groaned, and tried to frame some sort of idiotic sentence about being willing to give 'satisfaction.' But his interest in the woman was dead, had died out in the Rains, and, mentally, he was abusing her for her amazing indiscretion. It would have been so easy to have broken off the thing gently and by degrees, and now he was saddled with – Boulte's voice recalled him.

'I don't think I should get any satisfaction from killing you, and I'm pretty sure you'd get none from killing me.'

Then in a querulous tone, ludicrously disproportioned to his wrongs, Boulte added –

''Seems rather a pity that you haven't the decency to keep to the woman, now you've got her. You've been a true friend to *her* too, haven't you?'

Kurrell stared long and gravely. The situation was getting beyond him.

'What do you mean?' he said.

Boulte answered, more to himself than the questioner: 'My wife came over to Mrs Vansuythen's just now; and it seems you'd been telling Mrs Vansuythen that you'd never cared for Emma. I suppose you lied, as usual. What had Mrs Vansuythen to do with you, or you with her? Try to speak the truth for once in a way.'

Kurrell took the double insult without wincing, and replied by another question: 'Go on. What happened?'

'Emma fainted,' said Boulte simply. 'But, look here, what had you been saying to Mrs Vansuythen?'

Kurrell laughed. Mrs Boulte had, with unbridled tongue, made havoc of his plans; and he could at least retaliate by hurting the man in whose eyes he was humiliated and shown dishonourable.

'Said to her? What *does* a man tell a lie like that for? I suppose I said pretty much what you've said, unless I'm a good deal mistaken.'

'I spoke the truth,' said Boulte, again more to himself than Kurrell. 'Emma told me she hated me. She has no right in me.'

'No! I suppose not. You're only her husband, y'know. And what did Mrs Vansuythen say after you had laid your disengaged heart at her feet?'

Kurrell felt almost virtuous as he put the question.

'I don't think that matters,' Boulte replied; 'and it doesn't concern you.'

'But it does! I tell you it does' – began Kurrell shamelessly.

The sentence was cut by a roar of laughter from Boulte's lips. Kurrell was silent for an instant, and then he, too, laughed – laughed long and loudly, rocking in his saddle. It was an unpleasant sound – the mirthless mirth of these men on the long white line of the Narkarra Road. There were no strangers in Kashima, or they might have thought that captivity within the Dosehri hills had driven half the European population mad. The laughter ended abruptly, and Kurrell was the first to speak.

'Well, what are you going to do?'

Boulte looked up the road, and at the hills. 'Nothing,' said he quietly; 'what's the use? It's too ghastly for anything. We must let the old life go on. I can only call you a hound and a liar, and I can't go on calling you names forever. Besides which, I don't feel that I'm much better. We can't get out of this place. What *is* there to do?'

Kurrell looked round the rat-pit of Kashima and made no reply. The injured husband took up the wondrous tale.

'Ride on, and speak to Emma if you want to. God knows *I* don't care what you do.'

He walked forward, and left Kurrell gazing blankly after him. Kurrell did not ride on either to see Mrs Boulte or Mrs Vansuythen. He sat in his saddle and thought, while his pony grazed by the roadside.

The whir of approaching wheels roused him. Mrs Vansuythen was driving home Mrs Boulte, white and wan, with a cut on her forehead.

'Stop, please,' said Mrs Boulte, 'I want to speak to Ted.'

Mrs Vansuythen obeyed, but as Mrs Boulte leaned forward, putting her hand upon the splashboard of the dog-cart, Kurrell spoke.

'I've seen your husband, Mrs Boulte.'

There was no necessity for any further explanation. The man's eyes were fixed, not upon Mrs Boulte, but her companion. Mrs Boulte saw the look.

'Speak to him!' she pleaded, turning to the woman at her side. 'Oh, speak to him! Tell him what you told me just now. Tell him you hate him. Tell him you hate him!'

She bent forward and wept bitterly, while the *sais*, impassive, went forward to hold the horse. Mrs Vansuythen turned scarlet and dropped the reins. She wished to be no party to such unholy explanations.

'I've nothing to do with it,' she began coldly; but Mrs Boulte's sobs overcame her, and she addressed herself to the man. 'I don't know what I am to say, Captain Kurrell. I don't know what I can call you. I think you've – you've behaved abominably, and she has cut her forehead terribly against the table.'

'It doesn't hurt. It isn't anything,' said Mrs Boulte feebly. '*That* doesn't matter. Tell him what you told me. Say you don't care for him. Oh, Ted, *won't* you believe her?'

'Mrs Boulte has made me understand that you were – that you were fond of her once upon a time,' went on Mrs Vansuythen.

'Well!' said Kurrell brutally. 'It seems to me that Mrs Boulte had better be fond of her own husband first.'

'Stop!' said Mrs Vansuythen. 'Hear me first. I don't care – I don't want to know anything about you and Mrs Boulte; but I want *you* to know that I hate you, that I think you are a cur, and that I'll never, *never* speak to you again. Oh, I don't dare to say what I think of you, you – man!'

'I want to speak to Ted,' moaned Mrs Boulte, but the dog-cart rattled on, and Kurrell was left on the road, shamed, and boiling with wrath against Mrs Boulte.

He waited till Mrs Vansuythen was driving back to her own house, and, she being freed from the embarrassment of Mrs Boulte's presence, learned for the second time her opinion of himself and his actions.

In the evenings it was the wont of all Kashima to meet at the platform on the Narkarra Road, to drink tea and discuss the trivialities of the day. Major Vansuythen and his wife found themselves alone at the gathering-place for almost the first time in their remembrance; and the cheery Major, in the teeth of his wife's remarkably reasonable suggestion that the rest of the Station might be sick, insisted upon driving round to the two bungalows and unearthing the population.

'Sitting in the twilight!' said he, with great indignation, to the Boultes. 'That'll never do! Hang it all, we're one family here! You *must* come out, and so must Kurrell. I'll make him bring his banjo.'

So great is the power of honest simplicity and a good digestion over guilty consciences that all Kashima did turn out, even down to the banjo; and the Major embraced the company in one expansive grin. As he grinned, Mrs Vansuythen raised her eyes for an instant and looked at all Kashima. Her meaning was clear. Major Vansuythen would never know anything. He was to be the outsider in that happy family whose cage was the Dosehri hills.

'You're singing villainously out of tune, Kurrell,' said the Major truthfully. 'Pass me that banjo.'

And he sang in excruciating-wise till the stars came out and all Kashima went to dinner.

That was the beginning of the New Life of Kashima – the life that Mrs Boulte made when her tongue was loosened in the twilight.

Mrs Vansuythen has never told the Major; and since he insists upon keeping up a burdensome geniality, she has been compelled to break her vow of not speaking to Kurrell. This speech, which must of necessity preserve the semblance of politeness and interest, serves admirably to keep alight the flame of jealousy and dull hatred in Boulte's bosom, as it awakens the same passions in his wife's heart. Mrs Boulte hates Mrs Vansuythen because she has taken Ted from her, and, in some curious fashion, hates her because Mrs Vansuythen – and here the wife's eyes see far more clearly than the husband's – detests Ted. And Ted – that gallant captain and honourable man – knows now that it is possible to hate a woman once loved, to the verge of wishing to silence her for ever with blows. Above all, is he shocked that Mrs Boulte cannot see the error of her ways.

Boulte and he go out tiger-shooting together in all friendship. Boulte has put their relationship on a most satisfactory footing.

'You're a blackguard,' he says to Kurrell, 'and I've lost any self-respect I may ever have had; but when you're with me, I can feel certain that you are not with Mrs Vansuythen, or making Emma miserable.'

Kurrell endures anything that Boulte may say to him. Sometimes they are away for three days together, and then the Major insists upon his wife going over to sit with Mrs Boulte; although Mrs Vansuythen has repeatedly declared that she prefers her husband's company to any in the world. From the way in which she clings to him, she would certainly seem to be speaking the truth.

But of course, as the Major says, 'in a little Station we must all be friendly.'

THE HILL OF ILLUSION

What rendered vain their deep desire?
A God, a God their severance ruled,
And bade between their shores to be
The unplumbed, salt, estranging sea.
                              Matthew Arnold

HE: Tell your *jhampanies* not to hurry so, dear. They forget I'm fresh from the Plains.

SHE: Sure proof that *I* have not been going out with anyone. Yes, they *are* an untrained crew. Where do we go?

HE: As usual – to the world's end. No, Jakko.

SHE: Have your pony led after you, then. It's a long round.

HE: And for the last time, thank Heaven!

SHE: Do you mean *that* still? I didn't dare to write to you about it – all these months.

HE: Mean it! I've been shaping my affairs to that end since Autumn. What makes you speak as though it had occurred to you for the first time?

SHE: I? Oh! I don't know. I've had long enough to think, too.

HE: And you've changed your mind?

SHE: No. You ought to know that I am a miracle of constancy. What are your – arrangements?

HE: *Ours*, Sweetheart, please.

SHE: Ours, be it then. My poor boy, how the prickly heat has marked your forehead! Have you ever tried sulphate of copper in water?

HE: It'll go away in a day or two up here. The arrangements are simple enough. Tonga in the early morning – reach Kalka at twelve – Umballa at seven – down, straight by night train, to Bombay, and then the steamer of the 21st for Rome. That's my idea. The Continent and Sweden – a ten-week honeymoon.

SHE: Ssh! Don't talk of it in that way. It makes me afraid. Guy, how long have we two been insane?

HE: Seven months and fourteen days, I forget the odd hours exactly, but I'll think.

SHE: I only wanted to see if you remembered. Who are those two on the Blessington Road?

HE: Eabrey and the Penner Woman. What do they matter to *us*? Tell me everything that you've been doing and saying and thinking.

SHE: Doing little, saying less, and thinking a great deal. I've hardly been out at all.

HE: That was wrong of you. You haven't been moping?

SHE: Not very much. Can you wonder that I'm disinclined for amusement?

HE: Frankly, I do. Where was the difficulty?

SHE: In this only. The more people I know and the more I'm known here, the wider spread will be the news of the crash when it comes. I don't like that.

HE: Nonsense. We shall be out of it.

SHE: You think so?

HE: I'm sure of it, if there is any power in steam or horse-flesh to carry us away. Ha! ha!

SHE: And the *fun* of the situation comes in – where, my Lancelot?

HE: Nowhere, Guinevere. I was only thinking of something.

SHE: They say men have a keener sense of humour than women. Now *I* was thinking of the scandal.

HE: Don't think of anything so ugly. We shall be beyond it.

SHE: It will be there all the same – in the mouths of Simla – telegraphed over India, and talked of at the dinners – and when He goes out they will stare at Him to see how he takes it. And we shall be dead, Guy dear – dead and cast into the outer darkness where there is –

HE: Love at least. Isn't that enough?

SHE: I have said so.

HE: And you think so still?

SHE: What do *you* think?

HE: What have I *done?* It means equal ruin to me, as the world reckons it – outcasting, the loss of my appointment, the breaking off my life's work. I pay my price.

SHE: And are you so much above the world that you can afford to pay it. Am I?

HE: My Divinity – what else?

SHE: A very ordinary woman, I'm afraid, but so far, respectable. How d'you do, Mrs Middleditch? Your husband? I think he's riding down to Annandale with Colonel Statters. Yes, isn't it divine after the rain? – Guy, how long am I to be allowed to bow to Mrs Middleditch? Till the 17th?

HE: Frowsy Scotchwoman! What is the use of bringing her into the discussion? You were saying?

SHE: Nothing. Have you ever seen a man hanged?

HE: Yes. Once.

SHE: What was it for?

HE: Murder, of course.

SHE: Murder. Is *that* so great a sin after all? I wonder how he felt before the drop fell.

HE: I don't think he felt much What a gruesome little woman it is this evening! You're shivering. Put on your cape, dear.

SHE: I think I will. Oh! Look at the mist coming over Sanjaoli; and I thought we should have sunshine on the Ladies' Mile! Let's turn back.

HE: What's the good? There's a cloud on Elysium Hill, and that means it's foggy all down the Mall. We'll go on. It'll blow away before we get to the Convent, perhaps. 'Jove! It *is* chilly.'

SHE: You feel it, fresh from below. Put on your ulster. What do you think of my cape?

HE: Never ask a man his opinion of a woman's dress when he is desperately and abjectly in love with the wearer. Let me look. Like everything else of yours it's perfect. Where did you get it from?

SHE: He gave it me, on Wednesday – our wedding-day, you know.

HE: The Deuce He did! He's growing generous in his old age. D'you like all that frilly, bunchy stuff at the throat? I don't.

SHE: Don't you?

> Kind Sir, o' your courtesy,
> As you go by the town, Sir,
> 'Pray you o' your love for me,
> Buy me a russet gown, Sir.

HE: I won't say: 'Keek into the draw-well, Janet, Janet.' Only wait a little, darling, and you shall be stocked with russet gowns and everything else.

SHE: And when the frocks wear out you'll get me new ones – and everything else?

HE: Assuredly.

SHE: I wonder!

HE: Look here, Sweetheart, I didn't spend two days and two nights in the train to hear you wonder. I thought we'd settled all that at Shaifazehat.

SHE (*dreamily*): At Shaifazehat? Does the Station go on still? That was ages and *ages* ago. It must be crumbling to pieces. All except the Amirtollah *kutcha* road. I don't believe *that* could crumble till the Day of Judgment.

HE: You think so? What *is* the mood now?

SHE: I can't tell. How cold it is! Let us get on quickly.

HE: 'Better walk a little. Stop your *jhampanies* and get out. What's the matter with you this evening, dear?

SHE: Nothing. You must grow accustomed to my ways. If I'm boring you I can go home. Here's Captain Congleton coming, I daresay he'll be willing to escort me.

HE: Goose! Between *us*, too! *Damn* Captain Congleton.

SHE: Chivalrous Knight. Is it your habit to swear much in talking? It jars a little, and you might swear at me.

HE: My angel! I didn't know what I was saying; and you changed so quickly that I couldn't follow. I'll apologise in dust and ashes.

SHE: There'll be enough of those later on – Good-night, Captain Congleton. Going to the singing-quadrilles already? What dances am I giving you next week? No! You must have written them down wrong. Five and Seven, *I* said. If you've made a mistake, I certainly don't intend to suffer for it. You must alter your programme.

HE: I thought you told me that you had not been going out much this season?

SHE: Quite true, but when I do I dance with Captain Congleton. He dances very nicely.

HE: And sit out with him, I suppose?

SHE: Yes. Have you any objection? Shall I stand under the chandelier in future?

HE: What does he talk to you about?

SHE: What do men talk about when they sit out?

HE: Ugh! Don't! Well, now I'm up, you must dispense with the fascinating Congleton for a while. I don't like him.

SHE (*after a pause*): Do you know what you have said?

HE: 'Can't say that I do exactly. I'm not in the best of tempers.

SHE: So I see, – and feel. My true and faithful lover, where is your 'eternal constancy,' 'unalterable trust,' and 'reverent devotion'? I remember those phrases; you seem to have forgotten them. I mention a man's name –

HE: A good deal more than that.

SHE: Well, speak to him about a dance – perhaps the last dance that I shall ever dance in my life before I, – before I go away; and you at once distrust and insult me.

HE: I never said a word.

SHE: How much did you imply? Guy, is *this* amount of confidence to be our stock to start the new life on?

HE: No, of course not. I didn't mean that. On my word and honour, I didn't. Let it pass, dear. Please let it pass.

SHE: This once – yes – and a second time, and again and again, all through the years when I shall be unable to resent it. You want too much, my Lancelot, and, – you know too much.

HE: How do you mean?

SHE: That is a part of the punishment. There *cannot* be perfect trust between us.

HE: In Heaven's name, why not?

SHE: Hush! The Other Place is quite enough. Ask yourself.

HE: I don't follow.

SHE: You trust me so implicitly that when I look at another man – Never mind. Guy, have you ever made love to a girl – a *good* girl?

HE: Something of the sort. Centuries ago – in the Dark Ages, before I ever met you, dear.

SHE: Tell me what you said to her.

HE: What does a man say to a girl? I've forgotten.

SHE: *I* remember. He tells her that he trusts her and worships the ground she walks on, and that he'll love and honour and protect her till her dying day; and so she marries in that belief. At least, I speak of one girl who was *not* protected.

HE: Well, and then?

SHE: And then, Guy, and then, that girl needs *ten* times the love and trust and honour – yes, *honour* – that was enough when she was only a mere wife if – if – the other life she chooses to lead is to be made even bearable. Do you understand?

HE: Even bearable! It'll be Paradise.

SHE: Ah! Can you give me all I've asked for – not now, nor a few months later, but when you begin to think of what you might have done if you had kept your own appointment and your caste here – when you begin to look upon me as a drag and a burden? I shall want it most then, Guy, for there will be no one in the wide world but you.

HE: You're a little over-tired tonight, Sweetheart, and you're taking a stage view of the situation. After the necessary business in the Courts, the road is clear to –

SHE: 'The holy state of matrimony!' Ha! ha! ha!

HE: Ssh! Don't laugh in that horrible way!

SHE: I – I – c-c-c-can't help it! Isn't it too absurd! Ah! Ha! ha! ha! Guy, stop me quick or I shall – l-l-augh till we get to the Church.

HE: For goodness sake, stop! Don't make an exhibition of yourself. What *is* the matter with you?

SHE: N-nothing. I'm better now.

HE: That's all right. One moment, dear. There's a little wisp of hair got loose from behind your right ear and it's straggling over your cheek.

SHE: Thank'oo. I'm 'fraid my hat's on one side, too.

HE: What do you wear these huge dagger bonnet-skewers for? They're big enough to kill a man with.

SHE: Oh! don't kill *me*, though. You're sticking it into my head! Let *me* do it. You men are so clumsy.

HE: Have you had many opportunities of comparing us – in this sort of work?

SHE: Guy, what is my name?

HE: Eh! I don't follow.

SHE: Here's my card-case. Can you read?

HE: Yes. Well?

SHE: Well, that answers your question. You know the other's man's name. Am I sufficiently humbled, or would you like to ask me if there is anyone else?

HE: I see now. My darling, I never meant that for an instant. I was only joking. There! Lucky there's no one on the road. They'd be scandalised.

SHE: They'll be more scandalised before the end.

HE: Do-on't! I don't like you to talk in that way.

SHE: Unreasonable man! Who asked me to face the situation and accept it? – Tell me, do I look like Mrs Penner? *Do* I look like a naughty woman! *Swear* I don't! Give me your word of honour, my *honourable* friend, that I'm not like Mrs Buzgago. That's the way she stands, with her hands clasped at the back of her head. D'you like that?

HE: Don't be affected.

SHE: I'm not. I'm Mrs Buzgago. Listen!

Pendant une anne' toute entière
Le régiment n'a pas r'paru.
Au Ministère de la Guerre
On le r'porta comme perdu.

On se r'noncait à r'trouver sa trace,
Quand un matin subitement,
On le vit r'paraître sur la place
L'Colonel toujours en avant.

That's the way she rolls her r's. *Am* I like her?

HE: No, but I object when you go on like an actress and sing stuff of that kind. Where in the world did you pick up the *Chanson du Colonel?* It isn't a drawing-room song. It isn't proper.

SHE: Mrs Buzgago taught it me. She is both drawing-room and proper, and in another month she'll shut her drawing-room to me, and, thank God, she isn't as improper as I am. Oh, Guy, Guy! I wish I was like some women and had no scruples about – What is it Keene says? – 'Wearing a corpse's hair and being false to the bread they eat.'

HE: I am only a man of limited intelligence, and, just now, very bewildered. When you have *quite* finished flashing through all your moods tell me, and I'll try to understand the last one.

SHE: Moods, Guy! I haven't any. I'm sixteen years old and you're just twenty, and you've been waiting for two hours outside the school in the cold. And now I've met you, and now we're walking home together. Does *that* suit you, My Imperial Majesty?

HE: No. We aren't children. Why can't you be rational?

SHE: He asks me that when I'm going to commit suicide for his sake, and, and – I don't want to be French and rave about my mother, but have I ever told you that I have a mother, and a brother who was my pet before I married? He's married now. Can't you imagine the pleasure that the news of the elopement will give him? Have *you* any people at Home, Guy, to be pleased with your performances?

HE: One or two. One can't make omelets without breaking eggs.

SHE: (slowly): I don't see the necessity –

HE: Hah! What do you mean?

SHE: Shall I speak the truth?

HE: Under the circumstances, perhaps it *would* be as well.

SHE: Guy, I'm afraid.

HE: I thought we'd settled all that. What of?

SHE: Of you.

HE: Oh, damn it all! The old business! This is *too* bad!

SHE: Of you.

HE: And what now?

SHE: What do you think of me?

HE: Beside the question altogether. What do you intend to do?

SHE: I daren't risk it. I'm afraid. If I could only cheat –

HE: *À la Buzgago?* No, *thanks.* That's the one point on which I have any notion of Honour. I won't eat his salt and steal too. I'll loot openly or not at all.

SHE: I never meant anything else.

HE: Then, why in the world do you pretend not to be willing to come?

SHE: It's *not* pretence, Guy. I *am* afraid.

HE: Please explain.

SHE: It can't last, Guy. It can't last. You'll get angry, and then you'll swear, and then you'll get jealous, and then you'll mistrust me – you do *now* – and you yourself will be the best reason for doubting. And I – what shall *I* do? I shall be no better than Mrs Buzgago found out – no better than anyone. And you'll *know* that. Oh, Guy, can't you *see?*

HE: I see that you are desperately unreasonable, little woman.

SHE: There! The moment I begin to object, you get angry. What will you do when I am only your property – stolen property? It can't be, Guy. It can't be! I thought it could, but it *can't.* You'll get tired of me.

HE: I tell you I shall *not.* Won't anything make you understand that?

SHE: There, can't you see? If you speak to me like that now, you'll call me horrible names later, if I don't do everything as you like. And if you were cruel to me, Guy, where should I go? – where should I go? I can't trust you. Oh! I *can't* trust you!

HE: I suppose I ought to say that I *can* trust you. I've ample reason.

SHE: *Please* don't, dear. It hurts as much as if you hit me.

HE: It isn't exactly pleasant for *me*.

SHE: I can't help it. I wish I were dead! I can't trust you, and I don't trust myself. Oh, Guy, let it die away and be forgotten!

HE: Too late now. I don't understand you – I won't – and I can't trust myself to talk this evening. May I call tomorrow?

SHE: Yes. *No!* Oh, give me time! The day after. I get into my 'rickshaw here and meet Him at Peliti's. You ride.

HE: I'll go on to Peliti's too. I think I want a drink. My world's knocked about my ears and the stars are falling. Who are those brutes howling in the Old Library?

SHE: They're rehearsing the singing-quadrilles for the Fancy Ball. Can't you hear Mrs Buzgago's voice? She has a solo. It's quite a new idea. Listen!

MRS BUZGAGO (*in the Old Library, con. molt. exp.*).

> See-saw! Margery Daw!
> Sold her bed to lie upon straw.
> Wasn't she a silly slut
> To sell her bed and lie upon dirt?

Captain Congleton, I'm going to alter that to 'flirt.' It sounds better.

HE: No, I've changed my mind about the drink. Good-night, little lady. I shall see you tomorrow?

SHE: Ye – es. Good-night, Guy. *Don't* be angry with me.

HE: Angry! You *know* I trust you absolutely. Good-night and – God bless you!

(*Three seconds later. Alone.*) Hmm! I'd give something to discover whether there's another man at the back of all this.

A SECOND-RATE WOMAN

Est fuga, volvitur rota,
On we drift: where looms the dim port?
One Two Three Four Five contribute their quota:
Something is gained if one caught but the import,
Show it us, Hugues of Saxe-Gotha.
Master Hugues of Saxe-Gotha

'Dressed! Don't tell me that woman ever dressed in her life. She stood in the middle of the room while her *ayah* – no, her husband – it *must* have been a man – threw her clothes at her. She then did her hair with her fingers, and rubbed her bonnet in the flue under the bed. I *know* she did, as well as if I had assisted at the orgy. Who is she?' said Mrs Hauksbee.

'Don't!' said Mrs Mallowe feebly. 'You make my head ache. I'm miserable today. Stay me with *fondants*, comfort me with chocolates, for I am – Did you bring anything from Peliti's?'

'Questions to begin with. You shall have the sweets when you have answered them. Who and what is the creature? There were at least half-a-dozen men round her, and she appeared to be going to sleep in their midst.'

'Delville,' said Mrs Mallowe, '"Shady" Delville, to distinguish her from Mrs Jim of that ilk. She dances as untidily as she dresses, I believe, and her husband is somewhere in Madras. Go and call, if you are so interested.'

'What have I to do with Shigramitish women? She merely caught my attention for a minute, and I wondered at the attraction that a dowd has for a certain type of man. I expected to see her walk out of her clothes – until I looked at her eyes.'

'Hooks and eyes, surely,' drawled Mrs Mallowe.

'Don't be clever, Polly. You make my head ache. And round this hayrick stood a crowd of men – a positive crowd!'

'Perhaps *they* also expected –'

'Polly, don't be Rabelaisian!'

Mrs Mallowe curled herself up comfortably on the sofa, and turned her attention to the sweets. She and Mrs Hauksbee shared the same house at Simla; and these things befell two seasons after the matter of Otis Yeere, which has been already recorded.

Mrs Hauksbee stepped into the verandah and looked down upon the Mall, her forehead puckered with thought.

'Hah!' said Mrs Hauksbee shortly. 'Indeed!'

'What is it?' said Mrs Mallowe sleepily.

'That dowd and The Dancing Master – to whom I object.'

'Why to The Dancing Master? He is a middle-aged gentleman, of reprobate and romantic tendencies, and tries to be a friend of mine.'

'Then make up your mind to lose him. Dowds cling by nature, and I should imagine that this animal – how terrible her bonnet looks from above! – is specially clingsome.'

'She is welcome to The Dancing Master so far as I am concerned. I never could take an interest in a monotonous liar. The frustrated aim of his life is to persuade people that he is a bachelor.'

'O-oh! I think I've met that sort of man before. And isn't he?'

'No. He confided that to me a few days ago. Ugh! Some men ought to be killed.'

'What happened then?'

'He posed as the horror of horrors – a misunderstood man. Heaven knows the *femme incomprise* is sad enough and bad enough – but the other thing!

'And so fat too! *I* should have laughed in his face. Men seldom confide in me. How is it they come to you?'

'For the sake of impressing me with their careers in the past. Protect me from men with confidences!'

'And yet you encourage them?'

'What can I do? They talk, I listen, and they vow that I am sympathetic. I know I always profess astonishment even when the plot is – of the most old possible.'

'Yes. Men are so unblushingly explicit if they are once allowed to talk, whereas women's confidences are full of reservations and fibs, except –'

'When they go mad and babble of the unutterabilities after a week's acquaintance. Really, if you come to consider, we know a great deal more of men than of our own sex.'

'And the extraordinary thing is that men will never believe it. They say we are trying to hide something.'

'They are generally doing that on their own account. Alas! These chocolates pall upon me, and I haven't eaten more than a dozen. I think I shall go to sleep.'

'Then you'll get fat, dear. If you took more exercise and a more intelligent interest in your neighbours you would –'

'Be as much loved as Mrs Hauksbee. You're a darling in many ways, and I like you – you are not a woman's woman – but *why* do you trouble yourself about mere human beings?'

'Because in the absence of angels, who I am sure would be horribly dull, men and women are the most fascinating things in the whole wide world, lazy one. I am interested in The Dowd – I am interested in The Dancing Master – I am interested in the Hawley Boy – and I am interested in *you*.'

'Why couple me with the Hawley Boy? He is your property.'

'Yes, and in his own guileless speech, I'm making a good thing out of him. When he is slightly more reformed, and has passed his Higher Standard, or whatever the authorities think fit to exact from him, I shall select a pretty little girl, the Holt girl, I think, and' – here she waved her hands airily – '"whom Mrs Hauksbee hath joined together let no man put asunder." That's all.'

'And when you have yoked May Holt with the most notorious detrimental in Simla, and earned the undying hatred of Mamma Holt, what will you do with me, Dispenser of the Destinies of the Universe?'

Mrs Hauksbee dropped into a low chair in front of the fire, and, chin in hand, gazed long and steadfastly at Mrs Mallowe.

'I do not know,' she said, shaking her head, '*what* I shall do with you, dear. It's obviously impossible to marry you to someone else – your husband would object and the experiment might not be successful after all. I think I shall begin by preventing you from – what is it? – "sleeping on ale-house benches and snoring in the sun."'

'Don't! I don't like your quotations. They are so rude. Go to the Library and bring me new books.'

'While you sleep? *No!* If you don't come with me I shall spread your newest frock on my 'rickshaw-bow, and when anyone asks me what I am doing, I shall say that I am going to Phelps's to get it let out. I shall take care that Mrs MacNamara sees me. Put your things on, there's a good girl.'

Mrs Mallowe groaned and obeyed, and the two went off to the Library, where they found Mrs Delville and the man who went by the nickname of The Dancing Master. By that time Mrs Mallowe was awake and eloquent.

'That is the Creature!' said Mrs Hauksbee, with the air of one pointing out a slug in the road.

'No,' said Mrs Mallowe. 'The man is the Creature. Ugh! Good-evening, Mr Bent. I thought you were coming to tea this evening.'

'Surely it was for tomorrow, was it not?' answered The Dancing Master. 'I understood . . . I fancied . . . I'm so sorry . . . How very unfortunate!' . . .

But Mrs Mallowe had passed on.

'For the practised equivocator you said he was,' murmured Mrs Hauksbee, 'he strikes *me* as a failure. Now wherefore should he have preferred a walk with The Dowd to tea with us? Elective affinities, I suppose – both grubby. Polly, I'd never forgive that woman as long as the world rolls.'

'I forgive every woman everything,' said Mrs Mallowe. 'He will be a sufficient punishment for her. What a common voice she has!'

Mrs Delville's voice was not pretty, her carriage was even less lovely, and her raiment was strikingly neglected. All these things Mrs Mallowe noticed over the top of a magazine.

'Now *what* is there in her?' said Mrs Hauksbee. 'Do you see what I meant about the clothes falling off? If I were a man I would perish sooner than be seen with that rag-bag. And yet, she has good eyes, but – Oh!'

'What is it?'

'She doesn't know how to use them! On my honour, she does not. Look! Oh look! Untidiness I can endure, but ignorance never! The woman's a fool.'

'Hsh! She'll hear you.'

'All the women in Simla are fools. She'll think I mean someone else. Now she's going out. What a thoroughly objectionable couple she and The Dancing Master make! Which reminds me. Do you suppose they'll ever dance together?'

'Wait and see. I don't envy her the conversation of The Dancing Master – loathly man! His wife ought to be up here before long?'

'Do you know anything about him?'

'Only what he told me. It may be all a fiction. He married a girl bred in the country, I think, and, being an honourable, chivalrous soul, told me that he repented his bargain and sent her to her mother as often as possible – a person who has lived in the Doon since the memory of man and goes to Mussoorie when other people go Home. The wife is with her at present. So he says.'

'Babies?'

'One only, but he talks of his wife in a revolting way. I hated him for it. *He* thought he was being epigrammatic and brilliant.'

'That is a vice peculiar to men. I dislike him because he is generally in the wake of some girl, disappointing the Eligibles. He will persecute May Holt no more, unless I am much mistaken.'

'No. I think Mrs Delville may occupy his attention for a while.'

'Do you suppose she knows that he is the head of a family?'

'Not from his lips. He swore me to eternal secrecy. Wherefore I tell you. Don't you know that type of man?'

'Not intimately, thank goodness! As a general rule, when a man begins to abuse his wife to me, I find that the Lord gives me wherewith to answer him according to his folly; and we part with a coolness between us. I laugh.'

'I'm different. I've no sense of humour.'

'Cultivate it, then. It has been my mainstay for more years than I care to think about. A well-educated sense of humour will save a woman when Religion, Training, and Home influences fail; and we may all need salvation sometimes.'

'Do you suppose that the Delville woman has humour?'

'Her dress bewrays her. How can a Thing who wears her *supplément* under her left arm have any notion of the fitness of things – much less their folly? If she discards The Dancing Master after having once seen him dance, I may respect her. Otherwise –'

'But are we not both assuming a great deal too much, dear? You saw the woman at Peliti's – half an hour later you saw her walking with The Dancing Master – an hour later you met her here at the Library.'

'Still with The Dancing Master, remember.'

'Still with The Dancing Master, I admit, but why on the strength of that should you imagine –'

'I imagine nothing. I have no imagination. I am only convinced that The Dancing Master is attracted to The Dowd because he is objectionable in every way and she in every other. If I know the man as you have described him, he holds his wife in slavery at present.'

'She is twenty years younger than he.'

'Poor wretch! And, in the end, after he has posed and swaggered and lied – he has a mouth under that ragged moustache simply made for lies – he will be rewarded according to his merits.'

'I wonder what those really are,' said Mrs Mallowe.

But Mrs Hauksbee, her face close to the shelf of the new books, was humming softly: '*What shall he have who killed the Deer?*' She was a lady of unfettered speech.

One month later she announced her intention of calling upon Mrs Delville. Both Mrs Hauksbee and Mrs Mallowe were in morning wrappers, and there was a great peace in the land.

'I should go as I was,' said Mrs Mallowe. 'It would be a delicate compliment to her style.'

Mrs Hauksbee studied herself in the glass.

'Assuming for a moment that she ever darkened these doors, I should put on this robe, after all the others, to show her what a morning-wrapper ought to be. It might enliven her. As it is, I shall go in the dove-coloured – sweet emblem of youth and innocence – and shall put on my new gloves.'

'If you really are going, dirty tan would be too good; and you know that dove-colour spots with the rain.'

'I care not. I may make her envious. At least I shall try, though one cannot expect very much from a woman who puts a lace tucker into her habit.'

'Just Heavens! When did she do that?'

'Yesterday – riding with The Dancing Master. I met them at the back of Jakko, and the rain had made the lace lie down. To complete the effect, she was wearing an unclean *terai* with the elastic under her chin. I felt almost too well content to take the trouble to despise her.'

'The Hawley Boy was riding with you. What did he think?'

'Does a boy ever notice these things? Should I like him if he did? He stared in the rudest way, and just when I thought he had seen the elastic, he said, "There's something very taking about that face." I rebuked him on the spot. I don't approve of boys being taken by faces.'

'Other than your own. I shouldn't be in the least surprised if the Hawley Boy immediately went to call.'

'I forbade him. Let her be satisfied with The Dancing Master, and his wife when she comes up. I'm rather curious to see Mrs Bent and the Delville woman together.'

Mrs Hauksbee departed and, at the end of an hour, returned slightly flushed.

'There is no limit to the treachery of youth! I *ordered* the Hawley Boy, as he valued my patronage, not to call. The first person I stumble over – literally stumble over – in her poky, dark little drawing-room is, of course, the Hawley Boy. She kept us waiting ten minutes, and then emerged as though she had been tipped out of the dirty-clothes-basket. You know my way, dear, when I am at all put out. I was

Superior, *crrrrushingly* Superior! 'Lifted my eyes to Heaven, and had heard of nothing – 'dropped my eyes on the carpet and "really didn't know" – 'played with my card-case and "supposed so." The Hawley Boy giggled like a girl, and I had to freeze him with scowls between the sentences.'

'And she?'

'She sat in a heap on the edge of a couch, and managed to convey the impression that she was suffering from stomach-ache, at the very least. It was all I could do not to ask after her symptoms. When I rose, she grunted just like a buffalo in the water – too lazy to move.'

'Are you certain? –'

'Am I blind, Polly? Laziness, sheer laziness, nothing else – or her garments were only constructed for sitting down in. I stayed for a quarter of an hour trying to penetrate the gloom, to guess what her surroundings were like, while she stuck out her tongue.'

'Lu – *cy!*'

'Well – I'll withdraw the tongue, though I'm sure if she didn't do it when I was in the room, she did the minute I was outside. At any rate, she lay in a lump and grunted. Ask the Hawley Boy, dear. I believe the grunts were meant for sentences, but she spoke so indistinctly that I can't swear to it.'

'You are incorrigible, simply.'

'I am *not!* Treat me civilly, give me peace with honour, don't put the only available seat facing the window, and a child may eat jam in my lap before Church. But I resent being grunted at. Wouldn't you? Do you suppose that she communicates her views on life and love to The Dancing Master in a set of modulated "Grmphs"?'

'You attach too much importance to The Dancing Master.'

'He came as we went, and The Dowd grew almost cordial at the sight of him. He smiled greasily, and moved about that darkened dog-kennel in a suspiciously familiar way.'

'Don't be uncharitable. Any sin but that I'll forgive.'

'Listen to the voice of History. I am only describing what I saw. He entered, the heap on the sofa revived slightly, and the Hawley Boy and I came away together. *He* is disillusioned, but I felt it my duty to lecture him severely for going there. And that's all.'

'Now for Pity's sake leave the wretched creature and The Dancing Master alone. They never did you any harm.'

'No harm? To dress as an example and a stumbling-block for half Simla, and then to find this Person who is dressed by the hand of God – not that I wish to disparage *Him* for a moment, but you know the *tikka dhurzie* way He attires those lilies of the field – this Person draws the eyes of men – and some of them nice men? It's almost enough to make one discard clothing. I told the Hawley Boy so.'

'And what did that sweet youth do?'

'Turned shell-pink and looked across the far blue hills like a distressed cherub. *Am* I talking wildly, Polly? Let me say my say, and I shall be calm. Otherwise I may go abroad and disturb Simla with a few original reflections. Excepting always your own sweet self, there isn't a single woman in the land who understands me when I am – what's the word?'

'*Tête-fêlée,*' suggested Mrs Mallowe.

'Exactly! And now let us have tiffin. The demands of Society are exhausting, and as Mrs Delville says –' Here Mrs Hauksbee, to the horror of the *khitmatgars*, lapsed into a series of grunts, while Mrs Mallowe stared in lazy surprise.

'"God gie us a guid conceit of oorselves,"' said Mrs Hauksbee piously, returning to her natural speech. 'Now, in any other woman that would have been vulgar. I am consumed with curiosity to see Mrs Bent. I expect complications.'

'Woman of one idea,' said Mrs Mallowe shortly; 'all complications are as old as the hills! I have lived through or near all – *all* – ALL!'

'And yet do not understand that men and women never behave twice alike. I am old who was young – if ever I put my head in your lap, you dear, big sceptic, you will learn that my parting is gauze – but never, no never, have I lost my interest in men and women. Polly, I shall see this business out to the bitter end.'

'I am going to sleep,' said Mrs Mallowe calmly. 'I never interfere with men or women unless I am compelled,' and she retired with dignity to her own room.

Mrs Hauksbee's curiosity was not long left ungratified, for Mrs Bent came up to

Simla a few days after the conversation faithfully reported above, and pervaded the Mall by her husband's side.

'Behold!' said Mrs Hauksbee, thoughtfully rubbing her nose. 'That is the last link of the chain, if we omit the husband of the Delville, whoever he may be. Let me consider. The Bents and the Delvilles inhabit the same hotel; and the Delville is detested by the Waddy – do you know the Waddy? – who is almost as big a dowd. The Waddy also abominates the male Bent, for which, if her other sins do not weigh too heavily, she will eventually go to Heaven.'

'Don't be irreverent,' said Mrs Mallowe, 'I like Mrs Bent's face.'

'I am discussing the Waddy,' returned Mrs Hauksbee loftily. 'The Waddy will take the female Bent apart, after having borrowed – yes! – everything that she can, from hairpins to babies' bottles. Such, my dear, is life in a hotel. The Waddy will tell the female Bent facts and fictions about The Dancing Master and The Dowd.'

'Lucy, I should like you better if you were not always looking into people's back-bedrooms.'

'Anybody can look into their front drawing-rooms; and remember whatever I do, and whatever I look, I never talk – as the Waddy will. Let us hope that The Dancing Master's greasy smile and manner of the pedagogue will soften the heart of that cow, his wife. If mouths speak truth, I should think that little Mrs Bent could get very angry on occasion.'

'But what reason has she for being angry?'

'What reason! The Dancing Master in himself is a reason. How does it go? "If in his life some trivial errors fall, Look in his face and you'll believe them all." I am prepared to credit *any* evil of The Dancing Master, because I hate him so. And The Dowd is so disgustingly badly dressed –'

'That she, too, is capable of every iniquity? I always prefer to believe the best of everybody. It saves so much trouble.'

'Very good. I prefer to believe the worst. It saves useless expenditure of sympathy. And you may be quite certain that the Waddy believes with me.'

Mrs Mallowe sighed and made no answer.

The conversation was holden after dinner while Mrs Hauksbee was dressing for a dance.

'I am too tired to go,' pleaded Mrs Mallowe, and Mrs Hauksbee left her in peace till two in the morning, when she was aware of emphatic knocking at her door.

'Don't be *very* angry, dear,' said Mrs Hauksbee. 'My idiot of an *ayah* has gone home, and, as I hope to sleep tonight, there isn't a soul in the place to unlace me.'

'Oh, this is too bad!' said Mrs Mallowe sulkily.

''Cant help it. I'm a lone, lorn grass-widow, dear, but I will *not* sleep in my stays. And such news too! Oh, *do* unlace me, there's a darling! The Dowd – The Dancing Master – I and the Hawley Boy – You know the North verandah?'

'How can I do anything if you spin round like this?' protested Mrs Mallowe, fumbling with the knot of the laces.

'Oh, I forget. I must tell my tale without the aid of your eyes. Do you know you've lovely eyes, dear? Well, to begin with, I took the Hawley Boy to a *kala juggah*.'

'Did he want much taking?'

'Lots! There was an arrangement of looseboxes in *kanats*, and *she* was in the next one talking to *him*.'

'Which? How? Explain.'

'You know what I mean – The Dowd and The Dancing Master. We could hear every word, and we listened shamelessly – 'specially the Hawley Boy. Polly, I quite love that woman!'

'This is interesting. There! Now turn round. What happened?'

'One moment. Ah – h! Blessed relief. I've been looking forward to taking them off for the last half-hour – which is ominous at my time of life. But, as I was saying, we listened and heard The Dowd drawl worse than ever. She drops her final g's like a barmaid or a blue-blooded Aide-de-Camp. "Look he-ere, you're gettin' too fond o' me," she said, and The Dancing Master owned it was so in language that nearly made me ill. The Dowd reflected for a while. Then we heard her say, "Look he-ere, Mister Bent, why are you such an aw-ful liar?" I nearly exploded while The Dancing Master denied the charge. It seems that he never told her he was a married man.'

'I said he wouldn't.'

'And she had taken this to heart, on personal grounds, I suppose. She drawled along for five minutes, reproaching him with his perfidy, and grew quite motherly. "Now you've got a nice little wife of your own – you have," she said. "She's ten times too good for a fat old man like you, and, look he-ere, you never told me a word about her, and I've been thinkin' about it a good deal, and I think you're a liar." Wasn't that delicious? The Dancing Master maundered and raved till the Hawley Boy suggested that he should burst in and beat him. His voice runs up into an impassioned squeak when he is afraid. The Dowd must be an extraordinary woman. She explained that had he been a bachelor she might not have objected to his devotion; but since he was a married man and the father of a very nice baby, she considered him a hypocrite, and this she repeated twice. She wound up her drawl with: "An' I'm tellin' you this because your wife is angry with me, an' I hate quarrellin' with any other woman, an' I like your wife. You know how you have behaved for the last six weeks. You shouldn't have done it, indeed you shouldn't. You're too old an' too fat." Can't you imagine how The Dancing Master would wince at that! "Now go away," she said. "I don't want to tell you what I think of you, because I think you are not nice. I'll stay he-ere till the next dance begins." Did you think that the creature had so much in her?'

'I never studied her as closely as you did. It sounds unnatural. What happened?'

'The Dancing Master attempted blandishment, reproof, jocularity, and the style of the Lord High Warden, and I had almost to pinch the Hawley Boy to make him keep quiet. She grunted at the end of each sentence and, in the end, *he* went away swearing to himself, quite like a man in a novel. He looked more objectionable than ever. I laughed. I love that woman – in spite of her clothes. And now I'm going to bed. What do you think of it?'

'I shan't begin to think till the morning,' said Mrs Mallowe, yawning. 'Perhaps she spoke the truth. They do fly into it by accident sometimes.'

Mrs Hauksbee's account of her eavesdropping was an ornate one, but truthful in the main. For reasons best known to herself, Mrs 'Shady' Delville had turned upon Mr Bent and rent him limb from limb, casting him away limp and disconcerted ere she withdrew the light of her eyes from him permanently. Being a man of resource, and anything but pleased in that he had been called both old and fat, he gave Mrs

Bent to understand that he had, during her absence in the Doon, been the victim of unceasing persecution at the hands of Mrs Delville, and he told the tale so often and with such eloquence that he ended in believing it, while his wife marvelled at the manners and customs of 'some women.' When the situation showed signs of languishing, Mrs Waddy was always on hand to wake the smouldering fires of suspicion in Mrs Bent's bosom and to contribute generally to the peace and comfort of the hotel. Mr Bent's life was not a happy one, for if Mrs Waddy's story were true, he was, argued his wife, untrustworthy to the last degree. If his own statement was true, his charms of manner and conversation were so great that he needed constant surveillance. And he received it, till he repented genuinely of his marriage and neglected his personal appearance. Mrs Delville alone in the hotel was unchanged. She removed her chair some six paces towards the head of the table, and occasionally in the twilight ventured on timid overtures of friendship to Mrs Bent, which were repulsed.

'She does it for my sake,' hinted the virtuous Bent.

'A dangerous and designing woman,' purred Mrs Waddy.

Worst of all, every other hotel in Simla was full!

'Polly, are you afraid of diphtheria?'

'Of nothing in the world except small-pox. Diphtheria kills, but it doesn't disfigure. Why do you ask?'

'Because the Bent baby has got it, and the whole hotel is upside down in consequence. The Waddy has "set her five young on the rail" and fled. The Dancing Master fears for his precious throat, and that miserable little woman, his wife, has no notion of what ought to be done. She wanted to put it into a mustard bath – for croup!'

'Where did you learn all this?'

'Just now, on the Mall. Dr Howlen told me. The manager of the hotel is abusing the Bents, and the Bents are abusing the manager. They *are* a feckless couple.'

'Well. What's on your mind?'

'This; and I know it's a grave thing to ask. Would you seriously object to my bringing the child over here, with its mother?'

'On the most strict understanding that we see nothing of The Dancing Master.'

'He will be only too glad to stay away. Polly, you're an angel. The woman really is at her wits' end.

'And you know nothing about her, careless, and would hold her up to public scorn if it gave you a minute's amusement. Therefore you risk your life for the sake of her brat. No, Loo, *I'm* not the angel. I shall keep to my rooms and avoid her. But do as you please – only tell me why you do it.'

Mrs Hauksbee's eyes softened; she looked out of the window and back into Mrs Mallowe's face.

'I don't know,' said Mrs Hauksbee simply.

'You dear!'

'Polly! – and for aught you knew you might have taken my fringe off. Never do that again without warning. Now we'll get the rooms ready. I don't suppose I shall be allowed to circulate in society for a month.'

'And I also. Thank goodness I shall at last get all the sleep I want.'

Much to Mrs Bent's surprise she and the baby were brought over to the house almost before she knew where she was. Bent was devoutly and undisguisedly thankful, for he was afraid of the infection, and also hoped that a few weeks in the hotel alone with Mrs Delville might lead to explanations. Mrs Bent had thrown her jealousy to the winds in her fear for her child's life.

'We can give you good milk,' said Mrs Hauksbee to her, 'and our house is much nearer to the Doctor's than the hotel, and you won't feel as though you were living in a hostile camp. Where is the dear Mrs Waddy? She seemed to be a particular friend of yours.'

'They've all left me,' said Mrs Bent bitterly. 'Mrs Waddy went first. She said I ought to be ashamed of myself for introducing diseases there, and I am *sure* it wasn't my fault that little Dora –'

'How nice!' cooed Mrs Hauksbee. 'The Waddy is an infectious disease herself – "more quickly caught than the plague and the taker runs presently mad." I lived next door to her at the Elysium, three years ago. Now see, you won't give us the *least* trouble, and I've ornamented all the house with sheets soaked in carbolic. It smells comforting, doesn't it? Remember I'm always in call, and my *ayah's* at your service when yours goes to her meals, and – and – if you cry I'll *never* forgive you.'

Dora Bent occupied her mother's unprofitable attention through the day and the night. The Doctor called thrice in the twenty-four hours, and the house reeked with the smell of the Condy's Fluid, chlorine-water, and carbolic acid washes. Mrs Mallowe kept to her own rooms – she considered that she had made sufficient concessions in the cause of humanity – and Mrs Hauksbee was more esteemed by the Doctor as a help in the sick-room than the half-distraught mother.

'I know nothing of illness,' said Mrs Hauksbee to the Doctor. 'Only tell me what to do, and I'll do it.'

'Keep that crazy woman from kissing the child, and let her have as little to do with the nursing as you possibly can,' said the Doctor; 'I'd turn her out of the sick-room, but that I honestly believe she'd die of anxiety. She is less than no good, and I depend on you and the *ayahs*, remember.'

Mrs Hauksbee accepted the responsibility, though it painted olive hollows under her eyes and forced her to her oldest dresses. Mrs Bent clung to her with more than childlike faith.

'I *know* you'll make Dora well, won't you?' she said at least twenty times a day; and twenty times a day Mrs Hauksbee answered valiantly, 'Of course I will.'

But Dora did not improve, and the Doctor seemed to be always in the house.

'There's some danger of the thing taking a bad turn,' he said; 'I'll come over between three and four in the morning tomorrow.'

'Good gracious!' said Mrs Hauksbee. 'He never told me what the turn would be! My education has been horribly neglected; and I have only this foolish mother-woman to fall back upon.'

The night wore through slowly, and Mrs Hauksbee dozed in a chair by the fire. There was a dance at the Viceregal Lodge, and she dreamed of it till she was aware of Mrs Bent's anxious eyes staring into her own.

'Wake up! Wake up! Do something!' cried Mrs Bent piteously. 'Dora's choking to death! Do you mean to let her die?'

Mrs Hauksbee jumped to her feet and bent over the bed. The child was fighting for breath, while the mother wrung her hands despairingly.

'Oh, what can I do? What can you do? She won't stay still! I can't hold her. Why didn't the Doctor say this was coming?' screamed Mrs Bent. '*Won't* you help me? She's dying!'

'I – I've never seen a child die before!' stammered Mrs Hauksbee feebly, and then – let none blame her weakness after the strain of long watching – she broke down, and covered her face with her hands. The *ayahs* on the threshold snored peacefully.

There was a rattle of 'rickshaw wheels below, the clash of an opening door, a heavy step on the stairs, and Mrs Delville entered to find Mrs Bent screaming for the Doctor as she ran round the room. Mrs Hauksbee, her hands to her ears, and her face buried in the chintz of a chair, was quivering with pain at each cry from the bed, and murmuring, 'Thank God, I never bore a child! Oh! thank God, I never bore a child!'

Mrs Delville looked at the bed for an instant, took Mrs Bent by the shoulders, and said quietly, 'Get me some caustic. Be quick.'

The mother obeyed mechanically. Mrs Delville had thrown herself down by the side of the child and was opening its mouth.

'Oh, you're killing her!' cried Mrs Bent. 'Where's the Doctor? Leave her alone!'

Mrs Delville made no reply for a minute, but busied herself with the child.

'Now the caustic, and hold a lamp behind my shoulder. *Will* you do as you are told? The acid-bottle, if you don't know what I mean,' she said.

A second time Mrs Delville bent over the child. Mrs Hauksbee, her face still hidden, sobbed and shivered. One of the *ayahs* staggered sleepily into the room, yawning: '*Doctor Sahib* come.'

Mrs Delville turned her head.

'You're only just in time,' she said. 'It was chokin' her when I came, an' I've burnt it.'

'There was no sign of the membrane getting to the air-passages after the last steaming. It was the general weakness I feared,' said the Doctor half to himself, and he whispered as he looked, 'You've done what I should have been afraid to do without consultation.'

'She was dyin',' said Mrs Delville, under her breath. 'Can you do anythin'? What a mercy it was I went to the dance!'

Mrs Hauksbee raised her head.

'Is it all over?' she gasped. 'I'm useless – I'm worse than useless! What are *you* doing here?'

She stared at Mrs Delville, and Mrs Bent, realising for the first time who was the Goddess from the Machine, stared also.

Then Mrs Delville made explanation, putting on a dirty long glove and smoothing a crumpled and ill-fitting ball-dress.

'I was at the dance, an' the Doctor was tellin' me about your baby bein' so ill. So I came away early, an' your door was open, an' I – I – lost my boy this way six months ago, an' I've been tryin' to forget it ever since, an' I – I – I am very sorry for intrudin' an' anythin' that has happened.'

Mrs Bent was putting out the Doctor's eye with a lamp as he stopped over Dora.

'Take it away,' said the Doctor. 'I think the child will do, thanks to you, Mrs Delville. I should have come too late, but, I assure you' – he was addressing himself to Mrs Delville – 'I had not the faintest reason to expect *this*. The membrane must have grown like a mushroom. Will one of you help me, please?'

He had reason for the last sentence. Mrs Hauksbee had thrown herself into Mrs Delville's arms, where she was weeping bitterly, and Mrs Bent was unpicturesquely mixed up with both, while from the tangle came the sound of many sobs and much promiscuous kissing.

'Good gracious! I've spoilt all your beautiful roses!' said Mrs Hauksbee, lifting her head from the lump of crushed gum and calico atrocities on Mrs Delville's shoulder and hurrying to the Doctor.

Mrs Delville picked up her shawl, and slouched out of the room, mopping her eyes with the glove that she had not put on.

'I always said she was more than a woman,' sobbed Mrs Hauksbee hysterically, 'and *that* proves it!'

Six weeks later Mrs Bent and Dora had returned to the hotel. Mrs Hauksbee had come out of the Valley of Humiliation, had ceased to reproach herself for her collapse in an hour of need, and was even beginning to direct the affairs of the world as before.

'So nobody died, and everything went off as it should, and I kissed The Dowd, Polly. I feel so old. Does it show in my face?'

'Kisses don't as a rule, do they? Of course you know what the result of The Dowd's providential arrival has been.'

'They ought to build her a statue – only no sculptor dare copy those skirts.'

'Ah!' said Mrs Mallowe quietly. 'She has found another reward. The Dancing Master has been smirking through Simla, giving everyone to understand that she came because of her undying love for him – for him – to save *his* child, and all Simla naturally believes this.'

'But Mrs Bent –'

'Mrs Bent believes it more than anyone else. She won't speak to The Dowd now. *Isn't* The Dancing Master an angel?'

Mrs Hauksbee lifted up her voice and raged till bed-time. The doors of the two rooms stood open.

'Polly,' said a voice from the darkness, 'what did that American-heiress-globe-trotter girl say last season when she was tipped out of her 'rickshaw turning a corner? Some absurd adjective that made the man who picked her up explode.'

'"Paltry,"' said Mrs Mallowe. 'Through her nose – like this – "Ha-ow pahltry!"'

'Exactly,' said the voice. 'Ha-ow pahltry it all is!'

'Which?'

'Everything. Babies, Diphtheria, Mrs Bent and The Dancing Master, I whooping in a chair, and The Dowd dropping in from the clouds. I wonder what the motive was – *all* the motives.'

'Um!'

'What do *you* think?'

'Don't ask me. Go to sleep.'

Only a Subaltern

. . . Not only to enforce by command, but to encourage by example the energetic discharge of duty and the steady endurance of the difficulties and privations inseparable from Military Service.

Bengal Army Regulations

They made Bobby Wick pass an examination at Sandhurst. He was a gentleman before he was gazetted, so when the Empress announced that 'Gentleman-Cadet Robert Hanna Wick' was posted as Second Lieutenant to the Tyneside Tail Twisters at Krab Bokhar, he became an officer *and* a gentleman, which is an enviable thing; and there was joy in the house of Wick where Mamma Wick and all the little Wicks fell upon their knees and offered incense to Bobby by virtue of his achievements.

Papa Wick had been a Commissioner in his day, holding authority over three millions of men in the Chota-Buldana Division, building great works for the good of the land, and doing his best to make two blades of grass grow where there was but one before. Of course, nobody knew anything about this in the little English village where he was just 'old Mr Wick,' and had forgotten that he was a Companion of the Order of the Star of India.

He patted Bobby on the shoulder and said: 'Well done, my boy!'

There followed, while the uniform was being prepared, an interval of pure delight, during which Bobby took brevet-rank as a 'man' at the women-swamped tennis-parties and tea-fights of the village, and, I daresay, had his joining-time been extended, would have fallen in love with several girls at once. Little country villages at Home are very full of nice girls, because all the young men come out to India to make their fortunes.

'India,' said Papa Wick, 'is the place. I've had thirty years of it and, begad, I'd like to go back again. When you join the Tail Twisters you'll be among friends, if everyone hasn't forgotten Wick of Chota-Buldana, and a lot of people will be kind to you for our sakes. The mother will tell you more about outfit than I can; but remember this. Stick to your Regiment, Bobby – stick to your Regiment. You'll see men all round you going into the Staff Corps, and doing every possible sort of duty but regimental, and you may be tempted to follow suit. Now so long as you keep within your allowance, and I haven't stinted you there, stick to the Line, the whole Line, and nothing but the Line. Be careful how you back another young fool's bill, and if you fall in love with a woman twenty years older than yourself, don't tell *me* about it, that's all.'

With these counsels, and many others equally valuable, did Papa Wick fortify Bobby ere that last awful night at Portsmouth when the Officers' Quarters held more inmates than were provided for by the Regulations, and the liberty-men of the ships fell foul of the drafts for India, and the battle raged from the Dockyard Gates even to the slums of Longport, while the drabs of Fratton came down and scratched the faces of the Queen's Officers.

Bobby Wick, with an ugly bruise on his freckled nose, a sick and shaky detachment to manœuvre inship, and the comfort of fifty scornful females to attend to, had no time to feel home-sick till the *Malabar* reached mid-Channel, when he doubled his emotions with a little guard-visiting and a great many other matters.

The Tail Twisters were a most particular Regiment. Those who knew them least said that they were eaten up with 'side.' But their reserve and their internal arrangements generally were merely protective diplomacy. Some five years before, the Colonel commanding had looked into the fourteen fearless eyes of seven plump and juicy subalterns who had all applied to enter the Staff Corps, and had asked them why the three stars should he, a colonel of the Line, command a dashed nursery for double-dashed bottle-suckers who put on condemned tin spurs and rode qualified mokes at the hiatused heads of forsaken Black Regiments. He was a rude man and a terrible. Wherefore the remnant took measures [with the half-butt as an engine of public opinion] till the rumour went abroad that young men who used the Tail Twisters as a crutch to the Staff Corps had many and varied trials to endure. However, a regiment had just as much right to its own secrets as a woman.

When Bobby came up from Deolali and took his place among the Tail Twisters, it was gently but firmly borne in upon him that the Regiment was his father and his mother and his indissolubly wedded wife, and that there was no crime under the canopy of heaven blacker than that of bringing shame on the Regiment, which was the best-shooting, best-drilled, best-set-up, bravest, most illustrious, and in all respects most desirable Regiment within the compass of the Seven Seas. He was taught the legends of the Mess Plate, from the great grinning Golden Gods that had come out of the Summer Palace in Pekin to the silver-mounted markhor-horn snuff-mull presented by the last C. O. [he who spake to the seven subalterns]. And every one of those legends told him of battles fought at long odds, without fear as without support; of hospitality catholic as an Arab's; of friendships deep as the sea and steady as the fighting-line; of honour won by hard roads for honour's sake; and of instant and unquestioning devotion to the Regiment – the Regiment that claims the lives of all and lives for ever.

More than once, too, he came officially into contact with the Regimental colours, which looked like the lining of a bricklayer's hat on the end of a chewed stick. Bobby did not kneel and worship them, because British subalterns are not constructed in that manner. Indeed, he condemned them for their weight at the very moment that they were filling with awe and other more noble sentiments.

But best of all was the occasion when he moved with the Tail Twisters in review order at the breaking of a November day. Allowing for duty-men and sick, the Regiment was one thousand and eighty strong, and Bobby belonged to them; for was he not a Subaltern of the Line – the whole Line, and nothing but the Line – as the tramp of two thousand one hundred and sixty sturdy ammunition boots attested? He would not have changed places with Deighton of the Horse Battery, whirling by in a pillar of cloud to a chorus of 'Strong right! Strong left!' or Hogan-Yale of the White Hussars, leading his squadron for all it was worth, with the price of horseshoes thrown in; or 'Tick' Boileau, trying to live up to his fierce blue and gold turban while the wasps of the Bengal Cavalry stretched to a gallop in the wake of the long, lollopping Walers of the White Hussars.

They fought through the clear cool day, and Bobby felt a little thrill run down his spine when he heard the *tinkle-tinkle-tinkle* of the empty cartridge-cases hopping from the breech-blocks after the roar of the volleys; for he knew that he should live to hear that sound in action. The review ended in a glorious chase across the plain – batteries thundering after cavalry to the huge disgust of the White Hussars, and the Tyneside Tail Twisters hunting a Sikh Regiment, till the lean lathy Singhs panted with exhaustion. Bobby was dusty and dripping long before noon, but his enthusiasm was merely focused – not diminished.

He returned to sit at the feet of Revere, his 'skipper,' that is to say, the Captain of his Company, and to be instructed in the dark art and mystery of managing men, which is a very large part of the Profession of Arms.

'If you haven't a taste that way,' said Revere between his puffs of his cheroot, 'you'll never be able to get the hang of it, but remember, Bobby, 't isn't the best drill, though drill is nearly everything, that hauls a Regiment through Hell and out on the other side. It's the man who knows how to handle men – goat-men, swine-men, dog-men, and so on.'

'Dormer, for instance,' said Bobby, 'I think he comes under the head of fool-men. He mopes like a sick owl.'

'That's where you make your mistake, my son. Dormer isn't a fool *yet*, but he's a dashed dirty soldier, and his room corporal makes fun of his socks before kit-inspection. Dormer, being two-thirds pure brute, goes into a corner and growls.'

'How do you know?' said Bobby admiringly.

'Because a Company commander has to know these things – because, if he does *not* know, he may have crime – ay, murder – brewing under his very nose and yet not see that it's there. Dormer is being badgered out of his mind – big as he is – and he hasn't intellect enough to resent it. He's taken to quiet boozing, and, Bobby, when the butt of a room goes on the drink, or takes to moping by himself, measures are necessary to pull him out of himself.'

'What measures? 'Man can't run round coddling his men for ever.'

'No. The men would precious soon show him that he was not wanted. You've got to –'

Here the Colour-Sergeant entered with some papers; Bobby reflected for a while as Revere looked through the Company forms.

'Does Dormer do anything, Sergeant?' Bobby asked with the air of one continuing an interrupted conversation.

'No, sir. Does 'is dooty like a hortomato,' said the Sergeant, who delighted in long words. 'A dirty soldier and 'e's under full stoppages for new kit. It's covered with scales, sir.'

'Scales? What scales?'

'Fish-scales, sir. 'E's always pokin' in the mud by the river an' a-cleanin' them *muchly*-fish with 'is thumbs.' Revere was still absorbed in the Company papers, and the Sergeant, who was sternly fond of Bobby, continued – ''E generally goes down there when 'e's got 'is skinful, beggin' your pardon, sir, an' they *do* say that the more lush – in-*he*-briated 'e is, the more fish 'e catches. They call 'im the Looney Fishmonger in the Comp'ny, sir.'

Revere signed the last paper and the Sergeant retreated.

'It's a filthy amusement,' sighed Bobby to himself. Then aloud to Revere: 'Are you really worried about Dormer?'

'A little. You see he's never mad enough to send to hospital, or drunk enough to run in, but at any minute he may flare up, brooding and sulking as he does. He resents any interest being shown in him, and the only time I took him out shooting he all but shot *me* by accident.'

'I fish,' said Bobby with a wry face. 'I hire a country-boat and go down the river from Thursday to Sunday, and the amiable Dormer goes with me – if you can spare us both.'

'You blazing young fool!' said Revere, but his heart was full of much more pleasant words.

Bobby, the Captain of a *dhoni*, with Private Dormer for mate, dropped down the river on Thursday morning – the Private at the bow, the Subaltern at the helm. The Private glared uneasily at the Subaltern, who respected the reserve of the Private.

After six hours, Dormer paced to the stern, saluted, and said – 'Beg y' pardon, sir, but *was* you ever on the Durh'm Canal?'

'No,' said Bobby Wick. 'Come and have some tiffin.'

They ate in silence. As the evening fell, Private Dormer broke forth, speaking to himself –

'Hi was on the Durh'm Canal, jes' such a night, come next week twelve month, a-trailin' *of* my toes in the water.' He smoked and said no more till bedtime.

The witchery of the dawn turned the gray river-reaches to purple, gold, and opal; and it was as though the lumbering *dhoni* crept across the splendours of a new heaven.

Private Dormer popped his head out of his blanket and gazed at the glory below and around.

'Well – damn – my eyes!' said Private Dormer in an awed whisper. 'This 'ere is like a bloomin' gallantry-show!' For the rest of the day he was dumb, but achieved an ensanguined filthiness through the cleaning of big fish.

The boat returned on Saturday evening. Dormer had been struggling with speech since noon. As the lines and luggage were being disembarked, he found tongue.

'Beg y' pardon, sir,' he said, 'but would you – would you min' shakin' 'ands with me, sir?'

'Of course not,' said Bobby, and he shook accordingly. Dormer returned to barracks and Bobby to mess.

'He wanted a little quiet and some fishing, I think,' said Bobby. 'My aunt, but he's a filthy sort of animal! Have you ever seen him clean "them *muchly*-fish with 'is thumbs"?'

'Anyhow,' said Revere three weeks later, 'he's doing his best to keep his things clean.'

When the spring died, Bobby joined in the general scramble for Hill leave, and to his surprise and delight secured three months.

'As good a boy as I want,' said Revere the admiring skipper.

'The best of the batch,' said the Adjutant to the Colonel. 'Keep back that young skrim-shanker Porkiss, sir, and let Revere make him sit up.'

So Bobby departed joyously to Simla Pahar with a tin box of gorgeous raiment.

''Son of Wick – old Wick of Chota-Buldana? Ask him to dinner, dear,' said the aged men.

'What a nice boy!' said the matrons and the maids.

'First-class place, Simla. Oh, ri – ipping!' said Bobby Wick, and ordered new white cord breeches on the strength of it.

'We're in a bad way,' wrote Revere to Bobby at the end of two months. 'Since you left, the Regiment has taken to fever and is fairly rotten with it – two hundred in hospital, about a hundred in cells – drinking to keep off fever – and the Companies on parade fifteen file strong at the outside. There's rather more sickness in the out-villages than I care for, but then I'm so blistered with prickly-heat that I'm ready to hang myself. What's the yarn about your mashing a Miss Haverley up there? Not serious, I hope? You're over-young to hang millstones round your neck, and the Colonel will turf you out of that in double-quick time if you attempt it.'

It was not the Colonel that brought Bobby out of Simla, but a much-more-to-be-respected Commandant. The sickness in the out-villages spread, the Bazar was put out of bounds, and then came the news that the Tail Twisters must go into camp. The message flashed to the Hill stations. – 'Cholera – Leave stopped – Officers recalled.' Alas for the white gloves in the neatly-soldered boxes, the rides and the dances and picnics that were to be, the loves half spoken, and the debts unpaid! Without demur and without question, fast as tonga could fly or pony gallop, back to their Regiments and their Batteries, as though they were hastening to their weddings, fled the subalterns.

Bobby received his orders on returning from a dance at Viceregal Lodge where he had – But only the Haverley girl knows what Bobby had said, or how many waltzes he had claimed for the next ball. Six in the morning saw Bobby at the Tonga Office in the drenching rain, the whirl of the last waltz still in his ears, and an intoxication due neither to wine nor waltzing in his brain.

'Good man!' shouted Deighton of the Horse Battery through the mist. 'What you raise dat tonga? I'm coming with you. Ow! But I've a head and a half. *I* didn't sit out all night. They say the Battery's awful bad,' and he hummed dolorously –

> Leave the what at the what's-its-name,
> Leave the flock without shelter,
> Leave the corpse uninterred,
> Leave the bride at the altar!

'My faith! It'll be more bally corpse than bride, though, this journey. Jump in, Bobby. Get on, *Coachwan!*'

On the Umballa platform waited a detachment of officers discussing the latest news from the stricken cantonment, and it was here that Bobby learned the real condition of the Tail Twisters.

'They went into camp,' said an elderly Major recalled from the whist-tables at Mussoorie to a sickly Native Regiment, 'they went into camp with two hundred and ten sick in carts. Two hundred and ten fever cases only, and the balance looking like so many ghosts with sore eyes. A Madras Regiment could have walked through 'em.'

'But they were as fit as be-damned when I left them!' said Bobby.

'Then you'd better make them as fit as be-damned when you rejoin,' said the Major brutally.

Bobby pressed his forehead against the rain-splashed window-pane as the train lumbered across the sodden Doab, and prayed for the health of the Tyneside Tail Twisters. Naini Tal had sent down her contingent with all speed; the lathering ponies of the Dalhousie Road staggered into Pathankot, taxed to the full stretch of their strength; while from cloudy Darjiling the Calcutta Mail whirled up the last straggler of the little army that was to fight a fight in which was neither medal nor honour for the winning, against an enemy none other than 'the sickness that destroyeth in the noonday.'

And as each man reported himself, he said: 'This is a bad business,' and went about his own forthwith, for every Regiment and Battery in the cantonment was under canvas, the sickness bearing them company.

Bobby fought his way through the rain to the Tail Twisters' temporary mess, and Revere could have fallen on the boy's neck for the joy of seeing that ugly, wholesome phiz once more.

'Keep 'em amused and interested,' said Revere. 'They went on the drink, poor fools, after the first two cases, and there was no improvement. Oh, it's good to have you back, Bobby! Porkiss is a – never mind.'

Deighton came over from the Artillery camp to attend a dreary mess dinner, and contributed to the general gloom by nearly weeping over the condition of his beloved Battery. Porkiss so far forgot himself as to insinuate that the presence of the offi-cers could do no earthly good, and that the best thing would be to send the entire Regiment into hospital and 'let the doctors look after them.' Porkiss was demoralised with fear, nor was his peace of mind restored when Revere said coldly: 'Oh! The sooner *you* go out the better, if that's your way of thinking. Any public school could send us fifty *good* men in your place, but it takes time, time, Porkiss, and money, and a certain amount of trouble, to make a Regiment. 'S'pose *you're* the person we go into camp for, eh?'

Whereupon Porkiss was overtaken with a great and chilly fear which a drenching in the rain did not allay, and, two days later, quitted this world for another where, men do fondly hope, allowances are made for the weaknesses of the flesh. The Regimental Sergeant-Major looked wearily across the Sergeants' Mess tent when the news was announced.

'There goes the worst of them,' he said. 'It'll take the best, and then, please God, it'll stop.' The Sergeants were silent till one said: 'It couldn't be *him*!' and all knew of whom Travis was thinking.

Bobby Wick stormed through the tents of his Company, rallying, rebuking, mildly, as is consistent with the Regulations, chaffing the faint-hearted; hailing the sound into the watery sunlight when there was a break in the weather, and bidding them be of good cheer for their trouble was nearly at an end; scuttling on his dun pony round the outskirts of the camp, and heading back men who, with the innate perversity of British soldiers, were always wandering into infected villages, or drinking deeply from rain-flooded marshes; comforting the panic-stricken with rude speech, and more than once tending the dying who had no friends – the men without 'townies'; organising, with banjos and burnt cork, Sing-songs which should allow the talent of the Regiment full play; and generally, as he explained, 'playing the giddy garden-goat all round.'

'You're worth half-a-dozen of us, Bobby,' said Revere in a moment of enthusiasm. 'How the devil do you keep it up?'

Bobby made no answer, but had Revere looked into the breast-pocket of his coat he might have seen there a sheaf of badly-written letters which perhaps accounted for the power that possessed the boy. A letter came to Bobby every other day. The spelling was not above reproach, but the sentiments must have been most satisfactory, for on receipt Bobby's eyes softened marvellously, and he was wont to fall into a tender abstraction for a while ere, shaking his cropped head, he charged into his work.

By what power he drew after him the hearts of the roughest, and the Tail Twisters counted in their ranks some rough diamonds indeed, was a mystery to both skipper and C. O., who learned from the regimental chaplain that Bobby was considerably more in request in the hospital tents than the Reverend John Emery.

'The men seem fond of you. Are you in the hospitals much?' said the Colonel, who did his daily round and ordered the men to get well with a hardness that did not cover his bitter grief.

'A little, sir,' said Bobby.

''Shouldn't go there too often if I were you. They say it's not contagious, but there's no use in running unnecessary risks. We can't afford to have you down, y'know.'

Six days later, it was with the utmost difficulty that the post-runner splashed his way out to the camp with the mail-bags, for the rain was falling in torrents. Bobby received a letter, bore it off to his tent, and, the programme for the next week's Sing-song being satisfactorily disposed of, sat down to answer it. For an hour the unhandy pen toiled over the paper, and where sentiment rose to more than normal tide-level, Bobby Wick stuck out his tongue and breathed heavily. He was not used to letter-writing.

'Beg y' pardon, sir,' said a voice at the tent door; 'but Dormer's 'orrid bad, sir, an' they've taken him orf, sir.'

'Damn Private Dormer and you too!' said Bobby Wick, running the blotter over the half-finished letter. 'Tell him I'll come in the morning.'

''E's awful bad, sir,' said the voice hesitatingly. There was an undecided squelching of heavy boots.

'Well?' said Bobby impatiently.

'Excusin' 'imself before' and for takin' the liberty, 'e says it would be a comfort for to assist 'im, sir, if –'

'*Tattoo lao!* Get my pony! Here, come in out of the rain till I'm ready. What blasted nuisances you are! That's brandy. Drink some; you want it. Hang on to my stirrup and tell me if I go too fast.'

Strengthened by a four-finger 'nip' which he swallowed without a wink, the Hospital Orderly kept up with the slipping, mud-stained, and very disgusted pony as it shambled to the hospital tent.

Private Dormer was certainly ''orrid bad.' He had all but reached the stage of collapse and was not pleasant to look upon.

'What's this, Dormer?' said Bobby, bending over the man. 'You're not going out this time. You've got to come fishing with me once or twice more yet.'

The blue lips parted and in the ghost of a whisper said, – 'Beg y' pardon, sir, disturbin' of you now, but would you min' 'oldin' my 'and, sir?'

Bobby sat on the side of the bed, and the icy cold hand closed on his own like a vice, forcing a lady's ring which was on the little finger deep into the flesh. Bobby set his lips and waited, the water dripping from the hem of his trousers. An hour passed and the grasp of the hand did not relax, nor did the expression of the drawn face change. Bobby with infinite craft lit himself a cheroot with the left hand, his right arm was numbed to the elbow, and resigned himself to a night of pain.

Dawn showed a very white-faced Subaltern sitting on the side of a sick man's cot, and a Doctor in the doorway using language unfit for publication.

'Have you been here all night, you young ass?' said the Doctor.

'There or thereabouts,' said Bobby ruefully. 'He's frozen on to me.'

Dormer's mouth shut with a click. He turned his head and sighed. The clinging hand opened, and Bobby's arm fell useless at his side.

'He'll do,' said the Doctor quietly. 'It must have been a toss-up all through the night. 'Think you're to be congratulated on this case.'

'Oh, bosh!' said Bobby. 'I thought the man had gone out long ago – only – only I didn't care to take my hand away. Rub my arm down, there's a good chap. What a grip the brute has! I'm chilled to the marrow!' He passed out of the tent shivering.

Private Dormer was allowed to celebrate his repulse of Death by strong waters. Four days later he sat on the side of his cot and said to the patients mildly: 'I'd 'a' liken to 'a' spoken to 'im – so I should.'

But at that time Bobby was reading yet another letter – he had the most persistent correspondent of any man in camp – and was even then about to write that the sickness had abated, and in another week at the outside would be gone. He did not intend to say that the chill of a sick man's hand seemed to have struck into the heart whose capacities for affection he dwelt on at such length. He did intend to enclose the illustrated programme of the forthcoming Sing-song whereof he was not a little proud. He also intended to write on many other matters which do not concern us, and doubtless would have done so but for the slight feverish headache which made him dull and unresponsive at mess.

'You are overdoing it, Bobby,' said his skipper. 'Might give the rest of us credit of doing a little work. You go on as if you were the whole Mess rolled into one. Take it easy.'

'I will,' said Bobby. 'I'm feeling done up, somehow.' Revere looked at him anxiously and said nothing.

There was a flickering of lanterns about the camp that night, and a rumour that brought men out of their cots to the tent doors, a paddling of the naked feet of doolie-bearers and the rush of a galloping horse.

'Wot's up?' asked twenty tents; and through twenty tents ran the answer – 'Wick, 'e's down.'

They brought the news to Revere and he groaned. 'Any one but Bobby and I shouldn't have cared! The Sergeant-Major was right.'

'Not going out this journey,' gasped Bobby, as he was lifted from the doolie. 'Not going out this journey.' Then with an air of supreme conviction – 'I *can't*, you see.'

'Not if I can do anything!' says the Surgeon-Major, who had hastened over from the mess where he had been dining.

He and the Regimental Surgeon fought together with Death for the life of Bobby Wick. Their work was interrupted by a hairy apparition in a blue-gray dressing-gown who stared in horror at the bed and cried – 'Oh, my Gawd! It can't be '*im*!' until an indignant Hospital Orderly whisked him away.

If care of man and desire to live could have done aught, Bobby would have been saved. As it was, he made a fight of three days, and the Surgeon-Major's brow uncreased. 'We'll save him yet,' he said; and the Surgeon, who, though he ranked with the Captain, had a very youthful heart, went out upon the word and pranced joyously in the mud.

'Not going out this journey,' whispered Bobby Wick gallantly, at the end of the third day.

'Bravo!' said the Surgeon-Major. 'That's the way to look at it, Bobby.'

As evening fell a gray shade gathered round Bobby's mouth, and he turned his face to the tent wall wearily. The Surgeon-Major frowned.

'I'm awfully tired,' said Bobby, very faintly. 'What's the use of bothering me with medicine? I – don't – want – it. Let me alone.'

The desire for life had departed, and Bobby was content to drift away on the easy tide of Death.

'It's no good,' said the Surgeon-Major. 'He doesn't want to live. He's meeting it, poor child.' And he blew his nose.

Half a mile away the regimental band was playing the overture to the Sing-song, for the men had been told that Bobby was out of danger. The clash of the brass and the wail of the horns reached Bobby's ears.

> Is there a single joy or pain,
> That I should never kno – ow?
> You do not love me, 'tis in vain,
> Bid me goodbye and go!

An expression of hopeless irritation crossed the boy's face, and he tried to shake his head.

The Surgeon-Major bent down – 'What is it, Bobby?' – 'Not that waltz,' muttered Bobby. 'That's our own – our very ownest own . . . Mummy dear.'

With this he sank into the stupor that gave place to death early next morning.

Revere, his eyes red at the rims and his nose very white, went into Bobby's tent to write a letter to Papa Wick which should bow the white head of the ex-Commissioner of Chota-Buldana in the keenest sorrow of his life. Bobby's little store of papers lay in confusion on the table, and among them a half-finished letter. The last sentence ran: 'So you see, darling, there is really no fear, because as long as I know you care for me and I care for you, nothing can touch me.'

Revere stayed in the tent for an hour. When he came out his eyes were redder than ever.

Private Conklin sat on a turned-down bucket, and listened to a not unfamiliar tune. Private Conklin was a convalescent and should have been tenderly treated.

'Ho!' said Private Conklin. 'There's another bloomin' orf'cer da – ed.'

The bucket shot from under him, and his eyes filled with a smithyful of sparks. A tall man in a blue-gray bedgown was regarding him with deep disfavour.

'You ought to take shame for yourself, Conky! Orf'cer? – Bloomin' orf'cer? I'll learn you to misname the likes of 'im. Hangel! *Bloomin'* Hangel! That's wot 'e is!'

And the Hospital Orderly was so satisfied with the justice of the punishment that he did not even order Private Dormer back to his cot.

THE PHANTOM 'RICKSHAW

May no ill dreams disturb my rest,
Nor Powers of Darkness me molest.
Evening Hymn

One of the few advantages that India has over England is a great Knowability. After five years' service a man is directly or indirectly acquainted with the two or three hundred Civilians in his Province, all the Messes of ten or twelve Regiments and Batteries, and some fifteen hundred other people of the non-official caste. In ten years his knowledge should be doubled, and at the end of twenty he knows, or knows something about, every Englishman in the Empire, and may travel anywhere and everywhere without paying hotel bills.

Globe-trotters who expect entertainment as a right, have, even within my memory, blunted this open-heartedness, but none the less today, if you belong to the Inner Circle and are neither a Bear nor a Black Sheep, all houses are open to you, and our small world is very, very kind and helpful.

Rickett of Kamartha stayed with Polder of Kumaon some fifteen years ago. He meant to stay two nights, but was knocked down by rheumatic fever, and for six weeks disorganised Polder's establishment, stopped Polder's work, and nearly died in Polder's bedroom. Polder behaves as though he had been placed under eternal obligation by Rickett, and yearly sends the little Ricketts a box of presents and toys. It is the same everywhere. The men who do not take the trouble to conceal from you their opinion that you are an incompetent ass, and the women who blacken your character and misunderstand your wife's amusements, will work themselves to the bone in your behalf if you fall sick or into serious trouble.

Heatherlegh, the Doctor, kept, in addition to his regular practice, a hospital on his private account – an arrangement of loose boxes for Incurables, his friend called it – but it was really a sort of fitting-up shed for craft that had been damaged by stress of weather. The weather in India is often sultry, and since the tale of bricks is always a fixed quantity, and the only liberty allowed is permission to work overtime and get no thanks, men occasionally break down and become as mixed as the metaphors in this sentence.

Heatherlegh is the dearest doctor that ever was, and his invariable prescription to all his patients is, 'Lie low, go slow, and keep cool.' He says that more men are killed by overwork than the importance of this world justifies. He maintains that overwork slew Pansay, who died under his hands about three years ago. He has, of course, the right to speak authoritatively, and he laughs at my theory that there was a crack in Pansay's head and a little bit of the Dark World came through and pressed him to death. 'Pansay went off the handle,' says Heatherlegh, 'after the stimulus of long leave at Home. He may or he may not have behaved like a blackguard to Mrs Keith-Wessington. My notion is that the work of the Katabundi Settlement ran him off his legs, and that he took to brooding and making much of an ordinary P. & O. flirtation. He certainly was engaged to Miss Mannering, and she certainly broke off the engagement. Then he took a feverish chill and all that nonsense about ghosts developed. Overwork started his illness, kept it alight, and killed him, poor devil. Write him off to the System that uses one man to do the work of two and a half men.'

I do not believe this. I used to sit up with Pansay sometimes when Heatherlegh was called out to patients and I happened to be within claim. The man would make me most unhappy by describing, in a low, even voice, the procession that was always passing at the bottom of his bed. He had a sick man's command of language. When he recovered I suggested that he should write out the whole affair from beginning to end, knowing that ink might assist him to ease his mind.

He was in a high fever while he was writing, and the blood-and-thunder Magazine diction he adopted did not calm him. Two months afterwards he was reported fit for duty, but, in spite of the fact that he was urgently needed to help an undermanned Commission stagger through a deficit, he preferred to die; vowing at the last that he was hag-ridden. I got his manuscript before he died, and this is his version of the affair, dated 1885, exactly as he wrote it: –

My doctor tells me that I need rest and change of air. It is not improbable that I shall get both ere long – rest that neither the red-coated messenger nor the midday gun can break, and change of air far beyond that which any homeward-bound steamer can give me. In the meantime I am resolved to stay where I am; and, in flat defiance of my doctor's orders, to take all the world into my confidence. You shall learn for yourselves the precise nature of my malady, and shall, too, judge for yourselves whether any man born of woman on this weary earth was ever so tormented as I.

Speaking now as a condemned criminal might speak ere the drop-bolts are drawn, my story, wild and hideously improbable as it may appear, demands at least attention. That it will ever receive credence I utterly disbelieve. Two months ago I should have scouted as mad or drunk the man who had dared tell me the like. Two months ago I was the happiest man in India. Today, from Peshawar to the sea, there is no one more wretched. My doctor and I are the only two who know this. His explanation is, that my brain, digestion, and eyesight are all slightly affected; giving rise to my frequent and persistent 'delusions.' Delusions, indeed! I call him a fool; but he attends me still with the same unwearied smile, the same bland professional manner, the same neatly-trimmed red whiskers, till I begin to suspect that I am an ungrateful, evil-tempered invalid. But you shall judge for yourselves.

Three years ago it was my fortune – my great misfortune – to sail from Gravesend to Bombay, on return from long leave, with one Agnes Keith-Wessington, wife of an officer on the Bombay side. It does not in the least concern you to know what manner of woman she was. Be content with the knowledge that, ere the voyage had ended, both she and I were desperately and unreasoningly in love with one another.

Heaven knows that I can make the admission now without one particle of vanity. In matters of this sort there is always one who gives and another who accepts. From the first day of our ill-omened attachment, I was conscious that Agnes's passion was a stronger, a more dominant, and – if I may use the expression – a purer sentiment than mine. Whether she recognised the fact then, I do not know. Afterwards it was bitterly plain to both of us.

Arrived at Bombay in the spring of the year, we went our respective ways, to meet no more for the next three or four months, when my leave and her love took us both to Simla. There we spent the season together; and there my fire of straw burnt itself out to a pitiful end with the closing year. I attempt no excuse. I make no apology. Mrs Wessington had given up much for my sake, and was prepared to give up all. From my own lips, in August 1882, she learnt that I was sick of her presence, tired of her company, and weary of the sound of her voice. Ninety-nine women out of a hundred would have wearied of me as I wearied of them; seventy-five of that number would have promptly avenged themselves by active and obtrusive flirtation with other men. Mrs Wessington was the hundredth. On her neither my openly-expressed aversion nor the cutting brutalities with which I garnished our interviews had the least effect.

'Jack, darling!' was her one eternal cuckoo cry: 'I'm sure it's all a mistake – a hideous mistake; and we'll be good friends again some day. *Please* forgive me, Jack, dear.'

I was the offender, and I knew it. That knowledge transformed my pity into passive endurance and, eventually, into blind hate – the same instinct, I suppose, which prompts a man to savagely stamp on the spider he has but half killed. And with this hate in my bosom the season of 1882 came to an end.

Next year we met again at Simla – she with her monotonous face and timid attempts at reconciliation, and I with loathing of her in every fibre of my frame. Several times I could not avoid meeting her alone; and on each occasion her words were identically the same. Still the unreasoning wail that it was all a 'mistake'; and still the hope of eventually 'making friends.' I might have seen, had I cared to look, that that hope only was keeping her alive. She grew more wan and thin month by month. You will agree with me, at least, that such conduct would have driven anyone to despair. It was uncalled for; childish; unwomanly. I maintain that she was much to blame. And again, sometimes, in the black, fever-stricken night-watches, I have begun to think that I might have been a little kinder to her. But that really *is* a 'delusion.' I could not have continued pretending to love her when I didn't; could I? It would have been unfair to us both.

Last year we met again – on the same terms as before. The same weary appeals, and the same curt answers from my lips. At least I would make her see how wholly wrong and hopeless were her attempts at resuming the old relationship. As the season wore on, we fell apart – that is to say, she found it difficult to meet me, for I had other and more absorbing interests to attend to. When I think it over quietly in my sick-room, the season of 1884 seems a confused nightmare wherein light and shade were fantastically intermingled: my courtship of little Kitty Mannering; my hopes, doubts, and fears; our long rides together; my trembling avowal of attachment; her reply; and now and again a vision of a white face flitting by in the 'rickshaw with the black and white liveries I once watched for so earnestly; the wave of Mrs Wessington's gloved hand; and, when she met me alone, which was but seldom, the irksome monotony of her appeal. I loved Kitty Mannering; honestly, heartily loved her, and with my love for her grew my hatred for Agnes. In August Kitty and I were engaged. The next day I met those accursed 'magpie' *jhampanies* at the back of Jakko, and, moved by some passing sentiment of pity, stopped to tell Mrs Wessington everything. She knew it already.

'So I hear you're engaged, Jack, dear.' Then, without a moment's pause: 'I'm sure it's all a mistake – a hideous mistake. We shall be as good friends some day, Jack, as we ever were.'

My answer might have made even a man wince. It cut the dying woman before me like the blow of a whip. 'Please forgive me, Jack; I didn't mean to make you angry; but it's true, it's true!'

And Mrs Wessington broke down completely. I turned away and left her to finish her journey in peace, feeling, but only for a moment or two, that I had been an utterably mean hound. I looked back, and saw that she had turned her 'rickshaw with the idea, I suppose, of overtaking me.

The scene and its surroundings were photographed on my memory. The rain-swept sky (we were at the end of the wet weather), the sodden, dingy pines, the muddy road, and the black powder-riven cliffs formed a gloomy background against which the black and white liveries of the *jhampanies*, the yellow-panelled 'rickshaw, and Mrs Wessington's down-bowed golden head stood out clearly. She was holding her handkerchief in her left hand and was leaning back exhausted against the 'rickshaw cushions. I turned my horse up a bypath near the Sanjowlie Reservoir and literally ran away. Once I fancied I heard a faint call of 'Jack!' This may have been imagination. I never stopped to verify it. Ten minutes later I came across Kitty on horseback; and, in the delight of a long ride with her, forgot all about the interview.

A week later Mrs Wessington died, and the inexpressible burden of her existence was removed from my life. I went Plainsward perfectly happy. Before three months were over I had forgotten all about her, except that at times the discovery of some of her old letters reminded me unpleasantly of our bygone relationship. By January I had disinterred what was left of our correspondence from among my scattered belongings and had burnt it. At the beginning of April of this year, 1885, I was at Simla – semi-deserted Simla – once more, and was deep in lover's talks and walks with Kitty. It was decided that we should be married at the end of June. You will understand, therefore, that, loving Kitty as I did, I am not saying too much when I pronounce myself to have been, at that time, the happiest man in India.

Fourteen delightful days passed almost before I noticed their flight. Then, aroused to the sense of what was proper among mortals circumstanced as we were, I pointed out to Kitty that an engagement ring was the outward and visible sign of her dignity as an engaged girl; and that she must forthwith come to Hamilton's to be measured for one. Up to that moment, I give you my word, we had completely forgotten so trivial a matter. To Hamilton's we accordingly went on the 15th of April 1885. Remember that – whatever my doctor may say to the contrary – I was then in perfect health, enjoying a well-balanced mind and an *absolutely* tranquil spirit. Kitty and I entered Hamilton's shop together, and there, regardless of the order of affairs, I measured Kitty for the ring in the presence of the amused assistant. The ring was a sapphire with two diamonds. We then rode out down the slope that leads to the Combermere Bridge and Peliti's shop.

While my Waler was cautiously feeling his way over the loose shale, and Kitty was laughing and chattering at my side, – while all Simla, that is to say as much of it as had then come from the Plains, was grouped round the Reading-room and Peliti's verandah, – I was aware that someone, apparently at a vast distance, was calling me by my Christian name. It struck me that I had heard the voice before, but when and where I could not at once determine. In the short space it took to cover the road between the path from Hamilton's shop and the first plank of the Combermere Bridge I had thought over half-a-dozen people who might have committed such a solecism, and had eventually decided that it must have been some singing in my ears. Immediately opposite Peliti's shop my eye was arrested by the sight of four *jhampanies* in 'magpie' livery, pulling a yellow-panelled, cheap, bazar 'rickshaw. In a moment my mind flew back to the previous season and Mrs Wessington with a sense of irritation and disgust. Was it not enough that the woman was dead and done with, without her black and white servitors reappearing to spoil the day's happiness? Whoever employed them now I thought I would call upon, and ask as a personal favour to change her *jhampanies*' livery. I would hire the men myself, and, if necessary, buy their coats from off their backs. It is impossible to say here what a flood of undesirable memories their presence evoked.

'Kitty,' I cried, 'there are poor Mrs Wessington's *jhampanies* turned up again! I wonder who has them now?'

Kitty had known Mrs Wessington slightly last season, and had always been interested in the sickly woman.

'What? Where?' she asked. 'I can't see them anywhere.'

Even as she spoke, her horse, swerving from a laden mule, threw himself directly in front of the advancing 'rickshaw. I had scarcely time to utter a word of warning when, to my unutterable horror, horse and rider passed *through* men and carriage as if they had been thin air.

'What's the matter?' cried Kitty; 'what made you call out so foolishly, Jack? If I *am* engaged I don't want all creation to know about it. There was lots of space between the mule and the verandah; and, if you think I can't ride – There!'

Whereupon wilful Kitty set off, her dainty little head in the air, at a hand-gallop

303

in the direction of the Band-stand; fully expecting, as she herself afterwards told me, that I should follow her. What was the matter? Nothing indeed. Either that I was mad or drunk, or that Simla was haunted with devils. I reined in my impatient cob, and turned round. The 'rickshaw had turned too, and now stood immediately facing me, near the left railing of the Combermere Bridge.

'Jack! Jack, darling!' (There was no mistake about the words this time: they rang through my brain as if they had been shouted in my ear.) 'It's some hideous mistake, I'm sure. *Please* forgive me, Jack, and let's be friends again.'

The 'rickshaw-hood had fallen back, and inside, as I hope and pray daily for the death I dread by night, sat Mrs Keith-Wessington, handkerchief in hand, and golden head bowed on her breast.

How long I stared motionless I do not know. Finally, I was aroused by my syce taking the Waler's bridle and asking whether I was ill. From the horrible to the commonplace is but a step. I tumbled off my horse and dashed, half fainting, into Peliti's for a glass of cherry-brandy. There two or three couples were gathered round the coffee-tables discussing the gossip of the day. Their trivialities were more comforting to me just then than the consolations of religion could have been. I plunged into the midst of the conversation at once; chatted, laughed, and jested with a face (when I caught a glimpse of it in a mirror) as white and drawn as that of a corpse. Three or four men noticed my condition; and, evidently setting it down to the results of over-many pegs, charitably endeavoured to draw me apart from the rest of the loungers. But I refused to be led away. I wanted the company of my kind – as a child rushes into the midst of the dinner-party after a fright in the dark. I must have talked for about ten minutes or so, though it seemed an eternity to me, when I heard Kitty's clear voice outside inquiring for me. In another minute she had entered the shop, prepared to upbraid me for failing so signally in my duties. Something in my face stopped her.

'Why, Jack,' she cried, 'what *have* you been doing? What *has* happened? Are you ill?' Thus driven into a direct lie, I said that the sun had been a little too much for me. It was close upon five o'clock of a cloudy April afternoon, and the sun had been hidden all day. I saw my mistake as soon as the words were out of my mouth; attempted to recover it; blundered hopelessly, and followed Kitty in a regal rage out of doors, amid the smiles of my acquaintances. I made some excuse (I have forgotten what) on the score of my feeling faint; and cantered away to my hotel, leaving Kitty to finish the ride by herself.

In my room I sat down and tried calmly to reason out the matter. Here was I, Theobald Jack Pansay, a well-educated Bengal Civilian in the year of grace 1885, presumably sane, certainly healthy, driven in terror from my sweetheart's side by the apparition of a woman who had been dead and buried eight months ago. These were facts that I could not blink. Nothing was farther from my thought than any memory of Mrs Wessington when Kitty and I left Hamilton's shop. Nothing was more utterly commonplace than the stretch of wall opposite Peliti's. It was broad daylight. The road was full of people; and yet here, look you, in defiance of every law of probability, in direct outrage of Nature's ordinance, there had appeared to me a face from the grave.

Kitty's Arab had gone *through* the 'rickshaw: so that my first hope that some woman marvellously like Mrs Wessington had hired the carriage and the coolies with their old livery was lost. Again and again I went round this treadmill of thought; and again and again gave up baffled and in despair. The voice was as inexplicable as the apparition. I had originally some wild notion of confiding it all to Kitty; of begging her to marry me at once, and in her arms defying the ghostly occupant of the 'rickshaw. 'After all,' I argued, 'the presence of the 'rickshaw is in itself enough to prove the existence of a spectral illusion. One may see ghosts of men and women, but surely never coolies and carriages. The whole thing is absurd. Fancy the ghost of a hillman!'

Next morning I sent a penitent note to Kitty, imploring her to overlook my strange conduct of the previous afternoon. My Divinity was still very wroth, and a personal apology was necessary. I explained, with a fluency born of night-long pondering over a falsehood, that I had been attacked with a sudden palpitation of the heart – the result of indigestion. This eminently practical solution had its effect; and Kitty and I rode out that afternoon with the shadow of my first lie dividing us.

Nothing would please her save a canter round Jakko. With my nerves still unstrung from the previous night I feebly protested against the notion, suggesting Observatory Hill, Jutogh, the Boileau-gunge road – anything rather than the Jakko round. Kitty was

305

angry and a little hurt; so I yielded from fear of provoking further misunderstanding, and we set out together towards Chota Simla. We walked a greater part of the way, and, according to our custom, cantered from a mile or so below the Convent to the stretch of level road by the Sanjowlie Reservoir. The wretched horses appeared to fly, and my heart beat quicker and quicker as we neared the crest of the ascent. My mind had been full of Mrs Wessington all the afternoon; and every inch of the Jakko road bore witness to our old-time walks and talks. The boulders were full of it; the pines sang it aloud overhead; the rain-fed torrents giggled and chuckled unseen over the shameful story; and the wind in my ears chanted the iniquity aloud.

As a fitting climax, in the middle of the level men call the Ladies' Mile the Horror was awaiting me. No other 'rickshaw was in sight – only the four black and white *jhampanies*, the yellow-panelled carriage, and the golden head of the woman within – all apparently just as I had left them eight months and one fortnight ago! For an instant I fancied that Kitty *must* see what I saw – we were so marvellously sympathetic in all things. Her next words undeceived me – 'Not a soul in sight! Come along, Jack, and I'll race you to the Reservoir buildings!' Her wiry little Arab was off like a bird, my Waler following close behind, and in this order we dashed under the cliffs. Half a minute brought us within fifty yards of the 'rickshaw. I pulled my Waler and fell back a little. The 'rickshaw was directly in the middle of the road; and once more the Arab passed through it, my horse following. 'Jack! Jack dear! *Please* forgive me,' rang with a wail in my ears, and, after an interval: 'It's all a mistake, a hideous mistake!'

I spurred my horse like a man possessed. When I turned my head at the Reservoir works the black and white liveries were still waiting – patiently waiting – under the gray hillside, and the wind brought me a mocking echo of the words I had just heard. Kitty bantered me a good deal on my silence throughout the remainder of the ride. I had been talking up till then wildly and at random. To save my life I could not speak afterwards naturally, and from Sanjowlie to the Church wisely held my tongue.

I was to dine with the Mannerings that night, and had barely time to canter home to dress. On the road to Elysium Hill I overheard two men talking together in the dusk. – 'It's a curious thing,' said one, 'how completely all trace of it disappeared. You know my wife was insanely fond of the woman ('never could see anything in her myself), and wanted me to pick up her old 'rickshaw and coolies if they were to be got for love or money. Morbid sort of fancy I call it; but I've got to do what the *Memsahib* tells me. Would you believe that the man she hired it from tells me that all four of the men – they were brothers – died of cholera on the way to Hardwar, poor devils; and the 'rickshaw has been broken up by the man himself. 'Told me he never used a dead *Memsahib's* 'rickshaw. 'Spoilt his luck. Queer notion, wasn't it? Fancy poor little Mrs Wessington spoiling anyone's luck except her own!' I laughed aloud at this point; and my laugh jarred on me as I uttered it. So there *were* ghosts of 'rickshaws after all, and ghostly employments in the other world! How much did Mrs Wessington give her men? What were their hours? Where did they go?

And for visible answer to my last question I saw the infernal Thing blocking my path in the twilight. The dead travel fast, and by short cuts unknown to ordinary coolies. I laughed aloud a second time and checked my laughter suddenly, for I was afraid I was going mad. Mad to a certain extent I must have been, for I recollect that I reined in my horse at the head of the 'rickshaw, and politely wished Mrs Wessington 'Good-evening.' Her answer was one I knew only too well. I listened to the end; and replied that I had heard it all before, but should be delighted if she had anything further to say. Some malignant devil stronger than I must have entered into me that evening, for I have a dim recollection of talking the commonplaces of the day for five minutes to the Thing in front of me.

'Mad as a hatter, poor devil – or drunk. Max, try and get him to come home.'

Surely *that* was not Mrs Wessington's voice! The two men had overheard me speaking to the empty air, and had returned to look after me. They were very kind and considerate, and from their words evidently gathered that I was extremely drunk. I thanked them confusedly and cantered away to my hotel, there changed, and arrived at the Mannerings' ten minutes late. I pleaded the darkness of the night as an excuse; was rebuked by Kitty for my unlover-like tardiness; and sat down.

The conversation had already become general and, under cover of it, I was addressing some tender small talk to my sweetheart when I was aware that at the farther end of the table a short, red-whiskered man was describing, with much broidery, his encounter with a mad unknown that evening.

A few sentences convinced me that he was repeating the incident of half an hour ago. In the middle of the story he looked round for applause, as professional story-tellers do, caught my eye, and straightaway collapsed. There was a moment's awkward silence, and the red-whiskered man muttered something to the effect that he had 'forgotten the rest,' thereby sacrificing a reputation as a good story-teller which he had built up for six seasons past. I blessed him from the bottom of my heart, and – went on with my fish.

In the fulness of time that dinner came to an end; and with genuine regret I tore myself away from Kitty – as certain as I was of my own existence that It would be waiting for me outside the door. The red-whiskered man, who had been introduced to me as Dr Heatherlegh of Simla, volunteered to bear me company as far as our roads lay together. I accepted his offer with gratitude.

My instinct had not deceived me. It lay in readiness in the Mall, and, in what seemed devilish mockery of our ways, with a lighted head-lamp. The red-whiskered man went to the point at once, in a manner that showed he had been thinking over it all dinner-time.

'I say, Pansay, what the deuce was the matter with you this evening on the Elysium Road?' The suddenness of the question wrenched an answer from me before I was aware.

'That!' said I, pointing to It.

'*That* may be either D. T. or Eyes for aught I know. Now you don't liquor. I saw as much at dinner, so it can't be D. T. There's nothing whatever where you're pointing, though you're sweating and trembling with fright like a scared pony. Therefore, I conclude that it's Eyes. And I ought to understand all about them. Come along home with me. I'm on the Blessington lower road.'

To my intense delight the 'rickshaw, instead of waiting for us kept about twenty yards ahead – and this, too, whether we walked, trotted, or cantered. In the course of that long night ride I had told my companion almost as much as I have told you here.

'Well, you've spoilt one of the best tales I've ever laid tongue to,' said he, 'but I'll forgive you for the sake of what you've gone through. Now come home and do what

I tell you; and when I've cured you, young man, let this be a lesson to you to steer clear of women and indigestible food till the day of your death.'

The 'rickshaw kept steady in front; and my red-whiskered friend seemed to derive great pleasure from my account of its exact whereabouts. 'Eyes, Pansay – all Eyes, Brain, and Stomach. And the greatest of these three is Stomach. You've too much conceited Brain, too little Stomach, and thoroughly unhealthy Eyes. Get your Stomach straight and the rest follows. And all that's French for a liver pill. I'll take sole medical charge of you from this hour! for you're too interesting a phenomenon to be passed over.'

By this time we were deep in the shadow of the Blessington lower road, and the 'rickshaw came to a dead stop under a pine-clad, overhanging shale cliff. Instinctively I halted too, giving my reason. Heatherlegh rapped out an oath.

'Now, if you think I'm going to spend a cold night on the hillside for the sake of a Stomach-*cum*-Brain-*cum*-Eye illusion – Lord, ha' mercy! What's that?'

There was a muffled report, a blinding smother of dust just in front of us, a crack, the noise of rent boughs, and about ten yards of the cliff-side – pines, undergrowth, and all – slid down into the road below, completely blocking it up. The uprooted trees swayed and tottered for a moment like drunken giants in the gloom, and then fell prone among their fellows with a thunderous crash. Our two horses stood motionless and sweating with fear. As soon as the rattle of falling earth and stone had subsided, my companion muttered: 'Man, if we'd gone forward we should have been ten feet deep in our graves by now. "There are more things in heaven and earth" . . . Come home, Pansay, and thank God. I want a peg badly.'

We retraced our way over the Church Ridge, and I arrived at Dr Heatherlegh's house shortly after midnight.

His attempts towards my cure commenced almost immediately, and for a week I never left his sight. Many a time in the course of that week did I bless the good-fortune which had thrown me in contact with Simla's best and kindest doctor. Day by day my spirits grew lighter and more equable. Day by day, too, I became more and more inclined to fall in with Heatherlegh's 'spectral illusion' theory, implicating eyes, brain, and stomach. I wrote to Kitty, telling her that a slight sprain caused by a fall from my horse kept me indoors for a few days; and that I should be recovered before she had time to regret my absence.

Heatherlegh's treatment was simple to a degree. It consisted of liver pills, cold-water baths, and strong exercise, taken in the dusk or at early dawn – for, as he sagely observed: 'A man with a sprained ankle doesn't walk a dozen miles a day, and your young woman might be wondering if she saw you.'

At the end of the week, after much examination of pupil and pulse, and strict injunctions as to diet and pedestrianism, Heatherlegh dismissed me as brusquely as he had taken charge of me. Here is his parting benediction: 'Man, I certify to your mental cure, and that's as much as to say I've cured most of your bodily ailments. Now, get your traps out of this as soon as you can; and be off to make love to Miss Kitty.'

I was endeavouring to express my thanks for his kindness. He cut me short.

'Don't think I did this because I like you. I gather that you've behaved like a blackguard all through. But, all the same, you're a phenomenon, and as queer a phenomenon as you are a blackguard. No!' – checking me a second time – 'not a rupee, please. Go out and see if you can find the eyes-brain-and-stomach business again. I'll give you a lakh for each time you see it.'

Half an hour later I was in the Mannerings' drawing-room with Kitty – drunk with the intoxication of present happiness and the foreknowledge that I should never more be troubled with Its hideous presence. Strong in the sense of my new found security, I proposed a ride at once; and, by preference, a canter round Jakko.

Never had I felt so well, so overladen with vitality and mere animal spirits, as I did on the afternoon of the 30th of April. Kitty was delighted at the change in my appearance, and complimented me on it in her delightfully frank and outspoken manner. We left the Mannerings' house together, laughing and talking, and cantered along the Chota Simla road as of old.

I was in haste to reach the Sanjowlie Reservoir and there make my assurance doubly sure. The horses did their best, but seemed all too slow to my impatient mind. Kitty was astonished at my boisterousness. 'Why, Jack!' she cried at last, 'you are behaving like a child. What are you doing?'

We were just below the Convent, and from sheer wantonness I was making my Waler plunge and curvet across the road as I tickled it with the loop of my riding-whip.

'Doing?' I answered; 'nothing, dear. That's just it. If you'd been doing nothing for a week except lie up, you'd be as riotous as I.

> 'Singing and murmuring in your feastful mirth,
> Joying to feel yourself alive;
> Lord over Nature, Lord of the visible Earth,
> Lord of the senses five.'

My quotation was hardly out of my lips before we had rounded the corner above the Convent, and a few yards farther on could see across to Sanjowlie. In the centre of the level road stood the black and white liveries, the yellow-panelled 'rickshaw, and Mrs Keith-Wessington. I pulled up, looked, rubbed my eyes, and, I believe, must have said something. The next thing I knew was that I was lying face downward on the road, with Kitty kneeling above me in tears.

'Has it gone, child!' I gasped. Kitty only wept more bitterly.

'Has what gone, Jack dear? what does it all mean? There must be a mistake somewhere, Jack. A hideous mistake.' Her last words brought me to my feet – mad – raving for the time being.

'Yes, there *is* a mistake somewhere,' I repeated, 'a hideous mistake. Come and look at It.'

I have an indistinct idea that I dragged Kitty by the wrist along the road up to where It stood, and implored her for pity's sake to speak to It; to tell It that we were betrothed; that neither Death nor Hell could break the tie between us: and Kitty only knows how much more to the same effect. Now and again I appealed passionately to the Terror in the 'rickshaw to bear witness to all I had said, and to release me from a torture that was killing me. As I talked I suppose I must have told Kitty of my old relations with Mrs Wessington, for I saw her listen intently with white face and blazing eyes.

'Thank you, Mr Pansay,' she said, 'that's *quite* enough. *Syce ghora láo.*'

The syces, impassive as Orientals always are, had come up with the recaptured horses; and as Kitty sprang into her saddle I caught hold of her bridle, entreating her to hear me out and forgive. My answer was the cut of her riding-whip across my face from mouth to eye, and a word or two of farewell that even now I cannot write down. So I judged, and judged rightly, that Kitty knew all; and I staggered back to the side of the 'rickshaw. My face was cut and bleeding, and the blow of the riding-whip had raised a livid blue wheal on it. I had no self-respect. Just then, Heatherlegh, who must have been following Kitty and me at a distance, cantered up.

'Doctor,' I said, pointing to my face, 'here's Miss Mannering's signature to my order of dismissal and – I'll thank you for that lakh as soon as convenient.'

Heatherlegh's face, even in my abject misery, moved me to laughter.

'I'll stake my professional reputation –' he began.

'Don't be a fool,' I whispered. 'I've lost my life's happiness and you'd better take me home.'

As I spoke the 'rickshaw was gone. Then I lost all knowledge of what was passing. The crest of Jakko seemed to heave and roll like the crest of a cloud and fall in upon me.

Seven days later (on the 7th of May, that is to say) I was aware that I was lying in Heatherlegh's room as weak as a little child. Heatherlegh was watching me intently from behind the papers on his writing-table. His first words were not encouraging; but I was too far spent to be much moved by them.

'Here's Miss Kitty has sent back your letters. You corresponded a good deal, you young people. Here's a packet that looks like a ring, and a cheerful sort of a note from Mannering Papa, which I've taken the liberty of reading and burning. The old gentleman's not pleased with you.'

'And Kitty?' I asked dully.

'Rather more drawn than her father from what she says. By the same token you must have been letting out any number of queer reminiscences just before I met you. 'Says that a man who would have behaved to a woman as you did to Mrs Wessington ought to kill himself out of sheer pity for his kind. She's a hot-headed little virago, your mash. 'Will have it too that you were suffering from D. T. when that row on the Jakko road turned up. 'Says she'll die before she ever speaks to you again.'

I groaned and turned over on the other side.

'Now you've got your choice, my friend. This engagement has to be broken off; and the Mannerings don't want to be too hard on you. Was it broken through D. T. or epileptic fits? Sorry I can't offer you a better exchange unless you'd prefer hereditary insanity. Say the word and I'll tell 'em it's fits. All Simla knows about that scene on the Ladies' Mile. Come! I'll give you five minutes to think over it.'

During those five minutes I believe that I explored thoroughly the lowest circles of the Inferno which it is permitted man to tread on earth. And at the same time I myself was watching myself faltering through the dark labyrinths of doubt, misery, and utter despair. I wondered, as Heatherlegh in his chair might have wondered, which dreadful alternative I should adopt. Presently I heard myself answering in a voice that I hardly recognised –

'They're confoundedly particular about morality in these parts. Give 'em fits, Heatherlegh, and my love. Now let me sleep a bit longer.'

Then my two selves joined, and it was only I (half-crazed, devil-driven I) that tossed in my bed tracing step by step the history of the past month.

'But I am in Simla,' I kept repeating to myself. 'I, Jack Pansay, am in Simla, and there are no ghosts here. It's unreasonable of that woman to pretend there are. Why couldn't Agnes have left me alone? I never did her any harm. It might just as well have been me as Agnes. Only I'd never have come back on purpose to kill *her*. Why can't I be left alone – left alone and happy?'

It was high noon when I first awoke; and the sun was low in the sky before I slept – slept as the tortured criminal sleeps on his rack, too worn to feel further pain.

Next day I could not leave my bed. Heatherlegh told me in the morning that he had received an answer from Mr Mannering, and that, thanks to his (Heatherlegh's) friendly offices, the story of my affliction had travelled through the length and breadth of Simla, where I was on all sides much pitied.

'And that's rather more than you deserve,' he concluded pleasantly, 'though the

Lord knows you've been going through a pretty severe mill. Never mind; we'll cure you yet, you perverse phenomenon.'

I declined firmly to be cured. 'You've been much too good to me already, old man,' said I; 'but I don't think I need trouble you further.'

In my heart I knew that nothing Heatherlegh could do would lighten the burden that had been laid upon me.

With that knowledge came also a sense of hopeless, impotent rebellion against the unreasonableness of it all. There were scores of men no better than I whose punishments had at least been reserved for another world; and I felt that it was bitterly, cruelly unfair that I alone should have been singled out for so hideous a fate. This mood would in time give place to another where it seemed that the 'rickshaw and I were the only realities in a world of shadows; that Kitty was a ghost; that Mannering, Heatherlegh, and all the other men and women I knew were all ghosts; and the great gray hills themselves but vain shadows devised to torture me. From mood to mood I tossed backwards and forwards for seven weary days; my body growing daily stronger and stronger, until the bedroom looking-glass told me that I had returned to everyday life, and was as other men once more. Curiously enough my face showed no signs of the struggle I had gone through. It was pale indeed, but as expressionless and commonplace as ever. I had expected some permanent alteration – visible evidence of the disease that was eating me away. I found nothing.

On the 15th of May I left Heatherlegh's house at eleven o'clock in the morning; and the instinct of the bachelor drove me to the Club. There I found that every man knew my story as told by Heatherlegh, and was, in clumsy fashion, abnormally kind and attentive. Nevertheless I recognised that for the rest of my natural life I should be among but not of my fellows; and I envied very bitterly indeed the laughing coolies on the Mall below. I lunched at the Club, and at four o'clock wandered aimlessly down the Mall in the vague hope of meeting Kitty. Close to the Band-stand the black and white liveries joined me; and I heard Mrs Wessington's old appeal at my side. I had been expecting this ever since I came out, and was only surprised at her delay. The phantom 'rickshaw and I went side by side along the Chota Simla road in silence. Close to the bazar, Kitty and a man on horseback overtook and passed us. For any sign she gave I might have been a dog in the road. She did not even pay me the compliment of quickening her pace, though the rainy afternoon had served for an excuse.

So Kitty and her companion, and I and my ghostly Light-o'-Love, crept round Jakko in couples. The road was streaming with water; the pines dripped like roof-pipes on the rocks below, and the air was full of fine driving rain. Two or three times I found myself saying to myself almost aloud: 'I'm Jack Pansay on leave at Simla – at *Simla*! Everyday, ordinary Simla. I mustn't forget that – I mustn't forget that.' Then I would try to recollect some of the gossip I had heard at the Club: the prices of So-and-So's horses – anything, in fact, that related to the workaday Anglo-Indian world I knew so well. I even repeated the multiplication-table rapidly to myself, to make quite sure that I was not taking leave of my senses. It gave me much comfort, and must have prevented my hearing Mrs Wessington for a time.

Once more I wearily climbed the Convent slope and entered the level road. Here Kitty and the man started off at a canter, and I was left alone with Mrs Wessington. 'Agnes,' said I, 'will you put back your hood and tell me what it all means?' The hood dropped noiselessly, and I was face to face with my dead and buried mistress. She was wearing the dress in which I had last seen her alive; carried the same tiny handkerchief in her right hand, and the same card-case in her left. (A woman eight months dead with a card-case!) I had to pin myself down to the multiplication table, and to set both hands on the stone parapet of the road, to assure myself that that at least was real.

'Agnes,' I repeated, 'for pity's sake tell me what it all means.' Mrs Wessington leaned forward, with that odd, quick turn of the head I used to know so well, and spoke.

If my story had not already so madly overleaped the bounds of all human belief I should apologise to you now. As I know that no one – no, not even Kitty, for whom it is written as some sort of justification of my conduct – will believe me, I will go on. Mrs Wessington spoke, and I walked with her from the Sanjowlie road to the turning below the Commander-in-Chief's house as I might walk by the side of any living woman's 'rickshaw, deep in conversation. The second and most tormenting of my moods of sickness had suddenly laid hold upon me, and, like the Prince in Tennyson's poem, 'I seemed to move amid a world of ghosts.' There had been a garden-party at the Commander-in-Chief's, and we two joined the crowd of homeward-bound folk. As I saw them it seemed that *they* were the shadows – impalpable fantastic shadows – that divided for Mrs Wessington's 'rickshaw to pass through. What we said during the course of that weird interview I cannot – indeed, I dare not – tell. Heatherlegh's comment would have been a short laugh and a remark that I had been 'mashing a brain-eye-and-stomach chimera.' It was a ghastly and yet in some indefinable way a marvellously dear experience. Could it be possible, I wondered, that I was in this life to woo a second time the woman I had killed by my own neglect and cruelty?

I met Kitty on the homeward road – a shadow among shadows.

If I were to describe all the incidents of the next fortnight in their order, my story would never come to an end, and your patience would be exhausted. Morning after morning and evening after evening the ghostly 'rickshaw and I used to wander through Simla together. Wherever I went there the four black and white liveries followed me and bore me company to and from my hotel. At the Theatre I found them amid the crowd of yelling *jhampanies*; outside the Club verandah, after a long evening of whist; at the Birthday Ball, waiting patiently for my reappearance; and in broad daylight when I went calling. Save that it cast no shadow, the 'rickshaw was in every respect as real to look upon as one of wood and iron. More than once, indeed, I have had to check myself from warning some hard-riding friend against cantering over it. More than once I have walked down the Mall deep in conversation with Mrs Wessington, to the unspeakable amazement of the passers-by.

Before I had been out and about a week I learned that the 'fit' theory had been discarded in favour of insanity. However, I made no change in my mode of life. I called, rode, and dined out as freely as ever. I had a passion for the society of my kind which I had never felt before; I hungered to be among the realities of life; and at the same time I felt vaguely unhappy when I had been separated too long from my ghostly companion. It would be almost impossible to describe my varying moods from the 15th of May up to today.

The presence of the 'rickshaw filled me by turns with horror, blind fear, a dim sort of pleasure, and utter despair. I dared not leave Simla; and I knew that my stay there was killing me. I knew, moreover, that it was my destiny to die slowly and a little every day. My only anxiety was to get the penance over as quietly as might be. Alternately I hungered for a sight of Kitty, and watched her outrageous flirtations with my successor – to speak more accurately, my successors – with amused interest. She was as much out of my life as I was out of hers. By day I wandered with Mrs Wessington almost content. By night I implored Heaven to let me return to the world as I used to know it. Above all these varying moods lay the sensation of dull, numbing wonder that the seen and the unseen should mingle so strangely on this earth to hound one poor soul to its grave.

August 27. – Heatherlegh has been indefatigable in his attendance on me; and only yesterday told me that I ought to send in an application for sick leave. An application to escape the company of a phantom! A request that the Government would graciously permit me to get rid of five ghosts and an airy 'rickshaw by going to England! Heatherlegh's proposition moved me to almost hysterical laughter. I told him that I should await the end quietly at Simla; and I am sure that the end is not far off. Believe me that I dread its advent more than any word can say; and I torture myself nightly with a thousand speculations as to the manner of my death.

Shall I die in my bed decently and as an English gentleman should die; or, in one last walk on the Mall, will my soul be wrenched from me to take its place for ever and ever by the side of that ghastly phantasm? Shall I return to my old lost allegiance in the next world, or shall I meet Agnes loathing her and bound to her side through all eternity? Shall we two hover over the scene of our lives till the end of Time? As the day of my death draws nearer, the intense horror that all living flesh feels toward escaped spirits from beyond the grave grows more and more powerful. It is an awful thing to go down quick among the dead with scarcely one-half of your life completed. It is a thousand times more awful to wait as I do in your midst, for I know not what unimaginable terror. Pity me, at least on the score of my 'delusion,' for I know you will never believe what I have written here. Yet as surely as ever a man was done to death by the Powers of Darkness I am that man.

In justice, too, pity her. For as surely as ever woman was killed by man, I killed Mrs Wessington. And the last portion of my punishment is even now upon me.

MY OWN TRUE GHOST STORY

As I came through the Desert thus it was –
As I came through the Desert.
The City of Dreadful Night

This story deals entirely with ghosts. There are, in India, ghosts who take the form of fat, cold, pobby corpses, and hide in trees near the roadside till a traveller passes. Then they drop upon his neck and remain. There are also terrible ghosts of women who have died in childbed. These wander along the pathways at dusk, or hide in the crops near a village, and call seductively. But to answer their call is death in this world and the next. Their feet are turned backwards that all sober men may recognise them. There are ghosts of little children who have been thrown into wells. These haunt well-curbs and the fringes of jungles, and wail under the stars, or catch women by the wrist and beg to be taken up and carried. These and the corpse-ghosts, however, are only vernacular articles and do not attack Sahibs. No native ghost has yet been authentically reported to have frightened an Englishman; but many English ghosts have scared the life out of both white and black.

Nearly every other Station owns a ghost. There are said to be two at Simla, not counting the woman who blows the bellows at Syree dâk-bungalow on the Old Road; Mussoorie has a house haunted by a very lively Thing; a White Lady is supposed to

318

do night-watchman round a house in Lahore; Dalhousie says that one of her houses 'repeats' on autumn evenings all the incidents of a horrible horse-and-precipice accident; Murree has a merry ghost, and, now that she has been swept by cholera, will have room for a sorrowful one; there are Officers' Quarters in Mian Mir whose doors open without reason, and whose furniture is guaranteed to creak, not with the heat of June, but with the weight of Invisibles who come to lounge in the chairs; Peshawar possesses houses that none will willingly rent; and there is something – not fever – wrong with a big bungalow in Allahabad. The older Provinces simply bristle with haunted houses, and march phantom armies along their main thoroughfares.

Some of the dâk-bungalows on the Grand Trunk Road have handy little cemeteries in their compound – witnesses to the 'changes and chances of this mortal life' in the days when men drove from Calcutta to the North-West. These bungalows are objectionable places to put up in. They are generally very old, always dirty, while the *khansamah* is as ancient as the bungalow. He either chatters senilely, or falls into the long trances of age. In both moods he is useless. If you get angry with him, he refers to some Sahib dead and buried these thirty years, and says that when he was in that Sahib's service not a *khansamah* in the Province could touch him. Then he jabbers and mows and trembles and fidgets among the dishes, and you repent of your irritation.

Not long ago it was my business to live in dâk-bungalows. I never inhabited the same house for three nights running, and grew to be learned in the breed. I lived in Government-built ones with red brick walls and rail ceilings, an inventory of the furniture posted in every room, and an excited cobra on the threshold to give welcome. I lived in 'converted' ones – old houses officiating as dâk-bungalows – where nothing was in its proper place and there was not even a fowl for dinner. I lived in second-hand palaces where the wind blew through open-work marble tracery just as uncomfortably as through a broken pane. I lived in dâk-bungalows where the last entry in the visitors' book was fifteen months old, and where they slashed off the curry-kid's head with a sword. It was my good luck to meet all sorts of men, from sober travelling missionaries and deserters flying from British Regiments, to drunken loafers who threw whisky bottles at all who passed; and my still greater good fortune just to escape a maternity case. Seeing that a fair proportion of the tragedy of our lives in India acted itself in dâk-bungalows, I wondered that I had met no ghosts. A ghost that would voluntarily hang about a dâk-bungalow would be mad, of course; but so many men have died mad in dâk-bungalows that there must be a fair percentage of lunatic ghosts.

In due time I found my ghost, or ghosts rather, for there were two of them.

We will call the bungalow Katmal dâk-bungalow; but *that* was the smallest part of the horror. A man with a sensitive hide has no right to sleep in dâk-bungalows. He should marry. Katmal dâk-bungalow was old and rotten and unrepaired. The floor was of worn brick, the walls were filthy, and the windows were nearly black with grime. It stood on a bypath largely used by native Sub-Deputy Assistants of all kinds, from Finance to Forests; but real Sahibs were rare. The *khansamah*, who was bent nearly double with old age, said so.

When I arrived, there was a fitful, undecided rain on the face of the land, accompanied by a restless wind, and every gust made a noise like the rattling of dry bones in the stiff toddy-palms outside. The *khansamah* completely lost his head on my arrival. He had served a Sahib once. Did I know that Sahib? He gave me the name of a well-known man who has been buried for more than a quarter of a century, and showed me an ancient daguerreotype of that man in his prehistoric youth. I had seen a steel engraving of him at the head of a double volume of Memoirs a month before, and I felt ancient beyond telling.

The day shut in and the *khansamah* went to get me food. He did not go through the pretence of calling it 'khana,' – man's victuals. He said '*ratub*,' and that means, among other things, 'grub' – dog's rations. There was no insult in his choice of the term. He had forgotten the other word, I suppose.

While he was cutting up the dead bodies of animals, I settled myself down, after exploring the dâk-bungalow. There were three rooms besides my own, which was a corner kennel, each giving into the other through dingy white doors fastened with long iron bars. The bungalow was a very solid one, but the partition-walls of the rooms were almost jerry-built in their flimsiness. Every step or bang of a trunk echoed from my room down the other three, and every footfall came back tremulously from the far walls. For this reason I shut the door. There were no lamps – only candles in long glass shades. An oil wick was set in the bathroom.

For bleak, unadulterated misery that dâk-bungalow was the worst of the many that I had ever set foot in. There was no fireplace, and the windows would not open; so a brazier of charcoal would have been useless. The rain and the wind splashed and gurgled and moaned round the house, and the toddy-palms rattled and roared. Half-a-dozen jackals went through the compound singing, and a hyena stood afar off and mocked them. A hyena would convince a Sadducee of the Resurrection of the Dead – the worst sort of Dead. Then came the *ratub* – a curious meal, half native and half English in composition – with the old *khansamah* babbling behind my chair about dead-and-gone English people, and the wind-blown candles playing shadow-bo-peep with the bed and the mosquito-curtains. It was just the sort of dinner and evening to make a man think of every single one of his past sins, and of all the others that he intended to commit if he lived.

Sleep, for several hundred reasons, was not easy. The lamp in the bathroom threw the most absurd shadows into the room, and the wind was beginning to talk nonsense.

Just when the reasons were drowsy with blood-sucking I heard the regular – 'Let-us-take-and-heave-him-over' grunt of doolie-bearers in the compound. First one doolie came in, then a second, and then a third. I heard the doolies dumped on the ground, and the shutter in front of my door shook.

'That's someone trying to come in,' I said. But no one spoke, and I persuaded myself that it was the gusty wind. The shutter of the room next to mine was attacked, flung back, and the inner door opened. 'That's some Sub-Deputy Assistant,' I said, 'and he has brought his friends with him. Now they'll talk and spit and smoke for an hour.'

But there were no voices and no footsteps. No one was putting his luggage into the next room. The door shut, and I thanked Providence that I was to be left in peace. But I was curious to know where the doolies had gone. I got out of bed and looked into the darkness. There was never a sign of a doolie. Just as I was getting into bed again, I heard, in the next room, the sound that no man in his senses can possibly mistake – the whir of a billiard ball down the length of the slate when the striker is stringing for break. No other sound is like it. A minute afterwards there was another whir, and I got into bed. I was not frightened – indeed I was not. I was very curious to know what had become of the doolies. I jumped into bed for that reason.

Next minute I heard the double click of a cannon, and my hair sat up. It is a mistake to say that hair stands up. The skin of the head tightens, and you can feel a faint, prickly bristling all over the scalp. That is the hair sitting up.

There was a whir and a click, and both sounds could only have been made by one thing – a billiard ball. I argued the matter out at great length with myself; and the more I argued the less probable it seemed that one bed, one table, and two chairs – all the furniture of the room next to mine – could so exactly duplicate the sounds of a game of billiards. After another cannon, a three-cushion one to judge by the whir, I argued no more. I had found my ghost, and would have given worlds to have escaped from that dâk-bungalow. I listened, and with each listen the game grew clearer. There was whir on whir and click on click. Sometimes there was a double click and a whir and another click. Beyond any sort of doubt, people were playing billiards in the next room. And the next room was not big enough to hold a billiard table!

Between the pauses of the wind I heard the game go forward – stroke after stroke. I tried to believe that I could not hear voices; but that attempt was a failure.

Do you know what fear is? Not ordinary fear of insult, injury, or death, but abject, quivering dread of something that you cannot see – fear that dries the inside of the mouth and half of the throat – fear that makes you sweat on the palms of the hands, and gulp in order to keep the uvula at work? This is a fine Fear – a great cowardice, and must be felt to be appreciated. The very improbability of billiards in a dâk-bungalow proved the reality of the thing. No man – drunk or sober – could imagine a game at billiards, or invent the spitting crack of a 'screw cannon.'

A severe course of dâk-bungalows has this disadvantage – it breeds infinite credulity. If a man said to a confirmed dâk-bungalow-haunter: 'There is a corpse in the next room, and there's a mad girl in the next one, and the woman and man on that camel have just eloped from a place sixty miles away,' the hearer would not disbelieve, because he would know that nothing is too wild, grotesque, or horrible to happen in a dâk-bungalow.

This credulity, unfortunately, extends to ghosts. A rational person fresh from his own house would have turned on his side and slept. I did not. So surely as I was given up for a dry carcase by the scores of things in the bed, because the bulk of my blood was in my heart, so surely did I hear every stroke of a long game at billiards played in the echoing room behind the iron-barred door. My dominant fear was that the players might want a marker. It was an absurd fear; because creatures who could play in the dark would be above such superfluities. I only know that that was my terror; and it was real.

After a long, long while the game stopped, and the door banged. I slept because I was dead tired.

Otherwise I should have preferred to have kept awake. Not for everything in Asia would I have dropped the door-bar and peered into the dark of the next room.

When the morning came I considered that I had done well and wisely, and inquired for the means of departure.

'By the way, *khansamah*,' I said, 'what were those three doolies doing in my compound in the night?

'There were no doolies,' said the *khansamah*.

I went into the next room, and the daylight streamed through the open door. I was immensely brave. I would, at that hour, have played Black Pool with the owner of the big Black Pool down below.

'Has this place always been a dâk-bungalow?' I asked.

'No,' said the *khansamah*. 'Ten or twenty years ago, I have forgotten how long, it was a billiard room.'

'A what!'

'A billiard room for the Sahibs who built the Railway. I was *khansamah* then in the big house where all the Railway-Sahibs lived, and I used to come across with brandy-*shrab*. These three rooms were all one, and they held a big table on which the Sahibs played every evening. But the Sahibs are all dead now, and the Railway runs, you say, nearly to Kabul.'

'Do you remember anything about the Sahibs?'

'It is long ago, but I remember that one Sahib, a fat man, and always angry, was playing here one night, and he said to me: "Mangal Khan, brandy-*pani do*," and I filled the glass, and he bent over the table to strike, and his head fell lower and lower till it hit the table, and his spectacles came off, and when we – the Sahibs and I myself – ran to lift him he was dead. I helped to carry him out. Aha, he was a strong Sahib! But he is dead, and I, old Mangal Khan, am still living, by your favour.'

That was more than enough! I had my ghost – a first-hand, authenticated article. I would write to the Society for Psychical Research – I would paralyse the Empire with the news! But I would, first of all, put eighty miles of assessed crop-land between myself and that dâk-bungalow before nightfall. The Society might send their regular agent to investigate later on.

I went into my own room and prepared to pack, after noting down the facts of the case. As I smoked I heard the game begin again, – with a miss in balk this time, for the whir was a short one.

The door was open, and I could see into the room. *Click – click!* That was a cannon. I entered the room without fear, for there was sunlight within and a fresh breeze without. The unseen game was going on at a tremendous rate. And well it might, when a restless little rat was running to and fro inside the dingy ceiling-cloth, and a piece of loose window-sash was making fifty breaks off the window-bolt as it shook in the breeze!

Impossible to mistake the sound of billiard balls! Impossible to mistake the whir of a ball over the slate! But I was to be excused. Even when I shut my enlightened eyes the sound was marvellously like that of a fast game.

Entered angrily the faithful partner of my sorrows, Kadir Baksh.

'This bungalow is very bad and low-caste! No wonder the Presence was disturbed and is speckled. Three sets of doolie-bearers came to the bungalow late last night when I was sleeping outside, and said that it was their custom to rest in the rooms set apart for the English people! What honour has the *khansamah?* They tried to enter, but I told them to go. No wonder, if these *Oorias* have been here, that the Presence is sorely spotted. It is shame, and the work of a dirty man!'

Kadir Baksh did not say that he had taken from each gang two annas for rent in advance, and then, beyond my earshot, had beaten them with the big green umbrella whose use I could never before divine. But Kadir Baksh has no notions of morality.

There was an interview with the *khansamah*, but as he promptly lost his head, wrath gave place to pity, and pity led to a long conversation, in the course of which he put the fat Engineer-Sahib's tragic death in three separate stations – two of them fifty miles away. The third shift was to Calcutta, and there the Sahib died while driving a dog-cart.

I did not go away as soon as I intended. I stayed for the night, while the wind and the rat and the sash and the window-bolt played a ding-dong 'hundred and fifty up.' Then the wind ran out and the billiards stopped, and I felt that I had ruined my one genuine ghost story.

Had I only ceased investigating at the proper time I could have made *anything* out of it.

That was the bitterest thought of all.

THE STRANGE RIDE OF MORROWBIE JUKES

Alive or dead – there is no other way.
Native Proverb

There is no invention about this tale. Jukes by accident stumbled upon a village that is well known to exist, though he is the only Englishman who has been there. A somewhat similar institution used to flourish on the outskirts of Calcutta, and there is a story that if you go into the heart of Bikanir, which is in the heart of the Great Indian Desert, you shall come across, not a village, but a town where the Dead who did not die, but may not live, have established their headquarters. And, since it is perfectly true that in the same Desert is a wonderful city where all the rich money-lenders retreat after they have made their fortunes (fortunes so vast that the owners cannot trust even the strong hand of the Government to protect them, but take refuge in the waterless sands), and drive sumptuous C-spring barouches, and buy beautiful girls, and decorate their palaces with gold and ivory and Minton tiles and mother-o'-pearl, I do not see why Jukes's tale should not be true. He is a Civil Engineer, with a head for plans and distances and things of that kind, and he certainly would not take the trouble to invent imaginary traps. He could earn more by doing his legitimate work. He never varies the tale in the telling, and grows very hot and indignant when he thinks of the disrespectful treatment he received. He wrote this quite straightforwardly at first, but he has touched it up in places and introduced Moral Reflections: thus:

In the beginning it all arose from a slight attack of fever. My work necessitated my being in camp for some months between Pakpattan and Mubarakpur – a desolate sandy stretch of country as everyone who has had the misfortune to go there may know. My coolies were neither more nor less exasperating than other gangs, and my work demanded sufficient attention to keep me from moping, had I been inclined to so unmanly a weakness.

On the 23rd December 1884 I felt a little feverish. There was a full moon at the time, and, in consequence, every dog near my tent was baying it. The brutes assembled in twos and threes and drove me frantic. A few days previously I had shot one loud-mouthed singer and suspended his carcase *in terrorem* about fifty yards from my tent-door, but his friends fell upon, fought for, and ultimately devoured the body; and, as it seemed to me, sang their hymns of thanksgiving afterwards with renewed energy.

The light-headedness which accompanies fever acts differently on different men. My irritation gave way, after a short time, to a fixed determination to slaughter one huge black and white beast who had been foremost in song and first in flight throughout the evening. Thanks to a shaking hand and a giddy head I had already missed him twice with both barrels of my shot-gun, when it struck me that my best plan would be to ride him down in the open and finish him off with a hog-spear. This, of course, was merely the semi-delirious notion of a fever-patient; but I remember that it struck me at the time as being eminently practical and feasible.

I therefore ordered my groom to saddle Pornic and bring him round quietly to the rear of my tent. When the pony was ready, I stood at his head prepared to mount and dash out as soon as the dog should again lift up his voice. Pornic, by the way, had not been out of his pickets for a couple of days; the night air was crisp and chilly; and I was armed with a specially long and sharp pair of persuaders with which I had been rousing a sluggish cob that afternoon. You will easily believe, then, that when he was let go he went quickly. In one moment, for the brute bolted as straight as a die, the tent was left far behind, and we were flying over the smooth sandy soil at racing speed. In another we had passed the wretched dog, and I had almost forgotten why it was that I had taken horse and hog-spear.

The delirium of fever and the excitement of rapid motion through the air must have taken away the remnant of my senses. I have a faint recollection of standing upright in my stirrups, and of brandishing my hog-spear at the great white moon that looked down so calmly on my mad gallop; and of shouting challenges to the camel-thorn bushes as they whizzed past. Once or twice, I believe, I swayed forward on Pornic's neck, and literally hung on by my spurs – as the marks next morning showed.

The wretched beast went forward like a thing possessed, over what seemed to be a limitless expanse of moonlit sand. Next, I remember, the ground rose suddenly in front of us, and as we topped the ascent I saw the waters of the Sutlej shining like a silver bar below. Then Pornic blundered heavily on his nose, and we rolled together down some unseen slope.

I must have lost consciousness, for when I recovered I was lying on my stomach in a heap of soft white sand, and the dawn was beginning to break dimly over the edge of the slope down which I had fallen. As the light grew stronger I saw I was at the bottom of a horseshoe-shaped crater of sand, opening on one side directly on to the shoals of the Sutlej. My fever had altogether left me, and, with the exception of a slight dizziness in the head, I felt no bad effects from the fall overnight.

Pornic, who was standing a few yards away, was naturally a good deal exhausted, but had not hurt himself in the least. His saddle, a favourite polo one, was much knocked about, and had been twisted under his belly. It took me some time to put him to rights, and in the meantime I had ample opportunities of observing the spot into which I had so foolishly dropped.

At the risk of being considered tedious, I must describe it at length; inasmuch as an accurate mental picture of its peculiarities will be of material assistance in enabling the reader to understand what follows.

Imagine then, as I have said before, a horseshoe-shaped crater of sand with steeply-graded sand walls about thirty-five feet high. (The slope, I fancy, must have been about 65°.) This crater enclosed a level piece of ground about fifty yards long by thirty at its broadest part, with a rude well in the centre. Round the bottom of the crater, about three feet from the level of the ground proper, ran a series of eighty-three semicircular, ovoid, square, and multilateral holes, all about three feet at the mouth. Each hole on inspection showed that it was carefully shored internally with drift-wood and bamboos, and over the mouth a wooden drip-board projected, like the peak of a jockey's cap, for two feet. No sign of life was visible in these tunnels, but a most sickening stench pervaded the entire amphitheatre – a stench fouler than any which my wanderings in Indian villages have introduced me to.

Having remounted Pornic, who was as anxious as I to get back to camp, I rode round the base of the horseshoe to find some place whence an exit would be practicable. The inhabitants, whoever they might be, had not thought fit to put in an appearance, so I was left to my own devices. My first attempt to 'rush' Pornic up the steep sand-banks showed me that I had fallen into a trap exactly on the same model as that which the ant-lion sets for its prey. At each step the shifting sand poured down from above in tons, and rattled on the drip-boards of the holes like small shot. A couple of ineffectual charges sent us both rolling down to the bottom, half choked with the torrents of sand; and I was constrained to turn my attention to the river-bank.

Here everything seemed easy enough. The sand-hills ran down to the river edge, it is true, but there were plenty of shoals and shallows across which I could gallop Pornic, and find my way back to *terra firma* by turning sharply to the right or the left. As I led Pornic over the sands I was startled by the faint pop of a rifle across the river; and at the same moment a bullet dropped with a sharp '*whit*' close to Pornic's head.

There was no mistaking the nature of the missile – a regulation Martini-Henry 'picket.' About five hundred yards away a country-boat was anchored in mid-stream; and a jet of smoke drifting away from its bows in the still morning air showed me whence the delicate attention had come. Was ever a respectable gentleman in such an *impasse*? The treacherous sand-slope allowed no escape from a spot which I had visited most involuntarily, and a promenade on the river frontage was the signal for a bombardment from some insane native in a boat. I'm afraid that I lost my temper very much indeed.

Another bullet reminded me that I had better save my breath to cool my porridge;

and I retreated hastily up the sands and back to the horseshoe, where I saw that the noise of the rifle had drawn sixty-five human beings from the badger-holes which I had up till that point supposed to be untenanted. I found myself in the midst of a crowd of spectators – about forty men, twenty women, and one child who could not have been more than five years old. They were all scantily clothed in that salmon-coloured cloth which one associates with Hindu mendicants, and, at first sight, gave me the impression of a band of loathsome *fakirs*. The filth and repulsiveness of the assembly were beyond all description, and I shuddered to think what their life in the badger-holes must be.

Even in these days, when local self-government has destroyed the greater part of a native's respect for a Sahib, I have been accustomed to a certain amount of civility from my inferiors, and on approaching the crowd naturally expected that there would be some recognition of my presence. As a matter of fact there was, but it was by no means what I had looked for.

The ragged crew actually laughed at me – such laughter I hope I may never hear again. They cackled, yelled, whistled, and howled as I walked into their midst; some of them literally throwing themselves down on the ground in convulsions of unholy mirth. In a moment I had let go Pornic's head, and, irritated beyond expression at the morning's adventure, commenced cuffing those nearest to me with all the force I could. The wretches dropped under my blows like ninepins, and the laughter gave place to wails for mercy; while those yet untouched clasped me round the knees, imploring me in all sorts of uncouth tongues to spare them.

In the tumult, and just when I was feeling very much ashamed of myself for having thus easily given way to my temper, a thin high voice murmured in English from behind my shoulder: 'Sahib! Sahib! Do you not know me? Sahib, it is Gunga Dass, the telegraph-master.'

I spun round quickly and faced the speaker.

Gunga Dass (I have, of course, no hesitation in mentioning the man's real name) I had known four years before as a Deccanee Brahmin lent by the Punjab Government to one of the Khalsia States. He was in charge of a branch telegraph-office there, and when I had last met him was a jovial, full-stomached, portly Government servant with a marvelous capacity for making bad puns in English – a peculiarity which made me remember him long after I had forgotten his services to me in his official capacity. It is seldom that a Hindu makes English puns.

Now, however, the man was changed beyond all recognition. Caste-mark, stomach, slate-coloured continuations, and unctuous speech were all gone. I looked at a withered skeleton, turbanless and almost naked, with long matted hair and deep-set codfish-eyes. But for a crescent-shaped scar on the left cheek – the result of an accident for which I was responsible – I should never have known him. But it was indubitably Gunga Dass, and – for this I was thankful – an English-speaking native who might at least tell me the meaning of all that I had gone through that day.

The crowd retreated to some distance as I turned towards the miserable figure, and ordered him to show me some method of escaping from the crater. He held a freshly-plucked crow in his hand, and in reply to my question climbed slowly to a platform of sand which ran in front of the holes, and commenced lighting a fire there in silence. Dried bents, sand-poppies, and driftwood burn quickly; and I derived much consolation from the fact that he lit them with an ordinary sulphur match. When they were in a bright glow and the crow was neatly spitted in front thereof, Gunga Dass began without a word of preamble –

'There are only two kinds of men, Sar – the alive and the dead. When you are dead you are dead, but when you are alive you live.' (Here the crow demanded his attention for an instant as it twirled before the fire in danger of being burnt to a cinder.) 'If you die at home and do not die when you come to the ghât to be burnt you come here.'

The nature of the reeking village was made plain now, and all that I had known or read of the grotesque and the horrible paled before the fact just communicated by the ex-Brahmin. Sixteen years ago, when I first landed in Bombay, I had been told by a wandering Armenian of the existence, somewhere in India, of a place to which such Hindus as had the misfortune to recover from trance or catalepsy were conveyed and kept, and I recollect laughing heartily at what I was then pleased to consider a traveller's tale. Sitting at the bottom of the sand-trap, the memory of Watson's Hotel, with its swinging punkahs, white-robed servants, and the sallow-faced Armenian, rose up in my mind as vividly as a photograph, and I burst into a loud fit of laughter. The contrast was too absurd!

Gunga Dass, as he bent over the unclean bird, watched me curiously. Hindus seldom laugh, and his surroundings were not such as to move him that way. He removed the crow solemnly from the wooden spit and as solemnly devoured it. Then he continued his story, which I give in his own words –

'In epidemics of the cholera you are carried to be burnt almost before you are dead. When you come to the riverside the cold air, perhaps, makes you alive, and then, if you are only little alive, mud is put on your nose and mouth and you die conclusively. If you are rather more alive, more mud is put; but if you are too lively they let you go and take you away. I was too lively, and made protestation with anger against the indignities that they endeavoured to press upon me. In those days I was Brahmin and proud man. Now I am dead man and eat' – here he eyed the well-gnawed breast-bone with the first sign of emotion that I had seen in him since we met – 'crows, and – other things. They took me from my sheets when they saw that I was too lively and gave me medicines for one week, and I survived successfully. Then they sent me by rail from my place to Okara Station, with a man to take care of me; and at Okara Station we met two other men, and they conducted we three on camels, in the night, from Okara Station to this place, and they propelled me from the top to the bottom, and the other two succeeded, and I have been here ever since two and a half years. Once I was Brahmin and proud man, and now I eat crows.'

'There is no way of getting out?'

'None of what kind at all. When I first came I made experiments frequently, and all the others also, but we have always succumbed to the sand which is precipitated upon our heads.'

'But surely,' I broke in at this point, 'the river-front is open, and it is worth while dodging the bullets; while at night –'

I had already matured a rough plan of escape which a natural instinct of selfishness forbade me sharing with Gunga Dass. He, however, divined my unspoken thought almost as soon as it was formed; and, to my intense astonishment, gave vent to a long low chuckle of derision – the laughter, be it understood, of a superior or at least of an equal.

'You will not' – he had dropped the Sir after his first sentence – 'make any escape that way. But you can try. I have tried. Once only.'

The sensation of nameless terror which I had in vain attempted to strive against over-mastered me completely. My long fast – it was now close upon ten o'clock, and I had eaten nothing since tiffin on the previous day – combined with the violent agitation of the ride had exhausted me, and I verily believe that, for a few minutes, I acted as one mad. I hurled myself against the sand-slope. I ran round the base of the crater, blaspheming and praying by turns. I crawled out among the sedges of the river-front, only to be driven back each time in an agony of nervous dread by the rifle-bullets which cut up the sand round me – for I dared not face the death of a mad dog among that hideous crowd – and so fell, spent and raving, at the curb of the well. No one had taken the slightest notice of an exhibition which makes me blush hotly even when I think of it now.

Two or three men trod on my panting body as they drew water, but they were evidently used to this sort of thing, and had no time to waste upon me. Gunga Dass, indeed, when he had banked the embers of his fire with sand, was at some pains to throw half a cupful of fetid water over my head, an attention for which I could have fallen on my knees and thanked him, but he was laughing all the while in the same mirthless, wheezy key that greeted me on my first attempt to force the shoals. And so, in a half-fainting state, I lay till noon. Then, being only a man after all, I felt hungry, and said as much to Gunga Dass, whom I had begun to regard as my natural protector. Following the impulse of the outer world when dealing with natives, I put my hand into my pocket and drew out four annas. The absurdity of the gift struck me at once, and I was about to replace the money.

Gunga Dass, however, cried: 'Give me the money, all you have, or I will get help, and we will kill you!'

A Briton's first impulse, I believe, is to guard the contents of his pockets; but a moment's thought showed me the folly of differing with the one man who had it in his power to make me comfortable; and with whose help it was possible that I might eventually escape from the crater. I gave him all the money in my possession, Rs. 9-8-5 – nine rupees, eight annas, and five pie – for I always keep small change as *bakshish* when I am in camp. Gunga Dass clutched the coins, and hid them at once in his ragged loin-cloth, looking round to assure himself that no one had observed us.

'*Now* I will give you something to eat,' said he.

What pleasure my money could have given him I am unable to say; but inasmuch as it did please him I was not sorry that I had parted with it so readily, for I had no doubt that he would have had me killed if I had refused. One does not protest against the doings of a den of wild beasts; and my companions were lower than any beasts. While I ate what Gunga Dass had provided, a coarse *chapatti* and a cupful of the foul well-water, the people showed not the faintest sign of curiosity – that curiosity which is so rampant, as a rule, in an Indian village.

I could even fancy that they despised me. At all events they treated me with the most chilling indifference, and Gunga Dass was nearly as bad. I plied him with questions about the terrible village, and received extremely unsatisfactory answers. So far as I could gather, it had been in existence from time immemorial – whence I concluded that it was at least a century old – and during that time no one had ever been known to escape from it. [I had to control myself here with both hands, lest the blind terror should lay hold of me a second time and drive me raving round the crater.] Gunga Dass took a malicious pleasure in emphasising this point and in watching me wince. Nothing that I could do would induce him to tell me who the mysterious 'They' were.

'It is so ordered,' he would reply, 'and I do not yet know anyone who has disobeyed the orders.'

'Only wait till my servants find that I am missing,' I retorted, 'and I promise you that this place shall be cleared off the face of the earth, and I'll give you a lesson in civility, too, my friend.'

'Your servants would be torn in pieces before they came near this place; and, besides, you are dead, my dear friend. It is not your fault, of course, but none the less you are dead *and* buried.'

At irregular intervals supplies of food, I was told, were dropped down from the land side into the amphitheatre, and the inhabitants fought for them like wild beasts. When a man felt his death coming on he retreated to his lair and died there. The body was sometimes dragged out of the hole and thrown on to the sand, or allowed to rot where it lay.

The phrase 'thrown on to the sand' caught my attention, and I asked Gunga Dass whether this sort of thing was not likely to breed a pestilence.

'That,' said he, with another of his wheezy chuckles, 'you may see for yourself subsequently. You will have much time to make observations.'

Whereat, to his great delight, I winced once more and hastily continued the conversation: 'And how do you live here from day to day? What do you do?' The question elicited exactly the same answer as before – coupled with the information that 'this place is like your European heaven; there is neither marrying nor giving in marriage.'

Gunga Dass had been educated at a Mission School, and, as he himself admitted, had he only changed his religion 'like a wise man,' might have avoided the living grave which was now his portion. But as long as I was with him I fancy he was happy.

Here was a Sahib, a representative of the dominant race, helpless as a child and completely at the mercy of his native neighbours. In a deliberate lazy way he set himself to torture me as a schoolboy would devote a rapturous half-hour to watching the agonies of an impaled beetle, or as a ferret in a blind burrow might glue himself comfortably to the neck of a rabbit. The burden of his conversation was that there was no escape 'of no kind whatever,' and that I should stay here till I died and was 'thrown on to the sand.' If it were possible to forejudge the conversation of the Damned on the advent of a new soul in their abode, I should say that they would speak as Gunga Dass did to me throughout that long afternoon. I was powerless to protest or answer; all my energies being devoted to a struggle against the inexplicable terror that threatened to overwhelm me again and again. I can compare the feeling to nothing except the struggles of a man against the overpowering nausea of the Channel passage – only my agony was of the spirit and infinitely more terrible.

As the day wore on, the inhabitants began to appear in full strength to catch the rays of the afternoon sun, which were now sloping in at the mouth of the crater. They assembled by little knots, and talked among themselves without even throwing a glance in my direction. About four o'clock, so far as I could judge, Gunga Dass rose and dived into his lair for a moment, emerging with a live crow in his hands. The wretched bird was in a most draggled and deplorable condition, but seemed to be in no way afraid of its master. Advancing cautiously to the river-front, Gunga Dass stepped from tussock to tussock until he had reached a smooth patch of sand directly in the line of the boat's fire. The occupants of the boat took no notice. Here he stopped, and, with a couple of dexterous turns of the wrist, pegged the bird on its back with outstretched wings. As was only natural, the crow began to shriek at once and beat the air with its claws. In a few seconds the clamour had attracted the attention of a bevy of wild crows on a shoal a few hundred yards away, where they were discussing something that looked like a corpse. Half-a-dozen crows flew over at once to see what was going on, and also, as it proved, to attack the pinioned bird. Gunga Dass, who had lain down on a tussock, motioned to me to be quiet, though I fancy this was a needless precaution. In a moment, and before I could see how it happened, a wild crow, which had grappled with the shrieking and helpless bird, was entangled in the latter's claws, swiftly disengaged by Gunga Dass, and pegged down beside its companion in adversity.

Curiosity, it seemed, overpowered the rest of the flock, and almost before Gunga Dass and I had time to withdraw to the tussock, two more captives were struggling in the upturned claws of the decoys. So the chase – if I can give it so dignified a name – continued until Gunga Dass had captured seven crows. Five of them he throttled at once, reserving two for further operations another day. I was a good deal impressed by this, to me, novel method of securing food, and complimented Gunga Dass on his skill.

'It is nothing to do,' said he. 'Tomorrow you must do it for me. You are stronger than I am.'

This calm assumption of superiority upset me not a little, and I answered peremptorily: 'Indeed, you old ruffian? What do you think I have given you money for?'

'Very well,' was the unmoved reply. 'Perhaps not tomorrow, nor the day after, nor subsequently; but in the end, and for many years, you will catch crows and eat crows, and you will thank your European God that you have crows to catch and eat.'

I could have cheerfully strangled him for this, but judged it best under the circumstances to smother my resentment. An hour later I was eating one of the crows; and, as Gunga Dass had said, thanking my God that I had a crow to eat. Never as long as I live shall I forget that evening meal. The whole population were squatting on the hard sand platform opposite their dens, huddled over tiny fires of refuse and dried rushes. Death having once laid his hand upon these men and forborne to strike, seemed to stand aloof from them now; for most of our company were old men, bent and worn and twisted with years, and women aged to all appearance as the Fates themselves. They sat together in knots and talked – God only knows what they found to discuss – in low equable tones, curiously in contrast to the strident babble with which natives are accustomed to make day hideous. Now and then an access of that sudden fury which had possessed me in the morning would lay hold on a man or woman; and with yells and imprecations the sufferer would attack the steep slope until, baffled and bleeding, he fell back on the platform incapable of moving a limb. The others would never even raise their eyes when this happened, as men too well aware of the futility of their fellows' attempts and wearied with their useless repetition. I saw four such outbursts in the course of that evening.

Gunga Dass took an eminently business-like view of my situation, and while we were dining – I can afford to laugh at the recollection now, but it was painful enough at the time – propounded the terms on which he would consent to 'do' for me. My nine rupees eight annas, he argued, at the rate of three annas a day, would provide me with food for fifty-one days, or about seven weeks; that is to say, he would be willing to cater for me for that length of time. At the end of it I was to look after myself. For a further consideration – *videlicet* my boots – he would be willing to allow me to occupy the den next to his own, and would supply me with as much dried grass for bedding as he could spare.

'Very well, Gunga Dass,' I replied; 'to the first terms I cheerfully agree, but, as there is nothing on earth to prevent my killing you as you sit here and taking everything that you have' (I thought of the two invaluable crows at the time), 'I flatly refuse to give you my boots and shall take whichever den I please.'

The stroke was a bold one, and I was glad when I saw that it had succeeded.

Gunga Dass changed his tone immediately, and disavowed all intention of asking for my boots. At the time it did not strike me as at all strange that I, a Civil Engineer, a man of thirteen years' standing in the Service, and, I trust, an average Englishman, should thus calmly threaten murder and violence against the man who had, for a consideration it is true, taken me under his wing. I had left the world, it seemed, for centuries. I was as certain then as I am now of my own existence, that in the accursed settlement there was no law save that of the strongest; that the living dead men had thrown behind them every canon of the world which had cast them out; and that I had to depend for my own life on my strength and vigilance alone. The crew of the ill-fated *Mignonette* are the only men who would understand my frame of mind. 'At present,' I argued to myself, 'I am strong and a match for six of these wretches. It is imperatively necessary that I should, for my own sake, keep both health and strength until the hour of my release comes – if it ever does.'

Fortified with these resolutions, I ate and drank as much as I could, and made Gunga Dass understand that I intended to be his master, and that the least sign of insubordination on his part would be visited with the only punishment I had it in my power to inflict – sudden and violent death. Shortly after this I went to bed. That is to say, Gunga Dass gave me a double armful of dried bents which I thrust down the mouth of the lair to the right of his, and followed myself, feet foremost; the hole running about nine feet into the sand with a slight downward inclination, and being neatly shored with timbers. From my den, which faced the river-front, I was able to watch the waters of the Sutlej flowing past under the light of a young moon and compose myself to sleep as best I might.

The horrors of that night I shall never forget. My den was nearly as narrow as a coffin, and the sides had been worn smooth and greasy by the contact of innumerable naked bodies, added to which it smelt abominably. Sleep was altogether out of the question to one in my excited frame of mind. As the night wore on, it seemed that the entire amphitheatre was filled with legions of unclean devils that, trooping up from the shoals below, mocked the unfortunates in their lairs.

Personally I am not of an imaginative temperament – very few Engineers are – but on that occasion I was as completely prostrated with nervous terror as any woman.

After half an hour or so, however, I was able once more to calmly review my chances of escape. Any exit by the steep sand walls was, of course, impracticable. I had been thoroughly convinced of this some time before. It was possible, just possible, that I might, in the uncertain moonlight, safely run the gauntlet of the rifle shots. The place was so full of terror for me that I was prepared to undergo any risk in leaving it. Imagine my delight, then, when after creeping stealthily to the river-front I found that the infernal boat was not there. My freedom lay before me in the next few steps!

By walking out to the first shallow pool that lay at the foot of the projecting left horn of the horseshoe, I could wade across, turn the flank of the crater, and make my way inland. Without a moment's hesitation I marched briskly past the tussocks where Gunga Dass had snared the crows, and out in the direction of the smooth white sand beyond. My first step from the tufts of dried grass showed me how utterly futile was any hope of escape; for, as I put my foot down, I felt an indescribable drawing, sucking motion of the sand below. Another moment and my leg was swallowed up nearly to the knee. In the moonlight the whole surface of the sand seemed to be shaken with devilish delight at my disappointment. I struggled clear, sweating with terror and exertion, back to the tussocks behind me and fell on my face.

My only means of escape from the semicircle was protected by a quicksand!

How long I lay I have not the faintest idea; but I was roused at last by the malevolent chuckle of Gunga Dass at my ear. 'I would advise you, Protector of the Poor' (the ruffian was speaking English) 'to return to your house. It is unhealthy to lie down here. Moreover, when the boat returns you will most certainly be rifled at.' He stood over me in the dim light of the dawn, chuckling and laughing to himself. Suppressing my first impulse to catch the man by the neck and throw him on to the quicksand, I rose sullenly and followed him to the platform below the burrows.

Suddenly, and futilely as I thought while I spoke, I asked: 'Gunga Dass, what is the good of the boat if I can't get out *anyhow*?' I recollect that even in my deepest trouble I had been speculating vaguely on the waste of ammunition in guarding an already well-protected foreshore.

Gunga Dass laughed again and made answer: 'They have the boat only in daytime. It is for the reason that *there is a way*. I hope we shall have the pleasure of your company for much longer time. It is a pleasant spot when you have been here some years and eaten roast crow long enough.'

I staggered, numbed and helpless, towards the fetid burrow allotted to me, and fell asleep. An hour or so later I was awakened by a piercing scream – the shrill, high-pitched scream of a horse in pain. Those who have once heard that will never forget the sound. I found some little difficulty in scrambling out of the burrow. When I was in the open, I saw Pornic, my poor old Pornic, lying dead on the sandy soil. How they had killed him I cannot guess. Gunga Dass explained that horse was better than crow, and 'greatest good of greatest number is political maxim. We are now Republic, Mister Jukes, and you are entitled to a fair share of the beast. If you like, we will pass a vote of thanks. Shall I propose?'

Yes, we were a Republic indeed! A Republic of wild beasts penned at the bottom of a pit, to eat and fight and sleep till we died. I attempted no protest of any kind, but sat down and stared at the hideous sight in front of me. In less time almost than it takes me to write this, Pornic's body was divided, in some unclean way or other; the men and women had dragged the fragments on to the platform and were preparing their morning meal. Gunga Dass cooked mine. The almost irresistible impulse to fly at the sand walls until I was wearied laid hold of me afresh, and I had to struggle against it with all my might. Gunga Dass was offensively jocular till I told him that if he addressed another remark of any kind whatever to me I should strangle him where he sat. This silenced him till the silence became insupportable, and I bade him say something.

'You will live here till you die like the other Feringhi,' he said coolly, watching me over the fragment of gristle that he was gnawing.

'What other Sahib, you swine? Speak at once, and don't stop to tell me a lie.'

'He is over there,' answered Gunga Dass, pointing to a burrow-mouth about four doors to the left of my own. 'You can see for yourself. He died in the burrow as you will die, and I will die, and as all these men and women and the one child will also die.'

'For pity's sake tell me all you know about him. Who was he? When did he come, and when did he die?'

This appeal was a weak step on my part. Gunga Dass only leered and replied: 'I will not – unless you give me something first.'

Then I recollected where I was, and struck the man between the eyes, partially stunning him. He stepped down from the platform at once, and, cringing and fawning and weeping and attempting to embrace my feet, led me round to the burrow which he had indicated.

'I know nothing whatever about the gentleman. Your God be my witness that I do not. He was as anxious to escape as you were, and he was shot from the boat, though we all did all things to prevent him from attempting. He was shot here.' Gunga Dass laid his hand on his lean stomach and bowed to the earth.

'Well, and what then? Go on!'

'And then – and then, Your Honour, we carried him into his house and gave him water, and put wet cloths on the wound, and he laid down in his house and gave up the ghost.'

'In how long? In how long?'

'About half an hour after he received his wound. I call Vishnu to witness,' yelled the wretched man, 'that I did everything for him. Everything which was possible, that I did!'

He threw himself down on the ground and clasped my ankles. But I had my doubts about Gunga Dass's benevolence, and kicked him off as he lay protesting.

'I believe you robbed him of everything he had. But I can find out in a minute or two. How long was the Sahib here?'

'Nearly a year and a half. I think he must have gone mad. But hear me swear, Protector of the Poor! Won't Your Honour hear me swear that I never touched an article that belonged to him? What is Your Worship going to do?'

I had taken Gunga Dass by the waist and had hauled him on to the platform opposite the deserted burrow. As I did so I thought of my wretched fellow-prisoner's unspeakable misery among all these horrors for eighteen months, and the final agony of dying like a rat in a hole, with a bullet-wound in the stomach. Gunga Dass fancied I was going to kill him and howled pitifully. The rest of the population, in the plethora that follows a full flesh meal, watched us without stirring.

'Go inside, Gunga Dass,' said I, 'and fetch it out.'

I was feeling sick and faint with horror now. Gunga Dass nearly rolled off the platform and howled aloud.

'But I am Brahmin, Sahib – a high-caste Brahmin. By your soul, by your father's soul, do not make me do this thing!'

'Brahmin or no Brahmin, by my soul and my father's soul, in you go!' I said, and, seizing him by the shoulders, I crammed his head into the mouth of the burrow, kicked the rest of him in, and, sitting down, covered my face with my hands.

At the end of a few minutes I heard a rustle and a creak; then Gunga Dass in a sobbing, choking whisper speaking to himself; then a soft thud – and I uncovered my eyes.

The dry sand had turned the corpse entrusted to its keeping into a yellow-brown mummy. I told Gunga Dass to stand off while I examined it. The body – clad in an olive-green hunting-suit much stained and worn, with leather pads on the shoulders – was that of a man between thirty and forty, above middle height, with light sandy hair, long moustache, and a rough unkempt beard. The left canine of the upper jaw was missing, and a portion of the lobe of the right ear was gone. On the second finger of the left hand was a ring – a shield-shaped bloodstone set in gold, with a monogram that might have been either 'B. K.' or 'B. L.' On the third finger of the right hand was a silver ring in the shape of a coiled cobra, much worn and tarnished. Gunga Dass deposited a handful of trifles he had picked out of the burrow at my feet, and, covering the face of the body with my handkerchief, I turned to examine these. I give the full list in the hope that it may lead to the identification of the unfortunate man –

1. Bowl of a briarwood pipe, serrated at the edge; much worn and blackened; bound with string at the screw.

2. Two patent-lever keys; wards of both broken.

3. Tortoise-shell-handled penknife, silver or nickel, name-plate marked with monogram 'B. K.'

4. Envelope, postmark undecipherable, bearing a Victorian stamp, addressed to 'Miss Mon – (rest illegible) – 'ham' – 'nt.'

5. Imitation crocodile-skin notebook with pencil. First forty-five pages blank; four and a half illegible; fifteen others filled with private memoranda relating chiefly to three persons – a Mrs L. Singleton, abbreviated several times to 'Lot Single,' 'Mrs S. May,' and 'Garmison,' referred to in places as 'Jerry' or 'Jack.'

6. Handle of small-sized hunting-knife. Blade snapped short. Buck's horn, diamond-cut, with swivel and ring on the butt; fragment of cotton cord attached.

It must not be supposed that I inventoried all these things on the spot as fully as I have here written them down. The notebook first attracted my attention, and I put it in my pocket with a view to studying it later on. The rest of the articles I conveyed to my burrow for safety's sake, and there, being a methodical man, I inventoried them. I then returned to the corpse and ordered Gunga Dass to help me to carry it out to the river-front. While we were engaged in this, the exploded shell of an old brown cartridge dropped out of one of the pockets and rolled at my feet. Gunga Dass had not seen it; and I fell to thinking that a man does not carry exploded cartridge-cases, especially 'browns,' which will not bear loading twice, about with him when shooting. In other words, that cartridge-case had been fired inside the crater. Consequently there must be a gun somewhere. I was on the verge of asking Gunga Dass, but checked myself, knowing that he would lie. We laid the body down on the edge of the quicksand by the tussocks. It was my intention to push it out and let it be swallowed up – the only possible mode of burial that I could think of. I ordered Gunga Dass to go away.

Then I gingerly put the corpse out on the quicksand. In doing so – it was lying face downward – I tore the frail and rotten khaki shooting-coat open, disclosing a hideous cavity in the back. I have already told you that the dry sand had, as it were, mummified the body. A moment's glance showed that the gaping hole had been caused by a gunshot wound; the gun must have been fired with the muzzle almost touching the back. The shooting-coat, being intact, had been drawn over the body after death, which must have been instantaneous. The secret of the poor wretch's death was plain to me in a flash. Some one of the crater, presumably Gunga Dass, must have shot him with his own gun – the gun that fitted the brown cartridges. He had never attempted to escape in the face of the rifle-fire from the boat.

I pushed the corpse out hastily, and saw it sink from sight literally in a few seconds. I shuddered as I watched. In a dazed, half-conscious way I turned to peruse the notebook. A stained and discoloured slip of paper had been inserted between the binding and the back, and dropped out as I opened the pages. This is what it contained: '*Four out from crow-clump; three left; nine out; two right; three back; two left; fourteen out; two left; seven out; one left; nine back; two right; six back; four right; seven back.*' The paper had been burnt and charred at the edges. What it meant I could not understand. I sat down on the dried bents turning it over and over between my fingers, until I was aware of Gunga Dass standing immediately behind me with glowing eyes and outstretched hands.

'Have you got it?' he panted. 'Will you not let me look at it also? I swear that I will return it.'

'Got what? Return what?' I asked.

'That which you have in your hands. It will help us both.' He stretched out his long bird-like talons, trembling with eagerness.

'I could never find it,' he continued. 'He had secreted it about his person. Therefore I shot him, but nevertheless I was unable to obtain it.'

Gunga Dass had quite forgotten his little fiction about the rifle-bullet. I heard him calmly. Morality is blunted by consorting with the Dead who are alive.

'What on earth are you raving about? What is it you want me to give you?'

'The piece of paper in the notebook. It will help us both. Oh, you fool! You fool! Can you not see what it will do for us? We shall escape!'

His voice rose almost to a scream, and he danced with excitement before me. I own I was moved at the chance of getting away.

'Do you mean to say that this slip of paper will help us? What does it mean?'

'Read it aloud! Read it aloud! I beg and I pray to you to read it aloud.'

I did so. Gunga Dass listened delightedly, and drew an irregular line in the sand with his fingers.

'See now! It was the length of his gun-barrels without the stock. I have those barrels. Four gun-barrels out from the place where I caught crows. Straight out; do you mind me? Then three left. Ah! Now well I remember how that man worked it out night after night. Then nine out, and so on. Out is always straight before you across the quicksand to the north. He told me so before I killed him.'

'But if you knew all this why didn't you get out before?'

'I did *not* know it. He told me that he was working it out a year and a half ago, and how he was working it out night after night when the boat had gone away, and he could get out near the quicksand safely. Then he said that we would get away together. But I was afraid that he would leave me behind one night when he had worked it all out, and so I shot him. Besides, it is not advisable that the men who once get in here should escape. Only I, and *I* am a Brahmin.'

The hope of escape had brought Gunga Dass's caste back to him. He stood up, walked about, and gesticulated violently. Eventually I managed to make him talk soberly, and he told me how this Englishman had spent six months night after night in exploring, inch by inch, the passage across the quicksand; how he had declared it to be simplicity itself up to within about twenty yards of the river bank after turning the flank of the left horn of the horseshoe. This much he had evidently not completed when Gunga Dass shot him with his own gun.

In my frenzy of delight at the possibilities of escape I recollect shaking hands wildly with Gunga Dass, after we had decided that we were to make an attempt to get away that very night. It was weary work waiting throughout the afternoon.

About ten o'clock, as far as I could judge, when the moon had just risen above the lip of the crater, Gunga Dass made a move for his burrow to bring out the gun-barrels whereby to measure our path. All the other wretched inhabitants had retired to their lairs long ago. The guardian boat drifted down-stream some hours before, and we were utterly alone by the crow-clump. Gunga Dass, while carrying the gun-barrels, let slip the piece of paper which was to be our guide. I stooped down hastily to recover it, and, as I did so, I was aware that the creature was aiming a violent blow at the back of my head with the gun-barrels. It was too late to turn round. I must have received the blow somewhere on the nape of my neck, for I fell senseless at the edge of the quicksand.

When I recovered consciousness the moon was going down, and I was sensible of intolerable pain in the back of my head. Gunga Dass had disappeared and my mouth was full of blood. I lay down again and prayed that I might die without more ado. Then the unreasoning fury which I have before mentioned laid hold upon me, and I staggered inland towards the walls of the crater. It seemed that someone was calling to me in a whisper – 'Sahib! Sahib! Sahib!' exactly as my bearer used to call me in the mornings. I fancied that I was delirious until a handful of sand fell at my feet. Then I looked up and saw a head peering down into the amphitheatre – the head of Dunnoo, my dog-boy, who attended to my collies. As soon as he had attracted my attention, he held up his hand and showed a rope. I motioned, staggering to and fro the while, that he should throw it down. It was a couple of leather punkah-ropes knotted together, with a loop at one end. I slipped the loop over my head and under my arms; heard Dunnoo urge something forward; was conscious that I was being dragged, face downward, up the steep sand-slope, and the next instant found myself choked and half-fainting on the sand-hills overlooking the crater. Dunnoo, with his face ashy gray in the moonlight, implored me not to stay, but to get back to my tent at once.

It seems that he had tracked Pornic's footprints fourteen miles across the sands to the crater; had returned and told my servants, who flatly refused to meddle with anyone, white or black, once fallen into the hideous Village of the Dead; whereupon Dunnoo had taken one of my ponies and a couple of punkah ropes, returned to the crater, and hauled me out as I have described.

THE MAN WHO WOULD BE KING

Brother to a Prince and fellow to a beggar if he be found worthy

The Law, as quoted, lays down a fair conduct of life, and one not easy to follow. I have been fellow to a beggar again and again under circumstances which prevented either of us finding out whether the other was worthy. I have still to be brother to a Prince, though I once came near to kinship with what might have been a veritable King, and was promised the reversion of a Kingdom – army, law-courts, revenue, and policy all complete. But today ay, I greatly fear that my King is dead, and if I want a crown I must go hunt it for myself.

The beginning of everything was in a railway train upon the road to Mhow from Ajmir. There had been a Deficit in the Budget, which necessitated travelling, not Second-class, which is only half as dear as First-class, but by Intermediate, which is very awful indeed. There are no cushions in the Intermediate class, and the population are either Intermediate, which is Eurasian, or native, which for a long night journey is nasty, or Loafer, which is amusing though intoxicated. Intermediates do not buy from refreshment-rooms. They carry their food in bundles and pots, and buy sweets from the native sweetmeat-sellers, and drink the road-side water. That is why in the hot weather Intermediates are taken out of the carriages dead, and in all weathers are most properly looked down upon.

My particular Intermediate happened to be empty till I reached Nasirabad, when a big black-browed gentleman in shirt-sleeves entered, and, following the custom of Intermediates, passed the time of day. He was a wanderer and a vagabond like myself, but with an educated taste for whisky. He told tales of things he had seen and done, of out-of-the-way corners of the Empire into which he had penetrated, and of adventures in which he risked his life for a few days' food.

'If India was filled with men like you and me, not knowing more than the crows where they'd get their next day's rations, it isn't seventy millions of revenue the land would be paying – it's seven hundred millions,' said he; and as I looked at his mouth and chin I was disposed to agree with him.

We talked politics – the politics of Loaferdom, that sees things from the underside where the lath and plaster is not smoothed off – and we talked postal arrangements because my friend wanted to send a telegram back from the next station to Ajmir, the turning-off place from the Bombay to the Mhow line as you travel westward. My friend had no money beyond eight annas, which he wanted for dinner, and I had no money at all, owing to the hitch in the Budget before mentioned. Further, I was going into a wilderness where, though I should resume touch with the Treasury, there were no telegraph offices. I was, therefore, unable to help him in any way.

'We might threaten a Station-master, and make him send a wire on tick,' said my friend, 'but that'd mean inquiries for you and for me, and *I*'ve got my hands full these days. Did you say you are travelling back along this line within any days?'

'Within ten,' I said.

'Can't you make it eight?' said he. 'Mine is rather urgent business.'

'I can send your telegram within ten days if that will serve you,' I said.

'I couldn't trust the wire to fetch him now I think of it. It's this way. He leaves Delhi on the 23rd for Bombay. That means he'll be running through Ajmir about the night of the 23rd.'

'But I'm going into the Indian Desert,' I explained.

'Well *and* good,' said he. 'You'll be changing at Marwar Junction to get into Jodhpore territory – you must do that – and he'll be coming through Marwar Junction in the early morning of the 24th by the Bombay Mail. Can you be at Marwar Junction on that time? 'Twon't be inconveniencing you because I know that there's precious few pickings to be got out of these Central India States – even though you pretend to be correspondent of the *Backwoodsman*.'

'Have you ever tried that trick?' I asked.

'Again and again, but the Residents find you out, and then you get escorted to the Border before you've time to get your knife into them. But about my friend here. I *must* give him a word o' mouth to tell him what's come to me or else he won't know where to go. I would take it more than kind of you if you was to come out of Central India in time to catch him at Marwar Junction, and say to him: "He has gone South for the week." He'll know what that means. He's a big man with a red beard, and a great swell he is. You'll find him sleeping like a gentleman with all his luggage round him in a Second-class compartment. But don't you be afraid. Slip down the window, and say: "He has gone South for the week," and he'll tumble. It's only cutting your time of stay in those parts by two days. I ask you as a stranger – going to the West,' he said with emphasis.

'Where have *you* come from?' said I.

'From the East,' said he, 'and I am hoping that you will give him the message on the Square – for the sake of my Mother as well as your own.'

Englishmen are not usually softened by appeals to the memory of their mothers, but for certain reasons, which will be fully apparent, I saw fit to agree.

'It's more than a little matter,' said he, 'and that's why I asked you to do it – and now I know that I can depend on you doing it. A Second-class carriage at Marwar Junction, and a red-haired man asleep in it. You'll be sure to remember. I get out at the next station, and I must hold on there till he comes or sends me what I want.'

'I'll give the message if I catch him,' I said, 'and for the sake of your Mother as well as mine I'll give you a word of advice. Don't try to run the Central India States just now as the correspondent of the *Backwoodsman*. There's a real one knocking about here, and it might lead to trouble.'

'Thank you,' said he simply, 'and when will the swine be gone? I can't starve because he's ruining my work. I wanted to get hold of the Degumber Rajah down here about his father's widow, and give him a jump.'

'What did he do to his father's widow, then?'

'Filled her up with red pepper and slippered her to death as she hung from a beam.
I found that out myself, and I'm the only man that would dare go into the State to get
hush-money for it. They'll try to poison me, same as they did in Chortumna when I
went on the loot there. But you'll give the man at Marwar Junction my message?'

He got out at a little roadside station, and I reflected. I had heard, more than once,
of men personating correspondents of newspapers and bleeding small Native States
with threats of exposure, but I had never met any of the caste before. They led a hard
life, and generally die with great suddenness. The Native States have a wholesome
horror of English newspapers which may throw light on their peculiar methods of
government, and do their best to choke correspondents with champagne, or drive
them out of their mind with four-in-hand barouches. They do not understand that
nobody cares a straw for the internal administration of Native States so long as oppression and crime are kept within decent limits, and the ruler is not drugged, drunk, or
diseased from one end of the year to the other. They are the dark places of the earth,
full of unimaginable cruelty, touching the Railway and the Telegraph on one side,
and, on the other, the days of Harun-al-Raschid. When I left the train I did business
with divers Kings, and in eight days passed through many changes of life. Sometimes
I wore dress-clothes and consorted with Princes and Politicals, drinking from crystal
and eating from silver. Sometimes I lay out upon the ground and devoured what I
could get, from a plate made of leaves, and drank the running water, and slept under
the same rug as my servant. It was all in the day's work.

Then I headed for the Great Indian Desert upon the proper date, as I had promised, and the night Mail set me down at Marwar Junction, where a funny, little,
happy-go-lucky, native-managed railway runs to Jodhpore. The Bombay Mail from
Delhi makes a short halt at Marwar. She arrived as I got in, and I had just time to
hurry to her platform and go down the carriages. There was only one Second-class
on the train. I slipped the window and looked down upon a flaming red beard, half
covered by a railway rug. That was my man, fast asleep, and I dug him gently in the
ribs. He woke with a grunt, and I saw his face in the light of the lamps. It was a
great and shining face.

'Tickets again?' said he.

'No,' said I. 'I am to tell you that he is gone South for the week. He has gone South for the week!'

The train had begun to move out. The red man rubbed his eyes. 'He has gone South for the week,' he repeated. 'Now that's just like his impidence. Did he say that I was to give you anything? 'Cause I won't.'

'He didn't,' I said, and dropped away, and watched the red lights die out in the dark. It was horribly cold because the wind was blowing off the sands. I climbed into my own train – not an Intermediate Carriage this time – and went to sleep.

If the man with the beard had given me a rupee I should have kept it as a memento of a rather curious affair. But the consciousness of having done my duty was my only reward.

Later on I reflected that two gentlemen like my friends could not do any good if they forgathered and personated correspondents of newspapers, and might, if they black-mailed one of the little rat-trap states of Central India or Southern Rajputana, get themselves into serious difficulties. I therefore took some trouble to describe them as accurately as I could remember to people who would be interested in deporting them; and succeeded, so I was later informed, in having them headed back from the Degumber borders.

Then I became respectable, and returned to an Office where there were no Kings and no incidents outside the daily manufacture of a newspaper. A newspaper office seems to attract every conceivable sort of person, to the prejudice of discipline. Zenana-mission ladies arrive, and beg that the Editor will instantly abandon all his duties to describe a Christian prize-giving in a back-slum of a perfectly inaccessible village; Colonels who have been over-passed for command sit down and sketch the outline of a series of ten, twelve, or twenty-four leading articles on Seniority *versus* Selection; Missionaries wish to know why they have not been permitted to escape from their regular vehicles of abuse and swear at a brother-missionary under special patronage of the editorial We; stranded theatrical companies troop up to explain that they cannot pay for their advertisements, but on their return from New Zealand or Tahiti will do so with interest; inventors of patent punkah-pulling machines, carriage couplings, and unbreakable swords and axle-trees, call with specifications in their pockets and hours at their disposal; tea-companies enter and elaborate their prospectuses with the office pens; secretaries of ball-committees clamour to have the glories of their last dance more fully described; strange ladies rustle in and say, 'I want a hundred lady's cards printed *at once*, please,' which is manifestly part of an Editor's duty; and every dissolute ruffian that ever tramped the Grand Trunk Road makes it his business to ask for employment as a proof-reader. And, all the time, the telephone-bell is ringing madly, and Kings are being killed on the Continent, and Empires are saying, 'You're another,' and Mister Gladstone is calling down brimstone upon the British Dominions, and the little black copy-boys are whining, '*kaa-pi chay-ha-yeh*' (copy wanted) like tired bees, and most of the paper is as blank as Modred's shield.

But that is the amusing part of the year. There are six other months when none ever comes to call, and the thermometer walks inch by inch up to the top of the glass, and the office is darkened to just above reading-light, and the press-machines are red-hot of touch, and nobody writes anything but accounts of amusements in the Hill-stations or obituary notices. Then the telephone becomes a tinkling terror, because it tells you of the sudden deaths of men and women that you knew intimately, and the prickly-heat covers you with a garment, and you sit down and write: 'A slight increase of sickness is reported from the Khuda Janta Khan District. The outbreak is purely sporadic in its nature, and, thanks to the energetic efforts of the District authorities, is now almost at an end. It is, however, with deep regret we record the death, etc.'

Then the sickness really breaks out, and the less recording and reporting the better for the peace of the subscribers. But the Empires and the Kings continue to divert themselves as selfishly as before, and the Foreman thinks that a daily paper really ought to come out once in twenty-four hours, and all the people at the Hill-stations in the middle of their amusements say: 'Good gracious! Why can't the paper be sparkling? I'm sure there's plenty going on up here.'

That is the dark half of the moon, and, as the advertisements say, 'must be experienced to be appreciated.'

It was in that season, and a remarkably evil season, that the paper began running the last issue of the week on Saturday night, which is to say Sunday morning, after the custom of a London paper. This was a great convenience, for immediately after the paper was put to bed, the dawn would lower the thermometer from 96° to almost 84° for half an hour, and in that chill – you have no idea how cold is 84° on the grass until you begin to pray for it – a very tired man could get off to sleep ere the heat roused him.

One Saturday night it was my pleasant duty to put the paper to bed alone. A King or courtier or a courtesan or a Community was going to die or get a new Constitution, or do something that was important on the other side of the world, and the paper was to be held open till the latest possible minute in order to catch the telegram.

It was a pitchy black night, as stifling as a June night can be, and the *loo*, the red-hot wind from the westward, was booming among the tinder-dry trees and pretending that the rain was on its heels. Now and again a spot of almost boiling water would fall on the dust with the flop of a frog, but all our weary world knew that was only pretence. It was a shade cooler in the press-room than the office, so I sat there, while the type ticked and clicked, and the night-jars hooted at the windows, and the all but naked compositors wiped the sweat from their foreheads, and called for water. The thing that was keeping us back, whatever it was, would not come off, though the *loo* dropped and the last type was set, and the whole round earth stood still in the choking heat, with its finger on its lip, to wait the event. I drowsed, and wondered whether the telegraph was a blessing, and whether this dying man, or struggling people, might be aware of the inconvenience the delay was causing. There was no special reason beyond the heat and worry to make tension, but, as the clock-hands crept up to three o'clock, and the machines spun their fly-wheels two or three times to see that all was in order before I said the word that would set them off, I could have shrieked aloud.

Then the roar and rattle of the wheels shivered the quiet into little bits. I rose to go away, but two men in white clothes stood in front of me. The first one said: 'It's him!' The second said: 'So it is!' And they both laughed almost as loudly as the machinery roared, and mopped their foreheads. 'We seed there was a light burning across the road, and we were sleeping in that ditch there for coolness, and I said to my friend here, the office is open. Let's come along and speak to him as turned us back from the Degumber State,' said the smaller of the two. He was the man I had met in the Mhow train, and his fellow was the red-bearded man of Marwar Junction. There was no mistaking the eyebrows of the one or the beard of the other.

I was not pleased, because I wished to go to sleep, not to squabble with loafers. 'What do you want?' I asked.

'Half an hour's talk with you, cool and comfortable, in the office,' said the red-bearded man. 'We'd *like* some drink – the Contrack doesn't begin yet, Peachey, so you needn't look – but what we really want is advice. We don't want money. We ask you as a favour, because we found out you did us a bad turn about Degumber State.'

I led from the press-room to the stifling office with the maps on the walls, and the red-haired man rubbed his hands. 'That's something like,' said he. 'This was the proper shop to come to. Now, Sir, let me introduce to you Brother Peachey Carnehan, that's him, and Brother Daniel Dravot, that is *me*, and the less said about our professions the better, for we have been most things in our time. Soldier, sailor, compositor, photographer, proof-reader, street-preacher, and correspondents of the *Backwoodsman* when we thought the paper wanted one. Carnehan is sober, and so am I. Look at us first, and see that's sure. It will save you cutting into my talk. We'll take one of your cigars apiece, and you shall see us light up.'

I watched the test. The men were absolutely sober, so I gave them each a tepid whisky and soda.

'Well *and* good,' said Carnehan of the eyebrows, wiping the froth from his moustache. 'Let me talk now, Dan. We have been all over India, mostly on foot. We have been boiler-fitters, engine-drivers, petty contractors, and all that, and we have decided that India isn't big enough for such as us.'

They certainly were too big for the office. Dravot's beard seemed to fill half the room and Carnehan's shoulders the other half, as they sat on the big table. Carnehan continued: 'The country isn't half worked out because they that governs it won't let you touch it. They spend all their blessed time in governing it, and you can't lift a spade, nor chip a rock, nor look for oil, nor anything like that, without all the Government saying, "Leave it alone, and let us govern." Therefore, such *as* it is, we will let it alone, and go away to some other place where a man isn't crowded and can come to his own. We are not little men, and there is nothing that we are afraid of except Drink, and we have signed a Contrack on that. *Therefore*, we are going away to be Kings.'

'Kings in our own right,' muttered Dravot.

'Yes, of course,' I said. 'You've been tramping in the sun, and it's a very warm night, and hadn't you better sleep over the notion? Come tomorrow.'

'Neither drunk nor sunstruck,' said Dravot. 'We have slept over the notion half a year, and require to see Books and Atlases, and we have decided that there is only one place now in the world that two strong men can Sar-a-*whack*. They call it Kafiristan. By my reckoning it's the top right-hand corner of Afghanistan, not more than three hundred miles from Peshawar. They have two-and-thirty heathen idols there, and we'll be the thirty-third and fourth. It's a mountainous country, and the women of those parts are very beautiful.'

'But that is provided against in the Contrack,' said Carnehan. 'Neither Woman nor Liqu-or, Daniel.'

'And that's all we know, except that no one has gone there, and they fight, and in any place where they fight a man who knows how to drill men can always be a King. We shall go to those parts and say to any King we find – "D'you want to vanquish your foes?" and we will show him how to drill men; for that we know better than anything else. Then we will subvert that King and seize his Throne and establish a Dy-nasty.'

'You'll be cut to pieces before you're fifty miles across the Border,' I said. 'You have to travel through Afghanistan to get to that country. It's one mass of mountains and peaks and glaciers, and no Englishman has been through it. The people are utter brutes, and even if you reached them you couldn't do anything.'

'That's more like,' said Carnehan. 'If you could think us a little more mad we would be more pleased. We have come to you to know about this country, to read a book about it, and to be shown maps. We want you to tell us that we are fools and to show us your books.' He turned to the bookcases.

'Are you at all in earnest?' I said.

'A little,' said Dravot sweetly. 'As big a map as you have got, even if it's all blank where Kafiristan is, and any books you've got. We can read, though we aren't very educated.'

I uncased the big thirty-two-miles-to-the-inch map of India, and two smaller Frontier maps, hauled down volume INF-KAN of the *Encyclopædia Britannica*, and the men consulted them.

'See here!' said Dravot, his thumb on the map. 'Up to Jagdallak, Peachey and me know the road. We was there with Roberts' Army. We'll have to turn off to the right at Jagdallak through Laghmann territory. Then we get among the hills – fourteen thousand feet – fifteen thousand – it will be cold work there, but it don't look very far on the map.'

I handed him Wood on the *Sources of the Oxus*. Carnehan was deep in the *Encyclopædia*.

'They're a mixed lot,' said Dravot reflectively; 'and it won't help us to know the names of their tribes. The more tribes the more they'll fight, and the better for us. From Jagdallak to Ashang. H'mm!'

'But all the information about the country is as sketchy and inaccurate as can be,' I protested. 'No one knows anything about it really. Here's the file of the *United Services' Institute*. Read what Bellew says.'

'Blow Bellew!' said Carnehan. 'Dan, they're a stinkin' lot of heathens, but this book here says they think they're related to us English.'

I smoked while the men poured over Raverty, Wood, the maps, and the *Encyclopædia*.

'There is no use your waiting,' said Dravot politely. 'It's about four o'clock now. We'll go before six o'clock if you want to sleep, and we won't steal any of the papers. Don't you sit up. We're two harmless lunatics, and if you come tomorrow evening down to the Serai we'll say goodbye to you.'

'You *are* two fools,' I answered. 'You'll be turned back at the Frontier or cut up the minute you set foot in Afghanistan. Do you want any money or a recommendation down-country? I can help you to the chance of work next week.'

'Next week we shall be hard at work ourselves, thank you,' said Dravot. 'It isn't so easy being a King as it looks. When we've got our Kingdom in going order we'll let you know, and you can come up and help us to govern it.'

'Would two lunatics make a contrack like that?' said Carnehan, with subdued pride, showing me a greasy half-sheet of notepaper on which was written the following. I copied it, then and there, as a curiosity –

This Contract between me and you persuing witnesseth in the name of God –
Amen and so forth.

(One)   That me and you will settle this matter together; i.e. to be Kings of
Kafiristan.

(Two)   That you and me will not, while this matter is being settled, look at
any Liquor, nor any Woman black, white, or brown, so as to get mixed up with
one or the other harmful.

(Three)   That we conduct ourselves with Dignity and Discretion, and if one
of us gets into trouble the other will stay by him.

Signed by you and me this day.

Peachey Taliaferro Carnehan.

Daniel Dravot.

Both Gentlemen at Large.

'There was no need for the last article,' said Carnehan, blushing modestly; 'but it looks regular. Now you know the sort of men that loafers are – we *are* loafers, Dan, until we get out of India – and *do* you think that we would sign a Contrack like that unless we was in earnest? We have kept away from the two things that make life worth having.'

'You won't enjoy your lives much longer if you are going to try this idiotic adventure. Don't set the office on fire,' I said, 'and go away before nine o'clock.'

I left them still poring over the maps and making notes on the back of the 'Contrack.' 'Be sure to come down to the Serai tomorrow,' were their parting words.

The Kumharsen Serai is the great four-square sink of humanity where the strings of camels and horses from the North load and unload. All the nationalities of Central Asia may be found there, and most of the folk of India proper. Balkh and Bokhara there meet Bengal and Bombay, and try to draw eye-teeth. You can buy ponies, turquoises,

Persian pussy-cats, saddle-bags, fat-tailed sheep and musk in the Kumharsen Serai, and get many strange things for nothing. In the afternoon I went down to see whether my friends intended to keep their word or were lying there drunk.

A priest attired in fragments of ribbons and rags stalked up to me, gravely twisting a child's paper whirligig. Behind him was his servant bending under the load of a crate of mud toys. The two were loading up two camels, and the inhabitants of the Serai watched them with shrieks of laughter.

'The priest is mad,' said a horse-dealer to me. 'He is going up to Kabul to sell toys to the Amir. He will either be raised to honour or have his head cut off. He came in here this morning and has been behaving madly ever since.'

'The witless are under the protection of God,' stammered a flat-cheeked Usbeg in broken Hindi. 'They foretell future events.'

'Would they could have foretold that my caravan would have been cut up by the Shinwaris almost within shadow of the Pass!' grunted the Eusufzai agent of a Rajputana trading-house whose goods had been diverted into the hands of other robbers just across the Border, and whose misfortunes were the laughing-stock of the bazar. 'Ohé, priest, whence come you and whither do you go?'

'From Roum have I come,' shouted the priest, waving his whirligig; 'from Roum, blown by the breath of a hundred devils across the sea! O thieves, robbers, liars, the blessing of Pir Khan on pigs, dogs, and perjurers! Who will take the Protected of God to the North to sell charms that are never still to the Amir? The camels shall not gall, the sons shall not fall sick, and the wives shall remain faithful while they are away, of the men who give me place in their caravan. Who will assist me to slipper the King of the Roos with a golden slipper with a silver heel? The protection of Pir Khan be upon his labours!' He spread out the skirts of his gaberdine and pirouetted between the lines of tethered horses.

'There starts a caravan from Peshawar to Kabul in twenty days, *Huzrut*,' said the Eusufzai trader. 'My camels go therewith. Do thou also go and bring us good luck.'

'I will go even now!' shouted the priest. 'I will depart upon my winged camels, and be at Peshawar in a day! Ho! Hazar Mir Khan,' he yelled to his servant, 'drive out the camels, but let me first mount my own.'

He leaped on the back of his beast as it knelt, and, turning round to me, cried: 'Come thou also, Sahib, a little along the road, and I will sell thee a charm – an amulet that shall make thee King of Kafiristan.'

Then the light broke upon me, and I followed the two camels out of the Serai till we reached open road and the priest halted.

'What d'you think o' that?' said he in English. 'Carnehan can't talk their patter, so I've made him my servant. He makes a handsome servant. 'Tisn't for nothing that I've been knocking about the country for fourteen years. Didn't I do that talk neat? We'll hitch on to a caravan at Peshawar till we get to Jagdallak, and then we'll see if we can get donkeys for our camels, and strike into Kafiristan. Whirligigs for the Amir, O Lor! Put your hand under the camel-bags and tell me what you feel.'

I felt the butt of a Martini, and another and another.

'Twenty of 'em,' said Dravot placidly. 'Twenty of 'em and ammunition to correspond, under the whirligigs and the mud dolls.'

'Heaven help you if you are caught with those things!' I said. 'A Martini is worth her weight in silver among the Pathans.'

'Fifteen hundred rupees of capital – every rupee we could beg, borrow, or steal – are invested on these two camels,' said Dravot. 'We won't get caught. We're going through the Khaiber with a regular caravan. Who'd touch a poor mad priest?'

'Have you got everything you want?' I asked, overcome with astonishment.

'Not yet, but we shall soon. Give us a memento of your kindness, *Brother*. You did me a service, yesterday, and that time in Marwar. Half my Kingdom shall you have, as the saying is.' I slipped a small charm compass from my watch-chain and handed it up to the priest.

'Good-bye,' said Dravot, giving me hand cautiously. 'It's the last time we'll shake hands with an Englishman these many days. Shake hands with him, Carnehan,' he cried, as the second camel passed me.

Carnehan leaned down and shook hands. Then the camels passed away along the dusty road, and I was left alone to wonder. My eye could detect no failure in the disguises. The scene in the Serai proved that they were complete to the native mind. There was just the chance, therefore, that Carnehan and Dravot would be able to wander through Afghanistan without detection. But, beyond, they would find death – certain and awful death.

Ten days later a native correspondent giving me the news of the day from Peshawar, wound up his letter with: 'There has been much laughter here on account of a certain mad priest who is going in his estimation to sell petty gauds and insignificant trinkets which he ascribes as great charms to H.H. the Amir of Bokhara. He passed through Peshawar and associated himself to the Second Summer caravan that goes to Kabul. The merchants are pleased because through superstition they imagine that such mad fellows bring good fortune.'

The two, then, were beyond the Border. I would have prayed for them, but, that night, a real King died in Europe, and demanded an obituary notice.

The wheel of the world swings through the same phases again and again. Summer passed and winter thereafter, and came and passed again. The daily paper continued and I with it, and upon the third summer there fell a hot night, a night-issue, and a strained waiting for something to be telegraphed from the other side of the world, exactly as had happened before. A few great men had died in the past two years, the machines worked with more clatter, and some of the trees in the office garden were a few feet taller. But that was all the difference.

I passed over to the press-room, and went through just such a scene as I have already described. The nervous tension was stronger than it had been two years before, and I felt the heat more acutely. At three o'clock I cried, 'Print off,' and turned to go, when there crept to my chair what was left of a man. He was bent into a circle, his head was sunk between his shoulders, and he moved his feet one over the other like a bear. I could hardly see whether he walked or crawled – this rag-wrapped, whining cripple who addressed me by name, crying that he was come back. 'Can you give me a drink?' he whimpered. 'For the Lord's sake give me a drink!'

I went back to the office, the man following with groans of pain, and I turned up the lamp.

'Don't you know me?' he gasped, dropping into a chair, and he turned his drawn face, surmounted by a shock of gray hair, to the light.

I looked at him intently. Once before had I seen eyebrows that met over the nose in an inch-broad black band, but for the life of me I could not tell where.

'I don't know you,' I said, handing him the whisky. 'What can I do for you?'

He took a gulp of the spirit raw, and shivered in spite of the suffocating heat.

'I've come back,' he repeated; 'and I was the King of Kafiristan – me and Dravot – crowned Kings we was! In this office we settled it – you setting there and giving us the books. I am Peachey – Peachey Taliaferro Carnehan, and you've been setting here ever since – O Lord!'

I was more than a little astonished, and expressed my feelings accordingly.

'It's true,' said Carnehan, with a dry cackle, nursing his feet, which were wrapped in rags. 'True as gospel. Kings we were, with crowns upon our heads – me and Dravot – poor Dan – oh, poor, poor Dan, that would never take advice, not though I begged of him!'

'Take the whisky,' I said, 'and take your own time. Tell me all you can recollect of everything from beginning to end. You got across the Border on your camels, Dravot dressed as a mad priest and you his servant. Do you remember that?'

'I ain't mad – yet, but I shall be that way soon. Of course I remember. Keep looking at me, or maybe my words will go all to pieces. Keep looking at me in my eyes and don't say anything.'

I leaned forward and looked into his face as steadily as I could. He dropped one hand upon the table and I grasped it by the wrist. It was twisted like a bird's claw, and upon the back was a ragged red diamond-shaped scar.

'No, don't look there. Look at *me*,' said Carnehan. 'That comes afterwards, but for the Lord's sake don't distrack me. We left with that caravan, me and Dravot playing all sorts of antics to amuse the people we were with. Dravot used to make us laugh in the evenings when all the people was cooking their dinners – cooking their dinners, and . . . what did they do then? They lit little fires with sparks that went into Dravot's beard, and we all laughed – fit to die. Little red fires they was, going into Dravot's big red beard – so funny.' His eyes left mine and he smiled foolishly.

'You went as far as Jagdallak with that caravan,' I said at a venture, 'after you had lit those fires. To Jagdallak, where you turned off to try to get into Kafiristan.'

'No, we didn't neither. What are you talking about? We turned off before Jagdallak, because we heard the roads was good. But they wasn't good enough for our two camels – mine and Dravot's. When we left the caravan, Dravot took off all his clothes and mine too, and said we would be heathen, because the Kafirs didn't allow Mohammedans to talk to them. So we dressed betwixt and between, and such a sight as Daniel Dravot I never saw yet nor expect to see again. He burned half his beard, and slung a sheep-skin over his shoulder, and shaved his head into patterns. He shaved mine, too, and made me wear outrageous things to look like a heathen. That was in a most mountainous country, and our camels couldn't go along any more because of the mountains. They were tall and black, and coming home I saw them fight like wild goats – there are lots of goats in Kafiristan. And these mountains, they never keep still, no more than the goats. Always fighting they are, and don't let you sleep at night.'

'Take some more whisky,' I said very slowly. 'What did you and Daniel Dravot do when the camels could go no farther because of the rough roads that led into Kafiristan?'

'What did which do? There was a party called Peachey Taliaferro Carnehan that was with Dravot. Shall I tell you about him? He died out there in the cold. Slap from the bridge fell old Peachey, turning and twisting in the air like a penny whirligig that you can sell to the Amir. – No; they was two for three-ha'pence, those whirligigs, or I am much mistaken and woful sore . . . And then these camels were no use, and Peachey said to Dravot – "For the Lord's sake let's get out of this before our heads are chopped off," and with that they killed the camels all among the mountains, not having anything in particular to eat, but first they took off the boxes with the guns and the ammunition, till two men came along driving four mules. Dravot up and dances in front of them, singing – "Sell me four mules." Says the first man – "If you are rich enough to buy, you are rich enough to rob;" but before ever he could put his hand to his knife, Dravot breaks his neck over his knee, and the other party runs away. So Carnehan loaded the mules with the rifles that was taken off the camels, and together we starts forward into those bitter cold mountainous parts, and never a road broader than the back of your hand.'

He paused for a moment, while I asked him if he could remember the nature of the country through which he had journeyed.

'I am telling you as straight as I can, but my head isn't as good as it might be. They drove nails through it to make me hear better how Dravot died. The country was mountainous and the mules were most contrary, and the inhabitants was dispersed and solitary. They went up and up, and down and down, and that other party, Carnehan, was imploring of Dravot not to sing and whistle so loud, for fear of bringing down the tremenjus avalanches. But Dravot says that if a King couldn't sing it wasn't worth being King, and whacked the mules over the rump, and never took no heed for ten cold days. We came to a big level valley all among the mountains, and the mules were near dead, so we killed them, not having anything in special for them or us to eat. We sat upon the boxes, and played odd and even with the cartridges that was jolted out.

'Then ten men with bows and arrows ran down that valley, chasing twenty men with bows and arrows, and the row was tremenjus. They was fair men – fairer than you or me – with yellow hair and remarkable well built. Says Dravot, unpacking the guns – "This is the beginning of the business. We'll fight for the ten men," and with that he fires two rifles at the twenty men, and drops one of them at two hundred yards from the rock where he was sitting. The other men began to run, but Carnehan and Dravot sits on the boxes picking them off at all ranges, up and down the valley. Then we goes up to the ten men that had run across the snow too, and they fires a footy little arrow at us. Dravot he shoots above their heads and they all falls down flat. Then he walks over them and kicks them, and then he lifts them up and shakes hands all round to make them friendly like. He calls them and gives them the boxes to carry, and waves his hand for all the world as though he was King already. They takes the boxes and him across the valley and up the hill into a pine wood on the top, where there was half-a-dozen big stone idols. Dravot he goes to the biggest – a fellow they call Imbra – and lays a rifle and a cartridge at his feet, rubbing his nose respectful with his own nose, patting him on the head, and saluting in front of it. He turns round to the men and nods his head, and says – "That's all right. I'm in the know too, and all these old jim-jams are my friends." Then he opens his mouth and points down it, and when the first man brings him food, he says – "No"; and when the second man brings him food he says – "No"; but when one of the old priests and the boss of the village brings him food, he says – "Yes," very haughty, and eats it slow. That was how he came to our first village, without any trouble, just as though we had tumbled from the skies. But we tumbled from one of those damned rope-bridges, you see, and – you couldn't expect a man to laugh much after that?'

'Take some more whisky and go on,' I said. 'That was the first village you came into. How did you get to be King?'

'I wasn't King,' said Carnehan. 'Dravot he was the King, and a handsome man he looked with the gold crown on his head and all. Him and the other party stayed in that village, and every morning Dravot sat by the side of old Imbra, and the people came and worshipped. That was Dravot's order. Then a lot of men came into the valley, and Carnehan and Dravot picks them off with the rifles before they knew where they was, and runs down into the valley and up again the other side and finds another village, same as the first one, and the people all falls down flat on their faces, and Dravot says – "Now what is the trouble between you two villages?" and the people points to a woman, as fair as you or me, that was carried off, and Dravot takes her back to the first village and counts up the dead – eight there was. For each dead man Dravot pours a little milk on the ground and waves his arms like a whirligig, and "That's all right," says he. Then he and Carnehan takes the big boss of each village by the arm and walks them down into the valley, and shows them how to scratch a line with a spear right down the valley, and gives each a sod of turf from both sides of the line. Then all the people comes down and shouts like the devil and all, and Dravot says – "Go and dig the land, and be fruitful and multiply," which they did, though they didn't understand. Then we asks the names of things in their lingo – bread and water and fire and idols and such, and Dravot leads the priest of each village up to the idol, and says he must sit there and judge the people, and if anything goes wrong he is to be shot.

'Next week they was all turning up the land in the valley as quiet as bees and much prettier, and the priests heard all the complaints and told Dravot in dumb show what it was about. "That's just the beginning," says Dravot. "They think we're Gods." He and Carnehan picks out twenty good men and shows them how to click off a rifle, and form fours, and advance in line, and they was very pleased to do so, and clever to see the hang of it. Then he takes out his pipe and his baccy-pouch and leaves one at one village, and one at the other, and off we two goes to see what was to be done in the next valley. That was all rock, and there was a little village there, and Carnehan says – "Send 'em to the old valley to plant," and takes 'em there, and gives 'em some land that wasn't took before. They were a poor lot, and we blooded 'em with a kid before letting 'em into the new Kingdom. That was to impress the people, and then they settled down quiet, and Carnehan went back to Dravot who had got into another valley all snow and ice and most mountainous. There was no people there and the Army got afraid, so Dravot shoots one of them, and goes on till he finds some people in a village, and the Army explains that unless the people wants to be killed they had better not shoot their little matchlocks; for they had matchlocks. We makes friends with the priest, and I stays there alone with two of the Army, teaching the men how to drill, and a thundering big Chief comes across the snow with kettle-drums and horns twanging, because he heard there was a new God kicking about. Carnehan sights for the brown of the men half a mile across the snow and wings one of them. Then he sends a message to the Chief that, unless he wished to be killed, he must come and shake hands with me and leave his arms behind. The Chief comes alone first, and Carnehan shakes hands with him and whirls his arms about, same as Dravot used, and very much surprised that Chief was, and strokes my eyebrows. Then Carnehan goes alone to the Chief, and asks him in dumb show if he had an enemy he hated. "I have," says the Chief. So Carnehan weeds out the pick of his men, and sets the two of the Army to show them drill, and at the end of two weeks the men can manœuvre about as well as Volunteers. So he marches with the Chief to a great big plain on the top of a mountain, and the Chief's men rushes into a village and takes it; we three Martinis firing into the brown of the enemy. So we took that village too, and I gives the Chief a rag from my coat and says, "Occupy till I come"; which was scriptural. By way of a reminder, when me and the Army was eighteen hundred yards away, I drops a bullet near him standing on the snow, and all the people falls flat on their faces. Then I sends a letter to Dravot wherever he be by land or by sea.'

At the risk of throwing the creature out of train I interrupted – 'How could you write a letter up yonder?'

'The letter? – Oh! – The letter! Keep looking at me between the eyes, please. It was a string-talk letter, that we'd learned the way of it from a blind beggar in the Punjab.'

I remember that there had once come to the office a blind man with a knotted twig and a piece of string which he wound round the twig according to some cipher of his own. He could, after the lapse of days or hours, repeat the sentence which he had reeled up. He had reduced the alphabet to eleven primitive sounds, and tried to teach me his method, but I could not understand.

'I sent that letter to Dravot,' said Carnehan; 'and told him to come back because this Kingdom was growing too big for me to handle, and then I struck for the first valley, to see how the priests were working. They called the village we took along with the Chief, Bashkai, and the first village we took, Er-Heb. The priests at Er-Heb was doing all right, but they had a lot of pending cases about land to show me, and some men from another village had been firing arrows at night. I went out and looked for that village, and fired four rounds at it from a thousand yards. That used all the cartridges I cared to spend, and I waited for Dravot, who had been away two or three months, and I kept my people quiet.

'One morning I heard the devil's own noise of drums and horns, and Dan Dravot marches down the hill with his Army and a tail of hundreds of men, and, which was the most amazing, a great gold crown on his head. "My Gord, Carnehan," says Daniel, "this is a tremenjus business, and we've got the whole country as far as it's worth having. I am the son of Alexander by Queen Semiramis, and you're my younger brother and a God too! It's the biggest thing we've ever seen. I've been marching and fighting for six weeks with the Army, and every footy little village for fifty miles has come in rejoiceful; and more than that, I've got the key of the whole show, as you'll see, and I've got a crown for you! I told 'em to make two of 'em at a place called Shu, where the gold lies in the rock like suet in mutton. Gold I've seen, and turquoise I've kicked out of the cliffs, and there's garnets in the sands of the river, and here's a chunk of amber that a man brought me. Call up all the priests and, here, take your crown."

'One of the men opens a black hair bag, and I slips the crown on. It was too small and too heavy, but I wore it for the glory. Hammered gold it was – five pound weight, like a hoop of a barrel.

'"Peachey," says Dravot, "we don't want to fight no more. The Craft's the trick, so help me!" and he brings forward that same Chief that I left at Bashkai – Billy Fish we called him afterwards, because he was so like Billy Fish that drove the big tank-engine at Mach on the Bolan in the old days. "Shake hands with him," says Dravot, and I shook hands and nearly dropped, for Billy Fish gave me the Grip. I said nothing, but tried him with the Fellow Craft Grip. He answers all right, and I tried the Master's Grip, but that was a slip. "A Fellow Craft he is!" I says to Dan. "Does he know the word?" – "He does," says Dan, "and all the priests know. It's a miracle! The Chiefs and the priests can work a Fellow Craft Lodge in a way that's very like ours, and they've cut the marks on the rocks, but they don't know the Third Degree, and they've come to find out. It's Gord's Truth. I've known these long years that the Afghans knew up to the Fellow Craft Degree, but this is a miracle. A God and a Grand-Master of the Craft am I, and a Lodge in the Third Degree I will open, and we'll raise the head priests and the Chiefs of the villages."

'"It's against all the law," I says, "holding a Lodge without warrant from anyone; and you know we never held office in any Lodge."

'"It's a master-stroke o' policy," says Dravot. "It means running the country as easy as a four-wheeled bogie on a down grade. We can't stop to inquire now, or they'll turn against us. I've forty Chiefs at my heel, and passed and raised according to their merit they shall be. Billet these men on the villages, and see that we run up a Lodge of some kind. The temple of Imbra will do for the Lodge-room. The women must make aprons as you show them. I'll hold a levee of Chiefs tonight and Lodge tomorrow."

'I was fair run off my legs, but I wasn't such a fool as not to see what a pull this Craft business gave us. I showed the priests' families how to make aprons of the degrees, but for Dravot's apron the blue border and marks was made of turquoise lumps on white hide, not cloth. We took a great square stone in the temple for the Master's chair, and little stones for the officers' chairs, and painted the black pavement with white squares, and did what we could to make things regular.

'At the levee which was held that night on the hillside with big bonfires, Dravot gives out that him and me were Gods and sons of Alexander, and Past Grand-Masters in the Craft, and was come to make Kafiristan a country where every man should eat in peace and drink in quiet, and specially obey us. Then the Chiefs come round to shake hands, and they were so hairy and white and fair it was just shaking hands with old friends. We gave them names according as they was like men we had known in India – Billy Fish, Holly Dilworth, Pikky Kergan, that was Bazar-master when I was at Mhow, and so on, and so on.

'*The* most amazing miracles was at Lodge next night. One of the old priests was watching us continuous, and I felt uneasy, for I knew we'd have to fudge the Ritual, and I didn't know what the men knew. The old priest was a stranger come in from beyond the village of Bashkai. The minute Dravot puts on the Master's apron that the girls had made for him, the priest fetches a whoop and a howl, and tries to overturn the stone that Dravot was sitting on. "It's all up now," I says. "That comes of meddling with the Craft without warrant!" Dravot never winked an eye, not when ten priests took and tilted over the Grand-Master's chair – which was to say the stone of Imbra. The priests begins rubbing the bottom end of it to clear away the black dirt, and presently he shows all the other priests the Master's Mark, same as was on Dravot's apron, cut into the stone. Not even the priests of the temple of Imbra knew it was there. The old chap falls flat on his face at Dravot's feet and kisses 'em. "Luck again," says Dravot, across the Lodge to me; "they say it's the missing Mark that no one could understand the why of. We're more than safe now." Then he bangs the butt of his gun for a gavel and says: "By virtue of the authority vested in me by my own right hand and the help of Peachey, I declare myself Grand-Master of all Freemasonry in Kafiristan in this the Mother Lodge o' the country, and King of Kafiristan equally with Peachey!" At that he puts on his crown and I puts on mine – I was doing Senior Warden – and we opens the Lodge in most ample form. It was an amazing miracle! The priests moved in Lodge through the first two degrees almost without telling, as if the memory was coming back to them. After that, Peachey and Dravot raised such as was worthy – high priests and Chiefs of far-off villages. Billy Fish was the first, and I can tell you we scared the soul out of him. It was not in any way according to Ritual, but it served our turn. We didn't raise more than ten of the biggest men, because we didn't want to make the Degree common. And they was clamouring to be raised.

'"In another six months," says Dravot, "we'll hold another Communication, and see how you are working." Then he asks them about their villages, and learns that they was fighting one against the other, and were sick and tired of it. And when they wasn't doing that they was fighting with the Mohammedans. "You can fight those when they come into our country," says Dravot. "Tell off every tenth man of your tribes for a Frontier guard, and send two hundred at a time to this valley to be drilled. Nobody is going to be shot or speared any more so long as he does well, and I know that you won't cheat me, because you're white people – sons of Alexander – and not like common, black Mohammedans. You are *my* people, and by God," says he, running off into English at the end – "I'll make a damned fine Nation of you, or I'll die in the making!"

'I can't tell all we did for the next six months, because Dravot did a lot I couldn't see the hang of, and he learned their lingo in a way I never could. My work was to help the people plough, and now and again go out with some of the Army and see what the other villages were doing, and make 'em throw rope-bridges across the ravines which cut up the country horrid. Dravot was very kind to me, but when he walked up and down in the pine wood pulling that bloody red beard of his with both fists I knew he was thinking plans I could not advise about, and I just waited for orders.

'But Dravot never showed me disrespect before the people. They were afraid of me and the Army, but they loved Dan. He was the best of friends with the priests and the Chiefs; but anyone could come across the hills with a complaint, and Dravot would hear him out fair, and call four priests together and say what was to be done. He used to call in Billy Fish from Bashkai, and Pikky Kergan from Shu, and an old Chief we called Kafuzelum – it was like enough to his real name – and hold councils with 'em when there was any fighting to be done in small villages. That was his Council of War, and the four priests of Bashkai, Shu, Khawak, and Madora was his Privy Council. Between the lot of 'em they sent me, with forty men and twenty rifles and sixty men carrying turquoises, into the Ghorband country to buy those hand-made Martini rifles, that come out of the Amir's workshops at Kabul, from one of the Amir's Herati regiments that would have sold the very teeth out of their mouths for turquoises.

'I stayed in Ghorband a month, and gave the Governor there the pick of my baskets for hush-money, and bribed the Colonel of the regiment some more, and, between the two and the tribes-people, we got more than a hundred hand-made Martinis, a hundred good Kohat Jezails that'll throw to six hundred yards, and forty man-loads of very bad ammunition for the rifles. I came back with what I had, and distributed 'em among the men that the Chiefs sent in to me to drill. Dravot was too busy to attend to those things, but the old Army that we first made helped me, and we turned out five hundred men that could drill, and two hundred that knew how to hold arms pretty straight. Even those cork-screwed, hand-made guns was a miracle to them. Dravot talked big about powder-shops and factories, walking up and down in the pine wood when the winter was coming on.

'"I won't make a Nation," says he. "I'll make an Empire! These men aren't foreigners; they're English! Look at their eyes — look at their mouths. Look at the way they stand up. They sit on chairs in their own houses. They're the Lost Tribes, or something like it, and they've grown to be English. I'll take a census in the spring if the priests don't get frightened. There must be a fair two million of 'em in these hills. The villages are full o' little children. Two million people — two hundred and fifty thousand fighting men — and all English! They only want the rifles and a little drilling. Two hundred and fifty thousand men, ready to cut in on Russia's right flank when she tries for India! Peachey, man," he says, chewing his beard in great hunks, "we shall be Emperors — Emperors of the Earth! Rajah Brooke will be a suckling to us. I'll treat with the Viceroy on equal terms. I'll ask him to send me twelve picked English — twelve that I know of — to help us govern a bit. There's Mackray, Sergeant-pensioner at Segowli — many's the good dinner he's given me, and his wife a pair of trousers. There's Donkin, the Warder of Tounghoo Jail; there's hundreds that I could lay my hand on if I was in India. The Viceroy shall do it for me. I'll send a man through in the spring for those men, and I'll write for a dispensation from the Grand Lodge for what I've done as Grand-Master. That — and all the Sniders that'll be thrown out when the native troops in India take up the Martini. They'll be worn smooth, but they'll do for fighting in these hills. Twelve English, a hundred thousand Sniders run through the Amir's country in driblets – I'd be content with twenty thousand in one year – and we'd be an Empire. When everything was shipshape, I'd hand over the crown – this crown I'm wearing now – to Queen Victoria on my knees, and she'd say: 'Rise up, Sir Daniel Dravot.' Oh, it's big! It's big, I tell you! But there's so much to be done in every place – Bashkai, Khawak, Shu, and everywhere else."

"'What is it?' I says. "There are no more men coming in to be drilled this autumn. Look at those fat, black clouds. They're bringing the snow."

"'It isn't that,' says Daniel, putting his hand very hard on my shoulder; "and I don't wish to say anything that's against you, for no other living man would have followed me and made me what I am as you have done. You're a first-class Commander-in-Chief, and the people know you; but – it's a big country, and somehow you can't help me, Peachey, in the way I want to be helped."

"'Go to your blasted priests, then!' I said, and I was sorry when I made that remark, but it did hurt me sore to find Daniel talking so superior when I'd drilled all the men, and done all he told me. "Don't let's quarrel, Peachey," says Daniel without cursing. "You're a King too, and the half of this Kingdom is yours; but can't you see, Peachey, we want cleverer men than us now – three or four of 'em, that we can scatter about for our Deputies. It's a hugeous great State, and I can't always tell the right thing to do, and I haven't time for all I want to do, and here's the winter coming on and all." He put half his beard into his mouth, all red like the gold of his crown.

"'I'm sorry, Daniel,' says I. "I've done all I could. I've drilled the men and shown the people how to stack their oats better; and I've brought in those tinware rifles from Ghorband – but I know what you're driving at. I take it Kings always feel oppressed that way."

"'There's another thing too,' says Dravot, walking up and down. "The winter's coming and these people won't be giving much trouble, and if they do we can't move about. I want a wife."

"'For Gord's sake leave the women alone!' I says. "We've both got all the work we can, though I *am* a fool. Remember the Contrack, and keep clear o' women."

"'The Contrack only lasted till such time as we was Kings; and Kings we have been these months past," says Dravot, weighing his crown in his hand. "You go get a wife too, Peachey – a nice, strappin', plump girl that'll keep you warm in the winter. They're prettier than English girls, and we can take the pick of 'em. Boil 'em once or twice in hot water and they'll come out like chicken and ham."

"'Don't tempt me!" I says. "I will not have any dealings with a woman not till we are a dam' side more settled than we are now. I've been doing the work o' two men, and you've been doing the work o' three. Let's lie off a bit, and see if we can get some better tobacco from Afghan country and run in some good liquor; but no women."

"'Who's talking o' *women*?" says Dravot. "I said *wife* – a Queen to breed a King's son for the King. A Queen out of the strongest tribe, that'll make them your blood-brothers, and that'll lie by your side and tell you all the people thinks about you and their own affairs. That's what I want."

"'Do you remember that Bengali woman I kept at Mogul Serai when I was a platelayer?" says I. "A fat lot o' good she was to me. She taught me the lingo and one or two other things; but what happened? She ran away with the Station-master's servant and half my month's pay. Then she turned up at Dadur Junction in tow of a half-caste, and had the impidence to say I was her husband – all among the drivers in the running-shed too!"

"'We've done with that," says Dravot; "these women are whiter than you or me, and a Queen I will have for the winter months."

"'For the last time o' asking, Dan, do *not*," I says. "It'll only bring us harm. The Bible says that Kings ain't to waste their strength on women, 'specially when they've got a new raw Kingdom to work over."

"'For the last time of answering I will," said Dravot, and he went away through the pine-trees looking like a big red devil, the sun being on his crown and beard and all.

'But getting a wife was not as easy as Dan thought. He put it before the Council, and there was no answer till Billy Fish said that he'd better ask the girls. Dravot damned them all round. "What's wrong with me?" he shouts, standing by the idol Imbra. "Am I a dog or am I not enough of a man for your wenches? Haven't I put the shadow of my hand over this country? Who stopped the last Afghan raid?" It was me really, but Dravot was too angry to remember. "Who bought your guns? Who repaired the bridges? Who's the Grand-Master of the sign cut in the stone?" says he, and he thumped his hand on the block that he used to sit on in Lodge, and at Council, which opened like Lodge always. Billy Fish said nothing and no more did the others. "Keep your hair on, Dan," said I; "and ask the girls. That's how it's done at Home, and these people are quite English."

'"The marriage of the King is a matter of State," says Dan, in a white-hot rage, for he could feel, I hope, that he was going against his better mind. He walked out of the Council-room, and the others sat still, looking at the ground.

'"Billy Fish," says I to the Chief of Bashkai, "what's the difficulty here? A straight answer to a true friend."

'"You know," says Billy Fish. "How should a man tell you who knows everything? How can daughters of men marry Gods or Devils? It's not proper."

'I remembered something like that in the Bible; but if, after seeing us as long as they had, they still believed we were Gods, it wasn't for me to undeceive them.

'"A God can do anything," says I. "If the King is fond of a girl he'll not let her die." – "She'll have to," said Billy Fish. "There are all sorts of Gods and Devils in these mountains, and now and again a girl marries one of them and isn't seen any more. Besides, you two know the Mark cut in the stone. Only the Gods know that. We thought you were men till you showed the sign of the Master."

'I wished then that we had explained about the loss of the genuine secrets of a Master-Mason at the first go-off; but I said nothing. All that night there was a blowing of horns in a little dark temple half-way down the hill, and I heard a girl crying fit to die. One of the priests told us that she was being prepared to marry the King.

'"I'll have no nonsense of that kind," says Dan. "I don't want to interfere with your customs, but I'll take my own wife." – "The girl's a little bit afraid," says the priest. "She thinks she's going to die, and they are a-heartening of her up down in the temple."

'"Hearten her very tender, then," says Dravot, "or I'll hearten you with the butt of a gun so you'll never want to be heartened again." He licked his lips, did Dan, and stayed up walking about more than half the night, thinking of the wife that he was going to get in the morning. I wasn't any means comfortable, for I knew that dealings with a woman in foreign parts, though you was a crowned King twenty times over, could not but be risky. I got up very early in the morning while Dravot was asleep, and I saw the priests talking together in whispers, and the Chiefs talking together too, and they looked at me out of the corners of their eyes.

'"What is up, Fish?" I say to the Bashkai man, who was wrapped up in his furs and looking splendid to behold.

'"I can't rightly say," says he; "but if you can make the King drop all this nonsense about marriage, you'll be doing him and me and yourself a great service."

'"That I do believe," says I. "But sure, you know, Billy, as well as me, having fought against and for us, that the King and me are nothing more than two of the finest men that God Almighty ever made. Nothing more, I do assure you."

'"That may be," says Billy Fish, "and yet I should be sorry if it was." He sinks his head upon his great fur cloak for a minute and thinks. "King," says he, "be you man or God or Devil, I'll stick by you today. I have twenty of my men with me, and they will follow me. We'll go to Bashkai until the storm blows over."

'A little snow had fallen in the night, and everything was white except the greasy fat clouds that blew down and down from the north. Dravot came out with his crown on his head, swinging his arms and stamping his feet, and looking more pleased than Punch.

'"For the last time, drop it, Dan," says I in a whisper, "Billy Fish here says that there will be a row."

'"A row among my people!" says Dravot. "Not much. Peachey, you're a fool not to get a wife too. Where's the girl?" says he with a voice as loud as the braying of a jackass. "Call up all the Chiefs and priests, and let the Emperor see if his wife suits him."

'There was no need to call anyone. They were all there leaning on their guns and spears round the clearing in the centre of the pine wood. A lot of priests went down to the little temple to bring up the girl, and the horns blew fit to wake the dead. Billy Fish saunters round and gets as close to Daniel as he could, and behind him stood his twenty men with matchlocks. Not a man of them under six feet. I was next to Dravot, and behind me was twenty men of the regular Army. Up comes the girl, and a strapping wench she was, covered with silver and turquoises, but white as death, and looking back every minute at the priests.

'"She'll do," said Dan, looking her over. "What's to be afraid of, lass? Come and kiss me." He puts his arm round her. She shuts her eyes, gives a bit of a squeak, and down goes her face in the side of Dan's flaming red beard.

'"The slut's bitten me!" says he, clapping his hand to his neck, and, sure enough, his hand was red with blood. Billy Fish and two of his matchlock-men catches hold of Dan by the shoulders and drags him into the Bashkai lot, while the priests howls in their lingo – "Neither God nor Devil but a man!" I was all taken aback, for a priest cut at me in front, and the Army behind began firing into the Bashkai men.

'"God A'mighty!" says Dan. "What is the meaning o' this?"

'"Come back! Come away!" says Billy Fish. "Ruin and Mutiny is the matter. We'll break for Bashkai if we can."

'I tried to give some sort of orders to my men – the men o' the regular Army – but it was no use, so I fired into the brown of 'em with an English Martini and drilled three beggars in a line. The valley was full of shouting, howling creatures, and every soul was shrieking, "Not a God nor a Devil but only a man!" The Bashkai troops stuck to Billy Fish all they were worth, but their matchlocks wasn't half as good as the Kabul breech-loaders, and four of them dropped. Dan was bellowing like a bull, for he was very wrathy; and Billy Fish had a hard job to prevent him running out at the crowd.

'"We can't stand," says Billy Fish. "Make a run for it down the valley! The whole place is against us." The matchlock-men ran, and we went down the valley in spite of Dravot. He was swearing horrible and crying out he was a King. The priests rolled great stones on us, and the regular Army fired hard, and there wasn't more than six men, not counting Dan, Billy Fish, and Me, that came down to the bottom of the valley alive.

'Then they stopped firing and the horns in the temple blew again. "Come away – for God's sake come away!" says Billy Fish. "They'll send runners out to all the villages before ever we get to Bashkai. I can protect you there, but I can't do anything now."

'My own notion is that Dan began to go mad in his head from that hour. He stared up and down like a stuck pig. Then he was all for walking back alone and killing the priests with his bare hands; which he could have done. "An Emperor am I," says Daniel, "and next year I shall be a Knight of the Queen."

'"All right, Dan," says I; "but come along now while there's time."

'"It's your fault," says he, "for not looking after your Army better. There was mutiny in the midst, and you didn't know – you damned engine-driving, plate-laying, mission-ary's-pass-hunting hound!" He sat upon a rock and called me every foul name he could lay tongue to. I was too heart-sick to care, though it was all his foolishness that brought the smash.

'"I'm sorry, Dan," says I, "but there's no accounting for natives. This business is our Fifty-Seven. Maybe we'll make something out of it yet, when we've got to Bashkai."

'"Let's get to Bashkai, then," says Dan, "and, by God, when I come back here again I'll sweep the valley so there isn't a bug in a blanket left!"

'We walked all that day, and all that night Dan was stumping up and down on the snow, chewing his beard and muttering to himself.

'"There's no hope o' getting clear," said Billy Fish. "The priests will have sent runners to the villages to say that you are only men. Why didn't you stick on as Gods till things was more settled? I'm a dead man," says Billy Fish, and he throws himself down on the snow and begins to pray to his Gods.

'Next morning we was in a cruel bad country – all up and down, no level ground at all, and no food either. The six Bashkai men looked at Billy Fish hungry-way as if they wanted to ask something, but they said never a word. At noon we came to the top of a flat mountain all covered with snow, and when we climbed up into it, behold, there was an Army in position waiting in the middle!

'"The runners have been very quick," says Billy Fish, with a little bit of a laugh. "They are waiting for us."

'Three or four men began to fire from the enemy's side, and a chance shot took

Daniel in the calf of the leg. That brought him to his senses. He looks across the snow at the Army, and sees the rifles that we had brought into the country.

'"We're done for," says he. "They are Englishmen, these people, – and it's my blasted nonsense that has brought you to this. Get back, Billy Fish, and take your men away; you've done what you could, and now cut for it. Carnehan," says he, "shake hands with me and go along with Billy. Maybe they won't kill you. I'll go and meet 'em alone. It's me that did it. Me, the King!"

'"Go!" says I. "Go to Hell, Dan! I'm with you here. Billy Fish, you clear out, and we two will meet those folk."

'"I'm a Chief," says Billy Fish, quite quiet. "I stay with you. My men can go."

'The Bashkai fellows didn't wait for a second word, but ran off, and Dan and Me and Billy Fish walked across to where the drums were drumming and the horns were horning. It was cold – awful cold. I've got that cold in the back of my head now. There's a lump of it there.'

The punkah-coolies had gone to sleep. Two kerosene lamps were blazing in the office, and the perspiration poured down my face and splashed on the blotter as I leaned forward. Carnehan was shivering, and I feared that his mind might go. I wiped my face, took a fresh grip of the piteously mangled hands, and said: 'What happened after that?'

The momentary shift of my eyes had broken the clear current.

'What was you pleased to say?' whined Carnehan. 'They took them without any sound. Not a little whisper all along the snow, not though the King knocked down the first man that set hand on him – not though old Peachey fired his last cartridge into the brown of 'em. Not a single solitary sound did those swines make. They just closed up tight, and I tell you their furs stunk. There was a man called Billy Fish, a good friend of us all, and they cut his throat, Sir, then and there, like a pig; and the King kicks up the bloody snow and says: "We've had a dashed fine run for our money. What's coming next?" But Peachey, Peachey Taliaferro, I tell you, Sir, in confidence as betwixt two friends, he lost his head, Sir. No, he didn't neither. The King lost his head, so he did, all along o' one of those cunning rope-bridges. Kindly let me have the paper-cutter, Sir. It tilted this way. They marched him a mile across that snow to a rope-bridge over a ravine with a river at the bottom. You may have seen such. They prodded him behind like an ox. "Damn your eyes!" says the King. "D'you suppose I can't die like a gentleman?" He turns to Peachey – Peachey that was crying like a child. "I've brought you to this, Peachey," says he. "Brought you out of your happy life to be killed in Kafiristan, where you was late Commander-in-Chief of the Emperor's forces. Say you forgive me, Peachey." – "I do," says Peachey. "Fully and freely do I forgive you, Dan." – "Shake hands, Peachey," says he. "I'm going now." Out he goes, looking neither right nor left, and when he was plumb in the middle of those dizzy dancing ropes – "Cut, you beggars," he shouts; and they cut, and old Dan fell, turning round and round and round, twenty thousand miles, for he took half an hour to fall till he struck the water, and I could see his body caught on a rock with the gold crown close beside.

'But do you know what they did to Peachey between two pine-trees? They crucified him, Sir, as Peachey's hand will show. They used wooden pegs for his hands and his feet; and he didn't die. He hung there and screamed, and they took him down next day, and said it was a miracle that he wasn't dead. They took him down – poor old Peachey that hadn't done them any harm – that hadn't done them any –'

He rocked to and fro and wept bitterly, wiping his eyes with the back of his scarred hands and moaning like a child for some ten minutes.

'They was cruel enough to feed him up in the temple, because they said he was more of a God than old Daniel that was a man. Then they turned him out on the snow, and told him to go home, and Peachey came home in about a year, begging along the roads quite safe; for Daniel Dravot he walked before and said: "Come along, Peachey. It's a big thing we're doing." The mountains they danced at night, and the mountains they tried to fall on Peachey's head, but Dan he held up his hand, and Peachey came along bent double. He never let go of Dan's hand, and he never let go of Dan's head. They gave it to him as a present in the temple, to remind him not to come again, and though the crown was pure gold, and Peachey was starving, never would Peachey sell the same. You knew Dravot, Sir! You knew Right Worshipful Brother Dravot! Look at him now!'

He fumbled in the mass of rags round his bent waist; brought out a black horse-hair bag embroidered with silver thread, and shook therefrom on to my table – the dried, withered head of Daniel Dravot! The morning sun that had long been paling the lamps struck the red beard and blind sunken eyes; struck, too, a heavy circlet of gold studded with raw turquoises, that Carnehan placed tenderly on the battered temples.

'You be'old now,' said Carnehan, 'the Emperor in his 'abit as he lived – the King of Kafiristan with his crown upon his head. Poor old Daniel that was a monarch once!'

I shuddered, for, in spite of defacements manifold, I recognised the head of the man of Marwar Junction. Carnehan rose to go. I attempted to stop him. He was not fit to walk abroad. 'Let me take away the whisky, and give me a little money,' he gasped. 'I was a King once. I'll go to the Deputy Commissioner and ask to set in the Poorhouse till I get my health. No, thank you, I can't wait till you get a carriage for me. I've urgent private affairs – in the south – at Marwar.'

He shambled out of the office and departed in the direction of the Deputy Commissioner's house. That day at noon I had occasion to go down the blinding hot Mall, and I saw a crooked man crawling along the white dust of the roadside, his hat in his hand, quavering dolorously after the fashion of street-singers at Home. There was not a soul in sight, and he was out of all possible earshot of the houses. And he sang through his nose, turning his head from right to left –

'The Son of Man goes forth to war,
A golden crown to gain;
His blood-red banner streams afar –
Who follows in his train?'

I waited to hear no more, but put the poor wretch into my carriage and drove him off to the nearest missionary for eventual transfer to the Asylum. He repeated the hymn twice while he was with me whom he did not in the least recognise, and I left him singing it to the missionary.

Two days later I inquired after his welfare of the Superintendent of the Asylum.

'He was admitted suffering from sunstroke. He died early yesterday morning,' said the Superintendent. 'Is it true that he was half an hour bare-headed in the sun at midday?'

'Yes,' said I, 'but do you happen to know if he had anything upon him by any chance when he died?'

'Not to my knowledge,' said the Superintendent.

And there the matter rests.

WEE WILLIE WINKIE

An officer and a gentleman

His full name was Percival William Williams, but he picked up the other name in a nursery-book, and that was the end of the christened titles. His mother's *ayah* called him Willie-*Baba*, but as he never paid the faintest attention to anything that the *ayah* said, her wisdom did not help matters.

His father was the Colonel of the 195th, and as soon as Wee Willie Winkie was old enough to understand what Military Discipline meant, Colonel Williams put him under it. There was no other way of managing the child. When he was good for a week, he drew good-conduct pay; and when he was bad, he was deprived of his good-conduct stripe. Generally he was bad, for India offers many chances of going wrong to little six-year-olds.

Children resent familiarity from strangers, and Wee Willie Winkie was a very particular child. Once he accepted an acquaintance, he was graciously pleased to thaw. He accepted Brandis, a subaltern of the 195th, on sight. Brandis was having tea at the Colonel's, and Wee Willie Winkie entered strong in the possession of a good-conduct badge won for not chasing the hens round the compound. He regarded Brandis with gravity for at least ten minutes, and then delivered himself of his opinion.

'I like you,' said he slowly, getting off his chair and coming over to Brandis. 'I like you. I shall call you Coppy, because of your hair. Do you *mind* being called Coppy? It is because of ve hair, you know.'

Here was one of the most embarrassing of Wee Willie Winkie's peculiarities. He would look at a stranger for some time, and then, without warning or explanation, would give him a name. And the name stuck. No regimental penalties could break Wee Willie Winkie of this habit. He lost his good-conduct badge for christening the Commissioner's wife 'Pobs'; but nothing that the Colonel could do made the Station forego the nickname, and Mrs Collen remained 'Pobs' till the end of her stay. So Brandis was christened 'Coppy,' and rose, therefore, in the estimation of the regiment.

If Wee Willie Winkie took an interest in anyone, the fortunate man was envied alike by the mess and the rank and file. And in their envy lay no suspicion of self-interest. 'The Colonel's son' was idolised on his own merits entirely. Yet Wee Willie Winkie was not lovely. His face was permanently freckled, as his legs were permanently scratched, and in spite of his mother's almost tearful remonstrances he had insisted upon having his long yellow locks cut short in the military fashion. 'I want my hair like Sergeant Tummil's,' said Wee Willie Winkie, and, his father abetting, the sacrifice was accomplished.

Three weeks after the bestowal of his youthful affections on Lieutenant Brandis – henceforward to be called 'Coppy' for the sake of brevity – Wee Willie Winkie was destined to behold strange things and far beyond his comprehension.

Coppy returned his liking with interest. Coppy had let him wear for five rapturous minutes his own big sword – just as tall as Wee Willie Winkie. Coppy had promised him a terrier puppy; and Coppy had permitted him to witness the miraculous operation of shaving. Nay, more – Coppy had said that even he, Wee Willie Winkie, would rise in time to the ownership of a box of shiny knives, a silver soap-box, and a silver-handled 'sputter-brush,' as Wee Willie Winkie called it. Decidedly, there was no one except his father, who could give or take away good-conduct badges at pleasure, half so wise, strong, and valiant as Coppy with the Afghan and Egyptian medals on his breast. Why, then, should Coppy be guilty of the unmanly weakness of kissing – vehemently kissing – a 'big girl,' Miss Allardyce to wit? In the course of a morning ride Wee Willie Winkie had seen Coppy so doing, and, like the gentleman he was, had promptly wheeled round and cantered back to his groom, lest the groom should also see.

Under ordinary circumstances he would have spoken to his father, but he felt instinctively that this was a matter on which Coppy ought first to be consulted.

'Coppy,' shouted Wee Willie Winkie, reining up outside that subaltern's bungalow early one morning – 'I want to see you, Coppy!'

'Come in, young 'un,' returned Coppy, who was at early breakfast in the midst of his dogs. 'What mischief have you been getting into now?'

Wee Willie Winkie had done nothing notoriously bad for three days, and so stood on a pinnacle of virtue.

'*I've* been doing nothing bad,' said he, curling himself into a long chair with a studious affectation of the Colonel's languor after a hot parade. He buried his freckled nose in a tea-cup and, with eyes staring roundly over the rim, asked: 'I say, Coppy, is it pwoper to kiss big girls?'

'By Jove! You're beginning early. Who do you want to kiss?'

'No one. My muvver's always kissing me if I don't stop her. If it isn't pwoper, how was you kissing Major Allardyce's big girl last morning, by ve canal?'

Coppy's brow wrinkled. He and Miss Allardyce had with great craft managed to keep their engagement secret for a fortnight. There were urgent and imperative reasons why Major Allardyce should not know how matters stood for at least another month, and this small marplot had discovered a great deal too much.

'I saw you,' said Wee Willie Winkie calmly. 'But ve *sais* didn't see. I said, "*Hut jao!*"'

'Oh, you had that much sense, you young Rip,' groaned poor Coppy, half amused and half angry. 'And how many people may you have told about it?'

'Only me myself. You didn't tell when I twied to wide ve buffalo ven my pony was lame; and I fought you wouldn't like.'

'Winkie,' said Coppy enthusiastically, shaking the small hand, 'you're the best of good fellows. Look here, you can't understand all these things. One of these days – hang it, how can I make you see it! – I'm going to marry Miss Allardyce, and then she'll be Mrs Coppy, as you say. If your young mind is so scandalised at the idea of kissing big girls, go and tell your father.'

'What will happen?' said Wee Willie Winkie, who firmly believed that his father was omnipotent.

'I shall get into trouble,' said Coppy, playing his trump card with an appealing look at the holder of the ace.

'Ven I won't,' said Wee Willie Winkie briefly. 'But my faver says it's un-man-ly to be always kissing, and I didn't fink *you'd* do vat, Coppy.'

'I'm not always kissing, old chap. It's only now and then, and when you're bigger you'll do it too. Your father meant it's not good for little boys.'

'Ah!' said Wee Willie Winkie, now fully enlightened. 'It's like ve sputter-brush?'

'Exactly,' said Coppy gravely.

'But I don't fink I'll ever want to kiss big girls, nor no one, 'cept my muvver. And I *must* vat, you know.'

There was a long pause, broken by Wee Willie.

'Are you fond of vis big girl, Coppy?'

'Awfully!' said Coppy.

'Fonder van you are of Bell or ve Butcha – or me?'

'It's in a different way,' said Coppy. 'You see, one of these days Miss Allardyce will belong to me, but you'll grow up and command the Regiment and – all sorts of things. It's quite different, you see.'

'Very well,' said Wee Willie Winkie, rising. 'If you're fond of ve big girl I won't tell anyone. I must go now.'

Coppy rose and escorted his small guest to the door, adding – 'You're the best of little fellows, Winkie. I tell you what. In thirty days from now you can tell if you like – tell anyone you like.'

Thus the secret of the Brandis-Allardyce engagement was dependent on a little child's word. Coppy, who knew Wee Willie Winkie's idea of truth, was at ease, for he felt that he would not break promises. Wee Willie Winkie betrayed a special and unusual interest in Miss Allardyce, and, slowly revolving round that embarrassed young lady, was used to regard her gravely with unwinking eye. He was trying to discover why Coppy should have kissed her. She was not half so nice as his own mother. On the other hand, she was Coppy's property, and would in time belong to him. Therefore it behoved him to treat her with as much respect as Coppy's big sword or shiny pistol.

The idea that he shared a great secret in common with Coppy kept Wee Willie Winkie unusually virtuous for three weeks. Then the Old Adam broke out, and he made what he called a 'camp-fire' at the bottom of the garden. How could he have foreseen that the flying sparks would have lighted the Colonel's little hay-rick and consumed a week's store for the horses? Sudden and swift was the punishment – deprivation of the good-conduct badge and, most sorrowful of all, two days' confinement to barracks – the house and verandah – coupled with the withdrawal of the light of his father's countenance.

He took the sentence like the man he strove to be, drew himself up with a quivering under-lip, saluted, and, once clear of the room, ran to weep bitterly in his nursery – called by him 'my quarters.' Coppy came in the afternoon and attempted to console the culprit.

'I'm under awwest,' said Wee Willie Winkie mournfully, 'and I didn't ought to speak to you.'

Very early the next morning he climbed on to the roof of the house – that was not forbidden – and beheld Miss Allardyce going for a ride.

'Where are you going?' cried Wee Willie Winkie.

'Across the river,' she answered, and trotted forward.

Now the cantonment in which the 195th lay was bounded on the north by a river – dry in the winter. From his earliest years, Wee Willie Winkie had been forbidden to go across the river, and had noted that even Coppy – the almost almighty Coppy – had never set foot beyond it. Wee Willie Winkie had once been read to, out of a big blue book, the history of the Princess and the Goblins – a most wonderful tale of a land where the Goblins were always warring with the children of men until they were defeated by one Curdie. Ever since that date it seemed to him that the bare black and purple hills across the river were inhabited by Goblins, and, in truth, everyone had said that there lived the Bad Men. Even in his own house the lower halves of the windows were covered with green paper on account of the Bad Men who might, if allowed clear view, fire into peaceful drawing-rooms and comfortable bedrooms. Certainly, beyond the river, which was the end of all the Earth, lived the Bad Men. And here was Major Allardyce's big girl, Coppy's property, preparing to venture into their borders! What would Coppy say if anything happened to her? If the Goblins ran off with her as they did with Curdie's Princess? She must at all hazards be turned back.

The house was still. Wee Willie Winkie reflected for a moment on the very terrible wrath of his father; and then – broke his arrest! It was a crime unspeakable. The low sun threw his shadow, very large and very black, on the trim garden-paths, as he went down to the stables and ordered his pony. It seemed to him in the hush of the dawn that all the big world had been bidden to stand still and look at Wee Willie Winkie guilty of mutiny. The drowsy *sais* gave him his mount, and, since the one great sin made all others insignificant, Wee Willie Winkie said that he was going to ride over to Coppy Sahib, and went out at a foot-pace, stepping on the soft mould of the flower-borders.

The devastating track of the pony's feet was the last misdeed that cut him off from all sympathy of Humanity. He turned into the road, leaned forward, and rode as fast as the pony could put foot to the ground in the direction of the river.

But the liveliest of twelve-two ponies can do little against the long canter of a Waler. Miss Allardyce was far ahead, had passed through the crops, beyond the Police-posts, when all the guards were asleep, and her mount was scattering the pebbles of the river-bed as Wee Willie Winkie left the cantonment and British India behind him. Bowed forward and still flogging, Wee Willie Winkie shot into Afghan territory, and could just see Miss Allardyce, a black speck, flickering across the stony plain. The reason of her wandering was simple enough. Coppy, in a tone of too-hastily-assumed authority, had told her overnight that she must not ride out by the river. And she had gone to prove her own spirit and teach Coppy a lesson.

Almost at the foot of the inhospitable hills, Wee Willie Winkie saw the Waler blunder and come down heavily. Miss Allardyce struggled clear, but her ankle had been severely twisted, and she could not stand. Having fully shown her spirit, she wept, and was surprised by the apparition of a white, wide-eyed child in khaki, on a nearly spent pony.

'Are you badly, badly hurted?' shouted Wee Willie Winkie, as soon as he was within range. 'You didn't ought to be here.'

'I don't know,' said Miss Allardyce ruefully, ignoring the reproof. 'Good gracious, child, what are *you* doing here?'

'You said you was going acwoss ve wiver,' panted Wee Willie Winkie, throwing himself off his pony. 'And nobody – not even Coppy – must go acwoss ve wiver, and I came after you ever so hard, but you wouldn't stop, and now you've hurted yourself, and Coppy will be angwy wiv me, and – I've bwoken my awwest! I've bwoken my awwest!'

The future Colonel of the 195th sat down and sobbed. In spite of the pain in her ankle the girl was moved.

'Have you ridden all the way from cantonments, little man? What for?'

'You belonged to Coppy. Coppy told me so!' wailed Wee Willie Winkie disconsolately. 'I saw him kissing you, and he said he was fonder of you van Bell or ve Butcha or me. And so I came. You must get up and come back. You didn't ought to be here. Vis is a bad place, and I've bwoken my awwest.'

'I can't move, Winkie,' said Miss Allardyce, with a groan. 'I've hurt my foot. What shall I do?

She showed a readiness to weep anew, which steadied Wee Willie Winkie, who had been brought up to believe that tears were the depth of unmanliness. Still, when one is as great a sinner as Wee Willie Winkie, even a man may be permitted to break down.

'Winkie,' said Miss Allardyce, 'when you've rested a little, ride back and tell them to send out something to carry me back in. It hurts fearfully.'

The child sat still for a little time and Miss Allardyce closed her eyes; the pain was nearly making her faint. She was roused by Wee Willie Winkie tying up the reins on his pony's neck and setting it free with a vicious cut of his whip that made it whicker. The little animal headed towards the cantonments.

'Oh, Winkie, what are you doing?'

'Hush!' said Wee Willie Winkie. 'Vere's a man coming – one of ve Bad Men. I must stay wiv you. My faver says a man must *always* look after a girl. Jack will go home, and ven vey'll come and look for us. Vat's why I let him go.'

Not one man but two or three had appeared from behind the rocks of the hills, and the heart of Wee Willie Winkie sank within him, for just in this manner were the Goblins wont to steal out and vex Curdie's soul. Thus had they played in Curdie's garden – he had seen the picture – and thus had they frightened the Princess's nurse. He heard them talking to each other, and recognised with joy the bastard Pushto that he had picked up from one of his father's grooms lately dismissed. People who spoke that tongue could not be the Bad Men. They were only natives after all.

They came up to the boulders on which Miss Allardyce's horse had blundered.

Then rose from the rock Wee Willie Winkie, child of the Dominant Race, aged six and three-quarters, and said briefly and emphatically '*Jao!*' The pony had crossed the river-bed.

The men laughed, and laughter from natives was the one thing Wee Willie Winkie could not tolerate. He asked them what they wanted and why they did not depart. Other men with most evil faces and crooked-stocked guns crept out of the shadows of the hills, till, soon, Wee Willie Winkie was face to face with an audience some twenty strong. Miss Allardyce screamed.

'Who are you?' said one of the men.

'I am the Colonel Sahib's son, and my order is that you go at once. You black men are frightening the Miss Sahib. One of you must run into cantonments and take the news that the Miss Sahib has hurt herself, and that the Colonel's son is here with her.'

'Put our feet into the trap?' was the laughing reply. 'Hear this boy's speech!'

'Say that I sent you – I, the Colonel's son. They will give you money.'

'What is the use of this talk? Take up the child and the girl, and we can at least ask for the ransom. Ours are the villages on the heights,' said a voice in the background.

These *were* the Bad Men – worse than Goblins – and it needed all Wee Willie Winkie's training to prevent him from bursting into tears. But he felt that to cry before a native, excepting only his mother's *ayah*, would be an infamy greater than any mutiny. Moreover, he, as future Colonel of the 195th, had that grim regiment at his back.

'Are you going to carry us away?' said Wee Willie Winkie, very blanched and uncomfortable.

'Yes, my little *Sahib Bahadur*,' said the tallest of the men, 'and eat you afterwards.'

'That is child's talk,' said Wee Willie Winkie. 'Men do not eat men.'

A yell of laughter interrupted him, but he went on firmly – 'And if you do carry us away, I tell you that all my regiment will come up in a day and kill you all without leaving one. Who will take my message to the Colonel Sahib?'

Speech in any vernacular – and Wee Willie Winkie had a colloquial acquaintance with three – was easy to the boy who could not yet manage his 'r's' and 'th's' aright.

Another man joined the conference, crying: 'O foolish men! What this babe says is true. He is the heart's heart of those white troops. For the sake of peace let them go both, for if he be taken, the regiment will break loose and gut the valley. *Our* villages are in the valley, and we shall not escape. That regiment are devils. They broke Khoda Yar's breastbone with kicks when he tried to take the rifles; and if we touch this child they will fire and rape and plunder for a month, till nothing remains. Better to send a man back to take the message and get a reward. I say that this child is their God, and that they will spare none of us, nor our women, if we harm him.'

It was Din Mahommed, the dismissed groom of the Colonel, who made the diversion, and an angry and heated discussion followed. Wee Willie Winkie, standing over Miss Allardyce, waited the upshot. Surely his 'wegiment,' his own 'wegiment,' would not desert him if they knew of his extremity.

The riderless pony brought the news to the 195th, though there had been consternation in the Colonel's household for an hour before. The little beast came in through the parade-ground in front of the main barracks, where the men were settling down to play Spoil-five till the afternoon. Devlin, the Colour-Sergeant of E Company, glanced at the empty saddle and tumbled through the barrack-rooms, kicking up each Room Corporal as he passed. 'Up, ye beggars! There's something happened to the Colonel's son,' he shouted.

'He couldn't fall off! S'elp me, 'e *couldn't* fall off,' blubbered a drummer-boy. 'Go an' hunt acrost the river. He's over there if he's anywhere, an' maybe those Pathans have got 'im. For the love o' Gawd don't look for 'im in the nullahs! Let's go over the river.'

'There's sense in Mott yet,' said Devlin. 'E Company, double out to the river – sharp!'

So E Company, in its shirt-sleeves mainly, doubled for the dear life, and in the rear toiled the perspiring Sergeant, adjuring it to double yet faster. The cantonment was alive with the men of the 195th hunting for Wee Willie Winkie, and the Colonel finally overtook E Company, far too exhausted to swear, struggling in the pebbles of the river-bed.

Up the hill under which Wee Willie Winkie's Bad Men were discussing the wisdom of carrying off the child and the girl, a look-out fired two shots.

'What have I said?' shouted Din Mahommed. 'There is the warning! The *pulton* are out already and are coming across the plain! Get away! Let us not be seen with the boy.'

The men waited for an instant, and then, as another shot was fired, withdrew into the hills, silently as they had appeared.

'The wegiment is coming,' said Wee Willie Winkie confidently to Miss Allardyce, 'and it's all wight. Don't cwy!'

He needed the advice himself, for ten minutes later, when his father came up, he was weeping bitterly with his head in Miss Allardyce's lap.

And the men of the 195th carried him home with shouts and rejoicings; and Coppy, who had ridden a horse into a lather, met him, and, to his intense disgust, kissed him openly in the presence of the men.

But there was balm for his dignity. His father assured him that not only would the breaking of arrest be condoned, but that the good-conduct badge would be restored as soon as his mother could sew it on his blouse-sleeve. Miss Allardyce had told the Colonel a story that made him proud of his son.

'She belonged to you, Coppy,' said Wee Willie Winkie, indicating Miss Allardyce with a grimy forefinger. 'I *knew* she didn't ought to go acwoss ve wiver, and I knew ve wegiment would come to me if I sent Jack home.'

'You're a hero, Winkie,' said Coppy – 'a *pukka* hero!'

'I don't know what vat means,' said Wee Willie Winkie, 'but you mustn't call me Winkie any no more. I'm Percival Will'am Will'ams.'

And in this manner did Wee Willie Winkie enter into his manhood.

BAA BAA, BLACK SHEEP

Baa Baa, Black Sheep,
Have you any wool?
Yes, Sir, yes, Sir, three bags full.
One for the Master, one for the Dame –
None for the Little Boy that cries down the lane.

Nursery Rhyme

The First Bag

When I was in my father's house, I was in a better place

They were putting Punch to bed – the *ayah* and the *hamal* and Meeta, the big *Surti* boy, with the red and gold turban. Judy, already tucked inside her mosquito-curtains, was nearly asleep. Punch had been allowed to stay up for dinner. Many privileges had been accorded to Punch within the last ten days, and a greater kindness from the people of his world had encompassed his ways and works, which were mostly obstreperous. He sat on the edge of his bed and swung his bare legs defiantly.

'Punch-*baba* going to bye-lo?' said the *ayah* suggestively.

'No,' said Punch. 'Punch-baba wants the story about the Ranee that was turned into a tiger. Meeta must tell it, and the *hamal* shall hide behind the door and make tiger-noises at the proper time.'

'But Judy-*baba* will wake up,' said the *ayah*.

'Judy-*baba is* waked,' piped a small voice from the mosquito-curtains. 'There was a Ranee that lived at Delhi. Go on, Meeta,' and she fell fast asleep again while Meeta began the story.

Never had Punch secured the telling of that tale with so little opposition. He reflected for a long time. The *hamal* made the tiger-noises in twenty different keys.

''Top!' said Punch authoritatively. 'Why doesn't Papa come in and say he is going to give me *put-put?*'

'Punch-baba is going away,' said the *ayah*. 'In another week there will be no Punch-baba to pull my hair any more.' She sighed softly, for the boy of the household was very dear to her heart.

'Up the Ghauts in a train?' said Punch, standing on his bed. 'All the way to Nassick where the Ranee-Tiger lives?'

'Not to Nassick this year, little Sahib,' said Meeta, lifting him on his shoulder. 'Down to the sea where the cocoa-nuts are thrown, and across the sea in a big ship. Will you take Meeta with you to *Belait?*'

'You shall all come,' said Punch, from the height of Meeta's strong arms. 'Meeta and the *ayab* and the *hamal* and Bhini-in-the-Garden, and the salaam-Captain-Sahib-snake-man.'

There was no mockery in Meeta's voice when he replied – 'Great is the Sahib's favour,' and laid the little man down in the bed, while the *ayah*, sitting in the moonlight at the doorway, lulled him to sleep with an interminable canticle such as they sing in the Roman Catholic Church at Parel. Punch curled himself into a ball and slept.

Next morning Judy shouted that there was a rat in the nursery, and thus he forgot to tell her the wonderful news. It did not much matter, for Judy was only three and she would not have understood. But Punch was five; and he knew that going to England would be much nicer than a trip to Nassick.

Papa and Mamma sold the brougham and the piano, and stripped the house, and curtailed the allowance of crockery for the daily meals, and took long counsel together over a bundle of letters bearing the Rocklington postmark.

'The worst of it is that one can't be certain of anything,' said Papa, pulling his moustache. 'The letters in themselves are excellent, and the terms are moderate enough.'

'The worst of it is that the children will grow up away from me,' thought Mamma; but she did not say it aloud.

'We are only one case among hundreds,' said Papa bitterly. 'You shall go Home again in five years, dear.'

'Punch will be ten then – and Judy eight. Oh, how long and long and long the time will be! And we have to leave them among strangers.'

'Punch is a cheery little chap. He's sure to make friends wherever he goes.'

'And who could help loving my Ju?'

They were standing over the cots in the nursery late at night, and I think that Mamma was crying softly. After Papa had gone away, she knelt down by the side of Judy's cot. The *ayah* saw her and put up a prayer that the *memsahib* might never find the love of her children taken away from her and given to a stranger.

Mamma's own prayer was a slightly illogical one. Summarised it ran: 'Let strangers love my children and be as good to them as I should be, but let *me* preserve their love and their confidence for ever and ever. Amen.' Punch scratched himself in his sleep, and Judy moaned a little.

Next day they all went down to the sea, and there was a scene at the Apollo Bunder when Punch discovered that Meeta could not come too, and Judy learned that the *ayah* must be left behind. But Punch found a thousand fascinating things in the rope, block, and steam-pipe line on the big P. and O. Steamer long before Meeta and the *ayah* had dried their tears.

'Come back, Punch-*haha*,' said the *ayah*.

'Come back,' said Meeta, 'and be a *Burra Sahib*' (a big man).

'Yes,' said Punch, lifted up in his father's arms to wave goodbye. 'Yes, I will come back, and I will be a *Burra Sahib Bahadur*!' (a very big man indeed).

At the end of the first day Punch demanded to be set down in England, which he was certain must be close at hand. Next day there was a merry breeze, and Punch was very sick. 'When I come back to Bombay,' said Punch on his recovery, 'I will come by the road – in a broom-*gharri*. This is a very naughty ship.'

The Swedish boatswain consoled him, and he modified his opinions as the voyage went on. There was so much to see and to handle and ask questions about that Punch nearly forgot the *ayah* and Meeta and the *hamal*, and with difficulty remembered a few words of the Hindustani, once his second-speech.

But Judy was much worse. The day before the steamer reached Southampton, Mamma asked her if she would not like to see the *ayah* again. Judy's blue eyes turned to the stretch of sea that had swallowed all her tiny past, and she said: '*Ayah*! What *ayah*?'

Mamma cried over her and Punch marvelled. It was then that he heard for the first time Mamma's passionate appeal to him never to let Judy forget Mamma. Seeing that Judy was young, ridiculously young, and that Mamma, every evening for four weeks past, had come into the cabin to sing her and Punch to sleep with a mysterious rune that he called 'Sonny, my soul,' Punch could not understand what Mamma meant. But he strove to do his duty; for, the moment Mamma left the cabin, he said to Judy: 'Ju, you bemember Mamma?'

''Torse I do,' said Judy.

'Then *always* bemember Mamma, 'r else I won't give you the paper ducks that the red-haired Captain Sahib cut out for me.'

So Judy promised always to 'bemember Mamma.'

Many and many a time was Mamma's command laid upon Punch, and Papa would say the same thing with an insistence that awed the child.

'You must make haste and learn to write, Punch,' said Papa, 'and then you'll be able to write letters to us in Bombay.'

'I'll come into your room,' said Punch, and Papa choked.

Papa and Mamma were always choking in those days. If Punch took Judy to task for not 'bemembering,' they choked. If Punch sprawled on the sofa in the Southampton lodging-house and sketched his future in purple and gold, they choked; and so they did if Judy put up her mouth for a kiss.

Through many days all four were vagabonds on the face of the earth – Punch with no one to give orders to, Judy too young for anything, and Papa and Mamma grave, distracted, and choking.

'Where,' demanded Punch, wearied of a loathsome contrivance on four wheels with a mound of luggage atop – '*where* is our broom-*gharri*? This thing talks so much that I can't talk. Where is our *own* broom-*gharri*? When I was at Bandstand before we comed away, I asked Inverarity Sahib why he was sitting in it, and he said it was his own. And I said, "I will *give* it you" – I like Inverarity Sahib – and I said, "Can you put your legs through the pully-wag loops by the windows?" And Inverarity Sahib said No, and laughed. *I* can put my legs through the pully-wag loops. I can put my legs through *these* pully-wag loops. Look! Oh, Mamma's crying again! I didn't know I wasn't not to do *so*.'

Punch drew his legs out of the loops of the four-wheeler: the door opened and he slid to the earth, in a cascade of parcels, at the door of an austere little villa whose gates bore the legend 'Downe Lodge.' Punch gathered himself together and eyed the house with disfavour. It stood on a sandy road, and a cold wind tickled his knicker-bockered legs.

'Let us go away,' said Punch. 'This is not a pretty place.'

But Mamma and Papa and Judy had left the cab, and all the luggage was being taken into the house. At the doorstep stood a woman in black, and she smiled largely, with dry chapped lips. Behind her was a man, big, bony, gray, and lame as to one leg – behind him a boy of twelve, black-haired and oily in appearance. Punch surveyed the trio, and advanced without fear, as he had been accustomed to do in Bombay when callers came and he happened to be playing in the verandah.

'How do you do?' said he. 'I am Punch.' But they were all looking at the luggage – all except the gray man, who shook hands with Punch, and said he was 'a smart little fellow.' There was much running about and banging of boxes, and Punch curled himself up on the sofa in the dining-room and considered things.

'I don't like these people,' said Punch. 'But never mind. We'll go away soon. We have always went away soon from everywhere. I wish we was gone back to Bombay *soon*.'

The wish bore no fruit. For six days Mamma wept at intervals, and showed the woman in black all Punch's clothes – a liberty which Punch resented. 'But p'raps she's a new white *ayah*,' he thought. 'I'm to call her Antirosa, but she doesn't call *me* Sahib. She says just Punch,' he confided to Judy. 'What is Antirosa?'

Judy didn't know. Neither she nor Punch had heard anything of an animal called an aunt. Their world had been Papa and Mamma, who knew everything, permitted everything, and loved everybody – even Punch when he used to go into the garden at Bombay and fill his nails with mould after the weekly nail-cutting, because, as he explained between two strokes of the slipper to his sorely-tried Father, his fingers 'felt so new at the ends.'

In an undefined way Punch judged it advisable to keep both parents between himself and the woman in black and the boy in black hair. He did not approve of them. He liked the gray man, who had expressed a wish to be called 'Uncleharri.' They nodded at each other when they met, and the gray man showed him a little ship with rigging that took up and down.

'She is a model of the *Brisk* – the little *Brisk* that was sore exposed that day at Navarino.' The gray man hummed the last words and fell into a reverie. 'I'll tell you about Navarino, Punch, when we go for walks together; and you mustn't touch the ship, because she's the *Brisk*.'

Long before that walk, the first of many, was taken, they roused Punch and Judy in the chill dawn of a February morning to say Good-bye; and of all people in the wide earth to Papa and Mamma – both crying this time. Punch was very sleepy and Judy was cross.

'Don't forget us,' pleaded Mamma. 'Oh, my little son, don't forget us, and see that Judy remembers too.'

'I've told Judy to bemember,' said Punch, wriggling, for his father's beard tickled his neck, 'I've told Judy – ten – forty – 'leven thousand times. But Ju's so young – quite a baby – isn't she?'

'Yes,' said Papa, 'quite a baby, and you must be good to Judy, and make haste to learn to write and – and – and –'

Punch was back in his bed again. Judy was fast asleep, and there was the rattle of

397

a cab below. Papa and Mamma had gone away. Not to Nassick; that was across the sea. To some place much nearer, of course, and equally of course they would return. They came back after dinner-parties, and Papa had come back after he had been to a place called 'The Snows,' and Mamma with him, to Punch and Judy at Mrs Inverarity's house in Marine Lines. Assuredly they would come back again. So Punch fell asleep till the true morning, when the black-haired boy met him with the information that Papa and Mamma had gone to Bombay, and that he and Judy were to stay at Downe Lodge 'for ever.' Antirosa, tearfully appealed to for a contradiction, said that Harry had spoken the truth, and that it behoved Punch to fold up his clothes neatly on going to bed. Punch went out and wept bitterly with Judy, into whose fair head he had driven some ideas of the meaning of separation.

When a matured man discovers that he has been deserted by Providence, deprived of his God, and cast without help, comfort, or sympathy, upon a world which is new and strange to him, his despair, which may find expression in evil-living, the writing of his experiences, or the more satisfactory diversion of suicide, is generally supposed to be impressive. A child, under exactly similar circumstances as far as its knowledge goes, cannot very well curse God and die. It howls till its nose is red, its eyes are sore, and its head aches. Punch and Judy, through no fault of their own, had lost all their world. They sat in the hall and cried; the black-haired boy looking on from afar.

The model of the ship availed nothing, though the gray man assured Punch that he might pull the rigging up and down as much as he pleased; and Judy was promised free entry into the kitchen. They wanted Papa and Mamma gone to Bombay beyond the seas, and their grief while it lasted was without remedy.

When the tears ceased the house was very still. Antirosa had decided that it was better to let the children 'have their cry out,' and the boy had gone to school. Punch raised his head from the floor and sniffed mournfully. Judy was nearly asleep. Three short years had not taught her how to bear sorrow with full knowledge. There was a distant, dull boom in the air – a repeated heavy thud. Punch knew that sound in Bombay in the Monsoon. It was the sea – the sea that must be traversed before anyone could get to Bombay.

'Quick, Ju!' he cried, 'we're close to the sea. I can hear it! Listen! That's where they've went. P'raps we can catch them if we was in time. They didn't mean to go without us. They've only forgot.'

'Iss,' said Judy. 'They've only forgotted. Less go to the sea.'

The hall-door was open and so was the garden-gate.

'It's very, very big, this place,' he said, looking cautiously down the road, 'and we will get lost; but *I* will find a man and order him to take me back to my house – like I did in Bombay.'

He took Judy by the hand, and the two ran hatless in the direction of the sound of the sea. Downe Villa was almost the last of a range of newly-built houses running out, through a field of brick-mounds, to a heath where gypsies occasionally camped and where the Garrison Artillery of Rocklington practised. There were few people to be seen, and the children might have been taken for those of the soldiery who ranged far. Half an hour the wearied little legs tramped across heath, potato-patch, and sand-dune.

'I'se so tired,' said Judy, 'and Mamma will be angry.'

'Mamma's *never* angry. I suppose she is waiting at the sea now while Papa gets tickets. We'll find them and go along with them. Ju, you mustn't sit down. Only a little more and we'll come to the sea. Ju, if you sit down I'll *thmack* you!' said Punch.

They climbed another dune, and came upon the great gray sea at low tide. Hundreds of crabs were scuttling about the beach, but there was no trace of Papa and Mamma, not even of a ship upon the waters – nothing but sand and mud for miles and miles.

And 'Uncleharri' found them by chance – very muddy and very forlorn – Punch dissolved in tears, but trying to divert Judy with an 'ickle trab,' and Judy wailing to the pitiless horizon for 'Mamma, Mamma!' – and again 'Mamma!'

The Second Bag

Ah, well-a-day, for we are souls bereaved!
Of all the creatures under Heaven's wide scope
We are most hopeless, who had once most hope,
And most beliefless, who had most believed.
The City of Dreadful Night

All this time not a word about Black Sheep. He came later, and Harry the black-haired boy was mainly responsible for his coming.

Judy – who could help loving little Judy? – passed, by special permit, into the kitchen and thence straight to Aunty Rosa's heart. Harry was Aunty Rosa's one child, and Punch was the extra boy about the house. There was no special place for him or his little affairs, and he was forbidden to sprawl on sofas and explain his ideas about the manufacture of this world and his hopes for his future. Sprawling was lazy and wore out sofas, and little boys were not expected to talk. They were talked to, and the talking to was intended for the benefit of their morals. As the unquestioned despot of the house at Bombay, Punch could not quite understand how he came to be of no account in this his new life.

Harry might reach across the table and take what he wanted; Judy might point and get what she wanted. Punch was forbidden to do either. The gray man was his great hope and stand-by for many months after Mamma and Papa left, and he had forgotten to tell Judy to 'bemember Mamma.'

This lapse was excusable, because in the interval he had been introduced by Aunty Rosa to two very impressive things – an abstraction called God, the intimate friend and ally of Aunty Rosa, generally believed to live behind the kitchen-range because it was hot there – and a dirty brown book filled with unintelligible dots and marks. Punch was always anxious to oblige everybody. He therefore welded the story of the Creation on to what he could recollect of his Indian fairy tales, and scandalised Aunty Rosa by repeating the result to Judy. It was a sin, a grievous sin, and Punch was talked to for a quarter of an hour. He could not understand where the iniquity came in, but was careful not to repeat the offence, because Aunty Rosa told him that God had heard every word he had said and was very angry. If this were true why didn't God come and say so, thought Punch, and dismissed the matter from his mind. Afterwards he learned to know the Lord as the only thing in the world more awful than Aunty Rosa – as a Creature that stood in the background and counted the strokes of the cane.

But the reading was, just then, a much more serious matter than any creed. Aunty Rosa sat him upon a table and told him that A B meant ab.

'Why?' said Punch. 'A is a and B is bee. *Why* does A B meant ab?'

'Because I tell you it does,' said Aunty Rosa, 'and you've got to say it.'

Punch said it accordingly, and for a month, hugely against his will, stumbled through the brown book, not in the least comprehending what it meant. But Uncle Harry, who walked much and generally alone, was wont to come into the nursery and suggest to Aunty Rosa that Punch should walk with him. He seldom spoke, but he showed Punch all Rocklington, from the mud-banks and the sand of the back-bay to the great harbours where ships lay at anchor, and the dockyards where the hammers were never still, and the marine-store shops, and the shiny brass counters in the Offices where Uncle Harry went once every three months with a slip of blue paper and received sovereigns in exchange; for he held a wound-pension. Punch heard, too, from his lips the story of the battle of Navarino, where the sailors of the Fleet, for three days afterwards, were deaf as posts and could only sign to each other. 'That was because of the noise of the guns,' said Uncle Harry, 'and I have got the wadding of a bullet somewhere inside me now.'

Punch regarded him with curiosity. He had not the least idea what wadding was, and his notion of a bullet was a dockyard cannon-ball bigger than his own head. How could Uncle Harry keep a cannon-ball inside him? He was ashamed to ask, for fear Uncle Harry might be angry.

Punch had never known what anger – real anger – meant until one terrible day when Harry had taken his paint-box to paint a boat with, and Punch had protested. Then Uncle Harry had appeared on the scene and, muttering something about 'strangers' children,' had with a stick smitten the black-haired boy across the shoulders till he wept and yelled, and Aunty Rosa came in and abused Uncle Harry for cruelty to his own flesh and blood, and Punch shuddered to the tips of his shoes. 'It wasn't my fault,' he explained to the boy, but both Harry and Aunty Rosa said that it was, and that Punch had told tales, and for a week there were no more walks with Uncle Harry.

But that week brought a great joy to Punch.

He had repeated till he was thrice weary the statement that 'the Cat lay on the Mat and the Rat came in.'

'Now I can truly read,' said Punch, 'and now I will never read anything in the world.'

He put the brown book in the cupboard where his school-books lived and accidentally tumbled out a venerable volume, without covers, labelled *Sharpe's Magazine*. There was the most portentous picture of a griffin on the first page, with verses below. The griffin carried off one sheep a day from a German village, till a man came with a 'falchion' and split the griffin open. Goodness only knew what a falchion was, but there was the Griffin, and his history was an improvement upon the eternal Cat.

'This,' said Punch, 'means things, and now I will know all about everything in all the world.' He read till the light failed, not understanding a tithe of the meaning, but tantalised by glimpses of new worlds hereafter to be revealed.

'What is a "falchion"? What is a "e-wee lamb"? What is a "base *us*surper"? What is a "verdant me-ad"?' he demanded with flushed cheeks, at bedtime, of the astonished Aunty Rosa.

'Say your prayers and go to sleep,' she replied, and that was all the help Punch then or afterwards found at her hands in the new and delightful exercise of reading.

'Aunty Rosa only knows about God and things like that,' argued Punch. 'Uncle Harry will tell me.'

The next walk proved that Uncle Harry could not help either; but he allowed Punch to talk, and even sat down on a bench to hear about the Griffin. Other walks brought other stories as Punch ranged farther afield, for the house held large store of old books that no one ever opened – from *Frank Fairlegh* in serial numbers, and the earlier poems of Tennyson, contributed anonymously to *Sharpe's Magazine*, to '62 Exhibition Catalogues, gay with colours and delightfully incomprehensible, and odd leaves of *Gulliver's Travels*.

As soon as Punch could string a few pot-hooks together he wrote to Bombay, demanding by return of post 'all the books in all the world.' Papa could not comply with this modest indent, but sent *Grimm's Fairy Tales* and a Hans Andersen. That was enough. If he were only left alone Punch could pass, at any hour he chose, into a land of his own, beyond reach of Aunty Rosa and her God, Harry and his tease-ments, and Judy's claims to be played with.

'Don't disturbe me, I'm reading. Go and play in the kitchen,' grunted Punch. 'Aunty Rosa lets *you* go there.' Judy was cutting her second teeth and was fretful. She appealed to Aunty Rosa, who descended on Punch.

'I was reading,' he explained, 'reading a book I *want* to read.'

'You're only doing that to show off,' said Aunty Rosa. 'But we'll see. Play with Judy now, and don't open a book for a week.'

Judy did not pass a very enjoyable playtime with Punch, who was consumed with indignation. There was a pettiness at the bottom of the prohibition which puzzled him.

'It's what I like to do,' he said, 'and she's found out that and stopped me. Don't cry, Ju – it wasn't your fault – *please* don't cry, or she'll say I made you.'

Ju loyally mopped up her tears, and the two played in their nursery, a room in the basement and half underground, to which they were regularly sent after the midday dinner while Aunty Rosa slept. She drank wine – that is to say, something from a bottle in the cellaret – for her stomach's sake, but if she did not fall asleep she would sometimes come into the nursery to see that the children were really playing. Now bricks, wooden hoops, ninepins, and chinaware cannot amuse for ever, especially when all Fairyland is to be won by the mere opening of a book, and, as often as not, Punch would be discovered reading to Judy or telling her interminable tales. That was an offence in the eyes of the law, and Judy would be whisked off by Aunty Rosa, while Punch was left to play alone, 'and be sure that I hear you doing it.'

It was not a cheering employ, for he had to make a playful noise. At last, with infinite craft, he devised an arrangement whereby the table could be supported as to three legs on toy bricks, leaving the fourth clear to bring down on the floor. He could work the table with one hand and hold a book with the other. This he did till an evil day when Aunty Rosa pounced upon him unawares and told him that he was 'acting a lie.'

'If you're old enough to do that,' she said – her temper was always worst after dinner – 'you're old enough to be beaten.'

'But – I'm – I'm not a animal!' said Punch aghast. He remembered Uncle Harry and the stick, and turned white. Aunty Rosa had hidden a light cane behind her, and Punch was beaten then and there over the shoulders. It was a revelation to him. The room-door was shut, and he was left to weep himself into repentance and work out his own gospel of life.

Aunty Rosa, he argued, had the power to beat him with many stripes. It was unjust and cruel, and Mamma and Papa would never have allowed it. Unless perhaps, as Aunty Rosa seemed to imply, they had sent secret orders. In which case he was abandoned indeed. It would be discreet in the future to propitiate Aunty Rosa, but, then, again, even in matters in which he was innocent, he had been accused of wishing to 'show off.' He had 'shown off' before visitors when he had attacked a strange gentleman – Harry's uncle, not his own – with requests for information about the Griffin and the falchion, and the precise nature of the Tilbury in which Frank Fairlegh rode – all points of paramount interest which he was bursting to understand. Clearly it would not do to pretend to care for Aunty Rosa.

At this point Harry entered and stood afar off, eyeing Punch, a dishevelled heap in the corner of the room, with disgust.

'You're a liar – a young liar,' said Harry, with great unction, 'and you're to have tea down here because you're not fit to speak to us. And you're not to speak to Judy again till Mother gives you leave. You'll corrupt her. You're only fit to associate with the servant. Mother says so.'

Having reduced Punch to a second agony of tears, Harry departed upstairs with the news that Punch was still rebellious.

Uncle Harry sat uneasily in the dining-room. 'Damn it all, Rosa,' said he at last, 'can't you leave the child alone? He's a good enough little chap when I meet him.'

'He puts on his best manners with you, Henry,' said Aunty Rosa, 'but I'm afraid, I'm very much afraid, that he is the Black Sheep of the family.'

Harry heard and stored up the name for future use. Judy cried till she was bidden to stop, her brother not being worth tears; and the evening concluded with the return of Punch to the upper regions and a private sitting at which all the blinding horrors of Hell were revealed to Punch with such store of imagery as Aunty Rosa's narrow mind possessed.

Most grievous of all was Judy's round-eyed reproach, and Punch went to bed in the depths of the Valley of Humiliation. He shared his room with Harry and knew the torture in store. For an hour and a half he had to answer that young gentleman's questions as to his motives for telling a lie, and a grievous lie, the precise quantity of punishment inflicted by Aunty Rosa, and had also to profess his deep gratitude for such religious instruction as Harry thought fit to impart.

From that day began the downfall of Punch, now Black Sheep.

'Untrustworthy in one thing, untrustworthy in all,' said Aunty Rosa, and Harry felt that Black Sheep was delivered into his hands. He would wake him up in the night to ask him why he was such a liar.

'I don't know,' Punch would reply.

'Then don't you think you ought to get up and pray to God for a new heart?'

'Y-yess.'

'Get out and pray, then!' And Punch would get out of bed with raging hate in his heart against all the world, seen and unseen. He was always tumbling into trouble. Harry had a knack of cross-examining him as to his day's doings, which seldom failed to lead him, sleepy and savage, into half-a-dozen contradictions – all duly reported to Aunty Rosa next morning.

'But it *wasn't* a lie,' Punch would begin, charging into a laboured explanation that landed him more hopelessly in the mire. 'I said that I didn't say my prayers *twice* over in the day, and *that* was on Tuesday. *Once* I did. I *know* I did, but Harry said I didn't,' and so forth, till the tension brought tears, and he was dismissed from the table in disgrace.

'You usen't to be as bad as this,' said Judy, awe-stricken at the catalogue of Black Sheep's crimes. 'Why are you so bad now?'

'I don't know,' Black Sheep would reply. 'I'm not, if I only wasn't bothered upside down. I knew what I *did*, and I want to say so; but Harry always makes it out different somehow, and Aunty Rosa doesn't believe a word I say. Oh, Ju! don't you say I'm bad too.'

'Aunty Rosa says you are,' said Judy. 'She told the Vicar so when he came yesterday.'

'Why does she tell all the people outside the house about me? It isn't fair,' said Black Sheep. 'When I was in Bombay, and was bad – *doing* bad, not made-up bad like this – Mamma told Papa, and Papa told me he knew, and that was all. *Outside* people didn't know too – even Meeta didn't know.'

'I don't remember,' said Judy wistfully. 'I was all little then. Mamma was just as fond of you as she was of me, wasn't she?'

''Course she was. So was Papa. So was everybody.'

'Aunty Rosa likes me more than she does you. She says that you are a Trial and a Black Sheep, and I'm not to speak to you more than I can help.'

'Always? Not outside of the times when you mustn't speak to me at all?'

Judy nodded her head mournfully. Black Sheep turned away in despair, but Judy's arms were round his neck.

'Never mind, Punch,' she whispered. 'I *will* speak to you just the same as ever and ever. You're my own own brother though you are – though Aunty Rosa says you're bad, and Harry says you are a little coward. He says that if I pulled your hair hard, you'd cry.'

'Pull, then,' said Punch.

Judy pulled gingerly.

'Pull harder – as hard as you can! There! I don't mind how much you pull it *now*. If you'll speak to me same as ever I'll let you pull it as much as you like – pull it out if you like. But I know if Harry came and stood by and made you do it I'd cry.'

So the two children sealed the compact with a kiss, and Black Sheep's heart was cheered within him, and by extreme caution and careful avoidance of Harry he acquired virtue, and was allowed to read undisturbed for a week. Uncle Harry took him for walks, and consoled him with rough tenderness, never calling him Black Sheep. 'It's good for you, I suppose, Punch,' he used to say. 'Let us sit down. I'm getting tired.' His steps led him now not to the beach, but to the Cemetery of Rocklington, amid the potato-fields. For hours the gray man would sit on a tombstone, while Black Sheep would read epitaphs, and then with a sigh would stump home again.

'I shall lie there soon,' said he to Black Sheep, one winter evening, when his face showed white as a worn silver coin under the light of the lych-gate. 'You needn't tell Aunty Rosa.'

A month later he turned sharp round, ere half a morning walk was completed, and stumped back to the house. 'Put me to bed, Rosa,' he muttered. 'I've walked my last. The wadding has found me out.'

They put him to bed, and for a fortnight the shadow of his sickness lay upon the house, and Black Sheep went to and fro unobserved. Papa had sent him some new books, and he was told to keep quiet. He retired into his own world, and was perfectly happy. Even at night his felicity was unbroken. He could lie in bed and string himself tales of travel and adventure while Harry was downstairs.

'Uncle Harry's going to die,' said Judy, who now lived almost entirely with Aunty Rosa.

'I'm very sorry,' said Black Sheep soberly. 'He told me that a long time ago.'

Aunty Rosa heard the conversation. 'Will nothing check your wicked tongue?' she said angrily. There were blue circles round her eyes.

Black Sheep retreated to the nursery and read *Cometh up as a Flower* with deep and uncomprehending interest. He had been forbidden to open it on account of its 'sinfulness,' but the bonds of the Universe were crumbling, and Aunty Rosa was in great grief.

'I'm glad,' said Black Sheep. 'She's unhappy now. It wasn't a lie, though. *I* knew. He told me not to tell.'

That night Black Sheep woke with a start. Harry was not in the room, and there

BRITISH EMPIRE ADVENTURE STORIES

was a sound of sobbing on the next floor. Then the voice of Uncle Harry, singing the song of the Battle of Navarino, came through the darkness –

'Our vanship was the Asia –
The Albion and Genoa!'

'He's getting well,' thought Black Sheep, who knew the song through all its seventeen verses. But the blood froze at his little heart as he thought. The voice leapt an octave, and rang shrill as a boatswain's pipe –

'And next came on the lovely Rose,
The Philomel, her fire-ship, closed,
And the little Brisk was sore exposed
That day at Navarino.'

'That day at Navarino, Uncle Harry!' shouted Black Sheep, half wild with excitement and fear of he knew not what.

A door opened, and Aunty Rosa screamed up the staircase: 'Hush! For God's sake hush, you little devil. Uncle Harry is *dead!*'

The Third Bag

Journeys end in lovers' meeting,
Every wise man's son doth know.

'I wonder what will happen to me now,' thought Black Sheep, when semi-pagan rites peculiar to the burial of the Dead in middleclass houses had been accomplished, and Aunty Rosa, awful in black crepe, had returned to this life. 'I don't think I've done anything bad that she knows of. I suppose I will soon. She will be very cross after Uncle Harry's dying, and Harry will be cross too. I'll keep in the nursery.'

Unfortunately for Punch's plans, it was decided that he should be sent to a day-school which Harry attended. This meant a morning walk with Harry, and perhaps an evening one; but the prospect of freedom in the interval was refreshing. 'Harry'll tell everything I do, but I won't do anything,' said Black Sheep. Fortified with this virtuous resolution, he went to school only to find that Harry's version of his character had preceded him, and that life was a burden in consequence. He took stock of his associates. Some of them were unclean, some of them talked in dialect, many dropped their h's, and there were two Jews and a negro, or someone quite as dark, in the assembly. 'That's a *hubshi*,' said Black Sheep to himself. 'Even Meeta used to laugh at a *hubshi*. I don't think this is a proper place.' He was indignant for at least an hour, till he reflected that any expostulation on his part would be by Aunty Rosa construed into 'showing off,' and that Harry would tell the boys.

'How do you like school?' said Aunty Rosa at the end of the day.

'I think it is a very nice place,' said Punch quietly.

'I suppose you warned the boys of Black Sheep's character?' said Aunty Rosa to Harry.

'Oh yes,' said the censor of Black Sheep's morals. 'They know all about him.'

'If I was with my father,' said Black Sheep, stung to the quick, 'I shouldn't *speak* to those boys. He wouldn't let me. They live in shops. I saw them go into shops – where their fathers live and sell things.'

'You're too good for that school, are you?' said Aunty Rosa, with a bitter smile. 'You ought to be grateful, Black Sheep, that those boys speak to you at all. It isn't every school that takes little liars.'

Harry did not fail to make much capital out of Black Sheep's ill-considered remark; with the result that several boys, including the *hubshi*, demonstrated to Black Sheep the eternal equality of the human race by smacking his head, and his consolation from Aunty Rosa was that it 'served him right for being vain.' He learned, however, to keep his opinions to himself, and by propitiating Harry in carrying books and the like to get a little peace. His existence was not too joyful. From nine till twelve he was at school, and from two to four, except on Saturdays. In the evenings he was sent down into the nursery to prepare his lessons for the next day, and every night came the dreaded cross-questionings at Harry's hand. Of Judy he saw but little. She was deeply religious – at six years of age Religion is easy to come by – and sorely divided between her natural love for Black Sheep and her love for Aunty Rosa, who could do no wrong.

The lean woman returned that love with interest, and Judy, when she dared, took advantage of this for the remission of Black Sheep's penalties. Failures in lessons at school were punished at home by a week without reading other than schoolbooks, and Harry brought the news of such a failure with glee. Further, Black Sheep was then bound to repeat his lessons at bedtime to Harry, who generally succeeded in making him break down, and consoled him by gloomiest forebodings for the morrow. Harry was at once spy, practical Joker, inquisitor, and Aunty Rosa's deputy executioner. He filled his many posts to admiration. From his actions, now that Uncle Harry was dead, there was no appeal. Black Sheep had not been permitted to keep any self-respect at school: at home he was, of course, utterly discredited, and grateful for any pity that the servant girls – they changed frequently at Downe Lodge because they, too, were liars – might show. 'You're just fit to row in the same boat with Black Sheep,' was a sentiment that each new Jane or Eliza might expect to hear, before a month was over, from Aunty Rosa's lips; and Black Sheep was used to ask new girls whether they had yet been compared to him. Harry was 'Master Harry' in their mouths; Judy was officially 'Miss Judy'; but Black Sheep was never anything more than Black Sheep *tout court*.

As time went on and the memory of Papa and Mamma became wholly overlaid by the unpleasant task of writing them letters, under Aunty Rosa's eye, each Sunday, Black Sheep forgot what manner of life he had led in the beginning of things. Even Judy's appeals to 'try and remember about Bombay' failed to quicken him.

'I can't remember,' he said. 'I know I used to give orders and Mamma kissed me.'

'Aunty Rosa will kiss you if you are good,' pleaded Judy.

'Ugh! I don't want to be kissed by Aunty Rosa. She'd say I was doing it to get something more to eat.'

The weeks lengthened into months, and the holidays came; but just before the holidays Black Sheep fell into deadly sin.

Among the many boys whom Harry had incited to 'punch Black Sheep's head because he daren't hit back,' was one more aggravating than the rest, who, in an unlucky moment, fell upon Black Sheep when Harry was not near. The blows stung, and Black Sheep struck back at random with all the power at his command. The boy dropped and whimpered. Black Sheep was astounded at his own act, but, feeling the unresisting body under him, shook it with both his hands in blind fury and then began to throttle his enemy; meaning honestly to slay him. There was a scuffle, and Black Sheep was torn off the body by Harry and some colleagues, and cuffed home tingling but exultant. Aunty Rosa was out: pending her arrival, Harry set himself to lecture Black Sheep on the sin of murder – which he described as the offence of Cain.

'Why didn't you fight him fair? What did you hit him when he was down for, you little cur?'

Black Sheep looked up at Harry's throat and then at a knife on the dinner-table.

'I don't understand,' he said wearily. 'You always set him on me and told me I was a coward when I blubbed. Will you leave me alone until Aunty Rosa comes in? She'll beat me if you tell her I ought to be beaten; so it's all right.'

'It's all wrong,' said Harry magisterially. 'You nearly killed him, and I shouldn't wonder if he dies.'

'Will he die?' said Black Sheep.

'I daresay,' said Harry, 'and then you'll be hanged, and go to Hell.'

'All right,' said Black Sheep, picking up the table-knife. 'Then I'll kill *you* now. You say things and do things and – and I don't know how things happen, and you never leave me alone – and I don't care *what* happens!'

He ran at the boy with the knife, and Harry fled upstairs to his room, promising Black Sheep the finest thrashing in the world when Aunty Rosa returned. Black Sheep sat at the bottom of the stairs, the table-knife in his hand, and wept for that he had not killed Harry. The servant-girl came up from the kitchen, took the knife away, and consoled him. But Black Sheep was beyond consolation. He would be badly beaten by Aunty Rosa; then there would be another beating at Harry's hands; then Judy would not be allowed to speak to him; then the tale would be told at school, and then –

There was no one to help and no one to care, and the best way out of the business was by death. A knife would hurt, but Aunty Rosa had told him, a year ago, that if he sucked paint he would die. He went into the nursery, unearthed the now disused Noah's Ark, and sucked the paint off as many animals as remained. It tasted abominable, but he had licked Noah's Dove clean by the time Aunty Rosa and Judy returned. He went upstairs and greeted them with: 'Please, Aunty Rosa, I believe I've nearly killed a boy at school, and I've tried to kill Harry, and when you've done all about God and Hell, will you beat me and get it over?'

The tale of the assault as told by Harry could only be explained on the ground of possession by the Devil. Wherefore Black Sheep was not only most excellently beaten, once by Aunty Rosa and once, when thoroughly cowed down, by Harry, but he was further prayed for at family prayers, together with Jane who had stolen a cold rissole from the pantry, and snuffled audibly as her sin was brought before the Throne of Grace. Black Sheep was sore and stiff but triumphant. He would die that very night and be rid of them all. No, he would ask for no forgiveness from Harry, and at bed-time would stand no questioning at Harry's hands, even though addressed as 'Young Cain.'

'I've been beaten,' said he, 'and I've done other things. I don't care what I do. If you speak to me tonight, Harry, I'll get out and try to kill you. Now you can kill me if you like.'

Harry took his bed into the spare room, and Black Sheep lay down to die.

It may be that the makers of Noah's Arks know that their animals are likely to find their way into young mouths, and paint them accordingly. Certain it is that the common, weary next morning broke through the windows and found Black Sheep quite well and a good deal ashamed of himself, but richer by the knowledge that he could, in extremity, secure himself against Harry for the future.

When he descended to breakfast on the first day of the holidays, he was greeted with the news that Harry, Aunty Rosa, and Judy were going away to Brighton, while Black Sheep was to stay in the house with the servant. His latest outbreak suited Aunty Rosa's plans admirably. It gave her good excuse for leaving the extra boy behind. Papa in Bombay, who really seemed to know a young sinner's wants to the hour, sent, that week, a package of new books. And with these, and the society of Jane on board-wages, Black Sheep was left alone for a month.

The books lasted for ten days. They were eaten too quickly in long gulps of twelve hours at a time. Then came days of doing absolutely nothing, of dreaming dreams and marching imaginary armies up and downstairs, of counting the number of banisters, and of measuring the length and breadth of every room in handspans – fifty down the side, thirty across, and fifty back again. Jane made many friends, and, after receiving Black Sheep's assurance that he would not tell of her absences, went out daily for long hours. Black Sheep would follow the rays of the sinking sun from the kitchen to the dining-room and thence upward to his own bedroom until all was gray dark, and he ran down to the kitchen fire and read by its light. He was happy in that he was left alone and could read as much as he pleased. But, later, he grew afraid of the shadows of window-curtains and the flapping of doors and the creaking of shutters. He went out into the garden, and the rustling of the laurel-bushes frightened him.

He was glad when they all returned – Aunty Rosa, Harry, and Judy – full of news, and Judy laden with gifts. Who could help loving loyal little Judy? In return for all her merry babblement, Black Sheep confided to her that the distance from the hall-door to the top of the first landing was exactly one hundred and eighty-four handspans. He had found it out himself.

Then the old life recommenced; but with a difference, and a new sin. To his other iniquities Black Sheep had now added a phenomenal clumsiness – was as unfit to trust in action as he was in word. He himself could not account for spilling everything he touched, upsetting glasses as he put his hand out, and bumping his head against doors that were manifestly shut. There was a gray haze upon all his world, and it narrowed month by month, until at last it left Black Sheep almost alone with the flapping curtains that were so like ghosts, and the nameless terrors of broad daylight that were only coats on pegs after all.

Holidays came and holidays went, and Black Sheep was taken to see many people whose faces were all exactly alike; was beaten when occasion demanded, and tortured by Harry on all possible occasions; but defended by Judy through good and evil report, though she hereby drew upon herself the wrath of Aunty Rosa.

The weeks were interminable, and Papa and Mamma were clean forgotten. Harry had left school and was a clerk in a Banking-Office. Freed from his presence, Black Sheep resolved that he should no longer be deprived of his allowance of pleasure-reading. Consequently when he failed at school he reported that all was well, and conceived a large contempt for Aunty Rosa as he saw how easy it was to deceive her. 'She says I'm a little liar when I don't tell lies, and now I do, she doesn't know,' thought Black Sheep. Aunty Rosa had credited him in the past with petty cunning and stratagem that had never entered into his head. By the light of the sordid knowledge that she had revealed to him he paid her back full tale. In a household where the most innocent of his motives, his natural yearning for a little affection, had been interpreted into a desire for more bread and jam, or to ingratiate himself with strangers and so put Harry into the background, his work was easy. Aunty Rosa could penetrate certain kinds of hypocrisy, but not all. He set his child's wits against hers and was no more beaten. It grew monthly more and more of a trouble to read the school books, and even the pages of the open-print story-books danced and were dim. So Black Sheep brooded in the shadows that fell about him and cut him off from the world, inventing horrible punishments for 'dear Harry,' or plotting another line of the tangled web of deception that he wrapped round Aunty Rosa.

Then the crash came and the cobwebs were broken. It was impossible to foresee everything. Aunty Rosa made personal inquiries as to Black Sheep's progress and received information that startled her. Step by step, with a delight as keen as when she convicted an underfed housemaid of the theft of cold meats, she followed the trail of Black Sheep's delinquencies. For weeks and weeks, in order to escape banishment from the bookshelves, he had made a fool of Aunty Rosa, of Harry, of God, of all the world! Horrible, most horrible, and evidence of an utterly depraved mind.

Black Sheep counted the cost. 'It will only be one big beating and then she'll put a card with "Liar" on my back, same as she did before. Harry will whack me and pray for me, and she will pray for me at prayers and tell me I'm a Child of the Devil and give me hymns to learn. But I've done all my reading and she never knew. She'll say she knew all along. She's an old liar too,' said he.

For three days Black Sheep was shut in his own bedroom – to prepare his heart. 'That means two beatings. One at school and one here. *That* one will hurt most.' And it fell even as he thought. He was thrashed at school before the Jews and the *hubshi* for the heinous crime of carrying home false reports of progress. He was thrashed at home by Aunty Rosa on the same count, and then the placard was produced. Aunty Rosa stitched it between his shoulders and bade him go for a walk with it upon him.

'If you make me do that,' said Black Sheep very quietly, 'I shall burn this house down, and perhaps I'll kill you. I don't know whether I *can* kill you – you're so bony – but I'll try.'

No punishment followed this blasphemy, though Black Sheep held himself ready to work his way to Aunty Rosa's withered throat, and grip there till he was beaten off. Perhaps Aunty Rosa was afraid, for Black Sheep, having reached the Nadir of Sin, bore himself with a new recklessness.

In the midst of all the trouble there came a visitor from over the seas to Downe Lodge, who knew Papa and Mamma, and was commissioned to see Punch and Judy. Black Sheep was sent to the drawing-room and charged into a solid tea-table laden with china.

'Gently, gently, little man,' said the visitor, turning Black Sheep's face to the light slowly. 'What's that big bird on the palings?'

'What bird?' asked Black Sheep.

The visitor looked deep down into Black Sheep's eyes for half a minute, and then said suddenly: 'Good God, the little chap's nearly blind!'

It was a most businesslike visitor. He gave orders, on his own responsibility, that Black Sheep was not to go to school or open a book until Mamma came home. 'She'll be here in three weeks, as you know of course,' said he, 'and I'm Inverarity Sahib. I ushered you into this wicked world, young man, and a nice use you seem to have made of your time. You must do nothing whatever. Can you do that?'

'Yes,' said Punch in a dazed way. He had known that Mamma was coming. There was a chance, then, of another beating. Thank Heaven, Papa wasn't coming too. Aunty Rosa had said of late that he ought to be beaten by a man.

For the next three weeks Black Sheep was strictly allowed to do nothing. He spent his time in the old nursery looking at the broken toys, for all of which account must be rendered to Mamma. Aunty Rosa hit him over the hands if even a wooden boat were broken. But that sin was of small importance compared to the other revelations, so darkly hinted at by Aunty Rosa. 'When your Mother comes, and hears what I have to tell her, she may appreciate you properly,' she said grimly, and mounted guard over Judy lest that small maiden should attempt to comfort her brother, to the peril of her soul.

And Mamma came – in a four-wheeler – fluttered with tender excitement. Such a Mamma! She was young, frivolously young, and beautiful, with delicately-flushed cheeks, eyes that shone like stars, and a voice that needed no appeal of outstretched arms to draw little ones to her heart. Judy ran straight to her, but Black Sheep hesitated. Could this wonder be 'showing off'? She would not put out her arms when she knew of his crimes. Meantime was it possible that by fondling she wanted to get anything out of Black Sheep? Only all his love and all his confidence; but that Black Sheep did not know. Aunty Rosa withdrew and left Mamma, kneeling between her children, half laughing, half crying, in the very hall where Punch and Judy had wept five years before.

'Well, chicks, do you remember me?'

'No,' said Judy frankly, 'but I said, "God bless Papa and Mamma" ev'vy night.'

'A little,' said Black Sheep. 'Remember I wrote to you every week, anyhow. That isn't to show off, but 'cause of what comes afterwards.'

'What comes after? What should come after, my darling boy?' And she drew him to her again. He came awkwardly, with many angles. 'Not used to petting,' said the quick Mother-soul. 'The girl is.'

'She's too little to hurt anyone,' thought Black Sheep, 'and if I said I'd kill her, she'd be afraid. I wonder what Aunty Rosa will tell.'

There was a constrained late dinner, at the end of which Mamma picked up Judy and put her to bed with endearments manifold. Faithless little Judy had shown her defection from Aunty Rosa already. And that lady resented it bitterly. Black Sheep rose to leave the room.

'Come and say good-night,' said Aunty Rosa, offering a withered cheek.

'Huh!' said Black Sheep. 'I never kiss you, and I'm not going to show off. Tell that woman what I've done, and see what she says.'

Black Sheep climbed into bed feeling that he had lost Heaven after a glimpse through the gates. In half an hour 'that woman' was bending over him. Black Sheep flung up his right arm. It wasn't fair to come and hit him in the dark. Even Aunty Rosa never tried that. But no blow followed.

'Are you showing off? I won't tell you anything more than Aunty Rosa has, and *she* doesn't know everything,' said Black Sheep as clearly as he could for the arms round his neck.

'Oh, my son – my little, little son! It was my fault – *my* fault, darling – and yet how could we help it? Forgive me, Punch.' The voice died out in a broken whisper, and two hot tears fell on Black Sheep's forehead.

'Has she been making you cry too?' he asked. 'You should see Jane cry. But you're nice, and Jane is a Born Liar – Aunty Rosa says so.'

'Hush, Punch, hush! My boy, don't talk like that. Try to love me a little bit – a little bit. You don't know how I want it. Punch-*baba*, come back to me! I am your Mother – your own Mother – and never mind the rest. I know – yes, I know, dear. It doesn't matter now. Punch, won't you care for me a little?'

It is astonishing how much petting a big boy of ten can endure when he is quite sure that there is no one to laugh at him. Black Sheep had never been made much of before, and here was this beautiful woman treating him – Black Sheep, the Child of the Devil and the inheritor of undying flame – as though he were a small God.

'I care for you a great deal, Mother dear,' he whispered at last, 'and I'm glad you've come back; but are you sure Aunty Rosa told you everything?'

'Everything. What *does* it matter? But –' the voice broke with a sob that was also laughter – 'Punch, my poor, dear, half-blind darling, don't you think it was a little foolish of you?'

'*No*. It saved a lickin'.'

Mamma shuddered and slipped away in the darkness to write a long letter to Papa. Here is an extract –

. . . Judy is a dear, plump little prig who adores the woman, and wears with as much gravity as her religious opinions – only eight, Jack! – a venerable horse-

417

hair atrocity which she calls her Bustle! I have just burnt it, and the child is asleep in my bed as I write. She will come to me at once. Punch I cannot quite understand. He is well nourished, but seems to have been worried into a system of small deceptions which the woman magnifies into deadly sins. Don't you recollect our own upbringing, dear, when the Fear of the Lord was so often the beginning of falsehood? I shall win Punch to me before long. I am taking the children away into the country to get them to know me, and, on the whole, I am content, or shall be when you come home, dear boy, and then, thank God, we shall be all under one roof again at last!

Three months later, Punch, no longer Black Sheep, has discovered that he is the veritable owner of a real, live, lovely Mamma, who is also a sister, comforter, and friend, and that he must protect her till the Father comes home. Deception does not suit the part of a protector, and, when one can do anything without question, where is the use of deception?

'Mother would be awfully cross if you walked through that ditch,' says Judy, continuing a conversation.

'Mother's never angry,' says Punch. 'She'd just say, "You're a little *pagal*;" and that's not nice, but I'll show.'

Punch walks through the ditch and mires himself to the knees. 'Mother, dear,' he shouts, 'I'm just as dirty as I can pos-*sib*-ly be!'

'Then change your clothes as quickly as you pos-*sib*-ly can!' Mother's clear voice rings out from the house. 'And don't be a little *pagal*!'

'There! 'Told you so,' says Punch. 'It's all different now, and we are just as much Mother's as if she had never gone.'

Not altogether, O Punch, for when young lips have drunk deep of the bitter waters of Hate, Suspicion, and Despair, all the Love in the world will not wholly take away that knowledge; though it may turn darkened eyes for a while to the light, and teach Faith where no Faith was.

HIS MAJESTY THE KING

Where the word of a King is, there is power: And who may say unto
him – What doest thou?

'Yeth! And Chimo to sleep at ve foot of ve bed, and ve pink pikky-book, and
ve bwead – 'cause I will be hungwy in ve night – and vat's all, Miss Biddums.
And now give me one kiss and I'll go to sleep. – So! Kite quiet. Ow! Ve pink pikky-
book has slidded under ve pillow and ve bwead is cwumbling! Miss Biddums! Miss
Bid-dums! I'm *so* uncomfy! Come and tuck me up, Miss Biddums.'

His Majesty the King was going to bed; and poor, patient Miss Biddums, who had
advertised herself humbly as a 'young person, European, accustomed to the care of
little children,' was forced to wait upon his royal caprices. The going to bed was always
a lengthy process, because His Majesty had a convenient knack of forgetting which
of his many friends, from the *mehter's* son to the Commissioner's daughter, he had
prayed for, and, lest the Deity should take offence, was used to toil through his little
prayers, in all reverence, five times in one evening. His Majesty the King believed in
the efficacy of prayer as devoutly as he believed in Chimo the patient spaniel, or Miss
Biddums, who could reach him down his gun – 'with cursuffun caps – *reel* ones' –
from the upper shelves of the big nursery cupboard.

At the door of the nursery his authority stopped. Beyond lay the empire of his father and mother – two very terrible people who had no time to waste upon His Majesty the King. His voice was lowered when he passed the frontier of his own dominions, his actions were fettered, and his soul was filled with awe because of the grim man who lived among a wilderness of pigeon-holes and the most fascinating pieces of red tape, and the wonderful woman who was always getting into or stepping out of the big carriage.

To the one belonged the mysteries of the '*duftar*-room,' to the other the great, reflected wilderness of the 'Memsahib's room,' where the shiny, scented dresses hung on pegs, miles and miles up in the air, and the just-seen plateau of the toilet-table revealed an acreage of speckly combs, broidered 'hanafitch-bags,' and 'white-headed' brushes.

There was no room for His Majesty the King either in official reserve or worldly gorgeousness. He had discovered that, ages and ages ago – before even Chimo came to the house, or Miss Biddums had ceased grizzling over a packet of greasy letters which appeared to be her chief treasure on earth. His Majesty the King, therefore, wisely confined himself to his own territories, where only Miss Biddums, and she feebly, disputed his sway. From Miss Biddums he had picked up his simple theology and welded it to the legends of gods and devils that he had learned in the servants' quarters.

To Miss Biddums he confided with equal trust his tattered garments and his more serious griefs. She would make everything whole. She knew exactly how the Earth had been born, and had reassured the trembling soul of His Majesty the King that terrible time in July when it rained continuously for seven days and seven nights, and – there was no Ark ready and all the ravens had flown away! She was the most powerful person with whom he was brought into contact – always excepting the two remote and silent people beyond the nursery door.

How was His Majesty the King to know that, six years ago, in the summer of his birth, Mrs Austell, turning over her husband's papers, had come upon the intemperate letter of a foolish woman who had been carried away by the silent man's strength and personal beauty? How could he tell what evil the overlooked slip of notepaper had wrought in the mind of a desperately jealous wife? How could he, despite his wisdom, guess that his mother had chosen to make of it excuse for a bar and a division between herself and her husband, that strengthened and grew harder to break with each year; that she, having unearthed this skeleton in the cupboard, had trained it into a household God which should be about their path and about their bed, and poison all their ways?

These things were beyond the province of His Majesty the King. He only knew that his father was daily absorbed in some mysterious work for a thing called the *Sirkar*, and that his mother was the victim alternately of the *Nautch* and the *Burrakhana*. To these entertainments she was escorted by a Captain-Man for whom His Majesty the King had no regard.

'He *doesn't* laugh,' he argued with Miss Biddums, who would fain have taught him charity. 'He only makes faces wiv his mouf, and when he wants to o-muse me I am *not* o-mused.' And His Majesty the King shook his head as one who knew the deceitfulness of this world.

Morning and evening it was his duty to salute his father and mother – the former with a grave shake of the hand, and the latter with an equally grave kiss. Once, indeed, he had put his arms round his mother's neck, in the fashion he used towards Miss Biddums. The openwork of his sleeve-edge caught in an earring, and the last stage of His Majesty's little overture was a suppressed scream and summary dismissal to the nursery.

'It is w'ong,' thought His Majesty the King, 'to hug Memsahibs wiv fings in veir ears. I will amember.' He never repeated the experiment.

Miss Biddums, it must be confessed, spoilt him as much as his nature admitted, in some sort of recompense for what she called 'the hard ways of his Papa and Mamma.' She, like her charge, knew nothing of the trouble between man and wife – the savage contempt for a woman's stupidity on the one side, or the dull, rankling anger on the other. Miss Biddums had looked after many little children in her time, and served in many establishments. Being a discreet woman, she observed little and said less, and, when her pupils went over the sea to the Great Unknown, which she, with touching confidence in her hearers, called 'Home,' packed up her slender belongings and sought for employment afresh, lavishing all her love on each successive batch of ingrates. Only His Majesty the King had repaid her affection with interest; and in his uncomprehending ears she had told the tale of nearly all her hopes, her aspirations, the hopes that were dead, and the dazzling glories of her ancestral home in 'Calcutta, close to Wellington Square.'

Everything above the average was in the eyes of His Majesty the King 'Calcutta good.' When Miss Biddums had crossed his royal will, he reversed the epithet to vex that estimable lady, and all things evil were, until the tears of repentance swept away spite, 'Calcutta bad.'

Now and again Miss Biddums begged for him the rare pleasure of a day in the society of the Commissioner's child – the wilful four-year-old Patsie, who, to the intense amazement of His Majesty the King, was idolised by her parents. On thinking the question out at length, by roads unknown to those who have left childhood behind, he came to the conclusion that Patsie was petted because she wore a big blue sash and yellow hair.

This precious discovery he kept to himself. The yellow hair was absolutely beyond his power, his own tousled wig being potato-brown; but something might be done towards the blue sash. He tied a large knot in his mosquito-curtains in order to remember to consult Patsie on their next meeting. She was the only child he had ever spoken to, and almost the only one that he had ever seen. The little memory and the very large and ragged knot held good.

'Patsie, lend me your blue wiband,' said His Majesty the King.

'You'll bewy it,' said Patsie doubtfully, mindful of certain atrocities committed on her doll.

'No, I won't – twoofanhonour. It's for me to wear.'

'Pooh!' said Patsie. 'Boys don't wear sa-ashes. Zey's only for dirls.'

'I didn't know.' The face of His Majesty the King fell.

'Who wants ribands? Are you playing horses, chickabiddies?' said the Commissioner's wife, stepping into the verandah.

'Toby wanted my sash,' explained Patsie.

'I don't now,' said His Majesty the King hastily, feeling that with one of these terrible 'grown-ups' his poor little secret would be shamelessly wrenched from him, and perhaps – most burning descration of all – laughed at.

'I'll give you a cracker-cap,' said the Commissioner's wife. 'Come along with me, Toby, and we'll choose it.'

The cracker-cap was a stiff, three-pointed vermilion-and-tinsel splendour. His Majesty the King fitted it on his royal brow. The Commissioner's wife had a face that children instinctively trusted, and her action, as she adjusted the toppling middle spike, was tender.

'Will it do as well?' stammered His Majesty the King.

'As what, little one?'

'As ve wiban?'

'Oh, quite. Go and look at yourself in the glass.'

The words were spoken in all sincerity, and to help forward any absurd 'dressing-up' amusement that the children might take into their minds. But the young savage has a keen sense of the ludicrous. His Majesty the King swung the great cheval-glass down, and saw his head crowned with the staring horror of a fool's cap – a thing which his father would rend to pieces if it ever came into his office. He plucked it off, and burst into tears.

'Toby,' said the Commissioner's wife gravely, 'you shouldn't give way to temper. I am very sorry to see it. It's wrong.'

His Majesty the King sobbed inconsolably, and the heart of Patsie's mother was touched. She drew the child on to her knee. Clearly it was not temper alone.

'What is it, Toby? Won't you tell me? Aren't you well?'

The torrent of sobs and speech met, and fought for a time, with chokings and gulpings and gasps. Then, in a sudden rush, His Majesty the King was delivered of a few inarticulate sounds, followed by the words – 'Go a – way you – dirty – little debbil!'

'Toby! What do you mean?'

'It's what he'd say. I *know* it is! He said vat when were was only a little, little eggy mess, on my t-t-unic; and he'd say it again, and laugh, if I went in wif vat on my head.'

'Who would say that?'

'M-m-my Papa! And I fought if I had ve blue wiban, he'd let me play in ve waste-paper basket under ve table.'

'*What* blue riband, childie?'

''Ve same vat Patsie had – ve big blue wiban w-w-wound my t-t-tummy!'

'What is it, Toby? There's something on your mind. Tell me all about it, and perhaps I can help.'

'Isn't anyfing,' sniffed His Majesty, mindful of his manhood, and raising his head from the motherly bosom upon which it was resting. 'I only fought vat you – you petted Patsie 'cause she had ve blue wiban, and – and if I'd had ve blue wiban too, m-my Papa w-would pet me.'

The secret was out, and His Majesty the King sobbed bitterly in spite of the arms around him and the murmur of comfort on his heated little forehead.

Enter Patsie tumultuously, embarrassed by several lengths of the Commissioner's pet *mahseer*-rod. 'Tum along, Toby! Zere's a *chu-chu* lizard in ze *chick*, and I've told Chimo to watch him till we tum. If we poke him wiz zis his tail will go *wiggle-wiggle* and fall off. Tum along! I can't weach.'

'I'm comin',' said His Majesty the King, climbing down from the Commissioner's wife's knee after a hasty kiss.

Two minutes later, the *chu-chu* lizard's tail was wriggling on the matting of the verandah, and the children were gravely poking it with splinters from the *chick*, to urge its exhausted vitality into 'just one wiggle more, 'cause it doesn't hurt *chu-chu*.'

The Commissioner's wife stood in the doorway and watched – 'Poor little mite! A blue sash – and my own precious Patsie! I wonder if the best of us, or we who love them best, ever understood what goes on in their topsy-turvy little heads.'

She went indoors to devise a tea for His Majesty the King.

'Their souls aren't in their tummies at that age in this climate,' said the Commissioner's wife, 'but they are not far off. I wonder if I could make Mrs Austell understand. Poor little fellow!'

With simple craft, the Commissioner's wife called on Mrs Austell and spoke long and lovingly about children; inquiring specially for His Majesty the King.

'He's with his governess,' said Mrs Austell, and the tone showed that she was not interested.

The Commissioner's wife, unskilled in the art of war, continued her questionings.

'I don't know,' said Mrs Austell. 'These things are left to Miss Biddums, and, of course, she does not ill-treat the child.'

The Commissioner's wife left hastily. The last sentence jarred upon her nerves. 'Doesn't *ill-treat* the child! As if that were all! I wonder what Tom would say if I only "didn't ill-treat" Patsie!'

Thenceforward, His Majesty the King was an honoured guest at the Commissioner's house, and the chosen friend of Patsie, with whom he blundered into as many scrapes as the compound and the servants' quarters afforded. Patsie's Mamma was always ready to give counsel, help, and sympathy, and, if need were and callers few, to enter into their games with an *abandon* that would have shocked the sleek-haired subalterns who squirmed painfully in their chairs when they came to call on her whom they profanely nicknamed 'Mother Bunch.'

Yet, in spite of Patsie and Patsie's Mamma, and the love that these two lavished upon him, His Majesty the King fell grievously from grace, and committed no less a sin than that of theft – unknown, it is true, but burdensome.

There came a man to the door one day, when His Majesty was playing in the hall and the bearer had gone to dinner, with a packet for His Majesty's Mamma. And he put it upon the hall-table, and said that there was no answer, and departed.

Presently, the pattern of the dado ceased to interest His Majesty, while the packet, a white, neatly-wrapped one of fascinating shape, interested him very much indeed. His Mamma was out, so was Miss Biddums, and there was pink string round the packet. He greatly desired pink string. It would help him in many of his little businesses – the haulage across the floor of his small cane-chair, the torturing of Chimo, who could never understand harness – and so forth. If he took the string it would be his own, and nobody would be any the wiser. He certainly could not pluck up sufficient courage to ask Mamma for it. Wherefore, mounting upon a chair, he carefully untied the string and, behold, the stiff white paper spread out in four directions, and revealed a beautiful little leather box with gold lines upon it! He tried to replace the string, but that was a failure. So he opened the box to get full satisfaction for his iniquity, and saw a most beautiful Star that shone and winked, and was altogether lovely and desirable.

'Vat,' said His Majesty meditatively, 'is a 'parkle cwown, like what I will wear when I go to heaven. I will wear it on my head – Miss Biddums says so. I would like to wear it *now*.. I would like to play wiv it. I will take it away and play wiv it, very careful, until Mamma asks for it. I fink it was bought for me to play wiv – same as my cart.'

His Majesty the King was arguing against his conscience, and he knew it, for he thought immediately after: 'Never mind, I will keep it to play wiv until Mamma says where is it, and then I will say – 'I tookt it and I am sorry.' I will not hurt it because it is a 'parkle cwown. But Miss Biddums will tell me to put it back. I will not show it to Miss Biddums.'

If Mamma had come in at that moment all would have gone well. She did not, and His Majesty the King stuffed paper, case, and jewel into the breast of his blouse and marched to the nursery.

'When Mamma asks I will tell,' was the salve that he laid upon his conscience. But Mamma never asked, and for three whole days His Majesty the King gloated over his treasure. It was of no earthly use to him, but it was splendid, and, for aught he knew, something dropped from the heavens themselves. Still Mamma made no inquiries, and it seemed to him, in his furtive peeps, as though the shiny stones grew dim. What was the use of a 'parkle cwown if it made a little boy feel all bad in his inside? He had the pink string as well as the other treasure, but greatly he wished that he had not gone beyond the string. It was his first experience of iniquity, and it pained him after the flush of possession and secret delight in the ''parkle cwown' had died away.

Each day that he delayed rendered confession to the people beyond the nursery doors more impossible. Now and again he determined to put himself in the path of the beautifully-attired lady as she was going out, and explain that he and no one else was the possessor of a ''parkle cwown,' most beautiful and quite uninquired for. But she passed hurriedly to her carriage, and the opportunity was gone before His Majesty the King could draw the deep breath which clinches noble resolve. The dread secret cut him off from Miss Biddums, Patsie, and the Commissioner's wife, and – doubly hard fate – when he brooded over it Patsie said, and told her mother, that he was cross.

The days were very long to His Majesty the King, and the nights longer still. Miss Biddums had informed him, more than once, what was the ultimate destiny of 'fieves,' and when he passed the interminable mud flanks of the Central Jail, he shook in his little strapped shoes.

But release came after an afternoon spent in playing boats by the edge of the tank at the bottom of the garden. His Majesty the King went to tea, and, for the first time in his memory, the meal revolted him. His nose was very cold, and his cheeks were burning hot. There was a weight about his feet, and he pressed his head several times to make sure that it was not swelling as he sat.

'I feel vevy funny,' said His Majesty the King, rubbing his nose. 'Vere's a buzz-buzz in my head.'

He went to bed quietly. Miss Biddums was out and the bearer undressed him.

The sin of the ''parkle cwown' was forgotten in the acuteness of the discomfort to which he roused after a leaden sleep of some hours. He was thirsty, and the bearer had forgotten to leave the drinking-water. 'Miss Biddums! Miss Biddums! I'm so kirsty!'

No answer. Miss Biddums had leave to attend the wedding of a Calcutta school-mate. His Majesty the King had forgotten that.

'I want a dwink of water,' he cried, but his voice was dried up in his throat. 'I want a dwink! Vere is ve glass?'

He sat up in bed and looked round. There was a murmur of voices from the other side of the nursery door. It was better to face the terrible unknown than to choke in the dark. He slipped out of bed, but his feet were strangely wilful, and he reeled once or twice. Then he pushed the door open and staggered – a puffed and purple-faced little figure – into the brilliant light of the dining-room full of pretty ladies.

'I'm vevy hot! I'm vevy uncomfitivle,' moaned His Majesty the King, clinging to the portière, 'and vere's no water in ve glass, and I'm *so* kirsty. Give me a dwink of water.'

An apparition in black and white – His Majesty the King could hardly see distinctly – lifted him up to the level of the table, and felt his wrists and forehead. The water came, and he drank deeply, his teeth chattering against the edge of the tumbler. Then everyone seemed to go away – everyone except the huge man in black and white, who carried him back to his bed; the mother and father following. And the sin of the ''parkle cwown' rushed back and took possession of the terrified soul.

'I'm a fief!' he gasped. 'I want to tell Miss Biddums vat I'm a fief. Vere is Miss Biddums?'

Miss Biddums had come and was bending over him. 'I'm a fief,' he whispered. 'A fief – like ve men in ve pwison. But I'll tell now. I tookt – I tookt ve 'parkle cwown when ve man that came left it in ve hall. I bwoke ve paper and ve little bwown box, and it looked shiny, and I tookt it to play wif, and I was afwaid. It's in ve dooly-box at ve bottom. No one *never* asked for it, but I was afwaid. Oh, go an' get ve dooly-box!'

Miss Biddums obediently stooped to the lowest shelf of the *almirah* and unearthed the big paper box in which His Majesty the King kept his dearest possessions. Under the tin soldiers, and a layer of mud pellets for a pellet-bow, winked and blazed a diamond star, wrapped roughly in a half-sheet of notepaper whereon were a few words.

Somebody was crying at the head of the bed, and a man's hand touched the forehead of His Majesty the King, who grasped the packet and spread it on the bed.

'Vat is ve 'parkle cwown,' he said, and wept bitterly; for now that he had made restitution he would fain have kept the shining splendour with him.

'It concerns you too,' said a voice at the head of the bed. 'Read the note. This is not the time to keep back anything.'

The note was curt, very much to the point, and signed by a single initial. '*If you wear this tomorrow night I shall know what to expect.*' The date was three weeks old.

A whisper followed, and the deeper voice returned: 'And you drifted as far apart as *that!* I think it makes us quits now, doesn't it? Oh, can't we drop this folly once and for all? Is it worth it, darling?'

'Kiss me too,' said His Majesty the King dreamily. 'You isn't *vevy* angwy, is you?'

The fever burned itself out, and His Majesty the King slept.

When he waked, it was in a new world – peopled by his father and mother as well as Miss Biddums; and there was much love in that world and no morsel of fear, and more petting than was good for several little boys. His Majesty the King was too young to moralise on the uncertainty of things human, or he would have been impressed with the singular advantages of crime – ay, black sin. Behold, he had stolen the ''parkle cwown,' and his reward was Love, and the right to play in the waste-paper basket under the table 'for always.'

He trotted over to spend an afternoon with Patsie, and the Commissioner's wife would have kissed him. 'No, not vere,' said His Majesty the King, with superb insolence, fencing one corner of his mouth with his hand. 'Vat's my Mamma's place – vere *she* kisses me.'

'Oh!' said the Commissioner's wife briefly. Then to herself: 'Well, I suppose I ought to be glad for his sake. Children are selfish little grubs and – I've got my Patsie.'

THE DRUMS OF THE FORE AND AFT

In the Army List they still stand as 'The Fore and Fit Princess Hohenzollern-Sigmaringen-Auspach's Merthyr-Tydfilshire Own Royal Loyal Light Infantry, Regimental District 329A,' but the Army through all its barracks and canteens knows them now as the 'Fore and Aft.' They may in time do something that shall make their new title honourable, but at present they are bitterly ashamed, and the man who calls them 'Fore and Aft' does so at the risk of the head which is on his shoulders.

Two words breathed into the stables of a certain Cavalry Regiment will bring the men out into the streets with belts and mops and bad language; but a whisper of 'Fore and Aft' will bring out this regiment with rifles.

Their one excuse is that they came again and did their best to finish the job in style. But for a time all their world knows that they were openly beaten, whipped, dumb-cowed, shaking, and afraid. The men know it; their officers know it; the Horse Guards know it, and when the next war comes the enemy will know it also. There are two or three regiments of the Line that have a black mark against their names which they will then wipe out; and it will be excessively inconvenient for the troops upon whom they do their wiping.

The courage of the British soldier is officially supposed to be above proof, and, as a general rule, it is so. The exceptions are decently shovelled out of sight, only to be referred to in the freshest of unguarded talk that occasionally swamps a Mess-table at midnight. Then one hears strange and horrible stories of men not following their officers, of orders being given by those who had no right to give them, and of disgrace that, but for the standing luck of the British Army, might have ended in brilliant disaster. These are unpleasant stories to listen to, and the Messes tell them under their breath, sitting by the big wood fires, and the young officer bows his head and thinks to himself, please God, his men shall never behave unhandily.

The British soldier is not altogether to be blamed for occasional lapses; but this verdict he should not know. A moderately intelligent General will waste six months in mastering the craft of the particular war that he may be waging; a Colonel may utterly misunderstand the capacity of his regiment for three months after it has taken the field; and even a Company Commander may err and be deceived as to the temper and temperament of his own handful: wherefore the soldier, and the soldier of today more particularly, should not be blamed for falling back. He should be shot or hanged afterwards – to encourage the others; but he should not be vilified in newspapers, for that is want of tact and waste of space.

He has, let us say, been in the service of the Empress for, perhaps, four years. He will leave in another two years. He has no inherited morals, and four years are not sufficient to drive toughness into his fibre, or to teach him how holy a thing is his Regiment. He wants to drink, he wants to enjoy himself – in India he wants to save money – and he does not in the least like getting hurt. He has received just sufficient education to make him understand half the purport of the orders he receives, and to speculate on the nature of clean, incised, and shattering wounds. Thus, if he is told to deploy under fire preparatory to an attack, he knows that he runs a very great risk of being killed while he is deploying, and suspects that he is being thrown away to gain ten minutes' time. He may either deploy with desperate swiftness, or he may shuffle, or bunch, or break, according to the discipline under which he has lain for four years.

Armed with imperfect knowledge, cursed with the rudiments of an imagination, hampered by the intense selfishness of the lower classes, and unsupported by any regimental associations, this young man is suddenly introduced to an enemy who in eastern lands is always ugly, generally tall and hairy, and frequently noisy. If he looks to the right and the left and sees old soldiers – men of twelve years' service, who, he knows, know what they are about – taking a charge, rush, or demonstration without embarrassment, he is consoled and applies his shoulder to the butt of his rifle with a stout heart. His peace is the greater if he hears a senior, who has taught him his soldiering and broken his head on occasion, whispering: 'They'll shout and carry on like this for five minutes. Then they'll rush in, and then we've got 'em by the short hairs!'

But, on the other hand, if he sees only men of his own term of service turning white and playing with their triggers, and saying: 'What the Hell's up now?' while the Company Commanders are sweating into their sword-hilts and shouting: 'Front-rank, fix bayonets. Steady there – steady! Sight for three hundred – no, for five! Lie down, all! Steady! Front-rank kneel!' and so forth, he becomes unhappy; and grows acutely miserable when he hears a comrade turn over with the rattle of fire-irons falling into the fender, and the grunt of a pole-axed ox. If he can be moved about a little and allowed to watch the effect of his own fire on the enemy he feels merrier, and may be then worked up to the blind passion of fighting, which is, contrary to general belief, controlled by a chilly Devil and shakes men like ague. If he is not moved about, and begins to feel cold at the pit of the stomach, and in that crisis is badly mauled, and hear orders that were never given, he will break, and he will break badly; and of all things under the light of the Sun there is nothing more terrible than a broken British regiment. When the worst comes to the worst and the panic is really epidemic, the men must be e'en let go, and the Company Commanders had better escape to the enemy and stay there for safety's sake. If they can be made to come again they are not pleasant men to meet; because they will not break twice.

About thirty years from this date, when we have succeeded in half-educating everything that wears trousers, our Army will be a beautifully unreliable machine. It will know too much and it will do too little. Later still, when all men are at the mental level of the officer of today it will sweep the earth. Speaking roughly, you must employ either blackguards or gentlemen, or, best of all, blackguards commanded by gentlemen, to do butcher's work with efficiency and despatch. The ideal soldier should, of course, think for himself – the *Pocket-book* says so. Unfortunately, to attain this virtue he has to pass through the phase of thinking of himself, and that is misdirected

432

genius. A blackguard may be slow to think for himself, but he is genuinely anxious to kill, and a little punishment teaches him how to guard his own skin and perforate another's. A powerfully prayerful Highland Regiment, officered by rank Presbyterians, is, perhaps, one degree more terrible in action than a hard-bitten thousand of irresponsible Irish ruffians led by most improper young unbelievers. But these things prove the rule – which is that the midway men are not to be trusted alone. They have ideas about the value of life and an upbringing that has not taught them to go on and take the chances. They are carefully unprovided with a backing of comrades who have been shot over, and until that backing is re-introduced, as a great many Regimental Commanders intend it shall be, they are more liable to disgrace themselves than the size of the Empire or the dignity of the Army allows. Their officers are as good as good can be, because their training begins early, and God has arranged that a clean-run youth of the British middle classes shall, in the matter of backbone, brains, and bowels, surpass all other youths. For this reason a child of eighteen will stand up, doing nothing, with a tin sword in his hand and joy in his heart until he is dropped. If he dies, he dies like a gentleman. If he lives, he writes Home that he has been 'potted,' 'sniped,' 'chipped,' or 'cut over,' and sits down to besiege Government for a wound-gratuity until the next little war breaks out, when he perjures himself before a Medical Board, blarneys his Colonel, burns incense round his Adjutant, and is allowed to go to the Front once more.

Which homily brings me directly to a brace of the most finished little fiends that ever banged drum or tootled fife in the Band of a British Regiment. They ended their sinful career by open and flagrant mutiny and were shot for it. Their names were Jakin and Lew – Piggy Lew – and they were bold, bad drummer-boys, both of them frequently birched by the Drum-Major of the Fore and Aft.

Jakin was a stunted child of fourteen, and Lew was about the same age. When not looked after, they smoked and drank. They swore habitually after the manner of the Barrack-room, which is cold-swearing and comes from between clinched teeth; and they fought religiously once a week. Jakin had sprung from some London gutter and may or may not have passed through Dr Barnardo's hands ere he arrived at the dignity of drummer-boy. Lew could remember nothing except the regiment and the delight of listening to the Band from his earliest years. He hid somewhere in his grimy little soul a genuine love for music, and was most mistakenly furnished with the head of a cherub: insomuch that beautiful ladies who watched the Regiment in church were wont to speak of him as a 'darling.' They never heard his vitriolic comments on their manners and morals, as he walked back to barracks with the Band and matured fresh causes of offence against Jakin.

The other drummer-boys hated both lads on account of their illogical conduct. Jakin might be pounding Lew, or Lew might be rubbing Jakin's head in the dirt, but any attempt at aggression on the part of an outsider was met by the combined forces of Lew and Jakin; and the consequences were painful. The boys were the Ishmaels of the corps, but wealthy Ishmaels, for they sold battles in alternate weeks for the sport of the barracks when they were not pitted against other boys; and thus amassed money.

On this particular day there was dissension in the camp. They had just been convicted afresh of smoking, which is bad for little boys who use plug-tobacco, and Lew's contention was that Jakin had 'stunk so 'orrid bad from keepin' the pipe in pocket,' that he and he alone was responsible for the birching they were both tingling under.

'I tell you I 'id the pipe back o' barracks,' said Jakin pacifically.

'You're a bloomin' liar,' said Lew without heat.

'You're a bloomin little barstard,' said Jakin, strong in the knowledge that his own ancestry was unknown.

Now there is one word in the extended vocabulary of barrack-room abuse that cannot pass without comment. You may call a man a thief and risk nothing. You may even call him a coward without finding more than a boot whiz past your ear, but you must not call a man a bastard unless you are prepared to prove it on his front teeth.

'You might ha' kep' that till I wasn't so sore,' said Lew sorrowfully, dodging round Jakin's guard.

'I'll make you sorer,' said Jakin genially, and got home on Lew's alabaster forehead. All would have gone well and this story, as the books say, would never have been written, had not his evil fate prompted the Bazar-Sergeant's son, a long, employless man of five-and-twenty, to put in an appearance after the first round. He was eternally in need of money, and knew that the boys had silver.

'Fighting again,' said he. 'I'll report you to my father, and he'll report you to the Colour-Sergeant.'

'What's that to you?' said Jakin with an unpleasant dilation of the nostrils.

'Oh! nothing to *me*. You'll get into trouble, and you've been up too often to afford that.'

'What the Hell do you know about what we've done?' asked Lew the Seraph. '*You* aren't in the Army, you lousy, cadging civilian.'

He closed in on the man's left flank.

'Jes' 'cause you find two gentlemen settlin' their diff'rences with their fistes you stick in your ugly nose where you aren't wanted. Run 'ome to your 'arf-caste slut of a Ma – or we'll give you what-for,' said Jakin.

The man attempted reprisals by knocking the boys' heads together. The scheme would have succeeded had not Jakin punched him vehemently in the stomach, or had Lew refrained from kicking his shins. They fought together, bleeding and breathless, for half an hour, and, after heavy punishment, triumphantly pulled down their opponent as terriers pull down a jackal.

'Now,' gasped Jakin, 'I'll give you what-for.' He proceeded to pound the man's features while Lew stamped on the outlying portions of his anatomy. Chivalry is not a strong point in the composition of the average drummer-boy. He fights, as do his betters, to make his mark.

Ghastly was the ruin that escaped, and awful was the wrath of the Bazar-Sergeant. Awful, too, was the scene in Orderly-room when the two reprobates appeared to answer the charge of half-murdering a 'civilian.' The Bazar-Sergeant thirsted for a criminal action, and his son lied. The boys stood to attention while the black clouds of evidence accumulated.

'You little devils are more trouble than the rest of the Regiment put together,' said the Colonel angrily. 'One might as well admonish thistledown, and I can't well put you in cells or under stoppages. You must be birched again.'

'Beg y' pardon, Sir. Can't we say nothin' in our own defence, Sir?' shrilled Jakin.

'Hey! What? Are you going to argue with *me*?' said the Colonel.

'No, Sir,' said Lew. 'But if a man come to you, Sir, and said he was going to report you, Sir, for 'aving a bit of a turn-up with a friend, Sir, an' wanted to get money out o' *you*, Sir –'

The Orderly-room exploded in a roar of laughter. 'Well?' said the Colonel.

'That was what that measly *jarnwar* there did, Sir, and 'e'd 'a' *done* it, Sir, if we 'adn't prevented 'im. We didn't 'it 'im much, Sir. 'E 'adn't no manner o' right to interfere with us, Sir. I don't mind bein' birched by the Drum-Major, Sir, nor yet reported by *any* Corp'ral, but I'm – but I don't think it's fair, Sir, for a civilian to come an' talk over a man in the Army.'

A second shout of laughter shook the Orderly-room, but the Colonel was grave.

'What sort of characters have these boys?' he asked of the Regimental Sergeant-Major.

'Accordin' to the Bandmaster, Sir,' returned that revered official – the only soul in the regiment whom the boys feared – 'they do everything *but* lie, Sir.'

'Is it like we'd go for that man for fun, Sir?' said Lew, pointing to the plaintiff.

'Oh, admonished – admonished!' said the Colonel testily, and when the boys had gone he read the Bazar-Sergeant's son a lecture on the sin of unprofitable meddling, and gave orders that the Bandmaster should keep the Drums in better discipline.

'If either of you comes to practice again with so much as a scratch on your two ugly little faces,' thundered the Bandmaster, 'I'll tell the Drum-Major to take the skin off your backs. Understand that, you young devils.'

Then he repented of his speech for just the length of time that Lew, looking like a Seraph in red worsted embellishments, took the place of one of the trumpets – in hospital – and rendered the echo of a battle-piece. Lew certainly was a musician, and had often in his more exalted moments expressed a yearning to master every instrument of the Band.

'There's nothing to prevent your becoming a Bandmaster, Lew,' said the Bandmaster, who had composed waltzes of his own, and worked day and night in the interests of the Band.

'What did he say?' demanded Jakin after practice.

''Said I might be a bloomin' Bandmaster, an' be asked in to 'ave a glass o' sherry-wine on Mess-nights.'

'Ho!' Said you might be a bloomin' noncombatant, did 'e! That's just about wot 'e would say. When I've put in my boy's service – it's a bloomin' shame that doesn't count for pension – I'll take on as a privit. Then I'll be a Lance in a year – knowin' what I know about the ins an' outs o' things. In three years I'll be a bloomin' Sergeant. I won't marry then, not I! I'll 'old on and learn the orf'cers' ways an' apply for exchange into a reg'ment that doesn't know all about me. Then I'll be a bloomin' orf'cer. Then I'll ask you to 'ave a glass o' sherry-wine, *Mister* Lew, an' you'll bloomin' well 'ave to stay in the hanty-room while the Mess-Sergeant brings it to your dirty 'ands.'

''S'pose I'm going to be a Bandmaster? Not I, quite. I'll be a orf'cer too. There's nothin' like taking to a thing an' stickin' to it, the Schoolmaster says. The reg'ment don't go 'ome for another seven years. I'll be a Lance then or near to.'

Thus the boys discussed their futures, and conducted themselves piously for a week. That is to say, Lew started a flirtation with the Colour-Sergeant's daughter, aged thirteen – 'not,' as he explained to Jakin, 'with any intention o' matrimony, but by way o' keepin' my 'and in.' And the black-haired Cris Delighan enjoyed that flirtation more than previous ones, and the other drummer-boys raged furiously together, and Jakin preached sermons on the dangers of 'bein' tangled along o' petticoats.'

But neither love nor virtue would have held Lew long in the paths of propriety had not the rumour gone abroad that the Regiment was to be sent on active service, to take part in a war which, for the sake of brevity, we will call 'The War of the Lost Tribes.'

The barracks had the rumour almost before the Mess-room, and of all the nine hundred men in barracks not ten had seen a shot fired in anger. The Colonel had, twenty years ago, assisted at a Frontier expedition; one of the Majors had seen service at the Cape; a confirmed deserter in E Company had helped to clear streets in Ireland; but that was all. The Regiment had been put by for many years. The overwhelming mass of its rank and file had from three to four years' service; the non-commissioned officers were under thirty years old; and men and sergeants alike had forgotten to speak of the stories written in brief upon the Colours – the New Colours that had been formally blessed by an Archbishop in England ere the Regiment came away.

They wanted to go to the Front – they were enthusiastically anxious to go – but they had no knowledge of what war meant, and there was none to tell them. They were an educated regiment, the percentage of school-certificates in their ranks was high, and most of the men could do more than read and write. They had been recruited in loyal observance of the territorial idea; but they themselves had no notion of that idea. They were made up of drafts from an over-populated manufacturing district. The system had put flesh and muscle upon their small bones, but it could not put heart into the sons of those who for generations had done overmuch work for over-scanty pay, had sweated in drying-rooms, stooped over looms, coughed among white-lead, and shivered on lime-barges. The men had found food and rest in the Army, and now they were going to fight 'natives' – people who ran away if you shook a stick at them. Wherefore they cheered lustily when the rumour ran, and the shrewd, clerkly non-commissioned officers speculated on the chances of batta and of saving their pay. At Headquarters men said: 'The Fore and Fit have never been under fire within the last generation. Let us, therefore, break them in easily by setting them to guard lines of communication.' And this would have been done but for the fact that British Regiments were wanted – badly wanted – at the Front, and there were doubtful Native Regiments that could fill the minor duties. 'Brigade 'em with two strong Regiments,' said Headquarters. 'They may be knocked about a bit, but they'll learn their business before they come through. Nothing like a night-alarm and a little cutting-up of stragglers to make a Regiment smart in the field. Wait till they've had half-a-dozen sentries' throats cut.'

The Colonel wrote with delight that the temper of his men was excellent, that the Regiment was all that could be wished, and as sound as a bell. The Majors smiled with a sober joy, and the subalterns waltzed in pairs down the Mess-room after dinner, and nearly shot themselves at revolver-practice. But there was consternation in the hearts of Jakin and Lew. What was to be done with the Drums? Would the Band go to the Front? How many of the Drums would accompany the Regiment?

They took counsel together, sitting in a tree and smoking.

'It's more than a bloomin' toss-up they'll leave us be'ind at the Depot with the women. You'll like that,' said Jakin sarcastically.

''Cause o' Cris, y' mean? Wot's a woman, or a 'ole bloomin' depot o' women, 'long-side o' the chanst of field-service? You know I'm as keen on goin' as you,' said Lew.

''Wish I was a bloomin' bugler,' said Jakin sadly. 'They'll take Tom Kidd along, that I can plaster a wall with, an' like as not they won't take us.'

'Then let's go an' make Tom Kidd so bloomin' sick' 'e can't bugle no more. You 'old 'is 'ands an' I'll kick him,' said Lew, wriggling on the branch.

'That ain't no good neither. We ain't the sort o' characters to presoom on our rep'tations – they're bad. If they leave the Band at the Depot we don't go, and no error *there*. If they take the Band we may get cast for medical unfitness. Are you medical fit, Piggy?' said Jakin, digging Lew in the ribs with force.

'Yus,' said Lew with an oath. 'The Doctor says your 'eart's weak through smokin' on an empty stummick. Throw a chest an' I'll try yer.'

Jakin threw out his chest, which Lew smote with all his might. Jakin turned very pale, gasped, crowed, screwed up his eyes, and said – 'That's all right.'

'You'll do,' said Lew. 'I've 'eard o' men dying when you 'it 'em fair on the breastbone.'

'Don't bring us no nearer goin', though,' said Jakin. 'Do you know where we're ordered?'

'Gawd knows, an' 'E won't split on a pal. Somewheres up to the Front to kill Paythans – hairy big beggars that turn you inside out if they get 'old o' you. They say their women are good-looking, too.'

'Any loot?' asked the abandoned Jakin.

'Not a bloomin' anna, they say, unless you dig up the ground an' see what the natives 'ave 'id. They're a poor lot.' Jakin stood upright on the branch and gazed across the plain.

'Lew,' said he, 'there's the Colonel coming. Colonel's a good old beggar. Let's go an' talk to 'im.

Lew nearly fell out of the tree at the audacity of the suggestion. Like Jakin he feared not God, neither regarded he Man, but there are limits even to the audacity of drummer-boy, and to speak to a Colonel was –

439

But Jakin had slid down the trunk and doubled in the direction of the Colonel. That officer was walking wrapped in thought and visions of a C.B. – yes, even a K.C.B., for had he not at command one of the best Regiments of the Line – the Fore and Fit? And he was aware of two small boys charging down upon him. Once before it had been solemnly reported to him that 'the Drums were in a state of mutiny,' Jakin and Lew being the ringleaders. This looked like an organised conspiracy.

The boys halted at twenty yards, walked to the regulation four paces, and saluted together, each as well-set-up as a ramrod and little taller.

The Colonel was in a genial mood; the boys appeared very forlorn and unprotected on the desolate plain, and one of them was handsome.

'Well!' said the Colonel, recognising them. 'Are you going to pull me down in the open? I'm sure I never interfere with you, even though' – he sniffed suspiciously – 'you have been smoking.'

It was time to strike while the iron was hot. Their hearts beat tumultuously.

'Beg y' pardon, Sir,' began Jakin. 'The Reg'ment's ordered on active service, Sir?'

'So I believe,' said the Colonel courteously.

'Is the Band goin,' Sir?' said both together. Then, without pause, 'We're goin,' Sir, ain't we?'

'You!' said the Colonel, stepping back the more fully to take in the two small figures. 'You! You'd die in the first march.'

'No, we wouldn't, Sir. We can march with the Reg'ment anywheres – p'rade an' anywhere else,' said Jakin.

'If Tom Kidd goes 'e'll shut up like a clasp-knife,' said Lew. 'Tom 'as very-close veins in both 'is legs, Sir.'

'Very how much?'

'Very-close veins, Sir. That's why they swells after long p'rade, Sir. If 'e can go, we can go, Sir.'

Again the Colonel looked at them long and intently.

'Yes, the Band is going,' he said as gravely as though he had been addressing a brother officer. 'Have you any parents, either of you two?'

'No, Sir,' rejoicingly from Lew and Jakin. 'We're both orphans, Sir. There's no one to be considered of on our account, Sir.'

'You poor little sprats, and you want to go up to the Front with the Regiment, do you? Why?'

'I've wore the Queen's Uniform for two years,' said Jakin. 'It's very 'ard, Sir, that a man don't get no recompense for doin' of 'is dooty, Sir.'

'An' – an' if I don't go, Sir,' interrupted Lew, 'the Bandmaster 'e says 'e'll catch an' make a bloo – a blessed musician o' me, Sir. Before I've seen any service, Sir.'

The Colonel made no answer for a long time. Then he said quietly: 'If you're passed by the Doctor I daresay you can go. I shouldn't smoke if I were you.'

The boys saluted and disappeared. The Colonel walked home and told the story to his wife, who nearly cried over it. The Colonel was well pleased. If that was the temper of the children, what would not the men do?

Jakin and Lew entered the boys' barrack-room with great stateliness, and refused to hold any conversation with their comrades for at least ten minutes. Then, bursting with pride, Jakin drawled: 'I've bin intervooin' the Colonel. Good old beggar is the Colonel. Says I to 'im, "Colonel," says I, "let me go to the Front, along o' the Reg'ment." – "To the Front you shall go," says 'e, "an' I only wish there was more like you among the dirty little devils that bang the bloomin' drums." Kidd, if you throw your 'courtrements at me for tellin' you the truth to your own advantage, your legs'll swell.'

None the less there was a Battle-Royal in the barrack-room, for the boys were consumed with envy and hate, and neither Jakin nor Lew behaved in conciliatory wise.

'I'm goin' out to say adoo to my girl,' said Lew, to cap the climax. 'Don't none o' you touch my kit because it's wanted for active service; me bein' specially invited to go by the Colonel.'

He strolled forth and whistled in the clump of trees at the back of the Married Quarters till Cris came to him, and, the preliminary kisses being given and taken, Lew began to explain the situation.

'I'm goin' to the Front with the Reg'ment,' he said valiantly.

'Piggy, you're a little liar,' said Cris, but her heart misgave her, for Lew was not in the habit of lying.

'Liar yourself, Cris,' said Lew, slipping an arm round her. 'I'm goin'. When the Reg'ment marches out you'll see me with 'em, all galliant and gay. Give us another kiss, Cris, on the strength of it.'

'If you'd on'y a-stayed at the Depot – where you *ought* to ha' bin – you could get as many of 'em as – as you dam please,' whimpered Cris, putting up her mouth.

'It's 'ard, Cris. I grant you it's 'ard. But what's a man to do? If I'd a-stayed at the Depot, you wouldn't think anything of me.'

'Like as not, but I'd 'ave you with me, Piggy. An' all the thinkin' in the world isn't like kissin'.'

'An' all the kissin' in the world isn't like 'avin' a medal to wear on the front o' your coat.'

'*You* won't get no medal.'

'Oh yus, I shall though. Me an' Jakin are the only acting-drummers that'll be took along. All the rest is full men, an' we'll get our medals with them.'

'They might ha' taken anybody but you, Piggy. You'll get killed – you're so venture-some. Stay with me, Piggy darlin', down at the Depot, an' I'll love you true, for ever.'

'Ain't you goin' to do that *now*, Cris? You said you was.'

'O' course I am, but th' other's more comfortable. Wait till you've growed a bit, Piggy. You aren't no taller than me now.'

'I've bin in the Army for two years an' I'm not goin' to get out of a chanst o' seein' service, an' don't you try to make me do so. I'll come back, Cris, an' when I take on as a man I'll marry you – marry you when I'm a Lance.'

'Promise, Piggy?'

Lew reflected on the future as arranged by Jakin a short time previously, but Cris's mouth was very near to his own.

'I promise, s'elp me Gawd!' said he.

Cris slid an arm round his neck.

'I won't 'old you back no more, Piggy. Go away an' get your medal, an' I'll make you a new button-bag as nice as I know how,' she whispered.

'Put some o' your 'air into it, Cris, an' I'll keep it in my pocket so long's I'm alive.'

Then Cris wept anew, and the interview ended. Public feeling among the drummer-boys rose to fever pitch and the lives of Jakin and Lew became unenviable. Not only had they been permitted to enlist two years before the regulation boy's age – fourteen – but, by virtue, it seemed, of their extreme youth, they were allowed to go to the Front – which thing had not happened to acting-drummers within the knowledge of boy. The Band which was to accompany the Regiment had been cut down to the regulation twenty men, the surplus returning to the ranks. Jakin and Lew were attached to the Band as supernumeraries, though they would much have preferred being Company buglers.

''Don't matter much,' said Jakin, after the medical inspection. 'Be thankful that we're 'lowed to go at all. The Doctor 'e said that if we could stand what we took from the Bazar-Sergeant's son we'd stand pretty nigh anything.'

'Which we will,' said Lew, looking tenderly at the ragged and ill-made housewife that Cris had given him, with a lock of her hair worked into a sprawling 'L' upon the cover.

'It was the best I could,' she sobbed. 'I wouldn't let mother nor the Sergeants' tailor 'elp me. Keep it always, Piggy, an' remember I love you true.'

They marched to the railway station, nine hundred and sixty strong, and every soul in cantonments turned out to see them go. The drummers gnashed their teeth at Jakin and Lew marching with the Band, the married women wept upon the platform, and the Regiment cheered its noble self black in the face.

'A nice level lot,' said the Colonel to the Second-in-Command as they watched the first four companies entraining.

'Fit to do anything,' said the Second-in-Command enthusiastically. 'But it seems to me they're a thought too young and tender for the work in hand. It's bitter cold up at the Front now.'

'They're sound enough,' said the Colonel. 'We must take our chance of sick casualties.'

So they went northward, ever northward, past droves and droves of camels, armies of camp followers, and legions of laden mules, the throng thickening day by day, till with a shriek the train pulled up at a hopelessly-congested junction where six lines of temporary track accommodated six forty-waggon trains; where whistles blew, Babus sweated, and Commissariat officers swore from dawn till far into the night amid the wind-driven chaff of the fodder-bales and the lowing of a thousand steers.

'Hurry up – you're badly wanted at the Front,' was the message that greeted the Fore and Aft, and the occupants of the Red Cross carriages told the same tale.

''Tisn't so much the bloomin' fightin',' gasped a headbound trooper of Hussars to a knot of admiring Fore and Afts. ''Tisn't so much the bloomin' fightin', though there's enough o' that. It's the bloomin' food an' the bloomin' climate. Frost all night 'cept when it hails, and biling sun all day, and the water stinks fit to knock you down. I got my 'ead chipped like a egg; I've got pneumonia too, an' my guts is all out o' order. 'Tain't no bloomin' picnic in those parts, I can tell you.'

'Wot are the enemy like?' demanded a private.

'There's some prisoners in that train yonder. Go an' look at 'em. They're the aristoc-racy o' the country. The common folk are a dashed sight uglier. If you want to know what they fight with, reach under my seat an' pull out the long knife that's there.'

They dragged out and beheld for the first time the grim, bone-handled, triangular Afghan knife. It was almost as long as Lew.

'That's the thing to jint ye,' said the trooper feebly. 'It can take off a man's arm at the shoulder as easy as slicing butter. I halved the beggar that used that 'un, but there's more of his likes up above. They don't understand thrustin', but they're devils to slice.'

The men strolled across the tracks to inspect the Afghan prisoners. They were unlike any 'natives' that the Fore and Aft had ever met – these huge, black-haired, scowling sons of the Beni-Israel. As the men stared the Afghans spat freely and muttered one to another with lowered eyes.

'My eyes! Wot awful swine!' said Jakin, who was in the rear of the procession. 'Say, old man, how you got *puckrowed*, eh? *Kiswasti* you wasn't hanged for your ugly face, hey?'

The tallest of the company turned, his leg-irons clanking at the movement, and stared at the boy. 'See!' he cried to his fellows in Pushto. 'They send children against us. What a people, and what fools!'

'*Hya*!' said Jakin, nodding his head cheerily. 'You go down-country. *Khana* get, *peenikapanee* get – live like a bloomin' Raja *ke marfik*. That's a better *bandobust* than baynit get it in your innards. Good-bye, ole man. Take care o' your beautiful figure-'ed, an' try to look *kushy*.'

The men laughed and fell in for their first march, when they began to realise that a soldier's life was not all beer and skittles. They were much impressed with the size and bestial ferocity of the natives whom they had now learned to call 'Paythans,' and more with the exceeding discomfort of their own surroundings. Twenty old soldiers in the corps would have taught them how to make themselves moderately snug at night, but they had no old soldiers, and, as the troops on the line of march said, 'they lived like pigs.' They learned the heart-breaking cussedness of camp-kitchens and camels and the depravity of an E. P. tent and a wither-wrung mulc. They studied animalculæ in water, and developed a few cases of dysentery in their study.

At the end of their third march they were disagreeably surprised by the arrival in their camp of a hammered iron slug which, fired from a steady rest at seven hundred yards, flicked out the brains of a private seated by the fire. This robbed them of their peace for a night, and was the beginning of a long-range fire carefully calculated to that end. In the daytime they saw nothing except an unpleasant puff of smoke from a crag above the line of march. At night there were distant spurts of flame and occasional casualties, which set the whole camp blazing into the gloom and, occasionally, into opposite tents. Then they swore vehemently, and vowed that this was magnificent but not war.

Indeed it was not. The Regiment could not halt for reprisals against the sharp-shooters of the countryside. Its duty was to go forward and make connection with the Scotch and Gurkha troops with which it was brigaded. The Afghans knew this, and knew too, after their first tentative shots, that they were dealing with a raw regiment. Thereafter they devoted themselves to the task of keeping the Fore and Aft on the strain. Not for anything would they have taken equal liberties with a seasoned corps – with the wicked little Gurkhas, whose delight it was to lie out in the open on a dark night and stalk their stalkers – with the terrible, big men dressed in women's clothes, who could be heard praying to their God in the night-watches, and whose peace of mind no amount of 'sniping' could shake – or with those vile Sikhs, who marched so ostentatiously unprepared, and who dealt out such grim reward to those who tried to profit by that unpreparedness. This white regiment was different – quite different. It slept like a hog, and, like a hog, charged in every direction when it was roused. Its sentries walked with a footfall that could be heard for a quarter of a mile; would fire at anything that moved – even a driven donkey – and when they had once fired, could be scientifically 'rushed' and laid out a horror and an offence against the morning sun. Then there were camp-followers who straggled and could be cut up without fear. Their shrieks would disturb the white boys, and the loss of their services would inconvenience them sorely.

Thus, at every march, the hidden enemy became bolder and the regiment writhed and twisted under attacks it could not avenge. The crowning triumph was a sudden night-rush ending in the cutting of many tent-ropes, the collapse of the sodden canvas, and a glorious knifing of the men who struggled and kicked below. It was a great deed, neatly carried out, and it shook the already shaken nerves of the Fore and Aft. All the courage that they had been required to exercise up to this point was the 'two o'clock in the morning courage;' and, so far, they had only succeeded in shooting their comrades and losing their sleep.

Sullen, discontented, cold, savage, sick, with their uniforms dulled and unclean, the Fore and Aft joined their Brigade.

'I hear you had a tough time of it coming up,' said the Brigadier. But when he saw the hospital-sheets his face fell.

'This is bad,' said he to himself. 'They're as rotten as sheep.' And aloud to the Colonel – 'I'm afraid we can't spare you just yet. We want all we have, else I should have given you ten days to recover in.'

The Colonel winced. 'On my honour, Sir,' he returned, 'there is not the least necessity to think of sparing us. My men have been rather mauled and upset without a fair return. They only want to go in somewhere where they can see what's before them.'

'Can't say I think much of the Fore and Fit,' said the Brigadier in confidence to his Brigade-Major. 'They've lost all their soldiering, and, by the trim of them, might have marched through the country from the other side. A more fagged-out set of men I never put eyes on.'

'Oh, they'll improve as the work goes on. The parade gloss has been rubbed off a little, but they'll put on field polish before long,' said the Brigade-Major. 'They've been mauled, and they quite don't understand it.'

They did not. All the hitting was on one side, and it was cruelly hard hitting with accessories that made them sick. There was also the real sickness that laid hold of a strong man and dragged him howling to the grave. Worst of all, their officers knew just as little of the country as the men themselves, and looked as if they did. The Fore and Aft were in a thoroughly unsatisfactory condition, but they believed that all would be well if they could once get a fair go-in at the enemy. Pot-shots up and down the valleys were unsatisfactory, and the bayonet never seemed to get a chance. Perhaps it was as well, for a long-limbed Afghan with a knife had a reach of eight feet, and could carry away lead that would disable three Englishmen.

The Fore and Fit would like some rifle-practice at the enemy – all seven hundred rifles blazing together. That wish showed the mood of the men.

The Gurkhas walked into their camp, and in broken, barrack-room English strove to fraternise with them; offered them pipes of tobacco and stood them treat at the canteen. But the Fore and Aft, not knowing much of the nature of the Gurkhas, treated them as they would treat any other 'foreigners,' and the little men in green trotted back to their firm friends the Highlanders, and with many grins confided to them: 'That dam white regiment no dam use. Sulky – ugh! Dirty – ugh! Hya, any tot for Johnny?' Whereat the Highlanders smote the Gurkhas as to the head, and told them not to vilify a British Regiment, and the Gurkhas grinned cavernously, for the Highlanders were their elder brothers and entitled to the privileges of kinship. The common soldier who touches a Gurkha is more than likely to have his head sliced open.

Three days later the Brigadier arranged a battle according to the rules of war and the peculiarity of the Afghan temperament. The enemy were massing in inconvenient strength among the hills, and the moving of many green standards warned him that the tribes were 'up' in aid of the Afghan regular troops. A squadron and a half of Bengal Lancers represented the available Cavalry, and two screw-guns borrowed from a column thirty miles away, the Artillery at the General's disposal.

'If they stand, as I've a very strong notion that they will, I fancy we shall see an infantry fight that will be worth watching,' said the Brigadier. 'We'll do it in style. Each regiment shall be played into action by its Band, and we'll hold the Cavalry in reserve.'

'For *all* the reserve?' somebody asked.

'For all the reserve; because we're going to crumple them up,' said the Brigadier, who was an extraordinary Brigadier, and did not believe in the value of a reserve when dealing with Asiatics. Indeed, when you come to think of it, had the British Army consistently waited for reserves in all its little affairs, the boundaries of Our Empire would have stopped at Brighton beach.

That battle was to be a glorious battle.

The three regiments debouching from three separate gorges, after duly crowning the heights above, were to converge from the centre, left, and right upon what we will call the Afghan army, then stationed towards the lower extremity of a flat-bottomed valley. Thus it will be seen that three sides of the valley practically belonged to the English, while the fourth was strictly Afghan property. In the event of defeat the Afghans had the rocky hills to fly to, where the fire from the guerilla tribes in aid would cover their retreat. In the event of victory these same tribes would rush down and lend their weight to the rout of the British.

The screw-guns were to shell the head of each Afghan rush that was made in close formation, and the Cavalry, held in reserve in the right valley, were to gently stimulate the break-up which would follow on the combined attack. The Brigadier, sitting upon a rock overlooking the valley, would watch the battle unrolled at his feet. The Fore and Aft would debouch from the central gorge, the Gurkhas from the left, and the Highlanders from the right, for the reason that the left flank of the enemy seemed as though it required the most hammering. It was not every day that an Afghan force would take ground in the open, and the Brigadier was resolved to make the most of it.

'If we only had a few more men,' he said plaintively, 'we could surround the creatures and crumple 'em up thoroughly. As it is, I'm afraid we can only cut them up as they run. It's a great pity.'

The Fore and Aft had enjoyed unbroken peace for five days, and were beginning, in spite of dysentery, to recover their nerve. But they were not happy, for they did not know the work in hand, and had they known, would not have known how to do it. Throughout those five days in which old soldiers might have taught them the craft of the game, they discussed together their misadventures in the past – how such an one was alive at dawn and dead ere the dusk, and with what shrieks and struggles such another had given up his soul under the Afghan knife. Death was a new and horrible thing to the sons of mechanics who were used to die decently of zymotic disease; and their careful conservation in barracks had done nothing to make them look upon it with less dread.

Very early in the dawn the bugles began to blow, and the Fore and Aft, filled with a misguided enthusiasm, turned out without waiting for a cup of coffee and a biscuit; and were rewarded by being kept under arms in the cold while the other regiments leisurely prepared for the fray. All the world knows that it is ill taking the breeks off a Highlander. It is much iller to try to make him stir unless he is convinced of the necessity for haste.

The Fore and Aft waited, leaning upon their rifles and listening to the protests of their empty stomachs. The Colonel did his best to remedy the default of lining as soon as it was borne in upon him that the affair would not begin at once, and so well did he succeed that the coffee was just ready when – the men moved off, their Band leading. Even then there had been a mistake in time, and the Fore and Aft came out into the valley ten minutes before the proper hour. Their Band wheeled to the right after reaching the open, and retired behind a little rocky knoll still playing while the regiment went past.

It was not a pleasant sight that opened on the uninstructed view, for the lower end of the valley appeared to be filled by an army in position – real and actual regiments attired in red coats, and – of this there was no doubt – firing Martini-Henry bullets which cut up the ground a hundred yards in front of the leading company.

Over that pock-marked ground the regiment had to pass, and it opened the ball with a general and profound courtesy to the piping pickets; ducking in perfect time, as though it had been brazed on a rod. Being half-capable of thinking for itself, it fired a volley by the simple process of pitching its rifle into its shoulder and pulling the trigger. The bullets may have accounted for some of the watchers on the hillside, but they certainly did not affect the mass of enemy in front, while the noise of the rifles drowned any orders that might have been given.

'Good God!' said the Brigadier, sitting on the rock high above all. 'That regiment has spoilt the whole show. Hurry up the others, and let the screw-guns get off.'

But the screw-guns, in working round the heights, had stumbled upon a wasp's nest of a small mud fort which they incontinently shelled at eight hundred yards, to the huge discomfort of the occupants, who were unaccustomed to weapons of such devilish precision.

The Fore and Aft continued to go forward, but with shortened stride. Where were the other regiments, and why did the enemy use Martinis? They took open order instinctively, lying down and firing at random, rushing a few paces forward and lying down again, according to the regulations. Once in this formation, each man felt himself desperately alone, and edged in towards his fellow for comfort's sake.

Then the crack of his neighbour's rifle at his ear led him to fire as rapidly as he could – again for the sake of the comfort of the noise. The reward was not long delayed. Five volleys plunged the files in banked smoke impenetrable to the eye, and the bullets began to take ground twenty or thirty yards in front of the firers, as the weight of the bayonet dragged down and to the right arms wearied with holding the kick of the leaping Martini. The Company Commanders peered helplessly through the smoke, the more nervous mechanically trying to fan it away with their helmets.

'High and to the left!' bawled a Captain till he was hoarse. 'No good! Cease firing, and let it drift away a bit.'

Three and four times the bugles shrieked the order, and when it was obeyed the Fore and Aft looked that their foe should be lying before them in mown swaths of men. A light wind drove the smoke to leeward, and showed the enemy still in position and apparently unaffected. A quarter of a ton of lead had been buried a furlong in front of them, as the ragged earth attested.

That was not demoralising to the Afghans, who have not European nerves. They were waiting for the mad riot to die down, and were firing quietly into the heart of the smoke. A private of the Fore and Aft spun up his company shrieking with agony, another was kicking the earth and gasping, and a third, ripped through the lower intestines by a jagged bullet, was calling aloud on his comrades to put him out of his pain. These were the casualties, and they were not soothing to hear or see. The smoke cleared to a dull haze.

Then the foe began to shout with a great shouting, and a mass – a black mass – detached itself from the main body, and rolled over the ground at horrid speed. It was composed of, perhaps, three hundred men, who would shout and fire and slash if the rush of their fifty comrades who were determined to die carried home. The fifty were Ghazis, half-maddened with drugs and wholly mad with religious fanaticism. When they rushed the British fire ceased, and in the lull the order was given to close ranks and meet them with the bayonet.

Any one who knew the business could have told the Fore and Aft that the only way of dealing with a Ghazi rush is by volleys at long ranges; because a man who means to die, who desires to die, who will gain heaven by dying, must, in nine cases out of ten, kill a man who has a lingering prejudice in favour of life. Where they should have closed and gone forward, the Fore and Aft opened out and skirmished, and where they should have opened out and fired, they closed and waited.

A man dragged from his blankets half awake and unfed is never in a pleasant frame of mind. Nor does his happiness increase when he watches the whites of the eyes of three hundred six-foot fiends upon whose beards the foam is lying, upon whose tongues is a roar of wrath, and in whose hands are yard-long knives.

The Fore and Aft heard the Gurkha bugles bringing that regiment forward at the double, while the neighing of the Highland pipes came from the left. They strove to stay where they were, though the bayonets wavered down the line like the oars of a ragged boat. Then they felt body to body the amazing physical strength of their foes; a shriek of pain ended the rush, and the knives fell amid scenes not to be told.

The men clubbed together and smote blindly – as often as not at their own fellows. Their front crumpled like paper, and the fifty Ghazis passed on; their backers, now drunk with success, fighting as madly as they.

Then the rear-ranks were bidden to close up, and the subalterns dashed into the stew – alone. For the rear-rank had heard the clamour in front, the yells and the howls of pain, and had seen the dark stale blood that makes afraid. They were not going to stay. It was the rushing of the camps over again. Let their officers go to Hell, if they chose; they would get away from the knives.

'Come on!' shrieked the subalterns, and their men, cursing them, drew back, each closing into his neighbour and wheeling round.

Charteris and Devlin, subalterns of the last company, faced their death alone in the belief that their men would follow.

'You've killed me, you cowards,' sobbed Devlin and dropped, cut from the shoulder-strap to the centre of the chest, and a fresh detachment of his men retreating, always retreating, trampled him under foot as they made for the pass whence they had emerged.

> I kissed her in the kitchen and I kissed her in the hall.
> Child'un, child'un, follow me!
> Oh Golly, said the cook, is he gwine to kiss us all?
> Halla – Halla – Halla – Hallelujah!

The Gurkhas were pouring through the left gorge and over the heights at the double to the invitation of their Regimental Quick-step. The black rocks were crowned with dark green spiders as the bugles gave tongue jubilantly –

> In the morning! In the morning *by* the bright light!
> When Gabriel blows his trumpet in the morning!

The Gurkha rear-companies tripped and blundered over loose stones. The front-files halted for a moment to take stock of the valley and to settle stray bootlaces. Then a happy little sigh of contentment soughed down the ranks, and it was as though the land smiled, for behold there below was the enemy, and it was to meet them that the Gurkhas had doubled so hastily. There was much enemy. There would be amusement. The little men hitched their *kukris* well to hand, and gaped expectantly at their officers as terriers grin ere the stone is cast for them to fetch. The Gurkhas' ground sloped downward to the valley, and they enjoyed a fair view of the proceedings. They sat upon the boulders to watch, for their officers were not going to waste their wind in assisting to repulse a Ghazi rush more than half a mile away. Let the white men look to their own front.

'Hi! yi!' said the Subadar-Major, who was sweating profusely. 'Dam fools yonder, stand close-order! This is no time for close order, it is the time for volleys. Ugh!'

Horrified, amused, and indignant, the Gurkhas beheld the retirement of the Fore and Aft with a running chorus of oaths and commentaries.

'They run! The white men run! Colonel Sahib, may *we* also do a little running?' murmured Runbir Thappa, the Senior Jemadar.

But the Colonel would have none of it. 'Let the beggars be cut up a little,' said he wrathfully. 'Serves 'em right. They'll be prodded into facing round in a minute.' He looked through his field-glasses, and caught the glint of an officer's sword.

'Beating 'em with the flat – damned conscripts! How the Ghazis are walking into them!' said he.

The Fore and Aft, heading back, bore with them their officers. The narrowness of the pass forced the mob into solid formation, and the rear-rank delivered some sort of a wavering volley. The Ghazis drew off, for they did not know what reserves the gorge might hide. Moreover, it was never wise to chase white men too far. They returned as wolves return to cover, satisfied with the slaughter that they had done, and only stopping to slash at the wounded on the ground. A quarter of a mile had the Fore and Aft retreated, and now, jammed in the pass, was quivering with pain, shaken and demoralised with fear, while the officers, maddened beyond control, smote the men with the hilts and the flats of their swords.

'Get back! Get back, you cowards – you women! Right about face – column of companies, form – you hounds!' shouted the Colonel, and the subalterns swore aloud.

But the Regiment wanted to go – to go anywhere out of the range of those merciless knives. It swayed to and fro irresolutely with shouts and outcries, while from the right the Gurkhas dropped volley after volley of cripple-stopper Snider bullets at long range into the mob of the Ghazis returning to their own troops.

The Fore and Aft Band, though protected from direct fire by the rocky knoll under which it had sat down, fled at the first rush. Jakin and Lew would have fled also, but their short legs left them fifty yards in the rear, and by the time the Band had mixed with the regiment, they were painfully aware that they would have to close in alone and unsupported.

'Get back to that rock,' gasped Jakin. 'They won't see us there.'

And they returned to the scattered instruments of the Band, their hearts nearly bursting their ribs.

'Here's a nice show for *us*,' said Jakin, throwing himself full length on the ground. 'A bloomin' fine show for British Infantry! Oh, the devils! They've gone an' left us alone here! Wot'll we do?'

Lew took possession of a cast-off water bottle, which naturally was full of canteen rum, and drank till he coughed again.

'Drink,' said he shortly. 'They'll come back in a minute or two – you see.'

Jakin drank, but there was no sign of the regiment's return. They could hear a dull clamour from the head of the valley of retreat, and saw the Ghazis slink back, quickening their pace as the Gurkhas fired at them.

'We're all that's left of the Band, an' we'll be cut up as sure as death,' said Jakin.

'I'll die game, then,' said Lew thickly, fumbling with his tiny drummer's sword. The drink was working on his brain as it was on Jakin's.

''Old on! I know something better than fightin',' said Jakin, 'stung by the splendour of a sudden thought' due chiefly to rum. 'Tip our bloomin' cowards yonder the word to come back. The Paythan beggars are well away. Come on, Lew! We won't get hurt. Take the fife an' give me the drum. The Old Step for all your bloomin' guts are worth! There's a few of our men coming back now. Stand up, ye drunken little defaulter. By your right – quick march!'

He slipped the drum-sling over his shoulder, thrust the fife into Lew's hand, and the two boys marched out of the cover of the rock into the open making a hideous hash of the first bars of the 'British Grenadiers.'

As Lew had said, a few of the Fore and Aft were coming back sullenly and shame-facedly under the stimulus of blows and abuse; their red coats shone at the head of the valley, and behind them were wavering bayonets. But between this shattered line and the enemy, who with Afghan suspicion feared that the hasty retreat meant an ambush, and had not moved therefore, lay half a mile of level ground dotted only by the wounded.

The tune settled into full swing and the boys kept shoulder to shoulder, Jakin banging the drum as one possessed. The one fife made a thin and pitiful squeaking, but the tune carried far, even to the Gurkhas.

'Come on, you dogs!' muttered Jakin to himself. 'Are we to play forhever?' Lew was staring straight in front of him and marching more stiffly than ever he had done on parade.

And in bitter mockery of the distant mob, the old tune of the Old Line shrilled and rattled –

> Some talk of Alexander,
> And some of Hercules;
> Of Hector and Lysander,
> And such great names as these!

There was a far-off clapping of hands from the Gurkhas, and a roar from the Highlanders in the distance, but never a shot was fired by British or Afghan. The two little red dots moved forward in the open parallel to the enemy's front.

> But of all the world's great heroes
> There's none that can compare,
> With a tow-row-row-row-row-row,
> To the British Grenadier!

The men of the Fore and Aft were gathering thick at the entrance to the plain. The Brigadier on the heights far above was speechless with rage. Still no movement from the enemy. The day stayed to watch the children.

Jakin halted and beat the long roll of the Assembly, while the fife squealed despairingly.

'Right about face! Hold up, Lew, you're drunk,' said Jakin. They wheeled and marched back –

> Those heroes of antiquity
> Ne'er saw a cannon-ball,
> Nor knew the force o' powder,

'Here they come!' said Jakin. 'Go on, Lew' –

> To scare their foes withal!

The Fore and Aft were pouring out of the valley. What officers had said to men in that time of shame and humiliation will never be known; for neither officers nor men speak of it now.

'They are coming anew!' shouted a priest among the Afghans. 'Do not kill the boys! Take them alive, and they shall be of our faith.'

But the first volley had been fired, and Lew dropped on his face. Jakin stood for a minute, spun round and collapsed, as the Fore and Aft came forward, the curses of their officers in their ears, and in their hearts the shame of open shame.

Half the men had seen the drummers die, and they made no sign. They did not even shout They doubled out straight across the plain in open order, and they did not fire.

'This,' said the Colonel of Gurkhas, softly, 'is the real attack, as it should have been delivered. Come on, my children.'

'Ulu-lu-lu-lu!' squealed the Gurkhas, and came down with a joyful clicking of *kukris* – those vicious Gurkha knives.

On the right there was no rush. The Highlanders, cannily commending their souls to God (for it matters as much to a dead man whether he has been shot in a Border scuffle or at Waterloo), opened out and fired according to their custom, that is to say, without heat and without intervals, while the screw-guns, having disposed of the impertinent mud fort aforementioned, dropped shell after shell into the clusters round the flickering green standards on the heights.

'Charrging is an unfortunate necessity,' murmured the Colour-Sergeant of the right company of the Highlanders. 'It makes the men sweer so, but I am thinkin' that it will come to a charrge if these black devils stand much longer. Stewarrt, man, you're firing into the eye of the sun, and he'll not take any harm for Government ammu-neetion. A foot lower and a great deal slower! What are the English doing? They're very quiet there in the centre. Running again?'

The English were not running. They were hacking and hewing and stabbing, for though one white man is seldom physically a match for an Afghan in a sheepskin or wadded coat, yet, through the pressure of many white men behind, and a certain thirst for revenge in his heart, he becomes capable of doing much with both ends of his rifle. The Fore and Aft held their fire till one bullet could drive through five or six men, and the front of the Afghan force gave on the volley. They then selected their men, and slew them with deep gasps and short hacking coughs, and groanings of leather belts against strained bodies, and realised for the first time that an Afghan attacked is far less formidable than an Afghan attacking: which fact old soldiers might have told them.

But they had no old soldiers in their ranks.

The Gurkhas' stall at the bazar was the noisiest, for the men were engaged – to a nasty noise as of beef being cut on the block – with the *kukri*, which they preferred to the bayonet; well knowing how the Afghan hates the half-moon blade.

As the Afghans wavered, the green standards on the mountain moved down to assist them in a last rally. This was unwise. The Lancers chafing in the right gorge had thrice despatched their only subaltern as galloper to report on the progress of affairs. On the third occasion he returned, with a bullet-graze on his knee, swearing strange oaths in Hindustani, and saying that all things were ready. So that Squadron swung round the right of the Highlanders with a wicked whistling of wind in the pennons of its lances, and fell upon the remnant just when, according to all the rules of war, it should have waited for the foe to show more signs of wavering.

But it was a dainty charge, deftly delivered, and it ended by the Cavalry finding itself at the head of the pass by which the Afghans intended to retreat; and down the track that the lances had made streamed two companies of the Highlanders, which was never intended by the Brigadier. The new development was successful. It detached the enemy from his base as a sponge is torn from a rock, and left him ringed about with fire in that pitiless plain. And as a sponge is chased round the bath-tub by the hand of the bather, so were the Afghans chased till they broke into little detachments much more difficult to dispose of than large masses.

'See!' quoth the Brigadier. 'Everything has come as I arranged. We've cut their base, and now we'll bucket 'em to pieces.'

A direct hammering was all that the Brigadier had dared to hope for, considering the size of the force at his disposal; but men who stand or fall by the errors of their opponents may be forgiven for turning Chance into Design. The bucketing went forward merrily. The Afghan forces were upon the run – the run of wearied wolves who snarl and bite over their shoulders. The red lances dipped by twos and threes, and, with a shriek, up rose the lance-butt, like a spar on a stormy sea, as the trooper cantering forward cleared his point. The Lancers kept between their prey and the steep hills, for all who could were trying to escape from the valley of death. The Highlanders gave the fugitives two hundred yards' law, and then brought them down, gasping and choking, ere they could reach the protection of the boulders above. The Gurkhas followed suit; but the Fore and Aft were killing on their own account, for they had penned a mass of men between their bayonets and a wall of rock, and the flash of the rifles was lighting the wadded coats.

'We cannot hold them, Captain Sahib!' panted a Ressaldar of Lancers. 'Let us try the carbine. The lance is good, but it wastes time.'

They tried the carbine, and still the enemy melted away – fled up the hills by hundreds when there were only twenty bullets to stop them. On the heights the screw-guns ceased firing – they had run out of ammunition – and the Brigadier groaned, for the musketry fire could not sufficiently smash the retreat. Long before the last volleys were fired the doolies were out in force looking for the wounded. The battle was over, and, but for want of fresh troops, the Afghans would have been wiped off the earth. As it was they counted their dead by hundreds, and nowhere were the dead thicker than in the track of the Fore and Aft.

But the Regiment did not cheer with the Highlanders, nor did they dance uncouth dances with the Gurkhas among the dead. They looked under their brows at the Colonel as they leaned upon their rifles and panted.

'Get back to camp, you. Haven't you disgraced yourself enough for one day! Go and look to the wounded. It's all you're fit for,' said the Colonel. Yet for the past hour the Fore and Aft had been doing all that mortal commander could expect. They had lost heavily because they did not know how to set about their business with proper skill, but they had borne themselves gallantly, and this was their reward.

A young and sprightly Colour-Sergeant, who had begun to imagine himself a hero, offered his water-bottle to a Highlander, whose tongue was black with thirst. 'I drink with no cowards,' answered the youngster huskily, and, turning to a Gurkha, said, 'Hya, Johnny! Drink water got it?' The Gurkha grinned and passed his bottle. The Fore and Aft said no word.

They went back to camp when the field of strife had been a little mopped up and made presentable, and the Brigadier, who saw himself a Knight in three months, was the only soul who was complimentary to them. The Colonel was heart-broken, and the officers were savage and sullen.

'Well,' said the Brigadier, 'they are young troops of course, and it was not unnatural that they should retire in disorder for a bit.'

'Oh, my only Aunt Maria!' murmured a junior Staff Officer. 'Retire in disorder! It was a bally run!'

'But they came again, as we all know,' cooed the Brigadier, the Colonel's ashy-white face before him, 'and they behaved as well as could possibly be expected. Behaved beautifully, indeed. I was watching them. It's not a matter to take to heart, Colonel. As some German General said of his men, they wanted to be shooted over a little, that was all.' To himself he said – 'Now they're blooded I can give 'em responsible work. It's as well that they got what they did. 'Teach 'em more than half-a-dozen rifle flirtations, that will – later – run alone and bite. Poor old Colonel, though.'

All that afternoon the heliograph winked and flickered on the hills, striving to tell the good news to a mountain forty miles away. And in the evening there arrived, dusty, sweating, and sore, a misguided Correspondent who had gone out to assist at a trumpery village-burning, and who had read off the message from afar, cursing his luck the while.

'Let's have the details somehow – as full as ever you can, please. It's the first time I've ever been left this campaign,' said the Correspondent to the Brigadier, and the Brigadier, nothing loath, told him how an Army of Communication had been crumpled up, destroyed, and all but annihilated by the craft, strategy, wisdom, and foresight of the Brigadier.

But some say, and among these be the Gurkhas who watched on the hillside, that that battle was won by Jakin and Lew, whose little bodies were borne up just in time to fit two gaps at the head of the big ditch-grave for the dead under the heights of Jagai.

WITH CLIVE
IN INDIA

PREFACE

In the following pages I have endeavoured to give a vivid picture of the wonderful events of the ten years, which at their commencement saw Madras in the hands of the French – Calcutta at the mercy of the Nabob of Bengal – and English influence apparently at the point of extinction in India – and which ended in the final triumph of the English, both in Bengal and Madras. There were yet great battles to be fought, great efforts to be made, before the vast Empire of India fell altogether into British hands; but these were but the sequel of the events I have described.

The historical details are, throughout the story, strictly accurate, and for them I am indebted to the history of these events written by Mr. Orme, who lived at that time, to the 'Life of Lord Clive,' recently published by Lieutenant Colonel Malleson, and to other standard authorities. In this book I have devoted a somewhat smaller space to the personal adventures of my hero than in my other historical tales, but the events themselves were of such a thrilling and exciting nature that no fiction could surpass them.

A word as to the orthography of the names and places. An entirely new method of spelling Indian words has lately been invented by the Indian authorities. This is no doubt more correct than the rough-and-ready orthography of the early traders, and I have therefore adopted it for all little-known places. But there are Indian names which have become household words in England, and should never be changed; and as it would be considered a gross piece of pedantry and affectation on the part of

463

a tourist on the Continent, who should, on his return, say he had been to Genova, Firenze, and Wien, instead of Genoa, Florence, and Vienna; it is, I consider, an even worse offence to transform Arcot, Cawnpoor, and Lucknow, into Arkat, Kahnpur, and Laknao. I have tried, therefore, so far as possible, to give the names of well-known personages and places in the spelling familiar to Englishmen, while the new orthography has been elsewhere adopted.

G. A. Henty

Chapter 1

LEAVING HOME

A lady in deep mourning was sitting, crying bitterly, by a fire in small lodgings in the town of Yarmouth. Beside her stood a tall lad of sixteen. He was slight in build, but his schoolfellows knew that Charlie Marryat's muscles were as firm and hard as those of any boy in the school. In all sports requiring activity and endurance, rather than weight and strength, he was always conspicuous. Not one in the school could compete with him in long-distance running, and when he was one of the hares there was but little chance for the hounds. He was a capital swimmer, and one of the best boxers in the school. He had a reputation for being a leader in every mischievous prank; but he was honorable and manly, would scorn to shelter himself under the semblance of a lie, and was a prime favourite with his masters, as well as his schoolfellows. His mother bewailed the frequency with which he returned home with blackened eyes and bruised face; for between Dr. Willet's school and the fisher lads of Yarmouth there was a standing feud, whose origin dated so far back that none of those now at school could trace it. Consequently, fierce fights often took place in the narrow rows, and sometimes the fisher boys would be driven back on to the broad quay shaded by trees, by the river, and there being reinforced from the craft along the side, would reassume the offensive and drive their opponents back into the main street.

It was but six months since Charlie had lost his father, who was the officer in command at the coast guard station, and his scanty pension was now all that remained for the support of his widow and children. His mother had talked his future prospects

465

over, many times, with Charlie. The latter was willing to do anything, but could suggest nothing. His father had but little naval interest, and had for years been employed on coast guard service. Charlie agreed that, although he should have liked of all things to go to sea, it was useless to think of it now, for he was past the age at which he could have entered as a midshipman.

The matter had been talked over four years before, with his father; but the latter had pointed out that a life in the navy, without interest, is in most cases a very hard one. If a chance of distinguishing himself happened, promotion would follow; but if not, he might be for years on shore, starving on half pay and waiting in vain for an appointment, while officers with more luck and better interest went over his head.

Other professions had been discussed, but nothing determined upon, when Lieutenant Marryat suddenly died. Charlie, although an only son, was not an only child, as he had two sisters both younger than himself. After a few months of effort, Mrs. Marryat found that the utmost she could hope to do, with her scanty income, was to maintain herself and daughters, and to educate them until they should reach an age when they could earn their own living as governesses; but that Charlie's keep and education were beyond her resources. She had, therefore, very reluctantly written to an uncle, whom she had not seen for many years, her family having objected very strongly to her marriage with a penniless lieutenant in the navy. She informed him of the loss of her husband, and that, although her income was sufficient to maintain herself and her daughters, she was most anxious to start her son, who was now sixteen, in life; and therefore begged him to use his influence to obtain for him a situation of some sort. The letter which she now held in her hand was the answer to the appeal.

'My dear Niece,' it began, 'Since you, by your own foolish conduct and opposition to all our wishes, separated yourself from your family, and went your own way in life, I have heard little of you, as the death of your parents so shortly afterwards deprived me of all sources of information. I regret to hear of the loss which you have suffered. I have already taken the necessary steps to carry out your wishes. I yesterday dined with a friend, who is one of the directors of the Honorable East India Company, and at my request he has kindly placed a writership in the Company at your son's service.

He will have to come up to London to see the board, next week, and will probably have to embark for India a fortnight later. I shall be glad if he will take up his abode with me, during the intervening time. I shall be glad also if you will favour me with a statement of your income and expenses, with such details as you may think necessary. I inclose four five-pound bank notes, in order that your son may obtain such garments as may be immediately needful for his appearance before the board of directors, and for his journey to London. I remain, my dear niece, yours sincerely,

'Joshua Tufton.'

'It is cruel,' Mrs. Marryat sobbed, 'cruel to take you away from us, and send you to India, where you will most likely die of fever, or be killed by a tiger, or stabbed by one of those horrid natives, in a fortnight.'

'Not so bad as that, Mother, I hope,' Charlie said sympathizingly, although he could not repress a smile; 'other people have managed to live out there, and have come back safe.'

'Yes,' Mrs. Marryat said, sobbing; 'I know how you will come back. A little, yellow, shrivelled up old man with no liver, and a dreadful temper, and a black servant. I know what it will be.'

This time Charlie could not help laughing.

'That's looking too far ahead altogether, Mother. You take the two extremes. If I don't die in a fortnight, I am to live to be a shrivelled old man. I'd rather take a happy medium, and look forward to coming back before my liver is all gone, or my temper all destroyed, with lots of money to make you and the girls comfortable.

'There is only one thing. I wish it had been a cadetship, instead of a writership.'

'That is my only comfort,' Mrs. Marryat said. 'If it had been a cadetship, I should have written to say that I would not let you go. It is bad enough as it is; but if you had had to fight, I could not have borne it.'

Charlie did his best to console his mother, by telling her how everyone who went to India made fortunes, and how he should be sure to come back with plenty of money; and that, when the girls grew up, he should be able to find rich husbands for them; and at last he succeeded in getting her to look at matters in a less gloomy light.

'And I'm sure, Mother,' he said, 'Uncle means most kindly. He sends twenty pounds, you see, and says that that is for immediate necessities; so I have no doubt he means to help to get my outfit, or at any rate to advance money, which I can repay him out of my salary. The letter is rather stiff and businesslike, of course, but I suppose that's his way; and you see he asks about your income, so perhaps he means to help for the girls' education. I should go away very happy, if I knew that you would be able to get on comfortably. Of course it's a long way off, Mother, and I should have liked to stay at home, to be a help to you and the girls; but one can't have all one wishes. As far as I am concerned, myself, I would rather go out as a writer there, where I shall see strange sights and a strange country, than be stuck all my life at a desk in London.

'What is Uncle like?'

'He is a short man, my dear, rather stiff and pompous, with a very stiff cravat. He used to give me his finger to shake, when I was a child, and I was always afraid of him. He married a most disagreeable woman, only a year or two before I married, myself. But I heard she died not very long afterwards;' and so Mrs. Marryat got talking of her early days and relations, and was quite in good spirits again, by the time her daughters returned from school; and she told them what she was now coming to regard as the good fortune which had befallen their brother.

The girls were greatly affected. They adored their brother, and the thought that he was going away for years was terrible to them. Nothing that could be said pacified them in the slightest degree, and they did nothing but cry, until they retired to bed. Charlie was much affected by their sorrow; but when they had retired, he took his hat and went out to tell the news of his approaching departure to some of his chums.

The next day, Mrs. Marryat wrote thanking her uncle for his kindness, and saying that Charlie would go round to London by the packet which sailed on the following Monday; and would, if the wind were fair and all went well, reach London on the Wednesday.

School was, of course, at once given up, and the girls also had a holiday till their brother's departure. When the necessary clothes were ordered, there was little more to do; and Charlie spent the time, when his boy friends were in school, in walking with the girls along the shore, talking to them of the future, of the presents he would send them home, and of the life he should lead in India; while at other times he went out with his favourite schoolfellows, and joined in one last grand battle with the smack boys.

On Monday morning, after a sad farewell to his family, Charlie embarked on board the Yarmouth Belle, a packet which performed the journey to and from London once a fortnight. She was a roomy lugger, built for stowage rather than speed, and her hold was crammed and her deck piled with packages of salted fish. There were five or six other persons also bound for London, the journey to which was, in those days, regarded as an arduous undertaking.

As soon as the Yarmouth Belle issued from the mouth of the river, she began to pitch heavily; and Charlie, who from frequently going out with his father in the revenue cutter, was a good sailor, busied himself in doing his best for his afflicted fellow passengers. Towards evening the wind got up, and shifting ahead, the captain dropped anchor off Lowestoft. The next morning was finer, and the Yarmouth Belle continued her way. It was not, however, till Thursday afternoon that she dropped anchor in the Pool.

Charlie was soon on shore, and giving his trunk to a porter, desired him to lead the way to Bread Street, in which his uncle resided; for in the last century, such things as country villas were almost unknown, and the merchants of London for the most part resided in the houses where they carried on their business. Keeping close to the porter, to see that he did not make off with his trunk, for Charlie had received many warnings as to the extreme wickedness of London, he followed him through the busy streets, and arrived safely at his uncle's door.

It was now dusk, and Charlie, on giving his name, was shown upstairs to a large room, which was lighted by a fire blazing in the hearth. Standing with his back to this was a gentleman whom he at once recognized, from his mother's description, as her uncle, although he was a good deal more portly than when she had seen him last.

'So you are my grandnephew,' he said, holding out what Charlie considered to be a very limp and flabby hand towards him.

'Yes, Uncle,' Charlie said cheerfully; 'and we are very much obliged to you, Mamma and I, for your kindness.'

'Humph!' the old gentleman grunted.

'And how is it,' he asked severely, 'that you were not here yesterday? My niece's letter led me to expect that you would arrive yesterday.'

'We came as fast as we could, Uncle,' Charlie laughed; 'but of course the time depends upon the wind. The captain tells me that he has been as much as three weeks coming round.'

Mr. Tufton grunted again as if to signify that such unpunctuality was altogether displeasing to him.

'You are tall,' he said, looking up at Charlie, who stood half a head above him, 'and thin, very thin. You have a loose way of standing, which I don't approve of.'

'I'm sorry I'm loose, sir,' Charlie said gravely, 'if you do not approve of it; but you see, running about and playing games make one lissome. I suppose, now that's all over and I am going to spend my time in writing, I shall get stiffer.'

'I hope so, I hope so,' Mr. Tufton said encouragingly, and as if stiffness were one of the most desirable things in life. 'I like to see young men with a sedate bearing.

'And you left my niece and grandnieces well, I hope?'

'Quite well, thank you, sir,' Charlie said; 'but, of course, a good deal upset with parting from me.'

'Yes,' Mr. Tufton said; 'I suppose so. Women are so emotional. Now there's nothing I object to more than emotion.'

As Charlie thought that this was probably the case, he was silent, although the idea vaguely occurred to him that he should like to excite a little emotion in his uncle, by the sudden insertion of a pin, or some other such means. The silence continued for some little time, and then Mr. Tufton said:

'I always dine at two o'clock; but as probably you are hungry – I have observed that boys always are hungry – some food will be served you in the next room. I had already given my housekeeper orders. No doubt you will find it prepared. After that, you may like to take a walk in the streets. I have supper at nine, by which hour you will, of course, have returned.'

Charlie, as he ate his meal, thought to himself that his uncle was a pompous old gentleman, and that it would be very hard work getting on with him, for the next three weeks. However, he consoled himself by the thought:

'Kind is as kind does after all, and I expect the old gentleman is not as crusty as he looks.'

Charlie had handed to Mr. Tufton a letter which his mother had given him, and when he returned from a ramble through the streets, he found that gentleman sitting by the fire, with lights upon a small table beside him. Upon this Mrs. Marryat's letter lay open.

'So you have soon become tired of the streets of London, Grandnephew!' he said.

'There is not much to see, sir. The lamps do not burn very brightly, and the fog is coming on. I thought that, if it grew thicker, I might lose my way, and in that case I might not have been in at the hour you named for supper.'

'Humph!' the other gentleman grunted. 'So your mother has taught you to be punctual to meals. But, no; boys' appetites teach them to be punctual then, if never at any other time.

'And why, sir?' he asked severely, 'Did my niece not write to me before?'

'I don't know, sir,' Charlie said. 'I suppose she did not like – that is, she didn't think – that is –'

'Think, sir! Like, sir!' said his uncle. 'What right had she either to think or to like? Her duty clearly was to have made me acquainted, at once, with all the circumstances. I suppose I had a right to say whether I approved of my grandnieces going tramping about the world as governesses, or not. It isn't because a woman chooses, by her folly, to separate herself from her family, that they are to be deprived of their rights in a matter of this kind. Eh, sir, what do you say to that?' and Mr. Tufton looked very angry, indeed.

'I don't know, sir,' Charlie said. 'I have never thought the matter over.'

'Why, sir, suppose she had made you a tinker, sir, and you turned out a thief, as likely as not you would have done, and you'd been hung, sir, what then? Am I to have such discredit as this brought upon me, without my having any option in the matter?'

'I suppose not, sir,' Charlie said. 'I hope I shouldn't have turned out a thief, even if I'd been a tinker; but perhaps it was because my mother feared that this might be the case, that she did give you the option.'

His uncle looked at him keenly; but Charlie, though with some difficulty, maintained the gravest face.

'It is well she did so,' Mr. Tufton said; 'very well. If she had not done so, I should have known the reason why. And you, sir, do you like the thought of going to India?'

'Yes, Uncle, I like the thought very much, though I would rather, if I may say so, have gone as a cadet.'

'I thought so,' Mr. Tufton said, sarcastically. 'I was sure of it. You wanted to wear a red coat and a sword, and to swagger about the streets of Calcutta, instead of making an honorable living and acquiring a fortune.'

'I don't think, sir,' Charlie said, 'that the idea of the red coat and sword entered into my mind; but it seemed to me the choice of a life of activity and adventure, against one as a mere clerk.'

'Had you entered the military service of the Company, even if you didn't get shot, you could only hope to rise to the command of a regiment, ranking with a civilian very low down on the list. The stupidity of boys is unaccountable. It's a splendid career, sir, that I have opened to you; but if I'd known that you had no ambition, I would have put you into my own counting house; though there, that wouldn't have done either, for I know you would have blotted the ledger, and turned all the accounts topsy-turvy.

'And now, sir, supper is ready;' and the old gentleman led the way into the next room.

Upon the following day Charlie was introduced, by his uncle, to the director who had given him his nomination, and was told by him that the board would sit upon the following day, and that he must call at the India House, at eleven o'clock. The ordeal was not a formidable one. He was shown into a room where eight or ten elderly gentlemen were sitting round a large table. Among these was his friend of the day before. He was asked a question or two about his age, his father's profession, and his place of education. Then the gentleman at the head of the table nodded to him, and said he could go, and instructions would be sent to him, and that he was to prepare to sail in the Lizzie Anderson, which would leave the docks in ten days' time, and that he would be, for the present, stationed at Madras.

Much delighted at having got through the ordeal so easily, Charlie returned to his uncle's. He did not venture to penetrate into the latter's counting house, but awaited his coming upstairs to dinner, to tell him the news.

'Humph!' said his uncle; 'it is lucky they did not find out what a fool you were, at once. I was rather afraid that even the two minutes would do it. After dinner, I will send my clerk round with you, to get the few things which are necessary for your voyage.

'I suppose you will want to, what you call amuse yourself, to see the beasts at Exeter Change, and the playhouses. Here are two sovereigns. Don't get into loose company, and don't get drinking, sir, or out of the house you go.'

Charlie attempted to express his thanks, but his uncle stopped him abruptly.

'Hold your tongue, sir. I am doing what is right; a thing, sir, Joshua Tufton always has done, and doesn't expect to be thanked for it. All I ask you is, that if you rob the Company's till and are hung, don't mention that you are related to me.'

After dinner was over, Charlie went out under the charge of an old clerk, and visited tailors' and outfitters' shops, and found that his uncle's idea of the few necessaries for a voyage differed very widely from his own. The clerk, in each case, inquired from the tradesmen what was the outfit which gentlemen going to India generally took with them, and Charlie was absolutely appalled at the magnitude of the orders. Four dozen shirts, ten dozen pairs of stockings, two dozen suits of white cotton cloth, and everything else in proportion. Charlie in vain remonstrated, and even implored the clerk to abstain from ordering what appeared to him such a fabulous amount of things; and begged him, at any rate, to wait until he had spoken to his uncle. The clerk, however, replied that he had received instructions that the full usual outfit was to be obtained, and that Mr. Tufton never permitted his orders to be questioned. Charlie was forced to submit, but he was absolutely oppressed with the magnitude of his outfit, to carry which six huge trunks were required.

'It is awful,' Charlie said to himself, 'positively awful. How much it will all come to, goodness only knows; three or four hundred pounds, at least.'

In those days, before steam was thought of, and the journey to India was often of six months' duration, men never came home more than once in seven years, and often remained in India from the day of their arrival until they finally retired, without once revisiting England. The outfits taken out were, therefore, necessarily much larger than at the present time, when a run home to England can be accomplished in three weeks, and there are plenty of shops, in every town in India, where all European articles of necessity or luxury can be purchased.

After separating from the clerk, Charlie felt altogether unable to start out in search of amusement. He wandered about vaguely till supper time, and then attempted to address his uncle on the subject.

'My dear Uncle,' he began, 'you've been so awfully kind to me, that I really do not like to trespass upon you. I am positively frightened at the outfit your clerk has ordered. It is enormous. I'm sure I can't want so many things, possibly, and I would really rather take a much smaller outfit; and then, as I want them, I can have more things out from England, and pay for them myself.'

'You don't suppose,' Mr. Tufton said sternly, 'that I'm going to have my nephew go out to India with the outfit of a cabin boy. I ordered that you were to have the proper outfit of a gentleman, and I requested my clerk to order a considerable portion of the things to be made of a size which will allow for your growing, for you look to me as if you were likely enough to run up into a lanky giant, of six feet high. I suppose he has done as I ordered him. Don't let me hear another word on the subject.'

Chapter 2

THE YOUNG WRITER

For the next four days, Charlie followed his uncle's instructions and amused himself. He visited Exeter Change, took a boat and rowed down the river to Greenwich, and a coach and visited the palace of Hampton Court. He went to see the coaches make their start, in the morning, for all places in England, and marvelled at the perfection of the turnouts. He went to the playhouses twice, in the evening, and saw Mr. Garrick in his performance as Richard the Third.

On the fifth day, a great surprise awaited him. His uncle, at breakfast, had told him briefly that he did not wish him to go out before dinner, as someone might want to see him; and Charlie, supposing that a messenger might be coming down from the India House, waited indoors; and an hour later he was astonished, when the door of the room opened and his mother and sisters entered.

With a shout of gladness and surprise, Charlie rushed into their arms.

'My dear mother, my dear girls, this is an unexpected pleasure, indeed! Why, what has brought you here?'

'Didn't you know we were coming, Charlie? Didn't Uncle tell you?' they exclaimed.

'Not a word,' Charlie said. 'I never dreamt of such a thing. What, has he called you up here to stay till I go?'

'Oh, my dear, he has been so kind,' his mother said; 'and so funny! He wrote me such a scolding letter, just as if I had been a very naughty little girl. He said he wasn't going to allow me to bring disgrace upon him, by living in wretched lodgings at Yarmouth, nor by his grandnieces being sent out as governesses. So he ordered me at once – ordered me Charlie, as if I had no will of my own – to give up the lodgings, and to take our places in the coach, yesterday morning. He said we were not to shame him by appearing here in rags, and he sent me a hundred pounds, every penny of which, he said, was to be laid out in clothes. As to the future, he said it would be his duty to see that I brought no further disgrace upon the family.'

'Yes, and he's been just as kind to me, Mother. As I told you when I wrote, he had ordered an enormous outfit, which will, I am sure, cost hundreds of pounds. He makes me go to the playhouses, and all sorts of amusements; and all the time he has been so kind he scolds, and grumbles, and predicts that I shall be hanged.'

'I'm sure you won't,' Kate, his youngest sister, said indignantly. 'How can he say such a thing?'

'He doesn't mean it,' Charlie laughed. 'It's only his way. He will go on just the same way with you, I have no doubt; but you mustn't mind, you know, and mustn't laugh, but must look quite grave and serious.

'Ah! Here he is.

'Oh, Uncle, this is kind of you!'

'Hold your tongue, sir,' said his uncle, 'and try and learn not to speak to your elders, unless you are addressed.

'Niece Mary,' he said, kissing her upon the forehead, 'I am glad to see you again. You are not so much changed as I expected.

'And these are my grandnieces, Elizabeth and Kate, though why Kate I don't know. It is a fanciful name, and new to the family, and I am surprised that you didn't call her Susanna, after your grandmother.'

Kate made a little face at the thought of being called Susanna. However, a warning glance from Charlie closed her lips, just as she was about to express her decided preference for her own name. Mr. Tufton kissed them both, muttering to himself:

'I suppose I ought to kiss them. Girls always expect to be kissed at every opportunity.

'What are you laughing at, grandniece?'

'I don't think girls expect to be kissed, except by people they like,' Kate said; 'but we do like kissing you, Uncle,' throwing her arms round his neck, and kissing him heartily; 'because you have been so kind to Charlie, and have brought us up to see him again.'

'You have disarranged my white tie, Niece,' Mr. Tufton said, extricating himself from Kate's embrace.

'Niece Mary, I fear that you have not taught your daughters to restrain their emotions, and there is nothing so dreadful as emotional women.'

'Perhaps I have not taken so much pains with their education, in that way, as in some others,' Mrs. Marryat said, smiling. 'But of course, Uncle, if you object to be kissed, the girls will abstain from doing so.'

'No,' Mr. Tufton said, thoughtfully. 'It is the duty of nieces to kiss their uncles, in moderation – in moderation, mind – and it is the duty of the uncles to receive those salutations, and I do not know that the duty is altogether an unpleasant one. I am, myself, unaccustomed to be kissed, but it is an operation to which I may accustom myself, in time.'

'I never heard it called an operation, Uncle,' Lizzie said demurely; 'but I now understand the meaning of the phrase of a man's undergoing a painful operation. I used to think it meant cutting off a leg, or something of that sort, but I see it's much worse.'

Her uncle looked at her steadily.

'I am afraid, Grandniece, that you intend to be sarcastic. This is a hateful habit in a man, worse in a woman. Cure yourself of it as speedily as possible, or Heaven help the unhappy man who may some day be your husband.

'And now,' he said, 'ring the bell. The housekeeper will show you to your rooms. My nephew will tell you what are the hours for meals. Of course, you will want to be gadding about with him. You will understand that there is no occasion to be in to meals; but if you are not present when they are upon the table, you will have to wait for the next. I cannot have my house turned upside down, by meals being brought up at all sorts of hours.

'You must not expect me, Niece, to be at your beck and call during the day, as I have my business to attend to; but of an evening I shall, of course, feel it my duty to accompany you to the playhouse. It will not do for you to be going about with only the protection of a hare-brained boy.'

The remainder of Charlie's stay in London passed most pleasantly. They visited all the sights of town, Mr. Tufton performing what he called his duty with an air of protest, but showing a general thoughtfulness and desire to please his visitors, which was very apparent even when he grunted and grumbled the most.

On the evening before he started, he called Charlie down into his counting house.

'Tomorrow you are going to sail,' he said, 'and to start in life on your own account, and I trust that you will, as far as possible, be steady, and do your duty to your employers. You will understand that, although the pay of a writer is not high, there are opportunities for advancement. The Company have the monopoly of the trade of India, and in addition to their great factories at Bombay, Calcutta, and Madras, they have many other trading stations. Those who, by their good conduct, attract the attention of their superiors, rise to positions of trust and emolument. There are many who think that the Company will, in time, enlarge its operations; and as they do so, superior opportunities will offer themselves; and since the subject of India has been prominently brought before my notice, I have examined the question, and am determined to invest somewhat largely in the stock of the Company, a step which will naturally give me some influence with the board. That influence I shall, always supposing that your conduct warrants it, exercise on your behalf.

'As we are now at war with France, and it is possible that the vessel in which you are proceeding may be attacked by the way, I have thought it proper that you should be armed. You will, therefore, find in your cabin a brace of pistols, a rifle, and a double-barrel shotgun: which last, I am informed, is a useful weapon at close quarters. Should your avocations in India permit your doing so, you will find them useful in the pursuit of game. I hope that you will not be extravagant; but as a matter of business I find that it is useful to be able to give entertainments, to persons who may be in a position to benefit or advance you. I have, therefore, arranged that you will draw from the factor at Madras the sum of two hundred pounds, annually, in addition to your pay. It is clearly my duty to see that my nephew has every fair opportunity for making his way.

'Now, go upstairs at once to your mother. I have letters to write, and am too busy for talking.'

So saying, with a peremptory wave of his hand he dismissed his nephew.

'Well, Mother,' Charlie said, after telling her of his uncle's generosity, 'thank goodness you will be all right now, anyhow. No doubt Uncle intends to do something for you and the girls, though he has said nothing at present, beyond the fact that you are not to be in wretched lodgings, and they are not to go out as governesses. But even if he should change his mind, and I don't think he ever does that, I shall be able to help you.

'Oh, he is kind, isn't he?'

The parting was far less sad than that which had taken place at Yarmouth. Charlie was now assured that his mother and sisters would be comfortable, and well cared for in his absence; while his mother, happy in the lightening of her anxiety as to the future of her daughters, and as to the prospects of her son, was able to bear with better heart the thought of their long separation.

Mrs. Marryat and the girls accompanied him on board ship. Mr. Tufton declined to join the party, under the plea that, in the first place, he was busy; and in the second, that he feared there would be an emotional display. He sent, however, his head clerk with them, to escort the ladies on their return from the docks.

The Lizzie Anderson was a fine ship, of the largest size, and she was almost as clean and trim as a man of war. She carried twelve cannon, two of them thirty-two pounders, which were in those days considered large pieces of ordnance. All the ships of the Company, and, indeed, all ocean-going merchantmen of the day, were armed, as the sea swarmed with privateers, and the black flag of the pirates was still occasionally to be seen.

The girls were delighted with all they saw, as, indeed, was Charlie; for accustomed, as they were, only to the coasting vessels which frequented the port of Yarmouth, this floating castle appeared to them a vessel of stupendous size and power.

This was Charlie's first visit, also, to the ship, for his uncle had told him that all directions had been given, that the trunks with the things necessary for the voyage would be found in his cabin, at the time of starting, and the rest of the luggage in the hold. Everything was in order, and Charlie found that his cabin companion was a doctor in the service, returning to Madras. He was a pleasant man, of some five or six and thirty, and assured Mrs. Marryat that he would soon make her son at home on board ship, and would, moreover, put him up to the ways of things upon his arrival in India. There were many visitors on board, saying goodbye to their friends, and all sat down to lunch, served in the saloon.

When this was over, the bell rang for visitors to go ashore. There was a short scene of parting, in which Charlie was not ashamed to use his handkerchief as freely as did his mother and sisters. Five minutes later, the great vessel passed through the dock gates. Charlie stood at the stern, waving his handkerchief as long as he could catch a glimpse of the figures of his family; and then as, with her sails spread and the tide gaining strength every minute beneath her, the vessel made her way down the river, he turned round to examine his fellow passengers.

These were some twenty in number, and for the most part men. Almost all were, in some capacity or other, civil or military, in the service of the Company; for at that time their monopoly was a rigid one, and none outside its boundary were allowed to trade in India. The Company was, indeed, solely a great mercantile house of business. They had their own ships, their own establishments, and bought and sold goods like other traders. They owned a small extent of country, round their three great trading towns; and kept up a little army, composed of two or three white regiments; and as many composed of natives, trained and disciplined like Europeans, and known as Sepoys. Hence the clergyman, the doctor, a member of the council of Madras, four or five military officers, twice as many civilians, and three young writers, besides Charlie, were all in the employment of the Company.

'Well, youngster,' a cheery voice said beside him, 'take your last look at the smoke of London, for it will be a good many years before you see it again, my lad. You've blue skies and clear ones where you're going, except when it rains, and when it does there is no mistake about it.'

The speaker was the captain of the Lizzie Anderson, a fine sailor-like man of some fifty years, of which near forty had been spent in the service of the Company.

'I'm not a Londoner,' Charlie said, smiling, 'and have no regret for leaving its smoke. Do you think we shall make a quick voyage?'

'I hope so,' the captain said, 'but it all depends upon the wind. A finer ship never floated than the Lizzie Anderson; but the Company don't build their vessels for speed, and it's no use trying to run, when you meet a Frenchman. Those fellows understand how to build ships, and if they could fight them as well as they build them, we should not long be mistress of the sea.'

Most of the people on board appeared to know each other, and Charlie felt rather lonely, till the doctor came up and began to chat with him. He told him who most of his fellow passengers were:

'That gentleman there, walking on the other side of the deck, as if not only the ship but the river and banks on both sides belonged to him, is one of the council. That is his wife over there, with a companion holding her shawl for her. That pretty little woman, next to her, is the wife of Captain Tibbets, the tall man leaning against the bulwarks. Those two sisters are going out to keep house for their uncle, one of the leading men in Madras; and, I suppose, to get husbands, which they will most likely do before they have been there many weeks. They look very nice girls.

'But you soon get acquainted with them all. It is surprising how soon people get friendly on board ship, though, as a rule, they quarrel like cats and dogs before they get to the end of it.'

'What do they quarrel about?' Charlie asked, surprised.

'Oh, about anything or nothing,' the doctor said. 'They all get heartily sick of each other, and of the voyage, and they quarrel because they have nothing else to do. You will see, we shall be as happy a party as possible till we get about as far as the Cape. After that, the rows will begin, and by the time we get to India, half the people won't speak to each other.

'Have you been down the river before? That's Gravesend. I see the captain is getting ready to anchor. So, I suppose the tide has nearly run out. If this wind holds, we shall be fairly out at sea when you get up tomorrow.'

'You snore, I hope?'

'No, sir, I don't think so,' Charlie said.

'I hoped you did,' the doctor said, 'because I'm told I do, sometimes. However, as I usually smoke a cigar on deck, the last thing, I hope you will be fairly asleep before I am. If at any time I get very bad, and keep you awake, you must shake me.'

Charlie said it took a good deal to keep him awake, and that he should probably get accustomed to it, ere long.

'It's better to do that,' he said with a laugh, 'than to keep on waking you, for the next four or five months.'

A week later, the Lizzie Anderson was running down the Spanish coast, with all sail set. She was out of sight of land, and so far had seen nothing likely to cause uneasiness. They had met many vessels, homeward bound from the Mediterranean, and one or two big ships which the captain pronounced to be Indiamen. That morning, however, a vessel was seen coming out from the land. She seemed, to Charlie's eyes, quite a small vessel, and he was surprised to see how often the captain and officers turned their glasses towards her.

'I fancy our friend over there is a French privateer,' the doctor remarked to him; 'and I should not be surprised if we found ourselves exchanging shots with her, before many hours are over.'

'But she's a little bit of a thing,' Charlie said. 'Surely she would never venture to attack a ship like ours.'

'It's the size of the guns, not the size of the ship, that counts, my boy. She has the advantage of being able to sail three feet to our two; and probably, small as she is, she carries half as many men again as we do. However, we carry heavy metal, and can give a good account of ourselves. Those thirty-twos will astonish our friend, if she comes within range.'

The stranger was a large schooner, and the tautness of the spars and rigging showed that she was in beautiful order. She crossed the line upon which the merchantman was sailing, some two miles in her rear; and then, bearing up, followed in her wake.

Charlie stood near the captain, who, instead of watching her, was sweeping the horizon with his glass. Presently he paused, and gazed intently at a distant object.

'I thought so,' he said to the first officer. 'I fancied that fellow wasn't alone. He would hardly have ventured to try his strength with us, if he had been. Send a man up to the tops, and let him see what he can make her out to be. I can only see her topmasts, but I can make out no yards.'

Presently the lookout came down, and reported that the distant vessel appeared to be a large fore-and-aft schooner, bearing down upon them.

'She will not be up for two hours, yet,' the captain said. 'It will be getting dark, then. It is not likely they will engage at night, but they will keep close, and show their teeth at daybreak.'

It soon became known that the belief of the captain was that the vessel in their wake, and that which could be seen approaching on the beam, were French privateers; and soon all were preparing, in their own way, for what might happen. The sailors cleared the decks, and loosed the guns. The gentlemen went below, and shortly returned bringing up rifles and fowling pieces. Small arms and cutlasses were brought up, and piled round the masts.

'Why don't you put on more sail, sir?' Mr. Ashmead, the member of the council, said to the captain. 'My wife, sir, objects to the sound of firearms, and I must really beg that you will increase your speed. As it is, we are losing rather than gaining upon that vessel behind. The duty of the ships of the Company is to try not to fight.'

'If they can help it,' the captain added quietly. 'Not to fight, if they can help it, Mr. Ashmead. But unfortunately, the choice upon the present occasion lies with the gentlemen yonder, and not with us. It is not of the slightest use adding to the sail we carry, for at our very best speed, those schooners could sail round and round us. As night comes on I intend to shorten sail, and put the ship into fighting trim. In the morning I shall again increase it, but I shall not make any attempt to escape a combat which it depends entirely on those privateers to bring on, or not, as they choose. I am sorry that Mrs. Ashmead should be exposed to the unpleasantness of listening to the explosion of firearms, and that my other lady passengers should be exposed to the danger which cannot but arise, more or less, from a naval conflict.

'However, I hope, sir, that there need be no great anxiety as to the result. The

Company has given us a heavy armament, and you may be sure that we shall all do our best.'

Seeing the gentlemen go below for their guns, Charlie asked one of the other young writers, a lad of about his own age, named Peters, with whom he had become very friendly, to go below with him. He had not yet examined the arms that his uncle had given him, for he had not thought of them since he saw the gun cases under his berth, on his first arrival on board ship. He found the doctor already in his cabin, putting together a heavy double-barrelled gun.

'Well, youngster,' he said, 'so we're likely to have a brush. I see you have a couple of gun cases under your berth. You are a good deal better provided than most lads who go out as writers.

'Ah! That's a beautiful piece of yours,' he said, as Charlie unlocked one of the cases and took out a rifle, 'a small bore and a heavy barrel, and beautifully finished. With a greased patch and a heavy charge, that ought to carry a bullet far and true. Have you had any practice?'

'Not with this gun, sir. I used, sometimes, to practise shooting at gulls with a musket, on board the cutter my father commanded; and I got to be a fair shot with it.'

'Then you ought to be able to do good work, with such a piece as that. What is in the other case?

'Ah! That's a beauty, too,' he said, as he examined the double-barrelled gun. 'Made extra strong and heavy, I see, so as to carry bullets. You'll find your shoulder ache, at first; but you'll get accustomed to it, in time. I'm always in favour of heavy barrels. They shoot stronger and straighter than your light guns, are not so liable to get bent or bruised, if a stupid servant drops one across a stone; and, after all, two or three pounds difference in weight does not make any material difference, when you're accustomed to it. Although, I grant, a heavy gun does not come quite so quickly up to the shoulder, for a snap shot.'

'Now, Peters,' Charlie said, 'you take the double barrel. I will use the rifle. Mine will come into play first, but, as my uncle said when he gave it me, yours will do most execution at close quarters.'

At dusk the schooners, having exchanged some signals by flags, took up their positions, one on each quarter of the ship, at a distance of some two miles.

'Do not you think,' Charlie asked his friend the doctor, 'that they are likely to try and board us tonight?'

'No,' the doctor said. 'These privateers generally depend upon their long guns. They know that we shall be on the watch all night, and that, in a hand-to-hand fight, they would lose a considerable number of men; while by keeping at a distance, and maintaining a fire with their long guns, they rely upon crippling their opponents; and then, ranging up under their stern, pouring in a fire at close quarters until they surrender.

'Another thing is that they prefer daylight, as they can then see whether any other vessel is approaching. Were one of our cruisers to hear a cannonade in the night, she would come down and take them unaware. No, I think you will see that at daylight, if the coast is clear, they will begin.'

Such was evidently the captain's opinion also, as he ordered sail to be still further shortened, and all, save the watch on deck, to turn in at once. The lights were all extinguished, not that the captain had any idea of evading his pursuers, but that he wished to avoid offering them a mark for their fire, should they approach in the darkness.

Chapter 3

A BRUSH WITH PRIVATEERS

The night passed quietly. Once or twice lights were seen, as the schooners showed a lantern for a moment to notify their exact position to each other.

As soon as dawn broke, every man on board the Lizzie Anderson was at his post. The schooners had drawn up a little, but were still under easy sail. The moment that the day grew clear enough for it to be perceived that no other sail could be seen above the horizon, fresh sail was spread upon the schooners, and they began rapidly to draw up.

On the previous evening the four heavy guns had been brought aft, and the Indiaman could have made a long running fight with her opponents, had the captain been disposed. To this, however, he objected strongly, as his vessel was sure to be hulled and knocked about severely, and perhaps some of his masts cut down. He was confident in his power to beat off the two privateers, and he therefore did not add a stitch of canvas to the easy sail under which he had been holding on all night.

Presently a puff of smoke shot out from the bow of the schooner from the weather quarter, followed almost instantaneously by one from her consort. Two round shot struck up the water, the one under the Indiaman's stern, the other under her forefoot.

'The rascals are well within range,' the captain said quietly. 'See, they are taking off canvas again. They intend to keep at that distance, and hammer away at us. Just what I thought would be their tactics.'

Two more shots were fired by the schooners. One flew over the deck between the masts, and plunged harmlessly in the sea beyond. The other struck the hull with a dull crash.

'It is lucky the ladies were sent into the hold,' the captain said. 'That shot has gone right through their cabin.'

'Now, my lads, have you got the sights well upon them? Fire!'

The four thirty-two pounders spoke out almost at the same moment, and all gazed over the bulwarks anxiously to watch the effect, and a cheer arose as it was seen how accurate had been the aim of the gunners. One shot struck the schooner to windward in the bow, a foot or two above the water level. Another went through her foresail, close to the mast.

'A foot more, and you would have cut his foremast asunder.'

The vessel to leeward had been struck by only one shot, the other passing under her stern. She was struck just above her deck line, the shot passing through the bulwark, and, as they thought on board the merchantman, narrowly missing if not actually striking the mainmast.

'There is some damage done,' Dr. Rae said, keeping his glass fixed on the vessel. 'There is a good deal of running about on deck there.'

It was evident that the display of the heavy metal carried by the Indiaman was an unpleasant surprise to the privateers. Both lowered sail and ceased firing, and there was then a rapid exchange of signals between them.

'They don't like it,' the captain said, laughing. 'They see that they cannot play the game they expected, and that they've got to take as well as to give. Now it depends upon the sort of stuff their captains are made of, whether they give it up at once, or come straight up to close quarters.

'Ah! They mean fighting.'

As he spoke, a cloud of canvas was spread upon the schooners and, sailing more than two feet to the merchantman's one, they ran quickly down towards her, firing rapidly as they came. Only the merchantman's heavy guns replied, but these worked steadily and coolly, and did considerable damage. The bowsprit of one of their opponents was shot away. The sails of both vessels were pierced in several places, and several ragged holes were knocked in their hulls.

'If it were not that I do not wish to sacrifice any of the lives on board, unnecessarily,' the captain said, 'I would let them come alongside and try boarding. We have a strong crew, and with the sixty soldiers we should give them such a reception as they do not dream of. However, I will keep them off, if I can.

'Now, Mr. James,' he said to the first officer, 'I propose to give that vessel to leeward a dose. They are keeping about abreast, and by the course they are making will range alongside at about a cable's length. When I give the word, pour a broadside with the guns to port upon that weather schooner.

'At that moment, gentlemen,' he said, turning to the passengers, 'I shall rely upon you to pick off the steersman of the other vessel, and to prevent another taking his place. She steers badly now, and the moment her helm is free, she'll run up into the wind. As she does so, I shall bear off, run across her bow, and rake her deck with grape as we pass.

'Will you, Mr. Barlow, order your men to be in readiness to open fire with musketry upon her, as we pass?'

The schooners were now running rapidly down upon the Indiaman. They were only able to use the guns in their bows, and the fire of the Indiaman from the heavy guns on her quarter was inflicting more damage than she received.

'Let all hands lie down on deck,' the captain ordered. 'They will open with their broadside guns, as they come up. When I give the word, let all the guns on the port side be trained at the foot of her mainmast, and fire as you get the line. On the starboard side, lie down till I give the word.'

It was a pretty sight as the schooners, throwing the water high up from their sharp cut-waters, came running along, heeling over under the breeze. As they ranged alongside, their topsails came down, and a broadside from both was poured into the Indiaman. The great ship shook as the shot crashed into her, and several sharp cries told of the effect which had been produced.

Then the captain gave the word, and a moment afterwards an irregular broadside, as the captain of each gun brought his piece to bear, was poured into the schooner from the guns on the port side. As the privateer heeled over, her deck could be plainly seen, and the shot of the Indiaman, all directed at one point, tore up a hole around the foot of the mainmast. In an instant the spar tottered and, with a crash, fell alongside. At the same moment, three of the passengers took a steady aim over the bulwark at the helmsman of the other privateer and, simultaneously with the reports of their pieces, the man was seen to fall. Another sprang forward to take his place, but again the rifles spoke out, and he fell beside his comrade.

Freed from the strain which had counteracted the pressure of her mainsail, the schooner flew up into the wind. The Indiaman held on her course for another length, and then her helm was put up, and she swept down across the bows of the privateer. Then the men leaped to their feet, the soldiers lined the bulwarks, and as she passed along a few yards only distant from her foe, each gun poured a storm of grape along her crowded deck, while the troops and passengers kept up a continuous fire of musketry.

'That will do,' the captain said, quietly. 'Now we may keep her on her course. They have had more than enough of it.'

There was no doubt of that, for the effect of the iron storm had been terrible, and the decks of the schooner were strewn with dead and dying. For a time after the merchantman had borne upon her course, the sails of the schooner flapped wildly in the wind, and then the foremast went suddenly over the side.

'I should think you could take them both, Captain Thompson,' one of the passengers said.

'They are as good as taken,' the captain answered, 'and would be forced to haul down their flags, if I were to wear round and continue the fight. But they would be worse than useless to me. I should not know what to do with their crews, and should have to cripple myself by putting very strong prize crews upon them, and so run the risk of losing my own ship and cargo.

'No, my business is to trade and not to fight. If any one meddles with me, I am ready to take my own part; but the Company would not thank me, if I were to risk the safety of this ship and her valuable cargo for the sake of sending home a couple of prizes, which might be recaptured as they crossed the bay, and would not fetch any great sum if they got safely in port.'

An examination showed that the casualties on board the Lizzie Anderson amounted to three killed and eight wounded. The former were sewn in hammocks, with a round shot at their feet, and dropped overboard; the clergyman reading the burial service. The wounded were carried below, and attended to by the ship's surgeon and Doctor Rae. The ship's decks were washed, and all traces of the conflict removed. The guns were again lashed in their places, carpenters were lowered over the side to repair damages; and when the ladies came on deck an hour after the conflict was over, two or three ragged holes in the bulwarks, and a half dozen in the sails, were the sole signs that the ship had been in action; save that some miles astern could be seen the two crippled privateers, with all sails lowered, at work to repair damages.

Two or three days afterwards, Charlie Marryat and his friend Peters were sitting beside Doctor Rae, when the latter said:

'I hope that we sha'n't find the French in Madras, when we get there.'

'The French in Madras!' Charlie exclaimed in surprise. 'Why, sir, there's no chance of that, is there?'

'A very great chance,' the doctor said. 'Don't you know that they captured the place three years ago?'

'No, sir; I'm ashamed to say that I know nothing at all about India, except that the Company have trading stations at Bombay, Madras, and Calcutta.'

'I will tell you about it,' the doctor said. 'It is as well that you should understand the position of affairs, at the place to which you are going. You must know that the Company hold the town of Madras, and a few square miles of land around it, as tenants of the Nawab of the Carnatic, which is the name of that part of India. The French have a station at Pondicherry, eighty-six miles to the sou'west of Madras. This is a larger and more important town than Madras, and of course the greatest rivalry prevails between the English and French.

'The French are much more powerful than the English, and exercise a predominating influence throughout the Carnatic. The French governor, Monsieur Dupleix, is a man of very great ability, and far-seeing views. He has a considerable force of French soldiers at his command, and by the aid which he has given to the nawab, upon various occasions, he has obtained a predominating influence in his councils.

'When war was declared between England and France, in the year '44, the English squadron under Commodore Barnet was upon the coast, and the Company sent out orders to Mr. Morse, the governor of Madras, to use every effort to destroy the French settlement, of whose rising power they felt the greatest jealousy. Dupleix, seeing the force that could be brought against him, and having no French ships on the station, although he was aware that a fleet under Admiral La Bourdonnais was fitting out and would arrive shortly, dreaded the contest, and proposed to Mr. Morse that the Indian colonies of the two nations should remain neutral, and take no part in the struggle in which their respective countries were engaged. Mr. Morse, however, in view of the orders he had received from the Company, was unable to agree to this.

'Dupleix then applied to the nawab who, at his request, forbade his European tenants to make war on land with each other, an order which they were obliged to obey.

'In July, 1746, La Bourdonnais arrived with his fleet, and chased the small English squadron from the Indian seas. Dupleix now changed his tactics, and regardless of the injunction which he himself had obtained from the nawab, he determined to crush the English at Madras. He supplied the fleet with men and money, and ordered the admiral to sail for Madras. The fleet arrived before the town on the 14th of September; landed a portion of its troops, six hundred in number, with two guns, a short distance along the coast; and on the following day disembarked the rest, consisting of a thousand French troops, four hundred Sepoys, and three hundred African troops, and summoned Madras to surrender.

'Madras was in no position to offer any effectual resistance. The fort was weak and indefensible. The English inhabitants consisted only of a hundred civilians, and two hundred soldiers. Governor Morse endeavoured to obtain, from the nawab, the protection which he had before granted to Dupleix, a demand which the nawab at once refused.

'I was there at the time, and quite agreed with the governor that it was useless to attempt resistance to the force brought against us. The governor, therefore, surrendered on the 21st. The garrison, and all the civilians in the place not in the service of the Company, were to become prisoners of war; while those in the regular service of the Company were free to depart, engaging only not to carry arms against the French until exchanged. These were the official conditions; but La Bourdonnais, influenced by jealousy of Dupleix, and by the promise of a bribe of forty thousand pounds, made a secret condition with Mr. Morse, by which he bound himself to restore Madras in the future, upon the payment of a large sum of money. This agreement Dupleix, whose heart was set upon the total expulsion of the English, refused to ratify.

'A good many of us considered that, by this breach of the agreement, we were released from our parole not to carry arms against the French; and a dozen or so of us, in various disguises, escaped from Madras and made our way to Fort Saint David, a small English settlement twelve miles south of Pondicherry. I made the journey with a young fellow named Clive, who had come out as a writer about two years before. He was a fine young fellow; as unfitted as you are, I should think, Marryat, for the dull life of a writer, but full of energy and courage.

'At Fort Saint David we found two hundred English soldiers, and a hundred Sepoys, and a number of us, having nothing to do at our own work, volunteered to aid in the defence.

'After Dupleix had conquered Madras, the nawab awoke to the fact of the danger of allowing the French to become all-powerful, by the destruction of the English, and ordered Dupleix to restore the place. Dupleix refused, and the nawab sent his son Maphuz Khan to invest the town. Dupleix at once despatched a detachment of two hundred and thirty French, and seven hundred Sepoys, commanded by an engineer officer named Paradis, to raise the siege.

'On the 2nd of November, the garrison of Madras sallied out and drove away the cavalry of Maphuz Khan; and on the 4th, Paradis attacked his army, and totally defeated it.

'This, lads, was a memorable battle. It is the first time that European and Indian soldiers have come into contest, and it shows how immense is the superiority of Europeans. What Paradis did then opens all sorts of possibilities for the future; and it may be that either we or the French are destined to rise, from mere trading companies, to be rulers of Indian states.

'Such, I know, is the opinion of young Clive, who is a very long-headed and ambitious young fellow. I remember his saying to me one night, when we were, with difficulty, holding our own in the trenches, that if we had but a man of energy and intelligence at the head of our affairs in Southern India, we might, ere many years passed, be masters of the Carnatic. I own that it appears to me more likely that the French will be in that position, and that we shall not have a single establishment left there; but time will show.

'Having defeated Maphuz Khan, Dupleix resolved to make a great effort to expel us from Fort Saint David, our sole footing left in Southern India; and he despatched an army of nine hundred Frenchmen, six hundred Sepoys, and a hundred Africans, with six guns and mortars, against us. They were four to one against us, and we had hot work, I can tell you. Four times they tried to storm the place, and each time we drove them back; till at last they gave it up in disgust, at the end of June, having besieged us for six months.

'Soon after this Admiral Boscawen, with a great fleet and an army, arrived from England; and on 19th of August besieged Pondicherry. The besieging army was six thousand strong; of whom three thousand, seven hundred and twenty were English. But Pondicherry resisted bravely, and after two months the besiegers were forced to retire, having lost, in attacks or by fever, one thousand and sixty-five men.

'At the end of the siege, in which I had served as a medical officer, I returned to England. A few months after I left, peace was made between England and France, and by its terms Dupleix had to restore Madras to the English. I hear that fighting has been going on ever since, the English and French engaging as auxiliaries to rival native princes; and especially that there was some hot fighting round Devikota. However, we shall hear about that when we get there.'

'And what do you think will be the result of it all, Doctor Rae?'

'I think that undoubtedly, sooner or later, either the French or ourselves will be driven out. Which it will be remains to be seen. If we are expelled, the effect of our defeat is likely to operate disastrously at Calcutta, if not at Bombay. The French will be regarded as a powerful people, whom it is necessary to conciliate, while we shall be treated as a nation of whom they need have no fear, and whom they can oppress accordingly.

'If we are successful, and absolutely obtain possession of the Carnatic, our trade will vastly increase, fresh posts and commands of all sorts will be established, and there will be a fine career open to you young fellows, in the service of the Company.'

After rounding the Cape of Good Hope, the ship encountered a series of very heavy gales, which drove her far out of her course up the eastern coast of Africa. In the last gale her foremast was carried away, and she put in to a small island to refit. She had also sprung a leak, and a number of stores were landed, to enable her to be taken up into shallow water and heeled over, in order that the leak might be got at.

The captain hurried on the work with all speed.

'Had it not been for this,' Charlie heard him say to Mr. Ashmead, 'I would have rigged a jury-mast and proceeded; but I can't stop the leak from the inside, without shifting a great portion of the cargo, and our hold is so full that this would be difficult in the extreme. But I own that I do not like delaying a day longer than necessary, here. The natives have a very bad reputation, besides which it is suspected that one, if not more, pirates have their rendezvous in these seas. Several of our merchantmen have mysteriously disappeared, without any gale having taken place which would account for their loss.

'The captain of a ship which reached England, two or three days before we sailed, brought news that when she was within a fortnight's sail of the Cape, the sound of guns was heard one night, and that afterwards a ship was seen on fire, low down on the horizon. He reached the spot soon after daybreak, and found charred spars and other wreckage; but though he cruised about all day, he could find no signs of any boats. Complaints have been made to government, and I hear that there is an intention of sending two or three sloops out here to hunt the pirates up. But that will be of no use to us.'

Upon the day of their arrival at the island, a native sailing boat was seen to pass across the mouth of the bay. When half across, she suddenly tacked round and sailed back in the direction from which she had come.

Before proceeding to lighten the ship, the captain had taken steps to put himself in a position of defence. For some distance along the centre of the bay the ground rose abruptly, at a distance of some thirty yards from the shore, forming a sort of natural terrace. Behind this a steep hill rose. The terrace, which was forty feet above the water level, extended for about a hundred yards, when the ground on either side of the plateau dropped away, as steeply as in front.

The guns were the first things taken out of the ship, and, regardless of the remonstrances of the passengers at what they considered to be a waste of time, Captain Thompson had the whole of them taken up on the terrace. A small battery was thrown up by the sailors, at the two corners, and in each of these two of the thirty-two pounders were placed. The broadside guns were ranged in line along the centre of the terrace.

'Now,' the captain said when, at the end of the second day, the preparations were completed by the transport of a quantity of ammunition from the ship's magazine to the terrace, 'I feel comfortable. We can defend ourselves here against all the pirates of the South Seas. If they don't come, we shall only have lost our two days' work, and shall have easy minds for the remainder of our stay here; which we should not have had, if we had been at the mercy of the first of those scoundrels who happened to hear of our being laid up.'

The next morning the work of unloading the ship began, the bales and packages being lowered from the ship, as they were brought up from the hold, into boats alongside; and then taken to the shore, and piled there at the foot of the slope. This occupied three days, and at the end of that time the greater portion of the cargo had been removed. The ship, now several feet lighter in the water than before, was brought broadside to shore until her keel touched the ground. Then the remaining cargo was shifted, and by the additional aid of tackle and purchases on shore fastened to her masts, she was heeled over until her keel nearly reached the level of the water.

It was late one evening when this work was finished, and the following morning the crew were to begin to scrape her bottom, and the carpenters were to repair the leak, and the whole of the seams underwater were to be corked and repitched. Hitherto all had remained on board; but previous to the ship being heeled over, tents constructed of the sails were erected on the terrace, beds and other articles of necessity landed, and the passengers, troops, and crew took up their temporary abode there.

Chapter 4

THE PIRATES OF THE PACIFIC

A regular watch was set, both on the plateau and on board ship. Towards morning, one of the watch on board hailed the officer above:

'I have fancied, sir, for some time, that I heard noises. It seems to me like the splash of a very large number of oars.'

'I have heard nothing,' the officer said; 'but you might hear sounds down there, coming along on the water, before I do. I will go down to the water's edge, and listen.'

He did so, and was at once convinced that the man's ears had not deceived him. Although the night was perfectly still, and not a breath of wind was stirring, he heard a low rustling sound, like that of the wind passing through the dried leaves of a forest, in autumn.

'You are right, Johnson, there is something going on out at sea, beyond the mouth of the bay. I will call the captain, at once.'

Captain Thompson, on being aroused, also went down to the waterside to listen; and at once ordered the whole party to get under arms. He requested Mr. Barlow, the young lieutenant in charge of the troops, to place half his men across each end of the plateau. The back was defended by a cliff, which rose almost perpendicularly from it to a height of some hundred feet; the plateau being some thirty yards, in depth, from the sea face to its foot. The male passengers were requested to divide themselves into two parties, and to join the soldiers in defending the position against flank attacks. The guns were all loaded, and the sailors then set to work dragging up bales of goods from below, and placing them so as to form a sort of breastwork before the guns along the sea face.

The noise at sea had, by this time, greatly increased; and although it was still too dark to see what was passing, Captain Thompson said that he had no doubt, whatever, that the boats had one or more large ships in tow.

'Had it not been for that,' he said, 'they would long ago have been here. I expect that they hoped to catch us napping, but the wind fell and delayed them. They little dream how well we are prepared. Did they know of our fort here, I question whether they would have ventured upon attacking us at all, but would have waited till we were well at sea, and then our chance would have been a slight one.

'Well, gentlemen, you will allow that the two days were not wasted. I think, now, the pirates are well inside the bay. In half an hour we shall have light enough to see them.

'There, listen! There's the splash of their anchors. There, again! I fancy there are two ships moored broadside on, stem and stern.'

All this time, the work on shore had been conducted in absolute silence, and the pirates could have had no intimation that their presence was discovered. Presently, against the faintly dawning light in the east, the masts of two vessels could be seen. One was a large ship, the other a brig. Almost at the same time the rough sound of boats' keels grounding on the shore could be heard.

'Just as I thought,' the captain whispered. 'They have guessed that some of us will be ashore, and will make a rush upon us here, when the ships open fire.'

The word was passed along the guns that every one was to be double shotted, and that their fire was at first to be directed at the brig. They were to aim between wind and water, and strive to sink her as speedily as possible.

As the light gradually grew brighter, the party on the plateau anxiously watched for the moment when the hull of the Indiaman became plain to the enemy. These would open fire upon it, and so give the signal for the fight. At the first alarm the tents had all been levelled; and a thick barricade of bales erected, round a slight depression of the plateau at the foot of the cliff in its rear. Here the ladies were placed, for shelter.

As the light increased, it could be seen that in addition to the two ships were a large number of native dhows. Presently, from the black side of the ship, a jet of fire shot out; and at the signal a broadside was poured into the Indiaman by the two vessels. At the same moment, with a hideous yell, hundreds of black figures leaped to their feet on the beach, and rushed towards the, as yet, unseen position of the English.

The captain shouted 'Fire!' and the twenty guns on the plateau poured their fire simultaneously into the side of the brig. The captain then gave orders that two of the light guns should be run along the terrace, to take position on the flanks, and aid the soldiers against the attacks.

This time Charlie had lent his rifle to Peters, and was himself armed with his double-barrel gun.

'Steady, boys,' Mr. Hallam, the ensign who commanded the soldiers at the side where Charlie was stationed, cried; 'don't fire a shot till I give the word, and then aim low.'

With terrific yells the throng of natives, waving curved swords, spears, and clubs, rushed forward. The steep ascent checked them, but they rushed up until within ten yards of the line of soldiers on its brow. Then Mr. Hallam gave the word to fire, and the soldiers and passengers poured a withering volley into them.

At so short a distance, the effect was tremendous. Completely swept away, the leading rank fell down among their comrades; and these, for a moment, recoiled. Then gathering themselves together they again rushed forward, while those in their rear discharged volleys of arrows over their heads.

Among the defenders, every man now fought for himself, loading and firing as rapidly as possible. Sometimes the natives nearly gained a footing on the crest; but each time the defenders, with clubbed muskets, beat them back again.

The combat was, however, doubtful, for their assailants were many hundred strong; when the defenders were gladdened with a shout of 'Make way, my hearties. Let us come to the front, and give them a dose.' In a moment two ship's guns, loaded to the muzzle with bullets, were run forward, and poured their contents among the crowded masses below.

The effect was decisive. The natives, shaken by the resistance they had already experienced, and appalled by the destruction wrought by the cannon, turned and fled along the shore, followed by the shots of the defenders, and by two more rounds of grape, which the sailors poured into them before they could reach their boats.

Similar success had attended the defenders of the other flank of the position, and all hands now aided in swinging round the guns, which had done such good service, to enable them to bear their share in the fight with the ships. In the middle of the fight, the party had heard a great cheer from those working the seaward guns, and they now saw its cause. The brig had disappeared below the water, and the sailors were now engaged in a contest with the ship.

The pirates fought their guns well, but they were altogether over matched by the twenty guns playing upon them from a commanding position. Already the dhows were hoisting their sails, and one of the cables of the ship suddenly disappeared in the water, while a number of men sprang upon the ratlines.

'Fire at the masts,' Captain Thompson shouted. 'Cripple her if you can. Let all with muskets and rifles try to keep men out of the rigging.'

The ship was anchored within three hundred yards of the shore, and although the distance was too great for anything like accurate fire, several of the men dropped as they ran up the shroud. The sailors worked their guns with redoubled vigour, and a great shout arose as the mainmast, wounded in several places, fell over the side.

'Sweep her decks with grape,' the captain shouted, 'and she's ours.

'Mr. James, take all the men that can be spared from the guns, man the boats, and make a dash for the ship at once. I see the men are leaving her. They're crowding over the side into their boats. Most likely they'll set fire to her. Set all your strength putting it out. We will attend to the other boats.'

It was evident, now, that the pirates were deserting the ship. They had fallen into a complete trap, and instead of the easy prey on which they calculated, found themselves crushed by the fire of a heavy battery in a commanding position. Captain Thompson, seeing that the guns of the ship were silent, and that all resistance had ceased, now ordered the sailors to turn their guns on the dhows and sink as many as possible. These, crowded together in their efforts to escape, offered an easy mark for the gunners, whose shot tore through their sides, smashing and sinking them in all directions.

In ten minutes the last of those that floated had gained the mouth of the bay and, accompanied by the boats, crowded with the crews of the two pirate vessels, made off; followed by the shot of the thirty-two pounders, until they had turned the low promontory which formed the head of the bay. Long ere this Mr. James and the boats' crews had gained the vessel, and were engaged in combating the fire, which had broken out in three places.

The boats were sent back to shore, and returned with Captain Thompson and the rest of the sailors, and this reinforcement soon enabled them to get the mastery of the flames. The ship was found to be the Dover Castle, a new and very fast ship of the Company's service, of which all traces had been lost since she left Bombay two years before. She was now painted entirely black, and a snake had been added for her figurehead. The original name, however, still remained upon the binnacle and ship's bell. Her former armament had been increased and she now carried thirty guns, of which ten were thirty-two pounders.

A subsequent search showed that her hold was stored with valuable goods; which had, by the marks upon the bales, evidently belonged to several ships; which she had, no doubt, taken and sunk after removing the pick of their cargoes. The prize was a most valuable one, and the captain felt that the board of directors would be highly delighted at the recovery of their ship, and still more by the destruction of the two bands of pirates.

The deck of the ship was thickly strewn with dead. Among them was the body of a man who, by his dress, was evidently the captain. From some of the pirates who still lived, Captain Thompson learned that the brig was the original pirate, that she had captured the Dover Castle, that from her and subsequent prizes they had obtained sufficient hands to man both ships, all who refused to join being compelled to walk the plank. These were the only two pirate ships in those seas, so far as the men knew. Their rendezvous was at a large native town on the mainland, at the mouth of a river three days' sail distant.

The news of the Indiaman being laid up, refitting at the island, was brought by the native craft they had seen on the day after their arrival; and upon its being known, the natives had insisted in joining in the attack. The pirate captain, whose interest it was to keep well with them, could not refuse to allow them to join, although he would gladly have dispensed with their aid, believing his own force to be far more than sufficient to capture the vessel, which he supposed to be lying an easy prize at his hands.

Another ten days were spent in getting the cargo and guns on board the Lizzie Anderson, and in fitting out both ships for sea. Then, Mr. James and a portion of the crew being placed on board the prize, they sailed together for India. The Dover Castle proved to be much the faster sailer, but Captain Thompson ordered her to reduce sail, and to keep about a mile in his wake, as she could at any time close up when necessary; and the two, together, would be able to oppose a determined front, even to a French frigate, should they meet with one on their way.

The voyage passed without incident save that, when rounding the southern point of Ceylon, a sudden squall from the land struck them. The vessel heeled over suddenly, and a young soldier, who was sitting on the bulwarks to leeward, was jerked backwards and fell into the water.

Charlie Marryat was on the quarterdeck, leaning against the rail, watching a shoal of flying fish passing at a short distance. In the noise and confusion, caused by the sudden squall, the creaking of cordage, the flapping of sails, and the shouts of the officer to let go the sheets, the fall of the soldier was unnoticed; and Charlie was startled by perceiving, in the water below him, the figure of a struggling man.

He saw, at once, that he was unable to swim. Without an instant's hesitation Charlie threw off his coat, and kicked off his shoes, and with a loud shout of 'Man overboard!' sprang from the taffrail and, with a few vigorous strokes, was alongside the drowning man. He seized him by the collar, and held him at a distance.

'Now,' he said, 'don't struggle, else I'll let you go. Keep quiet, and I can hold you up till we're picked up.'

In spite of the injunction, the man strove to grasp him; but Charlie at once let go his hold, and swam a pace back as the man sunk. When he came up he seized him again, and again shouted:

'Keep quite quiet, else I'll leave go.'

This time the soldier obeyed him and, turning him on his back, and keeping his face above water, Charlie looked around at the vessel he had left.

The Indiaman was still in confusion. The squall had been sudden and strong. The sheets had been let go, the canvas was flapping in the wind, and the hands were aloft reducing sail. She was already some distance away from him. The sky was bright and clear, and Charlie, who was surprised at seeing no attempt to lower a boat, saw a signal run up to the masthead.

Looking the other way, he saw at once why no boat had been lowered. The Dover Castle was but a quarter of a mile astern. Carrying less sail than her consort, she had been better prepared for the squall, and was running down upon him at a great rate.

A moment later a boat was swung out on davits, and several men climbed into it. The vessel kept on her course, until scarcely more than her own length away. Then she suddenly rounded up into the wind, and the boat was let fall, and rowed rapidly towards him.

All this time, Charlie had made no effort beyond what was necessary to keep his own head, and his companion's face, above the water. He now lifted the soldier's head up, and shouted to him that aid was at hand. In another minute they were dragged into the boat. This was soon alongside the ship, and three minutes later the Dover Castle was pursuing her course, in the track of the Lizzie Anderson, having signalled that the pair had been rescued.

Charlie found that the soldier was an Irish lad, of some nineteen years old. His name, he said, was Tim Kelly, and as soon as he had recovered himself sufficiently to speak, he was profuse in his professions of gratitude to his preserver. Tim, like the majority of the recruits in the Company's service, had been enlisted while in a state of drunkenness; had been hurried on board a guard ship, where, when he recovered, he found a number of other unfortunates like himself. He had not been permitted to communicate with his friends on shore, but had been kept in close confinement, until he had been put in uniform and conveyed on board the Lizzie Anderson, half an hour before she sailed.

The Company's service was not a popular one. There was no fighting in India, and neither honor, glory, nor promotion to be won. The climate was unsuited to Europeans, and few, indeed, of those who sailed from England as soldiers in the Company's service ever returned. The Company, then, were driven to all sorts of straits to keep up even the small force which they then maintained in India, and their recruiting agents were, by no means, particular as to the means they employed to make up the tale of recruits.

The vessels did not again communicate until they came to anchor in Madras roads, as the wind was fair and Captain Thompson anxious to arrive at his destination. During these few days, Tim Kelly had followed Charlie about like a shadow. Having no duties to perform on board, he asked leave to act as Charlie's servant; and Charlie was touched by the efforts which the grateful fellow made to be of service to him.

Upon their arrival they saw, to their satisfaction, that the British flag was waving over the low line of earthworks, which constitute the British fort. Not far from this, near the water's edge, stood the white houses and stores of the Company's factors; and behind these, again, were the low hovels of the black town. The prospect was not an inviting one, and Charlie wondered how on earth a landing was to be effected, through the tremendous surf which broke upon the shore.

He soon found that, until the wind went down and the surf moderated somewhat, no communication could be effected. The next morning, however, the wind lulled, and a crowd of curious native boats were seen putting off from the shore.

Charlie had, after the vessel anchored, rejoined his ship with Tim Kelly, and he now bade goodbye to all on board; for only the doctor, two civilians, and the troops were destined for Madras; all the rest going on in the ship to Calcutta, after she had discharged that portion of her cargo intended for Madras. Charlie had, during the last twelve hours, been made a great deal of, on account of the gallantry he had displayed in risking his life for that of the soldier. Peters and one of the other young writers were also to land; and, taking his seat with these in a native boat, paddled by twelve canoe men, he started for the shore.

As they approached the line of surf, Charlie fairly held his breath; for it seemed impossible that the boat could live through it. The boatmen, however, ceased rowing outside the line of broken water, and lay on their paddles for three or four minutes.

At last a wave, larger than any of its predecessors, was seen approaching. As it passed under them, the steersman gave a shout. In an instant the rowers struck their paddles into the water, and the boat dashed along, with the speed of a racehorse, on the crest of the wave. There was a crash. For a moment the boat seemed, to the lads, engulfed in white foam; and then she ran high up upon the beach. The rowers seized the boys and, leaping out, carried them beyond the reach of the water, before the next wave broke upon them; and then triumphantly demanded a present, for their skilful management. This the lads were glad to give, for they considered that their escape had been something miraculous.

For a while they stood on the shore, watching other boats, with the soldiers and baggage, coming ashore; and then, being accosted by a gentleman in the employment of the Company, followed him to the residence of the chief factor. Here they were told that rooms would be given them, in one of the houses erected by the Company for the use of its employees; that they would mess with the other clerks residing in the same house; and that, at nine o'clock in the morning, they would report themselves as ready for work.

Charlie and his friends amused themselves by sauntering about in the native town, greatly surprised by the sights and scenes which met their eyes; for in those days very little was known of India, in England. They were, however, greatly disappointed. Visions of oriental splendour, of palaces and temples, of superbly dressed chiefs with bands of gorgeous retainers, had floated before their mind's eye. Instead of this they saw squalid huts, men dressed merely with a rag of cotton around them, everywhere signs of squalor and poverty.

Madras, however, they were told that evening, was not to be taken as a sample of India. It was a mere collection of huts, which had sprung up round the English factories. But when they went to a real Indian city, they would see a very different state of things.

Chapter 5

MADRAS

After the young writers had seen the native town, they returned to the beach, and spent the afternoon watching the progress of landing the cargo of the Lizzie Anderson. They were pleased to see their own luggage safely ashore; as it would have been greatly damaged, had the boat containing it been swamped; a misfortune which happened to several of the boats laden with cargo. It was very amusing, each time that one of these boats arrived, to see a crowd of natives rush down into the water, waist deep, seize it, and drag it up beyond the next wave. Many of them would be knocked down, and some swept out by the retreating wave, only to return on the next roller. All could swim like fish, and any of these events were greeted with shouts of laughter by the rest.

When the packages were landed a rope was put round them, and through this a long bamboo pole was inserted, which would be lifted on to the shoulders of two, four, or six porters, according to its weight; and these would go off, at a hobbling sort of trot, with their burden to the factory.

Their own baggage was taken up to the quarters allotted to them, and at the hour named for dinner the newcomers met, for the first time, those with whom they were to be associated. All were dressed in white suits, and Charlie was struck with the pallor of their faces, and the listless air of most of them. The gentleman to whom they had first been introduced made them acquainted with the others.

'How refreshingly healthy and well you look!' a young man of some six and twenty years old, named Johnson, said. 'I was something like that, when I first came out here, though you'd hardly think it now. Eight years of stewing, in this horrible hole, takes the life and spirits out of anyone.

'However, there's one consolation. After eight or ten years of quill driving in a stuffy room, one becomes a little more one's own master, and one's duties begin to be a little more varied and pleasant. One gets a chance of being sent up, occasionally, with goods; or on some message or other to one of the native princes, and then one gets treated like a prince, and sees that India is not necessarily so detestable as we have contrived to make it here. The only bearable time of one's life is the few hours after dinner, when one can sit in a chair in the veranda, and smoke and look at the sea. Some of the fellows play billiards and cards; but if you will take my advice, you won't go in for that sort of thing. It takes a lot out of one, and fellows that do it are, between you and me, in the bad books of the bigwigs. Besides, they lose money, get into debt, and all sorts of mischief comes of it.'

The speaker was sitting between Charlie and Peters, and was talking in a tone of voice which would not be overheard by the others.

'Thank you,' Charlie said. 'I, for one, will certainly take your advice. I suppose one can buy ponies here. I should think a good ride every morning early, before work, would do one good.'

'Yes, it is not a bad thing,' Johnson said. 'A good many fellows do it, when they first come out here. But after a time they lose their energy, you see, though some do keep it up.

'What appetites you fellows have! It does one good to see you eat.'

'I have not the least idea what we are eating,' Charlie said, laughing; 'but it's really very nice, whatever it is. But there seems an immense quantity of pepper, or hot stuff of some kind or other; which one would have thought, in this tremendous heat, would have made one hotter instead of cooler.'

'Yes,' their new friend answered. 'No doubt all this pepper and curry do heat the blood; but you see, it is done to tempt the appetite. Meat here is fearfully coarse and tasteless. Our appetites are poor, and were it not for these hot sauces, we should eat next to nothing.

'Will you have some bananas?'

'They are nice and cool,' Peters said as, having peeled the long fruit as he saw his companion doing, he took a bite of one; 'but they have very little taste.'

'Most of our fruit is tasteless,' Johnson said, 'except, indeed, the mango and mangostine. They are equal to any English fruit in flavour, but I would give them all for a good English apple. Its sharpness would be delicious here.

'And now, as you have done, if you will come and sit in the veranda of my room, we will smoke a cigar and have something cool to drink; and I will answer, as well as I can, the questions you've asked me about the state of things here.'

When they had seated themselves in the extremely comfortable cane chairs, in a veranda facing the sea, and had lit their cigars, their friend began:

'Madras isn't much of a place, now; but you should have seen it before the French had it. Our chiefs think of nothing but trade, and care nothing how squalid and miserable is the place in which they make money. The French have larger ideas. They transformed this place; cleared away that portion of the native town which surrounded the factory and fort, made wide roads, formed an esplanade, improved and strengthened the fortifications, forbade the natives to throw all their rubbish and offal on the beach; and made, in fact, a decent place of it. We hardly knew it when we came back, and whatever the Company may have thought, we were thoroughly grateful for the French occupation.

'One good result, too, is that our quarters have been greatly improved; for not only did the French build several new houses, but at present all the big men, the council and so on, are still living at Fort Saint David, which is still the seat of administration. So you see, we have got better quarters; we are rid of the stenches and nuisances of the native town; the plague of flies which made our life a burden is abated; and we can sit here and enjoy the cool sea breeze, without its being poisoned before it reaches us by the heaped up filth on the beach.

'It must have wrung Dupleix's heart to give up the place over which they expended so much pains, and after all it didn't do away with the fighting. In April we sent a force from Fort Saint David – before we came back here – four hundred and thirty white soldiers and a thousand Sepoys, under the command of Captain Cope, to aid a fellow who had been turned out of the Rajahship of Tanjore. I believe he was a great blackguard, and the man who had taken his place was an able ruler liked by the people.'

'Then why should we interfere on behalf of the other?' Charlie asked.

'My dear Marryat,' their host said compassionately, 'you are very young yet, and quite new to India. You will see, after a time, that right has nothing at all to do with the dealings of the Company, in their relations to the native princes. We are, at present, little people living here on sufferance, among a lot of princes and powers who are enemies and rivals of each other. We have, moreover, as neighbours, another European colony considerably stronger than we are. The consequence is, the question of right cannot enter into the considerations of the Company. It may be said that, for every petty kingdom in Southern India, there are at least two pretenders, very often half a dozen. So far we have not meddled much in their quarrels, but the French have been much more active that way. They always side with one or other of these pretenders, and when they get the man they support into power, of course he repays them for their assistance. In this manner, as I shall explain to you presently, they have virtually made themselves masters of the Carnatic, outside the walls of Fort Saint David and this place.

'Well, our people thought to take a leaf out of the French book, and as the ex-rajah offered us, in payment for our aid, the possession of Devikota, a town at the mouth of the river Kolrun, a place likely to be of great use to us, we agreed to assist him. Cope, with the land forces, had marched to the border of the Tanjore territory, and the guns and heavy baggage were to go by sea.

'But, unfortunately, we had a tremendous gale just after they sailed. The admiral's flagship, the Namur, of seventy-four guns; the Pembroke, of sixty; and the hospital ship, Apollo, were totally lost; and the rest of the fleet scattered in all directions. Cope entered the Tanjore territory, but found the whole population attached to the new rajah. It was useless for him, therefore, to march upon Tanjore, which is a really strong town, so he marched down to Devikota, where he hoped to find some of the fleet. Not a ship, however, was to be seen, and as without guns Cope could do nothing, he returned here, as we had just taken possession again.

'Then he went to Fort Saint David, and there was a great discussion among the bigwigs. It was clear, from what Cope said, that our man had not a friend in his own country. Still, as he pointed out, Devikota was a most important place for us. Neither Madras nor Fort Saint David has a harbour; and Devikota, therefore, where the largest ships could run up the river and anchor, would be of immense utility to us.

'As this was really the reason for which we had gone into the affair, it was decided to repeat the attempt. By this time Major Lawrence, who commands the whole of the Company's forces in India, and who had been taken a prisoner in one of the French sorties at the siege of Pondicherry, had been released. So he was put at the head of the expedition; and the whole of the Company's English troops, eight hundred in all, including the artillery; and fifteen hundred Sepoys, started on board ship for Devikota. I must tell you that Lawrence is a first-rate fellow, the only really good officer we have out here, and the affair couldn't have been in the hands of a better man.

'The ships arrived safely at the mouth of the Kolrun, and the troops were landed on the bank of the river opposite the town, where Lawrence intended to erect his batteries; as, in the first place, the shore behind the town was swampy, and in the second the Rajah of Tanjore, who had got news of our coming, had his army encamped there to support the place. Lawrence got his guns in position and fired away, across the river, at the earthen wall of the town. In three days he had a breach. The enemy didn't return our fire, but occupied themselves in throwing up an entrenchment across the side of the fort.

'We made a raft and crossed the river, but the enemy's matchlock men peppered us so severely that we lost thirty English and fifty Sepoys in getting over. The enemy's entrenchment was not finished, but in front of it was a deep rivulet, which had to be crossed.

'Lawrence gave the command of the storming party to Clive. He is one of our fellows; a queer, restless sort of chap, who was really no good here, for he hated his work and always seemed to think himself a martyr. He was not a favourite among us, for he was often gloomy and discontented, though he had his good points. He was straightforward and manly, and he put down two or three fellows here, who had been given to bully the young ones, in a way that astonished them.

'He would never have made a good servant of the Company, for he so hated his work that, when he had been out here about a year, he tried to blow out his brains. He snapped the pistol twice at his head, but it didn't go off, though it was loaded all right. Strange, wasn't it? So he came to the conclusion that he wasn't meant to kill himself, and went on living till something should turn up.'

'Yes,' Charlie said; 'Doctor Rae spoke to us about him during the voyage. He knew him at the siege of Fort Saint David, and Pondicherry.'

'Yes,' Johnson said. 'He came out there quite in a new light. He got transferred into the military service, and was always in the middle of the fighting. Major Lawrence had a very high opinion of him, and so selected him to lead the storming party. It really seems almost as if he had a charmed life. Lawrence gave him thirty-three English soldiers, and seven hundred Sepoys. The rest of the force were to follow as soon as Clive's party gained the entrenchments. Clive led the way with his Europeans, with the Sepoys supporting behind, and got across the rivulet with a loss of only four men. He waited on the other bank till he saw the Sepoys climbing up, and then again led the English on in advance towards the unfinished part of the entrenchment.

'The Sepoys, however, did not move, but remained waiting for the main body to come up. The enemy let Clive and his twenty-nine men get on some distance in advance, and then their cavalry, who had been hidden by a projection of the fort, charged suddenly down on him. They were upon our men before they had time to form, and in a minute twenty-six of them were cut to pieces. Clive and the other three managed to get through the Tanjore horsemen and rejoin the Sepoys. That was almost as narrow a shave for his life as with the pistol.

'Lawrence now crossed with his main body and advanced. Again the Tanjore horsemen charged; but this time we were prepared, and Lawrence let them come on till within a few yards, and then gave them a volley which killed fourteen and sent the rest scampering away. Lawrence pushed forward. The garrison, panic stricken at the defeat of their cavalry, abandoned the breach and escaped to the opposite side of the town, and Devikota was ours.

'A few days later we captured the fortified temple of Uchipuran. A hundred men were left there, and these were afterwards attacked by the Rajah of Tanjore, with five thousand men; but they held their own, and beat them off. A very gallant business, that!

'These affairs showed the rajah that the English could fight; a point which, hitherto, the natives had been somewhat sceptical about. They were afraid of the French, but they looked upon us as mere traders. He had, too, other things to trouble him as to the state of the Carnatic, and so hastened to make peace. He agreed to pay the expenses of the war, and to cede us Devikota and some territory round it; and to allow the wretched ex-rajah, in whose cause we had pretended to fight, a pension of four hundred a year, on condition that we kept him shut up in one of our forts.

'Not a very nice business on our side, was it? Still, we had gained our point, and, with the exception of the ex-rajah, who was a bad lot after all, no one was discontented.

'When the peace was signed, our force returned to Fort Saint David. While they had been away, there had been a revolution in the Carnatic. Now this was rather a complicated business; but as the whole situation at present turns upon it; and it will, not improbably, cause our expulsion from Southern India; I will explain it to you as well as I can.

'Now you must know that all Southern India, with the exception of a strip along the west coast, is governed by a viceroy, appointed by the emperor at Delhi. He was called the Subadar of the Deccan. Up till the end of 'forty-eight, Nizam Ul-Mulk was viceroy. About that time he died, and the emperor appointed his grandson, Muzaffar Jung, who was the son of a daughter of his, to succeed him. But the subadar had left five sons. Four of these lived at Delhi, and were content to enjoy their life there. The second son, however, Nazir Jung, was an ambitious man, who had rebelled even against his father. Naturally, he rebelled against his nephew.

'He was on the spot when his father died, while the new subadar was absent. Nazir, therefore, seized the reins of government, and all the resources of the state. The emperor has troubles enough of his own at Delhi, and Muzaffar had no hope of aid from him. He therefore went to Satarah, the court of the Mahrattas, to ask for their assistance.

'There he met Chunda Sahib. This man was the nephew of the last nawab of the

Carnatic, Dost Ali. Dost Ali had been killed in a battle with them, in 1739; and they afterwards captured Trichinopoli, and took Chunda Sahib, who commanded there, prisoner; and had since kept him at Satarah. Had he been at liberty he would, no doubt, have succeeded his uncle, whose only son had been murdered; but as he was at Satarah, the Subadar of the Deccan bestowed the government of the Carnatic upon Anwarud-din.

'Chunda Sahib and Muzaffar Jung put their heads together, and agreed to act in concert. Muzaffar, of course, desired the subadarship of the Deccan, to which he had been appointed by the court of Delhi. Chunda Sahib wanted the nawabship of the Carnatic, and advised his ally to abandon his intention of asking for Mahratta aid, and to ally himself with the French. A correspondence ensued with Dupleix, who, seeing the immense advantage it would be to him to gain what would virtually be the position of patron and protector of the Subadar of the Deccan, and the Nawab of the Carnatic, at once agreed to join them.

'Muzaffar raised thirty thousand men, and Chunda Sahib six thousand – it is always easy, in India, to raise an army; with a certain amount of money, and lavish promises – marched down and joined a French force of four hundred strong, commanded by D'Auteuil.

'The nawab advanced against them, but was utterly defeated at Ambur, the French doing pretty well the whole of the work. The nawab was killed, and one of his sons, Maphuz Khan, taken prisoner. The other, Muhammud Ali, bolted at the beginning of the fight. Arcot, the capital of the Carnatic, surrendered next day.

'Muzaffar Jung proclaimed himself Subadar of the Deccan, and appointed Chunda Sahib Nawab of the Carnatic. Muzaffar Jung conferred upon Dupleix the sovereignty of eighty-one villages adjoining the French territory. Muzaffar, after paying a visit to Pondicherry, remained in the camp with his army, twenty miles distant from that place. Chunda Sahib remained, as the guest of Dupleix, at Pondicherry.

'On the receipt of the news of the battle of Ambur, Mr. Floyer, who is governor at Fort Saint David, sent at once to Chunda Sahib to acknowledge him as nawab; which, in the opinion of everyone here, was a very foolish step. Muhammud Ali had fled to Trichinopoli, and sent word to Mr. Floyer that he could hold the place, and even reconquer the Carnatic, if the English would assist him. I know that Admiral Boscawen, who was with the fleet at Fort Saint David, urged Mr. Floyer to do so, as it was clear that Chunda Sahib would be a mere tool in the hands of the French.

'When Chunda Sahib delayed week after week at Pondicherry, Mr. Floyer began to hesitate, but he could not make up his mind, and Admiral Boscawen, who had received orders to return home, could no longer act in contravention to them, and was obliged to sail.

'The instant the fleet had left, and we remained virtually defenceless, Chunda Sahib, supplied with troops and money by Dupleix, marched out from Pondicherry and joined Muzaffar Jung, with the avowed intention of marching upon Trichinopoli. Had he done this at once, he must have taken the place, and it was a question of weeks and days only of our being turned altogether out of Southern India. Nothing, indeed, could have saved us.

'Muzaffar Jung and Chunda Sahib, however, disregarding the plan which Dupleix had marked out for them, resolved, before marching on Trichinopoli, to conquer Tanjore, which is the richest city in Southern India. The rajah had, only a few weeks before, made peace with us; and he now sent messengers to Nazir Jung, Muzaffar's rival in the Deccan, and to the English, imploring their assistance. Both parties resolved at once to grant it, for alone both must have been overwhelmed by the alliance between the two Indian princes and the French; and their only hope of a successful resistance to this combination was in saving Trichinopoli.

'The march of these allies upon Tanjore opened the road to Trichinopoli; and Captain Cope, with a hundred and twenty men, were at once despatched to reinforce Muhammud Ali's garrison. Of this little force, he sent off twenty men to the aid of the Rajah of Tanjore, and these, under cover of the night, passed through the lines of the besiegers and into the city, which was strongly fortified and able to stand a long siege.

'The English at once entered into a treaty with Nazir Jung, promising him six hundred English troops; to assist him in maintaining his sovereignty of the Deccan, and in aiding to place Muhammud Ali in the nawabship of the Carnatic.

'Tanjore held out bravely. For some weeks the rajah had thrown dust in the eyes of

Chunda Sahib, by pretending to negotiate. Then, when the allies attacked, he defended the city for fifty-two days, at the end of which one of the gates of the town had been captured, and the city was virtually at the mercy of the besiegers. He again delayed them by entering into negotiations for surrender. In vain Dupleix continued to urge Chunda Sahib to act energetically, and to enter Tanjore.

'Chunda Sahib, however, although he has a good head for planning, is irresolute in action. His troops were discontented at the want of pay. The French contingent also was demoralized, from the same cause. The troops feared to engage in a desperate struggle, in the streets of a town abounding with palaces, each of which was virtually a fortress; especially as it was known that Nazir Jung was marching, with all speed, to fall upon their rear. So at last the siege was broken up, and the army fell back upon Pondicherry.

'Meanwhile Cope's detachment of a hundred men, with six thousand native horsemen, escorted Muhammud Ali to join Nazir Jung at Valdaur, fifteen miles from Pondicherry. Lawrence was busy at work at Fort Saint David, organizing a force to go to his aid. Dupleix saw that it was necessary to aid his allies energetically. The army, on its return from the siege of Tanjore, was reorganized; the French contingent increased to two thousand men; and a supply of money furnished, from his private means.

'The army set out to attack Nazir Jung and his ally at Valdaur. When the battle began, however, the French contingent mutinied and refused to fight; and the natives, panic stricken by the desertion of their allies, fell back on Pondicherry. Chunda Sahib accompanied his men. Muzaffar Jung surrendered to his uncle, the usurper.

'In three or four days the discipline of the French army was restored, and on the 13th of April it attacked and defeated a detachment of Nazir Jung's army; and a few days later captured the strong temple of Tiruvadi, sixteen miles from Fort Saint David.

'Some months passed before the French were completely prepared; but on September the first, D'Auteuil, who commanded the French, and Chunda Sahib attacked the army of the native princes, twenty thousand strong, and defeated it utterly, the French not losing a single man. Muhammud Ali, with only two attendants, fled to Arcot, and the victory rendered Chunda Sahib virtual master of the Carnatic.

'Muzaffar Jung, after his surrender to his uncle, had been loaded with chains, and remained a prisoner in the camp; where, however, he managed to win over several of the leaders of his uncle's army. Gingee was stormed by a small French force, and the French officer there entered into a correspondence with the conspirators, and it was arranged that, when the French army attacked Nazir Jung, these should declare against him.

'On the 15th December the French commander, with eight hundred Europeans, three thousand Sepoys, and ten guns, marched against Nazir Jung, whose army of twenty-five thousand men opposed him. These, however, he defeated easily. While the battle was going on, the conspirators murdered Nazir Jung, released Muzaffar Jung, and saluted him as subadar. His escape was a fortunate one, for his uncle had ordered him to be executed that very day.

'Muzaffar Jung proceeded to Pondicherry, where he was received with great honors. He nominated Dupleix Nawab of the Carnatic and neighbouring countries, with Chunda Sahib as his deputy, conferred the highest dignities upon him, and granted the French possession of all the lands and forts they had conquered. He arranged with Dupleix a plan for common action, and agreed that a body of French troops should remain permanently at his capital.'

Chapter 6

THE ARRIVAL OF CLIVE

'I have nearly brought down the story to the present time,' Mr. Johnson said. 'One event has taken place, however, which was of importance. Muzaffar Jung set out for Hyderabad, accompanied by a French contingent under Bussy. On the way, the chiefs who had conspired against Nazir Jung mutinied against his successor. Muzaffar charged them with his cavalry. Two of the three chief conspirators were killed and, while pursuing the third, Muzaffar was himself killed.

'Bussy at once released from confinement a son of Nazir Jung, proclaimed him Subadar of the Deccan, escorted him to Hyderabad, and received from him the cession of considerable fresh grants of territory to the French. The latter were now everywhere triumphant, and Trichinopoli and Tanjore were, with the three towns held by the English, the sole places which resisted their authority. Muhammud Ali, deeming further resistance hopeless, had already opened negotiations with Dupleix for the surrender of Trichinopoli. Dupleix agreed to his conditions; but when Muhammud Ali found that Count Bussy, with the flower of the French force, had been despatched to Hyderabad, he gained time by raising fresh demands, which would require the ratification of the subadar.

'Luckily for us Mr. Floyer had been recalled, and his place taken by Mr. Saunders; who is, everyone says, a man of common sense and determination. Muhammud Ali urged upon him the necessity for the English to make common cause with him against the enemy, for if Trichinopoli fell, it would be absolutely impossible for the

English to resist the French and their allies. Early this year, then, Mr. Saunders assured him that he should be assisted with all our strength, and Muhammud Ali thereupon broke off the negotiations with the French.

'Most unfortunately for us, Major Lawrence had gone home to England on sick leave. Captain Gingen, who now commands our troops, is a wretched substitute for him. Captain Cope is no better.

'Early this year Mr. Saunders sent Cope, with two hundred and eighty English and three hundred Sepoys, to Trichinopoli. Benefiting by the delay which was caused before Dupleix, owing to the absence of his best troops at Hyderabad, could collect an army, Cope laid siege to Madura, but was defeated and had to abandon his guns. Three thousand of Muhammud Ali's native troops thereupon deserted to the enemy.

'The cause of the English now appeared lost. Dupleix planted the white flags, emblems of the authority of France, in the fields within sight of Fort Saint David. With immense efforts, Mr. Saunders put into the field five hundred English troops, a thousand Sepoys, a hundred Africans, and eight guns; under the command of Captain Gingen, whose orders were to follow the movements of the army with which D'Auteuil and Chunda Sahib were marching against Trichinopoli.

'Luckily Chunda Sahib, instead of doing so at once, moved northwards to confirm his authority in the towns of North and South Arcot, and to raise additional levies. Great delay was caused by this. On arriving before the important fortress of Valkonda, Chunda Sahib found before it the troops of Captain Gingen, who had been reinforced by sixteen hundred troops from Trichinopoli. The governor of the place, not knowing which party was the stronger, refused to yield to either; and for a fortnight the armies lay at a short distance from each other, near the fortress, with whose governor both continued their negotiations.

'Gingen then lost patience and attacked the place, but was repulsed, and the governor at once admitted the French within the fortress. The next day the main body of the French attacked us, the guns of the fortress opening fire upon us at the same time. Our men, a great portion of whom were recruits just joined from England, fell into a panic and bolted, abandoning their allies and leaving their guns, ammunition, and stores in the hands of the enemy.

'Luckily, D'Auteuil was laid up with gout. If he had pressed on, there remained only the two or three hundred men under Cope to offer the slightest resistance. Trichinopoli must have fallen at once; and we, without a hundred soldiers here, should have had nothing to do but pack up and go. As it was, Gingen's beaten men were allowed to retreat quietly towards Trichinopoli.

'The next day D'Auteuil was better, and followed in pursuit, and Gingen had the greatest difficulty in reaching Trichinopoli. There, at the present moment, we lie shut up, a portion of our force only remaining outside the walls.

'The place itself is strong. The town lies round a lofty rock, on which stands the fortress, which commands the country for some distance round. Still, there is no question that the French could take it, if they attacked it. Our men are utterly dispirited with defeat. Cope and Gingen have neither enterprise nor talent.

'At present the enemy, who are now under the command of Colonel Law, who has succeeded D'Auteuil, are contenting themselves with beleaguering the place. But as we have no troops whatever to send to its rescue, and Muhammud Ali has no friends elsewhere to whom to look for aid, it is a matter of absolute certainty that the place must fall, and then Dupleix will only have to request us to leave, and we shall have nothing else to do but to go at once. So I should advise you not to trouble yourself to unpack your luggage, for in all probability another fortnight will see us on board ship.

'There, that's a tremendous long yarn I've been telling you, and not a pleasant one. It's a history of defeat, loss of prestige and position. We have been out fought and out diplomatized, and have made a mess of everything we put our hand to. I should think you must be tired of it. I am. I haven't done so much talking, for years.'

Charlie and Peters thanked their new acquaintance, warmly, for the pains he had taken in explaining the various circumstances and events which had led to the present unfortunate position; and Charlie asked, as they stood up to say goodnight to Mr. Johnson, 'What has become of Clive, all this time?'

'After the conquest of Devikota,' Mr. Johnson said, 'the civilians in the service were called back to their posts; but to show that they recognized his services, the authorities allowed Clive to attain the rank of captain, which would have been bestowed upon him had he remained in the military service, and they appointed him commissary to the army, a post which would take him away from the office work he hated. Almost directly afterwards, he got a bad attack of fever, and was forced to take a cruise in the Bay of Bengal. He came back in time to go with Gingen's force; but after the defeat of Valkonda he resigned his office, I suppose in disgust, and returned to Fort Saint David. In July, some of the Company's ships came in with some reinforcements. There were no military officers left at Fort Saint David, so Mr. Pigot, a member of the council, started with a large convoy of stores, escorted by eighty English and three hundred Sepoys. Clive volunteered to accompany them. They had to march thirty or forty miles to Verdachelam, a town close to the frontier of Tanjore, through which the convoy to Trichinopoli would be able to pass unopposed, but the intervening country was hostile to the English.

'However, the convoy passed unmolested, and after seeing it safely to that point, Pigot and Clive set out to return, with an escort of twelve Sepoys. They were at once attacked, and for miles a heavy fire was kept up on them. Seven of the escort were killed, the rest reached Fort Saint David in safety. Pigot's report of Clive's conduct, strengthened by that previously made by Major Lawrence, induced the authorities to transfer him permanently to the army. He received a commission as captain and was sent off, with a small detachment remaining at Saint David's, to Devikota.

'There he placed himself under Captain Clarke, who commanded; and the whole body, numbering altogether a hundred English, fifty Sepoys, with a small field piece, marched up to Trichinopoli, and I hear managed to make its way in safety. He got in about a month ago.'

'And what force have we altogether, here and at Saint David's, in case Trichinopoli falls?'

'What with the detachment that came with you, and two others which arrived about ten days back, we have altogether about three hundred and fifty men. What on earth could these do against all the force of the nawab, the subadar, and three or four thousand French troops?'

The prospect certainly seemed gloomy in the extreme, and the young writers retired to their beds, on this, the first night of their arrival in India, with the conviction that circumstances were in a desperate position.

The next day they set to work, and at its end agreed that they should bear the loss of their situations, and their expulsion from the country, with more than resignation. It was now August, the heat was terrible, and as they sat in their shirtsleeves at their desks, bathed in perspiration, at their work of copying invoices, they felt that any possible change of circumstances would be for the better.

The next day, and the next, still further confirmed these ideas. The nights were nearly as hot as the days. Tormented by mosquitoes, they tossed restlessly in their beds for hours, dozing off towards morning and awaking unrefreshed and worn out. When released from work at the end of the third day, Charlie and Peters strolled down together to the beach, and bewailed their hard fate.

'There are two ships coming from the south,' Charlie said presently. 'I wonder whether they're from England, or Fort Saint David?'

'Which do you hope they will be?' Peters said.

'I hope they're from Saint David's,' Charlie answered. 'Even if they made a quick voyage, they couldn't have left England many weeks after us; and although I should be glad to get news from home, I am still more anxious, just at present, for news from Saint David's. Between ourselves, I long to hear of the fall of Trichinopoli. Everyone says it is certain to take place before long, and the sooner it does, the sooner we shall be out of this frightful place.'

After dinner they again went down to the beach, and were joined by Doctor Rae, who chatted with them as to the ships, which were now just anchoring. These had already signalled that they were from Saint David's, and that they had on board Mr. Saunders, the governor, and a detachment of troops. Already the soldiers from the Lizzie Anderson, aided by a number of natives, were at work pitching tents in the fort for the reception of the newcomers, and conjecture was busy on shore, among the civilians, as to the object of bringing troops from Saint David's to Madras, that is, directly away from the scene of action.

'It is one of two things,' Doctor Rae said: 'Either Trichinopoli has surrendered and they are evacuating Fort Saint David, or they have news that the nawab is marching to attack us here. I should think it to be the latter, for Fort Saint David is a great deal stronger than this place, though the French did strengthen it during their stay here.

If, then, the authorities have determined to abandon one of the two towns, and to concentrate all their force for the defence of the other, I should have thought they would have held on to Saint David's.

'There is a boat being lowered from one of the ships, so we shall soon have news.'

A signal from the ship announced that the governor was about to land, and the principal persons at the factory assembled on the beach to receive him. Doctor Rae and the two young writers stood, a short distance from the party. As the boat was beached, Mr. Saunders sprang out and, surrounded by those assembled to meet him, walked at once towards the factory. An officer got out from the boat and superintended the debarkation of the baggage, which a number of coolies at once placed on their heads and carried away.

The officer was following them, when his eye fell upon Doctor Rae.

'Ah! Doctor,' he said, 'how are you? When did you get out again from England?'

'Only three or four days since, Captain Clive. I did not recognize you, at first. I am glad to see you again.'

'Yes, I have cast my slough,' Captain Clive said, laughing, 'and have, thank God, exchanged my pen for a sword, for good.'

'You were able to fight, though, as a civilian,' Doctor Rae said, laughing.

'Yes, we had some tough fighting behind the ramparts of Saint David's, and in the trenches before Pondicherry; but we shall have sharper work, still before us, or I am mistaken.'

'What! Are they going to attack us here?' Doctor Rae exclaimed.

'Oh no, just the other way,' Captain Clive said. 'We are going to carry the war into their quarters. It is a secret yet, and must not go farther.'

And he included the two writers in his look.

'These are two fresh comers, Captain Clive. They came out in the same ship with me. This is Mr. Marryat, this Mr. Peters. They are both brave young gentlemen, and had an opportunity of proving it on the way out, for we were twice engaged; the first time with privateers; the second, a very sharp affair, with pirates. That ship lying off there is a pirate we captured.'

'Aha!' Captain Clive said, looking keenly at the lads. 'Well, young gentlemen, and how do you like what you have seen of your life here?'

'We hate it, sir,' Charlie said. 'We would, both of us, a thousand times rather enlist under you as private soldiers. Oh, sir, if there is any expedition going to take place, do you think there is a chance of our being allowed to go as volunteers?'

'I will see about it,' Captain Clive said, smiling. 'Trade must be dull enough here, at present, and we want every hand that can hold a sword or a musket in the field.'

'You are sure you can recommend them?' he said, turning to Doctor Rae with a smile.

'Most warmly,' the doctor said. 'They both showed great coolness and courage, in the affairs I spoke of. Have you any surgeons with you, Captain Clive? If not, I hope that I shall go with any expedition that will take place. The doctor here is just recovering from an attack of fever and will not be fit, for weeks, for the fatigues of active service.'

'May I ask who is to command the expedition?'

'I am,' Clive said quietly. 'You may well look surprised that an officer who has but just joined should have been selected; but in fact, there is no one else. Cope and Gingen are both at Trichinopoli, and even if they were not —' he paused, and a shrug of the shoulders expressed his meaning clearly. 'Mr. Saunders is good enough to feel some confidence in my capacity, and I trust that I shall not disappoint him.

'We are going — but this, mind, is a profound secret till the day we march — to attack Arcot. It is the only possible way of relieving Trichinopoli.'

'To attack Arcot?' Doctor Rae said, astonished. 'That does indeed appear a desperate enterprise, with such a small body as you have at your command, and these, entirely new recruits. But I recognize the importance of the enterprise. If you should succeed, it will draw off Chunda Sahib from Trichinopoli. It's a grand idea, Captain Clive, a grand idea, though I own it seems to me a desperate one.'

'In desperate times we must take desperate measures, Doctor,' Captain Clive said. 'Now I must be going on after the governor. I shall see you tomorrow.

'I will not forget you, young gentlemen.'

So saying, he proceeded to the factory.

It was afterwards known that the proposal, to effect a diversion by an expedition against Arcot, was the proposal of Clive himself. Upon arriving at Trichinopoli, he had at once seen that all was lost, there. The soldiers were utterly dispirited and demoralized. They had lost all confidence in themselves and their officers, who had also lost confidence in themselves. At Trichinopoli nothing was to be done, and it must be either starved out, or fall an easy prey should the enemy advance to the assault. Clive had, then, after a few days' stay, made his way out from the town, and proceeded to Fort Saint David, where he had laid before the governor the proposal, which he believed to be the only possible measure which could save the English in India.

The responsibility thus set before Mr. Saunders was a grave one. Upon the one hand, he was asked to detach half of the already inadequate garrisons of Fort Saint David and Madras upon an enterprise which, if unsuccessful, must be followed by the loss of the British possessions, of which he was governor. He would have to take this great risk, not upon the advice of a tried veteran like Lawrence, but on that of a young man, only a month or two back a civilian; and it was to this young man, untried in command, that the leadership of this desperate enterprise must be intrusted.

Upon the other hand, if he refused to take this responsibility the fall of Trichinopoli, followed by the loss of the three English ports, was certain. But for this no blame or responsibility could rest upon him. Many men would have chosen the second alternative; but Mr. Saunders had, since Clive's return, seen a good deal of him, and had been impressed with a strong sense of his capacity, energy, and good sense. Mr. Pigot, who had seen Clive under the most trying circumstances, was also his warm supporter; and Mr. Saunders at last determined to adopt Clive's plan, and to stake the fortunes of the English in India on this desperate venture.

Accordingly, leaving a hundred men only at Fort Saint David, he decided to carry the remainder to Madras; and that Clive, leaving only fifty behind as a garrison there, should, with the whole available force, march upon Arcot.

The next morning as Charlie and Peters were at breakfast, a native entered with a letter from the chief factor, to the effect that their services in the office would be dispensed with, and that they were, in accordance with their request, to report themselves to Captain Clive as volunteers. No words can express the joy of the two lads, at receiving the intelligence, and they created so much noise, in the exuberance of their delight, that Mr. Johnson came in from the next room to see what was the matter.

'Ah!' he said, when he heard the cause of the uproar; 'when I first came out here, I should have done the same, and should have regarded the certainty of being knocked on the head as cheerfully as you do. Eight years out here takes the enthusiasm out of a man, and I shall wait quietly to see whether we are to be transferred to Calcutta, or shipped back to England.'

A quarter of an hour later, Charlie and Peters joined Captain Clive in the camp.

'Ah!' he said, 'My young friends, I'm glad to see you. There is plenty for you to do, at once. We shall march tomorrow, and all preparations have to be made. You will both have the rank of ensign, while you serve with me. I have only six other officers, two of whom are civilians who, like yourselves, volunteered at Saint David's. They are of four or five year's standing and, as they speak the language, they will serve with the Sepoys under one of my military officers. Another officer, who is also an ensign, will take the command of the three guns. The Europeans are divided into two companies. One of you will be attached to each. The remaining officer commands both.'

During the day the lads had not a moment to themselves, and were occupied until late at night in superintending the packing of stores and tents; and the following morning, the 26th of August, 1751, the force marched from Madras. It consisted of two hundred of the Company's English troops, three hundred Sepoys, and three small guns. They were led, as has been said, by eight European officers, of whom only Clive and another had ever heard a shot fired in action, four of the eight being young men in the civil service, who had volunteered.

Charlie was glad to find that among the company to which he was appointed was the detachment which had come out with him on board ship; and the moment these heard that he was to accompany them, as their officer, Tim Kelly pressed forward and begged that he might be allowed to act as Charlie's servant, a request which the lad readily complied with.

The march the first day was eighteen miles, a distance which, in such a climate, was sufficient to try to the utmost the powers of the young recruits. The tents were soon erected, each officer having two or three native servants, that number being indispensable in India. Charlie and Peters had one tent between them, which was shared by two other officers, as the column had moved in the lightest order possible in India.

'Sure, Mr. Marryat,' Tim Kelly said to him confidentially, 'that black hathen of a cook is going to pison ye. I have been watching him, and there he is putting all sorts of outlandish things into the mate. He's been pounding them up on stones, for all the world like an apothecary, and even if he manes no mischief, the food isn't fit to set before a dog, let alone a Christian and a gintleman like yourself. If you give the word, sir, I knock him over with the butt end of my musket, and do the cooking for you, meself.'

'I'm afraid the other officers wouldn't agree to that, Tim,' Charlie said, laughing. 'The food isn't so bad as it looks, and I don't think an apprenticeship among the Irish bogs is likely to have turned you out a first rate cook, Tim; except, of course, for potatoes.'

'Sure, now, yer honor, I can fry a rasher of bacon with any man.'

'Perhaps you might do that, Tim, but as we've no bacon here, that won't help us. No, we must put up with the cook, and I don't think any of us will be the worse for the dinner.'

On the morning of the 29th Clive reached Conjeveram, a town of some size, forty-two miles from Madras. Here Clive gained the first trustworthy intelligence as to Arcot. He found the garrison outnumbered his own force by two to one; and that, although the defences were not in a position to resist an attack by heavy guns, they were capable of being defended against any force not so provided. Clive at once despatched a messenger to Madras, begging that two eighteen-pounders might be sent after him; and then, without awaiting their coming he marched forward against Arcot.

Chapter 7

THE SIEGE OF ARCOT

From Conjeveram to Arcot is twenty-seven miles, and the troops, in spite of a delay caused by a tremendous storm of thunder and lightning, reached the town in two days. The garrison, struck with panic at the sudden coming of a foe, when they deemed themselves in absolute security, at once abandoned the fort, which they might easily have maintained until Chunda Sahib was able to send a force to relieve it. The city was incapable of defence after the fort had been abandoned, and Clive took possession of both, without firing a shot.

He at once set to work to store up provisions in the fort, in which he found eight guns and an abundance of ammunition, as he foresaw the likelihood of his having to stand a siege there; and then, leaving a garrison to defend it in his absence, marched on the 4th of September with the rest of his forces against the enemy, who had retired from the town to the mud fort of Timari, six miles south of Arcot. After a few discharges with their cannon they retired hastily, and Clive marched back to Arcot.

Two days later, however, he found that they had been reinforced, and as their position threatened his line of communications, he again advanced towards them. He found the enemy about two thousand strong, drawn up in a grove under cover of the guns of the fort. The grove was inclosed by a bank and ditch, and some fifty yards away was a dry tank, inclosed by a bank higher than that which surrounded the grove. In this the enemy could retire, when dislodged from their first position.

Charlie's heart beat fast when he heard the order given to advance. The enemy outnumbered them by five to one, and were in a strong position. As the English advanced, the enemy's two field pieces opened upon them. Only three men were killed, and, led by their officers, the men went at the grove at the double. The enemy at once evacuated it, and took refuge in the tank, from behind whose high bank they opened fire upon the English.

Clive at once divided his men into two columns, and sent them round to attack the tank upon two sides. The movement was completely successful. At the same moment the men went with a rush at the banks, and upon reaching the top opened a heavy fire upon the crowded mass within. These at once fled in disorder.

Clive then summoned the fort to surrender; but the commander, seeing that Clive had no battering train, refused to do so; and Clive fell back upon Arcot again, until his eighteen-pounders should arrive.

For the next eight days, the troops were engaged in throwing up defences, and strengthening and victualling the fort. The enemy, gaining confidence, gathered to the number of three thousand, and encamped three miles from the town, proclaiming that they were about to besiege; and at midnight on the 14th Clive sallied out, took them by surprise, and dispersed them.

The two eighteen-pounders, for which Clive had sent to Madras, were now well upon the road, under the protection of a small body of Sepoys, and were approaching Conjeveram. The enemy sent a considerable body of troops to cut off the guns, and Clive found that the small number which he had sent out, to meet the approaching party, would not be sufficient. He therefore resolved to take the whole force, leaving only sufficient to garrison the fort.

The post which the enemy occupied was a temple near Conjeveram, and as this was twenty-seven miles distant, the force would be obliged to be absent for at least two days. As it would probably be attacked, and might have to fight hard, he decided on leaving only thirty Europeans and fifty Sepoys within the fort. He appointed Doctor Rae to the command of the post during his absence, and placed Charlie and Peters under his orders.

'I wonder whether they will have any fighting,' Charlie said, as the three officers looked from the walls of the fort after the departing force.

'I wish we had gone with them,' Peters put in; 'but it will be a long march, in the heat.'

'I should think,' Doctor Rae said, 'that they are sure to have fighting. I only hope they may not be attacked at night. The men are very young and inexperienced, and there is nothing tries new soldiers so much as a night attack. However, from what I hear of their own wars, I believe that night attacks are rare among them. I don't know that they have any superstition on the subject, as some African people have, on the ground that evil spirits are about at night; but the natives are certainly not brisk, after nightfall. They are extremely susceptible to any fall of temperature, and as you have, of course, noticed, sleep with their heads covered completely up. However, we must keep a sharp lookout here, tonight.'

'You don't think that we are likely to be attacked, sir, do you?'

'It is possible we may be,' the doctor said. 'They will know that Captain Clive has set out from here, with the main body, and has left only a small garrison. Of course they have spies, and will know that there are only eighty men here, a number insufficient to defend one side of this fort, to say nothing of the whole circle of the walls. They have already found out that the English can fight in the open, and their experience at Timari will make them shy of meeting us again. Therefore, it is just possible that they may be marching in this direction today, while Clive is going in the other, and that they may intend carrying it with a rush.

'I should say, today let the men repose as much as possible; keep the sentries on the gates and walls, but otherwise let them all have absolute quiet. You can tell the whites, and I will let the Sepoys know, that they will have to be in readiness all night, and that they had better, therefore, sleep as much as possible today. We will take it by turns to be on duty, one going round the walls and seeing that the sentries are vigilant, while the others sit in the shade and doze off, if they can. We must all three keep on the alert, during the night.'

Doctor Rae said that he, himself, would see that all went well for the first four hours, after which Charlie should go on duty; and the two subalterns accordingly made themselves as comfortable as they could in their quarters, which were high up in the fort, and possessed a window looking over the surrounding country.

'Well, Tim, what is the matter with you?' they asked that soldier, as he came in with an earthenware jar of water, which he placed to cool in the window. 'You look pale.'

'And it's pale I feel, your honor, with the life frightened fairly out of me, a dozen times a day. It was bad enough on the march, but this place just swarms with horrible reptiles. Shure an' it's a pity that the holy Saint Patrick didn't find time to pay a visit to India. If he'd driven the varmint into the sea for them, as he did in Ireland, the whole population would have become Christians, out of pure gratitude. Why, yer honor, in the cracks and crevices of the stones of this ould place there are bushels and bushels of 'em. There are things they call centipedes, with a million legs on each side of them, and horns big enough to frighten ye; of all sizes up to as long as my hand and as thick as my finger; and they say that a bite from one of them will put a man in a raging fever, and maybe kill him. Then there are scropions, the savagest looking little bastes ye ever saw, for all the world like a little lobster with his tail turned over his back, and a sting at the end of it. Then there's spiders, some of 'em nigh as big as a cat.'

'Oh, nonsense, Tim!' Charlie said; 'I don't think, from what I've heard, that there's a spider in India whose body is as big as a mouse.'

'It isn't their body, yer honor. It's their legs. They're just cruel to look at. It was one of 'em that gave me a turn, a while ago. I was just lying on my bed smoking my pipe, when I saw one of the creatures (as big as a saucer, I'll take my oath) walking towards me with his wicked eye fixed full on me. I jumped off the bed and on to a bench that stood handy.

'"What are ye yelling about, Tim Kelly?" said Corporal Jones to me.

'"Here's a riotous baste here, corporal," says I, "that's meditating an attack on me."

'"Put your foot on it, man," says he.

'"It's mighty fine," says I, "and I in my bare feet."

'So the corporal tells Pat Murphy, my right-hand man, to tackle the baste. I could see Pat didn't like the job ayther, yer honor, but he's not the boy to shrink from his duty; so he comes and he takes post on the form by my side, and just when the cratur is making up his mind to charge us both, Pat jumps down upon him and squelched it.

'Shure, yer honor, the sight of such bastes is enough to turn a Christian man's blood.'

'The spider had no idea of attacking you, Kelly,' Peters said, laughing. 'It might possibly bite you in the night, though I do not think it would do so; or if you took it up in your fingers.'

'The saints defind us, yer honor! I'd as soon think of taking a tiger by the tail. The corporal, he's an Englishman, and lives in a country where they've got snakes and reptiles; but it's hard on an Irish boy, dacently brought up within ten miles of Cork's own town, to be exposed to the like.

'And do ye know, yer honor, when I went out into the town yesterday, what should I see but a man sitting down against a wall, with a little bit of a flute in his hand, and a basket by his side. Well, yer honor, I thought maybe he was going to play a tune, when he lifts up the top of the basket and then began to play. Ye may call it music, yer honor, but there was nayther tune nor music in it.

'Then all of a suddint two sarpents in the basket lifts up their heads, with a great ear hanging down on each side, and began to wave themselves about.'

'Well, Tim, what happened then?' Charlie asked, struggling with his laughter.

'Shure it's little I know what happened after, for I just took to my heels, and I never drew breath till I was inside the gates.'

'There was nothing to be frightened at, Tim,' Charlie said. 'It was a snake charmer. I have never seen one yet, but there are numbers of them all over India. Those were not ears you saw, but the hood. The snakes like the music, and wave their heads about in time to it. I believe that, although they are a very poisonous snake and their bite is certain death, there is no need to be afraid of them, as the charmers draw out their poison fangs when they catch them.'

'Do they, now?' Tim said, in admiration. 'I wonder what the regimental barber would say to a job like that, now. He well nigh broke Dan Sullivan's jaw, yesterday, in getting out a big tooth; and then swore at the poor boy, for having such a powerful strong jaw. I should like to see his face, if he was asked to pull out a tooth from one of them dancing sarpents.

'I brought ye in some fruits, yer honors. I don't know what they are, but you may trust me, they're not poison. I stopped for half an hour beside the stall, till I saw some of the people of the country buying and ating them. So then I judged that they were safe for yer honors.'

'Now, Tim, you'd better go and lie down and get a sleep, if the spiders will let you, for you will have to be under arms all night, as it is possible that we may be attacked.'

The first part of the night passed quietly. Double sentries were placed at each of the angles of the walls. The cannons were loaded, and all ready for instant action. Doctor Rae and his two subalterns were upon the alert, visiting the posts every quarter of an hour to see that the men were vigilant.

Towards two o'clock a dull sound was heard and, although nothing could be seen, the men were at once called to arms, and took up the posts to which they had already been told of on the walls. The noise continued. It was slight and confused, but the natives are so quiet in their movements, that the doctor did not doubt that a considerable body of men were surrounding the place, and that he was about to be attacked.

Presently one of the sentries over the gateway perceived something approaching. He challenged, and immediately afterwards fired. The sound of his gun seemed to serve as the signal for an assault, and a large body of men rushed forward at the gate, while at two other points a force ran up to the foot of the walls, and endeavoured to plant ladders.

The garrison at once collected at the points of attack, a few sentries only being left at intervals on the wall, to give notice should any attempt be made elsewhere. From the walls, a heavy fire of musketry was poured upon the masses below; while from the windows of all the houses around, answering flashes of fire shot out, a rain of bullets being directed at the battlements. Doctor Rae himself commanded at the gate; one of the subalterns at each of the other points assailed.

The enemy fought with great determination. Several times the ladders were planted and the men swarmed up them, but as often these were hurled back upon the crowd below. At the gate the assailants endeavoured to hew their way, with axes, through it;

but so steady was the fire directed, from the loopholes which commanded it, upon those so engaged, that they were, each time, forced to recoil with great slaughter. It was not until nearly daybreak that the attack ceased, and the assailants, finding that they could not carry the place by a coup de main, fell back.

The next day, the main body of the British force returned with the convoy. News arrived, the following day, that the enemy were approaching to lay siege to the place.

The news of the capture of Arcot had produced the effect which Clive had anticipated from it. It alarmed and irritated the besiegers of Trichinopoli, and inspired the besieged with hope and exultation. The Mahratta chief of Gutti and the Rajah of Mysore, with whom Muhammud Ali had for some time been negotiating, at once declared in his favour. The Rajah of Tanjore and the chief of Pudicota, adjoining that state, who had hitherto remained strictly neutral, now threw in their fortunes with the English, and thereby secured the communications between Trichinopoli and the coast.

Chunda Sahib determined to lose not a moment in recovering Arcot, knowing that its recapture would at once cool the ardour of the new native allies of the English; and that, with its capture, the last hope of the besieged in Trichinopoli would be at an end. Continuing the siege, he despatched three thousand of his best troops, with a hundred and fifty Frenchmen, to reinforce the two thousand men already near Arcot, under the command of his son Riza Sahib. Thus the force about to attack Arcot amounted to five thousand men; while the garrison under Clive's orders had, by the losses in the defence of the fort, by fever and disease, been reduced to one hundred and twenty Europeans, and two hundred Sepoys; while four out of the eight officers were hors de combat.

The fort which this handful of men had to defend was in no way capable of offering a prolonged resistance. Its walls were more than a mile in circumference, and were in a very bad state of repair. The rampart was narrow and the parapet low, and the ditch, in many places, dry. The fort had two gates. These were in towers standing beyond the ditch, and connected with the interior by a causeway across it. The houses in the town in many places came close up to the walls, and from their roofs the ramparts of the forts were commanded.

On the 23rd September Riza Sahib, with his army, took up his position before

Arcot. Their guns had not, however, arrived, with the exception of four mortars; but they at once occupied all the houses near the fort, and from the walls and upper windows kept up a heavy fire on the besieged.

Clive determined to make an effort, at once, to drive them from this position, and he accordingly, on the same afternoon, made a sortie. So deadly a fire, however, was poured into the troops as they advanced, that they were unable to make any way, and were forced to retreat into the fort again, after suffering heavy loss.

On the night of the 24th, Charlie Marryat, with twenty men carrying powder, was lowered from the walls; and an attempt was made to blow up the houses nearest to them; but little damage was done, for the enemy were on the alert, and they were unable to place the powder in effective positions, and with a loss of ten of their number the survivors with difficulty regained the fort.

For the next three weeks the position remained unchanged. So heavy was the fire which the enemy, from their commanding position, maintained, that no one could show his head for a moment, without running the risk of being shot. Only a few sentinels were kept upon the walls, to prevent the risk of surprise, and these had to remain stooping below the parapet. Every day added to the losses.

Captain Clive had a series of wonderful escapes, and indeed the men began to regard him with a sort of superstitious reverence, believing that he had a charmed life. One of his three remaining officers, seeing an enemy taking deliberate aim at him through a window, endeavoured to pull him aside. The native changed his aim, and the officer fell dead. On three other occasions sergeants, who accompanied him on his rounds, were shot dead by his side. Yet no ball touched him.

Provisions had been stored in the fort, before the commencement of the siege, sufficient for sixty days; and of this a third was already exhausted when, on the 14th of October, the French troops serving with Riza Sahib received two eighteen-pounders, and seven smaller pieces of artillery. Hitherto the besiegers had contented themselves with harassing the garrison night and day, abstaining from any attack which would cost them lives, until the arrival of their guns. Upon receiving these, they at once placed them in a battery which they had prepared on the northwest of the fort, and opened fire.

So well was this battery placed, and so accurate the aim of its gunner, that the very first shot dismounted one of the eighteen-pounders in the fort. The second again struck the gun and completely disabled it. The besieged mounted their second heavy gun in its place, and were preparing to open fire on the French battery, when a shot struck it also and dismounted it. It was useless to attempt to replace it, and it was, during the night, removed to a portion of the walls not exposed to the fire of the enemy's battery. The besiegers continued their fire, and in six days had demolished the wall facing their battery, making a breach of fifty feet wide.

Clive, who had now only the two young subalterns serving under him, worked indefatigably. His coolness and confidence of bearing kept up the courage of his little garrison, and every night, when darkness hid them from the view of the enemy's sharpshooters, the men laboured to prepare for the impending attack. Works were thrown up inside the fort, to command the breach. Two deep trenches were dug, one behind the other; the one close to the wall, the other some distance farther back. These trenches were filled with sharp iron three-pointed spikes, and palisades erected extending from the ends of the ditches to the ramparts, and a house pulled down in the rear to the height of a breastwork, behind which the garrison could fire at the assailants, as they endeavoured to cross the ditches.

One of the three field pieces Clive had brought with him he mounted on a tower, flanking the breach outside. Two he held in reserve, and placed two small guns, which he had found in the fort when he took it, on the flat roof of a house in the fort commanding the inside of the breach.

From the roofs of some of the houses around the fort the besiegers beheld the progress of these defences; and Riza Sahib feared, in spite of his enormously superior numbers, to run the risk of a repulse. He knew that the amount of provisions which Clive had stored was not large, and thinking that famine would inevitably compel his surrender, shrank from incurring the risk of disheartening his army, by the slaughter which an unsuccessful attempt to carry the place must entail. He determined, at any rate, to increase the probability of success, and utilize his superior forces, by making an assault at two points, simultaneously. He therefore erected a battery on the south-west, and began to effect a breach on that side, also.

Clive, on his part, had been busy endeavouring to obtain assistance. His native emissaries, penetrating the enemy's lines, carried the news of the situation of affairs in the fort to Madras, Fort Saint David, and Trichinopoli. At Madras a few fresh troops had arrived from England, and Mr. Saunders, feeling that Clive must be relieved at all cost, however defenceless the state of Madras might be, despatched, on the 20th of October, a hundred Europeans and a hundred Sepoys, under Lieutenant Innis. These, after three days' marching, arrived at Trivatoor, twenty-two miles from Arcot.

Riza Sahib had heard of his approach; and sent a large body of troops, with two guns, to attack him. The contest was too unequal. Had the British force been provided with field pieces, they might have gained the day; but, after fighting with great bravery, they were forced to fall back; with a loss of twenty English and two officers killed and many more wounded, while the Sepoys suffered equally severely.

One of Clive's messengers reached Murari Reo, the Mahratta chief of Gutti. This man was a ferocious free-booting chief, daring and brave himself, and admiring those qualities in others. Hitherto, his alliance with Muhammud Ali was little more than nominal, for he had dreaded bringing upon himself the vengeance of Chunda Sahib and the French, whose ultimate success in the strife appeared certain. Clive's march upon Arcot, and the heroic defence which the handful of men there were opposing to overwhelming numbers, excited his highest admiration. As he afterwards said, he had never before believed that the English could fight, and when Clive's messenger reached him, he at once sent back a promise of assistance.

Riza Sahib learned, almost as soon as Clive himself, that the Mahrattas were on the move. The prospects of his communications being harassed, by these daring horsemen, filled him with anxiety. Murari Reo was encamped, with six thousand men, at a spot thirty miles to the west of Arcot; and he might, at any moment, swoop down upon the besiegers. Although, therefore, Riza Sahib had for six days been at work effecting a new breach, which was now nearly open to assault, he sent on the 30th of October a flag of truce, with an offer to Clive of terms, if he would surrender Arcot.

The garrison were to be allowed to march out with their arms and baggage, while to Clive himself he offered a large sum of money. In case of refusal, he threatened to storm the fort, and put all its defenders to the sword. Clive returned a defiant refusal, and the guns again opened on the second breach.

On the 9th of November, the Mahrattas began to show themselves in the neighbour-hood of the besieging army. The force under Lieutenant Innis had been reinforced, and was now under the command of Captain Kilpatrick, who had a hundred and fifty English troops, with four field guns. This was now advancing.

Four days later the new breach had attained a width of thirty yards, but Clive had prepared defences in the rear, similar to those at the other breach; and the difficulties of the besiegers would here be much greater, as the ditch was not fordable.

The fifty days which the siege had lasted had been terrible ones for the garrison. Never daring to expose themselves unnecessarily during the day, yet ever on the alert to repel an attack; labouring at night at the defences, with their numbers daily dwindling, and the prospect of an assault becoming more and more imminent, the work of the little garrison was terrible; and it is to the defences of Lucknow and Cawnpore, a hundred years later, that we must look to find a parallel, in English warfare, for their endurance and bravery.

Both Charlie Marryat and Peters had been wounded, but in neither case were the injuries severe enough to prevent their continuing on duty. Tim Kelly had his arm broken by a ball, while another bullet cut a deep seam along his check, and carried away a portion of his ear. With his arm in splints and a sling, and the side of his face covered with strappings and plaster, he still went about his business.

'Ah! Yer honors,' he said one day to his masters; 'I've often been out catching rabbits, with ferrits to drive 'em out of their holes, and sticks to knock 'em on the head, as soon as they showed themselves; and it's a divarshun I was always mightily fond of, but I never quite intered into the feelings of the rabbits. Now I understand them complately, for ain't we rabbits ourselves? The officers, saving your presence, are the ferrits who turn us out of our holes on duty; and the natives yonder, with their muskets and their matchlocks, are the men with sticks, ready to knock us on head, directly we show ourselves. If it plase Heaven that I ever return to the ould country again, I'll niver lend a hand at rabbiting, to my dying day.'

Chapter 8

THE GRAND ASSAULT

The 14th of November was a Mohammedan festival, and Riza Sahib determined to utilize the enthusiasm and fanatic zeal, which such an occasion always excites among the followers of the Prophet, to make his grand assault upon Arcot, and to attack at three o'clock in the morning. Every preparation was made on the preceding day, and four strong columns told off for the assault. Two of these were to attack by the breaches, the other two at the gates. Rafts were prepared to enable the party attacking by the new breach to cross the moat, while the columns advancing against the gates were to be preceded by elephants, who, with iron plates on their foreheads, were to charge and batter down the gates.

Clive's spies brought him news of the intended assault, and at midnight he learned full particulars as to the disposition of the enemy. His force was now reduced to eighty Europeans, and a hundred and twenty Sepoys. Every man was told off to his post, and then, sentries being posted to arouse them at the approach of the enemy, the little garrison lay down in their places, to get two or three hours' sleep before the expected attack.

At three o'clock, the firing of three shells from the mortars into the fort gave the signal for assault. The men leaped up and stood to their arms, full of confidence in their ability to resist the attack. Soon the shouts of the advancing columns testified to the equal confidence and ardour of the assailants.

Not a sound was heard within the walls of the fort, until the elephants advanced

537

towards the gates. Then suddenly a stream of fire leaped out from loophole and battlement. So well directed and continuous was the fire, that the elephants, dismayed at the outburst of fire and noise, and smarting from innumerable wounds, turned and dashed away, trampling in their flight multitudes of men in the dense columns packed behind them. These, deprived of the means upon which they had relied to break in the gates, turned and retreated rapidly.

Scarcely less prolonged was the struggle at the breaches. At the first breach, a very strong force of the enemy marched resolutely forward. They were permitted, without a shot being fired at them, to cross the dry ditch, mount the shattered debris of the wall, and pour into the interior of the fort. Forward they advanced until, without a check, they reached the first trench bristling with spikes.

Then, as they paused for a moment, from the breastwork in front of them, from the ramparts, and every spot which commanded the trench, a storm of musketry was poured on them; while the gunners swept the crowded mass with grape, and bags of bullets. The effect was tremendous. Mowed down in heaps, the assailants recoiled; and then, without a moment's hesitation, turned and fled. Three times, strongly reinforced, they advanced to the attack; but were each time repulsed, with severe slaughter.

Still less successful were those at the other breach. A great raft, capable of carrying seventy, conveyed the head of the storming party across the ditch; and they had just reached the foot of the breach, when Clive, who was himself at this point, turned two field pieces upon them, with deadly effect. The raft was upset and smashed, and the column, deprived of its intended means of crossing the ditch, desisted from the attack.

Among those who had fallen, at the great breach, was the commander of the storming party; a man of great valour. Four hundred of his followers had also been killed, and Riza Sahib, utterly disheartened at his repulse at all points, decided not to renew the attack. He had still more than twenty men to each of the defenders; but the obstinacy of their resistance, and the moral effect produced by it upon his troops; the knowledge that the Mahratta horse were hovering in his rear, and that Kilpatrick's little column was close at hand; determined him to raise the siege.

After the repulse of the assault, the heavy musketry fire from the houses around the fort was continued. At two in the afternoon he asked for two hours' truce, to bury the dead. This was granted, and on its conclusion the musketry fire was resumed, and continued until two in the morning. Then suddenly, it ceased. Under cover of the fire, Riza Sahib had raised the siege, and retired with his army to Vellore.

On the morning of the 15th, Clive discovered that the enemy had disappeared. The joy of the garrison was immense. Every man felt proud, and happy in the thought that he had taken his share in a siege, which would not only be memorable in English history till the end of time, but which had literally saved India to us. The little band made the fort re-echo with their cheers, when the news came in. Caps were thrown high in the air, and the men indulged in every demonstration of delight.

Clive was not a man to lose time. The men were at once formed up, and marched into the abandoned camp of the enemy; where they found four guns, four mortars, and a great quantity of ammunition. A cloud of dust was seen approaching, and soon a mounted officer, riding forward, announced the arrival of Captain Kilpatrick's detachment.

Not a moment was lost, for Clive felt the importance of, at once, following up the blow inflicted by the repulse of the enemy. Three days were spent, in continuous labour, in putting the fort of Arcot again in a position of defence; and, leaving Kilpatrick in charge there, he marched out with two hundred Europeans, seven hundred Sepoys, and three guns, and attacked and took Timari, the little fort which before baffled him.

This done, he returned towards Arcot to await the arrival of a thousand Mahratta horse, which Murari Reo had promised him. When these arrived, however, they proved unwilling to accompany him. Upon their way, they had fallen in with a portion of Riza Sahib's retreating force, and had been worsted in the attack; and as the chance of plunder seemed small, while the prospect of hard blows was certain, the free-booting horsemen refused, absolutely, to join in the pursuit of the retreating enemy.

Just at this moment, the news came in that reinforcements from Pondicherry were marching to meet Riza Sahib at Arni, a place seventeen miles south of Arcot, twenty south of Vellore. It was stated that, with these reinforcements, a large sum of money was being brought, for the use of Riza Sahib's army. When the Mahrattas heard the news, the chance of booty at once altered their intentions, and they declared themselves ready to follow Clive. The greater portion of them, however, had dispersed, plundering over the country, and great delay was caused before they could be collected. When six hundred of them had been brought together, Clive determined to wait no longer, but started at once for Arni.

The delay enabled Riza Sahib, marching down from Vellore, to meet his reinforcements; and when Clive, after a forced march of twenty miles, approached Arni, he found the enemy, composed of three hundred French troops, two thousand five hundred Sepoys, and two thousand horsemen, with four guns, drawn up before it. Seeing their immense superiority in numbers, these advanced to the attack.

Clive determined to await them where he stood. The position was an advantageous one. He occupied a space of open ground, some three hundred yards in width. On his right flank was a village, on the left a grove of palm trees. In front of the ground he occupied were rice fields, which, it being the wet season, were very swampy, and altogether impracticable for guns. These fields were crossed by a causeway which led to the village, but as it ran at an angle across them, those advancing upon it were exposed to the fire of the English front. Clive posted the Sepoys in the village, the Mahratta horsemen in the grove, and the two hundred English, with the guns, on the ground between them.

The enemy advanced at once. His native cavalry, with some infantry, marched against the grove; while the French troops, with about fifteen hundred infantry, moved along the causeway against the village.

The fight began on the English left. There the Mahratta cavalry fought bravely. Issuing from the palm grove, they made repeated charges against the greatly superior forces of the enemy. But numbers told, and the Mahrattas, fighting fiercely, were driven back into the palm grove; where they, with difficulty, maintained themselves.

In the meantime, the fight was going on at the centre. Clive opened fire with his guns on the long column marching, almost across his front, to attack the village. The enemy, finding themselves exposed to a fire which they were powerless to answer, quitted the causeway, and formed up in the rice fields fronting the English position. The guns, protected only by a few Frenchmen and natives, remained on the causeway.

Clive now despatched two of his guns, and fifty English, to aid the hard-pressed

Mahrattas in the grove; and fifty others to the village, with orders to join the Sepoys there, to dash forward on to the causeway, and charge the enemy's guns.

As the column issued from the village along the causeway, at a rapid pace, the French limbered up their guns and retired at a gallop. The infantry, dispirited at their disappearance, fell back across the rice fields; an example which their horsemen on their right, already dispirited by the loss which they were suffering, from the newly-arrived English musketry and the discharges of the field pieces, followed without delay.

Clive at once ordered a pursuit. The Mahrattas were despatched after the enemy's cavalry, while he himself, with his infantry, advanced across the causeway and pressed upon the main body. Three times the enemy made a stand, but each time failed to resist the impetuosity of the pursuers, and the night alone put a stop to the pursuit, by which time the enemy were completely routed.

The material loss had not been heavy, for but fifty French and a hundred and fifty natives were killed or wounded; but the army was broken up, the morale of the enemy completely destroyed; and it was proved to all Southern India, which was anxiously watching the struggle, that the English were, in the field of battle, superior to their European rivals. This assurance alone had an immense effect. It confirmed, in their alliance with the English, many of the chiefs whose friendship had hitherto been lukewarm; and brought over many waverers to our side.

In the fight, eight Sepoys and fifty of the Mahratta cavalry were killed or disabled. The English did not lose a single man. Many of Riza Sahib's soldiers came in, during the next few days, and enlisted in the British force. The Mahrattas captured the treasure, the prospect of which had induced them to join in the fight, and the governor of Arni agreed to hold the town for Muhammud Ali.

Clive moved on at once to Conjeveram, where thirty French troops and three hundred Sepoys occupied the temple, a very strong building. Clive brought up two eighteen-pounders from Madras, and pounded the walls; and the enemy, seeing that the place must fall, evacuated it in the night, and retired to Pondicherry. North Arcot being now completely in the power of the English, Clive returned to Madras; and then sailed to Fort Saint David, to concert measures with Mr. Saunders for the relief of Trichinopoli. This place still held out, thanks rather to the feebleness and indecision of Colonel Law, who commanded the besiegers, than to any effort on the part of the defenders.

Governor Dupleix, at Pondicherry, had seen with surprise the result of Clive's dash upon Arcot. He had, however, perceived that the operations there were wholly secondary, and that Trichinopoli was still the all-important point. The fall of that place would more than neutralize Clive's successes at Arcot; and he, therefore, did not suffer Clive's operations to distract his attention here. Strong reinforcements and a battering train were sent forward to the besiegers; and, by repeated messages, he endeavoured to impress upon Law and Chunda Sahib the necessity of pressing forward the capture of Trichinopoli.

But Dupleix was unfortunate in his instruments. Law was always hesitating and doubting. Chunda Sahib, although clever to plan, was weak in action; indecisive, at moments when it was most necessary that he should be firm. So then, in spite of the entreaties of Dupleix, he had detached a considerable force to besiege Clive. Dupleix, seeing this, and hoping that Clive might be detained at Arcot long enough to allow of the siege of Trichinopoli being brought to a conclusion, had sent the three hundred French soldiers to strengthen the force of Riza Sahib.

He had still an overpowering force at Trichinopoli, Law having nine hundred trained French soldiers, a park of fifty guns, two thousand Sepoys, and the army of Chunda Sahib, twenty thousand strong. Inside Trichinopoli were a few English soldiers under Captain Cope, and a small body of troops of Muhammud Ali; while outside the walls, between them and the besiegers, was the English force under Gingen, the men utterly dispirited, the officer without talent, resolution, or confidence.

Before leaving the troops with which he had won the battle of Arni, Clive had expressed, to the two young writers, his high appreciation of their conduct during the siege of Arcot; and promised them that he would make it a personal request, to the authorities at Fort Saint David, that they might be permanently transferred from the civil to the military branch of the service; and such a request, made by him, was certain to be complied with. He strongly advised them to spend every available moment of their time in the study of the native language; as, without that, they would be useless if appointed to command a body of Sepoys.

Delighted at the prospect, now open to them, of a permanent relief from the drudgery of a clerk's life in Madras, the young fellows were in the highest spirits; and Tim Kelly was scarcely less pleased, when he heard that Charlie was now likely to be always employed with him. The boys lost not a moment in sending down to Madras, to engage the services of a native 'moonshee' or teacher. They wrote to their friend Johnson, asking him to arrange terms with the man who understood most English, and to engage him to remain with them some time.

A few days later, Tim Kelly came in.

'Plase, yer honors, there's a little shrivelled atomy of a man outside, as wants to spake wid ye. He looks for all the world like a monkey, wrapped up in white clothes, but he spakes English after a fashion, and has brought this letter for you. The cratur scarce looks like a human being, and I misdoubt me whether you had better let him in.'

'Nonsense, Tim,' Charlie said, opening the letter; 'it's the moonshee we are expecting, from Madras. He has come to teach us the native language.'

'Moonshine, is it! By jabers, and it's a mighty poor compliment to the moon to call him so. And is it the language you're going to larn now? Shure, Mr. Charles, I wouldn't demane myself by larning the lingo of these black hathens. Isn't for them to larn the English, and mighty pleased they ought to be, to get themselves to spake like Christians.'

'But who's going to teach them, Tim?'

'Oh, they larn fast enough,' said Tim. 'You've only got to point to a bottle of water, or to the fire, or whatever else you want, and swear at them, and they understand directly. I've tried it myself, over and over again.'

'There, Tim, it's no use standing talking any longer. Bring in the moonshee.'

From that moment, the little man had his permanent post in a corner of the boys' room; and, when they were not on duty, they were constantly engaged in studying the language, writing down the names of every object they came across and getting it by heart, and learning every sentence, question, and answer which occurred to them as likely to be useful.

As for Tim, he quite lost patience at this devotion to study on the part of his master; who, he declared to his comrades, went on just as if he intended to become a native and a hathen himself.

'It's just awful to hear him, Corporal M'Bean, jabbering away in that foreign talk, with that little black monkey moonshine. The little cratur a-twisting his shrivelled fingers about, that looks as if the bones were coming through the skin. I wonder what the good father at Blarney, where I come from, you know, Corporal, would say to sich goings on. Faith, then, and if he were here, I'd buy a bottle of holy water, and sprinkle it over the little hathen. I suspict he'd fly straight up the chimney, when it touched him.'

'My opinion of you, Tim Kelly,' the corporal, who was a grave Scotchman, said; 'is that you're just a fule. Your master is a brave young gentleman, and is a deal more sensible than most of them, who spend all their time in drinking wine and playing cards. A knowledge of the language is most useful. What would you do, yourself, if you were to marry a native woman, and couldn't speak to her afterwards.'

'The saints defind us!' Tim exclaimed; 'and what put such an idea in yer head, Corporal? It's nayther more nor less than an insult to suppose that I, a dacent boy, and brought up under the teaching of Father O'Shea, should marry a hathen black woman; and if you weren't my suparior officer, corporal, I'd tach ye better manners.'

Fortunately, at this moment Charlie's voice was heard, shouting for his servant; and Tim was therefore saved from the breach of the peace, which his indignation showed that he meditated.

December passed quietly; and then, in January, 1752, an insurrection planned by Dupleix broke out. The governor of Pondicherry had been suffering keenly from disappointments; which, as time went on, and his entreaties and commands to Law to attack Trichinopoli were answered only by excuses and reasons for delay, grew to despair; and he resolved upon making another effort to occupy the attention of the man in whom he already recognized a great rival, and to prevent his taking steps for the relief of Trichinopoli. Law had over and over again assured him that, in the course of a very few weeks, that place would be driven by famine to surrender; and, as soon as Clive arrived at Fort Saint David, Dupleix set about taking steps which would again necessitate his return to the north, and so give to Law the time which he asked for.

Supplies of money were sent to Riza Sahib, together with four hundred French soldiers. These marched suddenly upon Punemalli and captured it, seized again the fortified temple of Conjeveram, and from this point threatened both Madras and Arcot.

Had this force possessed an active and determined commander, it could undoubtedly have carried out Dupleix's instructions, captured Madras, and inflicted a terrible blow upon the English. Fortunately, it had no such head. It marched indeed against Madras, plundered and burnt the factories, levied contributions, and obtained possession of everything but the fort; where the civilians, and the few men who constituted the garrison, daily expected to be attacked, in which case the place must have fallen. This, however, the enemy never even attempted, contenting themselves with ravaging the place outside the walls of the fort.

The little garrison of Arcot, two hundred men in all, were astonished at the news; that the province, which they had thought completely conquered, was again in flames; that the road to Madras was cut, by the occupation of Conjeveram by the French; and that Madras itself was, save the fort, in the hands of the enemy. The fort itself, they knew, might easily be taken, as they were aware that it was defended by only eighty men.

The change in the position was at once manifest, in the altered attitude of the fickle population. The main body of the inhabitants of Southern India were Hindoos, who had for centuries been ruled by foreign masters. The Mohammedans from the north had been their conquerors, and the countless wars which had taken place, to them signified merely whether one family or another were to reign over them. The sole desire was for peace and protection; and they, therefore, ever inclined towards the side which seemed strongest. Their sympathies were no stronger with their Mohammedan rulers than with the French or English, and they only hoped that whatever power was strongest might conquer; and that, after the hostilities were over, their daily work might be conducted in peace, and their property and possessions be enjoyed in security. The capture and defence of Arcot, and the battle of Arni, had brought them to regard the English as their final victors; and the signs of deep and even servile respect, which greeted the conquerors wherever they went, and which absolutely disgusted

Charlie Marryat and his friend, were really sincere marks of the welcome to masters who seemed able and willing to maintain their rule over them.

With the news of the successes of Riza Sahib, all this changed. The natives no longer bent to the ground, as the English passed them in the streets. The country people, who had flocked in with their products to the markets, absented themselves altogether, and the whole population prepared to welcome the French as their new masters.

In the fort, the utmost vigilance was observed. The garrison laboured to mend the breaches, and complete the preparations for defence. Provisions were again stored up, and they awaited anxiously news from Clive.

That enterprising officer was at Fort Saint David, busy in making his preparations for a decisive campaign against the enemy round Trichinopoli, when the news of the rising reached him. He was expecting a considerable number of fresh troops from England, as it was in January that the majority of the reinforcements despatched by the Company arrived in India; and Mr. Saunders had written to Calcutta, begging that a hundred men might be sent thence. These were now, with the eighty men at Madras, and the two hundred at Arcot, all the force that could be at his disposal, for at Fort Saint David there was not a single available man.

With all the efforts that Clive, aided by the authorities, could make, it was not until the middle of February that he had completed his arrangements. On the 9th, the hundred men arrived from Bengal, and, without the loss of a day, Clive started from Madras to form a junction with the garrison from Arcot, who, leaving only a small force to hold the fort, had moved down to meet him.

Chapter 9

THE BATTLE OF KAVARIPAK

The troops from Arcot had already moved some distance on their way to Madras, and Clive, therefore, with the new levies, joined them on the day after his leaving Madras. The French and Riza Sahib let slip the opportunity of attacking these bodies, before they united. They were well aware of their movements, and had resolved upon tactics, calculated in the first place to puzzle the English commander, to wear out his troops, and to enable them finally to surprise and take him entirely at a disadvantage.

The junction with the Arcot garrison raised the force under Clive's orders to three hundred and eighty English, thirteen hundred Sepoys, and six field guns, while the enemy at Vendalur, a place twenty-five miles south of Madras, where they had a fortified camp, had four hundred French troops, two thousand Sepoys, two thousand five hundred cavalry, and twelve guns.

Hoping to surprise them there, Clive marched all night. When the force approached the town they heard that the enemy had disappeared, and that they had started, apparently, in several directions.

The force was halted for a few hours, and then the news was obtained that the enemy had united their forces at Conjeveram, and that they had marched away from that place in a westerly direction. Doubting not that they were about to attack Arcot, which, weakened by the departure of the greater portion of its garrison, would be in no position to defend itself against a sudden coup de main by a strong force, Clive set his troops again in motion. The French, indeed, had already bribed some of the native soldiers within the fort; who were to reply to a signal made without, if they were in a position to open the gates. However, by good fortune their treachery had been discovered, and when the French arrived they received no reply to their signal; and as Arcot would be sure to fall if they defeated Clive, they marched away without attacking it, to take up the position which they had agreed upon beforehand.

It was at nine in the evening that Clive, at Vendalur, obtained intelligence that the enemy had assembled at Conjeveram. The troops had already marched twenty-five miles, but they had had a rest of five hours, and Clive started with them at once, and reached Conjeveram, twenty miles distant, at four in the morning. Finding that the enemy had again disappeared, he ordered the troops to halt for a few hours. They had already marched forty-five miles in twenty-four hours, a great feat when it is remembered that only the Arcot garrison were in any way accustomed to fatigue, the others being newly raised levies. The greater portion of the Sepoys had been enlisted within the fortnight preceding.

'I don't know, Mr. Marryat, whether the French call this fighting. I call it playing hide and seek,' Tim Kelly said. 'Shure we've bin marching, with only a halt of two or three hours, since yisterday morning; and my poor feet are that sore that I daren't take my boots off me, for I'm shure I'd never git 'em on agin. If the French want to fight us, why don't they do it square and honest, not be racing and chasing about like a lot of wild sheep.'

'Have you seen the moonshee, Tim? He is with the baggage.'

'Shure and I saw him,' Tim said. 'The cart come in just now, and there was he, perched up on the top of it like a dried monkey. You don't want him tonight, shure, yer honor.'

'Oh no, I don't want him, Tim. You'd better go now, and get to sleep at once, if you can. We may be off again, at any minute.'

Arcot is twenty-seven miles from Conjeveram. Clive felt certain that the enemy had gone on to that place; but, anxious as he was for its safety, it was absolutely necessary that the troops should have a rest before starting on such a march. They were, therefore, allowed to rest until twelve o'clock; when, refreshed by their eight hours' halt and breakfast, they started upon their long march towards Arcot, making sure that they should not find the enemy until they reached that place.

Had Clive possessed a body of cavalry, however small, he would have been able to scour the country, and to make himself acquainted with the real position of the French. Cavalry are to a general what eyes are to a man, and without these he is liable to tumble into a pitfall. Such was the case on the present occasion. Having no doubt that the enemy were engaged in attacking Arcot, the troops were plodding along carelessly and in loose order; when, to their astonishment, after a sixteen-mile march, as they approached the town of Kavaripak just as the sun was setting, a fire of artillery opened upon them from a grove upon the right of the road, but two hundred and fifty yards distant. Nothing is more confusing than a surprise of this kind, especially to young troops, and when no enemy is thought to be near.

The French general's plans had been well laid. He had reached Kavaripak that morning, and allowed his troops to rest all day, and he expected to obtain an easy victory over the tired men who would, unsuspicious of danger, be pressing on to the relief of Arcot. So far his calculations had been correct, and the English marched unsuspiciously into the trap laid for them.

The twelve French guns were placed in a grove, round whose sides, facing the point from which Clive was approaching, ran a deep ditch with a high bank forming a regular battery. A body of French infantry were placed in support of the guns, with some Sepoys in reserve behind the grove. Parallel with the road on the left ran a deep watercourse, now empty, and in this the rest of the infantry were stationed, at a point near the town of Kavaripak, and about a quarter of a mile further back than the grove. On either side of this watercourse the enemy had placed his powerful cavalry force.

For a moment, when the guns opened, there was confusion and panic among the British troops. Clive, however, ever cool and confident in danger, and well seconded by his officers, rallied them at once. The position was one of extreme danger. It was possible, indeed, to retreat, but in the face of an enemy superior in infantry and guns, and possessing so powerful a body of cavalry, the operation would have been a very dangerous one. Even if accomplished, it would entail an immense loss of morale and prestige to his troops. Hitherto, under his leading, they had been always successful; and a belief in his own superiority adds immensely to the fighting power of a soldier. Even should the remnant of the force fight its way back to Madras, the campaign would have been a lost one, and all hope of saving Trichinopoli would have been at an end.

'Steady, lads, steady,' he shouted. 'From up quietly and steadily. We have beaten the enemy before, you know, and we will do so again.'

While the troops, in spite of the artillery fire, fell into line, Clive rapidly surveyed the ground. He saw the enemy's infantry advancing up the watercourse, and so sheltered by it as to be out of the fire of his troops. He saw their cavalry sweeping down on the other side of the watercourse, menacing his left and threatening his baggage. The guns were at once brought up from the rear, but before these arrived the men were falling fast.

Three of the guns he placed to answer the French battery, two of them he hurried to his left, with a small body of English and two hundred Sepoys, to check the advance of the enemy's cavalry. The main body of his infantry he ordered into the watercourse, which afforded them a shelter from the enemy's artillery. The baggage carts and baggage he sent half a mile to the rear, under the protection of forty Sepoys and a gun.

While this was being done the enemy's fire was continuing, but his infantry advanced but slowly, and had not reached a point abreast of the grove when the British force in the watercourse met them. It would not seem to be a very important matter, at what point in the watercourse the infantry of the two opposing parties came into collision, but matters apparently trifling in themselves often decide the fate of battles; and, in fact, had the French artillery retained their fire until their infantry were abreast of the grove, the battle of Kavaripak would have been won by them, and the British power in Southern India would have been destroyed.

Clive moved confidently and resolutely among his men, keeping up their courage by cheerful words, and he was well seconded by his officers.

'Now, lads,' Charlie Marryat cried to the company of which he was in command, 'stick to it. You ought to be very thankful to the French, for saving you the trouble of having to march another twelve miles before giving you an opportunity of thrashing them.'

The men laughed, and redoubled their fire on the French infantry, who were facing them in the watercourse at a distance of eighty yards. Neither party liked to charge. The French commander knew that he had only to hold his position to win the day. His guns were mowing down the English artillerymen. The English party on the left of the watercourse, with difficulty, held their own against the charges of his horsemen, and were rapidly dwindling away under the artillery fire, while other bodies of his cavalry had surrounded the baggage, and were attacking the little force told off to guard it. He knew, too, that any attempt the English might make to attack the battery, with its strong defences, must inevitably fail.

The situation was becoming desperate. It was now ten o'clock. The fight had gone on for four hours. No advantage had been gained, the men were losing confidence, and the position grew more and more desperate. Clive saw that there was but one chance of victory. The grove could not be carried in the front, but it was just possible that it might be open in the rear.

Choosing a sergeant who spoke the native language well, he bade him leave the party in the watercourse, and make his way round to the rear of the grove, and discover whether it was strongly guarded there or not. In twenty minutes, the sergeant returned with the news that there was no strong force there.

Clive at once took two hundred of his English infantry, the men who had fought at Arcot, and quietly left the watercourse and made his way round towards the rear of the grove. Before he had gone far the main body in the watercourse, surprised at the sudden withdrawal of the greater portion of the English force, and missing the presence of Clive himself, began to lose heart. They no longer replied energetically to the fire of the French infantry. A movement of retreat began, the fire ceased, and in a minute or two they would have broken in flight.

At this moment, Clive returned. As he moved forward, he had marked the dying away of the English fire, and guessing what had happened, had given over the command of the column to Lieutenant Keene, the senior officer, and hurried back to the watercourse. He arrived there just as the troops had commenced to run away.

Throwing himself among them, with shouts and exhortations, he succeeded in arresting their flight; and, by assurance that the battle was as good as won elsewhere, and that they had only to hold their ground for a few minutes longer to ensure victory, he got them to advance to their former position; and to reopen fire on the French, who had, fortunately, remained inactive instead of advancing and taking advantage of the cessation of the English fire.

In the meantime, Lieutenant Keene led his detachment, making a long circuit, to a point three hundred yards immediately behind the grove. He then sent forward one of his officers, Ensign Symmonds, who spoke French perfectly, to reconnoitre the grove. Symmonds had proceeded but a little way, when he came upon a large number of French Sepoys, who were covering the rear of the grove; but who, as their services were not required, were sheltering themselves there from the random bullets which were flying about. They at once challenged; but Symmonds answering them in French they, being unable to see his uniform in the darkness, and supposing him to be a French officer, allowed him to advance.

He passed boldly forward into the grove. He proceeded nearly through it, until he came within sight of the guns, which were still keeping up their fire upon those of the English; while a hundred French infantry, who were in support, were all occupied in watching what was going on in front of them. Symmonds returned to the detachment, by a path to the right of that by which he had entered, and passed out without seeing a soul.

Lieutenant Keene gave the word to advance and, following the guidance of Mr. Symmonds, entered the grove. He advanced, unobserved, until within thirty yards of the enemy. Here he halted, and poured a volley into them.

The effect was instantaneous. Many of the French fell, and the rest, astounded at this sudden and unexpected attack, left their guns and fled. Sixty of them rushed for shelter into a building at the end of the grove, where the English surrounded them and forced them to surrender.

By this sudden stroke, the battle of Kavaripak was won. The sound of the musketry fire, and the immediate cessation of that of the enemy's guns, told Clive that the grove was captured. A few minutes later fugitives, arriving from the grove, informed the commander of the enemy's main body of infantry of the misfortune which had befallen them. The French fire at once ceased, and the troops withdrew.

In the darkness, it was impossible for Clive to attempt a pursuit. He was in ignorance of the direction the enemy had taken; his troops had already marched sixty miles in two days; and he would, moreover, have been exposed to sudden dashes of the enemy's cavalry. Clive, therefore, united his troops, joined his baggage, which the little guard had gallantly defended against the attacks of the enemy's cavalry, and waited for morning.

At daybreak, not an enemy was to be seen. Fifty Frenchmen lay dead on the field, and sixty were captives. Three hundred French Sepoys had fallen. There were, besides, many wounded. The enemy's artillery had been all captured. The British loss was forty English and thirty Sepoys killed, and a great number of both wounded.

The moral effect of the victory was immense. It was the first time that French and English soldiers had fought in the field against each other, in India. The French had proved to the natives that they were enormously their superiors in fighting power. Hitherto the English had not done so. The defence of Arcot had proved that they could fight behind walls; but the natives had, themselves, many examples of gallant defences of this kind. The English troops, under Gingen and Cope, had suffered themselves to be cooped up in Trichinopoli, and had not struck a blow in its defence.

At Kavaripak, the natives discovered that the English could fight as well, or better than the French. The latter were somewhat stronger, numerically, than their rivals. They had double the force of artillery, were half as strong again in Sepoys, and had two thousand five hundred cavalry, while the English had not a single horseman. They had all the advantages of surprise and position; and yet, they had been entirely defeated.

Thenceforth the natives of India regarded the English as a people to be feared and respected; and, for the first time, considered their ultimate triumph over the French to be a possibility. As the policy of the native princes had ever been to side with the strongest, the advantage thus gained to the English cause, by the victory of Kavaripak, was enormous.

On the following day, the English took possession of the fort of Kavaripak, and marched to Arcot. Scarcely had they arrived there when Clive received a despatch from Fort Saint David; ordering him to return there at once, with all his troops; to march to the relief of Trichinopoli, where the garrison was reported to be in the sorest straits, from want of provisions.

The force reached Fort Saint David on the 11th of March. Here preparations were hurried forward for the advance to Trichinopoli; and, in three days, Clive was ready to start. Just as he was about to set out, a ship arrived from England, having on board some more troops, together with Major Lawrence and several officers, some of whom were captains senior to Clive.

Major Lawrence, who had already proved his capacity and energy, of course took command of the expedition; and treated Clive, who had served under him at the siege of Pondicherry, and whose successes in the field had attracted his high admiration, as second in command, somewhat to the discontent of the officers senior to him in rank.

The force consisted of four hundred Europeans, eleven hundred Sepoys, and eight guns, and escorted a large train of provisions and stores. During these months which the diversion, caused by the attack of Riza Sahib and the French upon Madras, had given to the besiegers of Trichinopoli, they should have long since captured the town. In spite of all the orders of Dupleix, Law could not bring himself to attack the town; and the French governor of Pondicherry saw, with dismay, that the two months and a half, which his efforts and energy had gained for the besiegers, had been entirely wasted; and that it was probable the whole fruits of his labours would be thrown away.

He now directed Law to leave only a small force in front of Trichinopoli, and to march with the whole of his army, and that of Chunda Sahib, and crush the force advancing under Lawrence to the relief of Trichinopoli. Law, however, disobeyed orders; and, indeed, acted in direct contradiction to them. He maintained six hundred French troops and many thousands of native before Trichinopoli, and sent but two hundred and fifty French, and about three hundred and fifty natives – a force altogether inferior in numbers to that which it was sent to oppose – to arrest the progress of Lawrence's advancing column.

The position which this French force was directed to occupy was the fort of Koiladi, an admirable position. As the two branches of the Kavari were, here, but half a mile apart, had Law concentrated all his force here he could, no doubt, have successfully opposed the English.

Lawrence, however, when the guns of the fort opened upon him, replied to them by the fire of his artillery; and, as the French force was insufficient to enable its commander to fight him in the open, he was enabled to take his troops and convoy in safety past the fort. When Law heard this, he marched out and took his position round a lofty, and almost, inaccessible rock called Elmiseram, and prepared to give battle.

Lawrence, however, after passing Koiladi, had been joined by a hundred and fifty English dragoons, from Trichinopoli. These acted as guides, and led him by a route by which he avoided the French position; and effected a junction with two hundred Europeans, and four hundred Sepoys from Trichinopoli; and with a body of Mahratta cavalry, under Murari Reo.

Law, having failed to attack the English force upon its march, now, when its strength was nearly doubled, suddenly decided to give battle, and advanced against the force which, wearied with its long march, had just begun to prepare their breakfast. The French artillery at once put the Mahratta cavalry to flight.

Lawrence called the men again under arms, and sent Clive forward to reconnoitre. He found the French infantry drawn up, with twenty-two guns, with large bodies of cavalry on either flank. Opposite to the centre of their position was a large caravansary, or native inn, with stone buildings attached. It was nearer to their position than to that occupied by the English, and Clive saw at once that, if seized and held by the enemy's artillery, it would sweep the whole ground over which the English would have to advance.

He galloped back at full speed to Major Lawrence, and asked leave at once to occupy the building. Obtaining permission, he advanced with all speed to the caravansary, with some guns and infantry.

The negligence of the French, in allowing this movement to be carried out, was fatal to them. The English artillery opened upon them from the cover of the inn and buildings, and to this fire the French in the open could reply only at a great disadvantage. After a cannonade lasting half an hour, the French, having lost forty

European and three hundred native soldiers, fell back; the English having lost only twenty-one.

Disheartened at this result, utterly disappointed at the failure which had attended his long operations against Trichinopoli, without energy or decision, Law at once raised the siege of the town, abandoning a great portion of his baggage; and, destroying great stores of ammunition and supplies, crossed an arm of the Kavari and took post in the great fortified temple of Seringam.

The delight of the troops; so long besieged in Trichinopoli; inactive, dispirited, and hopeless, was extreme; and the exultation of Muhammud Ali and his native allies was no less.

Captain Cope, towards the end of the siege, had been killed, in one of the little skirmishes which occasionally took place with the French.

Charlie Marryat and Peters had, owing to some of the officers senior to them being killed or invalided, and to large numbers of fresh recruits being raised, received a step in rank. They were now lieutenants, and each commanded a body of Sepoys, two hundred strong. At Charlie's request, Tim Kelly was detached from his company, and allowed to remain with him as soldier servant. After the retreat of the French, and the settling down of the English force in the lines they had occupied, Charlie and his friend entered Trichinopoli, and were surprised at the temples and palaces there. Although very inferior to Tanjore, and in no way even comparable to the cities of the northwest of India, Trichinopoli was a far more important city than any they had hitherto seen. They ascended the lofty rock, and visited the fort on its summit, which looked as if, in the hands of a resolute garrison, it should be impregnable to attack.

The manner in which this rock, as well as that of Elmiseram and others lying in sight, rose sheer up from the plain, filled them with surprise; for, although these natural rock fortresses are common enough in India, they are almost without an example in Europe. After visiting the fort they rambled through the town, and were amused at the scene of bustle in its streets; and at the gay shops, full of articles new and curious to them, in the bazaars.

'They are wonderfully clever and ingenious,' Charlie said. 'Look what rough tools that man is working with, and what delicate and intricate work he is turning out. If these fellows could but fight as well as they work, and were but united among themselves, not only should we be unable to set a foot in India, but the emperor, with the enormous armies which he would be able to raise, would be able to threaten Europe. I suppose they never have been really good fighting men. Alexander, a couple of thousand years ago, defeated them; and since then the Afghans, and other northern peoples, have been always overrunning and conquering them.

'I can't make it out. These Sepoys, after only a few weeks' training, fight almost as well as our own men. I wonder how it is that, when commanded by their own countrymen, they are able to make so poor a fight of it.

'We had better be going back to camp again, Peters. At any moment, there may be orders for us to do something. With Major Lawrence and Clive together, we are not likely to stop here long, inactive.'

Chapter 10

THE FALL OF SERINGAM

Although called an island, Seringam is in fact a long narrow tongue of land, running between the two branches of the river Kavari. In some places these arms are but a few hundred yards apart, and the island can therefore be defended against an attack along the land. But the retreat of the French by this line was equally difficult, as we held the narrowest part of the neck, two miles from Koiladi.

Upon the south, our forces at Trichinopoli faced the French across the river. Upon the other side of the Kolrun, as the northern arm of the Kavari is called, the French could cross the river and make their retreat, if necessary, in any direction. The two principal roads, however, led from Paichandah, a strong fortified position on the bank of the river, facing the temple of Seringam.

Clive saw that a force crossing the river, and taking up its position on the north, would entirely cut off Law's army in the island; would intercept any reinforcements sent by Dupleix to its rescue; and might compel the surrender of the whole French army. The attempt would, of course, be a dangerous one. The French force was considerably stronger than the English, and were the latter divided into two portions, entirely cut off from each other, the central point between them being occupied by the French, the latter would have an opportunity of throwing his whole force upon one after the other.

This danger would have been so great that, had the French been commanded by an able and active officer, the attempt would never have been made. Law, however, had shown amply that he had neither energy nor intelligence, and Major Lawrence therefore accepted Clive's proposal.

But to be successful, it was necessary that both portions of the English force should be well commanded. Major Lawrence felt confident in his own capacity to withstand Law upon the southern bank, and in case of necessity he could fall back under the guns of Trichinopoli. He felt sure that he could, with equal certainty, confide the command of the other party to Captain Clive. There was, however, the difficulty that he was the junior captain present; and that already great jealousy had been excited, among his seniors, by the rank which he occupied in the councils of Lawrence.

Fortunately, the difficulty was settled by the native allies. Major Lawrence laid his plans before Muhammud Ali and his allies, whose cooperation and assistance were absolutely necessary. These, after hearing the proposal, agreed to give their assistance, but only upon the condition that Clive should be placed in command of the expeditionary party. They had already seen the paralysing effects of the incapacity of some English officers. Clive's defence of Arcot, and the victories of Arni and Kavaripak, had excited their intense admiration, and caused them to place unbounded confidence in him. Therefore they said:

'If Captain Clive commands, we will go – unless he commands, we do not.'

Major Lawrence was glad that the pressure thus placed upon him enabled him, without incurring a charge of favouritism, to place the command in the hands of the officer upon whom he most relied.

On the night of the 6th of April Clive set out; with a force composed of four hundred English, seven hundred Sepoys, three thousand Mahratta cavalry, a thousand Tanjore cavalry, six light guns and two heavy ones. Descending the river, he crossed the island at a point three miles to the east of Law's camping ground, and marched to Samieaveram, a town nine miles north of the island, and commanding the roads from the north and east.

The movement was just made in time. Dupleix, utterly disgusted with Law, had resolved to displace him. D'Auteuil, the only officer he had of sufficient high rank to take his place, had not, when previously employed, betrayed any great energy or capacity. It appeared, nevertheless, that he was at any rate superior to Law. On the

10th of April, therefore, he despatched D'Auteuil, with a hundred and twenty French, and five hundred Sepoys, with four guns and a large convoy, to Seringam, where he was to take the command. When he arrived within fifteen miles of Samieaveram, he learned that Clive had possession of that village, and he determined upon a circuitous route, by which he might avoid him. He therefore sent a messenger to Law, to acquaint him with his plans, in order that he might aid him by making a diversion.

Clive, in the meantime, had been at work. On the day after his arrival at Samieaveram, he attacked and captured the temple of Mansurpet, halfway between the village and the island. The temple was lofty, and stood on rising ground, and commanded a range of the country for many miles round.

On its top, Clive established a signal station. Upon the following day he carried the mud fort of Lalgudi, which was situated on the north bank of the river, two miles to the east of Paichandah, which now remained Law's only place of exit from the island.

D'Auteuil, after sending word to Law of his intentions, marched from Utatua, where he was lying, by a road to the west which would enable him to move round Samieaveram to Paichandah. Clive captured one of the messengers, and set off with his force to intercept him. D'Auteuil, however, received information by his spies of Clive's movement, and not wishing to fight a battle in the open, with a superior force, fell back to Utatua, while Clive returned to Samieaveram.

Law, too, had received news of Clive's movement. Here was a chance of retrieving the misfortunes of the campaign. Paichandah being still in his hands, he could sally out with his whole force and that of Chunda Sahib, seize Samieaveram in Clive's absence, and extend his hand to D'Auteuil, or fall upon Clive's rear. Instead of this, he repeated the mistake he had made before Trichinopoli; and, instead of marching out with his whole force, he sent only eighty Europeans, of whom forty were deserters from the English army, and seven hundred Sepoys.

The English returned from their march against D'Auteuil. The greater portion of the troops were housed in two temples, a quarter of a mile apart, known as the Large and Small Pagoda. Clive, with several of his officers, was in a caravansary close to the Small Pagoda.

Charlie's company were on guard, and after paying a visit to the sentries, and seeing that all were on the alert, he returned to the caravansary. The day had been a long one, and the march under the heat of the sun very fatiguing. There was therefore but little conversation, and Charlie, finding, on his return from visiting the sentries, that his leader and the other officers had already wrapped themselves in their cloaks and lain down to rest, imitated their example.

Half an hour later, the French column arrived at Samieaveram. The officer in command was a daring and determined man. Before reaching the place, he had heard that the English had returned; and, finding that he had been forestalled, he might well have returned to Law. He determined, however, to attempt to surprise the camp. He placed his deserters in front, and when the column, arriving near the Sepoy sentinel, was challenged, the officer in command of the deserters, an Irishman, stepped forward, and said that he had been sent by Major Lawrence to the support of Captain Clive. As the other English-speaking soldiers now came up, the sentry and native officer with him were completely deceived, and the latter sent a soldier to guide the column to the English quarter of the camp.

Without interruption, the column marched on through lines of sleeping Sepoys and Mahrattas until they reached the heart of the village. Here they were again challenged. They replied with a volley of musketry into the caravansary, and another into the pagoda. Then they rushed into the pagoda, bayoneting all they found there.

Charlie, who had just dropped off to sleep, sprang to his feet, as did the other officers. While, confused by the noise and suddenness of the attack, others scarcely understood what was happening, Clive's clear head and ready judgment grasped the situation at once.

'Gentlemen,' he said calmly, 'there is no firing going on in the direction of the Great Pagoda. Follow me there at once.'

Snatching up their arms, the officers followed him at a run. The whole village was a scene of wild confusion. The firing round the pagoda and caravansary were continuous. The Mahratta horsemen were climbing into their saddles, and riding away out into the plain; the Sepoys were running hither and thither.

At the pagoda he found the soldiers turning out under arms, and Clive, ordering his officers to do their best to rally the native troops in good order against the enemy, at once moved forward towards the caravansary, with two hundred English troops. On arriving there, he found a large body of Sepoys firing away at random. Believing them to be his own men, for the French and English Sepoys were alike dressed in white, he halted the English a few yards from them, and rushed among them, upbraiding them for their panic, striking them, and ordering them instantly to cease firing, and to form in order.

One of the Sepoy officers recognized Clive to be an Englishman, struck at him, and wounded him with his sword. Clive, still believing him to be one of his own men, was furious at what he considered an act of insolent insubordination; and, seizing him, dragged him across to the Small Pagoda to hand him over, as he supposed, to the guard there. To his astonishment he found six Frenchmen at the gate, and these at once summoned him to surrender.

Great as was his surprise, he did not for a moment lose coolness, and at once told them that he had come to beg them to lay down their arms, that they were surrounded by his whole army, and that, unless they surrendered, his troops would give no quarter. So impressed were the Frenchmen with the firmness of the speaker that three of them at once surrendered, while the other three ran into the temple to inform their commander.

Clive took the three men who had surrendered, and returned to the English troops he had left near the caravansary. The French Sepoys had discovered that the English were enemies, and had moved quietly off.

Confusion still reigned. Clive did not imagine, for a moment, that so daring an assault could have been made on his camp by a small body of enemies, and expected every moment an attack by Law's whole force. The commander of the French, in the pagoda, was disturbed by the news brought in by the three men from the gate, and despatched eight of his most intelligent men to ascertain exactly what was going on.

These, however, fell into the hands of the English; and the officer of the party, not knowing that the Small Pagoda was in the hands of the French, handed them over to a sergeant, and told him to take a party and escort his eight prisoners, and the three Captain Clive had captured, to that pagoda for confinement there.

Upon arrival at the gate the Frenchmen at once joined their comrades, and these latter were also so bewildered at the affair, that they allowed the English sergeant and his guard to march off again, unmolested.

By this time, owing to the absence of all resistance elsewhere, Clive had learnt that the whole of the party who had entered the camp were in the Lesser Pagoda; and, as he was still expecting, momentarily, to be attacked by Law's main army, he determined to rid himself of this enemy in his midst. The pagoda was very strong, and only two men could enter abreast. Clive led his men to the attack, but so well did the French defend themselves that, after losing an officer and fifteen men, Clive determined to wait till morning.

The French officer, knowing that he was surrounded, and beyond the reach of all assistance, resolved upon cutting a way through, and at daylight his men sallied out from the temple. So fierce, however, was the fire with which the English received him, that twelve of his men were instantly killed, and the rest ran back into the temple.

Clive, hoping that their commander would now surrender without further effusion of blood, advanced to the gateway and entered the porch to offer terms. He was himself so faint, from the loss of blood from his wounds, that he could not stand alone, but leaned against a wall, supported by two sergeants. The officer commanding the deserters came out to parley, but, after heaping abuse upon Clive, levelled his musket and discharged it at him. He missed Clive, but killed the two sergeants who were supporting him.

The French officer in command, indignant at this conduct, rushed forward at once to disavow it; and stated that he had determined to defend the post to the last, solely for the sake of the deserters, but that the conduct of their officer had released him from that obligation, and he now therefore surrendered at once.

The instant day broke, and Clive saw that Law was not, as he expected, at hand, he despatched the Mahratta horse in pursuit of the French Sepoys. These were overtaken and cut to pieces, and not one man, of the force which Law had despatched against Clive returned to the island.

The English loss was heavy. The greater portion of the occupants of the Small Pagoda were bayoneted by the French, when they entered; and, as fifteen others were killed in the attack, it is probable that at least one-fourth of the English force under Clive were killed.

Clive's own escapes were extraordinary. In addition to those of being killed by the French Sepoys, among whom he ran by mistake, and of death at the hands of the treacherous deserter, he had one almost as close, when the French fired their volley into the caravansary. A box at his feet was shattered, and a servant who slept close to him was killed.

Some days passed, after this attack, without any fresh movement on either side. Major Lawrence then determined to drive back D'Auteuil. He did not despatch Clive against him, as this would involve the risk that Law might again march out to surprise Samieaveram. He therefore directed Clive to remain at that place and watch the island, while he sent a force of a hundred and fifty English, four hundred Sepoys, five hundred Mahrattas, with four guns, to attack D'Auteuil; from his own force, under Captain Dalton. This officer, in the advance, marched his troops near Samieaveram; and, making as much show with them as he could, impressed D'Auteuil with the idea that the force was that of Clive.

Accordingly, he broke up his camp at Utatua in the night, abandoned his stores, and retreated hastily upon Valconda. Dalton then marched to Samieaveram, and placed his force at Clive's disposal; and, to prevent any disputes arising as to precedence and rank, offered himself to serve under him as a volunteer.

Not only D'Auteuil, but Law, was deceived by Dalton's march. From the lofty towers of Seringam he saw the force marching towards Utatua, believed that Clive with his whole force had left Samieaveram, and did now what he should have before done – crossed the river with all his troops.

Clive's lookout on the temple of Mansurpet perceived what was going on, and signalled the news to Clive, who at once set out with his whole force; and, before Law was prepared to issue out from Paichandah, Clive was within a mile of that place. Law might still have fought with a fair chance of success, as he was far stronger than his enemy, but he was again the victim of indecision and want of energy, and, covered by Paichandah, he fell back across the river again.

On the 15th of May Clive captured Paichandah, and then determined to give a final blow to D'Auteuil's force; which had, he learned, again set out to endeavour to relieve Law. He marched to Utatua to intercept him.

D'Auteuil, hearing of his coming, instantly fell back again to Valconda. The native chief of this town, however, seeing that the affairs of the French were desperate; and willing, like all his countrymen, to make his peace with the strongest, had already accepted bribes from the English; and upon D'Auteuil's return, closed the gates and refused to admit him. Clive soon arrived, and D'Auteuil, caught between two fires, surrendered with his whole force.

Had Law been a man of energy, he had yet a chance of escape. He had still seven or eight hundred French troops with him, two thousand Sepoys, and four thousand of Chunda Sahib's troops. He might, then, have easily crossed the Kavari at night and fallen upon Lawrence, whose force there now was greatly inferior to his own. Chunda Sahib, in vain, begged him to do so. His hesitation continued until, three days after the surrender of D'Auteuil, a battering train reached Lawrence; whereupon Law at once surrendered, his chief stipulation being that the life of Chunda Sahib should be spared.

This promise was not kept. The unfortunate prince had preferred to surrender to the Rajah of Tanjore, who had several times intrigued secretly with him, rather than to Muhammud Ali or the English, whom he regarded as his implacable enemies. Had he placed himself in our hands, his life would have been safe. He was murdered, by the treacherous rajah, within twenty-four hours of his surrender.

With the fall of Seringam terminated the contest for the supremacy of the Carnatic, between the English and French, fighting respectively on behalf of their puppets, Muhammud Ali and Chunda Sahib. This stage of the struggle was not a final one; but both by its circumstances, and by the prestige which we acquired in the eyes of the natives, it gave us a moral ascendency which, even when our fortunes were afterwards at their worst, was never lost again.

Muhammud Ali had, himself, gained but little in the struggle. He was, indeed, nominally ruler of the Carnatic, but he had to rely for his position solely on the support of the English bayonets. Indeed, the promises, of which he had been obliged to be lavish to his native allies, to keep them faithful to his cause, when that cause seemed all but lost, now came upon him to trouble him; and so precarious was his position, that he was obliged to ask the English to leave two hundred English troops, and fifteen hundred of their Sepoys, to protect the place against Murari Reo, and the Rajahs of Mysore and Tanjore.

The fatigues of the expedition had been great and, when the force reached the seacoast, Major Lawrence was forced to retire to Fort Saint David to recover his health; while Clive, whose health had now greatly broken down, betook himself to Madras; which had, when the danger of invasion by the French was at an end, become the headquarters of the government of the presidency.

There were, however, two French strongholds dangerously near to Madras, Covelong and Chengalpatt. Two hundred recruits had just arrived from England, and five hundred natives had been enlisted as Sepoys. Mr. Saunders begged Clive to take the command of these, and reduce the two fortresses. He took with him two twenty-four pounders, and four officers, of whom two were Charlie Marryat and Peters; to both of whom Clive was much attached, owing to their courage, readiness, and good humour.

Covelong was first attacked. It mounted thirty guns, and was garrisoned by fifty French, and three hundred Sepoys.

'I don't like the look o' things, Mr. Charles,' Tim Kelly said. 'There's nothing but boys altogether, white and black. Does it stand to reason that a lot of gossoons, who haven't learnt the goose step, and haven't as much as a shred of faith, ayther in themselves or their officers, are fit to fight the French?'

'Oh, I don't know, Tim,' Charlie said. 'Boys are just as plucky as men, in their way, and are ready to do all sorts of foolhardy things, which men would hesitate to attempt.'

'And that is so, Mr. Charles, when they've only other boys to dale with; but as they're growing up, they take some time before they're quite sure they're a match for men. That's what it is, yer honor, I tell ye, and you will see it, soon.'

Tim's predictions were speedily verified. The very morning after they arrived before the fort, the garrison made a sally, fell upon the troops, and killed one of their officers.

The whole of the new levies took to their heels, and fled away from the fight. Clive, with his three officers, threw himself among them and, for some time, in vain attempted to turn the tide. It was not, indeed, until several had been cut down that the rout was arrested, and they were brought back to their duty.

A day or two later a shot, striking a rock, killed or wounded fourteen men; and excited such a panic, that it was some time before the rest would venture near the front.

The enemy, with a considerable force, marched from Chengalpatt to relieve the place. Clive left half his force to continue the siege, and with the rest marched out and offered battle to the relieving force. Daring and confidence, as usual, prevailed. Had the enemy attacked, there is little doubt they would have put Clive's raw levies to flight. They were, however, cowed by his attitude of defiance, and retreated hastily.

The governor of Covelong at once lost heart and surrendered the place; which he might have maintained, for months, against the force before it; and on the fourth day of the siege, capitulated.

A few hours afterwards the enemy from Chengalpatt, ignorant of the fall of the fort, again advanced; and Clive met them with his whole force. Taken by surprise, they suffered heavily. Clive pursued them to the gates of their fort, to which he at once laid siege.

Fortunately for the English, the commander of this place, like him of Covelong, was cowardly and incapable. Had it not been so, the fort, which was very strong, well provisioned, and well garrisoned, might have held out for an indefinite time. As it was, it surrendered on the fourth day, and Clive took possession on the 31st of August.

He returned to Madras, and there, a short time afterwards, married Miss Maskelyne. Finding his health, however, continuing to deteriorate, he sailed for Europe in February, 1753. It was but five years since he had first taken up arms to defend Fort Saint David, an unknown clerk, without prospects and without fortune, utterly discontented and disheartened.

Madras was in the hands of the French. Everywhere their policy was triumphant, and the soil surrounded by the walls of Saint David's, alone, remained to the English in Southern India. In the five years which had elapsed, all had changed. The English were masters of the Carnatic. The French were broken and discredited. The English were regarded by the natives throughout the country as the coming power; and of this great change, no slight portion was due to the energy and genius of Clive, himself.

Chapter 11

AN IMPORTANT MISSION

A few days after the return of the expedition against Covelong and Chengalpatt, Charlie received a note from Governor Saunders, requesting him to call upon him at eleven o'clock. Charlie, of course, attended at Government House at the time named, and found Captain Clive with Mr. Saunders.

'I have sent for you, Mr. Marryat, to ask you if you are ready to undertake a delicate, and somewhat dangerous, mission. Captain Clive tells me that he is convinced that you will be able to discharge the duties satisfactorily. He has been giving me the highest report of your conduct and courage, and he tells me that you speak the language with some facility.'

'I have been working hard, sir,' Charlie said, 'and have had a moonshee for the last year; and as, except when on duty, I have spoken nothing but the native language with him, I can now speak it almost as fluently as I can English.'

'So Captain Clive has been telling me,' Mr. Saunders said; 'and it is, indeed, on that ground that I select you for the service. Your friend Mr. Peters has equally distinguished himself in the field, Captain Clive tells me, but he is greatly your inferior in his knowledge of the vernacular.'

This was indeed the case. Peters had but little natural aptitude for foreign languages; and after working hard, for a time, with the moonshee, he found that he was making so little progress, in comparison with Charlie, that he lost heart; and although he had continued his lessons with the moonshee, he had done so only to the extent of an hour or so a day, whereas Charlie had devoted his whole leisure time to the work.

'The facts of the case are these, Mr. Marryat. Owing to the failure, of Muhammud Ali, to fulfil the ridiculously onerous terms extorted from him, by some of his native allies, during the siege of Trichinopoli, several of them are in a state of discontent, which is likely soon to break out into open hostilities. The Rajahs of Mysore and Tanjore are, I have learned, already in communication with Pondicherry; and will, I believe, shortly acknowledge the son of Chunda Sahib, whom Dupleix has declared ruler of the Carnatic. Murari Reo has already openly joined the French. Their influence in the Deccan is now so great that Bussy may be said to rule there.

'Now, there is a chief named Boorhau Reo, whose territory lies among the hills, and extends from the plain nearly up to the plateau land of the Deccan. His position, like that of many of the other small rajahs, is precarious. In days like the present, when might makes right, and every petty state tries to make profit out of the constant wars, at the expense of its neighbour, the position of a chief, surrounded by half a dozen others more powerful than himself, is by no means pleasant. Boorhau Reo feels that he is in danger of being swallowed, by the nizam or by the Mahrattas, and he earnestly desires to ally himself with us; believing, as he says, that we are destined to be masters here. I have assured him that, although gratified at his expressions of friendship, we can enter into no alliance with him. The position of his territory would enable him to be of great assistance to us, in any war in which the whole force of the Deccan, controlled as it is at present at Bussy, might be utilized against us in the Carnatic. He would be able to harass convoys, cut communications, and otherwise trouble the enemy's movements. But, although we see that his aid would be very useful to us, in case of such a war; we do not see how, on our part, we could give him any protection. We have now, with the greatest difficulty, brought affairs to a successful conclusion in the Carnatic; but Dupleix is active and energetic, and well supported at home. Many of the chiefs lately our allies have, as I have just said, declared against us, or are about to do so; and it is out of the question, for us to think of supporting a chief so far removed from us as Boorhau. I have, therefore, told him that we greatly desire his friendship, but are at present powerless to protect him, should he be attacked by his northern neighbours.

'He is particularly anxious to train his men after the European fashion, as he sees that our Sepoys are a match for five times their number of the untrained troops of the Indian princes.

'This brings me to the subject before us. I have written to him, to say that I will send to him an English officer, capable of training and leading his troops, and whose advice may be useful to him upon all occasions; but that as, were it known that he had received a British officer, and was employing him to train his troops, it would excite the instant animosity of Bussy and of the Peishwar; I should send one familiar with the language, and who may pass as a native. Captain Clive has strongly recommended you for this difficult mission.'

'I fear, sir, that I could hardly pass as a native. The moonshee is constantly correcting mistakes which I make, in speaking.'

'That may be so,' Mr. Saunders said; 'but there are a score of dialects in Southern India, and you could be passed upon nineteen of the twenty peoples who speak them, as belonging to one of the other.'

'If you think, sir, that I shall do,' Charlie said; 'I shall be glad to undertake the mission.'

'Very well, Mr. Marryat, that is understood, then. You will receive full instructions in writing, and will understand that your duty is not only to drill the troops of this chief; but to give him such advice as may suit his and our interests; to strengthen his good feeling towards us; and to form, as far as possible, a compact little force which might, at a critical moment, be of immense utility. You will, of course, master the geography of the country, of which we are all but absolutely ignorant; find out about the passes, the mountain paths, the defensible positions. All these things may someday be of the highest importance.

'You will have a few days to make your arrangements, and settle as to the character you will adopt. This you had better do, in consultation with someone who thoroughly understands the country. It is intended that you shall go down to Trichinopoli, with the next convoy; and from there make your way to the stronghold of Boorhau.'

'Shall I take any followers with me?'

'Yes,' Mr. Saunders said. 'As you will go in the character of a military adventurer, who has served among our Sepoys long enough to learn European drill, you had better take two, three, or four men, as you like, with you as retainers. You might pick out two or three trusty men, from the Sepoys you command.'

Charlie left Government House in high spirits. It was certainly an honor, to have been selected for such a post. It was quite possible that it would be a dangerous one. It was sure to be altogether different from the ordinary life of a subaltern in the Company's army.

Peters was very sorry when he heard from Charlie that they were, at last, to be separated. It was now nearly two years since they had first met on board the Lizzie Anderson; and, since that time, they had been constantly together, and were greatly attached to each other.

Charlie, perhaps, had taken the lead. The fact of his having a stock of firearms, and being able to lend them to Peters, had given him, perhaps, the first slight and almost imperceptible advantage. His feat of jumping overboard, to rescue Tim Kelly, had been another step in advance; and, although Charlie would have denied it himself, there was no doubt that he generally took the lead, and that his friend was accustomed to lean upon him, and to look to him always for the initiative. It was, therefore, a severe blow to Peters, to find that Charlie was about to be sent on detached service.

As for Tim Kelly, he was uproarious in his grief, when he heard that he was to be separated from his master.

'Shure, Mr. Charlie, ye'll never have the heart to lave a poor boy, that sarved ye be night and day for eighteen months. Tim Kelly would gladly give his life for ye, and ye wouldn't go and lave him behind ye, and go all alone among these black thaves of the world.'

'But it is impossible that I can take you, Tim,' Charlie said. 'You know, yourself, that you cannot speak ten words of the language. How then could you possibly pass undetected, whatever disguise you put on?'

'But I'd never open my mouth at all, at all, yer honor, barring for mate and drink.'

'It's all very well for you to say so, Tim,' Charlie answered; 'but I do not think that anything, short of a miracle, would silence your tongue. But leave us now, Tim, and I will talk the matter over with Mr. Peters. I should be glad enough to have you with me, if we could arrange it.'

The moonshee was taken into their counsels, and was asked his opinion as to the disguise which Charlie could adopt, with least risk of detection. The moonshee replied that he might pass as a Bheel. These hill tribes speak a dialect quite distinct from that of the people around them, and the moonshee said that, if properly attired, Charlie would be able to pass anywhere for one of these people; provided, always, that he did not meet with another of the same race.

'You might assert,' he said, 'that your father had taken service with some rajah on the plain, and that you had there learned to speak the language. In this way, you would avoid having to answer any difficult questions regarding your native place; but as to that, you can get up something of the geography before you leave.'

'There are several Bheels among our Sepoys,' Charlie said. 'I can pick out three or four of them, who would be just the men for me to take. I believe they are generally very faithful, and attached to their officers.'

When Tim again entered the room, he inquired anxiously if his master hit upon any disguise which would suit him.

'What do you say, Mr. Moonshine?' Tim said.

The moonshee shook his head. Between these two a perpetual feud had existed, ever since the native had arrived at Arcot, to take his place as a member of Charlie's establishment. In obedience to Charlie's stringent orders, Tim never was openly rude to him; but he never lost an opportunity of making remarks, of a disparaging nature, as to the value of Charlie's studies.

The moonshee, on his part, generally ignored Tim's existence altogether; addressing him, when obliged to do so, with a ceremonious civility which annoyed Tim more than open abuse would have done.

'I think,' he said gravely, in reply to Tim's demand; 'that the very worshipful one would have most chance of escaping detection if he went in rags, throwing dust on his hair, and passing for one afflicted.'

'And what does he mean by afflicted, Mr. Charles?' the Irishman said wrathfully, as the two young officers laughed.

'He means one who is a born fool, Tim.'

Tim looked furiously at the moonshee.

'It would,' the latter said sententiously, 'be the character which the worshipful one would support with the greatest ease.'

'The black thief is making fun of me,' Tim muttered; 'but I'll be aven with him one of these days, or my name isn't Tim Kelly.'

'I was thinking, yer honor, that I might represent one deaf and dumb.'

'But you're always talking, Tim, and when you're not talking to others, you talk to yourself. It's quite impossible you could go as a dumb man; but you might go, as the moonshee suggests, as a half-witted sort of chap; with just sense enough to groom a horse and look after him, but with not enough to understand what's said to you, or to answer any questions.'

'I could do that asy enough, Mr. Charles.'

'And you have to keep from quarrelling, Tim. I hear you quarrelling, on an average, ten times a day; and as, in such a character as we're talking about, you would, of course, be exposed to all sorts of slights and unpleasantnesses, you would be in continual hot water.'

'Now, yer honor,' Tim said reproachfully, 'you're too hard on me, entirely. I like a bit of a row as well as any many, but it's all for divarsion; and I could go on, for a year, without quarrelling with a soul. Just try me, Mr. Charles. Just try me for a month, and if, at the end of that time, you find me in your way; or that I don't keep my character, then send me back agin to the regiment.'

It was arranged that the moonshee should remain with Peters, who, seeing that Charlie owed his appointment, to a post which promised excitement and adventure, to his skill in the native languages, was determined that he would again set to, in earnest, and try and master its intricacies. The moonshee went down to the bazaar, and purchased the clothes which would be necessary for the disguises; and Charlie found, in his company, four Sepoys who willingly agreed to accompany him, in the character of his retainers, upon his expedition. As to their costume, there was no difficulty. When off duty, the Sepoys in the Company's service were accustomed to dress in their native attire. Consequently, it needed only the addition of a tulwar, or short curved sword; a shield, thrown over one shoulder; a long matchlock; and two or three pistols and daggers, stuck into a girdle, to complete their equipment.

Charlie himself was dressed gaily, in the garb of a military officer in the service of an Indian rajah. He was to ride, and a horse, saddle, and gay housings were procured. He had, at last, given in to Tim's entreaties; and that worthy was dressed as a syce, or horse keeper.

Both Charlie and Tim had had those portions of their skin exposed to the air darkened, and both would pass muster, at a casual inspection. Charlie, in thus concealing his nationality, desired only to hide the fact that he was an officer in the Company's service. He believed that it would be impossible for him to continue to pass as a Bheel. This, however, would be of no consequence, after a time. Many of the native princes had Europeans in their service. Runaway sailors, deserters from the English, French, and Dutch armed forces in their possessions on the seacoast, adventurers influenced either by a love of a life of excitement, or whom a desire to escape the consequences of folly or crime committed at home had driven to a roving life – such men might be found in many of the native courts.

Once settled, then, in the service of the rajah, Charlie intended to make but little farther pretence, or secrecy, as to his nationality. Outwardly, he would still conform to the language and appearance of the character he had chosen; but he would allow it to be supposed that he was an Englishman, a deserter from the Company's service, and that his comrades were Sepoys in a similar position. His employment, then, at the court of the rajah, would have an effect the exact reverse of that which it would have done, had he appeared in his proper character.

Deserters were, of all men, the most opposed to their countrymen, to whom they had proved traitors. In battle they could be relied upon to fight desperately, for they fought with ropes round their necks. Therefore, while the appearance of an English officer, as instructor of the forces of the rajah, would have drawn upon himself the instant hostility of all opposed to the British; the circulation of a report that his troops were being disciplined by some English and native deserters, from the Company's forces, would excite no suspicion whatever.

To avoid attracting attention, Charlie Marryat and his party set out before daylight from Madras. Their appearance, indeed, would have attracted no attention, when they once had passed beyond the boundaries of the portion of the town occupied by the whites. In the native quarter, the appearance of a small zemindar, or landowner, attended by four or five armed followers on foot, was of such common occurrence as to attract no attention whatever; and, indeed, numbers of these come in to take service in the Sepoy regiments, the profession of arms being always considered honorable, in India.

For a fortnight they travelled, by easy stages, without question or suspicion being excited that they were not what they seemed. They were now among the hills, and soon arrived at Ambur, the seat of the rajah. The town was a small one, and above it rose the fortress, which stood on a rock rising sheer from the bottom of the valley, and standing boldly out from the hillside. The communication was effected by a shoulder which, starting from a point halfway up the rock, joined the hill behind it. Along this shoulder were walls and gateways. An enemy attacking these would be exposed to the fire from the summit of the rock. From the point where the shoulder joined the rock, a zigzag road had been cut, with enormous labour, in the face of the rock, to the summit.

'It is a strong place,' Charlie said to Tim Kelly, who was walking by his horse's head; 'and should be able to hold out against anything but starvation. That is to say, if properly defended.'

'It's a powerful place, surely,' Tim said; 'and would puzzle the ould boy himself to take. Even Captain Clive, who is afeard of nothing, would be bothered by it.'

As they rode up the valley, two horsemen were seen spurring towards them, from the town. They drew rein before Charlie; and one, bowing, said:

'My master, the rajah, sends his greeting to you, and begs to know if you are the illustrious soldier, Nadir Ali, for whom his heart has been longing.'

'Will you tell your lord that Nadir Ali is here,' Charlie said, 'and that he longs to see the face of the rajah.'

One of the horsemen at once rode off, and the other took his place by the side of Charlie; and, having introduced himself as captain of the rajah's bodyguard, rode with him through the town.

Had Charlie appeared in his character as English officer, the rajah and all his troops would have turned out to do honor to his arrival. As it was, a portion of the garrison, only, appeared at the gate and lined the walls. Through these the little party passed, and up the sharp zigzags, which were so steep that, had it not been that his dignity prevented him from dismounting, Charlie would gladly have got off and proceeded on foot; for it was as much as the animal could do, to struggle up the steep incline.

At each turn there was a gateway, with little flanking towers; on which jingalls, or small wall pieces, commanded the road.

'Faith, then, it's no fool that built this place. I shouldn't like to have to attack it, wid all the soldiers of the King's army, let alone those of the Company.'

'It is tremendously strong, Tim, but it is astonishing what brave men can do.'

In the after wars which England waged, in India, the truth of what Charlie said was over and over again proved. Numerous fortresses, supposed by the natives to be absolutely impregnable, and far exceeding in strength that just described, have been carried by assault, by the dash and daring of English troops.

They gained, at last, the top of the rock. It was uneven in surface, some portions being considerably more elevated than others. Roughly, its extent was about a hundred yards, either way. The lower level was covered with buildings, occupied by the garrison, and storehouses. On the upper level, some forty feet higher, stood the palace of the rajah. It communicated with the courtyard, below, by a broad flight of steps. These led to an arched gateway, with a wall and battlements; forming an interior line of defence, should an assailant gain a footing in the lower portion of the stronghold.

Alighting from his horse at the foot of the steps, Charlie, followed by his five retainers, mounted to the gateway. Here another guard of honor was drawn up. Passing through these, they entered a shady courtyard, on one side of which was a stone pavilion. The flat ceiling was supported by massive columns, closely covered with intricate sculpture. The roof was arabesqued with deeply cut patterns, picked out in bright colours. A fountain played in the middle.

On the farther side the floor, which was of marble, was raised; and two steps led to a wide recess, with windows of lattice stonework, giving a view over the town and valley below. In this recess were piles of cushions and carpets, and here reclined the rajah, a spare and active-looking man, of some forty years old. He rose, as Charlie approached, the soldiers and Sepoys remaining beyond the limits of the pavilion.

'Welcome, brave Nadir Ali,' he said courteously; 'my heart is glad, indeed, at the presence of one whose wisdom is said to be far beyond his years, and who has learned the arts of war of the infidels from beyond the seas.'

Then, inviting Charlie to take a seat on the divan with him, he questioned him as to his journey, and the events which were taking place in the plains; until the attendants, having handed round refreshments, retired at his signal.

'I am glad to see you, Sahib,' he said, when they were alone; 'though, in truth, I looked for one older than yourself. The great English governor of Madras tells me, however, in a letter which I received four days since, that you are skilled in war; that you fought by the side of that great Captain Clive at Arcot, Arni, Kavaripak, and at Trichinopoli; and that the great warrior, himself, chose you to come to me. Therefore, I doubt neither your valour nor your prudence, and put myself in your hands, wholly.

'The governor has already told you, doubtless, of the position in which I am placed here.'

'Governor Saunders explained the whole position to me,' Charlie said. 'You are, at present, menaced on all sides by powerful neighbours. You believe that the fortunes of the English are on the increase; and as you think the time may come, ere long, when they will turn the French out of the Deccan, and become masters there, as they have already become masters in the Carnatic, you wish to fight by their side, and share their fortunes. In the meantime, you desire to be able to defend yourself against your neighbours; for, at present, the English are too far away to assist you.

'To enable you to do this, I have been sent to drill and discipline your troops, like our Sepoys; and to give you such advice as may be best, for the general defence of your country. I have brought with me five soldiers; four Bheels, and one of my countrymen. The latter will be of little use in drilling your troops, for he is ignorant of the language, and has come as my personal attendant. The other four will assist me in my work.

'Your followers here will, no doubt, discover in a very short time that I am an Englishman. Let it be understood that I am a deserter, that I have been attracted to your court by the promise of high pay, and that I have assumed the character of a Bheel, lest my being here might put you on bad terms with the English.'

Charlie then asked the rajah as to the strength of his military force.

'In time of peace,' the rajah said, 'I keep three hundred men under arms. In case of taking the field, three thousand. To defend Ambur against an attack of an enemy, I could muster ten thousand men.'

'You could not call out three thousand men, without attracting the attention of your neighbours?' Charlie asked.

'No,' the rajah said; 'that would bring my neighbours upon me, at once.'

'I suppose, however, you might assemble another five hundred men, without attracting attention.'

'Oh, yes,' the rajah said; 'eight hundred men are not a force which could attract any great attention.'

'Then I should propose that we begin with eight hundred,' Charlie said. 'For a month, however, I will confine myself to the troops you at present have. We must, in the first place, train some officers. If you will pick out those to whom you intend to give commands, and subcommands; I will choose from the men, after drilling them for a few days, forty of the most intelligent as what we call noncommissioned officers.

'For the first month, we will work hard in teaching these officers and sub-officers their duties. Then, when the whole eight hundred assemble, we can divide them into four parties. There will be one of my drill instructors to each party, ten under officers, and four or five of the officers whom you will appoint. Six weeks' hard work should make these eight hundred men fairly acquainted with drill. The English Sepoys have often gone out to fight, with less. At the end of the six weeks, let the five hundred men you have called out, in addition to your bodyguard of three hundred, return to their homes; and replace them by an equal number of fresh levies, and so proceed until you have your three thousand fighting men, thoroughly trained. In nine months, all will have had their six weeks of exercise, and could take their places in the ranks again, at a day's notice.

'Two hundred of your men I will train in artillery; although I do not belong to that branch of the service, I learned the duties at Arcot.'

The rajah agreed, heartily, to Charlie's proposals; well pleased at the thought that he should, before the end of a year, be possessed of a trained force, which would enable him to hold his own against his powerful neighbours, until an opportunity might occur when, in alliance with the English, he should be able to turn the tables upon them, and to aggrandize himself at their expense.

Chapter 12

A MURDEROUS ATTEMPT

Handsome rooms, with a suite of attendants, were assigned to Charlie in the rajah's palace; and he was formally appointed commander of his forces. The four Sepoys were appointed to junior ranks, as was also Tim Kelly; who, however, insisted on remaining in the position of chief attendant upon his master; being, in fact, a sort of majordomo and valet in one, looking after his comforts when in the palace, and accompanying him as personal guard whenever he rode out.

'You niver know, yer honor, what these natives may be up to. They'll smile with you one day, and stab ye the next. They're treacherous varmint, yer honor, if you do but give 'em the chance.'

At first, Charlie perceived that his position excited some jealousy in the minds of those surrounding the rajah. He therefore did all in his power to show to them that he, in no way, aspired to interfere in the internal politics or affairs of the little state – that he was a soldier and nothing more. He urged upon the rajah, who wished to have him always by him, that it was far better that he should appear to hold aloof, and to avoid all appearance of favouritism, or of a desire to obtain dominance in the counsels of the rajah. He wished that the appointments to the posts of officers in the new force should be made by the rajah, who should lend an ear to the advice of his usual councillors; but that, once appointed, they should be under his absolute command and control, and that he should have power to dismiss those who proved themselves indolent and incapable, to promote active and energetic men, wholly regardless of influence or position.

The next morning, Charlie and his four assistants set to work to drill the three hundred men of the garrison, taking them in parties of twenty. They were thus able, in the course of a few days, to pick out the most active and intelligent for the sub-officers; and these, with the existing officers of the body, and the new ones appointed by the rajah, were at once taken in hand to be taught their duty.

For a month, the work went on steadily and without interruption, and from morn till night the courtyard echoed with the words of command. At the end of that time, the twenty officers and forty sub-officers had fairly learned their duty. The natives of India are very quick in learning drill, and a regiment of newly-raised Sepoys will perform manoeuvres and answer to words of command, in the course of a fortnight, as promptly and regularly as would one of English recruits in three months.

A good many changes had taken place during the month's work. Many of the officers became disgusted with hard and continuous work, to which they were unac-customed, while some of the sub-officers showed a deficiency of the quickness and intelligence needed for the work. Their places, however, were easily filled, and as the days went on, all took an increasing degree of interest, as they acquired facility of movement, and saw how quickly, according to the European methods, manoeuvres were gone through. At the end of a month, then, the sixty men were able in turn to instruct others; and, a body of five hundred men being called out, the work of drilling on a large scale began.

The drill ground now was a level space in the valley below the town, and the whole population assembled, day after day, to look on with astonishment at the exercises. The four great companies, or battalions, as Charlie called them, were kept entirely separate, each under the command of one of the Sepoys, under whom were a proportion of the officers and sub-officers. Every evening, Charlie came down for an hour, and put each body through its drill, distributing blame or praise as it was deserved, thus keeping up a spirit of emulation between the battalions. At the end of a fortnight, when the simpler manoeuvres had been learned, Charlie, for two hours each day, worked the whole together as one regiment; and was surprised, himself, to find how rapid was the progress which each day effected.

The rajah himself often came down to the drill ground, and took the highest interest in the work. He himself would fain have had regular uniforms, similar to those worn by the Sepoys in the service of the European powers, provided for the men; but Charlie strongly urged him not to do so. He admitted that the troops would look immensely better, if clad in regular uniform; than as a motley band, each dressed according to his own fancy. He pointed out, however, that while the news that the rajah was having some of his men drilled by European deserters would attract but little attention among his neighbours, the report that he was raising Sepoy battalions would certainly be received by them in a hostile spirit.

'By all means,' Charlie said, 'get the uniforms made for the whole force, and keep them by you in store. They can be at once served out in case of war, and the sight of a number of Sepoy battalions, where they expected only to meet an irregular force, will have an immense effect upon any force opposed to you.'

The rajah saw the force of this argument, and at once ordered five thousand suits of white uniforms, similar to those worn by the Sepoys in the English and French service, to be made and stored up in the magazines.

While his lieutenants were drilling the main body, Charlie himself took in hand a party of forty picked men, and instructed them in the use of field guns. The superiority of Europeans in artillery was one of the reasons which gave to them such easy victory, in their early battles with the native forces in India. The latter possessed a very powerful artillery, in point of numbers, but there was no regular drill nor manner of loading. They were in the habit, too, of allowing each gun to cool after it was fired, before being loaded again. It was thought, therefore, good practice if a gun were discharged once in a quarter of an hour. They were, then, utterly astounded and dismayed at the effects of the European guns, each of which could be loaded and fired twice, or even three times, a minute.

So month passed after month, until Rajah Boorhau was in a position to put, if necessary, five battalions of Sepoys, each seven hundred strong, into the field; with thirty guns, served by trained artillerymen. So quietly had the work gone on, that it attracted no attention among his neighbours. The mere rumour that the rajah had some European deserters in his service, and that these were drilling four or five hundred men, was considered of so little moment that it passed altogether unheeded.

The accounts of the state of affairs in the Carnatic, which reached Charlie, were not satisfactory – Dupleix, with his usual energy, was aiding the son of Chunda Sahib, with men and money, in his combat with the British protege; and most of the native allies of the latter had fallen away from him. Trichinopoli was again besieged, and the fortunes of England, lately so flourishing, were waning again. In the Deccan, French influence was supreme. Bussy, with a strong and well-disciplined French force, maintained Salabut Jung, whom the French had placed on the throne, against all opponents. At one time it was the Peishwar, at another the Mahrattas against whom Bussy turned his arms; and always with success, and the French had acquired the four districts on the coast, known as the Northern Sircas.

It was in vain that Charlie endeavoured to gain an accurate knowledge of the political position, so quickly and continually did this change. At one time the Peishwar and the Nizam, as the Subadar of the Deccan was now called, would be fighting in alliance against one or other of the Mahratta chiefs. At another time they would be in conflict with each other, while the Rajah of Mysore, Murari Reo, and other chiefs were sometimes fighting on one side, sometimes on another.

Proud of his rapidly increasing force, Boorhau Reo would, more than once in the course of the year, have joined in the warfare going on around. Charlie, however, succeeded in restraining him from doing so; pointing out that the victor of one day was the vanquished of the next, and that it was worse than useless to join in a struggle of which the conditions were so uncertain, and the changes of fortune so rapid, that none could count upon others for aid, however great the assistance they might have rendered only a short time before.

'Were you to gain territory, Rajah, which you might, perhaps, largely do, from the efficient aid which you might render to one party or the other, you would be the object of a hostile combination against which you could not hope to struggle.'

The rajah yielded at once to Charlie's arguments; but the influence of the latter added to the hostility, which the favour shown him by the rajah had provoked, among many of the leading men of the state. Where the sides were often so closely balanced as was the case in these intestine struggles, the aid of every rajah, however small his following, was sought by one or other of the combatants; and the counsellors of those able to place a respectable force in the field were heavily bribed, by one side or the other. Those around Rajah Boorhau found their efforts completely baffled by the influence of the English commander of his forces, and a faction of increasing strength and power was formed to overthrow him. The rajah himself had kept his secret well, and one or two, only, of his advisers knew that the Englishman was a trusted agent of the Company.

The soldiers were much attached to their English leader. They found him always just and firm. Complaints were always listened to, tyranny or ill treatment by the officers suppressed and punished, merit rewarded. Among the officers the strictness of the discipline alienated many, who contrasted the easy life which they had led before the introduction of the European system, with that which they now endured. So long as they were engaged in mastering the rudiments of drill they felt their disadvantage; but when this was acquired, each thought himself capable of taking the place of the English adventurer, and of leading the troops he had organized to victory. Already, Charlie had received several anonymous warnings that danger threatened him. The rajah was, he knew, his warm friend; and he, in his delight at seeing the formidable force which had been formed from his irregular levies, had presented him, as a token of his gratitude, with large sums of money.

In those days, this was the method by which Indian princes rewarded European officers who rendered them service, and it was considered by no means derogatory to the latter to accept the money. This was, indeed, the universal custom, and Charlie, knowing that Captain Clive had received large presents of this kind, had no hesitation in following his example. The treasures stored up by many of these Indian princes were immense, and a lac of rupees, equivalent to ten thousand pounds, was considered by no means a large present. Charlie, foreseeing that, sooner or later, the little state would become involved in hostilities, took the precaution of forwarding the money he had received down to Madras; sending it piecemeal, in charge of native merchants and traders. It was, by these, paid into the Madras treasury, where a large rate of interest, for all monies lent by its employees, was given by the Company.

For those at home he felt no uneasiness. It was very seldom that their letters reached him; but he learned that they were still in high favour with his uncle, that his mother continued installed at the head of the house, and that the girls were both at excellent schools.

Charlie mentioned, to the rajah, the rumours which had reached him of a plot against him. The rajah assured him of his own support, under all circumstances, and offered that a strong guard should be placed, night and day, over the apartments he occupied.

This Charlie declined.

'A guard can always be corrupted,' he said. 'My Irish servant sleeps in my ante-room, my four lieutenants are close at hand, and knowing that the soldiers are, for the most part, attached to me, I do not think that open force will be used. I will, however, cause a large bell to be suspended above my quarters. Its ringing will be a signal that I am attacked, in which case I rely upon your highness putting yourself at the head of the guard, and coming to my assistance.'

Tim Kelly was at once furious and alarmed, at the news that danger threatened his master, and took every precaution that he could imagine to ensure his safety. He took to going down to the town, himself, to purchase provisions; and, so far as possible, prepared these himself. He procured two or three monkeys, animals which he held in horror, and offered them a portion of everything that came on the table, before he placed it before his master.

Charlie at first protested against this, as his dinner became cold by waiting; but Tim had an oven prepared, and ordered dinner half an hour before the time fixed by his master. Each dish as brought in was, after a portion had been given to a monkey, placed in the oven, and thus half an hour was given to allow the poison to work. This was done without Charlie's knowledge, the oven being placed in the anteroom, and the dishes thence brought in, in regular order, by the body servant, whom even Tim allowed to be devoted to his master.

One day, Charlie was just sitting down to his soup, when Tim ran in.

'For the love of Heaven, Mr. Charles, don't put that stuff to your mouth. It's pisoned, or, at any rate, if it isn't, one of the other dishes is.'

'Poisoned, Tim! Nonsense, man. You are always thinking of poisonings and plots.'

'And it's lucky for your honor that I am,' Tim said. 'Jist come into the next room, and look at the monkeys.'

Charlie went in. One of the little creatures was lying upon the ground, evidently in a state of great agony. The other was sitting up, rocking itself backwards and forwards, like a human being in pain.

'They look bad, poor little beasts,' Charlie said; 'but what has that got to do with my soup?'

'Shure, yer honor, isn't that jist what I keep the cratures for, just to give them a taste of everything yer honor has, and I claps it into the oven there to kape it warm till I've had time to see, by the monkeys, whether it's good.'

'It looks very serious,' Charlie said, gravely. 'Do you go quietly out, Tim, call two men from the guardhouse, and seize the cook; and place one or two men as sentries over the other servants. I will go across to the rajah.'

The latter, on hearing what had happened, ordered the cook to be brought before him, together with the various dishes prepared for the dinner. The man, upon being interrogated, vehemently denied all knowledge of the affair.

'We shall see,' the rajah said. 'Eat up that plate of soup.'

The man turned pale.

'Your highness will observe,' he stammered, 'that you have already told me that one of these dishes is poisoned. I cannot say which, and whichever I eat may be the fatal one.'

The rajah made a signal to him to obey his orders, but Charlie interposed.

'There is something in what he says, your highness. Whether the man is innocent or guilty, he would shrink equally from eating any of them. It is really possible that he may know nothing of it. The poison may have been introduced into the materials beforehand. If the man is taken to a dungeon, I think I could suggest a plan by which we could test him.'

'I believe him to be guilty,' he said, when the prisoner had been removed.

'Then why not let him be beheaded at once?' the rajah asked.

'I would rather let ten guilty men escape,' Charlie replied, 'than run the risk of putting one innocent one to death. I propose, sir, that you order the eight dishes of food, which have been prepared for my dinner, to be carefully weighed. Let these be all placed in the cell of the prisoner, and there let him be left. In the course of two or three days he will, if guilty, endeavour to assuage his hunger by eating little bits of food, from every dish except that which he knows to be poisoned, but will take such a small portion from each that he will think it will not be detected. If he is innocent, and is really ignorant which dish is poisoned, he will not touch any of them, until driven to desperation by hunger. Then he will seize on one or more, and devour them to the end, running the chance of death by poison, rather than endure the pangs of hunger longer.'

'Your plan is a wise one,' the rajah said. 'It shall be tried. Let the dishes be taken to him, every morning, and removed every evening. Each evening they shall be weighed.'

These orders were carried out, and on the following morning the dishes were placed in the cell of the prisoner. When removed at night, they were found to be untouched. The next evening several of the dishes were found to have lost some ounces in weight. The third evening all but one had been tasted.

'Let the prisoner be brought in again,' the rajah ordered, when informed of this.

'Dog,' he said, 'you have betrayed yourself. Had you been innocent, you could not have known in which of the dishes the poison had been placed. You have eaten of all but one. If that one contains poison, you are guilty.'

Then, turning to an attendant, he ordered him to take a portion of the untouched food, and to throw it to a dog. Pending the experiment, the prisoner was removed. Half an hour later, the attendant returned with the news that the dog was dead.

'The guilt of the man is confirmed,' the rajah said. 'Let him be executed.'

'Will you give him to me, your highness?' Charlie asked. 'His death would not benefit me now, and to save his life, he may tell me who is my enemy. It is of no use punishing the instrument, and letting the instigator go free.'

'You are right,' the rajah agreed. 'If you can find out who bribed him, justice shall be done, though it were the highest in the state.'

Charlie returned to his own quarters, assembled his lieutenants and several other of his officers, and had the man brought before him.

'Hossein,' he said, 'you have taken money to take my life. I looked upon you as my faithful servant. I had done you no wrong. It has been proved that you attempted to poison me. You, when driven by hunger, ate small quantities, which you thought would pass unobserved, of all the dishes but one. That dish has been given to a dog, and he has died. You knew, then, which was the poisoned dish. The rajah has ordered your execution. I offer you life, if you will tell me who it was that tempted you.'

The prisoner preserved a stolid silence.

'We had better proceed to torture him, at once,' one of the rajah's officers said.

The man turned a little paler. He knew well the horrible tortures which would, in such an instance, be inflicted to extort the names of those who had bribed him.

'I will say nothing,' he said, firmly, 'though you tear me limb from limb.'

'I have no intention of torturing you,' Charlie said. 'A confession extorted by pain is as likely to be false as true, and even did you tell me one name, there might still be a dozen engaged in it who would remain unknown. No, Hossein, you have failed in your duty, you have tried to slay a master who was kind to you, and trusted you.'

'No, sahib,' the man exclaimed, passionately. 'You did not trust me. The food I sent you was tested and tried. I knew it; but I thought that the poison would not have acted on the monkeys, until you had eaten the dish. The fool who sold it me deceived me. Had you trusted me, I would never have done it. It was only when I saw that I was suspected and doubted, without cause, that my heart turned against you, and I took the gold which was offered to me to kill you. I swear it by the Prophet.'

Charlie looked at him steadily.

'I believe you,' he said. 'You were mistaken. I had no suspicions. My servant feared for me, and took these precautions without telling me. However, Hossein, I pardon you, and if you will swear to me to be faithful, in future, I will trust you. You shall again be my cook, and I will eat the food as you prepare it for me.'

'I am my lord's slave,' the man said in a low tone. 'My life is his.'

Charlie nodded, and the guard standing on either side of the prisoner stepped back, and without another word he left the room, a free man.

Charlie's officers remonstrated with him upon having not only pardoned the man, but restored him to his position of cook.

'I think I have done wisely,' Charlie said. 'I must have a cook, for Tim Kelly here is not famous that way; and although he might manage for me, when alone, he certainly could not turn out a dinner which would be suitable, when I have some of the rajah's kinsmen and officers dining with me. Did I get another cook, he might be just as open to the offers of my enemies as Hossein has been; and do you not think that, after what has passed, Hossein will be less likely to take bribes than any other man?'

Henceforth the oven was removed from the antechamber, and Charlie took his meals as Hossein prepared them for him. The man said little, but Charlie felt sure, from the glances that he cast at him, that he could rely upon Hossein now to the death.

Tim Kelly, who felt the strongest doubts as to the prudence of the proceeding, observed that Hossein no longer bought articles from men who brought them up to sell to the soldiers, but that every morning he went out early, and purchased all the supplies he desired from the shopkeepers in the town. Tim mentioned the fact to his master, who said:

'You see, Tim, Hossein has determined that I shall not be poisoned without his knowing it. The little peddlers who come up here with herbs, and spices, and the ingredients for curry, might be bribed to sell Hossein poisoned goods. By going down into the town, and buying in the open market, it is barely possible that the goods could be poisoned. You need have no more anxiety whatever, Tim, as to poison. If the attempt is made again, it will probably be by sword or dagger.'

'Well, yer honor,' said Tim, 'anything's better than pison. I've got to sleep almost with one eye open. And you've got sentries outside your windows. What a pity it is that we ain't in a climate where one can fasten the windows, and boult the shutters! But now the wet season is over again, ye might have yer bed put, as ye did last year, on the roof of your room, with a canopy over it to keep off the dew. Ye would be safe then, except from anyone coming through the room where I sleeps.'

Charlie's bedroom was at the angle of a wall, and on two sides he could look down from his windows, two hundred feet, sheer into the valley below. The view from the flat terraced roof was a charming one, and, as Tim said, Charlie had, in the fine weather, converted the terrace into a sleeping room. A broad canopy, supported by poles at the corner, stretched over it, and even in the hottest weather the nights were not unpleasant here.

Chapter 13

AN ATTEMPT AT MURDER

The house, of which the bedroom occupied by Charlie formed part, was elsewhere two stories higher; this room jutting out, alone, into the angle of the wall. The rest of the suite of rooms were in the house itself, but access could be obtained to this room through the window, which looked on to the terrace of the wall. Charlie's lieutenants always took pains to place men upon whom they could thoroughly rely as sentries, on this terrace.

One night, a fortnight after the events which have been described, Charlie was asleep on his bed, on the flats above his room. On one side the house rose straight beside it. On two others was the fall to the valley, on the fourth side was the wall, along which two sentries were pacing to and fro. From time to time, from a door some distance along the side of the house, opening on to the wall, a white figure came out, stretched himself as if unable to sleep, looked for a while over the parapet down into the valley, appeared to listen intently, and then sauntered into the house again.

It was the cook, Hossein. It was his custom. Successive sentries had, for many nights past, seen him do the same; but in a country where the nights are hot, a sleepless servant attracts but little attention. Upon the occasion of one of these visits to the parapet, he stood in an attitude of deep attention, longer than usual. Then he carelessly sauntered back. It was but a moment later that his face appeared at the window next to that of Charlie's bedroom. He stretched his head out, and again listened intently.

Then he went to Tim, who was sleeping heavily on a couch placed there, and touched him. He put his hand on his lips, as Tim sprang up.

'Take arm,' he said, in Hindostanee. 'Bad man coming.'

Tim understood the words and, seizing a sword and pistol which lay close to the bedside, followed Hossein, who had glided up the stairs, with a drawn tulwar in his hand. At the moment he did so, there was a noise of heavy bodies dropping, followed by a sudden shout from Charlie. There was a sound of clashing of arms, and the report of a pistol.

As Tim's eyes came on a level with the terrace, he saw Hossein bound with uplifted blade into the midst of a group of men in the corner. Three times the blade rose and fell, and each time a loud shriek followed. Then he disappeared in the midst.

Tim was but a few seconds behind him. Discharging his pistol into the body of one of the men, and running his sword into another, he, too, stood by the side of his master. Charlie, streaming with blood, was half sitting, half lying in the angle of the parapet. Hossein, his turban off, his long hair streaming down his back, was standing over him, fighting furiously against some ten men, who still pressed forward, while several others lay upon the ground.

In spite of the arrival of Charlie's two allies, they still pressed forward, but the shots of the pistols had been echoed by the muskets of the sentries. Loud shouts were heard, showing that the alarm was sounding through the palace.

One more desperate effort the assailants made, to beat the two men who opposed them over the parapet, but Hossein and the Irishman stood firm. The weight and numbers of their opponents, however, told upon them; when the first of the sentries appeared upon the platform, followed closely by his comrade; and both, with levelled bayonets, charged into the fray.

The assailants now thought only of escape, but their position was a desperate one. Some rushed to the end of the terrace, and tried to climb the ropes by which they had slid down from the upper roof of the house. Others endeavoured to rush down the staircase; but Tim, with one of the sentries, guarded this point, until a rush of feet below told that the guard were coming to their assistance.

It was well that help was at hand, for the conspirators, desperate at finding themselves in a trap, gathering themselves together, rushed with the fury of wild beasts upon Tim and the sentry. One was impaled upon a bayonet, another cut down by Tim, and then, borne back by the weight of their opponents, they were hurled backwards down the stairs. As the assailants followed them with a rush, the guard sprang through the open window, from the terrace below, into the room.

There was a short and desperate conflict. Then two of the conspirators bounded up the staircase on to the roof, ran to the parapet and leaped over into the valley, two hundred feet below. They were the last of the eighteen men who had lowered themselves, from the roof above, to attack Charlie.

As soon as Tim picked himself up, he hastened to ascend the stairs again, and to run to the side of his master. Charlie was insensible. Leaning against the parapet, too weak to stand, but still holding his sword, and ready to throw himself once more before him, stood Hossein; who now, seeing Tim approach, and that all danger was over, dropped his sword and sank upon the ground.

A minute or two later the rajah himself, sword in hand, hurried up. He was greatly concerned, and excited, at the sight which met his eyes. Charlie was at once lifted, and carried down to one of the rajah's own rooms, where he was instantly attended to.

A hasty examination showed that only two of the attacking party still breathed. None of those who had fallen above survived, so fiercely and deadly had been the blows struck by Hossein and Tim. Charlie himself had cut down one and shot another, before he fell, slashed in many places, just as Hossein bounded through his assailants.

The bodies of the dead were, by the rajah's orders, laid together for identification in the morning. The two who still lived were carried to the guardroom, and their wounds dressed, in order that the names of their employers might be obtained from them.

In the meantime, Charlie's lieutenants had hastily formed a body of their soldiers together, and these at once fell upon a number of men who were crowding up the steps to the palace, with shouts of 'Death to the Englishman.' A few volleys poured among these effactually scattered them, and they broke and hurried down the steep road, through the gates to the town, the sentries on the way offering no opposition, but many falling under the fire from the parapet of the fort.

In ten minutes, all was over. The gates were again closed, and a strong guard placed over them, and the attempted insurrection was at an end.

The native surgeon, who attended Charlie, pronounced that none of the five wounds he had received, although for the most part severe, were necessarily fatal; and that there was every chance of his recovery. Hossein's wounds, three in number, were pronounced to be more dangerous, one being a deep stab in the body, given by a man who had rushed at him, as he was guarding the blow of another. Tim's wounds were comparatively slight, and he suffered more from the bruises he had received, when hurled backwards down the stone staircase. However, with one arm in a sling, and his head bandaged, he was able to take his place by his master's bedside.

Having heard, from him, that it was entirely due to Hossein that Charlie's life had been saved, the rajah directed that every attention should be paid to him; and several times, during the night, Tim stole away to his bedside to press his hand, and call down blessings upon him.

The stanching of his wounds, and the application of strong restoratives, presently caused Charlie to open his eyes.

'The Lord be praised, Mr. Charles,' Tim said, 'that you're coming to yourself again. Don't you trouble, sir. We've done for the murdhering rascals; and, plase God, you'll soon be about again. Jist drink this draught, yer honor, and go off to sleep, if you can. In the morning I'll tell you all about it.

'You're in the rajah's own room,' he continued, seeing Charlie's eyes wander wonderingly around him, 'and all you've got to do is just to lie still, and get well as soon as you can.'

It was a fortnight before Charlie, still very weak and feeble, was able to totter from his room to that in which Hossein was lying. He himself knew nothing of what had passed after he fell. The conflict had, to him, been little more than a dream. Awakened from sleep by the sound of his assailants, as they dropped from the ropes, he had leaped up as a rush of figures came towards him, catching up his sword and pistol as he did so. He had shot the first, and cut down the next who rushed at him, but at the same moment he had felt a sharp pain, and remembered no more.

Tim heard from Hossein, when the latter, two days after the fight, was able to speak, that he had suspected that some renewed attempt might be made upon his master's life; and that for many nights he had not slept, contenting himself with such repose as he could snatch in the daytime, between the intervals of preparing meals. A few minutes before the attack, he fancied he heard a movement on the roof of the house; and running to Charlie's room he had, from the window, seen some dark figures sliding down the wall. Then he roused Tim, and rushed up to the rescue.

Tim eloquently described to his master the manner in which Hossein sprung upon his foes, and cut his way through, in time to drive back those who were hacking at him as he lay prostrate; and how he found him standing over him, keeping at bay the whole of his assailants.

Charlie, with difficulty, made his way to the bedside of the brave Mohammedan. The latter, however, did not know him. He was in the delirium of fever. He was talking rapidly to himself.

'He trusted me,' he said. 'He gave me my life. Should I not give mine for him? Anyone else would have had me hung as a dog. I will watch. I will watch. He shall see that Hossein is not ungrateful.'

Charlie's eyes filled with tears, as he looked at the wasted form of his follower.

'Is there any hope for him?' he asked the doctor.

'It is possible, just possible that he may live,' the latter said. 'Allah only knows.'

'Do all you can to save him,' Charlie said. 'I shall be ever grateful to you, if you do.'

Tim, now that his master could dispense with his services, transferred his attentions to the bedside of Hossein, and was unremitting in the care and attention with which he kept the bandages on his head cool with fresh water, and wetted his hot lips with refreshing drinks. It was another week before his illness took a turn. Then the fever left him, and he lay weak and helpless as an infant. Strong soups now took the place of the cooling drinks, and in a few days the native doctor was able to say, confidently, that the danger was passed, and that Hossein would recover.

In the meantime, the investigations of the rajah had brought to light the details of the conspiracy. The wounded men had confessed that they were employed by three of the principal persons at the rajah's court, one of them being the rajah's brother. The information, however, was scarcely needed; as it was found, in the morning, that their apartments were empty; they having fled with the men who had attacked the gates of the palace. These consisted partly of soldiers whom they had bribed, and of desperadoes from the town, who had singly entered the fort during the day, and had been concealed in the apartments of the conspirators, until the signal for attack was given.

The intention of the conspirators was not only to kill the Englishman, but to dethrone the rajah, and install his brother in his place. The attack had commenced with the attempt upon Charlie's life, because it was believed that his death would paralyse the troops who were faithful to the rajah.

At the end of six weeks, Charlie was able to resume his duties, and his appearance at the parade ground was hailed with enthusiastic shouts by the soldiers. The rajah was more attached to him than ever, and had again made him large presents, in token of the regret he felt at the sufferings he had endured in his cause.

Drilling was now carried on with redoubled energy, and large numbers of new levies had been summoned to the standard. A storm was gathering over Ambur. The rajah's brother was raising a force to attack him, and had, by means of large promises in case of success, persuaded Murari Reo to take up his cause; and he had, it was said, also sent messages to the nizam, pointing out that, in case of war with the English, the Rajah of Ambur would be a thorn in his side. He told of the numbers of troops who had been drilled, and how formidable such a force would be, if opposed to him at a critical moment; while if he, the claimant, gained power, the army of Ambur would be at the disposal of the nizam.

The rajah, on his side, had also sent messengers to Hyderabad, with assurances to the nizam of his fidelity and friendship. He urged that the preparations he had made were intended solely for the defence of his state, against marauding bands of Mahrattas, and especially against those of Murari Reo, who was a scourge to all his neighbours.

In the meantime, every effort was made to strengthen the defences of Ambur. The walls surrounding the town were repaired, and although these, in themselves, could have offered but a slight defence to a determined assault, the approaches to the town were all covered by the guns of the fort above.

The weak point of the defence was the hill behind the town. This sloped up, gradually, to a point higher than the level of the projecting rock upon which the castle stood. It then rose, in rugged cliffs, some two hundred feet higher; and then fell away again, steeply, to its summit. This was too far back for the fire of guns placed upon it to injure the castle or town. Guns placed, however, at the foot of the rocky wall, would dominate the castle and render it, at last, untenable.

Charlie had often looked, with an anxious eye, at this point; and one morning, accompanied by the rajah, he rode up to examine the position. The highest point of the slope, at the foot of the crag, was nearly opposite the castle; and it was here that an active enemy, making his way along the slope, would place his guns. Here, Charlie determined to establish a battery.

News had arrived that the rajah's brother had raised a force of three thousand men; and that, with seven thousand Mahrattas, he was about to march. This force, Charlie felt certain that he could meet and defeat, in the open. But more disquieting news was that Bussy, hearing that the rajah's troops had been trained by an Englishman, had advised the nizam to declare for his rival, and to send a considerable force to his assistance, if necessary. Fresh messengers were sent off, with new assurances of the rajah's loyalty to the nizam.

'It may not do much good,' Charlie said, 'but if we can induce him to remain quiet, until we have defeated Murari Reo, it will be so much gained.'

Charlie himself despatched a messenger to Mr. Saunders, begging that assistance might be sent to the rajah.

Having decided upon the position for a battery, energetic steps were taken to form it. A space large enough for the construction of the battery, and for the tents and stores of the artillerymen and two hundred infantry, was marked out; and the rajah ordered the whole population of Ambur, men, women, and children, to assist at the work. The troops, too, were all employed; and under Charlie's superintendence, a wondrous change was soon effected. The spot chosen was levelled, a strong earthwork was erected round it, and then the surrounding ground was removed. This was a work of immense labour, the ground consisting first of a layer of soil, then of debris which had fallen from the face of the rock above, stones and boulders, to the depth of some fifteen feet, under which was the solid earth.

The slope resembled an anthill. The soldiers and able-bodied men broke up the boulders and rock with sledgehammers; or, when necessary, with powder, and blasted the rock, when needed. The women and children carried away the fragments in baskets. The work lasted for a fortnight, at the end of which a position of an almost impregnable nature was formed. At the foot of the earthworks protecting the guns, both at the face and sides, the ground, composed of great boulders and stones, sloped steeply out, forming a bank fifteen feet deep. At its foot, again, the solid rock was blasted away, so as to form a deep chasm, thirty feet wide and ten feet high, round the foot of the fort. For a hundred yards on each side, the earth and stones had been entirely removed down to the solid rock.

Ten guns were placed in the battery, and the fire of these swept the slopes behind the town and castle, rendering it impossible, until the fort was carried, for an enemy to attack the town on that side; or to operate, in any way, against the only point at which an attack could be made upon the castle.

The rajah was delighted at this most formidable accession to the defensive power of his fortress, which was now in a position to defy any attack which could be made against it. A store of provisions and ammunition was collected there, and the command given to one of Charlie's Sepoy lieutenants, with a hundred trained artillerymen, and two hundred infantry. Numbers of cattle had been driven into the town and castle, and stores of provisions collected.

It was but two days after the battery was complete that the news arrived that the rajah's brother, with Murari Reo, had entered the rajah's dominions, and was marching up the valley to the assault. The rajah had, in the first place, wished to defend a strong gorge through which the enemy would have to pass; this having hitherto been considered the defensible point of his capital, against an invasion. Charlie pointed out, however, that although no doubt a successful defence might be made here, it would only be a repulse, which would leave the enemy but little weakened for further operations. He argued that it was better to allow them to advance to the point where the valley opened out into a plain, some two miles wide. He had no doubt whatever that the rajah's troops would be able to inflict a crushing defeat upon the invaders, who would be so disheartened, thereby, that they would be little likely to renew the attack.

Two bodies of troops, each three hundred strong, were sent down to the gorge, with orders to remain in hiding among the heights, to allow the invading army to pass unmolested, and then to inflict the greatest possible loss upon them, as they returned. These were under the command of another of Charlie's lieutenants, who received orders from him to erect breastworks of rock on the slopes above the entrance to the gorge, after the enemy had passed on; and to line these with a portion of his men, who should pour a heavy fire into the enemy as they came down the valley; while the rest were to line the heights above the gorge, and to roll down rocks upon those who passed through the fire of their comrades.

The uniforms were served out to the soldiers, and Charlie surveyed, with pride, the five battalions of trained troops which, with twelve guns, marched down into the valley and took up their post beyond it, at a point which he had carefully chosen, where the guns of the castle would be able to play upon an advancing body of troops. A body of trained artillerymen were told off for this service, and the last-raised levies were posted in the castle and on the walls of the town.

The position was so chosen that the flanks of the line rested on the slopes on either side. These were broken by inclosures and gardens; into which, on either side, half a battalion was thrown forward, so as to deliver a flanking fire upon an enemy advancing against the centre. Across the valley, two hundred yards in front of the position, the stream which watered it made a sharp turn, running for some distance directly across it, and several small canals for the irrigation of the fields rendered the ground wet and swampy. Across the line occupied by his troops, a breastwork had been thrown up, and in front of this rows of sharp-pointed stakes had been stuck in the ground. Altogether, the position was a formidable one.

An hour or two after the position so carefully prepared had been taken up, large bodies of Mahratta horse were seen dashing up the valley, and smoke rising from several points showed that they had begun their usual work, of plundering and destroying the villages on their way. A few discharges from the field pieces – those in the castle had been ordered to be silent until the raising of a white flag gave them the signal to open fire – checked the advance of the horsemen, and these waited until their infantry should arrive.

The force of Murari Reo was, at that time, the most formidable of any purely native army of Southern India. Recruited from desperadoes from all the Mahratta tribes, well disciplined by its leader, it had more than once fought, without defeat, against bodies of Europeans; while it had, in all cases, obtained easy victories over other native armies.

Presently the horsemen opened, and a compact body of three thousand Mahratta infantry, accompanied by an equal number of the irregulars of the rajah's brother, advanced to the attack; while the cavalry at their sides swept down upon the flanks of the rajah's position, and thirty pieces of artillery opened fire.

Not a shot was fired in return, Charlie ordering his men to lie down behind the breastworks, until they received the word of command to show themselves. The Mahratta horsemen, compelled by the bends of the stream to keep near the foot of the slopes, came forward in gallant style; until suddenly, from every wall and every clump of bushes on the slopes above them, a tremendous fire of musketry broke out, while the twelve field guns, six of which were posted on either side of Charlie's centre, poured a destructive fire into them. So deadly was the rain of iron and lead that the Mahratta horsemen instantly drew bridle and, leaving the ground strewn with their dead, galloped back.

By this time the infantry, covered by the fire of their artillery, had reached the stream. This was waist deep, and the banks were some two feet above its level. As they scrambled up after crossing it, from the line of embankment in front of them a tremendous fire was opened. Although mowed down in scores, the seasoned warriors of the Mahratta chief, cheered on by his voice as, recklessly exposing himself, he rode among them, pressed forward. Ever increasing numbers gained a footing across the stream, those in front keeping up a heavy fire at the breastwork, whose face was ploughed by their cannon shot.

As they advanced the guns of the castle opened fire, not upon those in front, for these were too near the line of entrenchment, but upon the struggling mass still crossing the stream, into which a ceaseless fire of musketry was poured from the slopes on their flanks. Still the Mahratta infantry struggled bravely on, until within a few yards of the entrenchments. Then, suddenly, with a mighty shout, the rajah's troops leaped to their feet, poured a volley from the crest of the breastwork into the enemy; and then, with fixed bayonets, flung themselves upon them.

The effect was decisive. The Mahrattas had, at the commencement of the fight, scarcely outnumbered the troops of the rajah in front of them, and had derived but little assistance from the levies of their ally; who, indeed, had contented themselves with keeping up a fire upon the defenders of the slopes. They had already suffered very severely, and the charge made upon them, along the whole line, was irresistible.

Before the bayonets crossed they broke and fled, hotly pursued by the troops of the rajah. These, in accordance with Charlie's orders, did not scatter, but kept in a close line, four deep, which advanced, pouring tremendous volleys into their foe.

In vain did Murari Reo endeavour to rally his men. His infantry, all order lost, fled at the top of their speed, their flight covered by their cavalry, who sacrificed themselves in two or three brilliant charges, right up to the line of pursuers, although suffering terribly from the withering volleys poured into their ranks.

The troops were now formed into heavy columns, and these rapidly marched down the valley, after their flying enemy. An hour later, the sound of heavy firing was heard in front, and at redoubled speed the troops pressed onward. When they arrived, however, at the gorge, they found that the last of the fugitives had passed through. The ground in front was strewn with dead and dying, for as the mass of fugitives had arrived at the gorge, the infantry from above had opened fire upon them. Several times the frightened throng had recoiled, but at last, impelled by the greater fear of their pursuers behind, they had dashed forward through the fire, only to fall in hundreds in the gorge, crushed beneath the rain of rocks showered down upon them from above.

Chapter 14

THE SIEGE OF AMBUR

The victory was a complete and decisive one. A thousand of the best troops of Murari Reo had fallen, besides some hundreds of their irregular allies, whose loss was incurred almost wholly at the gorge in the retreat. The rajah was in the highest state of delight at the splendid result, obtained by the European training of his troops; and these, proud of their victory over such formidable opponents, were full of enthusiasm for their young English leader. The rejoicings in Ambur that night were great, and all felt confident that the danger was at an end.

'What think you,' the rajah said to Charlie, as, the long feast at an end, they sat together in the divan, smoking their narghileys, 'will be the result, when the news of the defeat of Murari Reo reaches Hyderabad?'

'It is difficult to say,' Charlie replied. 'It is possible, of course, that it may be considered that it is better to leave you in peace; but, upon the other hand, it may be that they will consider that you are so formidable a power, that it is absolutely necessary to crush you at once, rather than to give you the chance of joining against them, in the war which must sooner or later take place between them and the English. In that case, it will be a very different affair from that which we have had today.

'Still, I should send off a messenger tomorrow, to acquaint the nizam with the defeat you inflicted upon the Mahrattas who have invaded you, to assure him again of your loyalty, and to beg him to lay his authority upon Murari Reo, not to renew the attack.'

Ten days later a messenger arrived from the nizam, ordering the rajah to repair, at once, to Hyderabad, to explain his conduct. The latter sent back a message of humble excuses, saying that his health was so injured, by the excitement of recent events, that he was unable to travel; but that, when he recovered, he would journey to Hyderabad to lay his respects at the feet of the nizam.

Two or three days later a messenger arrived from Mr. Saunders, with a letter to Charlie. In this he expressed his great satisfaction at the defeat Murari Reo had received; a defeat which would, for some time, keep him quiet, and so relieve the strain upon the English. Affairs had, he said, since the departure of Clive for England, been going badly. Dupleix had received large reinforcements, and the English had suffered several reverses. Mr. Saunders begged him to assure the rajah of the respect and friendship of England, and to give him the promise that, if he should be driven from his capital, he would be received with all honor at Madras, and should be reinstated in his dominions, with much added territory, when the English were again in a position to take the field in force, and to settle their long feud with the French.

Ten days later, they heard that the army of the nizam, of fifteen thousand troops, with eight hundred French under Bussy, were marching against them; and that the horsemen of Murari Reo were devastating the villages near the frontier. A council of war was held. Charlie would fain have fought in the open again, believing that his trained troops, flushed with their recent victory, would be a match even for the army of the nizam. But the rajah and the rest of the council, alarmed at the presence of the French troops, who had hitherto proved invincible against vastly superior forces of natives, shrank from such a course; and it was decided that they should content themselves with the defence of the town and castle.

Orders were accordingly issued that the old men, the women, and children should at once leave the town; and, under guard of one battalion of troops, take refuge in an almost impregnable hill fort some miles away. One battalion was placed in garrison in the castle. The other three, with the irregulars, took post in the town, whence they could, if necessary, retreat into the castle.

The day following the removal of the noncombatants the enemy appeared, coming down the valley, having marched over the hills; while the Mahratta cavalry again poured up from below.

Charlie had taken the command of the town, as it was against this that the efforts of the enemy would be first directed. It was an imposing sight, as the army of the nizam wound down the valley; the great masses of men with their gay flags, the elephants with the gold embroidery of their trappings glistening in the sun, the bands of horsemen careering here and there, the lines of artillery drawn by bullocks; and, less picturesque but far more menacing, the dark body of French infantry, who formed the nucleus and heart of the whole. The camp was pitched just out of range of the guns of the fort, and soon line after line of tents, gay with the flags that floated above them, rose across the valley.

Charlie had mounted to the castle, the better to observe the movements of the enemy, and he presently saw a small body of horsemen ride out of the camp, and mount the hillside across the valley. A glass showed that some of these were native officers, while others were in the dark uniform of the French.

'I have no doubt,' Charlie said to the rajah, 'that is the nizam himself, with Bussy, gone up to reconnoitre the position. I wonder how he likes the look of it. I wish we could have turfed the battery above, and the newly stripped land. We might, in that case, have given them a pleasant surprise. As it is, they are hardly likely to begin by an attack along the slopes in the rear of the town, and you will see that they will commence the attack at the farther face of the town. The battery above cannot aid us in our defence there; and although the castle may help, it will only be by a direct fire. If they try to carry the place by a coup de main, I think we can beat them off, but they must succeed by regular approaches.

'We must inflict as much loss as we can, and then fall back. However, it will be some time before that comes.'

The next morning, Charlie found that the enemy had, during the night, erected three batteries on the slopes facing the north wall of the town, that farthest removed from the castle. They at once opened fire, and the guns on the walls facing them replied, while those on the castle hurled their shot over the town into the enemy's battery. For three days, the artillery fire was kept up without intermission. The guns on the wall were too weak to silence the batteries of the besiegers, although these were much annoyed by the fire from the fort, which dismounted four of their guns, and blew up one of their magazines. Several times the town was set on fire by the shells from the French mortars; but Charlie had organized the irregulars into bands with buckets, and these succeeded in extinguishing the flames before they spread.

Seeing that the mud wall of the town was crumbling rapidly before the besiegers' fire, Charlie set his troops to work, and levelled every house within fifty yards of it, and with the stones and beams formed barricades across the end of the streets beyond. Many of the guns from other portions of the walls were removed, and placed on these barricades. The ends of the houses were loopholed, and all was prepared for a desperate defence.

Charlie's experience at Arcot stood him in good stead, and he imitated the measures taken by Clive at that place. When these defences were completed, he raised a second line of barricades some distance further back; and here, when the assault was expected, he placed one of his battalions, with orders that, if the inner line of entrenchments was carried, they should allow all the defenders of that post to pass through, and then resist until the town was completely evacuated, when they were to fall back upon the fort. He had, however, little fear that his position would be taken at the first assault.

Upon the evening of the third day, the besiegers' fire had done its work, and a gap in the wall some eighty yards wide was formed. The garrison were ordered to hold themselves in readiness, and a strict watch was set.

Towards morning, a distant hum in the nizam's camp proclaimed that the troops were mustering for the assault. The besiegers' guns had continued their fire all night, to prevent working parties from placing obstacles in the breach. As the first shades of daylight appeared the fire ceased, and a great column of men poured forward to the assault.

The few remaining guns upon the end wall opened upon them, as did the infantry who lined the parapet, while the guns in the castle at once joined in. The mighty column, however, composed of the troops of the nizam, pressed forward, poured over the fragments of the wall, and entered the clear space behind it.

Then, from housetop and loophole, and from the walls on either side, a concentrated fire of musketry was poured upon them, while twelve guns, four on each barricade, swept them with grape. The head of the column withered away under the fire, long lines were swept through the crowded mass; and, after a minute or two's wild firing at their concealed foes, the troops of the nizam, appalled and shattered by the tremendous fire, broke and fled.

The instant they had cleared the breach, the guns of the besiegers again opened furiously upon it, to check any sortie which the besieged might attempt.

An hour later, the besiegers hoisted a white flag, and requested to be allowed to bury their dead, and remove their wounded. This Charlie agreed to, with the proviso that these should be carried by his own men beyond the breach, as he did not wish that the enemy should have an opportunity of examining the internal defences. The task occupied some time, as more than five hundred dead and dying lay scattered in the open space.

During the rest of the day, the enemy showed no signs of resuming the assault. During the night they could be heard hard at work, and although a brisk fire was kept up to hinder them, Charlie found that they had pushed trenches, from the batteries, a considerable distance round each corner of the town.

For four days the besiegers worked vigorously, harassed as they were by the guns of the fort, and by those of the battery high up on the hillside, which were now able to take in flank the works across the upper angle of the town. At the end of that time, they had erected and armed two batteries, which at daylight opened upon the walls which formed the flanks of the clear space behind the breach. Although suffering heavily from the fire of the besieged, and losing many men, these batteries kept up their fire unceasingly, night and day, until great gaps had been made in the walls, and Charlie was obliged to withdraw his troops from them, behind the line of barricades.

During this time the fire of the batteries in front had been unceasing, and had destroyed most of the houses which formed the connecting line between the barricades. Each night, however, the besieged worked to repair damages, and to fill up the gaps thus formed with piles of stones and beams, so that, by the end of the fourth day after the repulse of the first assault, a line of barricades stretched across the line of defence.

The enemy, this time, prepared to attack by daylight, and early in the morning the whole army of the nizam marched to the assault. Heedless of the fire of the castle, they formed up in a long line of heavy masses, along the slope. One huge column moved forward against the main breach, two advanced obliquely towards the great gaps in the walls on either side. The latter columns were each headed by bodies of French troops.

In vain the guns of the fort, aided by those of the battery on the hill, swept them. The columns advanced without a check until they entered the breaches. Then a line of fire swept along the crest of the barricade from end to end, and the cannon of the besieged roared out. Pressed by the mass from behind, the columns advanced, torn and rent by the fire, and at last gained the foot of the barricade.

Here, those in front strove desperately to climb up the great mound of rubbish, while those behind covered them with a storm of bullets aimed at its summit. More than once the troops of the rajah, rushing down the embankment, drove back the struggling masses, but so heavily did they suffer from the fire, when they thus exposed themselves, that Charlie forbade them to repeat the attempt. He knew that there was safety behind, and was unwilling that his brave fellows should throw away their lives.

In the centre of the position the native troops, although they several times climbed some distance up the barricade, were yet unable to make way. But the French troops at the flanks were steadily forcing their way up. Many had climbed up by the ruins of the wall, and from its top were firing down on the defenders of the barricade. Inch by inch they won their way up the barricade, already thickly covered with dead; and then Charlie, seeing that his men were beginning to waver, gave the signal.

The long blast of a trumpet was heard even above the tremendous din. In an instant the barricades were deserted, and the defenders rushed into the houses. The partition walls between these on the lower floors had already been knocked down, and without suffering from the heavy fire which the assailants opened, as soon as they gained the crest of the barricade, the defenders retreated along these covered ways until in rear of the second line of defence.

This was held by the battalion placed there, until the whole of the defenders of the town had left it, by the gate leading up to the fort. Then Charlie withdrew this battalion also, and the town remained in the hands of the enemy; who had lost, Charlie reckoned, fully fifteen hundred men in the assault.

During the fight Tim and the faithful Hossein, now fully recovered and promoted to the rank of an officer, had remained close beside him; and were, with him, the last to leave the town.

The instant the evacuation was complete, the guns of the hill battery opened upon the town; and a tremendous fire of musketry was poured upon it from every point of the castle which commanded it; while the guns, which from their lofty elevation, could not be depressed sufficiently to bear upon the town, directed their fire upon the bodies of troops still beyond the walls. The enemy had captured the town, indeed, but its possession aided them but little in their assault upon the fort. The only advantage it gave them, would have been that it would have enabled them to attack the lower gate of the fort, protected by its outer wall from the fire of the hill battery. Charlie had, however, perceived that this would be the case, and had planted a number of mines under the wall at this point. These were exploded when the defenders of the town entered the fort, and a hundred yards of the wall were thus destroyed; leaving the space, across which the enemy must advance to the attack of the gate, exposed to the fire of the hill battery, as well as of the numerous guns of the fort bearing upon it.

Two days passed without any further operations on the part of the enemy; and then Bussy, seeing that nothing whatever could be done towards assaulting the fortress, so long as the battery remained in the hands of the besieged, determined to make a desperate effort to carry it, ignorant of its immense strength. At night, therefore, he ordered two bodies of men, each fifteen hundred strong, to mount the hillside, far to the right and left of the town; to move along at the foot of the wall of rock, and to carry the battery by storm at daybreak.

Charlie, believing that such an attempt would be made, had upon the day following the fall of the town taken his post there, and had ordered a most vigilant watch to be kept up, each night; placing sentries some hundred yards away, on either side, to give warning of the approach of an enemy.

Towards daybreak on the third morning a shot upon the left, followed a few seconds later by one on the right, told that the enemy were approaching. A minute or two afterwards the sentries ran in, climbed from the ditch by ladders which had been placed there for the purpose, and, hauling these up after them, were soon in the battery, with the news that large bodies of the enemy were approaching on either flank. Scarcely were the garrison at their posts, when the French were seen approaching. At once they broke into a run, and, gallantly led, dashed across the space of cleared rock, in spite of the heavy fire of musketry and grape.

When they came, however, to the edge of the deep gulf in the solid rock, they paused. They had had no idea of meeting with such an obstacle as this. It was easy enough to leap down, but impossible to climb up the steep face, ten feet high, in front of them; and which, in the dim light, could be plainly seen. It was, however, impossible for those in front to pause. Pressed upon by those behind, who did not know what was stopping them, large numbers were compelled to jump into the trench, where they found themselves unable either to advance or retreat.

By this time, every gun on the upper side of the castle had opened on the assailing columns, taking them in flank, while the fire of the battery was continued without a moment's intermission. Bussy himself, who was commanding one of the columns, pushed his way through his struggling soldiers to the edge of the trench; when, seeing the impossibility of scaling the sides, unprovided as he was with scaling ladders, he gave the orders to retreat; and the columns, harassed by the flanking fire of the guns of the castle, and pursued by that of the battery, retreated, having lost some hundreds of their number; besides a hundred and fifty of their best men, prisoners in the deep trench around the battery.

These were summoned to surrender; and, resistance being impossible, they at once laid down their arms. Ladders were lowered to them, and they were marched as prisoners to the fort.

The next morning, when the defenders of the fortress looked over the valley, the great camp was gone. The nizam and Bussy, despairing of the possibility of carrying the position, at once so enormously strong by nature, and so gallantly defended, had raised the siege; which had cost them over two thousand of their best soldiers, including two hundred French killed and prisoners, and retreated to the plateau of the Deccan.

The exultation of the rajah and his troops was unbounded. They felt that, now and henceforth, they were safe from another invasion; and the rajah saw that, in the future, he should be able to gain greatly increased territory, as the ally of the English. His gratitude to Charlie was unbounded, and he literally loaded him with costly presents.

Three weeks later, a letter was received by the latter from Mr. Saunders, congratulating him upon the inestimable service which he had rendered, and appointing him to the rank of captain in the Company's service. Now that the rajah would be able to protect himself, should any future assault be made upon him – an event most unlikely to happen, as Bussy and the nizam would be unwilling to risk a repetition of a defeat, which had already so greatly injured their prestige – he had better return to Madras, where, as Mr. Saunders said, the services of so capable an officer were greatly needed. He warned him, however, to be careful in the extreme how he made his way back, as the country was in a most disturbed state, the Mahratta bands being everywhere out plundering and burning.

Subsequent information, that the Mahrattas were swarming in the plains below, determined Charlie to accept an offer which the rajah made him; that he should, under a strong escort, cross the mountains, and make his way to a port on the west coast, in the state of a friendly rajah, where he would be able to take ship and coast round to Madras. The rajah promised to send Charlie's horses and other presents down to Madras, when an opportunity should offer; and Charlie, accompanied by the four Sepoys, all of whom had been promoted to the rank of officers; by Tim Kelly and Hossein, who would not separate himself a moment from his side, started from Ambur, with an escort of thirty horsemen.

The rajah was quite affected at the parting; and the army, which he had formed and organized, paraded before him for the last time, and then shouted their farewell.

Charlie himself, although glad to return among his countrymen, from whom he had been nearly two years separated, was yet sorry to leave the many friends he had made. His position was now a very different one from that which he held when he left

Madras. Then he was a newly made lieutenant, who had distinguished himself, indeed, under Clive, but who was as yet unknown save to his commander, and who was as poor as when he had landed, eighteen months before, in India. Now he had gained a name for himself, and his successful defence of Ambur had been of immense service to the Company. He was, too, a wealthy man; for the presents in money, alone, of the rajah, had amounted to over twenty-five thousand pounds; a sum which, in these days, may appear extraordinary, but which was small to that frequently bestowed, by wealthy native princes, upon British officers who had done them a good service. Clive himself, after his short campaign, had returned to England with a far larger sum.

For several days, the party rode through the hills without incident; and on the fifth day they saw, stretched at their feet, a rich flat country dotted with villages, beyond which extended the long blue line of the sea. The distance was greater than Charlie imagined, and 'twas only after two days' long ride that he reached Calicut, where he was received with great honor by the rajah, to whom the leader of the escort brought letters of introduction from the Rajah of Ambur.

For four days Charlie remained as his guest, and then took a passage in a large native vessel, bound for Ceylon, whence he would have no difficulty in obtaining passage to Madras.

These native ships are very high out of water, rising considerably towards the stem and stern, and in form they somewhat resemble the Chinese junk; but are without the superabundance of grotesque painting, carving, and gilding which distinguish the latter. The rajah accompanied Charlie to the shore, and a salute was fired, by his followers, in honor of the departure of the guest.

The weather was lovely, and the clumsy craft, with all sail set, was soon running down the coast. When they had sailed some hours from Calicut, from behind a head-land, four vessels suddenly made their appearance. They were lower in the water, and much less clumsy in appearance than the ordinary native craft, and were propelled not only by their sails, but by a number of oars on each side.

No sooner did the captain and crew of the ship behold these vessels, than they raised a cry of terror and despair. The captain, who was part owner of the craft, ran up and down the deck like one possessed, and the sailors seemed scarcely less terrified.

'What on earth is the matter?' Charlie exclaimed. 'What vessels are those, and why are you afraid of them?'

'Tulagi Angria! Tulagi Angria!' the captain cried, and the crew took up the refrain.

The name that they uttered fully accounted for their terror.

Chapter 15

THE PIRATES' HOLD

Sivagi, the founder of the Mahratta Empire, had, in 1662, seized and fortified Yijiyadrug; or, as the English call it, Gheriah, a town at the mouth of the river Kanui, one hundred and seventy miles south of Bombay; and also the island of Suwarndrug, about half way between Gheriah and Bombay. Here he established a piratical fleet. Fifty years later, Kanhagi Angria, the commander of the Mahratta fleet, broke off this connection with the successors of Sivagi, and set up as a pirate on his own account. Kanhagi not only plundered the native vessels, but boldly preyed upon the commerce of the European settlements. The ships of the East India Company, the French Company, and the Dutch were frequently captured by these pirates.

Tulagi Angria, who succeeded his father, was even bolder and more successful; and when the man-of-war brig, the Restoration, with twenty guns and two hundred men, was fitted out to attack him, he defeated and captured her. After this, he attacked and caputred the French man-of-war Jupitre, with forty guns; and had even the insolence to assail an English convoy guarded by two men-of-war; the Vigilant, of sixty-four guns, and the Ruby, of fifty.

The Dutch, in 1735, sent a fleet of seven ships of war, two bomb vessels, and a strong body of troops against Gheriah. The attack was, however, repulsed with considerable loss. From that date the pirates grew bolder and bolder, and were a perfect scourge to the commerce of Western India.

Charlie Marryat had, of course, frequently heard of the doings of these noted pirates, and the cry of 'Tulagi Angria' at once explained to him the terror of the master and crew.

'What is it, Mr. Charles, what on earth is the botheration about? Is it the little ships they're afeared of?'

'Those ships belong to a pirate called Tulagi Angria,' Charlie said, 'and I am very much afraid, Tim, that we are likely to see the inside of his fortress.'

'But shure, yer honor, we're not afeared of those four little boats.'

'We are, Tim, and very much afraid, too. Each of those boats, as you call them, carries four or five times as many men as this ship. They are well armed, while we have only those two little guns, which are useless except for show. If the crew were Englishmen, we might attempt a defence, although even then the odds would be terribly against us; but with these natives, it is hopeless to think of it, and the attempt would only ensure our throats being cut.'

It was clear that the idea of resistance did never even enter the minds of the crew of the trader. Some ran to and fro, with gesticulations and cries of despair. Some threw themselves upon the deck of the vessel, tore their hair, and rolled as if in convulsions. Some sat down quietly, with the air of apathetic resignation, with which the natives of India are used to meet what they consider the inevitable.

Hossein, who, at the first alarm, had bounded to his feet with his hand on his knife, subsided into an attitude of indifference, when he saw that Charlie did not intend making any defence.

'It's mighty lucky,' Tim said, 'that yer honor left all your presents to be forwarded to Madras. I thought you were wrong, Mr. Charles, when you advised me to send them thousand rupees the rajah gave me, along with your money. A hundred pounds wasn't a sum that Tim Kelly was likely to handle again in a hurry, and it went again the grain with me, to part with them out of my hands. Sure and it's well I took yer honor's advice.'

The four Sepoy officers also exchanged a few words with Charlie. They, too, would have resisted, had he given the word, hopeless though the effort would have been. But they acquiesced, at once, in his decision. They had little to lose; but the thought of a prolonged captivity, and of being obliged, perhaps, to enter the service of the

Mahratta freebooters, just when about to return to their wives and families at Madras, was a terrible blow to them.

'Keep up your spirits,' Charlie said. 'It is a bad business, but we must hope for the best. If we bide our time, we may see some chance of escape. You had better lay down your arms in a pile, here. Then we will sit down quietly, and await their coming on board. They will be here in a minute, now.'

Scarcely had the seven passengers taken their seats in a group, on the poop, when the freebooters ranged alongside, and swarmed over the sides onto the deck. Beyond bestowing a few kicks upon the crew, they paid no attention whatever to them; but tore off the hatches, and at once proceeded to investigate the contents of the hold. The greater portion of this consisted of native grains, but there were several bales of merchandise, consigned by traders at Calicut for Ceylon. The cargo was, in fact, rather more valuable than that generally found in a native coaster, and the pirates were satisfied.

The leader of the party, leaving to his followers the task of examining the hold, walked towards the group on the poop. They rose at his approach.

'Who are you?' the Mahratta asked.

'I am an officer in the English Company's service,' Charlie said, 'as are these five natives. The other Englishman is a soldier, under my orders.'

'Good,' the Mahratta said, emphatically. 'Tulagi Angria will be glad to have you. When your people capture any of our men, which is not often, they hang them. Tulagi is glad to have people he can hang, too.'

After being stripped of any small valuables on their persons, the captives were taken on board one of the pirate boats. A score of the Mahrattas remained in charge of the trader. Her head was turned north, and, accompanied by the four Mahratta boats, she proceeded up the coast again. Another trader was captured on the way, but two others evaded the pirates, by running into the port of Calicut.

The trader was a slow sailer, and they were eight days before they approached Gheriah. Early in the morning a heavy cannonade was heard in the distance, causing the greatest excitement among the Mahrattas. Every sail was hoisted, the sweeps got out and, leaving the trader to jog along in their rear, the four light craft made their way rapidly along the coast. The firing became heavier and heavier, and as it became light, three large ships could be seen, about two miles ahead, surrounded by a host of smaller craft.

'That's a big fight, Mr. Charles,' Tim exclaimed. 'It reminds me of three big bulls in a meadow, attacked by a host of little curs.'

'It does, Tim; but the curs can bite. What a fire they are keeping up. But those warships ought to thrash any number of them. Count the ports, I can see them now.'

'The biggest one,' Tim said, 'has got twenty-five.'

'Yes; and the others eighteen and nine. They are two frigates, one of fifty and the other of thirty-six guns; and a sloop of eighteen. I can't make out the colours, but I don't think they're English.'

'They're not English, yer honor,' Tim said confidently, 'or they would soon make an end of them varmint that's tormenting them.'

The scene, as the boats approached, was very exciting. The three ships were pouring their broadsides, without intermission, into the pirate fleet. This consisted of vessels of all sizes, from the Jupitre and Restoration, down to large rowing galleys. Although many were sunk, and more greatly damaged by the fire of the Dutch, they swarmed round the great ships with wonderful tenacity; and, while the larger vessels fought their guns against those of the men-of-war, the smaller ones kept close to them, avoiding as much as possible their formidable broadsides, but keeping up a perpetual musketry fire at their bulwarks and tops, throwing stink pots, and shooting burning arrows through the ports; and getting alongside under the muzzles of the guns, and trying to climb up into the ports.

The four newly arrived craft joined in the fray.

'This is mighty unpleasant, yer honor,' Tim said, as a shot from one of the Dutch men-of-war struck the craft they were in, crashing a hole through her bulwarks, and laying five or six of her crew upon the deck, killed or wounded by the splinters. 'Here we are, in the middle of a fight in which we've no consarn whatever, and which is carried on without asking our will or pleasure; and we are as likely to be killed by a Christian shot, as these hathen natives.'

'Hear them yell, yer honor. A faction fight's nothing to it. Look, yer honor, look! There's smoke curling up from a hatchway of the big ship. If they haven't set her afire!'

It was as Tim said. A cloud of black smoke was rising from the Dutch fifty-gun frigate. A wild yell of triumph broke from the Mahrattas. The fire of their guns upon her redoubled, while that from the man-of-war died away, as the crew were called off to assist in extinguishing the flames. Now the smaller boats pressed still more closely round her, and a rain of missiles was poured through the open ports. Several times the Mahrattas climbed on board, but each time were driven out again. The smoke rose thicker and thicker, and tongues of flame could be seen shooting up.

'She is doomed,' Charlie exclaimed. 'Even if unmolested, the crew could not extinguish the fire, now. It has got too much hold.'

'Ah! The other frigate is on fire now.'

Fresh yells of triumph rose from the Mahrattas. On board the sloop every sail was hoisted, in spite of the continued fire of muskets and arrows, which killed many of the sailors employed. The Jupitre, however, ran alongside her and grappled with her, and a furious combat could be seen proceeding on the decks. Meanwhile, the flames mounted higher and higher on board the two frigates. The crew now could be seen leaping overboard from the ports, choosing any death rather than that by fire.

It was but a choice. Many were drowned, the rest cut or shot down by the Mahrattas. Down came the Dutch flag, fluttering from the masthead of the sloop, and the wild Mahratta yell proclaimed that the victory was everywhere complete.

The frigates were now a sheet of flames, and the Mahratta craft drew away from them; until, with two tremendous explosions, their magazines blew up and they sank beneath the waters.

'I should scarcely have believed it possible,' Charlie said, 'that three fine ships of war, mounting a hundred and four guns, could be destroyed by a fleet of pirates, however numerous. Well, Tim, there is no doubt that these natives can fight, when well led. It is just as well, you see, that we did not attempt to offer any resistance, in that clumsy craft we were on board.'

'You're right there, yer honor. They would have aten us up in five minutes. It makes my heart bleed, to think of the sailors of those two fine ships. I don't believe that a soul has escaped; but in the small one, some may have been taken prisoners.'

When the fight was over, the craft in which were the captives ran alongside the flagship of the pirate leader, and the captain reported to him the capture he had made. Fortunately, Tulagi Angria was in a high state of delight, at the victory he had just won; and, instead of ordering them to be instantly executed, he told the captain to take them on to Suwarndrug, and to imprison them there until his arrival. He himself, with the rest of his fleet, and the captured Dutch sloop, sailed into Gheriah; and the craft, in which Charlie and his companions were imprisoned, continued her course to the island stronghold of the pirates.

Suwarndrug was built on a rocky island. It lay within gunshot of the shore. Here, when Kanhagi Angria had first revolted from the authority of the Mahratta kingdom, the ruler of the Deccan had caused three strong forts to be built, in order to reduce the island fort. The pirates, however, had taken the initiative, and had captured these forts; as well as the whole line of seacoast, a hundred and twenty miles in length; and the country behind, twenty or thirty miles broad, extending to the foot of the mountains.

On their arrival at Suwarndrug, the prisoners were handed over to the governor, and were imprisoned in one of the casemates of the fort. The next day, they were taken out and ordered to work; and, for weeks, they laboured at the fortifications, with which the pirates were strengthening their already naturally strong position. The labour was very severe, but it was a consolation to the captives that they were kept together.

By Charlie's advice they exerted themselves to the utmost, and thus succeeded in pleasing their masters, and in escaping with but a small share of the blows, which were liberally distributed among other prisoners, native and European, employed upon the work. Charlie, indeed, was appointed as a sort of overseer; having under him not only his own party, but thirty others, of whom twenty were natives, and ten English sailors, who had been captured in a merchantman. Although closely watched, he was able to cheer these men, by giving them a hope that a chance of escape from their captivity might shortly arrive. All expressed their readiness to run any risk to regain their liberty.

From what he heard the pirates say, Charlie learned that they were expecting an attack from an expedition which was preparing at Bombay. The English sailors were confined in a casemate, adjoining that occupied by Charlie and his companions. The guard kept over them was but nominal, as it was considered impossible that they could escape from the island, off which lay a large fleet of the pirate vessels.

One morning upon starting to work they perceived, by the stir in the fortress, that something unusual was taking place; and presently, on reaching the rampart, they saw in the distance a small squadron approaching. They could make out that it consisted of a ship of forty-four guns, one of sixteen, and two bomb vessels, together with a fleet of native craft.

The pirate fleet were all getting up sail.

'It's a bold thing, Tim, to attack this fortress with only two ships, when the pirates have lately beaten a Dutch squadron mounting double the number of guns.'

'Ah, yer honor, but then there is the Union Jack floating at the masthead. Do you think the creeturs don't know the differ?'

'But the Dutchmen are good sailors, and fought well, Tim. I think the difference is that in the last case they attacked the Dutch, while in the present we are attacking them. It makes all the difference in the world, with Indians. Let them attack you, and they'll fight bravely enough. Go right at them, and they're done for.

'Look, the pirate fleet are already sailing away.'

'And do you think the English will take the fort, yer honor?'

'I don't know, Tim. The place is tremendously strong, and built on a rock. There are guns which bear right down on the ships, if they venture in close, while theirs will do but little damage to these solidly built walls. Suwarndrug ought to resist a fleet ten times as strong as that before us.'

'Shure then, yer honor, and will we have to remain here all our lives, do ye think?'

'No, Tim, I hope not. Besides, I think that we ought to be able to render some assistance to them.'

'And how will we do it, yer honor? You have but to spake the word, and Tim Kelly is ready to go through fire and water; and so is Hossein. Ye may be shure of that.'

Seeing that the pirates were now mustering round their guns, and that the ships were ranging up for action, Charlie thought it prudent to retire. Hitherto no attention had been paid to them, but 'twas probable enough that, when the pirates' blood became heated by the fight, they would vent their fury upon their captives. He therefore advised not only the native officers, but the sailors, to retire to their casemates; which, as the guns placed in them did not command the position taken up by the ships, were at presented untenanted by any of the garrison.

Presently the noise of guns proclaimed that the engagement had begun. The boom of the cannon of the ships was answered by an incessant fire from the far more numerous artillery of the fortress, while now and then a heavy explosion, close at hand, told of the bursting of the bombs from the mortar vessels, in the fortress.

Charlie had been thinking of the best measures to be taken, to aid his friends, ever since the squadron came in sight; and, after sitting quietly for half an hour, he called his officers around him.

'I am convinced,' he said, 'that if unaided from within, the ships will have no chance whatever of taking this fortress; but I think that we may help them. The upper fort, which contains the magazine, commands the whole of the interior. But its guns do not bear upon the ships where they are anchored. Probably the place, at present, is almost deserted. As no one pays any attention to us, I propose, with Tim Kelly and the ten English sailors, to seize it. We can close the gate, and discharge the guns upon the defenders of the sea face. We could not, of course, defend it for five minutes if they attacked us; but we would threaten to blow up the magazine, if they did so.

'I propose that, tomorrow morning, you four and Hossein shall strip to your loincloths, and just before it becomes light go along the walls, and stop up, with pieces of wood, the touch holes of as many of the cannon as you can. It would not do to use nails, even if we had them. No one will notice, in the dark, that you are not Mahrattas; and if you scatter about, you may each manage to close up four or five guns, at least. It is, I know, a desperate service, and if discovered you will be instantly killed. But if it succeeds the pirates, scared by discovering, just as our ships open fire, that a number of their guns are disabled; while we take them in the rear, from the fort behind, may not improbably surrender at once. At any rate, it's worth trying; and I, for one, would rather run the risk of being killed, than be condemned to pass my life the slave of these pirates, who may at any moment cut our throats, in case of any reverse happening to them.'

The four native officers at once stated their willingness to join in the plan. Hossein did not consider any reply necessary. With him, it was a matter of course to do whatever Charlie suggested.

The latter then went into the next casemate, and unfolded his plan to the sailors, who heartily agreed to make an effort for their liberty.

The fire continued all day unabated; and at nightfall, when a man, as usual, brought the captives food, he exultingly told them that no damage whatever had been effected by the guns of the fleet.

In the evening, the party cut a number of pieces of wood; these, measuring by the cannon in the casemate, they made of just sufficient size and length to push down, with a slight effort, through the touch hole. When pushed down to their full length, they touched the interior of the cannon below, and were just level with the top of the touch hole. Thus, it would be next to impossible to extricate them in a hurry. They might, indeed, be broken and forced in by a solid punch, of the same size as the touch hole; but this would take time, and would not be likely to occur, on the moment, to the pirates.

The skewers, for this is what they resembled, were very strong and tough; being made of slips of bamboo. The prisoners had all knives, which they used for cutting their food. With these the work was accomplished.

Towards morning the five natives, with the skewers hidden away in their loincloths, and their turbans twisted in Mahratta fashion, stole out from the casemate. Charlie had ordered that, in case they should see that the ships had drawn off from the position they occupied on the preceding day, they should return without attempting to carry out their task.

He himself, with Tim, joined the sailors; and, first ascending the ramparts and seeing that the ships were still at anchor, abreast of the fort, he and his comrades strolled across the interior of the fort, in the direction of the magazine. They did not keep together, nor did all move directly towards the position which they wished to gain.

The place was already astir. Large numbers of the pirates thronged the interior. Groups were squatted round fires, busy in cooking their breakfasts. Numbers were coming from the magazine, with powder to fill up the small magazines on the walls. Others, again, were carrying shot from the pyramids of missiles, piled up here and there in the courtyard. None paid any attention to the English prisoners.

Presently a dull boom was heard. There was a whistling sound; and with a thud, followed by a loud explosion, a bomb fell and burst in the open space.

This was the signal for action. The pirates, in a moment, hurried down to the bastions overlooking the sea; and the Englishmen gathered, in a group, near the entrance to the magazine. Besides their knives they had no arms, but each had picked up two or three heavy stones.

A minute after the explosion of the shell, the cannonade of the ships broke out. It was answered by only a few guns from the fortress, and yells of astonishment and rage were heard to arise.

A moment later, five natives ran up to the group of Englishmen. Their work had been well done, and more than three-fourths of the guns on the sea face had been rendered temporarily useless.

Charlie gave the word, and with a rush they entered the upper fort. There were but two or three men there, who were just hurrying out with their bags of powder. These, before they realized the position, were instantly knocked down and bound. The gate of the fort was then shut and barred, and the party ran up to the bastion above.

Not a single pirate was to be seen there. The six guns, which stood there, were at once loaded with grape; and a heavy discharge was poured into the crowded masses of pirates, upon the bastions on the sea face. These, already greatly disturbed at finding that most of their guns had, in some way, been rendered useless; were panic stricken at this sudden and unexpected attack from the rear. Many of them broke from their guns and fled to shelter, others endeavoured to turn their cannon to bear upon the magazine.

The wildest confusion raged. At last some of their leaders rallied the men; and, with yells of fury, a rush was made towards the magazine. They were received with another discharge of grape, which took terrible effect. Many recoiled, but their leaders, shouting to them that the guns were discharged, and there were but a dozen men there, led them on again.

Charlie leaped upon the edge of the parapet, and shouted:

'If you attack us, we will blow up the magazine. I have but to lift my hand, and the magazine will be fired.'

The boldest of the assailants were paralysed by the threat. Confusion reigned throughout the fortress. The fleet kept up their fire with great vigour; judging, by the feebleness of the reply, that something unusual must be happening within the walls. The gunners, disheartened by finding their pieces useless, and unable to extract the wooden plugs, while Charlie's men continued to ply them with grape, left their guns and, with the greater portion of the garrison, disorganized and panic stricken, retired into shelter.

A shell from the ships, falling on to a thatched building, set it on fire. The flames rapidly spread, and soon all the small huts occupied by the garrison were in flames. The explosion of a magazine added to the terror of the garrison, and the greater portion of them, with the women and children, ran down to the water; and, taking boats, attempted to cross to Fort Goa, on the mainland. They were, however, cut off by the English boats, and captured.

Commodore James, who commanded the squadron, now directed his fire at Fort Goa; which was being feebly attacked, on the land side, by a Mahratta force; which had been landed from the Mahratta fleet, accompanying the English ships, a few miles down the coast. The fort shortly surrendered; but while the Mahrattas were marching to take possession, the governor, with some of his best men, took boat and crossed over to the island; of which, although the fire had ceased after the explosion of the magazine, the English had not taken possession.

The fire from its guns again opened, and as Commodore James thought it probable that the pirates would, in the night, endeavour to throw in large reinforcements, he determined to carry it by storm. The ships opened fire upon the walls; and under cover of this, half the seamen were landed. These ran up to the gate, and thundered at it with their axes.

Charlie and his companions aided the movement, by again opening a heavy fire of grape upon the guns which bore upon the sally port; and when the gates were forced the garrison, utterly dispirited by the crossfire to which they were subjected, at once laid down their arms.

Chapter 16

A TIGER HUNT

Commodore James was greatly astonished at the easy success which he had gained. The extraordinary cessation of fire from the sea face, and the sound of artillery within the walls, had convinced him that a mutiny among the garrison must have taken place; but upon entering the fort he was surprised, indeed, at being received with a hearty English cheer, from a little body of men on the summit of an interior work. The gate of this was at once thrown open, and Charlie, followed by his party, advanced towards the commodore.

'I am Captain Marryat, sir, of the Company's service in Madras; and was captured three months ago by these pirates. When you attacked the place, yesterday, I arranged to effect a small diversion; and with the assistance of these five native officers, of my soldier servant, here, and these ten men of the merchant service, we have, I hope, been able to do so. The native officers disabled the greater portion of the guns, during the night; and when you opened fire this morning we seized this inner work, which is also the magazine, and opened fire upon the rear of the sea defences. By dint of our guns, and of menaces to blow up the place if they assaulted it, we kept them at bay until their flag was hauled down.'

'Then, sir,' Commodore James said, warmly; 'I have to thank you, most heartily, for the assistance you have given. In fact, it is you who have captured the fortress. I was by no means prepared to find it so strong; and, indeed, had come to the conclusion, last night, that the force at my command was wholly insufficient for its capture.

Fortunately, I determined to try the effect of another day's fire. But, had it not been for you, this would assuredly have been as ineffectual as the first. You have, indeed, performed a most gallant action; and I shall have great pleasure in reporting your conduct to the authorities at home.'

The sailors had now landed in considerable force. The garrison were disarmed, and taken as prisoners on board the ships. Very large quantities of powder were found, stored up, and strong parties at once began to form mines, for the blowing up of the fortifications.

This was a labour of some days. When they were completed and charged, a series of tremendous explosions took place. Many of the bastions were completely blown to pieces. In others, the walls were shattered.

The prisoners were again landed, and set to work, aided by the sailors. The great stones, which composed the walls, were toppled over the steep faces of the rock on which the fort stood; and, at the end of a fortnight, the pirate hold of Suwarndrug, which had so long been the terror of the Indian Seas, had disappeared.

The fleet returned to Bombay; for it was, evidently, wholly insufficient to attempt an assault on Gheriah; defended, as that place would be, by the whole pirate fleet; which had, even without the assistance of its guns, proved itself a match for a squadron double the strength of that under the command of Commodore James.

The rejoicings at Bombay were immense, for enormous damage had been inflicted on the commerce of that place, by this pirate hold, situated but eighty miles from the port. Commodore James and his officers were feted, and Charlie Marryat had his full share of honor; the gallant sailor, everywhere, assigning to him the credit of its capture.

Charlie would now have sailed, at once, for Madras; but the authorities wished him to remain, as Clive was shortly expected to arrive, with a considerable force, which was destined to act against the French at Hyderabad. The influence of Bussy, with the nizam, rendered this important province little better than a French possession; and the territory of our rivals, upon the seacoast, had been immensely increased by the grant of the five districts, known as the Northern Sirdars, to Bussy.

It was all that the English could do to hold their own, around Madras; and it was out of the question for them to think of attempting, single handed, to dislodge Bussy from Hyderabad. Between the nizam, however, and the Peishwar of the Deccan, there was a longstanding feud; and the Company had proposed, to this prince, to aid him with a strong English force, in an attack upon Hyderabad.

Colonel Scott had, in the first place, been sent out to command this expedition; but when Clive, wearied with two years' life of inactivity in England, applied to be appointed to active service, the directors at once appointed him governor of Fort Saint David, and obtained for him the rank of lieutenant colonel in the royal army. They directed him to sail at once for Bombay, with three companies of the Royal Artillery, each a hundred strong, and three hundred infantry recruits. Upon his arrival there, he was to give Colonel Scott any assistance he required. That officer, however, had died before Clive arrived.

Upon reaching Bombay, Clive found that events had occurred, in the south, which would prevent the intended expedition from taking place. The French government had suddenly recalled Dupleix, the great man whose talent and statesmanship had sustained their cause. On his return to France, instead of treating him with honor for the work he had done for them, they even refused to repay him the large sums which he had advanced, from his private fortune, to carry on the struggle against the English; and Dupleix died in poverty and obscurity.

In his place, the French governor had sent out a man by the name of Godchen, who was weak and wholly destitute of ability. At the time of his arrival the English were hardly pressed, and a strong French fleet and force were expected on the coast. When, however, Mr. Saunders proposed to him a treaty of neutrality between the Indian possessions of the two powers, he at once accepted it; and thus threw away all the advantages, which Dupleix had struggled so hard to obtain. The result of this treaty, however, was that the English were unable to carry out their proposed alliance, with the peishwar, against the nizam and Bussy.

Upon Clive's arrival, Charlie at once reported himself to him. For a time, however, no active duty was assigned to him, as it was uncertain what steps would now be taken. Finally it was resolved that, taking advantage of the presence of Clive and his troops, and of a squadron which had arrived under Admiral Watson, the work commenced by Commodore James should be completed, by the capture of Gheriah and the entire destruction of the pirate power.

The peishwar had already asked them to aid him in his attack upon Angria, and Commodore James was now sent, with the Protector and two other ships, to reconnoitre Gheriah, which no Englishman then living had seen. The natives described it as of enormous strength, and it was believed that it was an Eastern Gibraltar.

Commodore James found the enemy's fleet at anchor in the harbour. Notwithstanding this, he sailed in until within cannon shot, and so completely were the enemy cowed and demoralized, by the loss of Suwarndrug, that they did not venture out to attack him.

After ascertaining the position and character of the defences, he returned, at the end of December, to Bombay; and reported that, while exceedingly strong, the place was by no means impregnable. The Mahratta army, under the command of Ramajee Punt, marched to blockade the place on the land side; and on the 11th of February, 1756, the fleet, consisting of four ships of the line, of seventy, sixty-four, sixty, and fifty guns; a frigate of forty-four, and three of twenty; a native ship called a grab, of twelve guns; and five mortar ships, arrived before the place. Besides the seamen, the fleet had on board a battalion of eight hundred Europeans and a thousand Sepoys.

The fortress of Gheriah was situated on a promontory of rock, a mile and a quarter broad; lying about a mile up a large harbour, forming the mouth of a river. The promontory projects to the southwest, on the right of the harbour on entering; and rises sheer from the water in perpendicular rocks, fifty feet high. On this stood the fortifications. These consisted of two lines of walls, with round towers, the inner wall rising several feet above the outer.

The promontory was joined to the land by a sandy slip, beyond which the town stood. On this neck of land, between the promontory and the town, were the docks and slips on which the pirate vessels were built or repaired; and ten of these, among which was the Derby, which they had captured from the Company, lay moored side by side, close by the docks, when the fleet arrived off the place.

Charlie Marryat had been sent, by Clive, as commissioner with the Mahratta army. A party of Mahratta horsemen came down to Bombay to escort him to Chaule, at which place the Mahratta army were assembled for their march. He was accompanied by Tim and Hossein, who were of course, like him, on horseback.

A long day's ride took them to their first halting place, a few miles from the foot of a splendid range of hills, which rise like a wall from the low land, for a vast distance along the coast. At the top of these hills – called in India, ghauts – lay the plateau of the Deccan, sloping gradually away to the Ganges, hundreds of miles to the east.

'Are we going to climb up to top of them mountains, your honor?'

'No, Tim, fortunately for our horses. We shall skirt their foot, for a hundred and fifty miles, till we get behind Gheriah.'

'You wouldn't think that a horse could climb them,' Tim said. 'They look as steep as the side of a house.'

'In many places they are, Tim, but you see there are breaks in them. At some points, either from the force of streams, or from the weather, the rocks have crumbled away; and the great slopes, which everywhere extend halfway up, reach the top. Zigzag paths are cut in these, which can be travelled by horses and pack animals.

'There must be quantities of game,' Charlie said to the leader of the escort, 'on the mountain sides.'

'Quantities?' the Mahratta said. 'Tigers and bears swarm there, and are such a scourge that there are no villages within miles of the foot of the hills. Even on the plateau above, the villages are few and scarce near the edge, so great is the damage done by wild beasts.

'But that is not all. There are numerous bands of Dacoits, who set the authority of the peishwar at defiance, plunder travellers and merchants going up and down, make raids into the Deccan, and plunder the low land nearly up to the gates of Bombay. Numerous expeditions have been sent against them, but the Dacoits know every foot of the hills. They have numerous, impregnable strongholds on the rocks; which you can see rising sheer up hundreds of feet, from among the woods on the slopes; and can, if pressed, shift their quarters, and move fifty miles away among the trees, while the troops are, in vain, searching for them.'

'I suppose there is no chance of their attacking us,' Charlie said.

'The Dacoit never fights if he can help it, and then only when driven into a corner, or when there appears a chance of very large plunder. He will always leave a strong party of armed men, from whom nothing but hard blows is to be got, in peace.'

The journey occupied five days, and was most enjoyable. The officer of the escort, as the peishwar's agent, would have requisitioned provisions at each of the villages; but Charlie insisted, under one pretence or another, on buying a couple of sheep or kids at each halting place, for the use of his own party and the escort. For a few copper coins an abundant supply of fruit and vegetables was obtainable; and as, each night, they spread their rugs under the shade of some overhanging tree, and smoked their pipes lazily after the very excellent meal which Hossein always prepared, Charlie and Tim agreed that they had spent no pleasanter time in India than that occupied by their journey.

Charlie was received with much honor by Ramajee Punt, and was assigned a gorgeous tent, next to his own.

'People in England, Mister Charles,' said Tim that evening, 'turn up their noses at the thought of living in tents, but what do they know of them? The military tent is an uncomfortable thing, and as for the gipsy tent, a dacent pig wouldn't look at it. Now this is like a palace, with its carpet under foot, and its sides covered with silk hangings, and its furniture fit for a palace. Father Murphy wouldn't believe me, if I told him about it on oath. If this is making war, yer honor, I shall be in no hurry for pace.'

The Mahratta force took up its position, beleaguering the town on the land side, some weeks before the arrival of the fleet; Commodore James, with his two ships, blockading it at sea. There was little to do, and Charlie accepted with eagerness an offer of Ramajee Punt, that they should go out for two or three days' tiger hunting, at the foot of the hills.

'Well, Mr. Charles,' Tim said, when he heard of the intention, 'if you want to go tiger hunting, Tim Kelly is not the boy to stay behind. But shure, yer honor, if the creeturs will lave ye alone, why should you meddle with them? I saw one in a cage at Arcot, and it's a baste I shouldn't wish to see on a lone road on a dark night. It had a way of wagging its tail that made you feel uncomfortable like, to the sole of yer boots; and after looking at me for some time, the baste opened its mouth, and gave a roar that shook the whole establishment. It's a baste safer to let alone than to meddle with.'

'But we shall be up on the top of an elephant. We shall be safe enough there, you know.'

'Maybe, yer honor,' Tim said doubtfully; 'but I mind me that, when I was a boy, me and my brother Peter was throwing sods at an old tomcat of my mother's, who had stolen our dinners, and it ran up a wall ten feet high. Well, yer honor, the tiger is as big as a hundred tomcats, and by the same token he ought to be able to run up a wall –'

'A thousand feet high, Tim? He can't do that. Indeed, I question whether he could run up much higher than a cat.

'We are to start this evening, and shall be there by midnight. The elephants have gone on ahead.'

At sunset the party started. It consisted of Ramajee Punt, one of his favourite officers, and a score of soldiers. An officer had already gone on, to enlist the services of the men of two or three villages as beaters. A small but comfortable tent had been erected for the party, and supper prepared.

The native shikari, or sportsman of the neighbourhood, had brought in the news that tigers were plentiful; and that one of unusual size had been committing great depredations; and had, only the day before, carried off a bullock into the thickets, a mile from the spot at which they were encamped.

'The saints preserve us!' Tim said, when he heard the news; 'a cat big enough to carry off a mouse in her mouth as big as a bullock.'

'It seems almost impossible, Tim, but it is a fact that tigers can carry in their mouths full-sized bullocks, for considerable distances, and that they can kill them with one stroke of their paw. However, they are not as formidable as you would imagine, as you will see, tomorrow.'

In the morning the elephants were brought out. Charlie took his place in the front of a howdah, with Tim behind him. Three rifles were placed in the seat, and these Tim was to hand to his master, as he discharged them. Ramajee Punt and his officer were also mounted on elephants, and the party started for their destination.

'It's as bad as being at sea, Mr. Charles,' Tim said.

'It does roll about, Tim. You must let your body go with the motion, just as on board ship. You will soon get accustomed to it.'

On reaching the spot, which was a narrow valley, with steep sides running up into the hill, the elephants came to a stand. The mouth of the valley was some fifty yards wide, and the animal might break from the trees at any point. The ground was covered with high, coarse grass.

Ramajee Punt placed himself in the centre, assigning to Charlie the position on his right, telling him that it was the best post, as it was on this side the tiger had been seen to enter. Soon after they had taken their places, a tremendous clamour arose near the head of the valley. Drums were beaten, horns blown, and scores of men joined in, with shouts and howls.

'What on arth are they up to, Mr. Charles?'

'They are driving the tiger this way, Tim. Now, sit quiet and keep a sharp lookout, and be ready to hand me a rifle, the instant I have fired.'

The noise increased, and was plainly approaching. The elephant fidgeted uneasily.

'That baste has more sinse than we have,' said Tim; 'and would be off, if that little black chap, astraddle of his neck, didn't keep on patting his head.'

Presently, the mahout pointed silently to the bushes ahead, and Charlie caught sight, for a moment, of some yellow fur. Apparently the tiger had heard or scented the elephants, for it again turned and made up the valley. Presently a redoubled yelling, with the firing of guns, showed that it had been seen by the beaters. Ramajee Punt held up his hand to Charlie, as a signal that next time the tiger might be expected.

Suddenly there was a movement among the bushes. A tiger sprang out, about halfway between Charlie's elephant and that of Ramajee Punt. It paused for a moment, on seeing them; and then, as it was about to spring forward, two balls struck it. It sprang a short distance, however, and then fell, rolling over and over. One ball had broken a foreleg, the other had struck it on the head. Another ball from Ramajee Punt struck it, as it rolled over and over, and it lay immovable.

'Why didn't you hand me the next rifle, Tim?' Charlie said sharply.

'It went clane out of my head, altogether. To think now, and you kilt it in a moment. The tiger is a poor baste, anyhow. I've seen a cat make ten times as strong a fight for its life.

'Holy Moses!'

The last exclamation was called from Tim's lips by a sudden jerk. A huge tiger, far larger than that which had fallen, had sprung up from the brushwood and leaped upon the elephant. With one forepaw he grasped the howdah, with the other clung to the elephant's shoulder, an inch or two only behind the leg of the mahout.

Charlie snatched the rifle from Tim's hand, and thrust the muzzle into the tiger's mouth, just as the elephant swerved round with sudden fright and pain. At the same moment the weight of the tiger on the howdah caused the girths to give way; and Charlie, Tim and the tiger fell together on the ground. Charlie had pulled his trigger, just as he felt himself going; and at the same moment he heard the crack of Ramajee Punt's rifle.

The instant they touched the ground, Tim and Charlie cast themselves over and over, two or three times; and then leaped to their feet, Charlie grasping his rifle, to make the best defence he could if the tiger sprang upon him. The creature lay, however, immovable.

'It is dead, Tim,' Charlie exclaimed. 'You needn't be afraid.'

'And no wonder, yer honor, when I pitched, head first, smack onto his stomach. It would have killed a horse.'

'It might have done, Tim, but I don't think it would have killed a tiger. Look there.'

Charlie's gun had gone off at the moment when the howdah turned round, and had nearly blown off a portion of the tiger's head; while, almost at the same instant, the ball of Ramajee Punt had struck it in the back, breaking the spine. Death had, fortunately for Tim, been instantaneous.

The tiger last killed was the great male which had done so much damage; the first, a female. The natives tied the legs together, placed long bamboos between them, and carried the animals off, in triumph, to the camp. The elephant on which Charlie had ridden ran some distance, before the mahout could stop him. He was, indeed, so terrified by the onslaught of the tiger, that it was not considered advisable to endeavour to get him to face another, that day. Ramajee Punt, therefore, invited Charlie to take his seat with him, on his elephant, an arrangement which greatly satisfied Tim, whose services were soon dispensed with.

'I'd rather walk on my own feet, Mister Charles, than ride any more on those great bastes. They're uncomfortable, anyhow. It's a long way to fall, if the saddle goes round; and next time one might not find a tiger handy, to light on.'

Two more tigers were killed that afternoon and, well pleased with his day's sport, Charlie returned to the hunting camp.

The next day, Hossein begged that he might be allowed to accompany Charlie in Tim's place; and as the Irishman was perfectly willing to surrender it, the change was agreed upon. The march was a longer one than it had been, on the previous morning. A notorious man-eating tiger was known to have taken up his abode, in a large patch of jungle, at the foot of an almost perpendicular wall of rock, about ten miles from the place where the camp was pitched. The patch of jungle stood upon a steep terrace, whose slopes were formed of boulders, the patch being some fifty or sixty yards long and thirty deep.

'It is a nasty place,' Ramajee Punt said, 'to get him from. The beaters cannot get behind to drive him out, and the jungle is too thick to penetrate.'

'How do you intend to proceed?' Charlie asked.

'We will send a party to the top of the hill, and they will throw down crackers. We have brought some rockets, too, which we will send in from the other side. We will take our places, on our elephants, at the foot of the terrace.'

The three elephants took their posts, at the foot of the boulder covered rise. As soon as they had done so, the men at the top of the rock began to throw down numbers of lighted crackers; while, from either side, parties sent rockets whizzing into the jungle.

For some time the tiger showed no signs of his presence, and Charlie began to doubt whether he could be really there. The shikaris, however, declared that he was certainly in the jungle. He had, on the day before, carried off a woman from a neighbouring village; and had been traced to the jungle, round which a watch had been kept all night.

Suddenly, uttering a mighty roar, the tiger bounded from the jungle, and stood at the edge of the terrace. Startled at his sudden appearance, the elephants recoiled, shaking the aim of their riders. Three shots were, however, fired almost at the same moment; and the tiger, with another roar, bounded back into the jungle.

'I think,' the rajah said, 'that he is badly hit. Listen to his roarings.'

The tiger, for a time, roared loudly at intervals. Then the sounds became lower and less frequent, and at last ceased altogether. In vain did the natives above shower down crackers. In vain were the rockets discharged into the jungle. An hour passed, since he had last been heard.

'I expect that he's dead,' Charlie said.

'I think so, too,' Ramajee Punt replied; 'but one can never be certain. Let us draw off a little, and take our luncheon. After that, we can try the fireworks again. If he will not move, then we must leave him.'

'But surely,' Charlie said, 'we might go in and see whether he's dead or not.'

'A wounded tiger is a terrible foe,' the Ramajee answered. 'Better leave him alone.'

Charlie, however, was anxious to get the skin to send home, with those of the others he had shot, to his mother and sisters. It might be very long before he had an opportunity of joining in another tiger hunt; and he resolved that, if the tiger gave no signs of life when the bombardment of the jungle with fireworks recommenced, he would go in and look for his body.

Chapter 17

THE CAPTURE OF GHERIAH

After having sat for an hour under the shade of some trees, and partaken of luncheon, the party again moved forward on their elephants to the jungle. The watchers declared that no sound, whatever, had been heard during their absence; nor did the discharge of fireworks, which at once recommenced, elicit the slightest response.

After this had gone on for half an hour, Charlie, convinced that the animal was dead, dismounted from his elephant. He had with him a heavy, double-barrelled rifle of the rajah's; and Hossein, carrying a similar weapon, and a curved tulwar which was sharpened almost to a razor edge, prepared to follow immediately behind him. Three or four of the most courageous shikaris, with cocked guns, followed in Hossein's steps.

Holding his gun advanced before him, in readiness to fire instantly, Charlie entered the jungle at the point where the tiger had retreated into it. Drops of blood spotted the grass, and the bent and twisted brushwood showed the path that the tiger had taken. Charlie moved as noiselessly as possible. The path led straight forward, towards the rocks behind, but it was not until within four or five yards of this that any sign of the tiger could be seen.

Then the bushes were burst asunder, and the great yellow body hurled itself forward upon Charlie. The attack was so sudden and instantaneous that the latter had not even time to raise his rifle to his shoulder. Almost instinctively, however, he discharged both of the barrels; but was, at the same moment, hurled to the ground, where he lay crushed down by the weight of the tiger, whose hot breath he could feel on his face. He closed his eyes, only to open them again at the sound of a heavy blow, while a deluge of hot blood flowed over him. He heard Hossein's voice, and then became insensible. When he recovered, he found himself lying with his head supported by Hossein, outside the jungle.

'Is he dead?' he asked faintly.

'He is dead, Sahib,' Hossein replied. 'Let the Sahib drink some brandy, and he will be strong again.'

Charlie drank some brandy and water, which Hossein held to his lips. Then the latter raised him to his feet.

Charlie felt his limbs and his ribs. He was bruised all over, but otherwise unhurt, the blood which covered him having flowed from the tiger. One of the balls which he had fired had entered the tiger's neck, the other had broken one of its forelegs, and Charlie had been knocked down by the weight of the animal, not by the blow of its formidable paw.

Hossein had sprung forward on the instant, and with one blow of his sharp tulwar, had shorn clear through skin and muscle and bone, and had almost severed the tiger's head from its body. It was the weight upon him which had crushed Charlie into a state of insensibility. Here he had lain, for four or five minutes, before Hossein could get the frightened natives to return, and assist him to lift the great carcass from his master's body.

Upon examination, it was found that two of the three bullets first fired had taken effect. One had broken the tiger's shoulder, and lodged in his body. The other had struck him fairly on the chest, and had passed within an inch or two of his heart.

'I thought,' Ramajee Punt said, as he viewed the body, 'that one of his legs must have been rendered useless. That was why he lay quiet so long, in spite of our efforts to turn him out.'

Charlie was too much hurt to walk, and a litter was speedily formed, and he was carried back to the camp, where his arrival in that state excited the most lively lamentations on the part of Tim. The next morning he was much recovered; and was able, in the cool of the evening, to take his place in a howdah, and to return to the camp before Gheriah.

A few days later the fleet made its appearance off the town, and the same evening Tulagi Angria rode up to Ramajee Punt's camp. Charlie was present at the interview, at which Angria endeavoured to prevail on Ramajee Punt, and Charlie, to accept a large ransom for his fort; offering them each great presents, if they would do their utmost to prevail on Admiral Watson, and Colonel Clive, to agree to accept it.

Charlie said at once that he was sure it was useless, that the English had now made a great effort to put a stop to the ravages which he, and his father before him, had for so many years inflicted upon their commerce; and that he was sure that nothing, short of the total destruction of the fort and fleet, would satisfy them. The meeting then broke up; and Charlie, supposing that Angria would return immediately, went back to his tent; where he directed Hossein at once to mingle with the men who had accompanied Angria, and to find out anything that he could concerning the state of things in the fort.

Hossein returned an hour later.

'Sahib,' he said, 'Ramajee Punt is thinking of cheating the English. He is keeping Angria a prisoner. He says that he came into his camp without asking for a safe conduct; and that, therefore, he shall detain him.

'But this is not all. Angria has left his brother in command of the fort; and Ramajee, by threatening Angria with instant execution, has induced him to send an order to deliver the fort at once to him. Ramajee wants, you see, Sahib, to get all the plunder of the fort for himself, and his Mahrattas.'

'This is very serious,' Charlie said, 'and I must let the admiral know, at once, what is taking place.'

When it became dark, Charlie, with Tim and Hossein, made his way through the Mahratta camp, down to the shore of the river. Here were numbers of boats, hauled up on the sand. One of the lightest of these was soon got into the water, and rowed gently out into the force of the stream. Then the oars were shipped, and they lay down perfectly quiet in the boat, and drifted past the fort without being observed.

When they once gained the open sea, the oars were placed in the rowlocks, and half an hour's rowing brought them alongside the fleet. Charlie was soon on board the flagship, and informed the admiral, and Colonel Clive, what Hossein had heard.

It was at once resolved to attack upon the following day. The two officers did not think it was likely that the pirates would, even in obedience to their chief's orders, surrender the place until it had been battered by the fleet.

The next morning, the fort was summoned to surrender. No answer was received, and as soon as the sea breeze set in, in the afternoon, the fleet weighed anchor and proceeded towards the mouth of the river. The men-of-war were in line, on the side nearest to the fort, to protect the mortar vessels and smaller ships from its fire.

Passing the point of the promontory, they stood into the river, and anchored at a distance of fifty yards from the north face of the fort. A gun from the admiral's ship gave the signal, and a hundred and fifty pieces of cannon at once opened fire, while the mortar vessels threw shell into the fort and town. In ten minutes after the fire began, a shell fell into one of Angria's large ships, and set her on fire. The flames soon spread to the others, fastened together on either side of her, and in less than an hour this fleet, which had for fifty years been the terror of the Malabar coast, was utterly destroyed.

In the meantime the fleet kept up their fire, with the greatest vigour, upon the enemy's works; and, before nightfall, the enemy's fire was completely silenced. No white flag, however, was hung up, and the admiral had little doubt that it was intended to surrender the place to the Mahrattas.

As soon, therefore, as it became quite dark, Colonel Clive landed with the troops, and took up a position between the Mahrattas and the fort; where, to his great disappointment and disgust, Ramajee Punt found him in the morning. The admiral again summoned the fort, declaring that he would renew the attack, and give no quarter, unless it was surrendered immediately. The governor sent back to beg the admiral to cease from hostilities until next day, as he was only waiting for orders from Angria to surrender. Angria declared that he had already sent the orders.

At four in the afternoon, therefore, the bombardment was renewed; and in less than half an hour, a white flag appeared above the wall. As, however, the garrison made no further sign of surrender, and refused to admit Colonel Clive with his troops, when he advanced to take possession, the bombardment was again renewed, more vigorously than ever. The enemy were unable to support the violence of the fire, and soon shouted over the walls, to Clive, that they surrendered; and he might enter and take possession. He at once marched in, and the pirates laid down their arms, and surrendered themselves prisoners.

It was found that a great part of the fortifications had been destroyed by the fire, but a resolute garrison might have held the fort, itself, against a long siege. Two hundred guns fell into the hands of the captors, together with great quantities of ammunition, and stores of all kinds. The money and effects amounted to a hundred and twenty thousand pounds, which was divided among the captors. The rest of Angria's fleet, among them two large ships on the stocks, was destroyed.

Ramajee Punt sent parties of his troops to attack the other forts held by the pirates. These, however, surrendered without resistance, and thus the whole country, which the pirates had held for seventy years, fell again into the hands of the Mahrattas, from whom they had wrested it.

Admiral Watson and the fleet then returned to Bombay, in order to repair the damages which had been inflicted upon them during the bombardment. There were great rejoicings upon their arrival there; the joy of the inhabitants, both European and native, being immense at the destruction of the formidable pirate colonies, which had so long ravaged the seas.

After the repairs were completed, the fleet, with the troops which had formed the expedition, were to sail for Madras. Charlie, however, did not wait for this; but, finding that one of the Company's ships would sail, in the course of a few days after their return to Bombay, he obtained leave from Colonel Clive to take a passage in her, and to proceed immediately to Madras. Tim and Hossein, of course, accompanied him; and the voyage down the west coast of India, and round Ceylon, was performed without any marked incident.

When within but a few hours of Madras, the barometer fell rapidly. Great clouds rose up upon the horizon, and the captain ordered all hands aloft to reduce sail.

'We are in,' he said, 'for a furious tempest. It is the breaking up of the monsoon. It is a fortnight earlier than usual. I had hoped that we should have got safely up the Hoogly before it began.'

Half an hour later the hurricane struck them, and for the next three days the tempest was terrible. Great waves swept over the ship, and every time that the captain attempted to show a rag of canvas, it was blown from the bolt ropes. The ship, however, was a stout one, and weathered the gale.

Upon the fourth morning the passengers, who had, during the tempest, been battened below, came on deck. The sky was bright and clear, and the waves were fast going down. A good deal of sail was already set, and the hands were at work to repair damages.

'Well, captain,' Charlie said to that officer, 'I congratulate you on the behaviour of the ship. It has been a tremendous gale, and she has weathered it stoutly.'

'Yes, Captain Marryat, she has done well. I have only once or twice been out in so severe a storm, since I came to sea.'

'And where are we now?' Charlie asked, looking round the horizon. 'When shall we be at Madras?'

'Well,' the captain said with a smile, 'I am afraid that you must give up all idea of seeing Madras, just at present. We have been blown right up the bay, and are only a few hours' sail from the mouth of the Hoogly. I have a far larger cargo for that place than for Madras, and it would be a pure waste of time for me to put back now. I intend, therefore, to go to Calcutta first, discharge and fill up there, and then touch at Madras on my way back.

'I suppose it makes no great difference to you.'

'No, indeed,' Charlie said. 'And I am by no means sorry of the opportunity of getting a glimpse of Calcutta, which I might never otherwise have done. I believe things are pretty quiet at Madras, at present; and I have been so long away, now, that a month or two sooner or later will make but little difference.'

A few hours later, Charlie noticed a change in the colour of the sea, the mud-stained waters of the Hoogly discolouring the Bay of Bengal, far out from its mouth. The voyage up was a tedious one. At times the wind fell altogether and, unable to stem the stream, the ship lay for days at anchor, the yellow tide running swiftly by it.

'The saints presarve us, Mr. Charles! Did you ever see the like?' Tim Kelly exclaimed. 'There's another dead body, floating down towards us, and that is the eighth I've seen this morning. Are the poor hathen craturs all committing suicide together?'

'Not at all, Tim,' Charlie said, 'the Hoogly is one of the sacred rivers of India, and the people on its banks, instead of burying their dead, put them into the river and let them drift away.'

'I calls it a bastly custom, yer honor, and I wonder it is allowed. One got athwart the cable this morning, and it frightened me nigh out of my sinses, when I happened to look over the bow, and saw the thing bobbing up and down in the water.

'This is tedious work, yer honor, and I'll be glad when we're at the end of the voyage.'

'I shall be glad, too, Tim. We have been a fortnight in the river already. But I think there is a breeze getting up, and there is the captain on deck, giving orders.'

In a few minutes, the ship was under way again, and the same night dropped her anchor in the stream, abreast of Calcutta. Charlie shortly after landed, and, proceeding to the Company's offices, reported his arrival, and that of the four Sepoy officers. Hossein, who was not in the Company's service, was with him merely in the character of a servant.

As the news of the share Charlie had had in the capture of Suwarndrug had reached Calcutta, he was well received; and one of the leading merchants of the town, Mr. Haines, who happened to be present when Charlie called upon the governor, at once invited him warmly to take up his residence with him, during his stay. Hospitality in India was profuse, and general. Hotels were unknown, and a stranger was always treated as an honored guest.

Charlie, therefore, had no hesitation whatever in accepting the offer. The four native officers were quartered in the barracks; and, returning on board ship, Charlie, followed by Tim and Hossein, and by some coolies bearing his luggage, was soon on his way to the bungalow of Mr. Haines.

On his way, he was surprised at the number and size of the dwellings of the merchants and officials, which offered a very strong contrast to the quiet and unpretending buildings round the fort of Madras. The house of Mr. Haines was a large one, and stood in a large and carefully kept garden. Mr. Haines received him at the door, and at once led him to his room, which was spacious, cool, and airy. Outside was a wide veranda, upon which, in accordance with the customs of the country, servants would sleep.

'Here is your bathroom,' Mr. Haines said, pointing to an adjoining room. 'I think you will find everything ready. We dine in half an hour.'

Charlie was soon in his bath, a luxury which, in India, every European indulges in at least twice a day. Then in his cool white suit, which at that time formed the regular evening dress, he found his way to the drawing room. Here he was introduced to the merchant's wife, and to his daughter, a girl of some thirteen years old, as well as to several guests who had arrived for dinner.

The meal was a pleasant one, and Charlie, after being cooped up for some weeks on board ship, enjoyed it much. A dinner in India is, to one unaccustomed to it, a striking sight. The punkah waving slowly to and fro, overhead, drives the cool air which comes in through the open windows down upon the table. Each guest brings his own servant, who, either in white or coloured robes, and in turbans of many different hues and shapes, according to the wearer's caste, stands behind his master's chair. The light is always a soft one, and the table richly garnished with bright-coloured tropical flowers.

Charlie was the hero of the hour, and was asked many questions concerning the capture of Suwarndrug; and also about the defence of Ambur, which, though now an old story, had excited the greatest interest through India. Presently, however, the conversation turned to local topics; and Charlie learned, from the anxious looks and earnest tones of the speakers, that the situation was considered a very serious one. He asked but few questions, then; but after the guests had retired, and Mr. Haines proposed to him to smoke one more quiet cigar, in the cool of the veranda, before retiring to bed; he took the opportunity of asking his host to explain to him the situation, with which he had no previous acquaintance.

'Up to the death of Ali Kerdy, the old viceroy of Bengal, on the 9th April, we were on good terms with our native neighbours. Calcutta has not been, like Madras, threatened by the rivalry of a European neighbour. The French and Dutch, indeed, have both trading stations like our own, but none of us have taken part in native affairs. Ali Kerdy has been all powerful, there have been no native troubles, and therefore no reason for our interference. We have just gone on as for many years previously, as a purely trading company.

'At his death, he was succeeded in the government by Suraja Dowlah, his grandson. I suppose, in all India, there is no prince with a worse reputation than this young scoundrel has already gained for himself, for profligacy and cruelty. He is constantly drunk, and is surrounded by a crew of reprobates, as wicked as himself. At the death of Ali Kerdy, Sokut Jung, another grandson of Ali, set up in opposition to him, and the new viceroy raised a large force to march against him. As the reputation of Sokut Jung was as infamous as that of his cousin, it would have made little difference to us which of the two obtained the mastery.

'Within the last few days, however, circumstances have occurred which have completely altered the situation. The town of Dacca was, about a year ago, placed under the governorship of Rajah Ragbullub, a Hindoo officer in high favour with Ali Kerdy. His predecessor had been assassinated and plundered, by order of Suraja Dowlah; and when he heard of the accession of that prince, he determined at once to fly, as he knew that his great wealth would speedily cause him to be marked out as a victim. He therefore obtained a letter of recommendation from Mr. Watts, the agent of the Company at their factory at Cossimbazar; and sent his son Kissendas, with a large retinue, his family and treasures, to Calcutta.

'Two or three days after his accession, Suraja Dowlah despatched a letter to Mr. Drake, our governor, ordering him to surrender Kissendas and the treasures immediately. The man whom he sent down arrived in a small boat, without any state or retinue; and Mr. Drake, believing that he was an impostor, paid no attention to the demand, but expelled him from the settlement. Two days ago a letter came from the viceroy; or, as we generally call him, the nabob, to Mr. Drake, ordering him instantly to demolish all the fortifications which he understood he had been erecting. Mr. Drake has sent word back, assuring the nabob that he is erecting no new fortifications, but simply executing some repairs in the ramparts facing the river, in view of the expected war between England and France.

'That is all that has been done, at present; but, seeing the passionate and overbearing disposition of this young scoundrel, there is no saying what will come of it.'

'But how do we stand here?' Charlie asked. 'What are the means of defence, supposing he should take it into his head to march, with the army which he has raised to fight against his cousin, to the attack of Calcutta?'

'Nothing could be worse than our position,' Mr. Haines said. 'Ever since the capture of Madras, nine years ago, the directors have been sending out orders that this place should be put in a state of defence. During the fifty years which have passed peacefully here, the fortifications have been entirely neglected. Instead of the space round them being kept clear, warehouses have been built close against them, and the fort is wholly unable to resist any attack. The authorities of the Company here have done absolutely nothing to carry out the orders from home. They think, I am sorry to say, only of making money with their own trading ventures; and although several petitions have been presented to them, by the merchants here, urging upon them the dangers which might arise at the death of Ali, they have taken no steps whatever, and indeed have treated all warnings with scorn and derision.'

'What force have we here?' Charlie asked.

'Only a hundred and seventy-four men, of whom the greater portion are natives.'

'What sort of man is your commander?'

'We have no means of knowing,' Mr. Haines said. 'His name is Minchin. He is a great friend of the governor's, and has certainly done nothing to counteract the apathy of the authorities. Altogether, to my mind, things look as bad as they possibly can.'

A week later, on the 15th of June, a messenger arrived with the news that the nabob, with fifty thousand men, was advancing against the town; and that, in two days, he would appear before it. All was confusion and alarm. Charlie at once proceeded to the fort, and placed his services at the disposal of Captain Minchin. He found that officer fussy, and alarmed.

'If I might be permitted to advise,' Charlie said, 'every available man in the town should be set to work, at once, pulling down all the buildings around the walls. It would be clearly impossible to defend the place when the ramparts are, on all sides, commanded by the musketry fire of surrounding buildings.'

'I know what my duty is, sir,' Captain Minchin said, 'and do not require to be taught it, by so very young an officer as yourself.'

'Very well, sir,' Charlie replied, calmly. 'I have seen a great deal of service, and have taken part in the defence of two besieged towns; while you, I believe, have never seen a shot fired. However, as you're in command you will, of course, take what steps you think fit; but I warn you that, unless those buildings are destroyed, the fort cannot resist an assault for twenty-four hours.'

Then, bowing quietly, he retired; and returned to Mr. Haines' house. That gentleman was absent, having gone to the governor's. He did not come back until late in the evening. Charlie passed the time in endeavouring to cheer up Mrs. Haines, and her daughter; assuring them that, if the worst came to the worst, there could be no difficulty in their getting on board ship.

Mrs. Haines was a woman of much common sense and presence of mind; and, under the influence of Charlie's quiet chat, she speedily recovered her tranquillity. Her daughter Ada, who was a very bright and pretty girl, was even sooner at her ease, and they were laughing and chatting brightly, when Mr. Haines arrived. He looked fagged and dispirited.

'Drake is a fool,' he said. 'Just as, hitherto, he has scoffed at all thought of danger, now he is prostrated at the news that danger is at hand. He can decide on nothing. At one moment he talks of sending messengers to Suraja Dowlah, to offer to pay any sum he may demand, in order to induce him to retire; the next he talks of defending the fort to the last. We can get him to give no orders, to decide on nothing, and the other officials are equally impotent and imbecile.'

On the 18th, the army of the nabob approached. Captain Minchin took his guns and troops a considerable distance beyond the walls, and opened fire upon the enemy. Charlie, enraged and disgusted at the folly of conduct which could only lead to defeat, marched with them as a simple volunteer.

The result was what he had anticipated. The enemy opened fire with an immensely superior force of artillery. His infantry advanced, and clouds of horsemen swept round the flanks, and menaced the retreat. In a very few minutes, Captain Minchin gave the order to retire; and, abandoning their guns, the English force retreated in all haste to the town.

Charlie had, on setting out, told Mr. Haines what was certain to occur; and had implored him to send all his valuables, at once, on board ship; and to retire instantly into the fort. Upon the arrival of the troops at the gate, they found it almost blocked with the throng of frightened Europeans, and natives, flying from their houses beyond it to its protection. Scarcely were all the fugitives within, and the gates closed, when the guns of Suraja Dowlah opened upon the fort; and his infantry, taking possession of the houses around it, began a galling musketry fire upon the ramparts.

Captain Minchin remained closeted with the governor; and Charlie, finding the troops bewildered and dismayed, without leading or orders, assumed the command, placed them upon the walls, and kept up a vigorous musketry fire in reply to that of the enemy.

Within, all was confusion and dismay. In every spot sheltered from the enemy's fire, Europeans and natives were huddled together. There was neither head nor direction. With nightfall the fire ceased, but still Mr. Drake and Captain Minchin were undecided what steps to take. At two o'clock in the morning, they summoned a council of war, at which Charlie was present, and it was decided that the women and children should at once be sent on board.

There should have been no difficulty in carrying this into effect. A large number of merchantmen were lying in the stream, opposite the fort, capable of conveying away in safety the whole of the occupants. Two of the members of the council had, early in the evening, been despatched on board ship to make arrangements for the boats being sent on shore; but these cowardly wretches, instead of doing so, ordered the ships to raise their anchors, and drop two miles farther down the stream. The boats, however, were sent up the river to the fort.

The same helpless imbecility, which had characterized every movement, again showed itself. There was no attempt, whatever, at establishing anything like order or method. The watergate was open, and a wild rush of men, women, and children took place down to the boats.

Charlie was on duty, on the walls. He had already said goodbye to Mrs. Haines and her daughter, and though he heard shouts and screams coming from the watergate, he had no idea what had taken place; until Mr. Haines joined him.

'Have you seen them safely off?' Charlie asked.

'My wife has gone,' Mr. Haines said. 'My daughter is still here. There has been a horrible scene of confusion. Although the boats were amply sufficient to carry all, no steps whatever had been taken to secure order. The consequence was, there was a wild rush. Women and children were knocked down and trampled upon. They leaped into the boats in such wild haste that several of these were capsized, and numbers of people drowned. I kept close to my wife and child, till we reached the side of the stream. I managed to get my wife into a boat, and then a rush of people separated me from my daughter; and before I could find her again, the remaining boats had all pushed off. Many of the men have gone with them, and among them, I am ashamed to say, several of the officers.

'However, I trust the boats will come up again tomorrow, and take away the rest. Two have remained, a guard having been placed over them, and I hope to get Ada off to her mother, in the morning.'

Towards morning, Mr. Haines again joined Charlie.

'What do you think?' he said. 'Those cowardly villains, Drake and Minchin, have taken the two boats, and gone off on board ship!'

'Impossible!' Charlie exclaimed.

'It is too true,' Mr. Haines said. 'The names of these cowards should be held as infamous, as long as the English nation exists.

'Come, now, we are just assembling to choose a commander. Mr. Peeks is the senior agent; but I think we shall elect Mr. Holwell, who is an energetic and vigorous man.'

It was as Mr. Haines had expected. Mr. Holwell was elected, and at once took the lead. He immediately assigned to Charlie the command of the troops. Little was done at the council, beyond speaker after speaker rising to express his execration of the conduct of the governor and Captain Minchin.

With daybreak, the enemy's fire recommenced. All day long Charlie hurried from post to post, encouraging his men, and aiding in working the guns. Two or three times, when the enemy showed in masses, as if intending to assault, the fire of the artillery drove them back; and up to nightfall they had gained but little success. The civilians as well as the soldiers had done their duty nobly, but the loss had been heavy, from the fire of the enemy's sharpshooters in the surrounding buildings; and it was evident that, however gallant the defence, the fort could not much longer resist.

All day long, signals had been kept flying for the fleet, two miles below, to come up to the fort; but although these could be plainly seen, not a ship weighed anchor.

Chapter 18

THE 'BLACK HOLE' OF CALCUTTA

When the fire of the enemy slackened, Charlie went to Mr. Holwell. 'It is impossible, sir,' he said, 'that the fort can hold out; for in another three or four days, the whole of the garrison will be killed. The only hope of safety is for the ships to come up, and remove the garrison, which they can do without the slightest danger to themselves. If you will allow me, sir, I will swim down to the ships, and represent our situation. Cowardly and inhuman as Mr. Drake has proved himself, he can hardly refuse to give orders for the fleet to move.'

'I don't know,' said Mr. Holwell. 'After the way in which he has behaved, there are no depths of infamy of which I believe him incapable. But you are my right hand here. Supposing Mr. Drake refuses, you could not return.'

'I will come back, sir,' Charlie answered. 'I will, if there be no other way, make my way along by the river bank. It is comparatively free of the enemy, as our guns command it. If you will place Mr. Haines at the corner bastion, with a rope, he will recognize my voice, and I can regain the fort.'

Mr. Holwell consented, and as soon as it was perfectly dark, Charlie issued out at the watergate, took off his coat, waistcoat, and boots, and entered the stream. The current was slack, but he had no difficulty in keeping himself afloat until he saw, close ahead of him, the lights of the ships.

He hailed that nearest him. A rope was thrown, and he was soon on board. Upon stating who he was, a boat was at once lowered, and he was taken to the ship upon which Mr. Drake and Captain Minchin had taken refuge. Upon saying that he was the bearer of a message from the gentleman now commanding the fort, he was conducted to the cabin, where Mr. Drake and Captain Minchin, having finished their dinner, were sitting comfortably over their wine with Captain Young, the senior captain of the Company's ships there.

'I have come, sir,' Charlie said to Mr. Drake, 'from Mr. Holwell; who has, in your absence, been elected to the command of the fort. He bids me tell you that our losses have been already very heavy, and that it is impossible that the fort can hold out for more than twenty-four hours longer. He begs you, therefore, to order up the ships tonight, in order that the garrison may embark.'

'It is quite out of the question,' Mr. Drake said coldly. 'Quite. It would be extremely dangerous.'

'You agree with me, Captain Young, that it would be most dangerous?'

'I consider that it would be dangerous,' Captain Young said.

'And you call yourself,' Charlie exclaimed indignantly, 'a British sailor! You talk of danger, and would desert a thousand men, women, and children, including two hundred of your own countrymen, and leave them at the mercy of an enemy!'

'You forget whom you are speaking to, sir,' Mr. Drake said, angrily.

'I forgot nothing, sir,' Charlie replied, trying to speak calmly. 'Then, sir, Mr. Holwell has charged me that if – which, however, he could not believe for a moment to be possible – you refuse to move up the ships to receive the garrison on board, that you would at least order all the boats up, as these would be amply sufficient to carry them away. Even in the daytime there would be no danger for the ships; and at night, at least, boats might come up, without being exposed to any risk whatever.'

'I shall certainly do nothing of the sort,' Mr. Drake said. 'The danger is even greater for the boats than for the ships.'

'And am I, sir, to return to the garrison of that fort, with the news that you utterly desert them, that you intend to remain quietly here, while they are sacrificed before your eyes? Is it possible that you are capable of such infamy as this?'

'Infamy!' exclaimed the three men, rising to their feet.

'I place you in arrest at once, for your insolence,' Mr. Drake said.

'I despise your arrest, as I do yourself.

'I did not believe it possible,' Charlie said, at last giving vent to his anger and scorn; 'and England will not believe, that three Englishmen so cowardly, so infamous as yourselves, are to be found.

'As for you, Captain Minchin, if ever after this I come across you, I will flog you publicly first, and shoot you afterwards like a dog, if you dare to meet me.

'As for you, Mr. Drake – as for you, Captain Young – you will be doomed to infamy, by the contempt and loathing which Englishmen will feel, when this deed is known.

'Cowards; base, infamous cowards!'

Charlie stepped back to go.

'Seize him!' Mr. Drake said, himself rushing forward.

Charlie drew back a step; and then, with all his strength, smote the governor between the eyes, and he fell in a heap beneath the table. Then Charlie grasped a decanter.

'Now,' he said, 'if either of you hounds move a finger, I'll brain you.'

The two officers stood paralysed. Charlie walked to the door, and sprang up the cabin stairs; and, as he did so, heard shouts for assistance from behind. He gained the deck, walked quietly to the bulwark and, placing his hand upon it, sprang over the side into the river. He swam to shore and, climbing up the bank, made his way along it back to the fort, where he arrived without any misadventure.

A fury of indignation seized all in the fort, when the result of Charlie's mission became known. With daybreak the attack recommenced; but the garrison, all day, bravely repulsed every attempt of the enemy to gain a footing. The fire from the houses was, however, so severe, that by nightfall nearly half the garrison were killed or wounded.

All day the signals to the fleet were kept flying, but not a ship moved. All night, an anxious watch was kept, in hopes that, at the last moment, some returning feeling of shame might induce the recreants to send up the boats of the ships. But the night passed without a movement on the river, and in the morning the fleet were seen, still lying at anchor.

The enemy recommenced the attack, even more vigorously than before. The men fell fast and, to Charlie's great grief, his friend Mr. Haines was shot by a bullet, as he was standing next to him. Charlie anxiously knelt beside him.

'It is all over with me,' he murmured. 'Poor little Ada. Do all you can for her, Marryat. God knows what fate is in store for her.'

'I will protect her with my life, sir,' Charlie said earnestly.

Mr. Haines pressed his hand feebly, in token of gratitude; and, two or three minutes later, breathed his last.

By midday, the loss had been so heavy that the men would no longer stand to their guns. Many of the European soldiers broke open the spirit stores, and soon drank to intoxication.

After a consultation with his officers, Mr. Holwell agreed that further resistance was hopeless. The flag of truce was therefore hoisted, and one of the officers at once started for the nabob's camp, with instructions to make the best terms he could for the garrison. When the gates were opened the enemy, seizing the opportunity, rushed in in great numbers; and as resistance was impossible, the garrison laid down their arms.

Charlie at once hurried to the spot where Ada, and the only other European lady who had not escaped, were anxiously awaiting news. Both were exhausted with weeping.

'Where is papa, Captain Marryat?' Ada asked.

Charlie knew that the poor girl would need all her strength, for what she might have to undergo; and at once resolved that, for the present at least, it would be better that she should be in ignorance of the fate of her father. He therefore said that, for the present, Mr. Haines was unable to come, and had asked him to look after her.

It was not until five o'clock that the nabob entered the fort. He was furious at hearing that only five lacs of rupees had been found in the treasury, as he had expected to become possessed of a vastly larger sum. Kissendas, the first cause of the present calamities, was brought before him; but the capricious tyrant, contrary to expectation, received him courteously, and told him he might return to Dacca. The whole of the Eurasians, or half castes, and natives found in the fort were also allowed to return to their homes.

Mr. Holwell was then sent for, and after the nabob had expressed his resentment at the small amount found in the treasury, he was dismissed, the nabob assuring him of his protection. Mr. Holwell returned to his English companions, who, one hundred and forty-six in number, including the two ladies, were drawn up under the veranda in front of the prison. The nabob then returned to his camp.

Some native officers went in search of some building where the prisoners could be confined, but every room in the fort had already been taken possession of, by the nabob's soldiers and officers. At eight o'clock, they returned with the news that they could find no place vacant, and the officer in command at once ordered the prisoners into a small room, used as a guardroom for insubordinate soldiers, eighteen feet square.

In vain they protested that it was impossible the room could contain them, in vain implored the officer to allow some of them to be confined in an adjoining cell. The wretch was deaf to their entreaties. He ordered his soldiers to charge the prisoners, and these, with blows of the butt ends of the muskets, and prods of the bayonets, were driven into the narrow cell.

Tim Kelly had kept close to his master, during the preceding days. The whole of the four native officers, who had so distinguished themselves under Charlie, were killed during the siege. Hossein, who would fain have shared his master's fortunes, was forcibly torn from him, when the English prisoners were separated from the natives.

The day had been unusually hot. The night was close and sultry, and the arched veranda, outside, further hindered the circulation of the air. This was still heavy with the fumes of powder, creating an intolerable thirst. Scarcely were the prisoners driven into their narrow cell where, even standing wedged closely together, there was barely room for them, than cries for water were raised.

'Tim, my boy,' Charlie said to his companion, 'we may say goodbye to each other now, for I doubt if one will be alive, when the door is opened in the morning.'

On entering, Charlie, always keeping Ada Haines by his side, had taken his place against the wall farthest from the window, which was closed with iron bars.

'I think, yer honor,' Tim said, 'that if we could get nearer to the window, we might breathe a little more easily.'

'Ay, Tim; but there will be a fight for life round that window, before long. You and I might hold our own, if we could get there, though it would be no easy matter where all are struggling for life; but this poor little girl would be crushed to death. Besides, I believe that what chance there is, faint as it may be, is greater for us here than there. The rush towards the window, which is beginning already, as you see, will grow greater and greater; and the more men struggle and strive, the more air they require.

'Let us remain where we are. Strip off your coat and waistcoat, and breathe as quietly and easily as you can. Every hour the crowd will thin, and we may yet hold on till morning.'

This conversation had been held in a low voice. Charlie then turned to the girl.

'How are you feeling, Ada?' he asked cheerfully. 'It's hot, isn't it!'

'It is dreadful,' the girl panted, 'and I seem choking from want of air; and oh, Captain Marryat, I am so thirsty!'

'It is hot, my dear, terribly hot, but we must make the best of it; and I hope, in a few days, you will join your mamma on board ship. That will be pleasant, won't it?'

'Where is papa?' the girl wailed.

'I don't know where he is now, my child. At any rate, we must feel very glad that he's not shut up here, with us. Now take your bonnet off, and your shawl, and undo the hooks of your dress, and loosen everything you can. We must be as quiet and cheerful as possible. I'm afraid, Ada, we have a bad time before us tonight. But try to keep cheerful and quiet; and above all, dear, pray God to give you strength to carry you through it, and to restore you safe to your mamma, in a few days.'

As time went on, the scene in the dungeon became terrible. Shouts, oaths, cries of all kinds, rose in the air. Round the window men fought like wild beasts, tearing each other down, or clinging to the bars for dear life, for a breath of the air without. Panting, struggling, crying, men sank exhausted upon the floor, and the last remnants of life were trodden out of them, by those who surged forward to get near the window.

In vain, Mr. Holwell implored them to keep quiet, for their own sakes. His voice was lost in the terrible din. Men, a few hours ago rich and respected merchants, now fought like maddened beasts for a breath of fresh air. In vain, those at the window screamed to the guards without, imploring them to bring water. Their prayers and entreaties were replied to only with brutal scoffs.

Several times Charlie and Tim, standing together against the wall behind, where there was now room to move, lifted Ada between them, and sat her on their shoulders in order that, raised above the crowd, she might breathe more freely. Each time, after sitting there for a while, the poor girl begged to come down again; the sight of the terrible struggle, ever going on at the window, being too much for her; and when released, leaning against Charlie, supported by his arm, with her head against his shoulder, and her hands over her ears to shut out the dreadful sounds which filled the cell.

Hour passed after hour. There was more room now, for already half the inmates of the place had succumbed. The noises, too, had lessened, for no longer could the parched lips and throats utter articulate sounds. Charlie and Tim, strong men as they were, leaned utterly exhausted against the wall, bathed in perspiration, gasping for air.

'Half the night must be gone, Tim,' Charlie said, 'and I think, with God's help, we shall live through it. The numbers are lessening fast, and every one who goes leaves more air for the rest of us.

'Cheer up, Ada dear, 'twill not be very long till morning.'

'I think I shall die soon,' the girl gasped. 'I shall never see papa or mamma again. You have been very kind, Captain Marryat, but it is no use.'

'Oh, but it is of use,' Charlie said cheerfully. 'I don't mean to let you die at all, but to hand you over to mamma, safe and sound. There, lay your head against me, dear, and say your prayers, and try and go off to sleep.'

Presently, however, Ada's figure drooped more and more, until her whole weight leaned upon Charlie's arm.

'She has fainted, Tim,' he said. 'Help me to raise her well in my arms, and lay her head on my shoulder. That's right. Now, you'll find her shawl somewhere under my feet; hold it up, and make a fan of it. Now, try to send some air into her face.'

By this time, not more than fifty out of the hundred and forty-six who entered the cell were alive. Suddenly a scream of joy, from those near the window, proclaimed that a native was approaching with some water. The struggle at the window was fiercer than ever. The bowl was too wide to pass through the bars, and the water was being spilt in vain; each man who strove to get his face far enough through to touch the bowl being torn back, by his eager comrades behind.

'Tim,' Charlie said, 'you are now much stronger than most of them. They are faint from the struggles. Make a charge to the window. Take that little shawl and dip it into the bowl, or whatever they have there, and then fight your way back with it.'

'I will do it, yer honor,' said Tim, and he rushed into the struggling group.

Weak as he was from exhaustion and thirst, he was as a giant to most of the poor wretches, who had been struggling and crying all night; and, in spite of their cries and curses, he broke through them and forced his way to the window.

The man with the bowl was on the point of turning away, the water being spilt in the vain attempts of those within to obtain it. By the light of the fire which the guard had lit without, Tim saw his face.

'Hossein,' he exclaimed, 'more water, for God's sake! The master's alive yet.'

Hossein at once withdrew, but soon again approached with the bowl. The officer in charge angrily ordered him to draw back.

'Let the infidel dogs howl,' he said. 'They shall have no more.'

Regardless of the order, Hossein ran to the window, and Tim thrust the shawl into the water at the moment when the officer, rushing forward, struck Hossein to the ground: a cry of anguish rising from the prisoners, as they saw the water dashed from their lips.

Tim made his way back to the side of his master. Had those who still remained alive been aware of the supply of water which he carried, in the shawl, they would have torn it from him; but none save those just at the window had noticed the act, and inside it was still entirely dark.

'Thank God, yer honor, here it is,' Tim said; 'and who should have brought it, but Hossein. Shure, yer honor, we both owe our lives to him this time, for I'm sure I should have been choked by thirst, before morning.'

Ada was now lowered to the ground and, forcing her teeth asunder, a corner of

WITH CLIVE IN INDIA

the folded shawl was placed between her lips, and the water allowed to trickle down. With a gasping sigh, she presently recovered.

'That is delicious,' she murmured. 'That is delicious.'

Raising her to her feet, Charlie and Tim both sucked the dripping shawl, until the first agonies of thirst were relieved. Then, tearing off a portion, in case Ada should again require it, Charlie passed the shawl to Mr. Holwell; who, after sucking it for a moment, again passed it on to several standing round; and in this way many of those, who would otherwise have succumbed, were enabled to hold on until morning.

Presently the first dawn of daylight appeared, giving fresh hopes to the few survivors. There were now only some six or eight standing by the window, and a few standing or leaning against the walls around. The room itself was heaped high with the dead.

It was not until two hours later that the doors were opened, and the guard entered; and it was found that, of the hundred and forty-six Englishmen inclosed there the night before, but twenty-three still breathed. Of these, very few retained strength to stagger out through the door. The rest were carried out, and laid in the veranda.

When the nabob came into the fort in the morning, he ordered Mr. Holwell to be brought before him. He was unable to walk, but was carried to his presence. The brutal nabob expressed no regret for what had happened, but loaded him with abuse, on account of the paucity of the treasure, and ordered him to be placed in confinement. The other prisoners were also confined in a cell. Ada, the only English female who had survived the siege, was torn, weeping, from Charlie's arms, and conveyed to the zenana, or ladies' apartments, of one of the nabob's generals.

A few days later, the English captives were all conveyed to Moorshedabad, where the rajah also returned, after having extorted large sums from the French and Dutch, and confiscated the whole of the property of the English in Bengal.

The prospect was a gloomy one for the captives. That the English would, in time, return and extort a heavy reckoning from the nabob, they did not doubt for a moment. But nothing was more likely than that, at the news of the first disaster which befell his troops, the nabob would order his captives to be put to death.

Upon the march up the country Charlie had, by his cheerfulness and good temper, gained the goodwill of the officer commanding the guard; and upon arriving at their

657

destination, he recommended him so strongly to the commander of the prison that the latter, instead of placing him in the apartment allotted to the remainder of the prisoners, assigned a separate room to him; permitting Tim, at his request, to occupy it with him. It was a room of fair size, in a tower on one of the angles of the walls. It had bars, but these did not prevent those behind them looking out at the country which stretched around. The governor of the prison, finding that Charlie spoke the language fluently, often came up to sit with him, conversing with him on the affairs of that unknown country, England.

Altogether, they were fairly treated. Their food was plentiful and, beyond their captivity, they had little to complain of. Over and over again, they talked about the possibilities of effecting an escape; but, on entering the prison, they had noticed how good was the watch, how many and strong the doors through which they had passed. They had meditated upon making a rope and escaping from the window; but they slept on the divan, each with a rug to cover them; and these, torn into strips and twisted, would not reach a quarter of the way from their window to the ground; and there was no other material of which a rope could possibly have been formed.

'Our only hope,' Charlie said one day, 'is in Hossein. I am sure he will follow us to the death; and if he did but know where we are confined, he would not, I am certain, rest day or night, till he had opened a communication with us.

'See, Tim, there is my regimental cap, with its gold lace. Let us fasten it outside the bars, with a thread from that rug. Of course, we must remove it when we hear anyone coming.'

This was speedily done and, for the next few days, one or other remained constantly at the window.

'Mr. Charles!' Tim exclaimed in great excitement, one day; 'there is a man I've been watching, for the last half hour. He seems to be picking up sticks, but all the while he keeps getting nearer and nearer, and two or three times it seems to me that he has looked up in this direction.'

Charlie joined Tim at the window.

'Yes, Tim, you are right. That's Hossein, I'm pretty sure.'

The man had now approached within two or three hundred yards of the corner of the wall. He was apparently collecting pieces of dried brushwood, for firing. Presently, he glanced in the direction of the window. Charlie thrust his arm through the bar, and waved his hand. The man threw up his arm with a gesture which, to a casual observer, would have appeared accidental; but which the watchers had no doubt, whatever, was intended for them. He was still too far off from them to be able to distinguish his features, but they had not the least doubt that it was Hossein.

Chapter 19

A DARING ESCAPE

'And what's to be done next, Mister Charles? That's Hossein, sure enough, but it don't bring us much nearer to getting out.'

'The first thing is to communicate with him in some way, Tim.'

'If he'd come up to the side of the moat, yer honor might spake to him.'

'That would never do, Tim. There are sure to be sentries on the walls of the prison. We must trust to him. He can see the sentries, and will know best what he can do.'

It was evident that Hossein did not intend doing anything, at present; for, still stooping and gathering brushwood, he gradually withdrew farther and farther from the wall. Then they saw him make his sticks into a bundle, put them on his shoulder, and walk away. During the rest of the day, they saw no more of Hossein.

'I will write,' Charlie said, '– fortunately I have a pencil – telling him that we can lower a light string down to the moat, if he can manage to get underneath with a cord which we can hoist up, and that he must have two disguises in readiness.'

'I don't think Hossein can read,' Tim said, 'any more than I can, myself.'

'I daresay not, Tim, but he will probably have friends in the town. There are men who were employed in the English factory at Kossimbazar, hard by. These will be out of employment, and will regret the expulsion of the English. We can trust Hossein. At any rate, I will get it ready.

'Now the first thing we have to do is to loosen one of these bars. I wish we had thought of doing it before. However, the stonework is pretty rotten, and we shall have no difficulty about that. The first thing is to get a tool of some sort.'

They looked round the room, and for some time saw nothing which could in any way serve. The walls, floor, and wide bench running round, upon which the cushions which served as their beds were laid, were all stone. There was no other furniture, of any kind.

'Divil a bit of iron do I see in the place, Mister Charles,' Tim said. 'They don't even give us a knife for dinner, but stew all their meats into a smash.'

'There is something, Tim,' Charlie said, looking at the door. 'Look at those long hinges.'

The hinges were of ornamented ironwork, extending half across the door. Upon one of the scrolls of this ironwork they set to work. Chipping a small piece of stone off an angle of the wall, outside the window; with great difficulty they thrust this under the end of the scroll, as a wedge. Another piece, slightly larger, was then pushed under it. The gain was almost imperceptible, but at last the piece of iron was raised from the woodwork sufficiently to allow them to get a hold of it, with their thumbs. Then, little by little, they bent it upward; until at last they could obtain a firm hold of it.

The rest was comparatively easy. The iron was tough and strong but, by bending it up and down, they succeeded at last in breaking it off. It was the lower hinge of the door, upon which they had operated, as the loss of a piece of iron there would be less likely to catch the eye of anyone coming in. They collected some dust from the corner of the room, moistened it, and rubbed it on to the wood so as to take away its freshness of appearance; and they then set to work with the piece of iron, which was of a curved shape, about three inches long, an inch wide, and an eighth of an inch thick.

Taking it by turns, they ground away the stone round the bottom of one of the bars. For the first inch, the stone yielded readily to the iron; but below that it became harder, and their progress was slow. They filled the hole which they had made with water, to soften the stone, and worked steadily away till night; when, to their great joy, they found that they had reached the bottom of the bar. They then enlarged the hole inwards, in order that the bar might be pulled back. Fortunately, it was much decayed by age; and they had no doubt that, by exerting all their strength, together they could bend it sufficiently to enable them to get through.

At the hour when their dinner was brought they had ceased their work, filled up the hole with dust collected from the floor, put some dust of the stone over it, and smoothed it down, so that it would not have been noticed by anyone casually looking from the window.

It was late at night before they finished their work. Their hands were sore and bleeding, and they were completely worn out with fatigue. They had saved, from their dinner, a good-sized piece of bread. They folded up into a small compass the leaf from his pocketbook, upon which Charlie had written in Hindostanee his letter to Hossein, and thrust this into the centre of the piece of bread. Then Charlie told Tim to lie down and rest for three hours, while he kept watch; as they must take it in turns, all night, to listen in case Hossein should come outside. The lamp was kept burning.

Just as Charlie's watch was over, he thought he heard a very faint splash in the water below. Two or three minutes later, he again thought he heard the sound. He peered out of the window anxiously, but the night was dark, and he could see nothing. Listening intently, it seemed to him, several times, that he heard the same faint sound.

Presently something whizzed by him, and looking round, to his delight he saw a small arrow, with a piece of very thin string attached. The arrow was made of very light wood. Round the iron point was a thick wrapping of cotton, which would entirely deaden its sound, as it struck a wall. It was soaked in water, and Charlie had no doubt that the sound he heard was caused by its fall into the moat, after ineffectual trials to shoot through the window.

Round the centre of the arrow a piece of greased silk was wrapped. Charlie took this off, and found beneath it a piece of paper, on which was written in Hindostanee:

'If you have a bar loosed, pull the string and haul up a rope. If not, throw the arrow down. I will come again, tomorrow night.'

Tim had by this time joined Charlie, and they speedily began to pull in the string. Presently a thicker string came up into their hands. They continued to pull, and soon the end of a stout rope, in which knots were tied every two feet, came up to them.

They fastened this to one of the bars, and then took hold of that which they had loosened; and, putting their feet against the wall, exerted themselves to the utmost. The iron was tougher than they had expected, but they were striving for liberty and, with desperate exertions, they bent it inwards until, at last, there was room enough for them to creep through.

'Can you swim, Tim?'

'Not a stroke, yer honor. Shure you should know that, when you fished me out of the water.'

'Very well, Tim. As I kept you up then, 'twill be easy enough for me, now, to take you across the moat. I will go first, and when I get into the water, will keep hold of the rope till you come down. Take off your boots, for they would be heard scraping against the wall. Be sure you make as little noise as possible, and lower yourself quietly into the water.'

Charlie then removed his own boots, squeezed himself through the bars and, grasping the rope tightly, began to descend. He found the knots of immense assistance, for had it not been for them, unaccustomed as he was to the work, he would have been unable to prevent himself from sliding down too rapidly. The window was fully sixty feet above the moat, and he was very thankful when, at last, he felt the water touch his feet. Lowering himself quietly into it, he shook the rope, to let Tim know that he could begin his descent.

Before Tim was halfway down, Charlie could hear his hard breathing, and muttered ejaculations to himself:

'Shure I'll never get to the bottom at all, my arms are fairly breaking. I shall squash Mr. Charles, if I fall on him.'

'Hold your tongue, Tim,' Charlie said in a loud whisper.

Tim was silent, but the panting and puffing increased, and Charlie swam a stroke or two away, expecting every moment that Tim would fall. The Irishman, however, held on; but let himself into the water with a splash, which aroused the attention of the sentry above, who instantly challenged.

Tim and Charlie remained perfectly quiet. Again the sentry challenged. Then there was a long silence. The sentry probably was unwilling to rouse the place by a false alarm, and the splash might have been caused by the fall of a piece of decayed stone from the face of the wall.

'Tim, you clumsy fellow,' whispered Charlie, 'you nearly spoiled all.'

'Shure, yer honor, I was kilt entirely, and my arms were pulled out of my sockets. Holy Mother, who'd have thought 'twould be so difficult to come down a rope! The sailors are great men, entirely.'

'Now, Tim, lie quiet. I will turn you on your back, and swim across with you.'

The moat was some twenty yards wide. Charlie swam across, towing Tim after him, and taking the greatest pains to avoid making the slightest splash. The opposite side was of stonework, and rose six feet above the water. As soon as they touched the wall, a stout rope was lowered to them.

'Now, Tim, you climb up first.'

'Is it climb up, yer honor? I couldn't do it, if it was to save my sowl. My arms are gone altogether, and I'm as weak as a child.

'You go, Mister Charles. I'll hould on by the rope till morning. They can but shoot me.'

'Nonsense, Tim! Here, I will fasten the rope round your body. Then I will climb up, and we will pull you up after me.'

In another minute, Charlie stood on the bank, and grasped the hand of his faithful follower. Hossein threw himself on his knees, and pressed his master to him. Then he rose and, at a word from Charlie, they hauled Tim to the top. The rope was taken off him and, noiselessly, they made their way across the country. Not a word was spoken, till they were at a considerable distance from the fort.

'Where are you taking us, Hossein?' Charlie asked, at last.

'I have two peasants' dresses, in a deserted cottage a quarter of a mile away.'

Not another word was spoken, until they reached the hut, which stood at the end of a small village. When they had entered this, Charlie first thanked, in the warmest terms, his follower for having rescued them.

'My life is my lord's,' Hossein answered simply. 'He gave it me. It is his again, whenever it is useful to him.'

'No, Hossein, the balance is all on your side, now. You saved my life that night at

Ambur. You saved it that night at Calcutta, for, without the water you brought us, I question whether we could have lived till morning. Now you have procured our freedom. The debt is all on my side now, my friend.'

'Hossein is glad that his lord is content,' the Mohammedan murmured. 'Now, what will my lord do?'

'Have you any place in the town to which we could go, Hossein?'

'Yes, Sahib. I hired a little house. I was dressed as a trader. I have been here for two months, but I could not find where you were confined, although I have tried all means, until I saw your cap.'

'It was foolish of me not to have thought of it before,' Charlie said. 'Well, Hossein, for a little time we had better take refuge in your house. They will not think of searching in the city; and, as Calcutta is in their hands, there is nowhere we could go. Besides, I must discover, if possible, where Miss Haines is kept a prisoner; and rescue her, if it can be done.'

'The white girl is in the zenana of Rajah Dulab Ram,' Hossein replied.

'Where is the rajah's palace?'

'He has one in the city, one at Ajervam, twenty miles from here. I do not know at which she is lodged.'

'We must find that out presently,' Charlie said. 'It is something to know she is in one of two houses.

'Now, about getting back into the town?'

'I have thought of that,' Hossein said. 'I have bought a quantity of plantains, and two large baskets. After the gates are opened, you will go boldly in with the baskets on your heads. No questions are asked of the country people who go in and out. I have some stain here, which will darken your skins.

'I will go in first in my merchant's dress, which I have here. I will stop a little way inside the gate, and when I see you coming, will walk on. Do you follow me, a little behind. My house is in a quiet street. When I reach the door, do you come up and offer to sell me plantains. If there are people about, I shall bargain with you until I see that no one is noticing us. Then you can enter. If none are about, you can follow me straight in.'

Hossein now set about the disguises. A light was struck, and both Tim and Charlie were shaved, up to the line which the turban would cover. Charlie's whiskers, which were somewhat faint, as he was still under twenty-one years old, gave but little trouble. Tim, however, grumbled at parting with his much more bushy appendages. The shaven part of the heads, necks, and faces were then rubbed with a dark fluid, as were the arms and legs.

They were next wrapped in dark blue clothes, in peasant fashion, and turbans wound round their heads. Hossein then, examining them critically, announced that they would pass muster anywhere.

'I feel mighty quare,' Tim exclaimed; 'and it seems to me downright ondacent, to be walking about with my naked legs.'

Charlie laughed.

'Why, Tim, you are accustomed to see thousands of men, every day, with nothing on but a loincloth.'

'Yes, yer honor, but then they're hathens, and it seems natural for them to do so; but for a dacent boy to go walking about in the streets, with a thing on which covers no more than his shirt, is onnatural altogether. Mother of Moses, what a shindy there would be, in the streets of Cork, if I were to show myself in such a state!'

Charlie now lay down for a sleep till morning; while Tim, who had had three hours' repose, settled himself for a comfortable chat with Hossein, to whom sleep appeared altogether unnecessary.

Between Hossein and Tim there was a sort of brotherly attachment, arising from their mutual love of their master. During the two years which Tim had spent apart from all Europeans, save Charlie, he had contrived to pick up enough of the language to make himself fairly intelligible; and, since the day when Hossein had saved Charlie's life at Ambur, the warmest friendship had sprung up between the good-humoured and warm-hearted Irishman, and the silent and devoted Mohammedan.

Tim's friendship even extended so far as to induce a toleration of Hossein's religion. He had come to the conclusion that a man who, at stated times in the day, would leave his employment, whatever it might be, spread his carpet, and be for some minutes lost in prayer, could not be altogether a hathen; especially when he learned, from Charlie, that the Mohammedans, like ourselves, worship one God. For the sake of his friend, then, he now generally excluded the Mohammedans from the general designation of heathen, which he still applied to the Hindoos.

He learned from Hossein that the latter, having observed from a distance the Europeans driven into the cell at Calcutta, perceived at once how fatal the consequences would be. He had, an hour or two after they were confined there, approached with some water, but the officer on guard had refused to let him give it. He had then gone into the native town, but being unable to find any fruit there, had walked out to the gardens, and had picked a large basketful. This he had brought as an offering to the officer, and the latter had then consented to his giving one bowl of water to the prisoners, among whom, as he had told him, was his master. For bringing a second bowl, contrary to his orders, Hossein had, as Tim saw, been struck down; but had the satisfaction of believing that his master, and Tim, had derived some benefit from his effort.

On the following morning, to his delight, he saw them issue among the few survivors from the dungeon; and had, when they were taken up the country, followed close behind them, arriving at the town on the same day as themselves. He had, ever since, been wandering round the prison. He had taken a house, so close to it that he could keep a watch on all the windows facing the town; and had, day after day, kept his eyes fixed upon these without success. He had, at last, found out from one of the soldiers that the white prisoners were confined on the other side of the prison; but until he saw Charlie's cap, he had been unable to discover the room in which they were confined.

In the morning, they started for the town. Groups of peasants were already making their way towards the gate, with fruit and grain; and, keeping near one of these parties, while sufficiently distant to prevent the chance of their being addressed, Charlie and Tim made their way to the gate; the latter suffering acutely, in his mind, from the impropriety of his attire.

No questions were asked, as they passed the guard. They at once perceived Hossein, standing a little way off, and followed him through the busy streets. They soon turned off into a quieter quarter, and stopped at a house, in a street in which scarcely anyone was stirring. Hossein glanced round, as he opened the door, and beckoned to them to enter at once. This they did, and were glad, indeed, to set down the heavy baskets of plantains.

'My lord's room is upstairs,' Hossein said, and led the way to a comfortably furnished apartment. 'I think that you might stay here, for months, unsuspected. A sweeper comes, every day, to do my rooms downstairs. He believes the rest of the house to be untenanted, and you must remain perfectly quiet, during the half hour he is here. Otherwise, no one enters the house but myself.'

Hossein soon set to work, and prepared an excellent breakfast. Then he left them, saying that he would now devote himself to finding out whether the young white lady was in the town palace of the rajah. He returned in the afternoon.

'She is here, Sahib,' he said. 'I got into conversation with one of the retainers of the rajah; and by giving him some wonderful bargains, in Delhi jewelry, succeeded in opening his lips. I dare not question him too closely, but I am to meet him tomorrow, to show him some more silver bracelets.'

'It is fortunate, Hossein, that you have some money, for neither Tim nor I have a rupee.'

'Thanks to the generosity of my lord,' Hossein said, 'I am well supplied.'

The next day, Hossein discovered that the windows of the zenana were at the back of the palace, looking into the large garden.

'I hear, however,' he said, 'that the ladies of the zenana are, next week, going to the rajah's other palace. The ladies will, of course, travel in palanquins; but upon the road I might get to talk with one of the waiting women, and might bribe her to pass a note into the hands of the white lady.'

'I suppose they will have a guard with them, Hossein?'

'Surely, a strong guard,' Hossein answered.

The time passed, until the day came for the departure of the rajah's zenana. Charlie wrote a note, as follows:

'My dear Ada,

'I am free, and am on the lookout for an opportunity to rescue you. Contrive to put a little bit of your handkerchief through the latticework of the window of your room, as a signal to us which it is. On the second night after your arrival, we will be under it with a ladder. If others, as is probable, sleep in your room, lie down without undressing more than you can help. When they are asleep, get up and go to the window, and open the lattice. If any of them wake, say you are hot and cannot sleep, and wait quietly till they are off again. Then stretch out your arm, and we shall know you are ready. Then we will put up the ladder, and you must get out, and come to us as quickly as possible. Once with us, you will be safe.'

This note was wrapped up very small, and put into a quill. As soon as the gates were open, Hossein and his companions left the town, and proceeded as far as a grove, halfway between the town and the rajah's country palace.

'They are sure to stop here, for a rest,' Hossein said. 'I will remain here, and try to enter into conversation with one of them. It will be better for you to go on, for some distance, and then turn aside from the road. When they have all passed, come back into the road again, and I will join you.'

After waiting two hours, Hossein saw two carts full of women approaching, and had no doubt that these were the servants of the zenana. As he had expected, the drivers halted their cattle in the shade of the trees; and the women, delighted to enjoy their liberty, alighted from the carts and scattered in the grove. Presently one of them, a middle-aged woman, approached the spot where Hossein had seated himself.

Hossein drew out a large and beautiful silver bracelet, of Delhi workmanship.

'Would you like to buy this?' he asked.

'How should I buy it?' she said. 'I am only a servant.'

'It is very beautiful;' and she looked at it, with longing eyes.

'I have two of them,' he said, 'and they will both be yours, if you will do me a service.'

'What is it?' she asked.

'They will be yours, if you will give this quill to the little white girl, who is in the zenana.'

The woman hesitated.

'It is dangerous,' she said.

'Not at all,' Hossein replied. 'It only gives her news of a friend, whom she thought was dead. It will cheer her heart, and will be a kind action. None can ever know it.'

'Give them to me,' the woman said, holding out her hand. 'I will do it.'

'No,' Hossein replied. 'I will give you one now, the other when I know that the note is delivered. I shall be watching, tomorrow. If she places her handkerchief in her lattice, I shall know that she has got it. When she does this, I will bury the other bracelet, a few inches in the ground, just under that window. You can dig it up when you will.'

'I understand,' the woman said. 'You can trust me. We all like the white girl. She is very gentle, but very sad. I would gladly give her pleasure.'

Hossein handed to her the bracelet, and the quill. She hid them in her dress, and sauntered away.

Hossein lay back, as if taking a sleep, and so remained until, half an hour later, he heard the shouts of the drivers to the women, to take their places in the carts. Then the sound of retreating wheels was heard.

Hossein was about to rise, when he heard the clatter of horses' hoofs. Looking round he saw eight elephants, each carrying a closed pavilion, moving along the road, escorted by a troop of horsemen. In the pavilions, as he knew, were the ladies of the rajah's zenana.

Chapter 20

THE RESCUE OF THE WHITE CAPTIVE

After the cavalcade had passed, Hossein rose to his feet and followed them, allowing them to go some distance ahead. Presently he was joined by Charlie and Tim, and the three walked quietly along the road, until within sight of the rajah's palace.

In front stood a great courtyard. Behind, also surrounded by a high wall, was the garden. As this was always devoted to the zenana, they had little doubt that the rooms of the ladies were on this side; and, two hours later, they were delighted at seeing a small piece of white stuff, thrust through one of the lattices. The woman had been faithful to her trust. Ada had received the letter.

They then retired to a distance from the palace, and at once set to work on the fabrication of a ladder. Hossein, followed by Charlie, who better enacted the part than Tim, went into a village and purchased four long bamboo poles, saying he wanted them for the carrying of burdens. Charlie placed these on his shoulder, and followed Hossein.

When they arrived at the grove they set to work, having brought with them all the necessary materials. The bamboos were spliced together, two and two; and while Charlie and Tim set to, to bore holes in these, Hossein chopped down a young tree and, cutting it into lengths, prepared the rungs.

It took them all that evening, and the greater part of the next day, before they had satisfactorily accomplished their work. They had, then, a ladder thirty feet long, the height which they judged the window to be above the terrace below. It was strong, and at the same time light.

They waited until darkness had completely fallen; and then, taking their ladder, went round to the back of the garden. They mounted the wall and, sitting on the top, dragged the ladder after them, and lowered it on the other side. It was of equal thickness the whole length; and could, therefore, be used indifferently either way.

They waited patiently, until they saw the lights in the zenana windows extinguished. Then they crept quietly up, and placed the ladder under the window at which the signal had been shown; and found that their calculations were correct, and that it reached to a few inches below the sill.

Half an hour later, the lattice above opened. They heard a murmur of voices, and then all was quiet again. After a few minutes, Charlie climbed noiselessly up the ladder and, just as he reached the top, an arm was stretched out above him; and, a moment afterwards, Ada's face appeared.

'I am here, dear,' he said, in a whisper. 'Lean out, and I will take you.'

The girl stretched out over the window. Charlie took her in his arms, and lifted her lightly out, and then slowly descended the ladder. No sooner did he touch the ground than they hurried away; Ada sobbing, with excitement and pleasure, on Charlie's shoulder; Tim and Hossein bearing the ladder; Hossein having already carried out his promise of concealing the second bracelet under the window.

In a few minutes they had safely surmounted the wall, and hurried across the country, with all speed. Before leaving the town, Hossein had purchased a cart with two bullocks; and had hired a man who was recommended to him, by one of his co-religionists there, as one upon whose fidelity he could rely. This cart was awaiting them at a grove.

Paying them the amount stipulated, Hossein took the ox goad and started the bullocks, Tim walking beside him, while Charlie and Ada took their places in the cart. They were sure that a hot pursuit would be set up. The rage of the nabob at the escape of Charlie and his servant had been extreme, and the whole country had been scoured by parties of horsemen; and they were sure that the rajah would use every possible means to discover Ada, before he ventured to report to the nabob that the prisoner committed to his charge had escaped.

'Of course, I can't see you very well,' Ada said, 'but I should not have known you, in the least.'

'No, I am got up like a peasant,' Charlie answered. 'We shall have to dress you so, before morning. We have got things here for you.'

'Oh, how delighted I was,' Ada exclaimed, 'when I got your note! I found it so difficult to keep on looking sad and hopeless, when I could have sung for joy. I had been so miserable. There seemed no hope, and they said, some day, I should be sent to the nabob's zenana – wretches! How poor mamma will be grieving for me, and papa! –

'Ah! Captain Marryat, he is dead, is he not?'

'Yes, my dear,' Charlie said gently. 'He was killed by my side, that afternoon. With his last breath, he asked me to take care of you.'

'I thought so,' Ada said, crying quietly. 'I did not think of it at the time. Everything was so strange, and so dreadful, that I scarcely thought at all. But afterwards, on the way here, when I turned it all over, it seemed to me that it must be so. He did not come to me, all that afternoon. He was not shut up with us in that dreadful place, and everyone else was there. So it seemed to me that he must have been killed, but that you did not like to tell me.'

'It was better for him, dear, than to have died in that terrible cell. Thank God your mamma is safe, and some day you will join her again.

'We have news that the English are coming up to attack Calcutta. A party are already in the Hoogly; and the nabob is going to start, in a few days, to his army there. I hope, in a very very short time, you will be safe among your friends.'

After travelling for several hours, they stopped. Charlie gave Ada some native clothes and ornaments, and told her to stain her face, arms, and legs, to put on the bangles and bracelets, and then to rejoin them. Half an hour later, Ada took her seat in the cart, this time transformed into a Hindoo girl, and the party again proceeded.

They felt sure that Ada's flight would not be discovered until daybreak. It would be some little time before horsemen could be sent off in all directions, in pursuit; and they could not be overtaken until between eleven and twelve.

The waggon was filled with grain, on the top of which Charlie and Ada were seated. When daylight came, Charlie alighted and walked by the cart. Unquestioned, they passed through several villages.

At eleven o'clock, Hossein pointed to a large grove, at some little distance from the road.

'Go in there,' he said, 'and stay till nightfall. Do you then come out, and follow me. I shall go into the next village, and remain there till after dark. I shall then start, and wait for you half a mile beyond the village.'

An hour after the waggon had disappeared from sight, the party in the grove saw ten or twelve horsemen galloping rapidly along the road. An hour passed, and the same party returned, at an equal speed. They saw no more of them and, after it became dark, they continued their way; passed through the village, which was three miles ahead; and found Hossein waiting, a short distance beyond. Ada climbed into the cart, and they again went forward.

'Did you put the rajah's men on the wrong track, Hossein? We guessed that you had done so, when we saw them going back.'

'Yes,' Hossein said. 'I had unyoked the bullocks, and had lain down in the cara-vanserai, when they arrived. They came in, and their leader asked who I was. I said that I was taking down a load of grain, for the use of the army at Calcutta. He asked where were the two men and the woman who were with me. I replied that I knew nothing of them. I had overtaken them on the road, and they had asked leave for the woman to ride in the cart. They said they were going to visit their mother, who was sick.

'He asked if I was sure they were natives, and I counterfeited surprise, and said that certainly they were; for which lie Allah will, I trust, be merciful, since it was told to an enemy. I said that they had left me, just when we had passed the last village; and had turned off by the road to the right, saying they had many miles to go.

'They talked together and decided that, as you were the only people who had been seen along the road, they must follow and find you; and so started at once, and I daresay they're searching for you now, miles away.'

Their journey continued without any adventure, until within a few miles of Calcutta. Hossein then advised them to take up their abode in a ruined mud hut, at a distance from the road. He had bought, at the last village, a supply of provisions, sufficient to last them for some days.

'I shall now,' he said, 'go into the town, sell my grain, bullocks, and cart, and find out where the soldiers are.'

As soon as the news of the nabob's advance against Calcutta reached Madras, Mr. Pigot, who was now governor there, despatched a force of two hundred and thirty men, under the orders of Major Kilpatrick. The party reached Falta, on the Hoogly, on the 2nd of August, and there heard of the capture of Calcutta. By detachments, who came down from some of the Company's minor posts, the force was increased to nearly four hundred. But sickness broke out among them and, finding himself unable to advance against so powerful an army as that of the nabob, Major Kilpatrick sent to Madras for further assistance.

When the news reached that place, Clive had recently arrived with a strong force, which was destined to operate against the French at Hyderabad. The news, however, of the catastrophe at Calcutta at once altered the destination of the force; and, on the 16th of October, the expedition sailed for Calcutta. The force consisted of two hundred and fifty men of the 39th Foot, the first regiment of the regular English army which had been sent out to India; five hundred and seventy men of the Madras European force; eighty artillerymen; and twelve hundred Sepoys.

Of the nine hundred Europeans, only six hundred arrived at that time at the mouth of the Hoogly, the largest ship, the Cumberland, with three hundred men on board, having grounded on the way. The remainder of the fleet, consisting of three ships of war, five transports, and a fire ship, reached Falta between the 11th and 20th of December.

Hossein had returned from Calcutta, with the news that the party commanded by Major Kilpatrick had been, for some weeks, at Falta; and the party at once set off towards that place, which was but forty miles distant. Travelling by night, and sleeping by day in the woods, they reached Falta without difficulty; and, learning that the force was still on board ship, they took possession of a boat, moored by the bank some miles higher up, and rowed down.

Great was their happiness, indeed, at finding themselves once more among friends. Here were assembled many of the ships which had been at Calcutta, at the time it was taken; and, to Ada's delight, she learned that her mother was on board one of these. They were soon rowed there, in a boat from the ship which they had first boarded; and Ada, on gaining the deck, saw her mother sitting among some other ladies, fugitives like herself.

With a scream of joy she rushed forward, and with a cry of, 'Mamma, Mamma!' threw herself into her mother's arms.

It was a moment or two before Mrs. Haines could realize that this dark-skinned Hindoo girl was her child, and then her joy equalled that of her daughter. It was some time before any coherent conversation could take place; and then Ada, running back to Charlie, drew him forward to her mother; and presented him to her as her preserver, the Captain Marryat who had stayed with them at Calcutta.

Mrs. Haines' gratitude was extreme, and Charlie was soon surrounded, and congratulated, by the officers on board, to many of whom, belonging as they did to the Madras army, he was well known. Foremost among them, and loudest in his expressions of delight, was his friend Peters.

'You know, Charlie, I suppose,' he said presently, 'that you are a major now?'

'No, indeed,' Charlie said. 'How is that?'

'When the directors at home received the report of Commodore James, that the fort of Suwarndrug had been captured entirely through you, they at once sent out your appointment as major.

'You are lucky, old fellow. Here are you a major, while I'm a lieutenant, still. However, don't think I'm jealous, for I'm not a bit, and you thoroughly deserve all, and more than you've got.'

'And this is Tim,' Charlie said. 'He has shared all my adventures with me.'

Tim was standing disconsolately by the bulwark, shifting uneasily from foot to foot, with the feeling of the extreme shortness of his garments stronger upon him than ever.

Peters seized him heartily by the hand.

'I am glad to see you, Tim, very glad. And so you've been with Major Marryat, ever since?'

'For the Lord's sake, Mr. Peters,' Tim said, in an earnest whisper, 'git me a pair of trousers. I'm that ashamed of myself, in the presence of the ladies, that I'm like to drop.'

'Come along below, Tim. Come along, Charlie. There are lots of poor fellows have gone down, and uniforms are plentiful. We'll soon rig you out again.'

'There is one more introduction, Peters. This is my man, Hossein. He calls himself my servant. I call him my friend. He has saved my life twice, and has been of inestimable service. Had it not been for him, I should still be in prison at Moorshedabad.'

Peters said a few hearty words to Hossein, and they then went below; returning on deck in half an hour, Charlie in the undress uniform of an officer, Tim in that of a private in the Madras infantry.

Mrs. Haines and Ada had gone below, where they could chat, unrestrained by the presence of others; and where an attempt could be made to restore Ada to her former appearance. Mrs. Haines had heard of her husband's death, on the day after the capture of Calcutta, Mr. Holwell having been permitted to send on board the ships a list of those who had fallen. She had learned that Ada had survived the terrible night in the dungeon, and that she had been sent up country, a captive. She almost despaired of ever hearing of her again, but had resolved to wait to see the issue of the approaching campaign.

Now that Ada was restored to her, she determined to leave for England; in a vessel which was to sail, in the course of a week, with a large number of fugitives. Mr. Haines was a very wealthy man, and had intended retiring, altogether, in the course of a few months; and she would, therefore, be in the enjoyment of an ample fortune in England.

Among those on board the ships at Falta was Mr. Drake, who at once, upon hearing of Charlie's arrival, ordered him to be arrested. Major Kilpatrick, however, firmly refused to allow the order to be carried out, saying that, as Charlie was under his orders as an officer in the Madras army, Mr. Drake had no control or authority over him. He could, however, upon Clive's arrival, lay the case before him.

A week later, Mrs. Haines and Ada sailed for England, the latter weeping bitterly at parting from Charlie, who promised them that, when he came home to England on leave, he would pay them a visit. He gave them his mother's address; and Mrs. Haines promised to call upon her, as soon as she reached England, and give her full news of him; adding that she hoped that his sisters, the youngest of whom was little older than Ada, would be great friends with her.

Very slowly and wearily the time passed at Falta. The mists from the river were deadly, and of the two hundred and thirty men whom Kilpatrick brought with him from Madras, in July, only about thirty remained alive; and of these, but ten were fit for duty when Clive, at last, arrived.

The fleet left Falta on the 27th of December, and anchored off Moiapur on the following day. The fort of Baj-baj, near this place, was the first object of attack; and it was arranged that, while Admiral Watson should bombard with the fleet, Clive should attack it on the land side.

Clive, who now held the rank of lieutenant colonel in the army, had manifested great pleasure at again meeting the young officer who had served under him at Arcot; and who had, in his absence, obtained a fame scarcely inferior to his own, by the defence of Ambur and the capture of Suwarndrug. A few hours after Clive's arrival, Mr. Drake had made a formal complaint of the assault which Charlie had committed; but after hearing, from Charlie, an account of the circumstances, Clive sent a contemptuous message to Mr. Drake, to the effect that Charlie had only acted as he should himself have done, under the same circumstances; and that, at the present time, he should not think of depriving himself of the services of one gallant soldier, even if he had maltreated a dozen civilians.

As Clive had been given paramount authority in Bengal, and as Mr. Drake had every reason to suppose that he, himself, would be recalled as soon as the circumstances attending the capture of Calcutta were known in England, he was unable to do anything further in the matter, and Charlie landed with Clive on the 28th. The force consisted of two hundred and fifty Europeans, and twelve hundred Sepoys, who were forced to drag with them, having no draft animals, two field pieces and a waggon of ammunition.

The march was an excessively fatiguing one. The country was swampy in the extreme, and intersected with watercourses; and, after a terribly fatiguing night march, and fifteen hours of unintermittent labour, they arrived, at eight o'clock in the morning, at the hollow bed of a lake, now perfectly dry. It lay some ten feet below the surrounding country, and was bordered with jungle. In the wet season it was full of water. On the eastern and southern banks lay an abandoned village, and it was situated about a mile and a half from the fort of Baj-baj.

Clive was ill, and unable to see after matters himself. Indeed, accustomed only to the feeble forces of Southern India, who had never stood for a moment against him in battle, he had no thought of danger. Upon the other hand the troops of the nabob, who had had no experience, whatever, of the superior fighting powers of the Europeans; and who had effected so easy a conquest at Calcutta, flushed with victory, regarded their European foes with contempt, and were preparing to annihilate them at a blow.

Manak Chand, the general commanding the nabob's forces, informed by spies of the movements of the English troops, moved out with fifteen hundred horses and two thousand foot. So worn out were the British upon their arrival at the dried bed of the lake that, after detaching a small body to occupy a village near the enemy's fort, from which alone danger was expected; while another took up the post in some jungles, by the side of the main road, the rest threw themselves down to sleep. Some lay in the village, some in the shade of the bushes along the sides of the hollow. Their arms were all piled in a heap, sixty yards from the eastern bank. The two field pieces stood deserted, on the north side of the village. Not a single sentry was posted.

Manak Chand, knowing that, after marching all night, they would be exhausted, now stole upon them, and surrounded the tank on three sides. Happily, he did not perceive that their arms were piled at a distance of sixty yards from the nearest man. Had he done so, the English would have been helpless in his hands. After waiting an hour, to be sure that the last of the English were sound asleep, he ordered a tremendous fire to be opened on the hollow and village.

Astounded at this sudden attack, the men sprang up from their deep sleep, and a rush was instantly made to their arms. Clive, ever coolest in danger, shouted to them to be steady, and his officers well seconded his attempts. Unfortunately the artillerymen, in their sudden surprise, instead of rushing to their cannon, joined the rest of the troops as they ran back to their arms, and the guns at once fell into the hands of the enemy.

These had now climbed the eastern bank, and a fire from all sides was poured upon the troops, huddled together in a mass.

'Major Marryat,' Clive said, 'if we fall back now, fatigued as the men are, and shaken by this surprise, we are lost. Do you take a wing of the Sepoy battalion, and clear the right bank. I will advance, with the main body, directly on the village.'

'Come on, my lads,' Charlie shouted, in Hindostanee; 'show them how the men of Madras can fight.'

The Sepoys replied with a cheer, advanced with a rush against the bank, drove the defenders at once from the point where they charged, and then swept round the tank towards the village, which Clive had already attacked in front.

The loss of Charlie's battalion was small, but the main body, exposed to the concentrated fire, suffered more heavily. They would not, however, be denied. Reaching the bank, they poured a volley into the village, and charged with the bayonet; just as Charlie's men dashed in at the side. The enemy fled from the village and, taking shelter in the jungles around, opened fire. The shouts of their officers could be heard, urging them again to sally out and fall upon the British; but at this moment, the party which had been sent forward along the road, hearing the fray, came hurrying up and poured their fire into the jungle.

Surprised at this reinforcement, the enemy paused as they were issuing from the wood, and then fell back upon their cavalry. The British artillerymen ran out, and seized the guns, and opened with them upon the retiring infantry. Clive now formed up his troops in line, and advanced against the enemy's cavalry, behind which their infantry had massed for shelter.

Manak Chand ordered his cavalry to charge, but just as he did so, a cannonball from one of Clive's field pieces passed close to his head. The sensation was so unplesant that he at once changed his mind. The order for retreat was given, and the beaten army fell back, in disorder, to Calcutta.

Chapter 21

THE BATTLE OUTSIDE CALCUTTA

After the defeat of the enemy, who had surprised and so nearly annihilated him, Clive marched at once towards the fort of Baj-baj. On the way he met Major Kilpatrick, who was advancing, with a force which had been landed from the ships when the sound of firing was heard, to his assistance.

The fleet had, at daybreak, opened a heavy fire upon the ramparts; and by the afternoon effected a breach. As his men were greatly fatigued, and had had but an hour's sleep, Clive determined upon delaying the attack until the morning; and a party of two hundred and fifty sailors, with two guns, were landed to take part in the storming.

Many of these sailors had drunk freely before landing, and as night fell, some of them strolled towards the fort. One of the number, named Strahan, moved along, unobserved by the enemy, to the foot of the breach, climbed up it, and came suddenly upon a party of its defenders sitting round a fire, smoking. Strahan immediately fired his pistol among them, with a shout of, 'The fort is mine!' and then gave three rousing cheers.

The enemy leaped to their feet and ran off for a little way. Then, seeing Strahan was alone, they rushed back and attacked him, firing as they came. Strahan, drawing his cutlass, defended himself vigorously for some time; but his weapon broke off at the hilt, just as a number of Sepoys and men of the 39th, who had been awakened from their sleep by the shouting and firing, came running up. Reinforcements of the garrison also joined their friends, but these were dispirited by the sudden and unexpected attack; and, as the troops continued to stream up the breach, the garrison were pressed; and, losing heart, fled through the opposite gate of the fort.

The only casualty on the British side was that Captain Campbell, marching up at the head of the Sepoys, was mistaken for an enemy by the sailors, and shot dead. Strahan was, in the morning, severely reprimanded by the admiral for his breach of discipline; and, retiring from the cabin, said to his comrades:

'Well, if I am flogged for this here action, I will never take another fort, by myself, as long as I live.'

Manak Chand was so alarmed at the fighting powers shown by the English in these two affairs, that, leaving only a garrison of five hundred men at Calcutta, he retired with his army to join the nabob at Moorshedabad. When the fleet arrived before the town, the enemy surrendered the fort at the first shot, and it was again taken possession of by the English.

Major Kilpatrick was at once sent up, with five ships and a few hundred men, to capture the town of Hoogly, twenty miles farther up. The defences of the place were strong. It was held by two thousand men, and three thousand horsemen lay around it. The ships, however, at once opened a cannonade upon it, and effected a breach before night, and at daybreak the place was taken by storm.

Two days after the capture of Calcutta, the news arrived that war had again been declared between England and France. It was fortunate that this was not known a little earlier; for had the French forces been joined to those under Manak Chand, the reconquest of Calcutta would not have been so easily achieved.

The nabob, furious at the loss of Calcutta, and the capture and sack of Hoogly, at once despatched a messenger to the governor of the French colony of Chandranagore, to join him in crushing the English. The governor, however, had received orders that, in the event of war being declared between England and France, he was, if possible, to arrange with the English that neutrality should be observed between them. He therefore refused the nabob's request, and then sent messengers to Calcutta, to treat.

The nabob had gathered an army of ten thousand foot and fifteen thousand horse, and advanced against Calcutta, arriving before the town on the 2nd February, 1757.

Clive's force had now, owing to the arrival of some reinforcements from Europe, and the enlisting of fresh Sepoys, been raised to seven hundred European infantry, a hundred artillerymen, and fifteen hundred Sepoys, with fourteen light field pieces.

The whole of the town of Calcutta was surrounded by a deep cut, with a bank behind, called the Mahratta Ditch. A mile beyond this was a large saltwater lake, so that an enemy advancing from the north would have to pass within a short distance of Clive's intrenched position outside the town, affording him great opportunities for a flank attack. On the day of their arrival Clive marched out, but the enemy opened a heavy fire, and he retired.

Clive determined to attack the enemy, next morning. Admiral Watson, at his request, at once landed five hundred and sixty sailors, under the command of Captain Warwick of the Thunderer. A considerable portion of the enemy had crossed the Mahratta Ditch, and encamped within it. The nabob himself pitched his tent in the garden of Omichund (a native Calcutta merchant who, though in the nabob's camp from motives of policy, sympathized entirely with the English), which occupied an advanced bastion within the Mahratta Ditch. The rest of the army were encamped between the ditch and the saltwater lake.

Clive's intentions were to march first against the battery which had played on him so effectually the day before; and, having carried this, to march directly against the garden in which the nabob was encamped. The force with which he started, at three o'clock in the morning of the 3rd, consisted of the five hundred and sixty sailors, who drew with them six guns, six hundred and fifty European infantry, a hundred European artillery, and eight hundred Sepoys. Half the Sepoys led the advance, the remainder covered the rear.

Soon after daybreak, the Sepoys came in contact with the enemy's advanced guard, placed in ditches along a road leading from the head of the lake to the Mahratta Ditch. These discharged their muskets, and some rockets, and took to flight. One of the rockets caused a serious disaster. The Sepoys had their ammunition pouches open, and the contents of one of these was fired by the rocket. The flash of the flame communicated the fire to the pouch of the next Sepoy, and so the flame ran along the line, killing, wounding, and scorching many, and causing the greatest confusion.

Fortunately the enemy were not near, and Captain Eyre Coote, who led the British infantry behind them, aided Charlie, who led the advance, in restoring order, and the forward movement again went on.

A new obstacle had, however, arisen. With the morning a dense fog had set in, rendering it impossible for the troops to see even a few yards in advance of them. Still they pushed on and, unopposed, reached a point opposite Omichund's garden, but divided from it by the Mahratta Ditch.

Presently they heard the thunder of a great body of approaching cavalry. They waited quietly until the unseen horse had approached within a few yards of them, and then poured a mighty volley into the fog. The noise ceased abruptly, and was followed by that of the enemy's cavalry in retreat.

The fog was now so dense that it was impossible even to judge of the directions in which the troops were moving. Clive knew, however, that the Mahratta Ditch was on his right and, moving a portion of his troops till they touched this, he again advanced, his object being to gain a causeway which, raised several feet above the country, led from Calcutta, across the Mahratta Ditch, into the country beyond. Towards this Clive now advanced, his troops firing, as they marched, into the fog ahead of them, and the guns firing from the flanks, obliquely, to the right and left.

Without experiencing any opposition Clive reached the causeway, and the Sepoys, turning to their right, advanced along this towards the ditch. As they crossed this, however, they came in the line of fire of their own guns, the officer commanding them being ignorant of what was taking place in front, and unable to see a foot before him. Charlie, closely accompanied always by Tim, was at the head of his troops when the iron hail of the English guns struck the head of the column, mowing down numbers of men. A panic ensued, and the Sepoys, terror stricken at this discharge, from a direction in which they considered themselves secure, leaped from the causeway into the dry ditch and sheltered themselves there. Charlie and his companion were saved by the fact that they were a few paces ahead of the column.

'Run back, Tim,' Charlie said. 'Find Colonel Clive, and tell him that we are being mowed down by our own artillery. If you can't find him, hurry back to the guns, and tell the officer what he is doing.'

Charlie then leaped down into the ditch, and endeavoured to rally the Sepoys. A few minutes later Clive himself arrived, and the Sepoys were induced to leave the ditch, and to form again by the side of the causeway, along which the British troops were now marching.

Suddenly, however, from the fog burst out the discharge of two heavy guns, which the enemy had mounted on a bastion flanking the ditch. The shouts of the officers, and the firing of the men, indicated precisely the position of the column. The grape-shot tore through it, and twenty-two of the English troops fell dead and wounded. Immediately afterwards another discharge followed, and the column, broken and confused, bewildered by the dense fog, and dismayed by the fire of these unseen guns, fell back.

Clive now determined to push on to the main road, which he knew crossed the fields half a mile in front of him. The country was, however, here laid out in rice fields, each inclosed by banks and ditches. Over these banks it was impossible to drag the guns, and the sailors could only get them along by descending into the ditches, and using these as roads. The labour was prodigious, and the men, fatigued and harassed by this battle in darkness, and by the fire from the unseen guns which the enemy continued to pour in their direction from either flank, began to lose heart.

Happily, however, the fog began to lift. The flanks of the columns were covered by bodies of troops, thrown out on either side, and after more than an hour's hard work, and abandoning two of the guns which had broken down, Clive reached the main road, again formed his men in column, and advanced towards the city.

The odds were overwhelmingly against him. There were guns, infantry, and cavalry, both in front and behind them. The column pressed on, in spite of the heavy fire, crossed the ditch, and attacked a strong body of the enemy drawn up on the opposite side. While it did so, a great force of the nabob's cavalry swept down on the rear, and for a moment captured the guns. Ensign Yorke, of the 39th Foot, faced the rear company about, and made a gallant charge upon the horsemen, drove them back, and recaptured the guns.

Clive's whole army was now across the ditch, and it was open to him either to carry out his original plan of attacking Omichund's garden, or of marching forward into the fort of Calcutta. Seeing that his men were fatigued, and worn out with six hours of labour and marching under the most difficult circumstances, he took the latter alternative, entered Calcutta, and then, following the stream, marched back to the camp he had left in the morning.

His loss amounted to thirty-nine Europeans killed, and eighteen Sepoys; eighty-two Europeans wounded, and thirty-five Sepoys; the casualties being caused almost entirely by the enemy's cannon.

The expedition, from a military point of view, had been an entire failure. He had carried neither the battery nor Omichund's garden. Had it not been for the fog he might have succeeded in both these objects; but, upon the other hand, the enemy were as much disconcerted by the fog as he was, and were unable to use their forces with any effect. Military critics have decided that the whole operation was a mistake; but although a mistake and a failure, its consequences were no less decisive.

The nabob, struck with astonishment at the daring and dash of the English, in venturing with so small a force to attack him, and to march through the very heart of his camp, was seized with terror. He had lost thirteen hundred men in the fight, among whom were twenty-four rajahs and lesser chiefs, and the next morning he sent in a proposal for peace.

A less determined man than Clive would, no doubt, have accepted the proposal. Calcutta was still besieged by a vastly superior force, supplies of all kinds were running short, the attack of the previous day had been a failure. He knew, however, the character of Asiatics, and determined to play the game of bounce. The very offer of the nabob showed him that the latter was alarmed. He therefore wrote to him, saying that he had simply marched his troops through his highness' camp to show him of what British soldiers were capable; but that he had been careful to avoid hurting anyone, except those who actually opposed his progress. He concluded by expressing his willingness to accede to the nabob's proposal, and to negotiate.

The nabob took it all in. If all this destruction and confusion had been wrought by a simple march through his camp, what would be the result if Clive were to take into his head to attack him in earnest? He therefore at once withdrew his army three miles to the rear, and opened negotiations. He granted all that the English asked: that all the property and privileges of the Company should be restored, that all their goods should pass into the country free of tax, that all the Company's factories, and all moneys and properties belonging to it or its servants, should be restored or made good, and that permission should be given to them to fortify Calcutta as they pleased.

Having agreed to these conditions, the nabob, upon the 11th of February, retired with his army to his capital; leaving Omichund with a commission to propose to the English a treaty of alliance, offensive and defensive, against all enemies. This proposal was a most acceptable one, and Clive determined to seize the opportunity to crush the French. His previous experiences, around Madras, had taught him that the French were the most formidable rivals of England in India. He knew that large reinforcements were on their way to Pondicherry, and he feared that the nabob, when he recovered from his panic, might regret the conditions which he had granted, and might ally himself with the French in an effort, again, to expel the English.

He therefore determined at once to attack the French. The deputies sent by Monsieur Renault, the governor of Chandranagore, had been kept waiting from day to day, under one pretence or another; and they now wrote to the governor that they believed that there was no real intention, on the part of the English, to sign an agreement of neutrality with him; and that they would be the next objects of attack. Monsieur Renault immediately sent messengers to the nabob, urging upon him that, if the English were allowed to annihilate the French, they would be more dangerous enemies than ever; and Suraja-u-Dowlah, having now recovered from his terror, wrote at once to Calcutta, peremptorily forbidding any hostilities against the French.

To show his determination, he despatched fifteen hundred men to Hoogly, which the English had abandoned after capturing it, with instructions to help the French if attacked; and he sent a lac of rupees to Monsieur Renault, to aid him in preparing for his defence.

Clive, unwilling to face a coalition between the French and the nabob, was in favour of acceding to the nabob's orders. The treaty of neutrality with the French was drawn up, and would have been signed, had it not been for the obstinate refusal of Admiral Watson to agree to it. Between that officer and Clive there had never been any cordial feeling, and from the time of their first connection, at the siege of

Gheriah, differences of opinion, frequently leading to angry disputes, had taken place between them. Nor was it strange that this should be so. Both were brave and gallant men; but while Watson had the punctilious sense of honor which naturally belongs to an English gentleman, Clive was wholly unscrupulous as to the means which he employed to gain his ends.

Between two such men, it is not singular that disagreements arose. Admiral Watson, impelled by feelings of personal dislike to Clive, often allowed himself to be carried to unwarrantable lengths. On the occasion of the capture of Calcutta, he ordered Captain Eyre Coote, who first entered it, to hold it in the king's name, and to disobey Clive's orders, although the latter had been granted a commission in the royal army as lieutenant colonel, and was, moreover, the chief authority of the Company in all affairs on land. Upon Clive's asserting himself, Admiral Watson absolutely threatened to open fire upon his troops. Apparently from a sheer feeling of opposition, he now opposed the signing of the treaty with the French, and several days were spent in stormy altercations.

Circumstances occurred, during this time, which strengthened the view he took, and changed those of Clive and his colleagues of the council. Just then, the news reached Suraja-u-Dowlah that Delhi had been captured by the Afghans; and, terrified at the thought that the victorious northern enemy might next turn their arms against him, he wrote to Clive, begging him to march to his assistance, and offering a lac of rupees a month towards the expense of his army.

On the same day that Clive received the letter, he heard that Commodore James and three ships, with reinforcements from Bombay, had arrived at the mouth of the Hoogly; and that the Cumberland, with three hundred troops, which had grounded on her way from Madras, was now coming up the river.

Almost at the same moment he heard, from Omichund, who had accompanied the nabob to Moorshedabad, that he had bribed the governor of Hoogly to offer no opposition to the passage of the troops up the river.

Clive was now ready to agree to Admiral Watson's views, and to advance at once against Chandranagore; but the admiral again veered round, and refused to agree to the measure, unless the consent of the nabob was obtained. He wrote, however, himself, a threatening, and indeed violent letter to the nabob, ordering him to give his consent. The nabob, still under the influence of his fears from the Afghans, replied in terms which amounted to consent, but the very next day, having received news which calmed his fears as to the Afghans, he wrote peremptorily, forbidding the expedition against the French. This letter, however, was disregarded, and the expedition prepared to start.

It consisted of seven hundred Europeans and fifteen hundred native infantry, who started by land; a hundred and fifty artillery proceeding in boats, escorted by three ships of war and several smaller vessels, under Admiral Watson.

The French garrison consisted only of a hundred and forty-six French, and three hundred Sepoys. Besides these were three hundred of the European population, and sailors of the merchant ships in port, who had been hastily formed into a militia.

The governor, indignant at the duplicity with which he had been treated, had worked vigorously at his defences. The settlement extended along the river banks for two miles. In the centre stood the fort, which was a hundred and twenty yards square, mounting ten thirty-two pounder guns on each of its four bastions. Twenty four-pounder guns were placed on the ramparts, facing the river on the south. On an outlying work commanding the watergate eight thirty-two pounders were mounted. Monsieur Renault set to work to demolish all the houses within a hundred yards of the fort, and to erect batteries commanding the approaches. He ordered an officer to sink several ships in the only navigable channel, about a hundred and fifty yards to the south of the fort, at a point commanded by the guns of one of the batteries.

The officer was a traitor. He purposely sank the ships in such a position as to leave a channel, through which the English ships might pass; and then, seizing his opportunity, deserted to them.

On approaching the town Clive, knowing that Charlie could speak the native language fluently, asked him whether he would undertake to reconnoitre the position of the enemy, with which he was entirely unacquainted. Charlie willingly agreed. When, on the night of the 13th of March, the army halted a few miles from the town, Charlie, disguising himself in a native dress and accompanied by Hossein, left the camp and made his way to the town. This he had no difficulty in entering. It extended a mile and a half back from the river, and consisted of houses standing in large gardens and inclosures. The whole of the Europeans were labouring at the erection of the batteries, and the destruction of the houses surrounding them; and Charlie and his companion, approaching closely to one of these, were pounced upon by the French officer in command of a working party, and set to work, with a number of natives, in demolishing the houses.

Charlie, with his usual energy, threw himself into the work, and would speedily have called attention to himself, by the strength and activity which he displayed, had not Hossein begged him to moderate his efforts.

'Native man never work like that, sahib. Not when he's paid ever so much. Work still less, no pay. The French would soon notice the sahib, if he laboured like that.'

Thus admonished, Charlie adapted his actions to those of his companions and, after working until dawn approached, he managed, with Hossein, to evade the attention of the officer; and, drawing off, hurried away to rejoin Clive. The latter was moving from the west, by a road leading to the northern face of the fort. It was at the battery which Renault was erecting upon this road that Charlie had been labouring. The latter informed Clive of the exact position of the work, and also, that although strong by itself, it was commanded by many adjoining houses; which the French, in spite of their efforts, had not time to destroy.

This news decided Clive to advance immediately, without giving the enemy further time to complete their operations.

Chapter 22

PLASSEY

As the English troops advanced, they were met on the outskirts of the settlement by the enemy, who contested bravely every garden and inclosure with them. The British force was, however, too strong to be resisted, and gradually the French were driven back, until they formed in the rear of the battery. Clive at once took possession of the houses surrounding it, and from them kept up, all day, a heavy fire upon the defenders; until, at nightfall, these fell back upon the fort, after spiking their guns. The loss of this position compelled the French to abandon the other outlying batteries, from which, during the night, they withdrew their guns into the fort.

The next four days Clive spent in bringing up the guns landed from the fleet, and establishing batteries round the fort; and on the 19th he opened fire against it. On the same day the three men of war; the Kent of sixty-four guns, the Tiger of sixty, and the Salisbury of fifty, anchored just below the channel, which the governor believed he had blocked up. The next four days were spent by the fleet in sounding, to discover whether the statements of the French deserter were correct.

During this time, a heavy cannonade was kept up unceasingly between Clive and the fort. In this the garrison had the best of it, silenced some of the English guns, killed many of the assailants, and would certainly have beaten off the land attack, had the fleet not been able to interfere in the struggle.

All this time, the governor was hoping that aid would arrive from the nabob. The latter, indeed, did send a force under Rajah Dulab Ram, but the governor of

691

Hoogly, bribed by Omichund, sent messages to this officer urging him to halt, as Chandranagore was about to surrender, and he would only incur the anger of the English, uselessly.

On the morning of the 23rd, having ascertained that a channel was free, the fleet advanced. The Tiger, leading, made her way through the passage and, taking up a position abreast of the northeast bastion of the fort, opened a heavy fire upon it with her guns, and harassed the besieged with a musketry fire from her tops. The Kent was on the point of anchoring opposite the watergate, when so heavy a fire was poured upon her that, in the confusion, the cable ran out; and the ship dropped down, till she anchored at a point exposed to a heavy crossfire from the southeast and southwest bastions. Owing to this accident, the Salisbury was forced to anchor a hundred and fifty yards below the fort.

The French fought with extreme bravery. Vastly superior as were the English force and guns, the French fire was maintained with the greatest energy and spirit, the gunners being directed and animated by Monsieur De Vignes, captain of one of the ships which had been sunk. No advantage was gained by the Tiger, in her struggle with the northeast bastion, and the guns of the southwest bastion galled the Kent so severely that the admiral, neglecting the southeast bastion, was forced to turn the whole of his guns upon it.

De Vignes concentrated his fire against one point in the Kent, and presently succeeded in setting her on fire. The conflagration spread, a panic ensued, and some seventy or eighty men jumped into the boats alongside.

The officers, however, rallied the rest of the crew. The fire was extinguished, the men returned to their duty, and the cannonade was recommenced.

After the battle had raged for two hours, the fire of the fort began to slacken, as one after another of the guns was dismounted. Monsieur Renault saw that the place could be no longer defended. Of his hundred and forty-six soldiers, over ninety had been killed and wounded. Collecting the remainder, and their officers, with twenty Sepoys, the governor ordered them to leave the fort immediately; making a detour to avoid the English, who were aiding the fleet by attacking the land side, and to march to Kossimbazar to join Monsieur Law, who commanded there. Then, there remaining in the fort only the clerks, women, and wounded, he hoisted a flag of truce.

Terms were speedily arranged. The governor, and all the civilians and natives, were allowed to go where they chose, with their clothes and linen. The wounded French soldiers were to remain, as prisoners of war.

Chandranagore cost the English two hundred and six men. The attack upon the French colony was blamed by many, at the time, for in the hour of English distress they had offered to remain neutral, instead of joining the nabob in crushing us. Upon the other hand, there was force in the arguments with which Admiral Watson had defended his refusal to sign the treaty of neutrality. That treaty would not be binding, unless ratified by Pondicherry; and to Pondicherry it was known that the most powerful fleet and army France had ever sent to India was on its way. It was also known that Bussy, at the court of the Nizam of the Deccan, was in communication with the nabob. Thus, then, in a short time English interests in India might be menaced more formidably than ever before, and the crushing out of the French colony, almost at the gates of Calcutta, was a measure of extreme importance. It was hard upon the gallant governor of Chandranagore, but public opinion generally agreed that the urgency of the case justified the course adopted by the English authorities at Calcutta.

Suraja-u-Dowlah was filled with fury, at the news of the capture of Chandranagore; but hearing a rumour, two days later, that the Afghans were upon their march to attack him, he wrote letters to Clive and Watson, congratulating them upon their success, and offering to them the territory of Chandranagore, on the same terms upon which it had been held by the French.

But the young tyrant of Moorshedabad was swayed by constantly fluctuating feeling. At one moment his fears were uppermost; the next, his anger and hate of the English. Instead of recalling the army of Rajah Dulab Ram, as he had promised, he ordered it to halt at Plassey, a large village twenty-two miles south of Moorshedabad.

The English were represented at his court by Mr. Watts, who had the greatest difficulty in maintaining his position, in the constantly changing moods of the nabob. One day the latter would threaten to order him to be led to instant execution, the next he would load him with presents.

Besides Mr. Watts, the English affairs were conducted by Omichund who, aided by the Sets, or native bankers, whom Suraja-u-Dowlah had plundered and despoiled, got up a conspiracy among the nabob's most intimate followers.

The history of these intrigues is the most unpleasant feature in the life of Clive. Meer Jaffier, the nabob's general, himself offered to Mr. Watts to turn traitor, if the succession to the kingdom was bestowed upon him. This was agreed to, upon his promise to pay, not only immense sums to the Company, but enormous amounts to the principal persons on the English side. So enormous, indeed, were these demands, that even Meer Jaffier, anxious as he was to conclude the alliance, was aghast. The squadron was to have two million and a half rupees, and the same amount was to be paid for the army. Presents amounting to six millions of rupees were to be distributed between Clive, Major Kilpatrick, the governor, and the members of the council. Clive's share of these enormous sums amounted to two million, eighty thousand rupees. In those days, a rupee was worth half a crown. Never did an English officer make such a bargain for himself.

But even this is not the most dishonorable feature of the transaction. Omichund had, for some time, been kept in the dark as to what was going forward; but, obtaining information through his agents, he questioned Mr. Watts concerning it. The latter then informed him of the whole state of affairs, and Omichund, whose services to the English had been immense, naturally demanded a share of the plunder.

Whether or not he threatened to divulge the plot to the nabob, unless his demands were satisfied, is doubtful. At any rate, it was considered prudent to pacify him, and he was accordingly told that he should receive the sum he named. Clive, and the members of the council, however, although willing to gratify their own extortionate greed, at the expense of Meer Jaffier, determined to rob Omichund of his share. In order to do this, two copies of the treaty with Meer Jaffier were drawn up, on different coloured papers. They were exactly alike, except that, in one, the amount to be given to Omichund was entirely omitted. This was the real treaty. The other was intended to be destroyed, after being shown to a friend of Omichund, in order to convince the latter that all was straight and honorable.

All the English authorities placed their signatures to the real treaty, but Admiral

Watson indignantly refused to have anything to do with the fictitious one; or to be a party, in any way, to the deceit practised on Omichund. In order to get out of the difficulty, Clive himself forged Admiral Watson's signature to the fictitious treaty.

A more disgraceful transaction was never entered into, by a body of English gentlemen. That Mr. Drake and the members of his council, the pitiful cowards who fled from Calcutta, and refused to allow the ships to draw off its brave garrison, should consent to such a transaction was but natural; but that Clive, the gallant and dashing commander, should have stooped to it, is sad, indeed.

It may be said that, to the end of his life, Clive defended his conduct in this transaction, under the excuse that Omichund was a scoundrel. The Indian was not, indeed, an estimable character. Openly, he was the friend and confidant of the nabob while, all the time, he was engaged in bribing and corrupting his officers, and in plotting with his enemies. This, however, in no way alters the facts that he rendered inestimable service to the English; and that the men who deceived and cheated him were, to the full, as greedy and grasping as himself; without, in the case of the governor and his council, having rendered any service whatever to the cause.

At last, the negotiations were complete. More and more severely did Clive press upon the nabob. Having compelled him to expel Law and the French, first from Moorshedabad and then from his dominions, he pressed fresh demands upon him; until the unfortunate prince, driven to despair, and buoyed up with the hope that he should receive assistance from Bussy, who had just expelled the English from their factory at Vizapatam, ordered Meer Jaffier to advance, with fifteen thousand men, to reinforce Rajah Dulab Ram at Plassey.

Clive, in fact, forced on hostilities. His presence, with that of a considerable portion of his army, was urgently required at Madras. He was sure, however, that the instant he had gone, and the English force was greatly weakened, the nabob would again commence hostilities; and the belief was shared by all in India. He was, therefore, determined to force on the crisis, as soon as possible; in order that, the nabob being disposed of, he should be able to send reinforcements to Madras.

While these negotiations had been going on, Charlie Marryat had remained in Calcutta. He had been severely wounded in the attack on Chandranagore, and was carried down to Calcutta in a boat. On arriving there, he heard that the Lizzie Anderson had just cast anchor off the fort. He caused himself at once to be conveyed on board, and was received with the greatest heartiness and pleasure, by his old friend, the captain; and assiduously attended by the doctor of the ship. In order that he might have as much air as possible, the captain had a sort of tent, with a double covering, erected on deck. During the daytime the sides of this were lifted, so that the air could pass freely across the bed.

Charlie's wound was a severe one and, had he been nursed in a hospital on shore, it is probable that it would have been fatal. Thanks, however, to the comforts on board ship, the freshness and coolness of the situation, and the care of all surrounding him, he was, after some weeks' illness, pronounced convalescent; and was sufficiently recovered to join the force with which Clive marched against Plassey.

This force consisted of nine hundred and fifty European infantry, a hundred artillerymen, fifty sailors, and two thousand one hundred Sepoys. The artillery consisted of eight six-pounders and two small howitzers. The army of the nabob was fifty thousand strong, and against such a force it was, indeed, an adventurous task for an army of three thousand men, of whom only one-third were Europeans, to advance to the attack. Everything depended, in fact, upon Meer Jaffier and his two colleagues in treachery, Rajah Dulab Ram and Yar Lutf Khan.

The nabob, on hearing of Clive's advance, had sent to Monsieur Law; who was, with a hundred and fifty men, at a place over a hundred miles distant; to which he had, in accordance with the orders of Clive, been obliged to retire; and begged him to advance to join him, with all speed. The nabob had with him forty or fifty Frenchmen, commanded by Monsieur Saint Frais, formerly one of the council of Chandranagore. These had some field pieces of their own, and also directed the native artillery, of fifty-three guns; principally thirty-two, twenty-four, and eighteen pounders.

Had Clive been sure of the cooperation of Meer Jaffier and his confederates, who commanded three out of the four divisions of the nabob's army, he need not have hesitated. But he was, till the last moment, in ignorance whether to rely upon them. The nabob, having become suspicious of Meer Jaffier, had obtained from him an oath, sworn on the Koran, of fidelity; and although the traitor continued his correspondence with Clive, his letters were of a very dubious character, and Clive was in total ignorance as to his real intentions. So doubtful, indeed, was he that, when only a few miles of ground and the river Bhagirathi lay between him and the enemy, Clive felt the position so serious that he called a council of war; and put to them the question whether they should attack the nabob, or fortify themselves at Katwa, and hold that place until the rainy season, which had just set in with great violence, should abate.

All the officers above the rank of subalterns, twenty in number, were present. Clive himself, contrary to custom, gave his vote first in favour of halting at Katwa. Major Kilpatrick, who commanded the Company's troops, Major Grant of the 37th, and ten other officers voted the same way. Major Eyre Coote declared in favour of an immediate advance. He argued that the troops were in high spirits, and had hitherto been everywhere successful, and that a delay would allow Monsieur Law and his troops to arrive. He considered that, if they determined not to fight, they should fall back upon Calcutta. Charlie Marryat supported him, as did five other officers, all belonging to the Indian service.

The decision taken, the council separated, and Clive strolled away to a grove, and sat down by himself. There he thought over, in his mind, the arguments which had been advanced by both sides. He saw the force of the arguments which had been adduced by Major Eyre Coote and Charlie Marryat; and his own experience showed him that the daring course is always the most prudent one, in fighting Asiatics. At last, he came to a conclusion. Rising, he returned to the camp; and, meeting Major Coote on the way, informed him that he had changed his mind, and would fight the next day.

Charlie returned to his tent after the council broke up, disheartened at the result. He was greeted by Tim.

'Shure, yer honor, Hossein is in despair. The water has filled up the holes, where he makes his fires, and the rain has soaked the wood. Yer dinner is not near cooked yet, and half the dishes are spoilt.'

'It does not matter a bit, Tim,' Charlie said. 'You know I'm not particular about my eating, though Hossein will always prepare a dinner fit for an alderman.'

'We are going to fight them tomorrow, yer honor, I hope,' Tim said. 'It's sick to death I am of wading about here in the wet, like a duck. It's as bare as the bogs of ould Ireland, without the blessings of the pigs and potatoes, to say nothing of the colleens.'

'No, Tim, I'm afraid we're going to stop where we are, for a bit. The council of war have decided not to fight.'

'Shure and that's bad news,' Tim said. 'The worst I've heard for many a day. What if there be fifty thousand of 'em, Mister Charles, haven't we bate 'em at long odds before, and can't we do it agin?'

'I think we could, Tim,' Charlie replied; 'but the odds of fifty-three heavy cannon, which the spies say they've got, to our ten popguns, is serious. However, I'm sorry we're not going to fight, and I'm afraid that you must make up your mind to the wet, and Hossein his to giving me bad dinners for some weeks to come; that is to say, if the enemy don't turn us out of this.'

A few minutes later, Lieutenant Peters entered the tent.

'Is it true, Charlie, that we are not going to fight, after all?'

'True enough,' Charlie said. 'We are to wait till the rains are over.'

'Rains!' Peters said, in disgust; 'what have the rains got to do with it? If we had a six weeks' march before us, I could understand the wet weather being a hindrance. Men are not water rats, and to march all day in these heavy downpours, and to lie all night in the mud, would soon tell upon our strength. But here we are, within a day's march of the enemy, and the men might as well get wet in the field as here. Everyone longs to be at the enemy, and a halt will have a very bad effect.

'What have you got to drink, Charlie?'

'I have some brandy and rum; nothing else,' Charlie said. 'But what will be better than either for you is a cup of tea. Hossein makes it as well as ever. I suppose you have dined?'

'Yes, half an hour ago.'

Just as Charlie finished his meal, Major Eyre Coote put his head into the tent.

'Marryat, the chief has changed his mind. We cross the river the first thing in the morning, and move at once upon Plassey.'

'Hurrah!' Charlie shouted; 'Clive is himself again. That is good news, indeed!'

'You will move your Sepoys down to the river at daybreak, and will be the first to cross. There is no chance of any opposition, as the spies tell us that the nabob has not arrived yet at Plassey.'

Several other officers afterwards dropped into the tent, for the news rapidly spread through the camp. There was, as had been the case at the council, considerable differences of opinion as to the prudence of the measure; but among the junior officers and men, the news that the enemy were to be attacked, at once, was received with hearty satisfaction.

'Here, major,' a fellow subaltern of Peters' said, as he entered the tent, followed by a servant; 'I have brought in half a dozen bottles of champagne. I started with a dozen from Calcutta, and had intended to keep these to celebrate our victory. But as, in the first place, all heavy baggage is to be left here; and in the second, it has occurred to me that possibly I may not come back to help to drink it; we may as well turn it to the good purpose of drinking success to the expedition.'

Some of the bottles were opened, and a merry evening was spent; but the party broke up early, for they had a heavy day's work before them, on the morrow.

At daybreak, the troops were in movement towards the banks of the Bhagirathi. They had brought boats with them from Chandranagore, and the work of crossing the river continued, without intermission, until four in the afternoon, when the whole force was landed on the left bank. Here Clive received another letter from Meer Jaffier, informing him that the nabob had halted at Mankarah, and intended to entrench himself there. He suggested that the English should undertake a circuitous march, and attack him in the rear; but as this march would have exposed Clive to being cut off from his communications, and as he was still very doubtful of the good faith of the conspirators, he determined to march straight forward; and sent word to Meer Jaffier, to that effect.

From the point where Clive had crossed the Bhagirathi it was fifteen miles to Plassey, following, as they did, the curves of the river. It was necessary to do this, as they had no carriage; and the men were obliged to tow their supplies in boats, against the stream.

Orders were issued that, as soon as the troops were across, they should prepare to eat their dinners, as the march was to be resumed at once. The rain was coming down in a steady pour as the troops, drenched to the skin, started upon their march. The stream, swollen by the rains, was in full flood, and the work of towing the heavy-laden barges was wearisome in the extreme. All took a share in the toil. In many cases the river had overflowed its banks, and the troops had to struggle through the water, up to their waists, while they tugged and strained at the ropes.

Charlie, as a mounted officer, rode at the head of his Sepoys; who formed the advance of the force. Three hundred men preceded the main body, who were towing the boats, to guard them from any sudden surprise. Tim marched beside him, occasionally falling back, and taking a turn at the ropes.

'This is dog's work, Mister Charles,' he said. 'It's lucky that it's raining, for the river can't make us wetter than we are. My hands are fairly sore, with pulling at the ropes.'

'Ah, Tim, you're not fond of ropes, you know. You remember that night at Moorshedabad.'

'Faith, yer honor, and I'll not forget it, if I live to be as old as Methuselah. Well, yer honor, it will be hard on us if we do not thrash them tomorrow, after all the trouble we are taking to be at them.'

At one o'clock in the morning, the weary troops reached the village of Plassey. They marched through it, and halted and bivouacked in a large mango grove, a short distance beyond.

Chapter 23

PLASSEY

Scarcely had the soldiers taken off their packs, when the sound of martial music was heard. Charlie was speaking, at the time, to Major Coote.

'There are the enemy, sure enough,' the latter said. 'That old rascal, Meer Jaffier, must have been deceiving us when he said that the nabob had halted at Mankarah. I'm afraid he means to play us false.'

'I expect,' Charlie remarked, 'that he does not know what he means, himself. These Asiatics are at any time ready to turn traitors, and to join the strongest. At present, Jaffier does not know what is the stronger; and I think it likely enough that he will take as little share as he can in the battle, tomorrow, till he sees which way it is going. Then, if we are getting the best of it, the rascal will join us, for the sake of the advantages which he expects to gain. If the day is going against us, he will do his best to complete his master's victory; and should proofs of his intended treachery ever come to light, he will clear himself by saying that he intended to deceive us all along, and merely pretended to treat with us, in order to throw us off our guard, and so deliver us into the hands of his master.'

'Yes,' Major Eyre Coote replied. 'These Mohammedan chiefs are indeed crafty and treacherous rascals. The whole history of India shows that gratitude is a feeling altogether unknown to them; and that, whatever favours a master may have lavished upon them, they are always ready to betray him, if they think that by so doing they will better their position.

'Now I shall lie down, and try to get a few hours' sleep before morning. I am wet to the skin, but fortunately in these sultry nights that matters little.'

'I must go my rounds,' Charlie said, 'and see that the sentries are on the alert. If the men were not so tired, I should have said that the best plan would have been to make a dash straight at the enemy's camp. It would take them quite unprepared, even if they know, as I daresay they do, that we are close at hand; and they would lose all the advantage of their artillery.'

'Yes, if we had arrived an hour before sunset, so as to be able to learn something of the nature of the ground, that would be our best course,' Major Coote agreed. 'But, even if the troops had been fresh, a night attack on an unknown position is a hazardous undertaking.'

'Good night. I must see Clive, and take his last orders.'

At daybreak the English were astir, and the position of the enemy became visible. He occupied strongly intrenched works, which the Rajah Dulab Ram had thrown up during his stay. The right of these works rested on the river; and extended inland, at a right angle to it, for about two hundred yards; and then swept round to the north, at an obtuse angle, for nearly three miles. At the angle was a redoubt, mounted with cannon. In advance of this was a mound, covered with jungle. Halfway between the intrenchments and the mango grove were two large tanks, near the river, surrounded by high mounds of earth. These tanks were about half a mile from the English position. On the river bank, a little in advance of the grove, was a hunting box belonging to the nabob, surrounded by a masonry wall. Clive took possession of this, immediately he heard the sound of the nabob's music, on his arrival.

Soon after daylight, the nabob's troops moved out from their intrenchments, and it was evident that he was aware of the position of the English. The French, with their four field guns, took up their post on the mound of the tank nearest to the grove, and about half a mile distant from it; and in the narrow space between them and the river two heavy guns, under a native officer, were placed.

Behind the French guns was the division of Mir Mudin Khan, the one faithful general of the nabob. It consisted of five thousand horse, and seven thousand foot. Extending, in the arc of a circle, towards the village of Plassey, were the troops of the three traitor generals Rajah Dulab Ram, Yar Lutf Khan, and Meer Jaffier. Thus, the English position was almost surrounded; and in advancing against the camp, they would have to expose themselves to an attack in the rear by the troops of the conspirators. These generals had, between them, nearly thirty-eight thousand troops.

From the roof of the hunting box, Clive watched the progress of the enemy's movements. He saw, at once, that the position which they had taken up was one which would entail the absolute destruction of his force, should he be defeated; and that this depended entirely upon the course taken by the conspirators. Against such a force as that opposed to him, if these remained faithful to their master, success could hardly be hoped for.

However, it was now too late to retreat, and the only course was to show a bold front. Clive accordingly moved his troops out, from the mango trees, to a line with the hunting box. The Europeans were formed in the centre, with three field pieces on each side. The native troops were on either flank. Two field guns, and the two howitzers, were placed a little in advance of the hunting box, facing the French position on the mound.

At eight o'clock in the morning, of the 23rd of June, a memorable day in the annals of India, the preparations on both sides were complete; and Saint Frais opened the battle, by the discharge of one of his guns at the English. At the signal, the whole of the artillery round the long curve opened their fire. The ten little guns replied to this overwhelming discharge, and for half an hour continued to play on the dense masses of the enemy. But, however well they might be handled, they could do little against the fire of the fifty pieces of cannon, concentrated upon them.

Had these been all served by European artillerymen, the British force would have been speedily annihilated as they stood. The natives of India, however, were extremely clumsy gunners. They fired but slowly, and had the feeblest idea of elevation. Consequently their balls, for the most part, went far over the heads of the English; and the four field guns of Saint Frais did more execution than the fifty heavy pieces of the nabob. At the end of half an hour, however, Clive had lost thirty of his men, and determined to fall back to the mango grove.

Leaving a party in the hunting box, and in the brick kilns in front of it, in which the guns had been posted, to harass Saint Frais' battery with their musketry fire, he withdrew the rest of his force into the grove. Here they were in shelter, for it was surrounded by a high and thick bank. Behind this the men sat down, while parties set to work, piercing holes through the banks as embrasures for the guns.

The enemy, on the retreat of the British within the grove, advanced with loud shouts of triumph; and, bringing their guns closer, again opened fire. The British had, by this time, pierced the holes for their field pieces; and these opened so vigorously that several of the enemy's cannon were disabled, numbers of their gunners killed, and some ammunition waggons blown up. On the other hand the English, now in perfect shelter, did not suffer at all, although the tops of the trees were cut off, in all directions, by the storm of cannon balls which swept through them.

Although the English fire was producing considerable loss among the enemy, this was as nothing in comparison to his enormous numbers; and, at eleven o'clock, Clive summoned his principal officers around him; and it was agreed that, as Meer Jaffier and his associates, of whose position in the field they were ignorant, showed no signs of drawing off, or of treachery to their master, it was impossible to risk an attack upon the front; since they would, as they pressed forward, be enveloped by the forces in the rear. It was determined, therefore, that unless any unexpected circumstance occurred, they should hold their present position till nightfall; and should, at midnight, attack the enemy's camp.

A quarter of an hour later, a tremendous tropical shower commenced, and for an hour the rain came down in torrents. Gradually the enemy's fire slackened. The English had tarpaulins to cover their ammunition, which, therefore, suffered no injury. The natives had no such coverings, and their powder was soon completely wetted, by the deluge of rain. Mir Mudin Khan, knowing that his own guns had been rendered useless, believed that those of the English were in a similar condition; and, leading out his cavalry, made a splendid charge down upon the grove.

The English were in readiness. As the cavalry swept up, a flash of fire ran from a thousand muskets, from the top of the embankments; while each of the field guns sent its load of grapeshot, through the embrasures, into the throng of horsemen.

The effect was decisive. The cavalry recoiled before the terrible fire, and rode back, with their brave leader mortally wounded. This blow was fatal to the fortunes of Suraja Dowlah. When the news of the death of his brave and faithful general reached him, he was struck with terror. He had long suspected Meer Jaffier of treachery, but he had now no one else to rely upon. Sending for that general he reminded him, in touching terms, of the benefits which he had received at the hands of his father; and conjured him to be faithful to him. Throwing his turban upon the ground, he said:

'Jaffier, you must defend that turban.'

'Jaffier responded with assurances of his loyalty and sincerity, and promised to defend his sovereign with his life. Then, riding off, he at once despatched a messenger to Clive, informing him of what had happened, and urging him to attack at once.

As long as Mir Mudin Khan lived, it is probable that Meer Jaffier was still undecided as to the part he should play. While that general lived it was possible, even probable, that the English would be defeated, even should the traitors take no part against them. His death, however, left the whole management of affairs in the hands of the three conspirators, and their course was now plain.

Scarcely had Meer Jaffier left the nabob, than the unhappy young man, who was still under twenty years old, turned to Rajah Dulab Ram for counsel and advice. The traitor gave him counsel that led to his destruction. He told him that the English could not be attacked in their position; that his troops, exposed to the fire of their guns, were suffering heavily and losing heart; and he advised him, at once, to issue orders for them to fall back within their intrenchments. He also advised him to leave the field himself, and to retire to Moorshedabad, leaving it to his generals to annihilate the English, should they venture to attack them.

Suraja Dowlah, at no time capable of thinking for himself, and now bewildered by the death of the general he knew to be faithful to him, and by his doubts as to the fidelity of the others, fell into the snare. He at once issued orders for the troops to retire within their intrenchments; and then, mounting a swift camel, and accompanied by two thousand horsemen, he left the field, and rode off to Moorshedabad.

The movement of retirement at once commenced. The three traitor generals drew off their troops, and those of Mir Mudin Khan also obeyed orders, and fell back.

Saint Frais, however, refused to obey. He saw the ruin which would follow upon the retreat, and he pluckily continued his fire.

Clive, after the council had decided that nothing should be done till nightfall, had lain down in the hunting box to snatch a little repose, his thoughts having kept him awake all night. Major Kilpatrick, seeing the retirement of the enemy; and that the French artillerymen remained, unsupported, on the mound; at once advanced, with two hundred and fifty Europeans, and two guns, against it; sending word to Clive what he was doing. Clive, angry that any officer should have taken so important a step, without consulting him, at once ran after the detachment, and severely reprimanded Major Kilpatrick, for moving from the grove without orders. Immediately, however, that he comprehended the whole position, he recognized the wisdom of the course Kilpatrick had taken, and sent him back to the grove, to order the whole force to advance.

Saint Frais, seeing that he was entirely unsupported, fired a last shot; and then, limbering up, fell back in perfect order to the redoubt at the corner of the intrenchment, where he again posted his field pieces, in readiness for action.

Looking round the field, Clive saw that two of the divisions which formed the arc of the circle were marching back towards the intrenchments; but that the third, that on the left of their line, had wheeled round and was marching towards the rear of the grove. Not having received the letter which Meer Jaffier had written to him, he supposed that this movement indicated an intention to attack his baggage; and he therefore detached some European troops, with a field gun, to check the advance. Upon the gun opening fire, the enemy's division halted. It ceased its advance, but continued apart from the rest of the enemy. In the meantime, Clive had arrived upon the mound which Saint Frais had left; and, planting his guns there, opened fire upon the enemy within their intrenchments.

The Indian soldiers and inferior officers, knowing nothing of the treachery of their chiefs, were indignant at being thus cannonaded in their intrenchments by a foe so inferior in strength; and horse, foot, and artillery poured out again from the intrenchments, and attacked the British.

The battle now raged in earnest. Clive posted half his infantry and artillery on the mound of the tank nearest to the enemy's intrenchments, and the greater part of the rest on rising ground, two hundred yards to the left of it; while he placed a hundred and sixty picked shots, Europeans and natives, behind the tank close to the intrenchments, with orders to keep up a continuous musketry fire upon the enemy, as they sallied out.

The enemy fought bravely. Saint Frais worked his guns unflinchingly at the redoubt, the infantry poured in volley after volley, the cavalry made desperate charges right up to the British lines. But they had no leader, and were fighting against men well commanded, and confident in themselves. Clive observed that the division on the enemy's extreme left remained inactive, and detached from the army; and it, for the first time, struck him that this was the division of Meer Jaffier. Relieved for the safety of his baggage, and from the attack which had hitherto threatened in his rear, he at once determined to carry the hill in advance of Saint Frais's battery, and the redoubt occupied by the French leader.

Strong columns were sent against each position. The hill was carried without opposition, and then so heavy and searching a fire was poured into the intrenched camp that the enemy began to fall back, in utter confusion. Saint Frais, finding himself isolated and alone in the redoubt, as he had before been on the mound, was forced to retire.

At five o'clock the battle was over, and the camp of the Nabob of Bengal in the possession of the English. The British loss was trifling. Seven European and sixteen native soldiers were killed, thirteen Europeans and thirty-six natives wounded. It was one of the decisive battles of the world, for the fate of India hung in the balance. Had Clive been defeated, and his force annihilated, as it must have been if beaten, the English would have been swept out of Bengal. The loss of that presidency would have had a decided effect on the struggle in Madras, where the British were, with the greatest difficulty, maintaining themselves against the French.

Henceforth Bengal, the richest province in India, belonged to the English; for although, for a time, they were content to recognize Meer Jaffier and his successors as its nominal rulers, these were but puppets in their hands, and they were virtual masters of the province.

After the battle, Meer Jaffier arrived. Conscious of his own double-dealing, he by no means felt sure of the reception he should meet with. It suited Clive, however, to ignore the doubtful part he had played, and he was saluted as Nabob of Bengal.

It would have been far better for him, had he remained one of the great chiefs of Bengal. The enormous debt, with which Clive and his colleagues had saddled him, crushed him. The sum was so vast that it was only by imposing the most onerous taxation upon his people that he was enabled to pay it, and the discontent excited proved his destruction.

Omichund had no greater reason for satisfaction, at the part which he had played in the ruin of his country. The fact that he had been deceived, by the forged treaty, was abruptly and brutally communicated to him; and the blow broke his heart. He shortly afterwards became insane, and died before eighteen months were over.

Suraja Dowlah fled to Moorshedabad, where the remnants of his army followed him. At first, the nabob endeavoured to secure their fidelity by issuing a considerable amount of pay. Then, overpowered by his fears of treachery, he sent off the ladies of the zenana, and all his treasures, on elephants; and, a few hours afterwards, he himself, accompanied by his favourite wife, and a slave with a casket of his most valuable jewels, fled in disguise.

A boat had been prepared, and lay in readiness at the wharf of the palace. Rowing day and night against the stream, the boat reached Rajmahal, ninety miles distant, on the night of the fourth day following his flight. Here the rowers were so knocked up, by their exertions, that it was impossible to proceed further; and they took refuge in a deserted hut, by the bank.

The following morning, however, they were seen by a fakir, whose ears the young tyrant had had cut off, thirteen months previously; and this man, recognizing the nabob even in his disguise, at once took the news to Meer Jaffier's brother, who happened to reside in the town. The latter immediately sent a party of his retainers, who captured the nabob without difficulty. He was again placed in the boat, and taken back to Moorshedabad, where he was led into the presence of Meer Jaffier.

The wretched young man implored the mercy of his triumphant successor, the man who owed station and rank and wealth to his grandfather; and who had, nevertheless, betrayed him to the English. His entreaties so far moved Meer Jaffier that he was irresolute, for a time, as to the course he should pursue. His son, however, Mirav, a youth of about the same age as the deposed nabob, insisted that it was folly to show mercy; as Meer Jaffier would never be safe, so long as Suraja Dowlah remained alive; and his father, at last, assigned the captive to his keeping, knowing well what the result would be.

In the night, Suraja Dowlah was murdered. His mangled remains were, in the morning, placed on an elephant, and exposed to the gaze of the populace and soldiery.

Suraja Dowlah was undoubtedly a profligate and rapacious tyrant. In the course of a few months, he alienated his people, and offended a great number of his most powerful chiefs. The war which he undertook against the English, although at the moment unprovoked, must still be regarded as a patriotic one; and, had he not soiled his victory by the massacre of the prisoners, which he first permitted and then approved, the English would have had no just cause of complaint against him.

From the day of the arrival of Clive at Calcutta, he was doomed. It is certain that the nabob would not have remained faithful to his engagements, when the danger which wrung the concessions from him had passed. Nevertheless, the whole of the circumstances which followed the signature of the treaty, the manner in which the unhappy youth was alternately cajoled and bullied to his ruin, the loathsome treachery in which those around him engaged, with the connivance of the English; and, lastly, the murder in cold blood, which Meer Jaffier, our creature, was allowed to perpetrate; rendered the whole transaction one of the blackest in the annals of English history.

Chapter 24

MOUNTED INFANTRY

A few days after Plassey, Colonel Clive sent for Charlie.

'Marryat,' he said, 'I must send you back, with two hundred men, to Madras. The governor there has been writing to me, by every ship which has come up the coast, begging me to move down with the bulk of the force, as soon as affairs are a little settled here. That is out of the question. There are innumerable matters to be arranged. Meer Jaffier must be sustained. The French under Law must be driven entirely out of Bengal. The Dutch must be dealt with. Altogether, I have need of every moment of my time, and of every man under my orders, for at least two years.

'However, I shall at once raise a Bengal native army, and so release the Sepoys of Madras. If there be any special and sore need, I must, of course, denude myself here of troops, to succour Madras; but I hope it will not come to that. In the meantime, I propose that you shall take back two hundred of the Madras Europeans. Lawrence will be glad to have you, and your chances of fighting are greater there than they will be here. Bengal is overawed, and so long as I maintain the force I now have, it is unlikely in the extreme to rise; whereas battles and sieges, great and small, are the normal condition of Madras.'

The next day Charlie, with two hundred European troops, marched down towards Calcutta. Clive had told him to select any officer he pleased to accompany him, as second in command; and he chose Peters, who, seeing that there were likely to be far more exciting times in Madras than in Bengal at present, was very glad to accompany him. Three days after reaching Calcutta, Charlie and his party embarked on board a ship, which conveyed them without adventure to Madras.

The authorities were glad, indeed, of the reinforcement; for the country was disturbed from end to end. Since the departure of every available man for Calcutta, the Company had been able to afford but little aid to Muhammud Ali, and the authority of the latter had dwindled to a mere shadow, in the Carnatic. The Mahrattas made incursions in all directions. The minor chiefs revolted and refused to pay tribute, and many of them entered into alliance with the French. Disorder everywhere reigned in the Carnatic, and Trichinopoli was, again, the one place which Muhammud Ali held.

The evening after landing, Charlie Marryat had a long chat with Colonel Lawrence; who, after explaining to him exactly the condition of affairs in the country, asked him to tell him, frankly, what command he would like to receive.

'I have thought for some time,' Charlie said, 'that the establishment of a small force of really efficient cavalry, trained to act as infantry, also, would be invaluable. The Mahratta horsemen, by their rapid movements, set our infantry in defiance; and the native horse of our allies are useless against them. I am convinced that two hundred horsemen, trained and drilled like our cavalry at home, would ride through any number of them. In a country like this, where every petty rajah has his castle, cavalry alone could, however, do little. They must be able to act as infantry, and should have a couple of little four-pounders to take about with them. A force like this would do more to keep order in the Carnatic than one composed of infantry, alone, of ten times its strength. It could act as a police force, call upon petty chiefs who refuse to pay their share of the revenue, restore order in disturbed places, and permit the peasants to carry on their agricultural work, upon which the revenue of the Company depends; and, altogether, render valuable services.

'Among the soldiers who came down with me is a sergeant who was at one time a trooper in an English regiment. He exchanged to come out with the 39th to India, and has again exchanged into the Company's service. I would make him drill instructor, if you will give him a commission as ensign. Peters I should like as my second in command; and, if you approve of the plan, I should be very much obliged if you would get him his step as captain. He's a good officer, but has not had such luck as I have.'

Colonel Lawrence was very much pleased at the idea, and gave Charlie full authority to carry it out. The work of enlistment at once commenced. Hossein made an excellent recruiting sergeant. He went into the native bazaars; and by telling of the exploits of Charlie at Ambur and Suwarndrug, and holding out bright prospects of the plunder which such a force would be likely to obtain, he succeeded in recruiting a hundred and fifty of his co-religionists. In those days, fighting was a trade in India; and in addition to the restless spirits of the local communities, great numbers of the hardy natives of northern India, Afghans, Pathans, and others, were scattered over India, ever ready to enlist in the service of the highest bidder. Among such men as these, Hossein had no difficulty in obtaining a hundred and fifty picked horsemen.

Charlie had determined that his force should consist of four troops, each of fifty strong. Of these, one would be composed of Europeans, and he was permitted to take this number from the party he had brought down. He had no difficulty in obtaining volunteers, for as soon as the nature of the force was known, the men were eager to engage in it. To this troop, the two little field pieces would be committed.

A few days after the scheme had been sanctioned, Ensign Anstey was at work drilling the recruits as cavalry. Charlie and Peters were instructed by him, also, in the drill and words of command, and were soon able to assist. Two months were spent in severe work and, at the end of that time, the little regiment were able to execute all simple cavalry manoeuvres with steadiness and regularity. The natives were all men who had lived on horseback from their youth, and therefore required no teaching to ride.

They were also, at the end of that time, able to act as infantry, with as much regularity as the ordinary Sepoys. When so engaged, four horses were held by one man, so that a hundred and fifty men were available for fighting on foot.

The work had been unusually severe, but as the officers did not spare themselves, and Charlie had promised a present to each man of the troop, when fit for service, they had worked with alacrity, and had taken great interest in learning their new duties. At the end of two months, they were inspected by Colonel Lawrence and Governor

Pigot, and both expressed their highest gratification and surprise at their efficiency, and anticipated great benefits would arise from the organization.

So urgent, indeed, was the necessity that something should be done for the restoration of order, that Charlie had with difficulty obtained the two months necessary to attain the degree of perfection which he deemed necessary.

The day after the inspection, the troop marched out from Madras. Ensign Anstey commanded the white troop, the other three were led by native officers. Captain Peters commanded the squadron composed of the white troop and one of the others. A Lieutenant Hallowes, whom Peters knew to be a hard working and energetic officer, was, at Charlie's request, appointed to the command of the other squadron. He himself commanded the whole.

They had been ordered, in the first place, to move to Arcot, which was held by a garrison of Muhammud Ali. The whole of the country around was greatly disturbed. French intrigues, and the sight of the diminished power of the English, had caused most of the minor chiefs in that neighbourhood to throw off their allegiance. A body of Mahratta horse were ravaging the country districts; and it was against these that Charlie determined, in the first place, to act.

He had been permitted to have his own way in the clothing and arming of his force. Each man carried a musket, which had been shortened some six inches, and hung in slings from the saddle, the muzzle resting in a piece of leather, technically termed a bucket. The ammunition pouch was slung on the other side of the saddle, and could be fastened in an instant, by two straps, to the belts which the troopers wore round their waists. The men were dressed in brown, thick cotton cloth, called karkee. Round their black forage caps was wound a long length of blue and white cotton cloth, forming a turban, with the ends hanging down to protect the back of the neck and spine from the sun.

Having obtained news that the Mahratta horse, two thousand strong, were pillaging at a distance of six miles from the town, Charlie set off the day following his arrival to meet them. The Mahrattas had notice of his coming; but hearing that the force consisted only of two hundred horse, they regarded it with contempt.

When Charlie first came upon them they were in the open country; and, seeing that they were prepared to attack him, he drew up his little force in two lines. The second line he ordered to dismount, to act as infantry. The two guns were loaded with grape, and the men of the first line were drawn up at sufficient intervals to allow an infantryman to pass between each horse.

With shouts of anticipated triumph, the Mahratta horse swept down. The front line of English horsemen had screened the movements of those behind, and when the enemy were within fifty yards, Charlie gave the word. The troopers already sat, musket in hand, and between each horse an infantry soldier now stepped forward; while towards each end, the line opened and the two field pieces were advanced.

The Mahratta horsemen were astonished at this sudden manoeuvre; but, pressed by the mass from behind, they still continued their charge. When but fifteen yards from the English line, a stream of fire ran along this, from end to end. Every musket was emptied into the advancing force, while the guns on either flank swept them with grape.

The effect was tremendous. Scarcely a man of the front line survived the fire, and the whole mass halted, and recoiled in confusion. Before they could recover themselves, another volley of shot and grape was fired into them. Then Charlie's infantry ran back; and the cavalry, closing up, dashed upon the foe, followed half a minute afterwards by the lately dismounted men of the other two troops; ten white soldiers, alone, remaining to work and guard the guns.

The effect of the charge of these two hundred disciplined horse, upon the already disorganized mob of Mahratta horsemen, was irresistible; and in a few minutes the Mahrattas were scattered, and in full flight over the plain, pursued by the British cavalry, now broken up into eight half troops. The rout was complete, and in a very short time the last Mahratta had fled, leaving behind them three hundred dead upon the plain.

Greatly gratified with their success; and feeling confident, now, in their own powers, the British force returned to Arcot.

Charlie now determined to attack the fort of Vellore, which was regarded as impregnable. The town lay at the foot of some very steep and rugged hills, which were surmounted by three detached forts. The rajah, encouraged by the French, had renounced his allegiance to Muhammud Ali, and had declared himself independent. As, however, it was certain that he was prepared to give assistance to the French, when they took the field against the English, Charlie determined to attack the place.

The French had received large reinforcements, and had already captured many forts and strong places, around Pondicherry. They were, however, awaiting the arrival of still larger forces, known to be on the way, before they made a decisive and, as they hoped, final attack upon the English.

The rajah's army consisted of some fifteen hundred infantry, and as many cavalry. These advanced to meet the English force. Charlie feigned a retreat, as they came on; and retired to a village, some thirty miles distant. The cavalry pursued at full speed, leaving the infantry behind.

Upon reaching the village, Charlie at once dismounted all his men, lined the inclosures, and received the enemy's cavalry, as they galloped up, with so heavy a fire that they speedily drew rein. After trying for some time to force the position, they began to fall back, and the English force again mounted, dashed upon them, and completed their defeat. The broken horsemen, as they rode across the plain, met their infantry advancing; and these, disheartened at the defeat of the cavalry, fell back in great haste; and, abandoning the town, which was without fortification, retired at once to the forts commanding it.

Charlie took possession of the town, and spent the next two days in reconnoitering the forts. The largest, and nearest, of these faced the right of the town. It was called Suzarow. The second, on an even steeper hill, was called Guzarow. The third, which lay some distance behind this, and was much smaller, was called Mortz Azur.

Charlie determined to attempt, in the first place, to carry Guzarow; as in this, which was considered the most inaccessible, the rajah himself had taken up his position, having with him all his treasure. Charlie saw that it would be next to impossible, with so small a force, to carry it by a direct attack, by the road which led to it, as this was completely covered by its guns. It appeared to him, however, that the rocks upon which it stood were, by no means, inaccessible.

He left twenty men to guard his guns, placed a guard of ten upon the road leading up to the fort, to prevent the inhabitants from sending up news of his intentions to the garrison, who had, with that of Suzarow, kept up a fire from their guns upon the town, since his arrival there. The moon was not to rise until eleven o'clock, and at nine Charlie marched, with a hundred and seventy men, from the town. Making a considerable detour, he found himself, at half past ten, at the foot of the rocks, rising almost sheer from the upper part of the hill.

He was well provided with ropes and ladders. The most perfect silence had been enjoined upon the men and, in the darkness, the march had been unseen by the enemy. While waiting for the moon to rise, the troopers all wound pieces of cloth, with which they had come provided, round their boots, to prevent these from making a noise, by slipping or stumbling on the rocks.

When the moon rose, the ascent of the rocks began at the point which Charlie had, after a close inspection through a telescope, judged to be most accessible. The toil was very severe. One by one, the men climbed from ledge to ledge, some of the most active hill men, from northern India, leading the way, and aiding their comrades to follow them, by lowering ropes, and placing ladders at the most inaccessible spots. All this time, they were completely hidden from the observation of the garrison, above.

At last, the leaders of the party stood at the foot of the walls, which rose a few feet from the edge of the cliff. The operation had been performed almost noiselessly. The ammunition pouches had been left behind, each man carrying ten rounds in his belt. Every piece of metal had been carefully removed from their uniforms, the very buttons having been cut off, lest these should strike against the rocks; and the muskets had been swathed up in thick coverings.

The men, as they gained the upper ridge, spread along at the foot of the walls, until the whole body had gathered there. They could hear the voices of the sentries, thirty feet above them; but these, having no idea of the vicinity of an enemy, did not look over the edge of the wall. Indeed, the parapets of the Indian fortifications were always so high, that it was only from projecting towers that the foot of the wall could be seen.

When the English force were assembled, the ladders, which, like everything else, had been muffled, were placed against the walls; and, headed by their officers, the troops ascended. The surprise was complete. Not until the leaders of the storming party stood upon the parapet was their presence perceived. The guards discharged their firelocks, and fled hastily.

As soon as twenty men were collected on the wall, Charlie took the command of these, and hurried forward towards the gate. Hallowes was to lead the next party along the opposite direction. Peters was to form the rest up, as they gained the wall, and to follow Charlie with fifty more; while Anstey was to hold the remainder in reserve, to be used as circumstances might demand.

The resistance, however, was slight. Taken absolutely by surprise, the enemy rushed out from their sleeping places. They were immediately fired upon from the walls. The greater part ran back into shelter, while some of the more determined, gathering together, made for the gate. But of this Charlie had already taken possession, and received them with so vigorous a fire that they speedily fell back.

When the whole circuit of the walls was in his possession, Charlie took a hundred of his men, and descended into the fort. Each building, as he reached it, was searched; and the garrison it contained made to come out, and lay down their arms, and were then allowed to depart through the gate.

Upon reaching the rajah's quarters, he at once came out and surrendered himself. Two guns were discharged, to inform the little body in the town of the complete success of the movement; and the guard on the road then fell back, and joined the party with the guns.

Thus, without losing a man, the fort of Guzarow, regarded by the natives as being impregnable, was carried. Fifteen lacs of rupees were found in the treasury. Of these, in accordance with the rules of the service, half was set aside for the Company, the remainder became the property of the force. Of this half fell to the officers, in proportion to their rank, and the rest was divided among the men. The share of each trooper amounted to nearly two hundred pounds.

Knowing how demoralizing the possession of such a sum would be, Charlie assembled his force next morning. He pointed out to them that, as the greater part of the plunder was in silver, it would be impossible for them to carry it on their persons. He advised them, then, to allow the whole sum to remain in the treasury, to be forwarded under an escort to Madras; each soldier to receive an order, for the amount of his share, upon the treasury there. This was agreed to, unanimously, and Charlie then turned his attention to the other forts.

The guns of Guzarow were turned against these, and a bombardment commenced. Suzarow, which extended partly down the slope, was much exposed to the fire from Guzarow; and although no damage could be done to the walls at so great a distance, the garrison, suffering from the fire, and intimidated by the fall of Guzarow, lost heart. Large numbers deserted, and the governor, in the course of two days, thought it prudent to obey the orders which the rajah had, upon being made captive, sent to him to surrender. The next day the governor of Mortz Azur followed his example; and Vellore, and its three strong forts, were thus in the possession of the English.

At Vellore, Charlie nearly lost one of his faithful followers. Early in the morning, Hossein came into Charlie's room.

'Sahib,' he said, 'something is the matter with Tim.'

'What is the matter?' Charlie said, sitting up in his bed.

'I do not know, sahib. When I went to him, he did not move. He was wide awake, and his eyes are staring. When I went beside him, he shook his head a little, and said, "S-s-s-h." He seems quite rigid, and is as pale as death.'

Charlie leaped out, and hurried to Tim. The latter was lying on the ground, in the next room. He had carried off three or four cushions, from the rajah's divan, and had thrown these down, and had spread a rug over him. He lay on his back, exactly as Hossein had described.

As Charlie hurried up, Tim again gave vent to the warning 'S-s-s-h.'

'What is the matter, Tim? What is the matter, my poor fellow?'

Tim made a slight motion, with his head, for his master to bend towards him. Charlie leant over him, and he whispered:

'There is a sarpent in bed with me.'

'Are you quite sure, Tim?'

'He woke me with his cold touch,' Tim whispered. 'I felt him crawling against my foot, and now he is laying against my leg.'

Charlie drew back for a minute, and consulted with Hossein.

'Lie quite still, Tim,' he said, 'and don't be afraid. We will try to kill him, without his touching you; but even if he should bite you, with help ready at hand, there will be no danger.'

Charlie now procured two knives; the one a sharp surgical knife, from a case which he had brought; the other he placed in a charcoal fire, which one of the men speedily fanned, until the blade had attained a white heat. Charlie had decided that, if the snake bit Tim, he would instantly make a deep cut through the line of the puncture of the fangs, cutting down as low as these could penetrate, and immediately cauterize it, by placing the hot knife in the gash so made. Six men were called in, with orders to seize Tim on the instant, and hold his leg firm, to enable the operation to be performed. Two others were to occupy themselves with the snake. These were armed with sticks.

Hossein now approached the bed, from which, hitherto, they had all kept well aloof. The snake, Tim said, lay against his leg, between the knee and the ankle, and the spot was marked by a slight elevation of the rug.

Hossein drew his tulwar, examined the edge to see that nothing had blunted its razor-like keenness, and then took his stand at the foot of the bed. Twice he raised his weapon; and then let it fall, with a drawing motion. The keen blade cut through the rug, as if it had been pasteboard; and, at the same instant, Tim sprang from the other side of the bed, and fainted in the arms of the men. Hossein threw off the rug, and there, severed in pieces, lay the writhing body of a huge cobra.

Tim soon recovered, under the administration of water sprinkled in his face, and brandy poured down his throat. But he was some time, ere he thoroughly recovered from the effects of the trying ordeal through which he had passed. Many of the buildings in the fort were in a very bad condition, and Charlie had several of the most dilapidated destroyed, finding in their walls several colonies of cobras, which were all killed by the troops.

Chapter 25

BESIEGED IN A PAGODA

A few days later Charlie received a message from the Rajah of Permacoil, saying that he was besieged by a strong native force, aided by the French. He at once moved his force to his assistance. He found that the besiegers, among whom were two hundred French troops, were too strong to be attacked. He therefore established himself in their rear, attacked and captured convoys, and prevented the country people from bringing in provisions. Several times the besieging infantry advanced against him, but before these he at once fell back, only to return as soon as they retired to their camp. Whenever their horse ventured out against him, he beat them back, with considerable loss.

Ten days after his arrival, the enemy, finding it impossible to maintain themselves in the face of so active an enemy, and suffering greatly from want of provisions, raised the siege and fell back.

As soon as they had drawn off, Charlie entered the fort. The rajah received him with the greatest warmth. He was, however, much distressed at the capture of a hill fort, at some distance from Permacoil. In this he had stowed his wives and treasure, thinking that it would be unmolested. The French, however, had, just before Charlie's arrival, detached a strong force with some guns, and these had captured the place. The force which had accomplished this had, he now heard, marched to Trinavody, a fort and town thirty miles away, upon the road by which the force which had besieged the town was retiring. The treasure was a considerable one, amounting to seven lacs of rupees, and as the rajah stated his willingness that the troops should take possession of this, if they could but rescue his women, Charlie at once determined to attempt the feat.

The main body of the enemy would not reach the place, until the afternoon of the following day. Charlie soon collected his men and, making a detour through the country, arrived next morning within a mile of Trinavody.

The town was a small one, and the fort one of the ordinary native forts, built in a parallelogram with flanking towers. The place, however, contained a very large and solidly built pagoda or temple. It was surrounded by a wall, forty feet high; and at the gateway stood an immense tower, with terraces rising one above the other.

Capturing a native, Charlie learnt that the fort was tenanted only by the troops of the native rajah of the place, the French detachment being encamped in the pagoda. He at once rode forward with his troops, dashed through the native town, and in through the wide gateway of the tower, into the courtyard within. Beyond two or three straggling shots from the sentries, he had so far encountered no opposition, and the native troops in the courtyard, thrown into wild confusion by this sudden appearance of a hostile force, threw down their arms and cried for mercy. From the temple within, however, the French infantry, a hundred strong, opened a brisk fire.

Charlie sent some of his men on to the tower, whence their fire commanded the flat roof of the temple, and these speedily drove the defenders from that post. The field pieces were unlimbered, and directed towards the gate of the inner temple, while a musketry fire was kept up against every window and loophole in the building. The gate gave way after a few shots had been fired, and Charlie led his party to the assault.

The French defended themselves bravely, but they were outnumbered and were driven, fighting, from room to room, until the survivors laid down their arms. The assault, however, had cost the British a loss of twenty-five men.

The Rajah of Permacoil's treasure, and his women, fell into the hands of the captors. Charlie ordered the chests to be brought down, and placed in bullock waggons. Just as he was about to order his men, who were scattered through the temple looting, to form up, he heard a shout from the tower; and, looking up, saw one of his men there gesticulating wildly. He ran up the tower, and on reaching the first terrace saw, to his surprise, the whole of the force which he believed to be fifteen miles distant, already entering the town.

The French officer in command, knowing the activity and dash of his opponent, and fearing that an attempt might be made to carry Trinavody and recapture the rajah's treasure, had marched all night. When within a mile of the place, he heard what had happened, and at once pushed forward.

Charlie saw that, already, his retreat was cut off; and, running to the edge of the terrace, shouted to Peters to hurry out with all the men already in the courtyard, to occupy the houses outside the gate, and to keep back the advancing enemy. Summoning another party to the tower, four guns upon the terrace were at once loaded, and these opened upon the head of the enemy's column, as they entered the street leading to the temple.

In a short time, a brisk fight began. The enemy planted guns to bear upon the tower. The cannon of the fort joined in the assault, the infantry pressed forward through the houses and inclosures to the temple, and were soon engaged with the men under Captain Peters, while the guns and musketry from the tower also opened upon them.

Having seen that the preparations to repulse an immediate attack were complete, Charlie again ran down to the courtyard. The weak point of the defences was the gateway. This was fifty feet wide, and unprovided with gates; and Charlie at once set a strong party to work, to form a barricade across it.

For some hours, the party outside the gates maintained their position, but they were gradually driven back; and towards evening, by Charlie's orders, they retired within the temple. The barricade was now eight feet high. The face was formed of large slabs of stone, piled one upon another, backed by a considerable thickness of earthwork. This, however, although capable of resisting a sudden rush of infantry, would, Charlie knew, be incapable of resisting artillery.

During the night, he divided his men in two parties, which alternately slept and worked at the inner defences which he had designed. These consisted of two walls, running from each side of the gateway to the temple. They were placed a few feet farther back than the edge of the gateway, so that an enemy advancing to the storm would not see them, until within the gate. These walls he intended to be eight feet high; and to be backed with earth, four feet high, so as to form a bank on which the defenders could stand, and fire into the space between them. To obtain materials, he pulled down several buildings forming a part of the temple. The distance from the gateway to the temple was fifty yards, and although the men worked without ceasing, the wall had made but little progress when daylight dawned.

During the night, Charlie lowered one of his men from the wall farthest from the enemy; with instructions to make his way, as fast as possible, to Madras to ask for succour. In the morning, Charlie found that the enemy had, on their side, been also busy. A house, which faced the end of the street leading to the temple, had been pulled down; and a battery of four guns erected there.

As soon as it was light, the combat began. The enemy had sixteen pieces of artillery, besides those on the fort; and while the four guns in front played unceasingly upon the barricade across the gateway, the others cannonaded the tower, whence the English guns kept up a fire on the battery in front. So well were these directed, and so heavy was the musketry, that the enemy's guns were several times silenced, and the artillerymen driven from them.

Behind the barricade, a working party threw up fresh earth, to strengthen the part most shaken by the enemy's fire, and then set to work to form a similar barricade, in a line with the back of the gateway. This was completed by nightfall, by which time the enemy's guns had completely shattered the stone facing of the outer barricade, rendering it possible for it to be carried with a rush. As, from the windows of the houses, they could see the new work behind it; they would, Charlie judged, not attempt an assault, until this also was destroyed.

During the night, large quantities of fresh earth were piled on the outer barricade, which was now useful as forming a screen to that behind it from the guns. All night the work at the parallel walls continued, and by morning these had reached a height of three feet.

During the next two days the fight continued, without much advantage on either side. Each day the enemy's guns shattered the outer barricade, but this was as regularly repaired at night, in spite of the heavy artillery and matchlock fire which they kept up towards the spot.

On the fourth day the enemy pulled down a house, standing just in the rear of their battery, and Charlie found that behind it they had erected another. It was a solidly built work, of fifteen feet in height, and the enemy must have laboured continuously at it, every night. It had a strong and high parapet, of sandbags, protecting the gunners from the musketry fire of the tower. The muzzles of four guns projected through embrasures, which had been left for them, and these opened fire over the heads of the gunners in the lower battery.

In spite of the efforts of the besieged, the enemy kept up so heavy a fire that, by the afternoon, the inner as well as the outer barricade was knocked to pieces. By this time, however, the inner walls were completed, and the English awaited the storm with confidence. The doorway of the temple had been closed, and blocked up behind; but the doors had been shattered to pieces, by the shot which had passed through the gateway, and the entrance now stood open.

Inside the temple, out of the line of fire, Charlie had the two little field pieces, each crammed to the muzzle with bullets, placed in readiness to fire. The lower floor of the tower had been pierced, above the gateway, and here two huge caldrons filled with boiling lead, stripped from the roof, stood ready for action.

At three in the afternoon, after a furious cannonade, the fire of the enemy's battery suddenly ceased. They had formed communications between the houses, on either side of the street; and, at the signal, the troops poured out from these in large bodies, and rushed to the assault.

The guns from the tower, which had been awaiting the moment, poured showers of grape among them; but, believing that the temple now lay at their mercy, the enemy did not hesitate, but rushed at the gateway.

Not a shot was fired, as they entered. Scrambling over the remains of the two barricades, the enemy poured with exulting shouts into the courtyard. Then those in front hesitated. On either hand, as far as the doorway of the temple, extended a massive wall, eight feet high; roughly built, certainly, but far too strong to be battered down, too steep to be scaled. They would have retreated, but they were driven forward by the mass which poured in through the gateway behind them; and, seeing that their only safety was in victory, they pressed forward again.

Not a defender showed himself, until the head of the column had reached a point two-thirds of the distance across the courtyard. Then suddenly, on either side, the wall was lined by the British, who at once opened a tremendous fire on the mass below. At the same moment, the guns were run into the doorway, and poured their contents into the struggling mass.

Pent up between the walls, unable to return the fire poured down upon them, with lanes torn through them by the discharge of the cannon, the greater portion of the mass strove to turn and retire. The officer in command, a gallant Frenchman, called upon the survivors of the fifty French infantry, who had led the attack, to follow him; and rushed forward upon the guns. Here, however, Charlie had posted his Europeans, and these, swarming out from the temple, poured a volley into the advancing French, and then charged them with the bayonet.

The pressure from behind had now ceased. Streams of boiling lead, poured through the holes above the archway, had effectually checked the advance; and through this molten shower, the shattered remnants of the assaulting column now fled for their lives, leaving two hundred and fifty of their best men dead behind them.

As the last of the column issued out, the guns of the battery again angrily opened fire. As Charlie had anticipated, the enemy, finding how strong were the inner defences, abandoned all further idea of attack by the gateway; and, leaving only two guns there to prevent a sortie, placed their whole artillery on the western side of the pagoda, and opened fire to prepare a breach there.

For a week the siege continued, and then Charlie determined to evacuate the place. The rajah's treasure was made up into small sacks, which were fastened to the horses' croups. Had it not been for these animals, he would have defended the place to the last, confident in his power to devise fresh means to repel fresh assaults. The store of forage, however, collected by the enemy for their own use in the temple, was now exhausted. Charlie directed Peters, with twenty men, to sally out from the gate at midnight, to enter the nearest house on the right hand side, and to follow the communications made by the enemy before the assault, until they came to the end of the street. Lieutenant Hallowes, with a similar party, was to take the left side. If they found any guards within the houses, they were to overpower these; and, rushing straight on, to attack the battery, and spike the guns. Should they find the houses deserted, they were to gather in the houses nearest the battery, when Peters was to fire his pistol as a signal to Hallowes, and both parties were to attack the battery.

One of the inner walls had been pulled down, and the main body of the force, having the wounded and the ladies of the rajah's zenana in their centre, were to sally out, the instant the guns were taken.

The plan was carried out with the greatest success. The houses on both sides of the street were found to be deserted, and as Peters fired his pistol, the party dashed at the flanks of the battery. The French gunners leaped to their feet and, believing that they were attacked in front, discharged their cannon. The grapeshot swept along the empty street, and through the gateway; and Charlie, leading one of the troops, at once dashed down the street.

At their first rush, Peters and Hallowes had carried the battery, cutting down the gunners. Immediately behind, however, the enemy had posted a support, several hundred strong, and these speedily advanced to recover the battery.

Leaving their horses in the charge of a small party, Charlie dismounted his men and joined Peters, and his fire quickly checked the assault. In the meantime, the rest of the defenders of the temple rode down the street and, leaving a few men with the horses of Peters' and Hallowes' detachments, rode out into the open country. After driving back his assailants, Charlie led his party back to their horses, mounted them, and speedily rejoined the main body. An hour later they were well on their way towards Permacoil, which they reached, next day.

The rajah was delighted at recovering his family. The treasure was divided, and the portion belonging to the troops was, with the Company's share, sent down under a strong escort to Madras.

For a considerable time, Charlie's force were occupied with small undertakings. Lally had now arrived, from France, and had taken the command. He had, at his orders, a European force considerably exceeding any that had hitherto been gathered in India, and he boasted that he was going to capture Madras, and drive the English out of

India. Nothing could have been more unfortunate for the French than the choice of such a man, and his appointment was destined to give the last blow to French influence in India, as the supercession of Dupleix had given the first.

Monsieur Lally had one virtue. He was personally brave; but he was arrogant, passionate, and jealous. He had no capacity, whatever, for either awing or conciliating those with whom he came in contact. He treated the natives with open contempt, and was soon as much hated, by them, as by his own soldiers.

His first step had been to order Bussy down, from Hyderabad, with the whole of his force. Bussy, a man of great genius, of extreme tact, of perfect knowledge of the Indian character; had, for eight years, maintained French influence supreme at that court, and had acquired for France the Northern Sirkars, a splendid and most valuable province, on the seacoast north of Madras. Salabut Jung, the ruler of Hyderabad, the protege of the French, heard with dismay the order which Bussy had received. To Bussy himself, the blow was a heavy one, and he saw that his departure would entail the ruin of the edifice of French influence, which he had built up by so many years of thought and toil.

However, he obeyed at once; and marched, with two hundred and fifty Europeans and five hundred native troops, into the Sirkars. He made over the charge of this treaty to the Marquis de Conflans, whom, although but just arrived from Europe, and entirely new to Indian affairs, Count de Lally had sent to replace Monsieur Moracin, who had, for years, ably managed the province. He then marched, with his troops, to join the main army under Count de Lally.

This force, having taken Fort Saint David, had operated against Tanjore, where it had suffered a repulse. The news of this reached the Northern Sirkars, soon after the departure of Bussy; and Anandraz, the most powerful chief of the country, rose in rebellion, and sent a messenger to Calcutta, begging the assistance of the English to drive out the French.

While the rest of the Bengal council, seeing that Bengal was, at the time, threatened with invasion from the north, and menaced with troubles within, considered that it would be an act little short of madness to send troops, at a time when they could be so little spared, to assist a chief, who, even from his own accounts, was only able to raise three thousand irregular followers, Clive thought otherwise. He saw the great value of the Northern Sirkars, whose possession would complete the line of British territory, along the seacoast, from Calcutta down to Madras. He saw, too, that a movement here would effect a diversion, in favour of Madras. The situation there appeared very serious, and he could spare no troops which would suffice to turn the scale. But even should Madras be lost, the gain of the Northern Sirkars would almost compensate for the disaster.

Having gained the council to his views, he sent Lieutenant Colonel Forde, who commanded the Company's troops in Bengal, with five hundred Europeans, two thousand natives, and six six-pounders, by sea to Vizagapatam, a port which Anandraz had seized. These landed on the 20th of October, 1758.

Had Conflans been an efficient officer, he could have crushed Anandraz long before the arrival of the English. He had, under his orders, a force composed of five hundred European troops, men trained by Bussy, and accustomed to victory; four thousand native troops, and a brigade of artillery. Instead of marching at once to crush the rebellion, he sent messenger after messenger to Lally, begging for assistance. It was only when he heard, from Lally, that he had directed Moracin, with three hundred European troops, to support him, that he moved against Anandraz.

His opportunity had, however, slipped from his hands. He had thrown away six weeks; and when, upon the march, the news reached him of the landing of the English, he took up the very strong position within sight of the fort Peddapur, and intrenched himself there.

Clive had sent to Madras the news that he was despatching Colonel Forde to the Sirkars, and begged that any body of troops who might be available might be forwarded. Charlie's corps had already been recalled towards Madras, to keep the bodies of French who were converging in that direction at a distance, as long as possible, so as to allow the victualling of Madras to go on uninterrupted. Mr. Pigot now instructed Charlie to hand over the command of that force to Peters; and, with fifty men, to make his way north and to effect a junction with Forde, who was entirely deficient in cavalry.

Avoiding the French force, Charlie reached Vizagapatam upon the 2nd of December, and found that Forde had marched on the previous day. He started at once, and on the evening of the 3rd came up to Forde, who had arrived in sight of the French position.

Charlie had already made the acquaintance of Colonel Forde in Bengal, and Forde was glad to obtain the assistance, and advice, of an officer who had seen so much service. An hour after arriving, Charlie rode out with his commander and reconnoitred the French position; which was, they concluded, too strong to be attacked. In point of numbers, the forces were about even. Conflans had, in addition to his five hundred Europeans, six thousand native infantry, five hundred native cavalry, and thirty guns. Forde had four hundred and seventy Europeans, one thousand nine hundred Sepoys, and six guns. Anandraz had forty Europeans, five thousand infantry, five hundred horsemen, and four guns. These five thousand men were, however, a mere ragged mob, of whom very few had firearms, and the rest were armed with bows and arrows. His horsemen were equally worthless, and Forde could only rely upon the troops he had brought with him from Calcutta, and the troop of fifty natives under Charlie Marryat.

Finding that the French position was too strong to be attacked, Forde fell back to a strong position at Chambol, a village nearly four miles from the French camp. Here, for four days, the two armies remained watching each other, the leaders of both sides considering that the position of the other was too strong to be attacked.

Chapter 26

THE SIEGE OF MADRAS

At last, weary of inactivity, the Marquis de Conflans and Colonel Forde arrived simultaneously, on the 8th of December, at a determination to bring matters to a crisis. Conflans had heard, from a deserter, that Forde had omitted to occupy a mound which, at a short distance from his camp, commanded the position. He determined to seize this during the night, and to open fire with his guns, and that his main army should take advantage of the confusion, which the sudden attack would occasion, to fall upon the English. Forde, on his part, had determined to march at four o'clock in the morning to a village named Condore, three miles distant, whence he could threaten the French flank.

Ignorant of each other's intentions, the English and French left their camps at night. Forde marched at a quarter past four, as arranged with Anandraz; but the rajah and his people, with the usual native aversion to punctuality, remained quietly asleep, and a few minutes after daybreak they were roughly awakened, by a deadly fire poured by six guns into the camp. The rajah sent messenger after messenger to Forde, urging him to return; and he himself, with his frightened army, hurried towards Condore. Forde had, indeed, retraced his steps immediately he heard the fire of the guns, and soon met the rajah's rabble in full flight; and, uniting with them, marched back to Condore.

Conflans supposed that the fire of his guns had driven the whole of his opponents in a panic from Chambol; and, determining to take advantage of the confusion, marched with his force against them. Forde at once prepared for the battle. In the centre he placed the English, including the rajah's forty Europeans. Next to these, on either side, he placed his Sepoys, and posted the troops of Anandraz on the right and left flanks. He then advanced towards the enemy.

The French guns opened fire. Forde halted. In the position in which he found himself, his centre occupied a field of Indian corn, so high that they were concealed from the enemy. Conflans had moved towards the English left, with the intention, apparently, of turning that flank; and after the artillery battle on both sides had continued for forty minutes, he ordered his troops to advance.

In Madras, both the English and French dress their Sepoys in white. In Bengal, however, since the raising of Sepoy regiments after the recapture of Calcutta, the English had clothed them in red. Conflans, therefore, thought that the force he was about to attack was the English contingent; and that, if he could defeat this, the rout of his enemy would be secured. The French advanced with great rapidity, and attacked the Sepoys in front and flank, so vigorously that they broke in disorder. The rajah's troops fled instantly; and, in spite of the exhortations of Forde, the Sepoys presently followed their example, and fled with the rajah's troops to Chambol, pursued by the enemy's horse.

They would have suffered even more severely than they did, in this pursuit, had not Charlie Marryat launched his little squadron at the enemy's horse. Keeping his men well together, he made repeated charges, several times riding through and through them; until at last they desisted from the pursuit and, forming in a compact body, fell back towards the field of battle; Charlie, who had already lost twelve men, not thinking it prudent again to attack so strong a force.

Conflans' easy success over the Sepoys was fatal to him. Believing that he had defeated the English, he gave orders to several companies of the French troops to press on in pursuit, without delay. They started off in hot speed, proceeding without much order or regularity, when they were suddenly confronted by the whole line of English troops, in solid order, advancing from the high corn to take the place lately occupied by the Sepoys. In vain, the scattered and surprised companies of the French endeavoured to reform, and make head against them. So heavy was the fire of musketry opened by the British line, immediately they had taken up their position, that the French broke their ranks, and ran back as fast as they could to regain their guns, which were fully half a mile in the rear.

In the meantime, the French Sepoys on their left had been gradually driving back the English right; but Forde, disregarding this, pressed forward in hot pursuit of the French with his English, behind whom the greater portion of the beaten Sepoys had already rallied. Keeping his men well together, he advanced at the fullest speed, following so closely upon the enemy that the latter had only time to fire one or two rounds, with their thirteen guns, before the English were upon them. The French, who had already lost heart by the serious check which had befallen them, were unable to stand the shock, and at once retreated, leaving their guns behind them.

As Forde had anticipated, the French Sepoys, seeing their centre and right defeated, desisted from their attack on the English right, and fell back upon their camp. The English Sepoys at once marched forward, and joined Forde's force. The rajah's troops, however, the whole of whom had fled, remained cowering in the shelter of a large dry tank.

Forde did not wait for them; but, leaving his guns behind him, pressed forward, an hour after the defeat of the French, against their camp. To reach this, he had to pass along a narrow valley, commanded by the French heavy guns. These opened fire, but the English pressed forward without wavering. The defenders, not yet recovered from the effects of their defeat in the plain, at once gave way, and retreated in the utmost confusion towards Rajahmahendri. Had the cavalry of Anandraz been at hand to follow up the advantage, great numbers might have been captured. As it was, Charlie Marryat, with his little force, harassed them for some miles; but was unable to effect any serious damage on so strong a body. The English captured thirty-two pieces of cannon, and all the stores, ammunition, and tents of the French.

Forde at once despatched a battalion of Sepoys, under Captain Knox, in pursuit; and this officer pressed on so vigorously that he approached Rajahmahendri the same evening. Two more native battalions reached Knox during the night.

So thoroughly dispirited were the enemy, that the sight of the red-coated Sepoys of Knox, whom they could not distinguish from English, induced them to abandon

Rajahmahendri in all haste, although it contained a strong mud fort, with several guns. The Godavery is two miles wide, and all night the passage of the river in boats continued; and when, at daybreak next morning, Knox broke into the town, he found fifteen Europeans still on the banks, expecting a returning boat. These he captured; and seeing, upon the opposite bank, a party about to disembark guns and stores from another boat, he opened fire from the guns of the fort towards it; and, although the shot could scarcely reach halfway across the river, such was the terror of the enemy that they forsook the boat, and fled. Knox at once sent a boat across, and brought back that containing the guns.

The French retreated to Masulipatam, the capital of the province, a port which rivalled Madras in its commerce. Forde determined to follow them there, but he was hindered by want of money to pay his troops. This the Rajah Anandraz, who had promised to supply money, now, excited and arrogant by the victory which he had done nothing towards gaining, refused to supply; and many weeks were spent in negotiations, before Forde was able to move forward.

Charlie was no longer with him. The very day before the fight of Condore, letters had arrived from Madras, stating the urgency of the position there; and, upon the night after the battle, Colonel Forde ordered Charlie to return to aid in the defence of that city, before which the French had appeared on the 29th of November.

Several skirmishes took place outside the city, and the English then retired within the fort. The force consisted of sixteen hundred white troops, and two thousand three hundred Sepoys. The nabob, who had also retired into the town, had two hundred horse and a huge retinue of attendants.

On the morning of the 14th the French occupied the town, and the next day the English made a sortie, with six hundred men. These, for a while, drove the French before them through the streets of Madras; but as the French gradually rallied, the fire upon the English was so heavy that the sortie was repulsed, with a loss of two hundred soldiers and six officers killed, wounded, and prisoners. The French loss had been about the same. Had not a large quantity of the French troops broken into the wine stores on their arrival, and drunk to a point of intoxication, it is probable that none of the British party would have returned to the fort. The sortie had, however, the effect that Saubinet, one of the best of the French officers, was killed, and Count D'Estaign, an able general, taken prisoner.

For some time, the siege proceeded slowly, the French waiting for the arrival of their siege artillery, by ship, from Pondicherry. The fort of Madras was now a far more formidable post than it had been when the French before captured it. In the year 1743 Mr. Smith, an engineer, had marked out the lines for a considerable increase in the fortifications. The ditch was dug and faced with brick, but on account of the expense, nothing further had been done. The French had added somewhat to the fortifications during their stay there in 1750. Nothing had been done by the English when they recovered the town, until the news of the preparations which the French were making for the siege of the place had been received. Four thousand natives were then set to work; and these, in eighteen months, had completed the fortifications, as designed by Mr. Smith, just before the arrival of the French.

The latter determined to attack from the northern side. Here the fort was protected by a demi-bastion, next to the sea; and by the Royal Bastion, the wall between the two being covered by a work known as the North Ravelin. The defence was also strengthened by the fire of the northwest lunette, and Pigot's Bastion.

Against these the French threw up four batteries. Lally's Battery, erected by the regiment of that name, was on the seashore directly facing the demi-bastion. To its right was the Burying Ground Battery, facing the Royal Bastion. Against the western face of this position the French regiment of Lorraine erected a strong work, while farther round to the west, on a rising ground, they threw up a battery called the Hospital Battery, which kept up a crossfire on the English position.

To prevent the French from pressing forward along the strip of shore between the fort and the sea, the English erected a strong stockade, behind which was a battery called the Fascine Battery.

A few days after the siege began, it was found that the numbers crowded up in the fort could scarcely be accommodated; and the rajah was, therefore, invited to leave by sea, on board a ship which would land him at the Dutch settlement of Negapatam, whence he might journey through the Tanjore country to Trichinopoli. This proposal he willingly accepted, and embarked with his wife, women, and children, his other followers leaving by the land side, opposite to that invested by the French. Thus the garrison were relieved of the embarrassment, and consumption of food, caused by four hundred men and two hundred horse.

Charlie rode, with his troop, without interruption through the country, avoiding all bodies of the enemy until he reached the sea, fifteen miles north of Madras. Here he hired a native boat and, leaving the troops under the command of Ensign Anstey, sailed for Madras; in order to inform the garrison of Forde's victory over the French, and to concert, with the governor, as to the measures which he wished him to carry out to harass the enemy. He was accompanied only by Tim and Hossein.

The wind was fair and, starting an hour before sunset, the boat ran into Madras roads two hours later. The Harlem, which had that day arrived with artillery for the French from Pondicherry, fired at the little craft; and the native boatmen were about to turn the head of the craft northward again. Charlie, however, drew his pistol, and Hossein took his place with his drawn tulwar by the helmsman. The boatmen, thereupon, again continued their course; and, though several shots fell near them, they escaped untouched, and anchored just outside the surf, abreast of the fort.

The English had taken the precaution of erecting a number of huts under the walls of the fort for the boatmen, in order to be able to communicate with any ship arriving, or to send messages in or out. As soon as the boat anchored, a catamaran put out, and brought Charlie and his followers to shore. There was great joy at the receipt of his news, and the guns of the fort fired twenty-one shots towards the enemy, in honor of the victory.

Governor Pigot was in general command of the defence, having under him Colonel Lawrence, in command of the troops. The latter, after inquiring from Charlie the character of the officer he had left in command of his troop, and finding that he was able and energetic, requested Charlie to send orders to him to join either the force under Captain Preston, at Chingalpatt, or that of a native leader, Mahomed Issoof, both of whom were ravaging and destroying the country about Conjeveram, whence the French besieging Madras drew most of their provisions. Charlie himself was requested to remain in the fort, where his experience in sieges would render him of great value.

At daybreak on the 2nd of January, the Lorraine and Lally Batteries opened fire. The English guns, however, proved superior in weight and number, dismounted two of the cannon, and silenced the others. The French mortars continued to throw heavy shell into the fort, and that night most of the European women and children were sent away, in native boats. The French batteries, finding the superiority of the English fire, ceased firing until the 6th, when seven guns and six large mortars from Lally's Battery, and eight guns and two mortars from the Lorraine Battery, opened upon the town.

The cannonade now continued without intermission, but the enemy gained but little advantage. Every day, however, added to their strength, as fresh vessels with artillery continued to arrive from Pondicherry. They were now pushing their approaches from Lally's Battery towards the demi-bastion. The losses on the part of the besieged were considerable, many being killed and wounded each day. This continued to the end of the month, in spite of many gallant sorties by parties of the besiegers, who repeatedly killed and drove out the working parties in the head of the French trenches. These progressed steadily, and reached to the outworks of the demi-bastion.

On the 25th the Shaftesbury, one of the Company's trading vessels, commanded by Captain Inglis, was seen approaching. The five French ships hoisted English colours. A catamaran was sent out to warn her, and at nine o'clock in the evening she came to anchor. She had on board only some invalids, but brought the welcome news that three other ships, with troops, would soon be up. She had on board, too, thirty-seven chests of silver, and many military stores, among them hand grenades and large shell, which were most welcome to the garrison, who had nearly expended their supply. The native boats went off from the fort, and brought on shore the ammunition and stores.

In the afternoon the Shaftesbury was attacked by the two French ships, the Bristol and the Harlem. She fought them for two hours, and then sailed in and anchored again near the fort. The French ships lay off at a distance, and these and one of their batteries played upon the Shaftesbury after she had anchored, and continued to do so for the next three days.

Many of the guns of the fort were dismounted by the artillery fire, which had continued, with scarcely any intermission, for a month. The parapets of the ramparts were in many places beaten down, and the walls exposed to the enemy's fire greatly damaged. The enemy now opened their breaching battery close to the works, and on the 7th two breaches had been effected, and Lally ordered his principal engineer and artillery officers to give their opinion as to the practicability of an assault.

These, however, considered that the assault would have no prospect of success, as the guns commanding the ditch were still uninjured, and the palisades which stormers must climb over before reaching the breach untouched. So heavy a crossfire could be brought to bear by the besieged upon an assaulting column, that it would be swept away before it could mount the breach. These officers added their opinion that, considering the number of men defending the fort in comparison with those attacking it, final success could not be looked for, and further prosecution of the works would only entail a useless loss of life.

On the 9th of February, the French attacked Mahomed Issoof's men and those of Captain Preston; the whole under the command of Major Calliaud, who had come up from Trichinopoli, and had taken station three miles in rear of the French position. The greater part of the natives, as usual, behaved badly; but Calliaud, with the artillery and a few Sepoys, defended himself till nightfall; and then drew off.

For the next week the French continued to fire, and their approaches were pushed on. Several sorties were made, but matters remained unchanged until the 14th, when six English ships were seen standing into the roads; and that night the French drew out from their trenches, and retreated. The next morning six hundred troops landed from the ships, and the garrison, who had so stoutly resisted the assaults made upon them for forty-two days, sallied out to inspect the enemy's works. Fifty-two cannon were left in them, and so great was the hurry with which the French retreated that they left forty-four sick in the hospital behind.

The fort fired, during the siege, 26,554 rounds from their cannon, 7,502 shells, threw 1,990 hand grenades, and expended 200,000 musketry cartridges. Thirty pieces of cannon and five mortars had been dismounted during the siege. Of the Europeans, the loss in killed, wounded, and prisoners was five hundred and seventy-nine. Three hundred and twenty-two Sepoys were killed and wounded, and four hundred and forty deserted during the siege.

In spite of the resolution with which the French had pushed the siege, it was, from the first, destined to failure. The garrison were well provisioned, had great stores of ammunition, and plenty of spare cannon to replace those disabled or dismounted. The works were strong, and the garrison not greatly inferior in number to the besiegers. The French, on the other hand, had to bring their artillery, ammunition, and stores by water from Pondicherry; and the activity of the English parties in their rear rendered it extremely difficult for them to receive supplies of food, by land. Lally had disgusted even the French officers and soldiers by his arrogance, and passionate temper; while by the Sepoys he was absolutely hated.

During the siege, Charlie had been most active in the defence. Colonel Lawrence had assigned no special post to him, but used him as what would now be called his chief of the staff. He was ever where the fire was thickest, encouraging the men; and, during the intervals of comparative cessation of fire, he went about the fort, seeing to the comforts of the men in their quarters, to the issue of stores, and other matters.

Upon the very morning after the French had withdrawn, he asked to be allowed to rejoin his troop, which was with Major Calliaud, and at once started to rejoin Colonel Forde. He wished to take the whole of his corps with him; but Colonel Lawrence considered that these would be of extreme use in following up the French, and in subsequent operations, as cavalry was an arm in which the English were greatly deficient.

Colonel Forde had been terribly delayed by the conduct of Rajah Anandraz, and the delay enabled the French again to recover heart. He was not able to move forward until the 1st of March. On the 6th he arrived before Masulipatam, and the following day Charlie joined him, with his troop.

The fort of Masulipatam stood in an extremely defensible position. It was surrounded by a swamp, on three sides. The other face rested on the river. From the land side, it was only approachable by a causeway across the swamp, and this was guarded by a strong ravelin, which is the military name for an outwork erected beyond the ditch of a fortress. It was, in all respects, capable of a prolonged defence. In form it was an irregular parallelogram, about eight hundred yards in length and

WITH CLIVE IN INDIA

six hundred yards wide, and on the walls were eleven strong bastions. The morass which surrounded it was of from three to eighteen feet in depth.

On the approach of Forde, Conflans evacuated the town; which, also surrounded by swamps, and lying two miles to the northwest of the fort, was itself a most defensible position; and retired across the narrow causeway, more than a mile long, to the fort.

Chapter 27

MASULIPATAM

'I am heartily glad that you have come, Marryat,' Colonel Forde said, as Charlie rode up. 'I have got here at last, as you see, but that is a very different thing from getting in. An uglier place to attack I never saw; and in other respects, matters are not bright.

'Anandraz is a constant worry and trouble to me. He has everything to gain by our success, and yet will do nothing to aid it. His men are worse than useless in fight, and the only thing which we want and he could give us – money – he will not let us have.

'Will you ride with me, to the spot where I'm erecting my batteries, and you will see the prospect for yourself?'

The prospect was, as Charlie found when he saw it, the reverse of cheerful. The point which Forde had selected to erect his batteries was on some sandbanks, eight hundred yards from the eastern face of the fort. It would be impossible to construct approaches against the walls; and, should a breach be made, there still remained a wide creek to be crossed, beyond which lay the deep, and in most parts absolutely impassable, swamp.

Charlie and his men were employed in bringing in provisions from the surrounding country; but a short distance in the rear, a French column under Du Rocher, with two hundred European and two thousand native troops, with four field pieces, watched the British, and rendered the collection of provisions difficult. Du Rocher had several strong places, with European and Sepoy garrisons, near him, in which to retire in case Forde should advance against him.

'Well, Mister Charles,' Tim said, one morning, 'this is altogether a quare sort of a siege. Here we are, with a place in front of us with ten times as many guns as we have got, and a force well nigh twice as large. Even if there were no walls, and no guns, I don't see how we could get at 'em, barring we'd wings, for this bog is worse than anything in the ould country. Then behind us we've got another army, which is, they say, with the garrisons of the forts, as strong as we are. We've got little food and less money, and the troops are grumbling mightily, I can tell you.'

On the 18th of March, while his batteries were still incomplete, Forde received certain news that the Nizam of the Deccan, the old ally of the French, was advancing with an army of forty thousand men to attack him. No British commander ever stood in a position of more imminent peril.

This completed the terror of Anandraz. Du Rocher had caused reports to be circulated that he intended to march against that chief's territories, and the news of the approach of the nizam, who was his suzerain lord, completed his dismay. He refused to advance another penny. Colonel Forde had already expended the prize money gained by the troops, his own private funds, and those of his officers, in buying food for his troops; and the men were several months in arrear of their pay.

'I'm afraid, yer honor,' Tim said that evening to Charlie, 'that there's going to be a shindy.'

'What do you mean by a shindy, Tim?'

'I mane, yer honor, that the men are cursing and swearing, and saying the divil a bit will they fight any longer. It's rank mutiny and rebellion, yer honor; but there's something to be said for the poor boys. They have seen all the prize money they have taken spent. Not a thraneen have they touched for months. Their clothes are in rags, and here they are before a place which there's no more chance of their taking than there is of their flying up to the clouds. And now they hear that, besides the French behind us, there's the nizam with forty thousand of his men marching against us. It's a purty kettle of fish altogether, yer honor.

'It isn't for myself I care, Mr. Charles. Haven't I got an order in my pocket, on the treasury at Madras, for three hundred pound and over; but it's mighty hard, yer honor, just when one has become a wealthy man, to be shut up in a French prison.'

'Well, Tim, I hope there will be no trouble; but I own that things look bad.'

'Hossein has been saying, yer honor, that he thinks that the best way would be for him and me to go out and chop off the heads of half a dozen of the chief ring-leaders. But I thought I'd better be after asking yer honor's pleasure in the affair, before I set about it.'

To Tim's great disappointment, Charlie told him that the step was one to which he could hardly assent, at present.

The next morning, the troops turned out with their arms, and threatened to march away. Forde spoke to them gently, but firmly. He told them that he could not believe that men who had behaved so gallantly, at Condore, would fail now in their duty. He begged them to return to their tents, and to send two of their number, as deputies, to him.

This they did. The deputies came to the colonel's tent, and told him that all were resolved to fight no more; unless they were immediately paid the amount of prize money due to them, and were assured of the whole booty, in case Masulipatam should be taken. Colonel Forde promised that they would receive their prize money out of the very first funds which reached him. As to the booty which might be taken in Masulipatam, he said he had no power to change the regulations of the Company, but that he would beg them, under consideration of the hardships which the troops had endured, and their great services, to forego their half of the plunder. Directly Masulipatam was taken, he said, he would divide one half among them, and hold the other until he obtained the Company's answer to his request. Then he would distribute it, at once. With this answer the troops were satisfied, and returned at once to their duty.

On the 25th, the guns of the battery opened fire upon the fort, but the damage which they did was inconsiderable. On the 27th, news came that the French army of observation had retaken Rajahmahendri; and that the nizam, with his army, had arrived at Baizwara, forty miles distant. Letters came in, from the nizam to Anandraz, ordering him instantly to quit the English camp, and join him. The rajah was so terrified that, that night, he started with his troops without giving any information of his intentions to Colonel Forde; and dilatory as were his motions in general, he, on this occasion, marched sixteen miles before daybreak.

The instant Colonel Forde heard that he had left, he sent for Charlie Marryat.

'I suppose you have heard, Marryat, that that scoundrel Anandraz has bolted. Ride off to him with your troop, and do your best to persuade him to return.'

'I will do so, sir,' Charlie said; 'but really, it seems to me that we are better without him than with him. His men only consume our provisions, and cause trouble, and they are no more good fighting than so many sheep.'

'That is so,' Colonel Forde said. 'But in the first place, his five thousand men, absolutely worthless as they are, swell our forces to a respectable size. If Conflans and Du Rocher saw how small is our real fighting body, they would fall upon us together, and annihilate us. In the second place, if Anandraz goes to the nizam he will at once, of course, declare for the French, and will give up Vizapatam and the rest of the ground we won by the battle of Condore. The whole of the fruits of the campaign would be lost, and we should only hold that portion of the Northern Sirkars on which our troops here are encamped.'

'I beg your pardon, Colonel,' Charlie said. 'You are right, and I am wrong. I will start at once.'

Putting himself at the head of his five-and-twenty men, Charlie rode off at once in pursuit of the rajah. He found him encamped in a village. Charlie had already instructed his men as to the course which they were to pursue, and halted them at a distance of fifty yards from the rajah's tent. Then dismounting, and followed by Tim as his orderly, and Hossein as his body servant, he walked to the tent.

He found Anandraz surrounded by his chief officers. The rajah received him coldly; but Charlie, paying no attention to this, took a seat close to him.

'I am come, Rajah,' he said, 'from Colonel Forde, to point out to you the folly of the course which you have pursued. By the line which you have taken so far, it is evidently your intention to cross the Godavery, and retire to your own country. What chance have you of accomplishing this? By this time, the cavalry of the nizam will be scattered over the whole country between this and the Godavery. At Rajahmahendri is Du Rocher, with his army, who will take you in flank. Even supposing that you reach your own country, what is the future open to you? If the English are finally successful, they will deprive you of your rank and possessions for deserting them now. If the French are victorious, they and the nizam will then turn their attention to you; and you cannot hope to escape with life, when your treason has brought such troubles upon them.'

The rajah looked for a minute doubtful; and then, encouraged by the murmurs of the officers around him, who were weary of the expedition and its labours, although their troops had not fired a single shot, he said obstinately:

'No more words are needed. I have made up my mind.'

'And so have I,' Charlie said, and with a sudden spring he leaped upon the rajah, seized him by the throat, and placed a pistol to his ear.

Hossein drew his sword, and rushed to his side. Tim ran outside and held up his arm, and the little body of cavalry at once rode up; and, half of them dismounting, entered the tent with drawn swords.

So astounded were the officers of the rajah, at Charlie's sudden attack, that for a moment they knew not what to do; and before they could recover from their surprise, Charlie's troopers entered.

'Take this man,' Charlie said, pointing to the rajah, 'to that tree, and hang him at once. Cut down any of these fellows who move a finger.'

The rajah was dragged to the tree, almost lifeless with terror.

'Now, Rajah,' Charlie said, 'you either give instant orders for your army to march back to Masulipatam, or up you go on that branch above there.'

The terrified rajah instantly promised to carry out Charlie's orders, and to remain faithful to the English. The officers were brought out from the tent, and received orders from the rajah to set his troops instantly in motion on their way back. The rajah was led to his tent, and there kept under a guard, until the army was in motion. When the whole of it was well on its way, Charlie said:

'Now, Rajah, we will ride on. We will say no more about this little affair, and I will ask Colonel Forde to forgive your ill behaviour in leaving him. But mind, if at any future time you attempt to disobey his orders, or to retire from the camp, I will

744

blow out your brains; even if I have to follow you, with my men, into the heart of your own palace.'

Upon their return to the British camp, Charlie explained to Colonel Forde the measures which he was obliged to take, to convince the rajah of the soundness of his arguments; and of these Colonel Forde entirely approved. He told Charlie that he had sent off, to open negotiations with Salabut Jung, so as to detain him as long as possible at Baizwara.

Without any intermission, the batteries continued to play on the fort from the 25th of March to the 6th of April. Several houses had been destroyed, and some breaches effected; but these the French repaired in the night, as fast as they were made. They were aware of the position of the English, and regarded the siege with contempt.

On the morning of the 7th, news came that the nizam was advancing from Baizwara to attack the English; and that Du Rocher was hurrying from Rajahmahendri, to effect a junction with him. The same morning, the senior artillery officer reported to Colonel Forde that only two days' ammunition for the batteries remained in store. He learned, too, that a ship with three hundred French soldiers would arrive, in the course of a day or two.

The position was, indeed, a desperate one, and there remained only the alternatives of success against the fort, or total destruction. He determined to attack. All day, his batteries kept up a heavier fire than ever, maintaining an equal fire against all the bastions in order that, if the enemy should obtain any information of the projected attack, they would not know against which point it was directed. Colonel Forde had ascertained that fishermen were in the habit of making their way, across the swamp, to the southwest angle of the fort, that on the sea face opposite to the British frontiers. He determined to effect a diversion, by an attack upon that side; and therefore ordered Captain Knox, with seven hundred Sepoys, to make a detour to cross the swamp, and to attack upon that side. Still further to distract the attention of the garrison, he instructed Anandraz to advance with his men along the causeway, and to open fire against the ravelin. The main attack, which consisted of the rest of the force, composed of three hundred and twenty European infantry, thirty gunners, thirty sailors, and seven hundred Sepoys, was to be delivered against the breach in the bastion, mounting ten guns, in the northeast angle of the fort.

At ten o'clock, the force drew up under arms. The fire of the batteries was kept up, much later than usual, in order that the enemy should have no time to repair the breaches. The hour of midnight was fixed for the attack, as at that time the tide was at its lowest, and the water in the ditches round the ramparts not more than three feet deep.

Captain Knox and his party started first. The main body should have set out half an hour later, but were detained, owing to the unaccountable absence of Captain Callender, the officer who was to command it. As this officer was afterwards killed, the cause of his absence was never explained. The party started without him, and before they could reach the ditch, they heard the sound of firing from the farther corner of the fort, telling that Knox was already at work.

'Shure, yer honor,' muttered Tim, as he made his way through the swamp, knee deep, beside his master, 'this is worse than the day before Plassey. It was water then, but this thick mud houlds one's legs fast at every step. I've lost one of my boots, already.'

It was indeed hard work; but at last, the head of the column reached the ditch, just as a fresh burst of firing told that the Rajah Anandraz was attacking the ravelin. The French, in their belief in the absolute security of the place, had taken but few precautions against an attack; and it was not until the leading party had waded, nearly breast high, through the ditch; and began to break down the palisade beyond it, that they were discovered. Then a heavy artillery and musketry fire from the bastions on the right and left was opened upon the assailants.

Captain Fisher with the first division attacked the breach; Captain Maclean with the second covered them, by opening fire upon the bastion on their right; while the third, led by Captain Yorke, replied to that on their left. Charlie, although superior in rank to any of these officers, had no specific command, but accompanied the party as a simple volunteer.

The storming party soon mounted the breach, and Yorke's division joined it on the top. Yorke, turning to the left, seized the bastion which was firing on Maclean;

while Fisher turned along the ramparts to the right, to secure the bastions in that direction.

Just as Yorke was setting out he saw a strong body of French Sepoys, advancing between the foot of the ramparts and the buildings of the town. These had been sent, directly the firing was heard, to reinforce the bastion just carried. Without a moment's hesitation, Yorke ran down the rampart, seized the French officer who commanded, and ordered him to surrender at once, as the place was already taken. Confused and bewildered, the officer gave up his sword, and ordered the Sepoys to lay down their arms. They were then sent, as prisoners, into the bastion.

Yorke now pushed forward, with his men, at the foot of the rampart; and carried two out of three of the bastions on that side. The men, however, separated from the rest, and alone in the unknown town, were beginning to lose heart. Suddenly they came upon a small magazine, and some of the men called out, 'A mine!' Seized with a sudden panic, the whole division ran back, leaving Yorke alone with two native drummer boys, who continued to beat the advance. The soldiers, however, did not stop running until they reached the bastion.

Captain Yorke went back, and found that many of the soldiers were proposing to leave the fort, altogether. He swore that he would cut down the first man who moved, and some of the men who had served with him in the 39th, ashamed of their conduct, said that they would follow him. Heading the thirty-six men who had now come to their senses, Captain Yorke again advanced, with the drummer boys.

Just as he was setting out, Charlie, who had at first gone with Fisher's division, hearing an entire cessation of fire on the other side, ran up to see what was going on.

'Major Marryat,' Captain Yorke said, 'will you rally these fellows, and bring them after me. They've been frightened with a false alarm of a mine, and have lost their heads altogether.'

Charlie, aided by Tim, exerted himself to the utmost to encourage and command the soldiers, shaming them by telling them that while they, European soldiers, were cowering in the bastion, their Sepoy comrades were winning the town.

'Unless,' he said, 'in one minute the whole of you are formed up ready to advance,

I will take care that not one shall have a share in the prize money that will be won tonight.'

The men now fell in, and Charlie led them after Captain Yorke. The first retreat of the latter's division had given the French time to rally a little, and as he now made along the rampart towards the bastion on the river, the French officer in command there, having turned a gun and loaded it with grape, discharged it when the English were within a few yards. Captain Yorke fell, badly wounded. The two black drummer boys were killed, as were several of the men, and sixteen others were wounded.

Charlie, hurrying along with the rest of the party, met the survivors of Captain Yorke's little band coming back, carrying their wounded officer.

'There,' Charlie shouted to his men, 'that is your doing. Now retrieve yourselves. Show you are worthy of the name of British soldiers.'

With a shout, the men rushed forward and carried the bastion, and this completed the capture of the whole of the wall, from the northeast angle to the river.

In the meantime Captain Fisher, with his division, was advancing to the right along the rampart. Maclean's men had joined him, and they were pushing steadily forward. Colonel Forde continued with the reserve at the bastion first taken, receiving reports from both divisions as they advanced, and sending the necessary orders. As fast as the prisoners were brought in, they were sent down the breach into the ditch, where they were guarded by Sepoys, who threatened to shoot any that tried to climb up.

Meanwhile, all was disorder in the town. Greatly superior as were the besieged to their assailants in number, they could, if properly handled, have easily driven them back. Instead, however, of disregarding the attack by Knox at the southwest angle, which was clearly only a feint; and that of Anandraz on the ravelin, which might have been disregarded with equal safety; and concentrating all their forces against the main attack, they made no sustained effort against either of the columns, which were rapidly carrying bastion after bastion. Conflans appeared to have completely lost his head, as messenger after messenger arrived at his house, by the river, with news of the progress of the English columns.

As Fisher's division advanced towards the bastion in which was the great gate, the French who had gathered there again attempted to check his progress. But his men reserved their fire, until close to the enemy; and then, discharging a volley at a few yards' distance, they rapidly cleared the bastion. Fisher at once closed the great gates, and thus cut off all the defenders of the ravelin, and prevented any of the troops within from joining these, and cutting their way through the rajah's troops, which would have been no difficult matter.

Just as the division were again advancing, Captain Callender, to the astonishment of everyone, appeared and took his place at its head. A few shots only were fired after this, and the last discharge killed Captain Callender.

By this time Conflans, bewildered and terrified, had sent a message to Colonel Forde, offering to surrender on honorable terms. Colonel Forde sent back to say that he would give no terms whatever; that the town was in his power and further resistance hopeless; and that, if it continued longer, he would put all who did not surrender to the sword. On the receipt of this message, Conflans immediately sent round orders that all his men were to lay down their arms, and to fall in, in the open space by the water.

The English assembled, on the parade, by the bastion of the gateway. Captain Knox's column was marched round, from the southwest, into the town. A strong body of artillery kept guard over the prisoners till morning. Then the gate was opened, and the French in the ravelin entered the fort, and became prisoners with the rest of the garrison. The whole number of prisoners exceeded three thousand, of whom five hundred were Europeans and the rest Sepoys. The loss of the English was twenty-two Europeans killed, and sixty-two wounded. The Sepoys had fifty killed and a hundred and fifty wounded. The rajah's people, who had kept up their false attack upon the ravelin with much more bravery and resolution than had been expected, also lost a good many men.

Considering the natural strength of the position, that the garrison was, both in European troops and Sepoys, considerably stronger than the besiegers, that the fort mounted a hundred and twenty guns, and that a relieving army, enormously superior to that of the besiegers, was within fifteen miles at the time the assault was made, the capture of Masulipatam may claim to rank among the very highest deeds ever performed by British arms.

Chapter 28

THE DEFEAT OF LALLY

A large quantity of plunder was obtained at Masulipatam. Half was at once divided among the troops, according to promise, and the other half retained until the permission, applied for by Colonel Forde, was received from Madras for its division among them.

The morning after the capture of the town, the Mahratta horse of Salabut Jung appeared. The nizam was furious when he found that he had arrived too late; but he resolved that when the three hundred French troops, daily expected by sea, arrived, he would besiege Forde in his turn; as, with the new arrivals, Du Rocher's force would alone be superior to that of Forde, and there would be, in addition, his own army of forty thousand men.

The ships arrived off the port three days later, and sent a messenger on shore to Conflans. Finding that no answer was returned, and that the fire had entirely ceased, they came to the conclusion that the place was captured by the English, and sailed away to Pondicherry again. Had Du Rocher taken the precaution of having boats in readiness to communicate with them, inform them of the real state of affairs, and order them to land farther along the coast and join him, Forde would have been besieged in his turn, although certainly the siege would have been ineffectual.

Rajah Anandraz, greatly terrified at the approach of the nizam, had, two days after the capture of the place, received a portion of the plunder as his share, and marched away to his own country; Forde, disgusted with his conduct throughout the campaign, making no effort whatever to retain him.

When Salabut Jung heard that the French had sailed away to Pondicherry, he felt that his prospects of retaking the town were small; and, at the same time receiving news that his own dominions were threatened by an enemy, he concluded a treaty with Forde, granting Masulipatam and the Northern Sirkars to the English, and agreeing never again to allow any French troops to enter his dominions. He then marched back to his own country.

Colonel Forde sailed with a portion of the force to Calcutta, where he shortly afterwards commanded at the battle of Chinsurah, where the Dutch, who had made vast preparations to dispute the supremacy of the English, were completely defeated; and thenceforth they, as well as the French, sunk to the rank of small trading colonies under British protection, in Bengal.

Charlie returned to Madras, and journeying up the country he joined the main body of his troop, under Peters. They had been engaged in several dashing expeditions, and had rendered great service; but they had been reduced in numbers, by action and sickness; and the whole force, when reunited, only numbered eighty sabres – Lieutenant Hallowes being killed. Peters had been twice wounded. The two friends were greatly pleased to meet again, and had much to tell each other of their adventures, since they parted.

The next morning, a deputation of four of the men waited upon Charlie. They said that, from their share of the booty of the various places they had taken, all were now possessed of sums sufficient, in India, to enable them to live in comfort for the rest of their lives. They hoped, therefore, that Charlie would ask the authorities at Madras to disband the corps, and allow them to return home. Their commander, however, pointed out to them that the position was still a critical one; that the French possessed a very powerful army at Pondicherry, which would shortly take the field; and that the English would need every one of their soldiers, to meet the storm. If victorious, there could be no doubt that a final blow would be dealt to French influence, and that the Company would then be able to reduce its forces. A few months would settle the event, and it would, he knew, be useless to apply for their discharge before that time. He thought he could promise them, however, that by the end of the year, at latest, their services would be dispensed with.

The men, although rather disappointed, retired, content to make the best of the circumstances. Desertions were very frequent in the Sepoy force of the Company, as the men, returning to their native villages and resuming their former dress and occupation, were in no danger whatever of discovery. But in Charlie's force not a single desertion had taken place since it was raised; as the men knew that, by leaving the colours, they would forfeit their share of the prize money, held for them in the Madras treasury.

'Have you heard from home lately?' Peters asked.

'Yes,' Charlie said. 'There was a large batch of letters lying for me, at Madras. My eldest sister, who has now been married three years, has just presented me with a second nephew. Katie and my mother are well.'

'Your sister is not engaged yet?' Peters asked.

'No. Katie says she's quite heart whole at present. Let me see – how old is she now? It is just eight years and a half since we left England, and she was twelve years old then. She is now past twenty.

'She would do nicely for you, Peters, when you go back. It would be awfully jolly, if you two were to fall in love with each other.'

'I feel quite disposed to do so,' Peters said, laughing, 'from your descriptions of her. I've heard so much of her, in all the time we've been together; and she writes such bright merry letters, that I seem to know her quite well.'

For Charlie, during the long evenings by the campfires, had often read to his friend the lively letters which he received from his sisters. Peters had no sisters of his own; and he had more than once sent home presents, from the many articles of jewelry which fell to his share of the loot of captured fortresses, to his friend's sisters, saying to Charlie that he had no one in England to send things to, and that it kept up his tie with the old country; for he had been left an orphan, as a child.

The day after the deputation from his men had spoken to Charlie, Tim said:

'I hope, yer honor, that whin the troop's disbanded, you will be going home for a bit, yourself.'

'I intend to do so, Tim. I have been wanting to get away, for the last two years, but I did not like to ask for leave until everything was settled here. And what is more, when I once get back, I don't think they will ever see me in India again. I have sufficient means to live as a wealthy man in England, and I've seen enough fighting to last a lifetime.'

'Hooroo!' shouted Tim. 'That's the best word I've heard for a long time. And I shall settle down as yer honor's butler, and look after the grand house, and see that you're comfortable.'

'You must never leave me, Tim, that's certain,' Charlie said. 'At least, till you marry and set up an establishment of your own.'

'If I can't marry without leaving yer honor, divil a wife will Tim Kelly ever take.'

'Wait till you see the right woman, Tim. There is no saying what the strongest of us will do, when he's once caught in a woman's net. However, we'll talk of that when the time comes.'

'And there's Hossein, yer honor. Fire and water wouldn't keep him away from you, though what he'll do in the colds of the winter at home is more than I know. It makes me laugh to see how his teeth chatter, and how the creetur shivers of a cold morning, here. But, cold or no cold, he'd follow you to the north pole, and climb up it if yer honor told him.'

Charlie laughed.

'He is safe not to be put to the test there, Tim. However, you may be sure that if Hossein is willing to go to England with me, he shall go. He has saved my life more than once; and you and he shall never part from me, so long as you are disposed to stay by my side.'

For some months, no great undertaking was attempted on either side. Many petty sieges and skirmishes took place, each party preparing for the great struggle, which was to decide the fate of Southern India.

At last, in January, 1760, the rival armies approached each other. Captain Sherlock, with thirty Europeans and three hundred Sepoys, were besieged by the French in the fort of Vandivash, which had shortly before been captured by them from the French.

Lally was himself commanding the siege, having as his second in command Monsieur Bussy, of whom, however, he was more jealous than ever. Lally's own incapacity was so marked that the whole army, and even Lally's own regiment, recognized the superior talents of Bussy. But although Lally constantly asked the advice of his subordinate, his jealousy of that officer generally impelled him to neglect it.

When the English, under Colonel Coote, who now commanded their forces in Madras, were known to be advancing against him, Bussy strongly advised that the siege should be abandoned, and a strong position taken up for the battle. The advice was unquestionably good, but Lally neglected it, and remained in front of Vandivash until the English were seen approaching. The French cavalry, among whom were three hundred European dragoons, and a cloud of Mahratta horse moved forward against the English, whose troops were scattered on the line of march.

Colonel Coote brought up two guns, and these, being kept concealed from the enemy until they came within two hundred yards, opened suddenly upon them, while the Sepoys fired heavily with their muskets. The Mahrattas rapidly turned and rode off, and the French cavalry, finding themselves alone, retired in good order.

Colonel Coote now drew up his army in order of battle, and marched his troops so as to take up a position in front of some gardens, and other inclosures, which extended for some distance from the foot of the mountains out on to the plain. These inclosures would serve as a defence, in case the army should be forced to retire from the open.

The French remained immovable in their camp. Seeing this, Colonel Coote marched his troops to the right, the infantry taking up their post in the stony ground at the foot of the mountain, at a mile and a half from the French camp. Some of the French cavalry came out to reconnoitre; but, being fired upon, returned.

Finding that the French would not come out to attack, Colonel Coote again advanced until he reached a point where, swinging round his right, he faced the enemy in a position of great strength. His right was now covered by the fire of the fort, his left by the broken ground at the foot of the hills.

As soon as the English had taken up their position, the French sallied out from their camp and formed in line of battle. The French cavalry were on their right; next to these was the regiment of Lorraine, four hundred strong; in the centre the battalion of India, seven hundred strong. Next to these was Lally's regiment, four hundred strong, its left resting upon an intrenched tank, which was held by three hundred marines and sailors from their fleet, with four guns. Twelve other guns were in line, three between each regiment. Four hundred Sepoys were in reserve, at a tank in rear of that held by the marines. Nine hundred Sepoys held a ridge behind the position, but in front of the camp, and at each end of this ridge was an intrenchment, guarded by fifty Europeans. A hundred and fifty Europeans and three hundred Sepoys remained in the batteries, facing Vandivash. The whole force consisted of two thousand four hundred Europeans, and sixteen hundred Sepoys. The Mahrattas, three thousand strong, remained in their own camp, and did not advance to the assistance of their allies.

The English army consisted of nineteen hundred Europeans, of whom eighty were cavalry, two thousand one hundred Sepoys, twelve hundred and fifty irregular horse, and twenty-six field guns. The Sepoys were on the flanks, the Company's two battalions in the centre, with Coote's regiment on their right and Draper's on their left. The four grenadier companies of the white regiments were withdrawn from the fighting line; and, with two hundred Sepoys on each flank, were held as a reserve. Ten field pieces were in line with the troops; two, with two companies of Sepoys, were posted a little on the left; the rest were in reserve. The English line was placed somewhat obliquely across that of the French, their left being the nearest to the enemy.

As the English took up their position, Lally led out his cavalry, made a wide sweep round the plain, and then advanced against the English horse, who were drawn up some little distance behind the reserve. Upon seeing their approach, the whole of the irregular horse fled at once, leaving only Charlie's troop remaining. The Sepoys with the two guns on the left were ordered to turn these round, so as to take the advancing French in flank; but the flight of their horse had shaken the natives, and the French cavalry would have fallen, unchecked, on Charlie's little troop, which was already moving forward to meet them, had not Captain Barlow, who commanded the British artillery, turned two of his guns and opened fire upon them.

Fifteen men and horses fell at the first discharge, throwing the rest into some confusion; and at the next deadly discharge, the whole turned and rode off. Seeing the enemy retreating, many of the irregular horse rode back, and, joining Charlie's troop, pursued them round to the rear of their own camp.

For a short time a cannonade was kept up by the guns on both sides, the English fire, being better directed, causing some damage. Upon Lally's return to his camp with the cavalry, he at once gave the order to advance. Coote ordered the Europeans of his force to do the same, the Sepoys to remain on their ground.

The musketry fire began at one o'clock. The English, according to Coote's orders, retained theirs until the enemy came close at hand. Following the tactics which were afterwards repeated many times in the Peninsula, the Lorraine regiment, forming a column twelve deep, advanced against that of Coote, which received them in line. The French came on at the double. When within a distance of fifty yards, Coote's regiment poured a volley into the front and flanks of the column. Although they suffered heavily from this fire, the French bravely pressed on with levelled bayonets, and the head of the column, by sheer weight, broke through the English line.

The flanks of the English, however, closed in on the sides of the French column, and a desperate hand-to-hand fight ensued. In this, the English had all the advantage, attacking the French fiercely on either side, until the latter broke and ran back to the camp.

Colonel Coote, who was with his regiment, ordered it to form in regular order again, before it advanced, and rode off to see what was going on in the rest of the line. As he was passing on, a shot struck an ammunition waggon in the intrenched tank held by the French. This exploded, killing and wounding eighty men, among whom was the commander of the post. The rest of its occupants, panic stricken by the explosion, ran back to the next tank. Their panic communicated itself to the Sepoys there, and all ran back together to the camp.

Colonel Coote at once sent orders to Major Brereton, who commanded Draper's regiment, to take possession of the tank, before the enemy recovered from the confusion which the explosion would be sure to cause. The ground opposite that which Draper's regiment occupied was held by Lally's regiment, and in order to prevent his men being exposed to a flanking fire from these, Draper ordered them to file off to the right. Bussy, who commanded at this wing, endeavoured to rally the fugitives, and gathering fifty or sixty together, added two companies of Lally's regiment to them, and posted them in the tank; he then returned to the regiment.

As Major Brereton, moving up his men, reached the intrenchment, a heavy fire was poured upon him. Major Brereton fell, mortally wounded, and many of his men were killed. The rest, however, with a rush carried the intrenchment, and firing down from the parapet on the guns on Lally's left, drove the gunners from them. Two companies held the intrenchment, and the rest formed in the plain on its left, to prevent Lally's regiment attacking it on this side.

Bussy wheeled Lally's regiment, detached a portion of it to recover the intrenchment, and with the rest marched against Draper's troops in the plain. A heavy musketry fire was kept up on both sides, until the two guns, posted by Draper's regiment, and left behind when they attacked the intrenchment, came up and opened on the French. These began to waver. Bussy, as the only chance of gaining the day, put himself at their head, and endeavoured to lead them forward to attack the English with the bayonet. His horse, however, was struck with a ball and soon fell; the English fire was redoubled, and but twenty of Lally's men kept round him.

Two companies of the English rushed forward and surrounded the little party, who at once surrendered. Bussy was led a prisoner to the rear, and as he went was surprised at the sight of the three hundred grenadiers, the best troops in the English army, remaining quietly in reserve.

While on either flank the French were now beaten, the fight in the centre, between the European troops of the English and French Companies, had continued, but had been confined to a hot musketry and artillery fire. But upon seeing the defeat of their flanks, the enemy's centre likewise fell back to their camp.

From the moment when the Lorraine regiment had been routed, four field pieces kept up an incessant fire into their camp, to prevent them from rallying. The three English regiments now advanced in line, and entered the enemy's camp without the least opposition. The Lorraine regiment had passed through it, a mass of fugitives. The India regiment and Lally's went through rapidly, but in good order.

Lally had, in vain, endeavoured to bring the Sepoys forward to the attack, to restore the day. The French cavalry, seeing the defeat of Lorraine's regiment, advanced to cover it, their appearance completely intimidating the English irregular horse. Charlie's troop were too weak to charge them single handed.

Reanimated by the attitude of their cavalry, the men of the Lorraine regiment rallied, yoked up four field pieces which were standing in the rear of the camp, and moved off in fair order. They were joined in the plain by Lally's regiment and the India battalion, and the whole, setting fire to their tents, moved off in good order. The four field pieces kept in the rear, and behind these moved the cavalry. As they retired, they were joined by the four hundred and fifty men from the batteries opposite Vandivash.

Colonel Coote sent orders to his cavalry to harass the enemy. These followed them for five miles, but as the native horse would not venture within range of the enemy's field guns, Charlie, to his great disappointment, was able to do nothing.

Upon neither side did the Sepoys take any part in the battle of Vandivash. It was fought entirely between the two thousand two hundred and fifty French, not including those in their battery, and sixteen hundred English, excluding the grenadiers, who never fired a shot. Twenty-four pieces of cannon were taken, and eleven waggons of ammunition, and all the tents, stores, and baggage that were not burned. The French left two hundred dead upon the field. A hundred and sixty were taken prisoner, of whom thirty died of their wounds before the next morning. Large numbers dropped upon the march, and were afterwards captured. The English had sixty-three killed, and a hundred and twenty-four wounded.

The news of this victory reached Madras on the following morning, and excited as much enthusiastic joy as that of Plassey had done at Calcutta; and the event was almost as important a one. There was no longer the slightest fear of danger, and the Madras authorities began to meditate an attack upon Pondicherry. So long as the great French settlement remained intact, so long would Madras be exposed to fresh invasions; and it was certain that France, driven now from Bengal, would make a desperate effort to regain her shaken supremacy in Madras.

The force, however, at the disposal of the Madras authorities, was still far too weak to enable them to undertake an enterprise like the siege of Pondicherry; for their army did not exceed, in numbers, that which Lally possessed for its defence. Accordingly, urgent letters were sent to Clive to ask him to send down, in the summer, as many troops as he could spare, other reinforcements being expected from England at that time. The intervening time was spent in the reduction of Chittapett, Karical, and many other forts which held out for the French.

After the battle of Vandivash, Charlie kept his promise to his men. He represented to Mr. Pigot that they had already served some months over the time for which they were enlisted, that they had gone through great hardships, and performed great services, and that they were now anxious to retire to enjoy the prize money they had earned. He added that he had given his own promise that they should be allowed to retire, if they would extend their service until after a decisive battle with the French. Mr. Pigot at once assented to Charlie's request, and ordered that a batta of six months' pay should be given to each man, upon leaving.

The troop, joined by many of their comrades, who had been at different times sent down sick and wounded to Madras, formed up there on parade for the last time. They responded with three hearty cheers to the address which Charlie gave them, thanking them for their services, bidding them farewell, and hoping that they would long enjoy the prize money which they had gallantly won. Then they delivered over their horses to the authorities, drew their prize money from the treasury, and started for their respective homes, the English portion taking up their quarters in barracks, until the next ship should sail for England.

'I am sorry to leave them,' Charlie said to Peters, as they stood alone upon the parade. 'We have gone through a lot of stirring work together, and no fellows could have behaved better.'

'No,' Peters agreed. 'It is singular that, contemptible as are these natives of India when officered by men of their own race and religion, they will fight to the death when led by us.'

Chapter 29

THE SIEGE OF PONDICHERRY

As the health of the two officers was shaken by their long and arduous work, and their services were not, for the moment, needed, they obtained leave for three months, and went down in a coasting ship to Columbo, where several English trading stations had been established. Here they spent two months, residing for the most part among the hills, at the town of a rajah very friendly to the English; and with him they saw an elephant hunt, the herd being driven into a great inclosure, formed by a large number of natives who had, for weeks, been employed upon it. Here the animals were fastened to trees by natives, who cut through the thick grass unobserved; and were one by one reduced to submission, first by hunger, and then by being lustily belaboured by the trunks of tamed elephants. Tim highly appreciated the hunt, and declared that tiger shooting was not to be compared to it.

Their residence in the brisk air of the hills completely restored their health, and they returned to Madras perfectly ready to take part in the great operations which were impending. Charlie, on his return, was appointed to serve as chief of the staff to Colonel Coote; Captain Peters being given the command of a small body of European horse, who were, with a large body of irregulars, to aid in bringing in supplies to the British army, and to prevent the enemy from receiving food from the surrounding country.

Early in June, the British squadron off the coast was joined by two ships of the line, the Norfolk and Panther, from England; and a hundred Europeans, and a detachment of European and native artillery came down from Bombay.

Around Pondicherry ran a strong cactus hedge, strengthened with palisades, and the French retired into this at the beginning of July. They were too strongly posted there to be attacked by the force with which the English at first approached them, and they were expecting the arrival of a large body of troops from Mysore, with a great convoy of provisions.

On the 17th these approached. Major Moore, who was guarding the English rear, had a hundred and eighty European infantry; fifty English horse, under Peters; sixteen hundred irregular horse; and eleven hundred Sepoys. The Mysoreans had four thousand good horse, a thousand Sepoys, and two hundred Europeans, with eight pieces of cannon.

The fight lasted but a few minutes. The British native horse and Sepoys at once gave way; and the English infantry retreated, in great disorder, to the fort of Trivadi, which they gained with a loss of fifteen killed and forty wounded. Peters' horse alone behaved well. Several times they charged right through the masses of Mysorean horse; but when five-and-twenty were killed, and most of the rest, including their commander, severely wounded, they also fell back into the fort.

Colonel Coote, when the news of the disaster reached him, determined, if possible, to get possession of the fort of Vellenore, which stood on the river Ariangopang, some three miles from Pondicherry, and covered the approaches of the town from that side. The English encampment was at Perimbe, on the main road leading, through an avenue of trees, to Pondicherry. Colonel Coote threw up a redoubt on the hill behind Perimbe, and another on the avenue, to check any French force advancing from Pondicherry. These works were finished on the morning of the 19th of July.

The next morning the French army advanced along the river Ariangopang, but Coote marched half his force to meet them, while he moved the rest as if to attack the redoubts, interspersed along the line of hedge. As the fall of these would have placed the attacking force in his rear, Lally at once returned to the town. The same evening the Mysoreans, with three thousand bullocks carrying their artillery and drawing their baggage, and three thousand more laden with rice and other provisions, arrived on the other bank of the Ariangopang river, crossed under the guns of the redoubt of that name, and entered the town.

The fort of Vellenore was strong, but the road had been cut straight through the glacis to the gate, and the French had neglected to erect works to cover this passage. Coote took advantage of the oversight, and laid his two eighteen-pounders to play upon the gate, while two others were placed to fire upon the parapet. The English batteries opened at daybreak on the 16th, and at nine o'clock the whole of the French army, with the Mysoreans, advanced along the bank of the river.

Coote at once got his troops under arms, and advanced towards the French, sending a small detachment of Europeans to reinforce the Sepoys firing at the fort of Vellenore. By this time the batteries had beaten down the parapet, and silenced the enemy's fire. Two companies of Sepoys set forward, at full run, up to the very crest of the glacis.

The French commander of the place had really nothing to fear, as the Sepoys had a ditch to pass, and a very imperfect breadth to mount, and the fort might have held out for two days, before the English could have been in a position to storm it. The French army was in sight, and in ten minutes a general engagement would have begun. In spite of all this, the coward at once hoisted a flag of truce, and surrendered. The Europeans and Sepoys ran in through the gate, and the former instantly turned the guns of the fort upon the French army. This halted, struck with amazement and anger, and Lally at once ordered it to retire upon the town.

A week afterwards six ships, with six hundred fresh troops from England, arrived.

The Mysoreans, who had brought food into Pondicherry, made many excursions in the country, but were sharply checked. They were unable to supply themselves with food, and none could be spared them from the stores in the magazines. Great distress set in among them, and this was heightened by the failure of a party, with two thousand bullocks with rice, to enter the town. This party, escorted by the greater portion of the Mysorean horse from Pondicherry, was attacked and defeated, and nine hundred bullocks, laden with baggage, captured. Shortly afterwards the rest of the Mysorean troops left Pondicherry, and marched to attack Trinomany.

Seeing that there was little fear of their returning to succour Pondicherry, the English now determined to complete the blockade of that place. In order to have any chance of reducing it by famine, it was necessary to obtain possession of the country within the hedge; which, with its redoubts, extended in the arc of a circle from the river Ariangopang to the sea. The space thus included contained an area of nearly seven square miles, affording pasture for the bullocks, of which there were sufficient to supply the troops and inhabitants for many months. Therefore, although the army was not yet strong enough to open trenches against the town, and indeed the siege artillery had not yet sailed from Madras, it was determined to get possession of the hedge and its redoubts.

Before doing this, however, it was necessary to capture the fort of Ariangopang. This was a difficult undertaking. The whole European force was but two thousand strong, and if eight hundred of these were detached across the river to attack the fort, the main body would be scarcely a match for the enemy, should he march out against them. If, on the other hand, the whole army moved round to attack the fort, the enemy would be able to send out and fetch in the great convoy of provisions collected at Jinji.

Mr. Pigot therefore requested Admiral Stevens to land the marines of the fleet. Although, seeing that a large French fleet was expected, the admiral was unwilling to weaken his squadron; he complied with the request, seeing the urgency of the case, and four hundred and twenty marines were landed.

On the 2nd of September two more men-of-war, the America and Medway, arrived, raising the fleet before Pondicherry to seventeen ships of the line. They convoyed several Company's ships, who had brought with them the wing of a Highland regiment.

The same evening Coote ordered four hundred men to march to invest the fort of Ariangopang; but Colonel Monson, second in command, was so strongly against the step that, at the last moment, he countermanded his orders. The change was fortunate, for Lally, who had heard from his spies of the English intentions, moved his whole army out to attack the – as he supposed – weakened force.

At ten at night fourteen hundred French infantry, a hundred French horse, and nine hundred Sepoys marched out to attack the English, who had no suspicion of their intent. Two hundred marines and five hundred Sepoys proceeded, in two columns. Marching from the Valdore redoubt, one party turned to the right to attack the Tamarind redoubt, which the English had erected on the Red Hill. Having taken this, they were to turn to their left and join the other column. This skirted the foot of the Red Hill, to attack the redoubt erected on a hillock at its foot, on the 18th July.

Four hundred Sepoys and a company of Portuguese were to take post at the junction of the Valdore and Oulgarry avenues. The regiments of Lorraine and Lally were to attack the battery in this avenue, Lorraine's from the front, while Lally's, marching outwards in the fields, was to fall on its right flank. The Indian battalion, with the Bourbon volunteers, three hundred strong, were to march from the fort of Ariangopang, across the river, to the villages under the fort of Vellenore; and, as soon as the fire became general, were to fall upon the right rear of the English encampment.

At midnight a rocket gave the signal, and the attack immediately commenced. The attack on the Tamarind redoubt was repulsed, but the redoubt on the hillock was captured, and the guns spiked. At the intrenchment on the Oulgarry Road the fight was fierce, and Colonel Coote himself brought down his troops to its defence. The attack was continued, but as, owing to some mistake, the column intended to fall upon the English rear had halted, and did not arrive in time, the regiments of Lorraine and Lally drew off, and the whole force retired to the town.

The ships arriving from England brought a commission appointing Monson to the rank of Colonel, with a date prior to that of Colonel Coote; ordering him, however, not to assert his seniority, so long as Coote remained at Madras. Coote, however, considered that it was intended that he should return to Bengal, and so handing over the command to Monson, he went back to Madras.

Colonel Monson at once prepared to attack the hedge, and its redoubts. Leaving sufficient guards for the camp, he advanced at midnight, with his troops divided into two brigades, the one commanded by himself, the other by Major Smith. Major Smith's division was first to attack the enemy, outside the hedge in the village of Oulgarry; and, driving them hence, to carry the Vellenore redoubt, while the main body were to make a sweep round the Red Hill, and come down to the attack of the Valdore redoubt.

Smith, moving to the right of the Oulgarry avenue, attacked that position on the left; and the advance, led by Captain Myers, carried by storm a redoubt in front of the village, and seized four pieces of cannon. Major Smith, heading his grenadiers, then charged the village, tore down all obstacles, and carried the place.

The day had begun to dawn when Colonel Monson approached the Valdore redoubt. But at the last moment, making a mistake in their way, the head of the column halted. At this moment the enemy perceived them, and discharged a twenty-four pounder, loaded with small shot, into the column. Eleven men were killed and twenty-six wounded by this terrible discharge, among the latter Colonel Monson himself, his leg being broken. The grenadiers now rushed furiously to the attack, swarmed round the redoubt and, although several times repulsed, at last forced their way through the embrasures and captured the position.

The defenders of the village of Oulgarry had halted outside the Vellenore redoubt; but, upon hearing the firing to their right, retreated hastily within it. Major Smith pressed them hotly with his brigade, and followed so closely upon their heels that they did not stop to defend the position, but retreated to the town. Major Smith was soon joined by the Highlanders, under Major Scott, who had forced a way through the hedge between the two captured redoubts.

Thus the whole line of the outer defence fell into the hands of the English, with the exception of the Ariangopang redoubt on the left, which was held by the India regiment. Major Gordon, who now took the command, placed the Bombay detachment, of three hundred and fifty men, in the captured redoubts; and encamped the whole of the force in the fields to the right of Oulgarry.

Major Smith advised that at least a thousand men should be left, near at hand, to succour the garrisons of the redoubts; which, being open at the rear, were liable to an attack. Major Gordon foolishly refused to follow his advice, and the same night the French attacked the redoubts. The Bombay troops, however, defended themselves with extreme bravery until assistance arrived.

Three days later the French evacuated and blew up the fort of Ariangopang, which the English were preparing to attack, and the India regiment retired into the town, leaving, however, the usual guard in the Ariangopang redoubt.

Colonel Coote had scarcely arrived at Madras when he received a letter from Colonel Monson, saying that he was likely to be incapacitated by his wound for some months, and requesting that he would resume the command of the army. The authorities of Madras strongly urged Coote to return, representing the extreme importance of the struggle in which they were engaged. He consented, and reached camp on the night of the 20th. He at once ordered the captured redoubts to be fortified, to prevent the enemy again taking the offensive; and erected a strong work, called the North Redoubt, near the seashore and facing the Madras redoubt.

A few days later, on a party of Sepoys approaching the Ariangopang redoubt, the occupants of that place were seized with a panic, abandoned the place, and went into the town. The English had now possession of the whole of the outward defences of Pondicherry, with the exception of the two redoubts by the seashore.

A day or two later Colonel Coote, advancing along the sea beach as if with a view of merely making a reconnaissance, pushed on suddenly, entered the village called the Blancherie, as it was principally inhabited by washerwomen, and attacked the Madras redoubt. This was carried, but the same night the garrison sallied out again, and fell upon the party of Sepoys posted there. Ensign MacMahon was killed, but the Sepoys, although driven out from the redoubt, bravely returned and again attacked the French; who, thinking that the Sepoys must have received large reinforcements, fell back into the village; from which, a day or two later, they retired into the town.

The whole of the ground outside the fort, between the river Ariangopang and the sea, was now in the hands of the English. The French still maintained their communications with the south by the sandy line of coast. By this time the attacks, which the English from Trichinopoli and Madura had made upon the Mysoreans, had compelled the latter to make peace, and recall their army, which was still hovering in the neighbourhood of Pondicherry.

Charlie, who had been suffering from a slight attack of fever, had for some time been staying on board ship, for change. In the road of Pondicherry three of the French Indiamen, the Hermione, Baleine, and the Compagnie des Indes, were at anchor, near the edge of the surf, under the cover of a hundred guns mounted on the sea face of the fort. These ships were awaiting the stormy weather, at the breaking of the monsoon, when it would be difficult for the English fleet to maintain their position off the town. They then intended to sail away to the south, fill up with provisions, and return to Pondicherry.

Admiral Stevens, in order to prevent this contingency, which would have greatly delayed the reduction of the place, determined to cut them out. Charlie's health being much restored by the sea breezes, he asked leave of the admiral to accompany the expedition, as a volunteer. On the evening of the 6th, six-and-twenty of the boats of the fleet, manned by four hundred sailors, were lowered and rowed to the Tiger, which was at anchor within two miles of Pondicherry, the rest of the fleet lying some distance farther away.

When, at midnight, the cabin lights of the Hermione were extinguished, the expedition started. The boats moved in two divisions, one of which was to attack the Hermione, the other the Baleine. The third vessel lay nearer in shore, and was to be attacked if the others were captured.

The night was a very dark one, and the boats of each division moved in line, with ropes stretched from boat to boat, to ensure their keeping together in the right direction. Charlie was in one of the boats intended to attack the Hermione. Tim accompanied him, but the admiral had refused permission for Hossein to do so, as there were many more white volunteers for the service than the boats would accommodate. They were within fifty yards of the Hermione before they were discovered, and a scattering musket fire was at once opened upon them.

The crews gave a mighty cheer and, casting off the ropes, separated; five making for each side of the ship, while two rowed forward to cut the cables at her bows. The Compagnie des Indes opened fire upon the boats, but these were already alongside the ship, and the sailors swarmed over the side at ten points.

The combat was a short one. The seventy men on board fought bravely, for a minute or two, but they were speedily driven below. The hatches were closed over them, and the cables being already cut, the mizzen topsail, the only sail bent, was hoisted; and the boats, taking towropes, began to row her away from shore.

The instant, however, that the cessation of fire informed the garrison the ship was captured, a tremendous cannonade was opened by the guns of the fortress. The lightning was flashing vividly, and this enabled the gunners to direct their aim upon the ship. Over and over again she was struck, and one shot destroyed the steering wheel, cut the tiller rope, and killed two men who were steering. The single sail was not sufficient to assist in steering her, and the men in the boats rowed with such energy that the ropes continually snapped.

The fire continued from the shore, doing considerable damage; and the men in the boats, who could not see that the ship was moving through the water, concluded that she was anchored by a concealed cable and anchor. The officer in command, therefore, called up the Frenchmen from below, telling them he was about to fire the ship. They came on deck and took their places in the boats, which rowed back to the Tiger.

Upon arriving there Captain Dent, who commanded her, sternly rebuked the officer; and said that, unless the boats returned instantly and brought the Hermione out, he should send his own crew in their boats to fetch her. The division thereupon returned, and met the ship half a mile off shore, the land wind having now sprung up.

The Baleine had been easily captured and, having several sails bent, she was brought out without difficulty. No attempt was made to capture the third vessel.

The rains had now set in, but the English laboured steadily at their batteries. The French were becoming pressed for provisions, and Lally turned the whole of the natives remaining in the town, to the number of fourteen hundred men and women, outside the fortifications. On their arrival at the English lines they were refused permission to pass, as Colonel Coote did not wish to relieve the garrison of the consumption of food caused by them. They returned to the French lines, and begged to be again received; but they were, by Lally's orders, fired upon, and several killed.

For seven days the unhappy wretches remained without food, save the roots they could gather in the fields. Then Colonel Coote, seeing that Lally was inflexible, allowed them to pass.

On the 10th of November the batteries opened, and every day added to the strength of the fire upon the town. The fortifications, however, were strong, and the siege progressed but slowly. On the 30th of December a tremendous storm burst, and committed the greatest havoc, both at land and sea. The Newcastle, man-of-war; the Queenborough, frigate; and the Protector, fire ship were driven ashore and dashed to pieces; but the crews, with the exception of seven, were saved. The Duke of Aquitaine, the Sunderland, and the Duke, store ship, were sunk, and eleven hundred sailors drowned. Most of the other ships were dismasted.

Chapter 30

HOME

The fire of the batteries increased, and by the 13th of January the enemy's fire was completely silenced. The provisions in the town were wholly exhausted, and on the 16th the town surrendered, and the next morning the English took possession. Three days afterwards Lally was embarked on board ship, to be taken a prisoner to Madras; and so much was he hated that the French officers and civilians assembled, and hissed and hooted him; and, had he not been protected by his guard, would have torn him to pieces. After his return to France he was tried for having, by his conduct, caused the loss of the French possessions in India, and being found guilty of the offence, was beheaded.

At Pondicherry two thousand and seventy-two military prisoners were taken, and three hundred and eighty-one civilians. Five hundred cannon and a hundred mortars, fit for service; and immense quantities of ammunition, arms, and military stores fell into the hands of the captors.

Pondicherry was handed over to the Company; who, a short time afterwards, entirely demolished both the fortress and town. This hard measure was the consequence of a letter which had been intercepted, from the French government to Lally, ordering him to raze Madras to the ground, when it fell into his hands.

Charlie, after the siege, in which he had rendered great services, received from the Company, at Colonel Coote's earnest recommendation, his promotion to the step of lieutenant colonel; while Peters was raised to that of major. A fortnight after the fall of Pondicherry, they returned to Madras, and thence took the first ship for England. It was now just ten years since they had sailed, and in that time they had seen Madras and Calcutta rise, from the rank of two trading stations, in constant danger of destruction by their powerful neighbours, to that of virtual capitals of great provinces. Not as yet, indeed, had they openly assumed the sovereignty of these territories; but Madras was, in fact, the absolute master of the broad tract of land extending from the foot of the mountains to the sea, from Cape Comorin to Bengal; while Calcutta was master of Bengal and Oressa, and her power already threatened to extend itself as far as Delhi. The conquest of these vast tracts of country had been achieved by mere handfuls of men, and by a display of heroic valour and constancy scarce to be rivalled in the history of the world.

The voyage was a pleasant one, and was, for the times, quick, occupying only five months. But to the young men, longing for home after so long an absence, it seemed tedious in the extreme.

Tim and Hossein were well content with their quiet, easy life, after their long toils. They had nothing whatever to do, except that they insisted upon waiting upon Charlie and Peters, at meals. The ship carried a large number of sick and wounded officers and men, and as these gained health and strength, the life on board ship became livelier, and more jovial. Singing and cards occupied the evenings, while in the daytime they played quoits, rings of rope being used for that purpose, and other games with which passengers usually wile away the monotony of long voyages.

It was late in June when the Madras sailed up the Thames; and, as soon as she came to anchor, the two officers and their followers landed. The din and bustle of the streets seemed almost as strange, to Charlie, as they had done when he came up a boy, from Yarmouth. Hossein was astonished at the multitude of white people, and inquired of Charlie why, when there were so many men, England had sent so few soldiers to fight for her in India; and for once, Charlie was unable to give a satisfactory reply.

'It does seem strange,' he said to Peters, 'that when such mighty interests were at stake, a body of even ten thousand troops could not have been raised, and sent out. Such a force would have decided the struggle at once; and in three months the great possessions, which have cost the Company twelve years' war, would have been at their feet. It would not have cost them more; indeed, nothing like as much as it now has done, nor one tithe of the loss in life. Somehow, England always seems to make war in driblets.'

Charlie knew that his mother and Kate had, for some years, been residing at a house which their uncle had taken, in the fashionable quarter of Chelsea. They looked in at the office, however, to see if Charlie's uncle was there; but found that he was not in the city, and, indeed, had now almost retired from the business. They therefore took a coach, placed the small articles of luggage which they had brought with them, from the ship, on the front seats; and then, Hossein and Tim taking their places on the broad seat beside the driver, they entered the coach and drove to Chelsea.

Charlie had invited Peters, who had no home of his own, to stay with him, at least for a while. Both were now rich men, from their shares of the prize money of the various forts and towns, in whose capture they had taken part; although Charlie possessed some twenty thousand pounds more than his friend, this being the amount of the presents he had received, from the Rajah of Ambur.

Alighting from the carriage, Charlie ran up to the door and knocked. Inquiring for Mrs. Marryat, he was shown into a room in which a lady, somewhat past middle age, and three younger ones were sitting. They looked up, in surprise, as the young man entered. Ten years had changed him almost beyond recognition, but one of the younger ones at once leaped to her feet, and exclaimed, 'Charlie!'

His mother rose with a cry of joy, and threw herself into his arms. After rapturously kissing her, he turned to the others. Their faces were changed, yet all seemed equally familiar to him, and in his delight he equally embraced them all.

'Hullo!' he exclaimed, when he freed himself from their arms. 'Why, there are three of you! What on earth am I doing? I have somebody's pardon to beg; and yet, although your faces are changed, they seem equally familiar to me. Which is it?

'But I need not ask,' he said, as a cloud of colour flowed over the face of one of the girls, while the others smiled mischievously.

'You are Katie,' he said, 'and you are Lizzie, certainly, and this is – why, it is Ada! 'This is a surprise, indeed; but I sha'n't beg your pardon, Ada, for I kissed you at parting, and quite intended to do so when I met again, at least if you had offered no violent objection.

'How you are all grown and changed, while you, Mother, look scarcely older than when I left you.

'But there, I have quite forgotten Peters. He has come home with me, and will stay till he has formed his own plans.'

He hurried out and brought in Peters; who, not wishing to be present at the family meeting, had been paying the coachman, and seeing to the things being brought into the house. He was warmly received, by the ladies, as the friend and companion of Charlie in his adventures; scarcely a letter having been received, from the latter, without mention having been made of his comrade.

In a minute or two Mr. Tufton, who had been in the large garden behind the house, hurried in. He was now quite an old man; and under the influence of age, and the cheerful society of Mrs. Marryat and her daughters, he had lost much of the pomposity which had before distinguished him.

'Ah! Nephew,' he said, when the happy party had sat down to dinner, their number increased by the arrival of Mrs. Haines, who had a house close by; 'wilful lads will go their own way. I wanted to make a rich merchant of you, and you have made of yourself a famous soldier. But you've not done badly for yourself after all; for you have, in your letters, often talked about prize money.'

'Yes, Uncle. I have earned, in my way, close upon a hundred thousand pounds; and I certainly shouldn't have made that if I had stuck to the office at Madras, even with the aid of the capital you offered to lend me, to trade with on my own account.'

There was a general exclamation of surprise and pleasure, at the mention of the sum; although this amount was small, in comparison to that which many acquired, in those days, in India.

'And you're not thinking of going back again, Charlie?' his mother said, anxiously. 'There can be no longer any reason for your exposing yourself to that horrible climate, and that constant fighting.'

'The climate is not so bad, Mother, and the danger and excitement of a soldier's life there, at present, render it very fascinating. But I have done with it. Peters and I intend, on the expiration of our leave, to resign our commissions in the Company's service, and to settle down under our own vines and fig trees. Tim has already elected himself to the post of my butler, and Hossein intends to be my valet and body servant.'

Immediately after their arrival, Charlie had brought in his faithful followers and introduced them to the ladies; who, having often heard of their devotion and faithful services, had received them with a kindness and cordiality which had delighted them.

Lizzie, whose appearance at home had been unexpected by Charlie, for her husband was a landed gentleman at Seven Oaks, in Kent, was, it appeared, paying a visit of a week to her mother; and her three children, two boys and a little girl, were duly brought down to be shown to, and admired by, their Uncle Charles.

'And how is it you haven't married, Katie? With such a pretty face as yours, it is scandalous that the men have allowed you to reach the mature age of twenty-two, unmarried.'

'It is the fault of the hussy herself,' Mr. Tufton said. 'It is not from want of offers, for she has had a dozen, and among them some of the nobility at court; for it is well known that John Tufton's niece will have a dowry such as many of the nobles could not give, to their daughters.'

'This is too bad, Kate,' Charlie said, laughing. 'What excuse have you to make for yourself for remaining single, with all these advantages of face and fortune?'

'Simply that I didn't like any of them,' Katie said. 'The beaux of the present day are contemptible. I would as soon think of marrying a wax doll. When I do marry; that is, if ever I do, it shall be a man, and not a mere tailor's dummy.'

'You are pert, miss,' her uncle said.

'Do what I will, Charlie, I cannot teach the hussy to order her tongue.'

'Katie's quite right, Uncle,' Charlie laughed. 'And I must make it my duty to find a man who will suit her taste; though, according to your account of her, he will find it a hard task to keep such a Xanthippe in order.'

Katie tossed her head.

'He'd better not try,' she said saucily, 'or it will be worse for him.'

Two days later, Charlie's elder sister returned with her family to her house at

Sevenoaks; where Charlie promised, before long, to pay her a visit. After she had gone, Charlie and Peters, with Katie, made a series of excursions to all the points of interest, round London; and on these occasions Ada usually accompanied them.

The natural consequences followed. Charlie had, for years, been the hero of Ada's thoughts; while Katie had heard so frequently of Peters that she was, from the first, disposed to regard him in the most favourable light. Before the end of two months, both couples were engaged; and as both the young officers possessed ample means, and the ladies were heiresses, there was no obstacle to an early union.

The weddings took place a month later; and Tim was, in the exuberance of his delight, hilariously drunk for the first and only time during his service with Charlie. Both gentlemen bought estates in the country, and later took their seats in Parliament, where they vigorously defended their former commander, Lord Clive, in the assaults which were made upon him.

Tim married, seven or eight years after his master, and settled down in a nice little house upon the estate. Although, henceforth, he did no work whatever; he insisted, to the end of his life, that he was still in Colonel Marryat's service.

Hossein, to the great amusement of his master and mistress, followed Tim's example. The pretty cook of Charlie's establishment made no objection to his swarthy hue. Charlie built a snug cottage for them, close to the house, where they took up their residence; but Hossein, though the happy father of a large family, continued, to the end of a long life, to discharge the duties of valet to his master.

Both he and Tim were immense favourites with the children of Charlie and Peters, who were never tired of listening to their tales of the exploits of their fathers, when with Clive in India.